TALE Of The FOX

HARRY TURTLEDOVE

TALE OF THE FOX

This is a work of fiction. All the characters and events portrayed in this book are fictional, and any resemblance to real people or incidents is purely coincidental.

A Baen Books Original Omnibus

Baen Publishing Enterprises
P.O. Box 1403
Riverdale, NY 10471
www.baen.com

ISBN: 0-671-57874-X

Cover art by Bob Eggleton

First printing, June 2000

Distributed by Simon & Schuster
1230 Avenue of the Americas
New York, NY 10020

Typeset by Brilliant Press
Printed in the United States of America

She was beautiful.

But *he* was the Fox.

In the middle of the clearing stood a comely naked woman with long dark hair, twice as tall as the Fox, who held in her right hand an axe of Gradi style.

"Voldar," Gerin whispered. In the silence of his mind, he thanked his own gods that the Gradi goddess had chosen to meet him in a dream rather than manifesting herself in the material world.

She looked at him—through him—with eyes pale as ice, eyes in which cold fire flickered. And he, abruptly, was cold, chilled in the heart, chilled from the inside out. Her lips moved. "You meddle in what does not concern you," she said. He did not think the words were Elabonian, but he understood them anyhow. That left him awed but unsurprised. Gods—and, he supposed, goddesses—had their own ways in such matters.

"The northlands are my land, the land of my people, the land of my gods," he answered, bold as he dared. "Of course what happens here concerns me."

That divinely chilling gaze pierced him again. Voldar tossed her head in fine contempt. Her hair whipped out behind her, flying back as if in a breeze—but there was no breeze. In face and form, the Gradi goddess was stunningly beautiful, more perfect than any being the Fox had imagined, but even had she been his size, he would have known no stir of desire for her. Whatever her purpose, love had nothing to do with it.

She said, "Obey me now and you may yet survive. Give over your vain resistance and you will be able to live out your full span most honored among all those not lucky enough to be born of the blood of my folk."

He said, "I'll take my chances. I may end up dead, but that strikes me as better than living under your people—and under you. Or I may end up alive and free. Till the time comes, you never know—and we Elabonians have gods, too."

BAEN BOOKS by HARRY TURTLEDOVE

The Fox novels:

Wisdom of the Fox
Tale of the Fox

Sentry Peak (forthcoming)
The Case of the Toxic Spell Dump
Thessalonica
Alternate Generals, editor
Down in the Bottomlands
(with L. Sprague de Camp)

CONTENTS

King of the North

King of the North

I

Gerin the Fox looked down his long nose at the two peasants who'd brought their dispute before him. "Now, Trasamir, you say this hound is yours, am I right?"

"Aye, that's right, lord prince." Trasamir Longshanks' shaggy head bobbed up and down. He pointed to several of the people who helped crowd the great hall of Fox Keep. "All these folks from my village, they'll say it's so."

"Of course they will," Gerin said. One corner of his mouth curled up in a sardonic smile. "They'd better, hadn't they? As best I can tell, you've got two uncles, a cousin, a nephew, and a couple of nieces there, haven't you?" He turned to the other peasant. "And you, Walamund, you claim the hound belongs to you?"

"That I do, lord prince, on account of it's so." Walamund Astulf's son had a typical Elabonian name, but dirty blond hair and light eyes said there were a couple of Trokmoi in the family woodpile. Like Gerin, Trasamir was swarthy, with brown eyes and black hair and beard—though the Fox's beard had gone quite gray the past few years. Walamund went on, "These here people will tell you that there dog is mine."

Gerin gave them the same dubious look with which he'd favored Trasamir's supporters. "That's your father and your brother and two of your brothers-in-law I see, one of them with your sister alongside—for luck, maybe."

Walamund looked as unhappy as Trasamir Longshanks had a moment before. Neither man seemed to have expected their overlord to be so well versed about who was who in their village. That marked them both for fools: any man who did not know Gerin kept close track of as many tiny details as he could wasn't keeping track of details himself.

Hesitantly, Trasamir pointed to the hound in question—a rough-coated, reddish brown beast with impressive fangs, now tied to a table leg and given a wide berth by everybody in the hall. "Uh, lord prince, you're a wizard, too, they say. Couldn't you use your magic to show whose dog Swifty there really is?"

"I could," Gerin said. "I won't. More trouble than it's worth." As far as he was concerned, most magic was more trouble than it was worth. His sorcerous training was more than half a lifetime old now, and had always been incomplete. A partially trained mage risked his own skin every time he tried a conjuration. The Fox had got away with it a few times over the years, but picked with great care the spots where he'd take the chance.

He turned to his eldest son, who stood beside him listening to the two peasants' arguments. "How would you decide this one, Duren?"

"Me?" Duren's voice broke on the word. He scowled in embarrassment. When you had fourteen summers, the world could be a mortifying place. But Gerin had put questions like that to him before: the Fox was all too aware he wouldn't last forever, and wanted to leave behind a well-trained successor. As Trasamir had, Duren pointed to the hound. "There's the animal. Here are the two men who say it's theirs. Why not let them both call it and see which one it goes to?"

Gerin plucked at his beard. "Mm, I like that well enough. Better than well enough, in fact—they should have thought of it for themselves back at their village instead of coming here and wasting my time with it." He looked to Trasamir and Walamund. "Whichever one of you can call the dog will keep it. Do you agree?"

Both peasants nodded. Walamund asked, "Uh, lord prince, what about the one the dog doesn't go to?"

The Fox's smile grew wider, but less pleasant. "He'll have to yield up a forfeit, to make sure I'm not swamped with this sort of foolishness. Do you still agree?"

Walamund and Trasamir nodded again, this time perhaps less enthusiastically. Gerin waved them out to the courtyard. Out they went, along with their supporters, his son, a couple of his vassals, and all the cooks and serving girls. He started out himself, then realized the bone of contention—or rather, the bone-gnawer of contention—was still tied to the table.

The hound growled and bared its teeth as he undid the rope holding it. Had it attacked him, he would have drawn his sword and solved the problem by ensuring that neither peasant took possession of it thereafter. But it let him lead it out into the afternoon sunlight.

"Get back, there!" he said, and the backers of Trasamir and Walamund retreated from their principals. He glared at them. "Any of you who speaks or moves during the contest will be sorry for it, I promise." The peasants might suddenly have turned to stone. Gerin nodded to the two men who claimed the hound. "All right—go ahead."

"Here, Swifty!" "Come, boy!" "Come on—good dog!" "That's my Swifty!" Walamund and Trasamir both called and chirped and whistled and slapped the callused palms of their hands against their woolen trousers.

At first, Gerin thought the dog would ignore both of them. It sat on its haunches and yawned, displaying canines that might almost have done credit to a longtooth. The Fox hadn't figured out what he'd do if Swifty wanted no part of either peasant.

But then the hound got up and began to strain against the rope. Gerin let go, hoping the beast wouldn't savage one of the men calling it. It ran straight to Trasamir Longshanks and let him pat and hug it. Its fluffy tail wagged back and forth. Trasamir's relatives clapped their hands and shouted in delight. Walamund's stood dejected.

So did Walamund himself. "Uh—what are you going to do to me, lord prince?" he asked, eyeing Gerin with apprehension.

"Do you admit to trying to take the hound when it was not yours?" the Fox asked, and Walamund reluctantly nodded. "You knew your claim wasn't good, but you made it anyhow?" Gerin persisted. Walamund nodded again, even more reluctantly. Gerin passed sentence: "Then you can kiss the dog's backside, to remind you to keep your hands off what belongs to your neighbors."

"Grab Swifty's tail, somebody!" Trasamir shouted with a whoop of glee. Walamund Astulf's son stared from Gerin to the dog and back again. He looked as if somebody had hit him in the side of the head with a board. But almost everyone around him—including some of his own kinsfolk—nodded approval at the Fox's rough justice. Walamund started to stoop, then stopped and sent a last glance of appeal toward his overlord.

Gerin folded his arms across his chest. "You'd better do it," he said implacably. "If I come up with something else, you'll like that even less, I promise you."

His own gaze went to the narrow window that gave light to his bedchamber. As he'd hoped, Selatre stood there, watching what was going on in the courtyard below. When he caught his wife's eye, she nodded vigorously. That made him confident he was on the right course. He sometimes doubted his own good sense, but hardly ever hers.

One of Trasamir's relatives lifted the hound's tail. Walamir got down on all fours, did as the Fox had required of him, and then spat in the dirt and grass again and again, wiping his lips on his sleeve all the while.

"Fetch him a jack of ale, to wash his mouth," Gerin told one of the serving girls. She hurried away. The Fox looked a warning to Trasamir and his relatives. "Don't hang an ekename on him on account of this," he told them. "It's over and done with. If he comes back here and tells me you're all calling him Walamund Hound-Kisser or anything like that, you'll wish you'd never done it. Do you understand me?"

"Aye, lord prince," Trasamir said, and his kinsfolk nodded solemnly. He didn't know whether they meant it. He knew he did, though, so if they didn't they'd be sorry.

The girl brought out two tarred-leather jacks of ale. She

gave one to Walamund and handed the Fox the other. "Here, lord prince," she said with a smile.

"Thank you, Nania," he answered. "That was kindly done." Her smile got wider and more inviting. She was new to Fox Keep; maybe she had in mind slipping into Gerin's bed, or at least a quick tumble in a storeroom or some such. In a lot of castles, that would have been the quickest way to an easy job. Gerin chuckled to himself as he poured out a small libation to Baivers, the god of barley and brewing. No reason for Nania to know yet that she'd found herself an uxorious overlord, but she had. He hadn't done any casual wenching since he'd met Selatre. *Eleven years, more or less*, he thought in some surprise. It didn't feel that long.

Walamund had also let a little ale slop over the rim of his drinking jack and drip onto the ground: only a fool slighted the gods. Then he raised the jack to his mouth. He spat out the first mouthful, then gulped down the rest in one long draught.

"Fill him up again," Gerin told Nania. He turned back to Walamund and Trasamir and their companions. "You can sup here tonight, and sleep in the great hall. The morning is time enough to get back to your village." The peasants bowed and thanked him, even Walamund.

By the time the man who'd wrongly claimed the hound had got outside of his second jack of ale, his view of the world seemed much improved. Duren stepped aside with Gerin and said, "I thought he'd hate you forever after that, but he doesn't seem to."

"That's because I let him down easy once the punishment was done," the Fox said. "I made sure he wouldn't be mocked, I gave him ale to wash his mouth, and I'll feed him supper same as I will Trasamir. Once you've done what you need to do, step back and get on with things. If you stand over him gloating, he's liable to up and kick you in the bollocks."

Duren thought about it. "That's not what Lekapenos' epic tells a man to do," he said. " 'Be the best friend your friends have, and the worst foe to your foes,' or so the poet says."

Gerin frowned. Whenever he thought of Lekapenos, he thought of Duren's mother; Elise had been fond of quoting the Sithonian poet. Elise had also run off with a traveling horse doctor, about the time Duren was learning to stand on his feet. Even with so many years gone by, remembering hurt.

The Fox stuck close to the point his son had raised: "Walamund's not a foe. He's just a serf who did something wrong. Father Dyaus willing, he won't take the chance of falling foul of me again, and that's what I was aiming at. There's more gray in life, son, than you'll find in an epic."

"But the epic is grander," Duren said with a grin, and burst into Sithonian hexameters. Gerin grinned, too. He was glad to see knowledge of Sithonian preserved here in the northlands, cut off these past fifteen years and more from the Empire of Elabon. Few hereabouts could read even Elabonian, the tongue in their mouths every day.

Gerin also smiled because Selatre, having first learned Sithonian herself, was the one who'd taught Duren the language. The boy—no, not a boy any more: the youth—didn't remember his birth mother. Selatre was the one who'd raised him, and he got on so well with her and with his younger half brothers and half sister that they might have been full-blooded kin.

Duren pointed eastward. "There's Elleb, coming up over the stockade," he said. "Won't be too long till sunset." Gerin nodded. Ruddy Elleb—actually, a washed-out pink with the sun still in the sky—was a couple of days before full. Pale Nothos floated high in the southeast, looking like half a coin at first quarter. Golden Math wasn't up yet: she'd be full tonight, Gerin thought. And swift-moving Tiwaz was lost in the skirts of the sun.

Walamund had his drinking jack filled yet again. The Fox brewed strong ale; he wondered if the peasant would fall asleep before supper. Well, if Walamund did, it was his business, no one else's. He'd hike back to his village in the morning with a thick head, nothing worse.

From the watchtower atop the keep, a sentry shouted, "A chariot approaches, lord prince." On the palisade surrounding Castle Fox, soldiers looked to their bows and bronze-headed spears. In these troubled times, you never could tell who might be coming. After a short pause, the sentry said, "It's Van of the Strong Arm, with Geroge and Tharma."

The soldiers relaxed. Van had been Gerin's closest friend since before the great werenight, and that had been . . . Gerin glanced up toward Elleb and Nothos once more. Those two moons, and Tiwaz and Math, had all been full together nearly sixteen years before. Sometimes, that night of terror seemed impossibly distant. Sometimes, as now, it might have been day before yesterday.

Chains creaked as the gate crew lowered the drawbridge to let Van and his companions into Fox Keep. The bridge thumped down onto the dirt on the far side of the ditch surrounding the palisade. Not for the first time, Gerin told himself he ought to dig a trench from the River Niffet and turn that ditch to a moat. *When I have time*, he thought, knowing that likely meant *never*.

Horses' hooves drummed on the oak planks as the chariot rattled over the drawbridge and into the courtyard. "Ho, Fox!" Van boomed. The outlander was driving the two-horse team, and in his fine bronze corselet and helm with tall crest could easily have been mistaken for a god visiting the world of men. He was half a foot taller than Gerin—who was not short himself—and broad through the shoulders in proportion. His hair and beard were still almost all gold, not silver, though he was within a couple of years of the Fox's age, one way or the other. But the scars seaming his face and arms and hands gave proof he was human, not divine.

Yet however impressive the figure he cut, Walamund and Trasamir and all the peasants who'd accompanied them to Castle Fox stared not at him but at Geroge and Tharma, who rose behind him in the car. Trasamir's eyes got very big. "Father Dyaus," he muttered, and made an apotropaic sign with his right hand. "I thought we were rid of those horrible things for good."

Van glared at him. "You watch your mouth," he said, a warning not to be taken lightly. He turned back to Geroge and Tharma and spoke soothingly: "Don't get angry. He doesn't mean anything by it. He just hasn't seen any like you for a long time."

"It's all right," Geroge said, and Tharma nodded to show

she agreed. He went on, "We know we surprise people. It's just the way things are."

"How'd the hunting go?" Gerin asked, hoping to distract Geroge and Tharma from the wide eyes of the serfs. They couldn't help their looks. As far as monsters went, in fact, they were very good people.

Tharma bent down and slung the gutted carcass of a stag out of the chariot. Geroge grinned proudly. "I caught it," he said. His grin made the peasants draw back in fresh alarm, for his fangs were at least as impressive as those of Swifty the hound. His face and Tharma's sloped forward, down to the massive jaws needed to contain such an imposing collection of ivory.

Neither monster was excessively burdened with forehead, but both, under their hairy hides, had thews as large and strong as Van's, which was saying a great deal. They wore baggy woolen trousers in a checked pattern of ocher and woad blue: a Trokmê style.

Pretty soon, Gerin realized, he was going to have to put them in tunics, too, for Tharma would start growing breasts before too much time went by. The Fox didn't know how long monsters took to reach puberty. He did know Geroge and Tharma were about eleven years old.

Monsters like them had overrun the northlands then, after a fearsome earthquake released them from the caverns under the temple of the god Biton, where they'd been confined for hundreds, maybe thousands, of years. The efforts of mere mortals hadn't sufficed to drive the monsters back, either; Gerin had had to evoke both Biton, who saw past and future, and Mavrix, the Sithonian god of wine, fertility, and beauty, to rout them from the land.

Before he'd done that, he'd found a pair of monster cubs and had not killed them, though he and his comrades had slain their mother. When Mavrix banished the monsters from the surface of the world, Biton had mocked his sloppy work, implying some of the creatures still remained in the northlands. Gerin had wondered then if they were the pair he'd spared, and wondered again a year later when a shepherd who'd apparently raised Geroge and Tharma as pets till then brought them to him. He thought it likely, but had no way to prove it. The shepherd had been maddeningly vague. He did know no other monsters had ever turned up, not in all these years.

Having two monsters around was interesting, especially since they seemed bright for their kind, which made them about as smart as stupid people. They'd grown up side by side with his own children, younger than Duren but older than Dagref, the Fox's older son by Selatre. They were careful with their formidable strength, and never used their fearsome teeth for anything but eating.

But soon Tharma would be a woman—well, an adult female monster—and Geroge mature as well. The Fox was anything but certain he wanted more than two monsters in the northlands, and just as uncertain what, if anything, to do about it. He'd kept putting off a decision by telling himself he didn't yet need to worry. That was still true, but wouldn't be much longer.

"Take that in to the cooks," he told Geroge. "Venison steaks tonight, roast venison, venison ribs—" Geroge slung the gutted deer over his shoulder and carried it into the castle. Tharma followed him, as she usually did, although sometimes he followed her. She ran her tongue across her wide, thin lips at the prospect of plenty of meat.

"I need more ale," Walamund muttered. "We're supposed to eat alongside those horrible things?"

"They don't mind," Gerin said. "You shouldn't, either."

Walamund sent him a resentful glare, but the memory of recent punishment remained fresh enough to keep the serf from saying anything. Geroge and Tharma came out into the courtyard again, this time accompanied by Dagref and his younger sister Clotild, and by Van's daughter Maeva and his son Kor.

Behind the children strode Fand. "You might have told me you were back," she said to Van, a Trokmê lilt to her Elabonian though she'd lived south of the Niffet since shortly after the werenight. A breeze blew a couple of strands of coppery hair in front of her face. She brushed them aside with her hand. She was perhaps five years younger than Van, but beginning to go gray.

He stared over toward her. "I might have done lots of things," he rumbled.

Fand set hands on hips. "Aye, you might have. But did

you, now? No, not a bit of a bit. Hopped in the car you did instead, and went off a-hunting with not a thought in your head for aught else."

"Who would have room for thoughts, with your eternal din echoing round in his head?" Van retorted. They shouted at each other.

Gerin turned to Nania. "Fetch them each the biggest jack of ale we have," he said quietly. The serving girl hurried away and returned with two jacks, each filled so full ale slopped over the side to make its own libation. Gerin knew he was gambling. If Van and Fand were still angry at each other by the time they got to the bottom of the jacks, they'd quarrel harder than ever because of the ale they'd drunk. A lot of the time, though, their fights were like rain squalls: blowing up suddenly, fierce while they lasted, and soon gone.

Maeva gave Dagref a shove. He staggered, but stayed on his feet. The two of them were very much of a size, though he had a year on her. Maeva showed every promise of having much of her father's enormous physical prowess. Gerin wondered if the world was ready for a woman warrior able to best almost any man. Ready or not, the world was liable to face the prospect in a few years.

Clotild said, "No, Kor, don't put that rock in your mouth."

Instead of putting it in his mouth, he threw it at her. Fortunately, he missed. He had a temper he'd surely acquired from Fand. Four-year-olds were not the most self-controlled people under any circumstances. A four-year-old whose mother was Fand was a conflagration waiting to happen.

Van and Fand upended their drinking jacks at about the same time. Gerin waited to see what would happen next. When what happened next was nothing, he allowed himself a tiny pat on the back. He glanced over at Fand. Hard to imagine these days that he and Van had once shared her favors. Getting to know Selatre afterwards was like coming into a calm harbor after a storm at sea.

The Fox shook his head. That that image occurred to him proved only that he'd done more reading than just about anyone else in the northlands (which, though undoubtedly true, wasn't saying much). He'd never been on the Orynian Ocean—which lapped against the shore of the northlands far to the west—or any other sea.

Shadows lengthened and began to gray toward twilight. A bronze horn sounded a long, hoarse, sour note in the peasant village a few hundred yards from Fox Keep: a signal for the serfs to come to their huts from out of the fields, both for supper and to keep themselves safe from the ghosts that roamed and ravened through the night.

Van looked around to gauge the hour. He nodded approval. "The new headman keeps 'em at it longer than Besant Big-Belly did," he said. "There were times when he'd blow the horn halfway through the afternoon, seemed like."

"That's so," Gerin agreed. "The peasants mourned for days after that tree fell on him last winter. Not surprising, is it? They knew they'd have to work harder with anybody else over them."

"Lazy buggers," Van said.

The Fox shrugged. "Nobody much likes to work. Sometimes you have to, though, or you pay for it later. Some people never do figure that out, so they need a headman who can get the most from 'em without making 'em hate him." He was happy to talk about work with his friend: anything to distract Van from yet another squabble with Fand.

Fand, however, didn't feel like being distracted. "And some people, now," she said, "are after calling others lazy while they their ownselves do whatever it is pleases them and not a lick of aught else."

"I'll give you a lick across the side of your head," Van said, and took a step toward her.

"Aye, belike you will, and one fine day you'll wake up beside me all nice and dead, with a fine slim dagger slid between your ribs," Fand said, now in grim earnest. Van did hit her every once in a while; brawling, for him, was a sport. She hit him, too, and clawed, and bit. The outlander was generally mindful of his great strength, and did not use all of it save in war and hunting. When Fand was in a temper, she was mindful of nothing and no one save her own fury.

Van said, "By all the gods in all the lands I've ever seen, I'll wake up beside somebody else, then."

"And I pity the poor dear, whoever she is," Fand shot back. "Sure and it's nobbut fool's luck—the only kind a fool like you's after having—you've not brought me back a sickness, what with your rutting like a stoat."

"As if I'm the only one, you faithless—!" Van clapped a hand to his forehead, speechless despite the many languages he knew.

Gerin turned to Trasamir, who happened to be standing closest to him. "Isn't love a wonderful thing?" he murmured.

"What?" Trasamir scratched his head.

Another one who wouldn't recognize irony if it came up and bit him on the leg, the Fox thought sadly. He wished he had the wisdom of a god, to say the perfect thing to make Van and Fand stop quarreling. With that, he'd probably need other divine powers, to make sure they didn't start up again the moment his back was turned.

Selatre came out to the entrance to the great hall. "Supper's ready," she called to the people gathered in the courtyard. Everyone, Van and Fand included, trooped toward the castle. Gerin chuckled under his breath. He hadn't known what to say to get Van and Fand to break off their fight, but Selatre had. Maybe she was divinely wise.

The notion wasn't altogether frivolous. Selatre had been Biton's Sibyl at Ikos, delivering the prophecies of the far-seeing god to those who sought his wisdom, until the earthquake that released the monsters tumbled the god's shrine in ruins. Had Gerin and Van not rescued her while she lay in entranced sleep, the creatures from the caverns below would have made short work of her.

Biton's Sybil had to be a maiden. Not only that, she was forbidden so much as to touch an entire man; eunuchs and women attended her. Selatre had reckoned herself profaned by Gerin's touch. Plainly, she would have preferred him to leave her in her bed for the monsters to devour.

So matters had stood then. Now, eleven years, three living children, and one small grave later, Selatre tilted up her face as Gerin came back into Castle Fox. He brushed his lips against hers. She smiled and took his hand. They walked back toward the Fox's place of honor near the hearth and near the altar to Dyaus close by it. The fat-wrapped thighbones of the stag Van, Geroge, and Tharma had killed smoked on the altar.

Selatre pointed to them. "So the king of the gods gets venison tonight."

"He'd better not be the only one," Gerin said in a voice intended to carry back to the kitchens, "or there'll be some cooks fleeing through the night with ghosts baying at their heels to drive them mad."

A serving girl set rounds of thick, chewy bread on the table in front of each feaster. When another servitor plopped a couple of still-sizzling ribs on Gerin's flatbread, it sopped up the grease and juices. The Fox reached out to a wooden saltcellar in front of him and sprinkled some salt onto the meat.

"I wish we had pepper," he said, fondly remembering the spices that had come up from the south till the Empire of Elabon sealed off the last mountain pass just before the werenight.

"Be thankful we still have salt," Selatre said. "We're beginning to run low on that. It hasn't been coming up the Niffet from the coast as it used to since the Gradi started raiding a couple of years ago."

"The Gradi," Gerin muttered under his breath. "As if the northlands didn't have troubles enough without them." North of the Niffet lay the forests in which the Trokmoi dwelt: or rather, had dwelt, for the fair-haired barbarians had swarmed south over the Niffet near the time of the were-night, and many still remained: some, like Fand, among Elabonians; others, such as Gerin's vassal Adiatunnus, in place of the locals, whom they had subjected, driven away, or slain.

The homeland of the Gradi lay north of the Trokmê country. Before coming down into Elabon, Van had been through the lands of both the Gradi and the Trokmoi. Gerin had seen a couple of Gradi at Ikos once, too: big, pale-skinned men with black hair, sweltering in furs. But, for the most part, the Trokmoi had kept the Elabonians from learning much about the Gradi and having much to do with them.

So it had been for generations. As Selatre had said, though, the Gradi had lately begun harrying the northlands' coastal regions by sea. Maybe they'd got word of disorder in the northlands and decided to take advantage of it. Maybe, too, their raids had nothing to do with whatever was going on locally, but had been spawned by some convulsion in their own country. Gerin did not know.

"Too much we don't know about the Gradi," he said, more to himself than to anyone else. Though he styled himself prince of the north, his power did not extend to the coast: none of the barons and dukes and petty lordlets by the sea acknowledged his suzerainty. If they were learning about the seaborne raiders, they kept that knowledge to themselves.

Selatre said, "I've been through the scrolls and codices in the library. Trouble is, they don't say anything about the Gradi except that there is such a people and they live north of the Trokmoi."

Gerin set his hand on hers. "Thanks for looking." When he'd brought her back to Fox Keep from Ikos, he'd taught her letters and set her in charge of the motley collection of volumes he called a library, more to give her a place of her own here than in the expectation she would make much of it.

But make something of it she had. She was as zealous now as he in finding manuscripts and adding them to the collection, and even more zealous in going through the ones they had and squeezing knowledge from them. If she said the books told little about the Gradi, she knew whereof she spoke.

She glanced down at the table. Compliments of any sort made her nervous, a trait she shared with Gerin and one that set them apart from most Elabonians, for whom bragging came natural as breathing.

"What are we going to do about the Gradi, Father?" Duren asked from across the table. "What can we do about them?"

"Watch and wait and worry," Gerin answered.

"Are they just raiding, do you suppose, or will they come to settle when they see how fragmented that part of the northlands is?" Selatre asked.

The Fox picked up his drinking jack and raised it in salute. "Congratulations," he told his wife. "You've given me something brand new to worry about. Here I spend half my time trying to figure out how to bundle the Trokmoi back across the Niffet from what ought to be a purely Elabonian land, and now I have to think about adding Gradi to the mix." He gulped ale and spat into the bosom of his tunic to avert the evil omen.

Selatre sent him a look he could not fathom until she murmured, "A purely Elabonian land?"

"Well, in a manner of speaking," he said, feeling his cheeks heat. Selatre's ancestors had dwelt in the northlands for years uncounted before Ros the Fierce added the province to the Empire of Elabon. They'd taken on Elabonian ways readily enough, and most of them spoke Elabonian these days, which was what had led him to make his remark. Still, differences lingered. Selatre's features were finer and more delicate than they would have been had she sprung of Elabonian stock: her narrow, pointed chin was a marker for those of her blood.

"I know what you meant," she said, her voice mischievous, "but since you pride yourself on being so often right, I thought surely you would take the correction in good part."

Gerin enjoyed being told he was wrong, even by his wife, no more than most other men. But before he could come back with a reply sardonic enough to suit him, one of Walamund's relatives shouted at Trasamir, "I know how you got that cursed dog to come when you called it. You—" The suggestion was remarkable for both its originality and its obscenity.

The Fox sprang to his feet. He could feel a vein pulse in his forehead, and was sure the old scar above one eye had gone pale, a sure sign he was furious. And furious he was. "You!" he snapped, his voice slicing through the racket in the great hall. Walamund's kinsman looked over to him in surprise. The Fox jerked a thumb toward the doorway. "Out! You can sleep in the courtyard on the grass and wash your mouth with water, not my good ale, for I'll waste no more of that on you. On your way home tomorrow, think about keeping your mind out of the midden."

"But, lord prince, I only meant—" the fellow began.

"I don't care what you meant. I care what you said," Gerin told him. "And I told you, out, and out I meant. One more word and it won't be out of the castle, it'll be out of the keep, and you can take your chances with wolves and night ghosts where no torches and sacrifices hold them at bay."

The foul-mouthed peasant gulped, nodded, and did not speak. He hurried out into the night, leaving thick, clotted silence behind him.

"Now," Gerin said into it, "where were we?"

No one seemed to remember, or to feel like hazarding a guess. Van said, "I don't know where we were, but I know where I'm going." He picked up Kor, who'd fallen asleep on the bench beside him, and headed for the stairs. Fand and Maeva followed, off to the big bed they all shared. The quarrel between Van and Fand hadn't flared again, so maybe it would be forgotten . . . till the next time, tomorrow or ten days down the road.

Once upon a time, Duren had been in the habit of falling asleep at feasts. Gerin sighed; remembering things like that and comparing them to how matters stood these days was a sign he wasn't getting any younger.

He looked around for Duren and didn't see him. He wouldn't be out in the courtyard, not with only a drunken, swill-mouthed peasant for company. More likely, he was back in the kitchens or in a corridor leading off from them, trying to slip his hands under a serving girl's tunic. He'd probably succeed, too: he was handsome, reasonably affable, and the son of the local lord to boot. Gerin remembered his own fumblings along those lines.

"Dyaus, what a puppy I was," he muttered.

Selatre raised one eyebrow. He didn't think she'd done that when he first brought her to Fox Keep; she must have got it from him. "What's that in aid of?" she asked.

"Not much, believe me," he answered with a wry chuckle. "Shall we follow Van and bring our children up to bed, too?"

Their younger son, named Blestar after Selatre's father (Gerin having named Duren and Dagref for his own brother and father, whom the Trokmoi had slain), lay snoring in her lap: he had only a couple of years to him. Dagref and Clotild were both trying to pretend they hadn't just yawned. The Fox gathered them up by eye. "Upstairs we go," he declared.

"Oh, Papa, do we have to?" Dagref said through another yawn. Along with belief in the gods, all children seemed to share an abiding faith that they had to deny the need for sleep under any and all circumstances.

Gerin did his best to look severe. Where his children were concerned, his best was none too good, and he knew it. He said, "Do you know what would happen to anyone else who presumed to argue with the prince of the north?"

"You'd cut off his head, or maybe stew him with prunes," Dagref said cheerfully. Gerin, who'd been taking a last swig from his drinking jack, sprayed ale onto the tabletop. Dagref said, "If Duren argued with you, would you stew *him* with prunes? Or isn't he part of 'everybody else'?"

Down in the City of Elabon, they'd had special schools to train the officials who interpreted the ancient and complex code of laws by which the Empire of Elabon functioned. The hairsplitting in which those schools indulged had once struck Gerin, who reveled in minutiae himself, as slightly mad: who could not only make such minute distinctions but enjoy doing it? Watching Dagref grow, he regretted being unable to send the boy south for legal training.

When he got upstairs, he opened the door to the chamber he shared with his wife and children and went inside to bring out a lamp. He lighted it at one of the torches flickering in a bronze wall sconce in the hallway, then used its weak glow to let Selatre go into the chamber and set Blestar at the edge of the big bed. Dagref and Clotild took turns using the chamber pot that stood by the side of the bed before getting in themselves, muttering sleepy good-nights. The straw in the mattress rustled as they lay down.

"Don't blow out the lamp," Selatre said quietly. "I need the pot myself."

"So do I, as a matter of fact," the Fox answered. "Ale."

He wondered if Duren would disturb them, coming

back later in the night. He didn't think so; he doubted his elder son would be sleeping in this bed tonight. Just in case, though, he shut the door without barring it. After he shoved the chamber pot against the wall so Duren wouldn't knock it over if he did come in, he blew out the lamp. Darkness and the heavy smell of hot fat filled the bedchamber.

The night was mild, not so much so that he felt like getting out of tunic and trousers and sleeping in his drawers, as he would when summer came, but enough that he didn't drag a thick wool blanket up over his chin and put a hot stone wrapped in flannel by his feet. He sighed and wriggled and twisted away from a stem of straw that was poking him in the ribs. Beside him, Selatre was making the same small adjustments.

Blestar snored on a surprisingly musical note. Dagref and Clotild wiggled around like their parents, also trying to get comfortable. "Stop poking me," Clotild complained.

"I wasn't poking you, I was just stretching out," Dagref answered, maddeningly precise as usual. "If I poke you, that's something I do on purpose." Usually, he would add, *like this*, and demonstrate. Tonight he didn't. That proved he was tired. Clotild didn't snap back at him, either.

Before long, their breathing smoothed out. Gerin yawned and stretched himself—carefully, so as not to bother anyone else. He yawned again, trying to lure sleep by sympathetic magic. Sleep declined to be lured.

Selatre was breathing very quietly, which meant she too was likely to be awake. When she slept, she sometimes snored. Gerin had never said anything about it. He wondered if he did the same. If he did, Selatre hadn't mentioned it. *Wonderful woman*, he thought.

Her voice reached him, a tiny thread of whisper: "Have you fallen asleep?"

"Yes, quite a while ago," he answered, just as softly. Dagref hadn't poked Clotild. Selatre did poke him now, right in the ribs, and found a sensitive spot. He had all he could do not to writhe and kick one of his children.

She started to poke him again. He grabbed her arm and pulled her close to him, that being the fastest way he could think of to keep her questing finger from making him jerk again. "You cheat," she said. "That's the only ticklish spot you have, and you won't let me get to it."

"I cheat," he agreed, and covered her right breast with his left hand. Through the thin linen of her long tunic, her nipple stiffened at his touch. The feel of her body pressed against his made him stiffen, too. He felt one eyebrow quirk upward into a question, but she couldn't see that in the dark. He put it into words: "Do you think they're sleeping soundly enough yet?"

"All we can do is find out," she answered. "If they do wake up, it would fluster you more than me. I grew up in a peasant's hut, remember: the whole of it about the size of this room. I never imagined having so much space as I found first at Ikos and then here at Fox Keep."

Thinking of the raised eyebrow he'd wasted, he said, "Well, if my ears turn red, it'll be too dark for the children to notice." He kissed her then, which struck him as a better idea under the circumstances—and, indeed, generally—than talking about his ears. His hand slid down from her breast to tug up the hem of her tunic.

They didn't hurry, both because they didn't want to wake the children and because, after a good many years together, friendly familiarity had taken the edge off passion. Presently, Selatre rolled over onto her side, facing away from Gerin. She lifted her top leg a little to let him slide in from behind, a quiet way of joining in more ways than one. Her breath sighed out as he entered her to the hilt. He reached over her to tease at her nipple again. The edge might have gone from their passion, but a solid core remained.

After they'd finished, Selatre said, "Did you put the pot by the wall? I think I'd better use it again." She slid out of bed and groped her way toward it. Gerin, meanwhile, separated his clothes from hers and got back into them. He suspected he had his drawers on backward, but resolved not to worry about it till morning.

When Selatre came back to bed, she put her drawers and tunic back on, too, then leaned over and unerringly planted a kiss on the end of his nose. He squeezed her. "If I wasn't sleepy before," he said, "I am now—or pleasantly tired, anyhow."

Selatre laughed at him. "You saved yourself in the nick of time there, didn't you?"

"Considering the history of this place since I took the rule after my father was killed, how could I do it any other way?" Gerin replied, and settled down to sleep. Laughing still, almost without voice, Selatre snuggled against him.

His eyelids were growing heavy when the bed frame in the next chamber started to creak. Selatre giggled, a sound different from her earlier laughter. "Maeva must have stayed awake longer than our brood did."

"Or maybe Kor woke up, just to be difficult," Gerin answered. "He has his mother's temper, all the way through. He'd better be a good swordsman when he grows up, because I have the feeling he'll need to be."

Selatre listened to the noises from the far side of the wall for a moment, then said, "His father's quite the mighty swordsman, by all I've seen."

"That's true any way you care to have it mean," Gerin agreed. "It's because of that, I suppose, that he and Fand are able to make up their quarrels. I almost wonder if they have them for the sake of making up."

"You're joking," Selatre said. After she'd thought it over, though, she shook her head against his chest. "No, you're not joking. But what an appalling notion. I couldn't live like that."

"Neither could I," he said, remembering fights he'd had with Fand back in the days when she was his lover as well as Van's. "My hair and beard would be white, not going gray, if I tried. But one of the things I've slowly come to figure out through the years is that not everybody works the same way I do."

"Some people never do figure that out." Selatre yawned. "One of the things I've slowly come to figure out over the years is that I can't do without sleep. Good night."

"Good night," Gerin said. He wasn't sure his wife even heard him: now her breathing was as deep and regular and—he smiled a little—raspy as that of their children. Sleep swallowed him moments later.

The peasants set out for their village early the next morning, Trasamir Longshanks leading Swifty the hound on a rope leash. Walamund's relative, rather to the Fox's disappointment, seemed not much worse for wear after his night in the courtyard. Uncharitably, Gerin wondered how often he'd passed out drunk between houses in his hamlet.

Bread and ale and cheese and an apple did for Gerin's breakfast. He was going down to see how the apples were holding out in the cellar when the lookout yelled, "A horseman approaching from out of the south, lord prince."

Gerin went out to the doorway of the great hall. "A horseman?" he called up. "Not a chariot?"

"A horseman," the sentry repeated. "One of our men, without a doubt."

He was right about that. The idea of getting up on a horse's back rather than traveling in wagon or chariot or cart was new in the northlands. As far as Gerin could discover, as far as widely traveled Van could say, it was new in all the world. One of the Fox's vassals, Duin the Bold, had come up with a trick that made staying mounted much easier: wooden rings that hung down from either side of a pad strapped around the horse's girth, so a man could use his hands for bow or spear without the risk of going over the animal's back.

Duin, though, had died fighting the Trokmoi just after the werenight. Without his driving energy, the device he invented advanced more slowly than it would have otherwise. If your father had ridden to war in a chariot, and your grandfather, and *his* grandfather . . . .

"It's Rihwin the Fox, lord prince," the sentry reported when the rider came close enough to recognize him.

"I might have known," Gerin muttered. That was true for a couple of reasons. For one, Rihwin had been some time away from Fox Keep. A couple of times a year, he went out to see how his numerous bastards were doing, and, no doubt, to try to sire some more of them. He had a fair-sized troop of by-blows scattered widely over the lands where Gerin's suzerainty ran, so his expeditions ate up a good deal of time.

And, for another, his love for the new extended to more than women. He'd come north with Gerin from the civilized heart of the Empire of Elabon bare days before the werenight for no better reason than that he craved adventure. Had riding horses been old and chariotry new, he would no doubt have become an enthusiastic advocate for the chariot. As things were, he probably spent more time on horseback than any other man in the northlands.

The gate crew let down the drawbridge. Rihwin rode into the courtyard of Fox Keep. He waved a salute to Gerin, saying, "I greet you, lord prince, my fellow Fox, valiant for your vassals, protector of your peasants, mild to merchants, and fierce against your foes."

"You've been in the northlands fifteen years and more now," Gerin said as Rihwin dismounted, "and you still talk like a toff from the city." Not only did Rihwin have a soft southern accent, he also remained fond of the elaborate phrasing and archaic vocabulary nobles from the City of Elabon used to show they had too much time on their hands.

A stable boy came up to lead Rihwin's horse to its stall. "Thank you, lad," he murmured before turning back to Gerin. "And why should I not proclaim my essence to the world at large?" A hand went up to the large gold hoop he wore in his left ear. So far as Gerin knew—and he likely knew more of the northlands than anyone else alive—no other man north of the High Kirs followed that style.

"Rihwin, save for keeping you out of the alepot as best I can, I've long since given up trying to make you over," he said.

Rihwin bowed, his handsome, mobile features twisting into a sly smile. "No small concession that, lord prince, and in good sooth I know it well, for where else has the victorious and puissant prince of the north retreated from any venture to which he set his hand?"

"I hadn't looked at it so," Gerin said thoughtfully. "You tempt me to go back to trying to reform you." Rihwin made a face at him. They both laughed. Gerin went on, "And how is your brood faring these days?"

"I have a new daughter—the mother says she's mine, anyhow, and since I lay with her at around the proper time, I'm willing to believe her—but I lost a son." Rihwin's face clouded. "Casscar had only three years: scarlet fever, his mother said. The gods be kind to his ghost. His mother was crying still, though it happened not long after I saw her last."

"She'll be grieving till they bury her," Gerin said, remembering the loss he and Selatre had had. He shook his head. "You know you shouldn't risk loving a child when it's very small, for so many of them never do live to grow big. But you can't help it: it's how the gods made us, I suppose."

About half the time, maybe more, a remark like that would have led Rihwin to make a philosophical rejoinder, and he and Gerin could have killed a pleasant stretch of time arguing about the nature of the gods and the reasons they'd made men and women as they had. The two of them were the only men in the northlands of whom Gerin knew who'd had a proper education down in the City of Elabon. That perforce kept them friendly even when they wore on each other: in an important way, they spoke the same language.

But now Rihwin said, "The other thing I wanted to tell you, lord prince, is something interesting I heard when I was out in the west, out well past Schild Stoutstaff's holding. When I went that way a few years ago, I met this yellow-haired Trokmê wench named Grainne and, one thing leading to another, these days I have myself a daughter in that village. The gods grant she does live to grow up, for she'll delight many a man's eye. She—"

Gerin stared down his nose at him. "Has this tale a point? Beyond the charm and grace of your daughter, I mean? If not, you'll have to listen to me going on about my children in return."

"Oh, I do that all the time anyhow," Rihwin said blithely, "whereas you need only put up with me a couple of times a year." Gerin staggered back as if he'd taken a thrust mortal. Chuckling, Rihwin said, "As a matter of fact, though, lord prince, the tale indeed has a point, though I own to being unsure precisely what it is. This village, you see, lies hard by the Niffet, and—"

"Did you get word of more Trokmoi planning to raid or, worse, settle?" Gerin demanded. "I'll hit them if you did, and hit them hard. Too cursed many woodsrunners this side of the Niffet already."

"If you will let me finish the tale, lord prince, rather than consistently interrupting, some of these queries may perhaps be answered," Rihwin replied. Gerin kicked at the grass, annoyed at himself. Rihwin had caught him out twice running now. The southerner went on, "Grainne told me that, not so long before I came to visit, she'd seen a new kind of boat on the river, like nothing on which she'd ever set eyes before."

"Well, what does she know of boats?" Gerin said. "She wouldn't have been down to the City of Elabon, now would she, to watch galleys on the Greater Inner Sea? All she'll have ever seen are little rowboats and rafts and those round little coracle things the Trokmoi make out of hides stretched over a wicker frame. You'd have to be a Trokmê to build a boat that doesn't know its front from its backside." He held up his hands. "No. Wait. I'm *not* interrupting. Tell me how this one was different."

"The Niffet bends a trifle, a few furlongs west of Grainne's village," Rihwin said. "There's a grove of beeches at the bend, with mushrooms growing under them. She was out gathering them with a wicker basket—which she showed me as corroborating evidence, for whatever it may be worth—when, through a screening of ferns, she spied this boat."

"Eventually, my fellow Fox, you're going to tell me about it," Gerin said. "Why not now?"

Rihwin gave him a hurt look before going on, "As you say, lord prince. By her description, it was far larger than anything that moved on the water she'd ever seen before, with a mast and sail and with some large but, I fear, indeterminate number of rowers laboring to either side."

"A war galley of some sort," Gerin said, and Rihwin nodded. Gerin continued, "You say she saw it through ferns? Lucky the rowers didn't spot her, or they'd likely have grabbed her and held her down and had their fun before they cut her throat. That'd be so no matter who they were—and, so far as I know, nobody's ever put a war galley on the Niffet. Do you suppose the Empire of Elabon has decided it wants the northlands back after all?"

"Under His indolent Majesty Hildor III?" Rihwin's

mobile features assumed a dubious expression. "It is, lord prince, improbable." But then he looked thoughtful. "On the other hand, we've had no word, or next to it, out of Elabon proper since the werenight, which is, by now, most of a generation past. Who can say with certainty whether the indolent posterior of Hildor III still warms the Elabonian throne?"

"A distinct point," Gerin said. "If it is the imperials—"

Rihwin raised a forefinger. "As you have several times in the course of this conversation, lord prince, you break in before I was able to impart salient information. While the ship and men Grainne saw may have been Elabonians, two significant features make me doubt it. First, while her Elabonian is fluent—much on the order of Fand's, including the spice thereof—she could not follow the sailors' speech. Admittedly, the ship was out on the river, so this is not decisive. But have you ever heard of an Elabonian ship mounting the shields of oarsmen and warriors between rowing benches?"

Gerin thought back to his days in the City of Elabon, and to the galleys he'd seen on the sea and tied up at the quays. He shook his head. "No. They always stow them down flat. Which leaves—"

He and Rihwin spoke together: "The Gradi."

"That's bad," Gerin said. He kicked again at the dirt and paced back and forth. "That's very bad, as a matter of fact. Having them raid the seacoast is one thing. But if they start bringing ships up the Niffet . . . Father Dyaus, a flotilla of them could beach right there, a few furlongs from Fox Keep, and land more men than we could hope to hold away from the walls. And we'd have scant warning of it, too. I need to send out messengers right away, to start setting up a river watch."

"It will not happen tomorrow, lord prince," Rihwin said soothingly. "Grainne watched this vessel turn around at the river bend and make its way back toward the west. The Gradi have not found Castle Fox."

"Not yet," Gerin answered; he borrowed trouble as automatically as he breathed, having seen from long experience that it came to him whether he borrowed or not, and that it was better met ahead of time when that proved possible. The Gradi, however, were not the only trouble he had, nor the most urgent. He asked Rihwin, "When you rode out to visit all your lady loves, did you go through Adiatunnus' holding?"

"Lord prince, I had intended to," Rihwin answered, "but when I came up to the margins of the lands he rules as your vassal, his guardsmen turned me away, calling me nothing but a stinking southron spy."

"He's not yet paid his feudal dues this year, either." Gerin's dark eyebrows lowered like stormclouds. "My guess is, he doesn't intend to pay them. He's spent the last ten years being sorry he ever swore me fealty, and he'll try breaking loose if he sees the chance."

"I would praise your wisdom more were what you foresee less obviously true," Rihwin answered.

"Oh, indeed," Gerin said. "All I had to do to gain his allegiance last time was work a miracle." Adiatunnus had made alliance with the monsters from under the temple at Ikos; when, at Gerin's urging, Mavrix and Biton routed them from the northlands, the proud Trokmê chieftain was overawed into recognizing the Fox as his overlord. Now Gerin sighed. "And if I want to keep that allegiance, all I have to do is work another one."

"Again, you have delivered an accurate summary of the situation," Rihwin agreed, "provided you mean keeping that allegiance through peaceable means. He may well prove amenable to persuasion by force, however."

"Always assuming we win the war, yes." Gerin's scowl grew blacker still. "We'll need to gather together a goodly force before we try it, though. Adiatunnus has made himself the biggest man among the Trokmoi who came over the Niffet in the time of the werenight; a whole great host of them will fight for him."

"I fear you have the right of it once more," Rihwin said. "He has even retained his stature among the woodsrunners while remaining your vassal, no mean application of the political art. As you say, suppressing him, can it be done, will involve summoning up all your other retainers."

"Which might give Grand Duke Aragis the excuse he needs to hit my southern frontier," Gerin said. "The Archer will recognize weakness when he sees it. The only reason he and I don't fight is that he's never seen it from me—till now."

"Will you then let Adiatunnus persist in his insolence?" Rihwin asked. "That would be unlike you."

"So it would," Gerin said, "and if I do, he'll be attacking me by this time next year. What choice have I, my fellow Fox? If I don't enforce my suzerainty, how long will I keep it?"

"Not long," Rihwin answered.

"Too right." Gerin kicked at the dirt once more. "I've always known I'd sooner have been a scholar than a baron, let alone a prince." With old friends, Gerin refused to take his title seriously. "There are times, though, when I think I'd sooner have run an inn like Turgis son of Turpin down in the City of Elabon than be a prince—or practiced any other honest trade, and some of the dishonest ones, too."

"Well, why not run off and start yourself an inn, then?" Rihwin poked his tongue into his cheek to show he didn't intend to be taken seriously. His hands deftly sketched the outlines of a big, square building. "By the gods, I can see it now: the hostelry of Gerin the Fox, all complaints cheerfully ignored! How the dour Elabonians and woad-dyed Trokmoi would throng to it as a haven from their journeys across the northlands to plunder one another!"

"You, sirrah, are a desperately deranged man," Gerin said. Rihwin bowed as if he'd just received a great compliment, which was not the effect Gerin had wanted to create. He plunged ahead: "And if I did start an inn, who'd keep the Trokmoi and the Elabonians—to say nothing of the Gradi—from plundering *me*?"

"By all means, let us say nothing of the Gradi," Rihwin said. "I wish my lady love there had never set eyes on that ship of theirs. Father Dyaus willing, none of us will see such ships with our own eyes."

But Gerin refused to turn aside from the inn he did not and never would have. "The only way to keep such a place is to have an overlord strong enough to hold bandits at bay and wise enough not to rob you himself. And where is such a fellow to be found?"

"Aragis the Archer is strong enough," Rihwin said

teasingly. "Were I a bandit in his duchy, I'd sooner leap off a cliff than let him get his hands on me."

Gerin nodded. "If he were less able, I'd worry about him less. But one fine day he'll die, and all his sons and all his barons will squabble over his lands in a war that'll make the unending mess in Bevon's holding look like a children's game by comparison. We'll not have that here, I think, when I'm gone."

"There I think you have reason, lord prince," Rihwin said, "and so, being the best of rulers, needs must continue in that present post without regard for your obvious and sadly wasted talents as taverner."

"Go howl!" Gerin said, throwing his hands in the air. "I know too well I'm stuck with the bloody job. It *is* a hardship, you know: on account of it, I have to listen to loons like you."

"Oh! I am cut to the quick!" Rihwin staggered about as if pierced by an arrow, then miraculously recovered. "Actually, I believe I shall go in and drink some ale. That accomplished, I shall take more pleasure in howling." With a bow to Gerin, he hied himself off toward the great hall.

"Try not to drink so much you forget your name," Gerin called after him. The only answer Rihwin gave was a finger-twiddling wave. Gerin sighed. Short of locking up the ale jars, he couldn't cut Rihwin off. His fellow Fox didn't turn sullen or vicious when he drank; he remained cheerful, amiable, and quite bright—but he could be bright in the most alarmingly foolish ways. Gerin worried about how often he got drunk, but Gerin, by nature, worried about everything that went on around him.

Right now, though, worrying about Rihwin went into the queue along with worrying about the Gradi. Both were a long way behind worrying about Adiatunnus. The Trokmê chieftain was liable to have the strength to set up on his own if he chose to repudiate Gerin's overlordship, and if he did set up on his own, the first thing he'd do would be to start raiding the lands of Gerin's vassals . . . even more than he was already.

The Fox muttered something unpleasant into his beard. Realizing he never was going to be able to drive all the Trokmoi out of the northlands and back across the Niffet into their gloomy forests came hard. One of the bitter things life taught you was that not all your dreams came true, no matter how you worked to make them real.

Up in the watchtower atop Castle Fox, the lookout shouted, "A chariot approaches, lord prince!"

"Just one?" Gerin asked. Like any sensible ruler, he made sure trees and undergrowth were trimmed well away from the keep and from the roads in his holding, the better to make life difficult for bandits and robbers.

"Aye, lord prince, just the one," the sentry answered. Gerin had chosen his lookouts from among the longer-sighted men in his holding. As it had a few times before, that proved valuable now. After a few heartbeats, the lookout said, "It's Widin Simrin's son, lord prince."

The drawbridge had not gone up after Rihwin arrived. Widin's driver guided his two-horse team into the keep. Widin jumped out of the car before it stopped rolling. He was a strong, good-looking young man in his late twenties, and had held a barony southwest of Fox Keep for more than half his life: his father had died in the chaos after the werenight. Whenever Gerin saw him, he was reminded of Simrin.

"Good to see you," Gerin said, and then, because Widin's keep was a couple of days' travel away and men seldom traveled without urgent need, he added, "What's toward?"

"Lord prince, it's that thieving, skulking demon of an Adiatunnus, that's what," Widin burst out. Worrying about the Trokmoi was already at the head of Gerin's list, which was the only thing that kept it from vaulting higher. Widin went on, "He's run off cattle and sheep both, and burned a peasant village for the sport of it, best I can tell."

"Has he?" Gerin asked. Widin, who had never studied philosophy, did not know a rhetorical question when he heard one, and so nodded vigorously. Gerin was used to such from his vassals; it no longer depressed him as it once had. He said, "If Adiatunnus is at war with one of my vassals, he's also at war with me. He will pay for what he's done to you, and pay more than he ever expected."

His voice held such cold fury that even Widin, who'd

brought him this word in hope of raising a response, drew back a pace. "Lord prince, you sound like you aim to tumble his keep down around his ears. That would be—"

"—A big war?" Gerin broke in. Widin nodded again, this time responsively. Gerin went on, "Sooner or later, Adiatunnus and I are going to fight a big war. I'd rather do it now, on my terms, than later, on his. The gods have decreed that we can't send all the woodsrunners back over the Niffet. Be it so, then. But we can—I hope—keep them under control. If we can't do even that much, what's left of civilization in the northlands?"

"Not much," Widin said. Now Gerin nodded, but as he did so he reflected that, even with the Trokmoi beaten, not much civilization was left in the northlands.

II

Chariots and a few horsemen rolled out of Fox Keep over the next couple of days, heading east and west and south to summon Gerin's vassals and their retainers to his castle for the war against Adiatunnus. He sent out the men heading west with more than a little apprehension: they would have to pass through Schild Stoutstaff's holding on the way to the rest of the barons who recognized the Fox as their overlord, and Schild, sometimes, was almost as balky a vassal as Adiatunnus himself.

Duren went wild with excitement when Gerin decided on war. "Now I can fight beside you, Father!" he said, squeezing the Fox in a tight embrace. "Now, maybe, I can earn myself an ekename."

"Duren the Fool, perhaps?" Gerin suggested mildly. Duren stared at him. He sighed, feeling like a piece of antiquity unaccountably left adrift in the present-day world. "I don't suppose there's any use telling you this isn't sport we're talking about. You really maim, you really kill. You can really get maimed, you can really get killed."

"You can prove your manhood!" No, Duren wasn't listening. "Tumbling a serving girl is all very well—better than all very well—but to fight! 'To battle your enemy with bright-edged bronze'—isn't that what the poet says?"

"That's what Lekapenos says, all right. You quoted him very well." Gerin looked up to the sky. What was he supposed to do with a boy wild for war? Did justifying being wild for war by quoting from the great Sithonian epic poem mean Duren was properly civilized himself, or did it mean he, as the Trokmoi sometimes did, had acquired a civilized veneer with which to justify his barbaric impulses? Father Dyaus gave no answers.

Van came out of Castle Fox. Duren ran over to him, saying, "It'll be war! Isn't that wonderful!"

"Oh, aye, it's wonderful, if you come through in one piece," Van answered. Duren took the half of the answer he was hoping to hear and went into the hall, singing a bloodthirsty song that had nothing to do with Lekapenos: Gerin knew the minstrel who, fool that he was, had translated it from the tongue of the Trokmoi. Van turned round to look after Duren. He chuckled. "The fire burns hot in him, Fox."

"I know." Gerin didn't try hiding that the fire didn't burn hot in him. He said, "This is needful, but—" and shrugged.

"Ahh, what's the matter? You don't want to be a hero?" Van teased.

"I've *been* a hero, over and over again," Gerin answered. "And what has it brought me, besides always another war? Not bloody much."

"You hadn't decided to be a hero when you went to rescue Selatre from the monsters, you wouldn't have the wife you've got now," his friend pointed out. "You'd not have three of your children, either. You might still be sharing Fand with me instead, you know." Van rolled his eyes.

"Now you've given me a defense of heroism indeed!" Gerin said. Both men laughed. Gerin went on, "But I don't see you rushing toward the fight the way you once did, either."

Van looked down at his toes. "I'm not so young as I used to be, either," he said, as if the admission embarrassed him. "Some days, I'm forced to remember it. My bones creak, my sight is getting long, my wind is shorter than it used to be, I can't futter three times a night every night any more—" He shook his head. "If you knew how long you were going to be old, you'd enjoy the time when you're younger more."

Gerin snorted. "If you'd done any more enjoying while you were younger, either you or the world wouldn't have lived through it. Maybe you and the world both."

"Ah, well, you have something there," Van answered. "But it's like you said, Captain: I've been a hero, too, and now what am I? I'm the fellow who, if some Trokmê brings me down and takes my head to nail over his doorposts, I turn him into a hero. So they come after me, whatever fight I happen to be in, and after a while it starts to wear thin."

"There you have it," Gerin agreed. "After a while, it starts to wear thin. And the ones who do come after you, they're always the young, hot, eager ones. And when you're not so young any more, and not so eager any more, and it has to be done anyhow, then it turns into work, as if we were serfs going out to weed the fields, except we pull up lives instead of nettles."

"But nettles don't uproot themselves and try pulling you up if you leave 'em in the fields," Van observed. He looked thoughtful. "Can't you magic Adiatunnus to death, if you don't fancy fighting him?"

"Not you too!" The Fox gave his friend a massively dubious look. Hearing vassals and peasants plead cases before him for years had given him a first-rate look of that description. Hardened warrior though Van was, he gave back a pace before it. Gerin said, "I could try spelling Adiatunnus, I suppose. I would try it, if I didn't think I was likelier to send myself to the five hells than the cursed Trokmê. Putting a half-trained wizard to work is like turning a half-trained cook loose in the kitchen: you don't know what he'll do, but you have a pretty good idea it'll turn out bad."

"Honh!" Van shook his head again. "All this time as a prince, and you still don't think you're as good as you really are. All the magics you've tried that I know of, they've worked fine."

"That's only because you don't know everything there is to know," Gerin retorted. "Ask Rihwin about his ear one day. It's not a story he's proud of, but he may tell it to you. And if you try working a spell with death in it, you'll get a death, all right, one way or another."

"What's the good of having all those what-do-you-call-'ems—grimoires—in your book-hoard if you won't use 'em?"

"I didn't say I wouldn't use them," Gerin snapped. "I do use them—for small things, safe things, where even if I go wrong the disaster will be small, too . . . and for things so great that having the magic fail won't be a bigger catastrophe than not trying it. Putting paid to Adiatunnus is neither the one nor the other."

"Honh!" Van repeated. "I may be turning into an old man, but you're turning into an old woman."

"You'll pay for that, by Dyaus!" Gerin sprang at the bigger man, got a foot behind his ankle, shoved, and knocked Van to the ground. With an angry roar, the outlander hooked an arm around the Fox's leg and dragged him down, too, but Gerin managed to land on top.

Men came running from all parts of the keep to watch them wrestle. As Gerin tried to keep Van from tearing his shoulder out of its socket, he reflected that they'd been grappling with each other for too many years. When they'd first begun, his tricks had let him beat Van as often as he lost. Now Van knew all the tricks, and he was still bigger and stronger than the Fox.

"I'm the prince, curse it," Gerin panted. "Doesn't that entitle me to win?" Van laughed at him. Any ruler in the northlands who tried to make more of his rank than was due him got laughed at, even Aragis.

Strength wouldn't serve, the usual tricks wouldn't serve, which left—what? Van tried to throw Gerin away. To the outlander's surprise, Gerin let him. The Fox flew through the air and landed with a thud and a groan, as if he'd had the wind knocked out of him. Blood up, Van leaped onto him to finish the job of pinning him to the dirt.

Gerin stuck an elbow right into the pit of the outlander's stomach. Van folded up. It wasn't anything he wanted to do, but he couldn't help himself; he had to fight to breathe, and, for the first moments of that fight, you always seemed to yourself to be losing. Gerin had no trouble pinning him instead of the other way round.

Van finally managed to suck in a couple of hissing gasps.

"Fox, you—cheat," he wheezed, his face a dusky red because he was so short of air.

"I know," Gerin said cheerfully. When his friend could breathe again, he helped pull him to his feet. "Most of the time, they pay off on what you do, not how you do it."

"And I thought I had all your tricks down." Van sounded chagrined, not angry. "It got to the point where you hadn't come up with anything new in so long, I didn't think you could. Shows what I know."

"Shows I got tired of having that great tun you call a body squashing me flat every time we wrestled," Gerin answered. "Actually, I used that ploy of seeming helpless against Aengus the Trokmê—remember him? The chief of the clan Balamung the wizard came from? I let the air out of him with my sword, not my elbow."

"Felt like your sword," Van grumbled, lifting up his tunic as if to see whether he was punctured. He had a red mark where Gerin's elbow had got home; it would probably turn into a bruise. But, considering the scars that furrowed his skin, reminders of a lifetime of wandering and strife, the mark was hardly worth noting. He rubbed at himself and let the tunic fall. "I should have been wearing my corselet. Then you'd have banged your elbow and not my poor middle."

"And you talk about me cheating!" Gerin said, full of mock dudgeon.

"So I do," Van said. "D'you care to wrestle again, to see if you can befool me twice?"

"Are you daft?" Gerin answered. "These days, it's a gift from the gods when I can fool you once. I'm going in for a jack of ale to celebrate." Van trailed after him, undoubtedly having in mind a jack of ale with which to drown his own discomfiture.

Before Gerin got to the entrance of the great hall, someone small came dashing out and kicked him in the shin. "Don't you hurt my papa!" Kor shouted. When Gerin bent down and tried to move him aside, he snapped at the Fox's hand.

"Easy there, boy." Van picked up his son. "He didn't do me any great harm, and it was a fair fight." No talk of illicit elbows now. Van carefully gentled Kor down: his son took after Fand in temperament, and Gerin supposed the patience Van needed to live with her—when he did live with her—came in handy for trying to keep the boy somewhere near calm, too.

After his ale, Gerin went out to the peasant village close by the keep. He had a pretty good notion of how the village stood for supplies and how much it could spare when his vassals and their retainers started arriving for the fight against Adiatunnus. The short answer was, not much. He wanted to see by how much the long answer differed from the short one.

The old village headman, Besant Big-Belly, would have whined and wheezed and pleaded poverty. His replacement, Carlun Vepin's son, was working in the fields as Gerin approached. The Fox nodded approvingly. Besant hadn't been fond of work of any description. Since his passing, yields from the village had gone up. That probably meant Gerin should have replaced him years before, but far too late to worry about that now. One of the five hells was said to have enormous water wheels in which lazy men had to tread forever, emptying buckets of boiling water onto themselves. For Besant's sake, Gerin hoped that wasn't so.

When Carlun spotted Gerin, he came trotting over to him. "Lord prince!" he called, giving the Fox something between a nod and a bow. "How may I serve you this afternoon?"

"How's your store of grain and beans and smoked meat and such holding up?" Gerin asked, hoping he sounded casual but doubting he sounded casual enough to make Carlun give him a quick, rash answer.

He didn't. The headman's face was thin and clever. "Not so well as I'd like, lord prince," he answered. "We had a long, hard winter, as you must recall, and so didn't get to plant till late this spring. The apples haven't been all they should on account of that, either, and the plums are coming in slow, too, so we've been drawing on the stores more than I would if I had other choices. Cabbages have done well, I will say," he added, as if to throw the Fox a bone of consolation.

"Let's have a look at the tallies for what you've used up," Gerin said.

"I'll fetch them, lord prince." Carlun trotted off toward the wattle-and-daub hut he shared with his wife and their four—or was it five?—children. He came out a moment later with a couple of sheets of parchment.

Even before the werenight, Gerin had begun teaching a few of the brighter peasants in his holding to read. His time in the City of Elabon had convinced him ignorance was an enemy as dangerous as the Trokmoi. When he'd begun his scheme, he hadn't thought of its also having thoroughly practical uses: a man who could read could keep records much more accurate than those proffered by a man relying solely on his memory.

Carlun probably inked his pen with blackberry juice, but that didn't bother the Fox. Neither did the headman's shaky scrawl. Here was the barley, here was the wheat— Gerin took a look at the records, took a look around the village, and started to laugh.

"Lord prince?" Did Carlun sound a trifle apprehensive? If he didn't, he should have. But he did: he was clever enough to know he hadn't been clever enough with the records.

"You'll have to do better than that if you're going to cheat me," Gerin said. "Not mentioning the storage pits off to the east there and hoping I wouldn't notice doesn't do the job. I remember you have them even if you didn't write anything about them here."

"Ah, a pestilence!" Carlun said. Like the Fox, he kicked at the dirt in anger and frustration. Carlun World-Bestrider, for whom he was named, had been the greatest emperor in Elabonian history. Now he saw even his little headmanship in danger. If Gerin raised someone else to take his place, he'd never live it down, not if he stayed in the village till he was ninety. "What—what will you do with me, lord prince?"

"Hush. I'm not finished here yet," Gerin said, and then fell silent again while he methodically went through the rest of the parchment. Carlun waited and squirmed. The Fox looked up. "You're right. The cabbages have done well."

Carlun jerked as if a wasp had stung him. Then he realized Gerin hadn't ordered him cast down from his small height. Gerin, in fact, hadn't said anything about his fate at all. "Lord prince?" he asked in a tiny voice, as if not willing to admit hope still lived in him.

"Oh, aye—about you." The matter might have slipped Gerin's mind. He turned brisk: "Well, it's simple enough. You can't be headman here any more. That's pikestaff plain."

Carlun took the blow like a warrior. "As you wish, lord prince," he said tonelessly. "Dare I ask you to give me leave to travel to some village far away in the lands you hold? That way, maybe, my family and I will be able to hold up our heads."

"No, that's impossible," Gerin said, and, for the first time, Carlun's shoulders slumped in dismay. Gerin went on, "Can't do it, I'm afraid. No, I'm going to move you into Fox Keep instead."

"Lord prince, I—" Carlun suddenly seemed to hear what the Fox had said. He gaped. "Into Fox Keep?" His gaze swung toward the timbers of the palisade. "Why?"

With a lot of lords, the question wouldn't have needed asking. You brought a peasant inside a keep so you could take all the time you wanted tormenting him with all the tools you had. But Gerin did not operate that way, and never had. He took a certain somber pride that his serfs understood as much.

It was, evidently, the only thing Carlun understood. In an exasperation partly feigned and partly quite genuine, Gerin said, "Father Dyaus above, man, don't you see you're the first of all the peasants I've taught who's ever tried to cheat me with words and numbers?"

"I'm sorry, lord prince," Carlun said miserably. "If only I could have another chance, I'd serve you well."

"I'll give you another chance," Gerin told him, "and a proper one this time. How would you like to keep accounts for all the lands I hold, not for this one little village? I've been doing it myself, but each day is only so long. Oh, I'll look over your shoulder, and so will Selatre, but I've dreamt for years of finding a man at home with numbers to whom I could give the job. If you're at home enough with numbers to try cheating with them, you may be the man to try. If you make good, you'll be better off there than you ever could be here, headman or no. Are you game for it?"

"Lord prince!" Carlun fell to his knees. "I'll be your man forever. I'll never cheat again, not by so much as a bean. I'll do whatever you ask of me, learn whatever you set before me—"

Gerin believed the last part. He was less sure of the rest. He'd been down to the City of Elabon and seen how arrogant imperial treasury officials—indeed, all imperial officials—could get. He didn't want men acting in his name behaving like that. Going through histories and chronicles, though, warned him they were liable to behave like that no matter what he wanted them to do. Despite Carlun's fervent protestations, they were also likely to see to it that silver and grain and other good things ended up in their hands rather than in the treasury.

"Get up," he told Carlun, his voice rough. "You're already my man forever. I'll thank you to remember it in better ways than this." He shook the offending parchments in Carlun's face. The headman quailed again. Gerin went on, "The other thing to keep in mind is, you're like a dog that's bitten once. If you cheat again and I find out about it, you'll wish you'd never been born, I promise you that. I've never crucified a man in all the years I've ruled this holding, but that would tempt me to change my mind."

"I already swore, lord prince, I'd not take even a bean that wasn't mine, and I meant every word of what I said." Carlun gabbled out the words. Was he trying to convince himself as well as the Fox? No, probably not, Gerin decided. He meant what he said—now. But it was a rare treasurer who died poor. Gerin shrugged. Time would tell the tale.

"I didn't mean to frighten you—too much," Gerin said, with a grin lacking only Geroge's fangs to make it truly fearsome. Carlun had picked a stupid way to cheat the first time. As he got more familiar with the numbers he juggled, he was liable to get more adept at concealing his thefts, too. Again, though, time would tell. "Go on, go let your wife know what we're going to do, then head up to the keep. Tell Selatre what I've sent you for—and why."

"Y-yes, lord prince," the newly promoted larcenous headman said.

But when he turned to go, Gerin held up a hand. "Wait. If you're leaving the village, with whom should I replace you?"

An evil gleam kindled in Carlun's eyes. "The one who complains most is Tostrov Waterdrinker. I'd like to see how he'd shape in the job if he had it."

"Tostrov?" Gerin rubbed his chin. "Aye, he does complain a lot, doesn't he? But no, he has no other virtues I can think of. No one would pay him any mind. Try again, and seriously this time."

"Aye, lord prince." Carlun hesitated, then said, "The man my sister married, Herris Bigfoot, is no fool, and he works hard. People respect him, too. You could do worse."

"Mm, so I could. I'll think on that," Gerin said. He slapped the parchments against his knee. They made a dry, rustling sound, as if they were dead leaves rubbing one another. "Now, back to the business I came here for. With that stored grain you didn't bother writing down" —he watched in some satisfaction as Carlun went pink— "how are you fixed for stores?"

He thought about adding something like, *If you still tell me you're starving, I'm going to open up those storage pits and see for myself*. In the end, he didn't; he wanted to see how Carlun would react without the goad. The headman hesitated, visibly thinking through the answers he might give. Gerin hid a smile: no, Carlun wasn't used to dealing with someone who was liable to be trickier than he. After a pause that stretched a couple of heartbeats too long, he replied, "Lord prince, we're—not too badly off, though I hate to say that so early in the year."

"And you have plenty of cabbages," the Fox added. Carlun squirmed. "Well, never mind that. We'll need some of what you have, to feed the warriors who'll be gathering here for war against Adiatunnus."

Carlun licked his lips. "You'll be drawing more than the customary dues from us, then?"

Was that a hint of reproach in his voice? It was, the Fox decided. He eyed Carlun with a mixture of annoyance and admiration. The headman would not have dared protest to any other ruler in the northlands: of that Gerin was sure. Most overlords thought, *What does ruling mean but taking what I want and what I'm strong enough to grab?* But the Fox, so far as he could, tried to substitute custom and even the beginning of law for naked theft.

He fixed Carlun with an unpleasant stare. "I could say the overage is forfeit as punishment for trying to cheat me." After watching the serf writhe, though, he said, "I won't. It's not the village's fault you cheated. It had better not be, anyhow." He stared again.

"Oh, no, lord prince," Carlun said quickly. "My idea. All mine."

No one from the village had come to complain he was cheating the Fox. Maybe the other peasants hadn't known. Maybe they'd hoped he'd get away with it. No proof, and Gerin didn't feel like digging. "I'll believe you," he said, "No, I won't simply take it. For whatever we exact over the set dues, I'll ease your labor in the forests and on the Elabon Way and such."

"Thank you, lord prince," Carlun said. Before Gerin could find any other awkward questions with which to tax him, he hurried back toward the village. The Fox had told him to do so, after all, and didn't take offense.

Still holding the parchments, Gerin stood a while in thought. From what he knew of Herris Bigfoot, Carlun's brother-in-law wouldn't make a bad headman. The only trouble he foresaw was that he hadn't taught Herris to read. Record-keeping here would go downhill for a while.

Or would it? Herris wasn't stupid. Maybe he could learn. You didn't need to know much in the way of reading and writing to keep track of livestock and produce. The Fox shaded his eyes with one hand and peered out over the fields. He was starting to have trouble reading these days, having to hold manuscripts farther from his eyes because his sight was lengthening. Out past arm's length, though, nothing was wrong with the way he saw.

There stood Herris, talking and laughing with a woman who, Gerin saw, was not Carlun's sister. He shrugged. He hadn't heard anything to make him think Herris was doing anything scandalous, so he wouldn't worry about this. He went over to Herris, noting as he did so that the barley was coming in well.

Carlun's brother-in-law watched him approach. Herris' friend quickly got back to work weeding. "You want something with me, lord prince?" Herris asked. "I saw you talking with Carlun, and—"

"How would you like his job?" the Fox asked bluntly.

The woman busy pulling weeds let out a startled gasp. Herris scratched his head. He didn't look or act as sharp as Carlun, but Gerin knew that didn't necessarily mean anything. After the pause for thought, Herris said, "It depends, lord prince. How come you don't want him there no more?"

Gerin nodded in approval—loyalty to your kin seldom went to waste. He explained the new post for which he wanted Carlun (though not the cheating that made him think Carlun might be right for it), finishing, "And he said you'd do for headman here. Thinking about it, I'd say he's likely right, if you want the job."

"I do, lord prince, and thank you," Herris said. "I'd've felt different, I expect, if you were giving him the sack for no good reason."

"No," Gerin said, again not mentioning he had a good reason if he wanted to use it. He smacked the rolled-up parchments against his leg once more. "There is one other thing—I know you don't have your letters, so I'm going to want you to learn them if you can. That way, you'll have an easier time keeping track of things here."

Herris pointed to the accounts Carlun had kept. "May I see those, lord prince?" Gerin handed them to him. He unrolled them and, to the Fox's surprise, began to read them out. He stumbled a couple of times, but did well enough on the whole.

"I *know* I didn't teach you your letters," Gerin said. "Where did you learn them?"

Herris looked worried. "Am I in trouble, lord prince?" Only after the Fox shook his head did the peasant say, "Carlun taught 'em to me. He didn't know he was doing anything wrong, swear by Dyaus he didn't. He learned 'em to me and a couple-three others, he did. It was a way to pass the time, nothin' more, that's for true."

"It's all right," Gerin said absently. "Don't worry about it." He shook his head, altogether bemused. So they'd been learning letters in the peasant huts, had they, instead of rolling dice and drinking ale? No, more likely alongside of rolling dice and drinking ale. A lot of nobles in the northlands reckoned serfs nothing more than domestic animals that chanced to walk on two legs. The Fox had never been of that school, but this caught him off guard. If you let learning put down one root, it would put out half a dozen on its own—unless, of course, the Trokmoi yanked them all out of the ground. "Can you write as well as read?" he asked Herris.

"Not as good as Carlun can," the peasant answered, "but maybe good enough so you can make out the words. The numbers, they're not hard."

"No, eh?" Was he boasting? Gerin decided to find out. "Take a look at the numbers on these sheets here. Tell me what you think is interesting about them."

Herris scratched his head thoughtfully, then went over the records his brother-in-law had kept. Gerin didn't say anything, but rocked from heels to toes and back again, giving Herris all the time he wanted. He couldn't think of a better test for the prospective headman's wits and honesty both.

He was beginning to think Herris either less honest or less bright than he'd hoped when the peasant coughed and said, "Uh, lord prince, is there another sheet somewheres?"

"No." The Fox kept his voice neutral. "Should there be?"

"You said you were giving Carlun this fancy spot at Fox Keep?" Herris asked. Gerin nodded. Herris looked worried. "Him and me, we've always got on well. I'd hate to have him think I was telling tales, but . . . we've got more grain than these here parchments show."

"Herris!" The woman who was weeding spoke his name reproachfully. Then, too late, she remembered with whom he was talking. She bent down and started pulling plants out of the ground as fast as she could.

"Good," Gerin said. "You'll do. You'll definitely do."

"Lord prince?" Herris was floundering.

"I never told Carlun not to cheat me," the Fox explained. "Of course, that was only because it hadn't occurred to me he'd try, but still, the fact remains, so how am I to blame him? In a way, I'm glad to see learning take hold, with him and with you. But only in a way—bear that in mind. I've warned him what will happen if he tries any more cheating, and I would advise you to think very hard about that, too. Do we understand each other?"

"Oh, yes, lord prince," Herris said, so sincerely that he either meant it or was a better liar than Gerin thought. One way or the other, the Fox would find out.

Chariots began rattling into Fox Keep, by ones and twos and sometimes by fours and fives. As they arrived, Gerin's vassals hung their armor on the walls of the great hall. The firelight from the hearth and torches made the shining bronze molten, almost bloody. That seemed fitting, for bloody work lay ahead.

Bevander Bevon's son said, "Lord prince, is all quiet with Aragis the Archer? If the grand duke gets wind of what we're about here, he's liable to jump us while we're busy."

"I've worried about the same thing myself," the Fox agreed, eyeing Bevander with considerable respect. The man was not the greatest warrior the gods ever made, but he knew intrigue. He and his father and brothers had fought a multicornered civil war for years; any man who couldn't keep track of who'd last betrayed whom soon paid the price.

Bevander went on, in meditative tones, "Or, on the other hand, Aragis might want to let us fight Adiatunnus and *then* attack. If we and the Trokmoi were both weakened, he might sweep us all into the Niffet and style himself king."

"If he wants the title, he's a fool, and whatever else Aragis is, he's no fool," Gerin answered. "I have a better claim to call myself king than he does, by the gods, but you don't see me doing it. If any man styles himself king, that'll be a signal for all the other nobles in the northlands to join together and pull him down."

"If any man styles himself king who hasn't earned it, you mean," Bevander said. "If Aragis beats you and the woodsrunners both, who could say he has no right to the title?

You should use some of your magic powers, lord prince, and see what Aragis intends when you move against the Trokmoi."

Like so many other people in the northlands, Bevander was convinced Gerin had strong magical powers because he'd cleared the land of the monsters from under Biton's shrine at Ikos. The Fox knew only too well that had been two parts desperation to one part sorcery. He hadn't advertised the fact, wanting his foes to think him more fearsome than he was. That created another problem, as solutions have a way of doing: his friends also thought him more fearsome than he was.

Now, though, he paused thoughtfully. "I may do that," he said at last. Scrying was not likely to be a form of magic particularly dangerous to his health. He didn't know how accurate the spells would prove; in peering into the future, you tried to navigate through a web of possibilities expanding so rapidly that even a god had trouble following the links.

Bevander beamed. "May you have good fortune with it," he said. He swelled with the self-importance of a man who's had a suggestion taken.

Gerin eyed him as he walked away, strutting just a little. He had wit enough to be dangerous had his ambition matched it. Having obtained the lion's share of Bevon's barony for backing the Fox in the last fight against Adiatunnus, though, he'd been satisfied with that—and with finally getting the upper hand on his brothers—ever since.

For his part, Gerin was satisfied to remain prince rather than king. The only trouble was, no one believed him when he said as much.

Selatre came into the library. "Hello," she said to the Fox. "I didn't expect to find you here." Ever since he'd taught her to read, she'd taken the chamber where he stored his scrolls and codices as her private preserve.

"I'm getting away from the racket of my barons," he said, and then, because he didn't like telling her half-truths, "and I'm looking in the grimoires to see what sort of scrying spell I can cast that's least likely to turn me into a salamander."

"I wouldn't want that," Selatre said seriously. "Salamanders aren't good at raising children, let alone running a principality." She walked over and ran a hand down his arm. "I suspect they're also, mm, less than desirable in certain other areas."

"I daresay you're right," Gerin answered. "The gods only know how we'd manage to put a pond in the bedchamber." As Selatre snorted, he went on, warming to the theme, "Or we could go up to the Niffet and make sport there, always hoping no big pike came along at the worst possible moment."

"I'm leaving," Selatre said with more dignity than the words really needed. "It's plain enough you won't keep your mind on what you're doing if I'm here to distract you."

The Fox grinned over his shoulder, then returned to the grimoires. If half what they said was true, seeing into the future was so easy, no one should ever have needed to consult Biton's Sibyl down at Ikos. Of course, if half what the grimoires said was true, anyone who read them would have more gold than he knew what to do with and live to be three hundred years old. Knowing which grimoire to trust was as important as anything else when it came to sorcery.

"Here, this ought to do it," the Fox said at last, picking a spell from a codex he'd brought back from the City of Elabon. He closed the book, tucked it under his arm, and carried it out of Castle Fox and over to the small hut near the stables where he worked his magic.

Every time he went in there, even if it was for nothing more elaborate than trying to divine where a sheep had strayed, he wondered if he would come out again. He knew how much he knew—just enough to be dangerous—and also how much he didn't know, which gave him pause about using the knowledge he had.

He opened the grimoire. The divining spell he'd chosen, unlike a lot of them, required no wine. Wine grapes would not grow in the northlands. Even if they had, he would have been leery of using what they yielded. His previous encounters with Mavrix, the Sithonian god of wine, made him anxious never to have another.

"Oh, a pestilence," he muttered. "I should have brought

fire with me." After filling a lamp with perfumed linseed oil, he went back to the castle, got the lamp going at a torch, and carried it over to the hut. He felt stares at his back; if his vassals hadn't noticed before what he was doing, they did now. Whatever enthusiasm they had, they hid very well.

He set the lamp on a wooden stand above his worktable. That done, he rummaged in a drawer under the table till he found and pulled out a large quartz crystal. The grimoire said the crystal was supposed to be flawlessly pure. He looked at it, shrugged, and started to chant. It was what he had. If he didn't use it, he couldn't work the spell.

As with a lot of spells, this one had the more difficult passes for the left hand. The Fox suspected that was intentional, to make the spells more likely to fail. It bothered him not at all, since he was left-handed. His magic did not go wrong on account of clumsiness. Lack of training and lack of talent, however, were something else again.

"Reveal, reveal, reveal!" Gerin shouted in tones of command, holding the crystal between the elevated lamp and the table.

A rainbow sprang into being on the grimy tabletop—getting it spotlessly white, as the grimoire suggested, had struck the Fox as more trouble than it was worth. As the magic began to unfold, he reckoned himself vindicated. He had seen, over the years, that the men who wrote tomes on magic had a way of worrying more about form than about function.

The rainbow vanished. A white light filled the crystal. Gerin almost dropped it in alarm, but held on when he realized it wasn't hot. Surely the little smudges and chips that white light revealed would not matter to the spell.

He concentrated his own formidable wits on Aragis the Archer, visualizing the grand duke's craggy, arrogant features: by his face, Aragis might have been half hawk on his father's side. The brain behind that harsh mask was alarmingly keen—nearly as good as Gerin's, if focused more on the short term and the immediate vicinity.

So what was Aragis plotting now? If the Fox locked

himself in battle with Adiatunnus, what would the grand duke do?

As soon as Gerin fully formed the question, a beam of light stabbed out from the glowing crystal down onto the tabletop. The Fox sucked in a quick, startled breath. There sat Aragis, with what looked like a mixture of distaste and intense concentration on his face. Gerin looked closely, trying to be sure he was reading the expression correctly. His rival seemed shrouded in shadow.

Aragis suddenly rose. The perspective shifted. The strings of oaths Gerin let out had nothing to do with the spell. Maybe purity of materials and cleanliness of scrying surface mattered more than he'd thought. A view of Aragis grunting in the smelly castle latrine was less edifying than the Fox had hoped. No wonder the grand duke's expression had been as it was. Had he obtained relief for the problem troubling him? Gerin would never know.

The light from the crystal faded. Evidently that was the only glimpse of Aragis Gerin would get. He swore again, half in anger, half in resignation. Sometimes his magics worked, sometimes he made an idiot of himself and wondered why he ever bothered trying. At least he hadn't come close to burning down the hut, as had happened before.

Unlike most of Gerin's vassals, Bevander could guess why Gerin had gone into the hut in the first place. Looking very full of himself, he walked up to the Fox and asked, "What news of Aragis, lord prince? Will he bedevil us if we war with Adiatunnus?"

"I don't really know, worse luck," the Fox answered. "The spell I tried turned out to be full of shit." He wasn't often able to tell literal and symbolic truth at the same time, and savored this chance the way a litterateur savored a well-turned verse. All the same, he would have traded the witticism for a real look into the future.

Every time his vassals rode away from Fox Keep at the end of a campaign, Gerin forgot how much chaos they brought while they were there. Part of that came from packing a lot of fighting men into a compact space and then having to wait for the latecomers before everyone could go out and fight. If they couldn't battle their foes, a lot of the Fox's troopers were willing, even eager, to battle one another.

Some of those fights were good-natured affrays that sprang from nothing more than high spirits and a couple of mugs of ale too many. Some had the potential for being more serious. Not all of Gerin's vassals loved one another. Not all of them loved him, either. Schild Stoutstaff was not the only man who would have liked nothing better than to renounce his allegiance to the Fox—had he not had Adiatunnus hanging over his southern border.

Gerin did his best to keep known enemies among his vassals as far from each other as he could. For years, he'd been doing his best to keep those vassals from going on with their own private wars. "And you've done well at it, too," Van said when he complained aloud one day: "better nor I ever thought you could. A lot of the feuds that were hot as a smith's fire when first I came here have cooled down in the years since."

"And a lot of them haven't, too," Gerin said. "Drungo Drago's son remembers that Schild's great-great-grandfather killed his own great-great-great-grandfather in a brawl a hundred years ago, and he wants to pay Schild back. And Schild remembers, too, and he's proud of what his flea-bitten brigand of an ancestor managed to do."

"Isn't that—what do you call it?—history, that's the word I want?" Van said. "You always say we have to know history if we're going to be civilized, whatever that means. Do you want Drungo and Schild to forget their blood feud?"

"I want them to forget their blood vengeance," Gerin answered. "The old quarrels get in the way, because the new one we have is more important—or it ought to be more important. The way some of my vassals eye some of the others, you'd think they came here for their own private wars. As far as they're concerned, fighting mine is a nuisance."

"Only one way to deal with that," Van said. "So long as they're more afraid of you than they are of each other, they'll do as you like."

"Oh, they know I can thump them like a drum if I have

to, and they're too fractious to join together and cast me down, for which the gods be praised," the Fox replied. "But that isn't what brings them together here. The one they're really afraid of is the cursed Trokmê."

Van scratched a scar that wandered down into his beard. Himself afraid of nothing this side of angry gods, he found fear of a foe hard to fathom. At last, he said, "There's that, too, I suppose. Anyone who thinks the woodsrunners make good neighbors has been chewing the wrong leaves and berries: I give you so much."

Vassals hastily moved aside from the doorway to the great hall. Gerin understood that a moment later, when Geroge walked outside. Even without armor, the monster was a match for men who wore bronze-scaled corselets and helms and carried spears and shields. A couple of minor barons had already urged the Fox to get rid of Geroge and Tharma both. He'd invited them to try it, with no more additions to nature than the monsters enjoyed. They hadn't urged twice.

Geroge came up to Gerin at a sort of lumbering trot. "Something wrong?" the Fox asked. As best he could tell, Geroge looked troubled. The monster's features were hard to read. The forward stretch of the lower half of his face made his nose low and flat, and heavy brow ridges shadowed his eyes. Had a creature half-wolf, half-bear walked like a man, it would have looked a lot like him.

He was also right on the edge of the transition from child to adult, and no more easy with that than anyone else. "They laugh at me," he said in his rough, growly voice, pointing with a clawed forefinger back toward the great hall. "They should be used to me by now, but they call me names."

"Why don't you grab one of them and eat him?" Van said. "He won't call you names after that, by the gods."

"Oh, no!" Geroge sounded horrified. As best the Fox could tell, he looked horrified, too. "Gerin taught Tharma and me never to eat people. And we couldn't eat enough of them to keep the rest from hurting us."

"That's right," Gerin said firmly, giving Van a dirty look. He'd worked hard trying to humanize the monsters, and didn't appreciate having his work undermined. "That's just right, Geroge," he repeated, "and you reasoned it out very well, too." For their kind, Geroge and Tharma were both clever. He never failed to let them know it.

Geroge said, "What do we do, then? I don't like it when they call us names. It makes me mad." He opened his mouth very wide. Examining the sharp ivory within, Gerin knew he would not have wanted the monster annoyed at him.

He said, "If they bother you again, *I* will eat them."

"Really?" Geroge's narrow eyes widened.

"Er—no," the Fox admitted. He had to keep reminding himself that, even though Geroge was bigger and much more formidably equipped than he, the monster was also as literal-minded as a child half his age. "But I will make them very sorry they insulted you. They have no business doing it, and I won't stand for it."

"All right," Geroge said. Like a child with its father, he was convinced Gerin always could and would do exactly as he promised. Gerin had to bear that in mind when he spoke with the monster. If he didn't deliver on a promise . . . he didn't know what would happen then, or want to find out.

"Anyone who bothers you will answer to me, too," Van rumbled. That made the monster happy; unlike most mere mortals, Van was still stronger than Geroge, and also unintimidated by his fearsome looks. That made him a hero in the monster's eyes.

"Let's go hunting," Geroge said. "We need more meat with all these people crowding the keep. We always need more meat." His tongue, long and red and rough like a cat's, flicked out to moisten his lips. He didn't just need meat—he needed to hunt more meat.

"You won't hear me say no," Van answered. He went back into the great hall, emerging a moment later with a stout bow and a quiver slung over his back. He affected to despise archery when fighting men—he preferred a long, heavy spear that he handled as if it were a twig used for picking teeth—but proved his skill as a bowman whenever he went after game.

Geroge hurried away, too, returning momentarily with Tharma. Both monsters were chattering excitedly; they were about to go off and do something they loved. With so many warriors in the keep, the drawbridge was down. Flanked on either side by a monster, Van tromped out of the keep and headed for the woods.

No one would call Geroge and Tharma names while they were out hunting. Even if a warrior came upon them in the woods, he would think several times before drawing their notice, much less their anger. Gerin had hunted with them, many times. Out among the trees, they sloughed off a lot of the cloak of humanity they wore inside Fox Keep. They were more purely predators in the woods, and less inclined to put up with nonsense from people.

Gerin, much to his own regret, had to put up with a lot of nonsense. He sometimes thought that the hardest part of the ruler's art. He'd never been one to suffer fools gladly. In his younger days, he'd never been one to suffer fools at all. He would either ignore them or insult them till they went away. First as baron, though, and then as self-styled prince, he'd gradually become convinced the number of fools was so high, he made too many enemies by treating them all as they deserved. Little by little, he'd learned patience, though he'd never learned to like it.

Rihwin the Fox and Carlun Vepin's son came out of the great hall together. Seeing them so sent alarm through Gerin. Carlun had already figured out on his own how to get into trouble, and if by some chance he hadn't, Rihwin would have taken care of that small detail for him. Rihwin could get anyone, from himself up to and including gods, into trouble.

To Gerin's relief, his fellow Fox said something to Carlun that seemed to rub the ex-headman the wrong way. Rihwin laughed out loud at that. Carlun looked angry, but didn't do anything about it. In his place, Gerin wouldn't have done anything, either. Carlun had spent a lifetime with hoe and shovel and plow, Rihwin just as long with sword and bow and spear. If you weren't trained from childhood as a warrior, you were a fool to take on a man who was.

Laughing still, Rihwin gave Carlun a mocking bow and went on his way. Carlun saw Gerin and hurried over to him. "Lord prince!" he cried, his face red with frustrated, impotent fury. "They scorn me, lord prince!"

He might have been Geroge, though he expressed himself better. On the other hand, the warriors could twit him with impunity; he wasn't liable to tear them limb from limb if they pushed him too far. "What are they calling you?" Gerin asked.

"They've given me an ekename," Carlun said indignantly. "One of them called me Carlun Inkfingers, and now they're all doing it." He held out his hands to the Fox. Sure enough, the right one was stained with ink.

Gerin held out his hands in return. "I have those stains, too, you'll note," he said, "and rather worse than you: being left-handed, I drag the side of my hand through what I've written while that's still wet."

"But they don't call you Gerin Inkfingers," Carlun said.

"That's true. I've given them reason to hang a different sobriquet on me," Gerin said. "You could do that. Or you could take pride in the one they've given you, instead of letting them make you angry with it. Most of them, you know, couldn't find their own name on a piece of parchment if it stood up and waved to them."

"I don't like trying to deal with so many of your warriors," Carlun said, sticking out his lower lip like a sulky child.

"Then it's back to a village for you—a village far away," Gerin told him. "You won't be headman there, either—you know that. You'd just be a serf among serfs for the rest of your life. If that's truly what you want, I'll put you and your family on the road tomorrow."

Carlun shook his head. "I don't want that, lord prince. What I want is revenge, and I can't take it. They'd kill me if I tried." His eyes swung in the direction Rihwin had gone.

"If you tried sticking a knife into one of them, he would kill you," the Fox agreed. "There are other ways, though, if you think for a bit. A man with armor can stand off several without. And a man who knows reading and numbers, if you put him in with folk who don't—"

He watched Carlun's eyes catch fire. That amused him; clever as the ex-headman was, he hadn't yet learned to conceal his thoughts. And, a moment later, the fire faded. Carlun said, "You warned me, lord prince, what would happen if you caught me cheating. I don't like the warriors' mocking me, but you would do worse than mock."

Though he did not smile, the Fox was pleased he'd put a healthy dose of fear in Carlun's soul. He answered, "I didn't say anything about cheating—certainly not about cheating me out of my due. But if a man insults you, he should hardly be surprised if you reckon up what he owes his overlord with very close attention to every detail. Do you understand what I'm saying?" He waited for Carlun to nod, then went on, "It's not as satisfying as smashing a man in the face with an axe, maybe, but you're not there so he can smash you in the face, either."

Carlun went down on one knee and seized Gerin's right hand in both of his. "Lord prince," he said, "now I understand why you have gone from victory to victory. You see farther ahead than any man now living. Teach me!"

That evening, in some bemusement, Gerin said to Selatre, "There I was, explaining how to avenge yourself on someone who'd offended you without getting killed in the process, and he ate it up like a bear in a honey tree. Have I made him someone who will aid me better, or am I turning him into a monster more dangerous than any of Geroge and Tharma's unlamented cousins?"

"You can't be sure, one way or the other," she answered, sensible as usual. "For all you know, you may be doing both at once. He may end up being a useful monster, if you know what I mean."

"Which is fine for me, but not so good for him," Gerin answered. "Maybe I should have just sent him off to another village and had done with it. That would have been simplest, and it wouldn't have shown poor Carlun temptations the likes of which he's never seen before."

"Nonsense," Selatre said crisply. "If he hadn't known about temptations like that, he wouldn't have tried cheating you in the first place. Now you have him working for you, not against you."

"People like Carlun, the only ones they work for are themselves," Gerin replied with a shake of the head. "The way you get them to do what you want is to make them see that going your way sends them along their own path better than anything else they could do."

Selatre nodded. "Aye, I can see that. You've done it for Carlun, plain enough. By the time he's through with your vassals, they'll be lucky if they have a tunic and a pot of beans apiece to call their own."

She laughed, but the Fox began to worry. "Can't have that. If he squeezes them too hard, they'll blame me. Just what I'd need—rebellions from men who've always been solid backers."

"You'll curb him before it comes to that," Selatre said confidently. She had more confidence in Gerin, sometimes, than he had in himself.

"The gods grant you're right," he said.

From Fox Keep, the land sloped down to the Niffet a few furlongs away. Gerin drilled his vassals on the expanse of grass and bushes where sheep and cattle usually grazed. Some of the warriors grumbled at that. Drungo Drago's son complained, "This practicing is a silly notion, lord prince. We go off, we find the cursed Trokmoi, and we smash 'em into the ground. Nothing to worry about in any of that." He folded massive arms across a wide chest.

"You're your father come again," Gerin said. Drungo beamed, but Gerin had not meant it altogether as a compliment. Drago the Bear had been strong and brave, but up to the day he clutched his chest and keeled over dead he'd not been long on thought.

"Aye," several men said together. "Turn us loose on the Trokmoi. We'll take care of what happens next."

"You practice with the bow, don't you?" the Fox asked them. They nodded. He tried again: "You practice with the spear and the sword, too?" More nods. He did his best to drive the lesson home: "You practice in your chariots, I expect, so you can do the best job of fighting from them?" When he got still more nods, he bellowed, "Then why in the five hells don't you want to practice with a whole swarm of chariots together?"

He should have known better than to expect logic to have anything to do with their answer. Drungo said, "On account of we already know how to do that, on account of we've all been in a bunch of fights already."

"Brawls," Gerin said scornfully. "Every car for itself, every man for himself. The woodsrunners fight the same way. If we have an idea of what we're going to do before we do it, we'll have a better chance of winning than if we make it up as we go along. And besides" —he pointed off to the right wing— "we'll be trying something new on this campaign."

"Yes, and those fools on horses' backs aren't worth anything, either," Drungo said, eloquently dubious, as his gaze followed the Fox's finger.

"You *are* your father's son," Gerin told him, feeling old. Sixteen years ago now, back before the werenight, Drago had mocked Duin the Bold, claiming the art of equitation was more trouble than it would ever be worth. They'd almost brawled then. Now Gerin was going to find out whether Duin had known what he was talking about.

When his overlord pointed to him, Rihwin the Fox waved from the stallion on whose back he perched. He led a couple of dozen mounted men, most of them only half his age. His years were the main reason Gerin, halfway against his better judgment, had placed him in command of the riders. With luck, he would have more sense than the hotheads he led, but he was also living proof that experience did not necessarily bring maturity.

"We'll try another practice charge," Gerin said to Drungo. "Maybe you'll see what I'm driving at." He had thought about giving up the chariot himself and going over to riding a horse, but his long partnership with Van and their driver Raffo had kept him in the car.

He brought down his arm. The chariots jounced across the meadow in a line less ragged than it had been a few days before. And over on the right flank, the horses moved faster than any team hauling car and warriors both. They also made their way without effort over ground that would surely have made a chariot flip over. Rihwin even leaped his horse across a gully: you would have had to be mad to urge a team to try such a stunt (which might not have deterred Rihwin, but would have given anyone else pause).

"There," Gerin said when the exercise was over. "Do the lot of you think this business of riding horses may have something to it after all?"

Again, Drungo spoke for the conservative majority, just as Drago had in his day: "Maybe a small something, lord prince, but no more than that. Horses for scouts and for flank attacks: aye, I'll give you so much. But it's the chariots that'll finish the foe."

As he was still fighting from a chariot himself, Gerin could not very well argue with that. In fact, he more or less agreed. Having stood up against a chariot charge, he knew how it turned opponents' blood to water and their bones to gelatin. The drum of the hooves, the rattle and bang of the cars as they thundered down on you, the fierce cries of the warriors standing upright in them, weapons ready to hand . . . If you could stand up against such without quailing, you were a man indeed. Cavalry alone would not be nearly so fearsome.

What he said, then, was, "We will be using the cavalry on the flanks, to disrupt the charge our foes try to make against us. We've not done that before, not in war. That's why I've been bringing us out here the past few days: so we could see how it would go, see how the flank chariots need to stick close to the riders and how the riders can't get too far out in front of the chariotry—"

"Well, why didn't you say so, lord prince?" Drungo demanded.

The Fox couldn't decided whether to throttle his literal-minded vassal or merely to pound his own head against the side rail of his car. By Drungo's self-righteous tones, the notion that they had been out there for any reason save Gerin's perverse obstinacy had till that moment not penetrated his thick skull and actually reached his brain.

After a long sigh, the Fox said, "We'll try it again, this time charging down toward the Niffet. If the woodsrunners on the north side are peering across, as they likely are, we'll give them something new to think on, too."

They pounded down toward the Niffet, as he'd ordered, and then, after a pause to let the horses rest, back up toward Fox Keep. The men on the palisade there gave them a cheer. Gerin took that as a good omen. Very often, looking bloodthirsty was a sign you would fight well.

"You know something, Fox?" Van said as Raffo drove the chariot at a slow walk toward the drawbridge. "By the time Duren's son is the big man here, most of his warriors will be on horseback, and they'll listen to the minstrels' old songs about chariot battles and wonder why the singers couldn't get it right."

"D'you think so?" Gerin said. Van's big head bobbed up and down. That surprised Gerin; in matters military, the outlander was for the most part as conservative as Drungo. "Well, you may be right, but I'd bet on the bards to change their tunes by then."

He thought about what he'd just said, then shook his head. "No, I take that back. You're likelier to be right than I am. The minstrels have a whole great store of stock phrases and lines about chariots, same as they do about keeps and love and everything else you can think of. If they have to start singing about horses instead of chariots, their verses won't scan."

"And most of 'em, being lazy as everybody else, won't have the wit to come up with anything new on their own, so we'll hear the same songs a bit longer yet, aye." Van cocked his head to one side, studying the Fox. "Not everybody would up and own he was wrong like that."

"What's the point to defending a position you can't hold?" Gerin asked. Put that way, it made sense to the outlander. He nodded again, jumped down from the chariot, and headed into Castle Fox afoot.

Gerin let Raffo drive him into the stables. There, his lungs full of the green, grassy smell of horse manure, he said to Rihwin, "You did well in the practice. I want to see how well your lads fare at charging home with the spear and at archery from horseback, too."

"I'd not care to be a man afoot trying to stand against me when I have a leaf-pointed spear of shining bronze aimed at his belly," Rihwin replied, sounding a bit like a bard himself. "Riding him down or putting the point through his vitals should be no harder than gigging trout from a stream."

Gerin shook his head in bemusement; he'd been on the other end of this same conversation with Van a few days before. "Except the trout aren't trying to gig you, too," he pointed out, his voice dry. "And except that you mostly won't be going up against men afoot. How will you do against chariotry?"

"We'll ride over them like—" Rihwin paused to catch

an elusive simile and caught sight of Gerin drumming the fingers of one hand into the palm of the other. His flight of fancy came back to earth with a thud. "When we fight the battle, we'll know, lord prince. With luck, we'll come at them from directions they'll not expect."

Gerin thumped him on the shoulder. "Good. That's what I'm hoping you do. I don't ask miracles, you know: just that you do what you can."

"Ah, but, my fellow Fox, miracles are so much more dramatic—the stuff of which the minstrels sing for generations yet unborn."

"Aye, with formulas that should have died of old age but haven't," Gerin said, now picking up the discussion he'd just been having with Van as if it hadn't stopped. "Besides, the trouble with miracles is that, even if you do get 'em, you'd almost rather not: getting 'em is a sign of how bad you need 'em, as much as anything else."

He did not mention the couple he'd pulled off, though they went a long way toward proving his point. By the gleam in Rihwin's eye, he was about to bring them up, but he suddenly thought better of it; if it hadn't been for him, at least one and maybe both of them would have been unnecessary.

What he did say, after a few heartbeats' hesitation, was, "For a man who has accomplished as much as you have, lord prince, you've left the bards surprisingly little about which to sing."

The converse of that was, *For a man who's accomplished as little as you, Rihwin, you've given the bards all too much fodder*. Gerin did not say that. Rihwin was as he was, charm and flaws engagingly blended. You enjoyed him, admired his courage, and hoped he was seldom in a position to do you much harm. That hope, however, did not always work out.

"Let's go into the great hall," Gerin said, also a little more slowly than he should have. "We'll drink some ale and hash over how best we can make horses and chariots work together."

"I'm for that," Rihwin said. "I have several ideas we've yet to try, which, if they work as I hope, bid fair to make that cooperation easier to effect." Rihwin always had several ideas. Out of any given batch, some would work. The trouble was figuring out which ones before you tried them all, because those that failed had a way of failing spectacularly.

In the courtyard, Duren was patiently standing alongside Dagref, helping his half brother improve his form at archery. Under Duren's tutelage, Dagref let fly. He whooped in delight when he hit the target.

Watching them, Rihwin sighed. "There are times, my fellow Fox, when I envy you—oh, not so much your children, but having them all here so you can see them every moment as they grow. It's not like that with my brood of bastards."

Gerin exhaled through his nose. "If you'd wanted a wife, plenty of barons had daughters or sisters they'd have pledged to you. We both know that's so." He didn't come any closer to mentioning that Rihwin would have been betrothed to Elise, back before the werenight, if he hadn't gone and disgraced himself as the betrothal was about to be announced. Instead, he went on, "Plenty of barons would pledge you a daughter or sister even now. You have but to seek a bit."

Rihwin sighed again, on a different note. "You, my fellow Fox, are fortunate enough to enjoy waking in the same bed each morning, and to enjoy the company of the same lady—and an excellent lady she is; mistake me not—when not in that bed. In my opinion, the chances of finding a woman who both makes a pleasing bedmate and is interesting when vertical as well as horizontal are lamentably low. Were I wed, I fear I should be bored."

"You don't know till you look," Gerin said stubbornly. "If you're unhappy with your life as it is, wringing your hands and moaning won't make it better."

" 'Unhappy' perhaps takes the point too far," Rihwin answered. "Say rather I recognize its imperfections, but also realize it would have other imperfections, likely worse ones, did I change it."

"And you the one who usually plunges ahead without the least thought of consequences," Gerin exclaimed. "You'd best have a care, or you'll get a name for prudence."

"Father Dyaus avert such a twisted fate!" Rihwin cried. Both men laughed.

In the great hall, the kitchen servants had set a big jar of ale in the middle of the floor, the pointed tip stabbed through the rushes strewn there and into the dirt below. Gerin and Rihwin got drinking jacks, filled them with the dipper, and joined a crowd of warriors at a table arguing over what they'd done and what still needed doing.

"A good strong spear thrust into a man from horseback, now—that'd do some damage," Schild Stoutstaff declared. He pointed to his own weapon hanging on the wall, which had given him his sobriquet. His thinking lived up to the ekename. He nodded to Gerin. "This time, lord prince, maybe we'll be rid of that cursed Trokmê for good."

"Aye, maybe," Gerin said. He suspected that, if Adiatunnus was beaten, Schild would promptly forget as many of his own feudal obligations as he could. He'd done that before. The only time he remembered he owed service was when he needed protection.

Well, he was here now. That would do. Gerin poured out a small libation to Baivers, then stuck his forefinger into the drinking jack and used ale to draw cryptic lines on the tabletop in front of him. "Here—these are the chariots," he told Rihwin, pointing. "And *these* are your horses. What you need to—"

He didn't get to finish explaining what Rihwin needed to do. The lookout's horn blew, a higher, clearer note than the one the village horn used to call the serfs back from the fields at close of day. Normally, the sentry up in the watchtower just called out when he spied someone. He saved the horn for times he really needed it.

After he sounded the warning note, he shouted something. Through the racket and chatter in the great hall, Gerin couldn't hear what he said. He got to his feet and started for the doorway. He hadn't gone more than a few steps when a man came running in, yelling, "Lord prince! Lord prince! There's boats in the Niffet—big boats—and they're heading this way!"

III

"Oh, a pestilence," Gerin said as men exclaimed and cried out all around him. Unlike his vassals, he was angry at himself. After Rihwin had told him of the galley his leman had seen on the Niffet, he'd intended to station riders along the river to bring word if more such came up it. As sometimes happens, what he'd intended to do didn't match what he'd actually done.

Too late for self-reproach now. He ran outside and hurried up onto the palisade. One of the warriors already up there pointed out to the Niffet. Gerin had to choke down sardonic thanks. The ships out there, all five of them, were quite easy enough to find without help.

He saw at first glance that they weren't Elabonian war galleys. Instead of the bronze-clad rams those carried, these ships had high prows carved into the shapes of snarling animals and painted to look more ferocious. *Grainne might have mentioned that*, he thought, absurdly aggrieved the woman had left out an important detail.

The galleys strode briskly up the Niffet, propelled against the current by a couple of dozen oars on either side. They turned sharply toward the riverbank as they drew nearest to Fox Keep, and grounded themselves on that muddy bank harder than Gerin would have liked to endure were he aboard one of them. As soon as they were aground, men started spilling out of them.

"Arm yourselves!" Gerin shouted to his vassals, some of whom had followed him out into the courtyard to see what the fuss was about. "The Gradi are attacking us!"

That sent the nobles running back into the great hall—or trying to, for at the doorway they collided with others trying to get outside. After much screaming and gesticulating, pushing and shoving, that straightened itself out.

Meanwhile, the warriors from the ships pounded toward Fox Keep at a steady, ground-eating trot. As they drew nearer, Gerin got his first good look at them: big, bulky fellows with fair skins and dark hair. They wore bronze helms and leather jerkins and tall boots, and carried a shield on one arm and a long-hafted axe in the other hand.

"Gradi, sure enough," Van said from beside the Fox. Gerin jumped; his attention on the invaders, he hadn't noticed the outlander ascending to the palisade.

Rihwin the Fox had been right behind Van. "My leman surely saw one of those ships, lord prince," he said, pointing out toward the Niffet.

"If I thought you were wrong, I would argue with you," Gerin said. For a moment, gloom threatened to overwhelm him. "This is what I feared worst when I heard your woman's news: these cursed raiders sweeping down on us by surprise, hitting us with no warning—"

To his amazement, both Van and Rihwin burst into raucous laughter. Van said, "Mm, Captain, don't you think it's the Gradi who're liable to get the surprise?" He half turned and waved down into the courtyard, which was aboil with a great host of the most ferocious—or at least the most effective—warriors the northlands knew.

"Just so, lord prince," Rihwin agreed. "Had they chosen another time to come, they might have done you grievous harm: truth. But now, with so many bold and valiant men assembled here, they are more apt to find themselves in the position of a man who bites down hard on a stone, thinking it a piece of fruit."

"Put that way—it could be so," Gerin said, that choking depression lifting almost as fast as it had settled on him. He looked out over the wall again. The Gradi had got close enough for him to hear them singing. He had no idea what the words meant, but the song sounded fierce. Some of the raiders carried long ladders. A corner of the Fox's mouth quirked upwards. "Aye, let 'em try to storm the keep, and see how much joy they have of it." He thumped Rihwin on the shoulder. "And you, my fellow Fox, gather up your horse-riders and prepare your mounts. Readying the chariots would take a long time, but we can loose you against the foe at a moment's notice."

Rihwin's eyes shone. "Just as you say, lord prince." He hurried down off the walkway, shouting for his horsemen.

Gerin's eyes went to the peasant village not far from Fox Keep and the fields surrounding it. Not since the year of the werenight, most of a generation before, had the serfs come under attack. The older men and women, though, knew what to do, and the younger ones didn't take long to figure it out: as soon as they spied the war galleys landing, they all ran for the woods not far away. The Fox hoped they wouldn't peep out from the edge of the forest, either, but would keep running to get away from the invaders.

Some of the Gradi peeled off toward the villages. "They'll steal the animals and burn the huts," Gerin said mournfully.

"Let's make 'em thoughtful about the keep," Van answered. "They haven't got the strength to coop us up in here, though they don't know that yet, either. We'll give 'em one set of lumps, then another."

The Gradi started shooting fire arrows at Fox Keep. A good many of the logs of the palisade, though, were still painted with the gunk Siglorel Shelofas' son had used to keep Balamung the Trokmê from burning the keep with magic fire during the chaos after the werenight. Even all these years later, flames would not catch on them.

Elabonians on the walkway shot back at the Gradi. A couple of the big, burly men out on the grass crumpled. One of them thrashed about, clutching at his shoulder. The other lay very still; the arrow must have found a vital spot.

"Ladders! Ladders!" The cry came from two sides of the palisade at once. One of the ladders peeked over the top of the log fence only a few yards from where Gerin stood. He rushed toward it, and reached it at the same moment as a Gradi swarmed up and tried to scramble onto the walkway.

The raider bawled something at him in an unintelligible language—and swung his axe through a deadly arc. But the Fox ducked under the stroke and thrust the point of his sword through the Gradi's throat before the fellow could fully protect himself with his shield.

The Gradi had eyes bright and blue as a lightning bolt. They went wide in horror and shock. The heavy axe dropped from his hand. He clutched at the spurting wound as he slipped and slid down the ladder. Cries of dismay from below said he was fouling the men behind him.

Gerin leaned forward and shoved at the top of the ladder with all his strength. Two arrows whipped past his head; the fletching on one of them brushed his cheek as it flew past. He ducked away, fast as he could. The Gradi on the bottom part of the ladder shouted as it leaned away from the wall and toppled over with a crash. He looked again. Three or four of them were writhing at the bottom of the ditch. If he had any luck, they'd broken bones.

The cry of "Ladders!" rose again and again, now from all four sides of the square palisade. Three of the ladders went over faster and more easily than the one Gerin toppled—his men had remembered the forked poles kept on the walkway against just such an emergency. At the fourth one, though, around the far side of Castle Fox from Gerin, cries of alarm and the clash of metal against shields and metal against metal said the Gradi had gained a lodgement. Elabonian warriors rushed toward the fighting to hold them in check.

Down in the courtyard, trying to reach the drawbridge through chaos, came Rihwin the Fox and most of his horseriders. "Let down the bridge!" Gerin yelled to the gate crew. He had to shout several times to gain the crew's attention, and several more to make them believe him. With a squeal of chains, the bridge fell.

The Gradi outside Fox Keep roared in triumph when the drawbridge came down. Maybe they thought their own folk were opening it, to let them into the keep. If they did, they discovered their mistake in short order. A few of them started over the bridge. Rihwin, leading his riders out, skewered the leading Gradi on his spear. His followers rode down the others, trampling them or knocking them into the ditch around the palisade. The shouts of triumph turned to shouts of alarm.

Rihwin and his horsemen smashed through the Gradi who swarmed near the drawbridge and then galloped off toward the stragglers who'd decided to plunder the peasant village. Some they rode down, some they shot with arrows, some they speared. Had the Gradi stuck together in a tight formation, they might have been able to fight back. Instead, they scattered. A running man was no match for a man aboard a speeding horse.

With the riders gone, the Gradi tried once more to rush in over the drawbridge. Gerin's men met them at the gate, slashing with swords, thrusting with spears, and putting their bodies between the invaders and the courtyard.

Gerin hurried down to the yard to help drive away the Gradi. And, step by step, he and his men did exactly that, forcing their bigger foes back across the drawbridge and then gaining the grass on the far side.

That seemed to discomfit the Gradi. Instead of sweeping all before them, here they were swept instead. Gerin pointed toward the Niffet. "Get torches!" he cried. "We'll burn the bastards' boats and see if they can swim home!" His vassals roared in fierce approval. As he'd hoped, some of the Gradi understood Elabonian. They yelled in alarm. Some of them, at first a trickle and then a great flow, began streaming away from Fox Keep and toward the great river.

Gerin looked southward. He wished Rihwin would come galloping back and hit the invaders while they were in disorder. It was probably too much to ask for, but—

No sooner had he wished for it than Rihwin, at the head of most of his riders, charged down on the Gradi. Every once in a while, Rihwin did something right, and, when he did, it was as magnificent as any of his failures. As he'd predicted and as he'd proved by the village, foot soldiers had enormous trouble standing against onrushing horses with armored men on top of them. Neither he nor Gerin had imagined how much alarm the horses would create in a foe. The Gradi were seeing mounted men for the first time, and did not like what they saw.

Neat as you please, Rihwin snatched a torch out of the hand of a running Elabonian and urged his horse ahead until the animal seemed to be all but flying over the ground. He darted past the Gradi as if their rawhide boots had been nailed to the grass and flung the torch into one of the war galleys.

They still had men aboard their ships, to protect them if something went wrong with the attack on Fox Keep. Gerin expected one of those men to douse the torch before the ship caught. But Rihwin's spirit was rewarded with a gift of luck. The torch must have landed in a bucket of pitch or something equally inflammable, for a great pillar of black smoke rose from the galley.

The Gradi howled as if they were being burned. Gerin's men, for their part, howled too, but with fierce joy in their voices. Not all the Gradi gave way to despair, though. A big fellow turned and slashed at the Fox with his axe. Gerin turned the blow with his shield, and felt it all the way up his arm to his shoulder. He knew he had to be careful; the axehead, if it squarely met the facing of the shield, was liable to bite straight through and into his arm.

He thrust at the invader with his sword. The Gradi also got his shield up in time to block the stroke, although he seemed cautious and tentative in meeting a left-handed swordsman.

Clank! A rock the size of a man's fist bounced off the side of the Gradi's helmet. He staggered. His blue, blue eyes suddenly looked distant, his face blank, as if he were drunk. Taking advantage of a stunned man was anything but sporting. The Fox cut him down without a qualm.

"Well done, Father!"

Gerin whirled around. There stood Duren, a helm on his head, a shield on his arm, a sword in his hand—his right hand, for he hadn't taken after his father there. The blade had blood on it.

"Get back to the keep," Gerin snapped. "You've no business here."

"Who says I haven't?" his son retorted. "Who do you think threw that rock at the Gradi? You'd still be fighting him if I hadn't."

Gerin started to shout at Duren, but closed his mouth with a snap before angry words came out. If his son was big enough to do a man's job on the battlefield—and evidently he was—how could the Fox order him back like a boy? The plain truth was, he couldn't.

"Be careful," he said gruffly, and then, "come on."

A pig darted across the field, squealing and threatening with its tushes anyone who came near. Gerin wondered whether some Gradi had hoped to take it away as loot, or whether they'd simply broken the pen confining it to let it run wild. It headed off toward the woods. If one of the villagers didn't track it down there pretty soon, it would be a wild animal again; the difference between domestic swine and wild boars wasn't great.

As the Gradi neared their galleys, they found a shield wall, behind which the men not fighting pushed the surviving ships back into the Niffet and began boarding them. The warriors of the shield wall refused to give ground, but fought in place till they were killed. Their stubborn resistance let most of their comrades escape.

The torches the Elabonians flung at the galleys fell short and died, hissing, in the Niffet. A couple of archers had fire arrows ready to shoot. Most of those missed, too, but one stuck in the timbers at the stern of a ship. Gerin's men cheered at that. The Fox hoped the Gradi wouldn't note the little fire till it had grown into a big one. A bend of the Niffet carried the raiders out of sight before he could find out.

Wearily, he turned and looked back toward Fox Keep. The meadows his chariotry had been churning into a rutted mess now had bodies scattered over them. Some of his men were methodically going from one Gradi on the ground to the next, making sure those bodies were dead ones.

"Take prisoners!" he shouted.

"Why?" Drungo Drago's son shouted back. He was about to smash in the head of a fair-skinned Gradi down with an arrow through the thigh.

"So we can squeeze answers out of them," Gerin told him. "You need to be a patient man to go around questioning corpses." Drungo stared at him, then decided it was a joke and laughed. Had Gerin been the Gradi writhing on the ground in front of him, he didn't think he would have found that laugh pleasing to the ear.

His own men had taken hurts, too. Parol Chickpea, who was a good enough warrior to have lived through a lot of fights but not good enough to come through them unscathed, was binding up a cut on his shield arm. One of the northerners' axes must have hacked right through the shield, as had almost happened to Gerin.

Schild Stoutstaff was hobbling around, using his spear as a stick. When Gerin asked how he was, he gritted his teeth and answered, "I expect I'll heal. The cut runs up and down" —he pointed to his calf— "not straight across. If I'd got it that way, the bastard would have hamstrung me."

"Go back to the keep and have them wash it out with ale," Gerin told him. "It'll burn like fire, but it makes the wound less likely to rot."

"I'll do that, lord prince," Schild said. "You're clever about those things, I can't deny." He limped back toward the castle, blood soaking the bandage he'd ripped from his tunic and trickling down his heel onto the grass.

Gerin headed back to Fox Keep at a pace no better than Schild's. Not only was he weary past belief, almost past comprehension, but he also wanted a closer look at the damage his holding and his army had suffered. Hagop son of Hovan, his neighbor to the east, whose holding had acknowledged his suzerainty since not long after the werenight, crouched by a corpse that looked like him—maybe a younger brother, maybe a son. He did not look up as the Fox walked by.

The thump of hooves on turf made Gerin turn his head. Rihwin the Fox was having a little trouble controlling his horse, which might not have cared for the stink of blood so thick in the air even human nostrils could smell it. The animal kept rolling its eyes and trying to sidestep, almost as if it were skipping. It snorted, and looked for a moment as if it would rear, but Rihwin, leaning forward and speaking to it in a coaxing voice, persuaded it to keep all four feet on the ground.

"By Dyaus All-Father, my fellow Fox, you couldn't have done that better if we'd done nothing but practice it for the past year," Gerin told him. He turned and pointed back toward the war galley Rihwin had fired, which still crackled and burned and sent a great cloud of smoke into the sky. "And that—that was better than I'd dared hope."

"It did work rather well, didn't it?" Rihwin said. "We were here, we were there, with almost no time between being one place and the other. And wherever we were, the Gradi gave way before us, though they have a name for ferocity." He looked back at the carnage on the field and shook his head. "So much happened so fast. Astonishing, lord prince."

It wasn't done happening yet, either. Not quite all the Gradi had been flushed out of the village south of Fox Keep. There was fighting on the winding lanes that ran through the huts of the village. Gerin watched a couple of raiders flee into the forest with Elabonians pounding after them. "If the troopers don't get them, the serfs likely will," he said. "If they don't have ambushes set already, I miss my guess. And they know those woods the way they know the feel of their wives' backsides in their hands."

"Or maybe the backsides of their neighbors' wives," Rihwin said.

"If they're at all like you, that's probably the way of it," Gerin agreed.

Rihwin glared, then started to laugh. "That barb has too much truth in it for me to deny."

"Hasn't stopped you before," Gerin said, which got him another glare.

Back at Fox Keep, the men on the palisade raised a cheer when they recognized their overlord. "We beat the bastards back," one of them shouted, and in a moment they all took up the cry. The ditch around the palisade was full of dead Gradi. A few live men were trapped down there, too. They'd leaped in to try to swarm up the scaling ladders, only to find that those went down almost as fast as they went up.

Gerin looked with some curiosity from them to his troopers who peered over the top of the palisade to watch them. "I'd have expected you to have finished them by now," he called to his men.

"If you want us to, we will, lord prince," Bevander Bevon's son called back. "Your wife said you'd be likely to want them alive for questioning, and when the lady Selatre says something, we know it's best to listen to her."

That might have been because the warriors respected Selatre's own good sense, or because they still felt awe for the god who had spoken through her and wondered whether Biton might still inform her thoughts. Gerin sometimes wondered that himself. He said, "She's right, of course." However she did it, she knew him almost better than he knew himself. Walking up to the edge of the ditch, he called down to the Gradi, "Surrender and you'll live."

For a moment, the big men down in there did not respond. He wondered if they knew Elabonian. Then one of them said, "We live, you make us slaves?"

"Well, of course," Gerin answered. "What else am I going to do with you? Give you a barony? Turn out my peasants so you can have a farm?"

"You make us slaves, what we do?" the Gradi asked.

"Whatever I tell you to do," the Fox snapped. "If you're a slave, that's the end of the stick you're holding. If I put you in the mines to grub out copper or tin, you do that. And if I have you walking a water wheel, you walk it and thank the gods you're alive to do the walking."

"My gods, Voldar and comrades, they ashamed if I do these things," the raider replied. Drawing a dagger from a sheath on his belt, he muttered something in his own guttural language and plunged the knife into his chest. He tried to cry out, but blood pouring from his mouth and nose drowned his words. Slowly, he crumpled.

As if watching him inspired them, the rest of the Gradi also slew themselves—except for two who slew each other, each ramming his knife into the other's throat at the same instant. "Voldar!" each cried the moment before his end came.

"Father!" Duren said, gulping. He'd come through his

first battle fine—better than Gerin had, at about the same age—but this . . .

"I've never seen anything like it in all my life," the Fox said. He was sickened, too. Facing death on the field was one thing. If you were a warrior, that was what you did, not least so you could reap the rewards of triumph. But to embrace death as if it were a lover . . . you had to be mad to do that, he thought.

"Is Voldar their chief god?" Duren asked, seeking, as men will, an explanation for the inexplicable.

"I don't know," Gerin said. "Too much about the Gradi I don't know. Van went through their country; maybe he can tell us something of what gods they have." Something else occurred to him. He raised his voice to a great shout: "Bind the prisoners well. Don't let them harm themselves."

From the palisade, Bevander said, "None of the warriors who made it up to the walkway by that one ladder yielded. They all fell fighting."

"That, at least, doesn't surprise me," Gerin answered. "Their blood was up, and so was ours. Even if they had tried to surrender, we might have slain them out of hand. This, though—" He pointed down into the ditch, then shook his head. The most articulate man in the northlands save perhaps Rihwin, he was speechless in the face of the self-murdered Gradi.

He looked over the battlefield till he spotted Van of the Strong Arm. He waved to him, but the outlander did not see. The Fox turned to Duren. "Go fetch Van here. Because he went through the country of the Gradi, he's two ahead of anyone else around."

"Aye, Father." Duren loped off. Gerin looked at him with a small stir of jealousy for his son's limber youth. He could feel himself stiffening up already; for the next couple of days he'd be hobbling around like an old man.

Van came trotting back with the Fox's son. If he felt any twinges, he didn't let on. "They killed themselves?" he called to Gerin. "That's the tale the lad here tells."

"See for yourself." Gerin pointed down into the ditch. "Some of them called on Voldar as they did it. Is he their chief god?"

"She—goddess," Van answered. "She's cold as ice, any

way you care to take that. They love her madly, the Gradi do, though they know she doesn't love them." He shrugged. "If they didn't love her, they say, the land they live in would be bleaker yet, though how that could be, I tell you, is past anything my poor wits can fathom. But she's that kind of goddess. If I were one of hers, I'd not want to make her angry at me, and that's for true."

"Surrendering after you've lost a fight would anger her?" the Fox asked.

"So it would, to hear the Gradi tell it." Van frowned. "Or so I thought I heard it, not knowing their tongue any too well, and so I remember it, not having been in the Gradi country for going on twenty years now."

"As I told Duren, you may not know much, but whatever you do know puts you ahead of everyone else here," Gerin told him. "Do you still remember any of what you learned of their speech?"

Van's frowned deepened. "A few words come back, no more—no surprise, when for so long I've used Elabonian and a bit of the Trokmê tongue and none of the rest of the languages I once knew."

"Let's go talk to a prisoner." Gerin headed toward a Gradi down on the ground with one of his own men squatting beside the fellow. Not far away lay a bronze axe. The Gradi tried to hitch himself toward it, but the Elabonian wouldn't let him. The blood-soaked bandage on the raider's thigh showed why he couldn't do more.

He glared up at Gerin, gray-blue eyes blazing. But the blaze slowly faded, to be replaced by a puzzled look. The Fox had seen that before, on the faces of men who would bleed to death soon. He said, "Why did you strike Fox Keep?"

The Gradi didn't answer. Maybe he didn't understand Elabonian. Maybe he didn't understand anything, not any more. He nudged Van. The outlander spoke, haltingly, in a language that seemed to be pronounced farther back in the throat than Elabonian.

Something like intelligence came back into the Gradi's face. He answered in the same tongue. "He says it doesn't matter what he tells us now. He's died in battle. Voldar's handmaidens will carry him off to the golden couches of the afterworld and lie with him whenever he likes, and give him roast meat and beer when he doesn't feel like futtering."

"If it doesn't matter what he tells us, ask him again why he and his comrades hit Fox Keep," Gerin said.

Van repeated what he'd said before, whatever that was. Again, the Gradi answered without hesitation. Van translated: "He says, to kill you and take your land and—something." The outlander scowled. "Bring it under Voldar and his other goddesses and gods, I think he means."

"Just what we need," Gerin said unhappily. "The Trokmoi are already here in the northlands in numbers enough to let their bloodthirsty gods contend with Dyaus and the other Elabonian deities. Will we have a three-cornered war among gods as well as men?"

No sooner were the words out of his mouth than he realized the war might have more than three corners. Selatre's Biton was ancient in the northlands, far more ancient than the Elabonian presence here. And Mavrix, originally from far Sithonia, manifested himself in this land as a fertility god even if wine grapes would not grow here.

The Gradi spoke again, dreamily, as if from far away. Gerin caught the name Voldar, but had no idea what else the raider was saying. Van asked a question that sounded as if he were choking on a piece of meat. The Gradi answered. Van said, "He says Voldar and the rest like this land. They will make it their home, and change it to suit them even better." He ground up some turf with the sole of his hobnailed boot as he twisted a foot back and forth. "I think that's what he says. It's been a demon of a long time, Fox."

Whatever the Gradi had said, they weren't going to get anything more out of him. He slumped forward, took a last few rattling breaths, and lay still. The blood from the thigh wound had not only soaked the rough bandage Gerin's man had given him, it also puddled beneath his body.

"Let's go on to another one, Captain," Van said to the Fox. "We need to nail that down. If their gods are fighting for them right out in the open, like I thought from what he said, we've got troubles. Your Dyaus and the rest, they let people do more unless you really shout to draw their notice."

"I wish I could say you were wrong," Gerin answered. "The other half of the loaf is, when you have drawn their notice, you almost wish you hadn't. I don't like dealing with gods."

"You don't like dealing with anything stronger than you," Van said shrewdly.

"You're right about that, too." The Fox paused thoughtfully. "You know, I've never truly evoked an Elabonian god. Mavrix is Sithonian, and Biton got adopted into our pantheon. I'm not eager to start, mind, but I haven't."

"Don't blame you," Van said. "But if the Gradi do and you don't, what does that leave? Leaves you in a bad place, you ask me."

"I'm already in a bad place," Gerin told him. Van looked a question his way. He explained: "Somewhere in there between being born and dying, I mean."

"Oh, that bad place," Van said. "The others are worse yet, I hear, but I'm in no hurry to find out."

Over the next few days, several of the wounded Gradi found ways to kill themselves. One threw himself down a stairway and broke his neck, one hanged himself with his belt, one bit through his tongue and choked to death on his own blood. The determination required for that chilled Gerin. Was he supposed to stuff rags into the mouths of all the prisoners?

A few of the raiders, though, lacked the fortitude of their fellows and seemed to resign themselves to captivity. They did not ask the Fox what he would do with them after they healed, as if, not hearing it from his lips, they could pretend they did not know.

He didn't push the issue. Instead, he asked them as many questions as he could, using Van's halting command of their speech and the smattering of Elabonian some of them had acquired. The picture he got from them was more detailed than the one the first dying Gradi had given him, but not substantially different: they'd come to stay, they like the northlands fine, and their goddesses and gods had every intention of establishing themselves here.

"You yield to them, they let you be their slave in this world, in next world, too," said one of the prisoners, a warrior named Kapich. Like his countrymen, he took their victory and the victory of their deities for granted.

"Look around," the Fox suggested. "Look where you are. Look who is the lord here." He phrased that carefully, not wanting to remind the Gradi of his status so strongly that he would be inspired to kill himself.

The raider looked at the underground storeroom where he was confined. He shrugged. "All will change when this is the Gradihome." He used Elabonian, but ran that together, as his people seemed to do in their own language. His eyes were clear and innocent and confident. He believed what he was saying, believed it so strongly he'd never thought to question it.

Gerin, by his nature, questioned everything. That made him perhaps a broader and deeper man than any other in the northlands. But the Gradi's pure and simple faith in what he said was like an armor the arrows of reason could not pierce. That frightened the Fox.

He waited unhappily for Adiatunnus to take advantage of the disruption of the planned Elabonian attack to launch one of his own. Had he been in Adiatunnus' boots, that was what he would have done, and the Trokmê's mental processes were less alien to him than those of the Gradi.

And, when from the watchtower the lookout spied Widin Simrin's son approaching in his chariot, Gerin was sure the blow had fallen. The only reason Widin and his men weren't already at Fox Keep was so they could absorb Adiatunnus' first onslaught and keep him and his woodsrunners from penetrating too deeply into territory the Fox held.

The drawbridge came down with a thud: now, although Castle Fox bulged with men, the bridge stayed up till newcomers were identified. Gerin waited impatiently at the gatehouse. "What word?" he called before Widin had even entered Fox Keep.

His vassal, almost as urgent, jumped out of the chariot and hurried over to him. "Lord prince, the Trokmoi have suffered a great defeat!" he said.

"That's wonderful!" Gerin said, as all the men who heard

burst into cheers and swarmed round to pound Widin on the back. Then the Fox, with a keener ear for detail than his comrade, noticed what Widin had said—and what he hadn't. "You didn't beat the woodsrunners yourself, did you?"

"No, lord prince," Widin answered. "Some of them have entered my fief, but as refugees and bandits, not an army."

"Well, who did beat them, then?" Drungo Drago's son demanded, bushy eyebrows pulling together in puzzlement. He was brave and strong and honest and had not a dram of imagination in his head or concealed anywhere else about his person.

"The Gradi, they said," Widin replied. "Four boatloads came down a tributary of the Niffet, grounded themselves, and out poured warriors grim enough, by all accounts, to have turned even Adiatunnus' stomach."

"I wonder if those were the four boatloads who got away from us," Gerin said, and then, in thoughtful tones, "I wonder whether I want the answer to that to be yes or no. Yes, I suppose: if they have enough warriors to assail Adiatunnus and us at the same time, they've put a lot of men into the northlands these past few years."

"Don't know the answer either way, lord prince," Widin said. "From what the Trokmoi who fled 'em told me, they landed, stole everything that wasn't roped down, killed all the men they could, kidnapped some women, and sailed off with the wenches still screaming on their ships. Adiatunnus' men couldn't very well go after them."

"No more than we could." Gerin pointed toward the Niffet. "I wish that Gradi ship hadn't burned altogether. We need to start learning more about how to make such ships for ourselves."

"As may be, lord prince," Widin said with a shrug. "What matters is, the woodsrunners got badly hurt. But then, I hear the same thing happened here."

"If I hadn't been mustering men to move against Adiatunnus, you'd be telling your story to the Gradi here," Gerin said.

"That wouldn't be so good," Widin said; the Fox thought the understatement commendable. His vassal went on, "If the Gradi hadn't hit the Trokmoi, though, I might not be around to tell you my tale, so I suppose it evens out, in a way."

"I suppose it does," Gerin agreed. His scowl was directed at the world at large, and especially at the western part of it where the Gradi congregated. "What's really happened is that the raiders have knocked me and Adiatunnus both back on our heels. That's bad. If they're doing the moving and we're being moved, that makes them the strongest power in the northlands right now."

"You'll check 'em, lord prince," Widin said with the unbounded faith of a man who had watched the Fox overcome every obstacle since he himself was a boy.

Gerin sighed. "I wish I knew how."

The underground storerooms of Castle Fox made good places to stash prisoners, as Gerin had long since found. He had several Gradi down there now, and had not lost any of them in a good many days. He'd counted on that. One of the things he'd seen over the years was that not everyone could live up to a strict code of conduct. The Gradi came closer to managing than most, but they were human, too.

It was dark underground, dark and dank. Gerin carried a lamp as he headed down to a makeshift cell for another round of questioning with one of the captured raiders. As the Gradi was nearly Van's size and not of the sort of temper given to inspiring trust, Gerin also brought along Geroge and Tharma. If anything or anybody could intimidate the prisoner, the monsters were the likeliest candidates.

He unbarred the door to the chamber where the Gradi was confined and went in. The raider had a lamp inside, a small, flickering one that filled the room with swooping shadows but didn't really illuminate it. Gerin half expected the Gradi's eyes to reflect the light he carried, as a wolf's would have, but his prisoner was merely human after all.

"I greet you, Kapich," Gerin said in Elabonian.

"I greet you, Gerin the Fox," Kapich returned in the same language. He was more fluent in it than any other Gradi at Fox Keep, which was one reason Gerin kept interrogating him.

He walked farther into the chamber. That let Geroge and Tharma come in behind him. Their eyes did give back the lamplight, redly. Their kind had lived in caverns subterranean for uncounted generations; they needed to be able to seize on any tiny speck of light they could.

Even Gerin's lamp, though, was not very bright. Kapich needed a moment to realize the Fox hadn't just brought a couple of bravos with him, as he'd done on earlier visits. The Gradi sat up on his straw pallet. "Voldar," he muttered, and then something unintelligible in his own language.

"These are my friends, Geroge and Tharma," the Fox said cheerfully. "They're here to make sure you stay friendly and talkative."

Kapich didn't look friendly and he'd never been what anyone would have reckoned talkative. Staring toward the two monsters, he said, "You have bad friends."

"I have bad taste in all sorts of things," Gerin agreed, cheerful still. "I'm keeping you alive, for instance." That brought Kapich's pale glare back to him. He went on, "Now tell me more of what you Gradi aim to do with the land here once you have it."

"There is to tell not so much," Kapich answered. "We make this land into a new Gradihome, we live here, our goddess and gods live here, we all happy, all you other people serve us in life, Voldar and others torment you forever when you die. It is good."

"I'm glad someone thinks so, but it doesn't sound any too good to me," the Fox said. If that bothered Kapich, he did an astonishingly good job of concealing it. Gerin said, "Why do you think you and your jolly crew of gods and goddesses can settle down here without regard for anybody else?"

"Because we are stronger," the Gradi said, with the irksome self-assurance of his kind. "We beat you people at every fight—"

"What are you doing here, then?" Gerin broke in.

"Almost every fight," Kapich corrected himself. "Here, you were lucky. We beat the Trokmoi at every fight, too. Voldar and the gods beat down their gods, too, drive them away. Your gods—" For a moment, his self-assurance cracked. "If your gods let you rule over things like that"

—he pointed to the two monsters— "they must have some strength."

"I'm not a thing," Geroge said indignantly. "Do you hear me calling you a thing? You should know better than to call names." Had Gerin been admonished to mind his manners by anyone with such an impressive set of dental work, he would have seriously considered it.

"It talks!" Kapich said to him. "It is not a hound only. It talks. Your gods will indeed be more trouble than the . . . holy foretellers said."

"And what did the holy foretellers foretell wholly wrong?" Gerin asked.

The wordplay made Kapich frown and mutter; Gerin resolved not to waste his wit on those who couldn't follow it. After puzzling out what he meant, the Gradi said, "They said your gods were foolish and they were weak because this was not their proper home and they had no traffic with that home."

Gerin plucked at his beard. The holy foretellers had a point. In a way, the Elabonian gods were immigrants here, as were those of the Gradi pantheon. And, indeed, the northlands had been cut off from the Elabonian heartland for most of a generation now. But if Dyaus and Baivers and Astis the goddess of love and the rest of the deities who had made their way north with Ros the Fierce were not at home here by now, then they were nowhere at home. They'd had centuries to grow acclimated to the northlands and have the landscape accept them. The Fox was sure the Gradi foretellers had blundered there. How to make them pay for the error?

Had he been one of the heroes of whom the minstrels sang, he would have come up with an answer on the instant and been able to use it within days, if not right away. As he was, however, an ordinary man in the real world, nothing occurred to him. He asked the Gradi, "What do you mean, you'll make the northlands into another Gradihome? What does that entail?" He'd heard the phrase before; he wanted to be sure he understood its meaning.

Kapich stared at him, plainly thinking the question either foolish or having an answer so obvious, it needed no explaining. But explain he did, in condescending tones: "We make this country over, to suit us better. It is too hot now, too sunny. Our gods do not like this; it makes them squint and sweat. When they are at home here, they will shield us from the nasty heat."

Were the Gradi gods strong enough to do that? Gerin didn't know. He didn't want to find out, either. Kapich thought they were. That probably meant they thought they were, too, which meant they'd try.

What little he knew of the land from which the Gradi came derived from Van's accounts of his travels through it. By the outlander's tales, it was a country of snow and rock and stunted trees, where the farmers grew oats and rye because wheat and barley wouldn't ripen in the short, cool summers, a place where berries took the place of tree fruit and wolves and great white bears prowled through the winters.

"I thought you were coming here because you liked our land and our weather better than your own," he said to Kapich. He had a hard time imagining anyone not wanting to escape from the grim conditions Van had described.

But the Gradi shook his head. "No. Voldar hates this hot country. When it is ours, she will make it comfortable. Some of our rowers, in working the oars, fall into a faint from the heat. How do we do a man's deeds while we bake in an oven?"

"If you wanted a cold country, you should have stayed in the one you had." That was not Gerin, or even Geroge: that was Tharma, who usually held her tongue.

"If we are strong enough to take this one, our gods are strong enough to make it fit what we want—and what they want," Kapich answered.

"Do your gods ever want something different from what you want?" the Fox asked, probing for weaknesses.

Kapich shook his head again. "How could that be? They are strong. We are weak. We are their thralls, to do as they will with us. Is it not the same among you here, you and the Trokmoi?"

Gerin thought of his own efforts, some even successful, to trick the gods into doing what he wanted rather than the other way round. "You might say that," he answered, "and then again you might not." Kapich stared at him in incomprehension.

He left the Gradi and went up to the great hall, Geroge and Tharma following. Geroge asked, "Can his gods really do that, what he said they could?" The monster sounded like a boy asking his father for reassurance the sky couldn't really freeze and shatter and fall on his head during a cold winter.

Gerin was as close to a father as Geroge had among the world of men. As far as he was concerned, that meant he had a father's obligation to be honest with the young monster. He said, "I don't know. I've never had to deal with the gods the Gradi follow till now."

"You'll find a way around them." Tharma spoke confidently. As children are convinced their fathers can do anything, she was certain the Fox would be able to fend off Voldar and the rest of the dark deities from the dark, gloomy land the Gradi called their own.

As Widin Simrin's son had shown, most of Gerin's subjects felt that same confidence in him. He wished he had more of it himself. As far as he could see, he'd been lucky in his dealings with gods up to now. When you were dealing with beings far more powerful than you were, how long could your luck last? Could you make it stretch for a whole lifetime? *Of course you can*, Gerin thought wryly. *If you make a mistake while you're treating with a god, you don't have any more lifetime after that.*

Van got up from the table where he'd been sitting. "You look like a man who could use a jack of ale, or maybe three," he said.

"One, maybe," Gerin said while the outlander plied the dipper. "If I drink three, I'll drink myself gloomy."

"Honh!" Van said. "How would anyone else tell the difference?"

"To the crows with you, too," the Fox said, and poured down the ale Van had given him. "These Gradi, you know, they're going to be nothing but trouble."

"No doubt," Van said, but more as if relishing than abhorring the prospect. "You ask me, life gets dull without trouble."

"No one asked you," Gerin said pointedly.

His friend went on as if he hadn't spoken: "Aye, betimes life gets dull. I've put down so many roots here at Fox Keep, oftentimes I think I'm all covered with moss and dust. Life here can be a bore, for true."

"If things get too boring, you can always fight with Fand," the Fox said.

Van tried to ignore that, too, but found he couldn't. "So I do," he said, shaking his head as if to shake off a wasp buzzing around it. "So I do. But she fights with me as much as I fight with her."

That, Gerin knew from experience, was also true. "Maybe it's love," he murmured, which drew an irate glare from Van. The outlander's eyes didn't quite focus and were tracked with red, which made Gerin wonder how many jacks of ale Van had had. His friend didn't test his enormous capacity as often as he once had, but today looked to be an exception.

"If it is love, why do we go on sticking knives into each other year after year?" Van demanded. Given Fand's habits—she'd stabbed a Trokmê who'd mistreated her—Gerin wasn't so sure his friend was using a metaphor till the outlander went on, "You and Selatre, a year'll go by between harsh words. Me and Fand, every peaceful day is a battle won. And you call that love?"

"If it weren't, you'd leave it," Gerin answered. "Every time you have left, though, you've come back." He raised a sardonic eyebrow. "And wouldn't you be bored if you didn't quarrel? You just said you thought peace and staying in one place for years were boring."

"Ahh, Fox, you don't fight fair, hitting a man on the head with his own words like that." Van hiccuped. "Most people—Fand, f'r instance—you say something to 'em and they pay it no mind. But you, now, you listen and you save it and you give it back just so as it'll hurt worst when you do."

"Thank you," Gerin said.

That got him another dirty look from the outlander. "I didn't mean it for praise."

"I know," the Fox answered, "but I'll take it for such all the same. If you don't listen and remember, you can't do much." He turned the subject: "Do you think the Gradi can do as they say they will—them and their gods, I mean?"

"That's the question, sure as sure," Van said, "the one we've been scratching our heads about since they tried to tear the keep down around our ears." He peered down into his jack of ale, as if trying to use it as a scrying tool. "If I had to guess, Captain, I'd say they likely can . . . unless somebody stops them, that is."

"Unless *I* stop them, you mean," the Fox said, and Van nodded, his hard features unwontedly somber.

Gerin muttered something coarse under his breath. Even Van of the Strong Arm, who'd traveled far more widely than he himself ever would, who'd done things and dared things that would have left him quivering in horror, looked to him for answers. He was sick of having the weight of the whole world pressed down on his shoulder. Even a god would break under a burden like that, let alone a man likely more than half through his appointed skein of days. Whenever he wished he could rest, something new and dreadful came along to keep him hopping.

"Lord prince?"

He looked up. There stood Herris Bigfoot, his expression nervous. The new village headman often looked nervous. Gerin wondered whether that was because he worried about his small job as the Fox did about his larger one or because he had something going on the side. "Well?" he said, his voice neutral.

"Lord prince, the village suffered when the Gradi came here," Herris said. "We had men killed, as you know, and fields trampled, and animals run off or wantonly slain, and some of our houses burned down, too—lucky for us it wasn't all of 'em."

"Not just luck, headman." Gerin waved to the warriors sitting here and there in the great hall, some repairing the leather jerkins they covered with scales of bronze to make corselets of them, others fitting points to arrows, still others sharpening sword blades against whetstones. "Luck had a bit of help here. If we hadn't driven the Gradi away, you'd have had a thin time of it."

"That's so." Herris bobbed his head in his eagerness to agree—or at least to be seen agreeing. "Dyaus praise all your brave vassals who kept those robbers from hauling everything back to their big boats. Still and all, though, some bad things happened to us in spite of how brave they fought."

"Ah, now I see which way the wind blows," Gerin said. "You'll want me to take that into account come fall, when I'm reckoning up your dues. You'll be missing people and animals, you'll have spent time you could have been weeding on making repairs, and so forth."

"That's it. That's right," Herris exclaimed. Then he noticed Gerin hadn't promised anything. "Uh, lord prince—will you?"

"How in the five hells do I know?" the Fox shouted. Herris sprang back a couple of paces in alarm. Several of the warriors looked up to see why Gerin was yelling. A little more quietly, he went on, "Have you noticed, sirrah, I have rather more to worry about than you or your village? I was going to fight a war against the Trokmoi. Now I'll have to fight the Gradi first, and maybe Aragis the Archer off to the side. If anything is left of this principality come fall, I'll worry over what to do about your dues. Ask me then, if we're both alive. Till then, don't joggle my elbow over such things, not when I'm trying to figure out how to fight gods. Do you understand?"

Herris gulped and nodded and fled. His sandals thumped on the drawbridge as he hurried back to the village. No doubt he was disappointed; no doubt the rest of the serfs would be. Gerin resolved to bear up under that. As he'd told the headman, he had more important things to worry about.

To his own surprise, he burst out laughing. "What's funny, Fox?" Van demanded.

"Now I understand what the gods must feel like when I ask them for something," Gerin said. "They're really doing things that matter more to them, and they don't like being nagged by some piddling little mortal who's going to up and disappear in a few years no matter what they do or don't do for him. As far as they're concerned, I'm an annoyance, nothing more."

"Ah, well, you're good at the job," Van said. Gerin wondered whether his friend intended that as a compliment or a sly dig. After a moment, he shrugged. However Van intended it, it was true.

Gerin drew his bow back to his ear and let fly. The sinew bowstring lashed his wrist. The arrow flew straight and true, into the flank of a young deer that had wandered too close to the bushes behind which he sheltered. The deer bounded away through the underbrush.

"After him!" Gerin shouted, bursting from concealment. He and Van and Geroge and Tharma pounded down the trail of blood the deer left.

"You got him good, Fox," Van panted. "He won't run far, and we'll feast tonight. Venison and onions, and ale to wash 'em down." He smacked his lips.

"There!" Gerin pointed. The deer had hardly been able to run even a bowshot. It lay on the ground, looking reproachfully back at the men who had brought it down. As always when he saw a deer's liquid black eyes fixed on his, the Fox knew a moment's guilt.

Not so Geroge. With a hoarse cry, the monster threw himself on the fallen deer and tore out its throat with his fangs. The deer's hooves thrashed briefly. Then it lay still.

Geroge got to his feet. His mouth was bloody; he ran his tongue around his lips to clean them. More blood dripped from his massive jaws down onto the brownish hair that grew thick on his chest.

"You didn't need to do that," Gerin said, working hard to keep his voice mild. "It would have been dead soon anyhow."

"But I *liked* killing it," Geroge answered. By the way his deep-set eyes glittered, by the way the breath whistled in and out of his lungs, he'd more than liked it. It had excited him. The suddenly rampant and quite formidable bulge in his trousers suggested the same thing. He didn't yet realize the excitement of the hunt could be transmuted to other excitements, but he would soon.

And what then? Gerin asked himself. It was another question that refused to wait for an answer, especially when he saw how Tharma looked at Geroge. Everything seemed to be descending on his head at the same time: the Trokmoi, the Gradi, the gods, and now the awakening of the monsters. It wasn't fair. You could deal with troubles when they came singly. But how were you supposed to deal with them when you couldn't handle one before the next upped and bit you?

Maybe you couldn't. He'd learned a long time before that life wasn't fair. You had to go on any way you could. But having all his problems so compressed seemed . . . inartistic, somehow. Whatever gods were responsible for his fate should have had more consideration.

Van drew his bronze dagger. "After I gut the beast, what say we make a fire and roast the liver and kidneys right here? Meat doesn't get any fresher than that."

Geroge and Tharma agreed so readily and so enthusiastically that, even had Gerin been inclined to argue, he would have thought twice. But he wasn't inclined to argue. Turning to the monsters, he said, "Gather me some tinder, would you?"

While they scooped up dry leaves and tiny twigs, Gerin found a stout branch on the ground and a good, straight stick. He used the point of his own dagger to bore a hole in the branch, then wound a spare bowstring around the stick and twirled it rapidly with the string. Van was even better with a fire bow than he was, but the outlander was also busy butchering the deer, and Gerin had made plenty of fires on his own. If you were patient . . .

He worked the string back and forth, back and forth. The stick went round and round, round and round in the hole. After a while, smoke began to rise from it. "Tinder," he said softly, not breaking his rhythm.

"Here." Geroge fed some crumpled leaves into the hole—not too many, or he would have snuffed out the sparks Gerin had brought to life. He'd done that before, and Gerin had shouted at him for it just as if he weren't physically far more formidable than the Fox. Gerin breathed gently on the sparks: blowing them out was another risk you took. Presently, they grew to flames.

"There ought to be a way to do that by magic," Van said, impaling a chunk of liver on a stick and handing it to Geroge.

"I know several, as a matter of fact," Gerin answered.

"The easiest will leave you exhausted for half a day. . . . No, that's not so; the one for the flaming sword won't, but that one takes ingredients that aren't always easy to come by and, if you do it wrong, you're liable to burn yourself up. Sometimes the simplest way is the best one."

"Aye, well, summat to that, I suppose," the outlander admitted. "But still, a clever fellow like you ought to be able to figure out an easy way to make the kind of magic you need."

"I have trouble enough working magic," Gerin exclaimed. "Expecting me to come up with new kinds is asking too much." Wizards who could do things like that wrote grimoires; they didn't go from one book of spells to another picking out the simplest things to try and hoping they worked.

Geroge toasted his chunk of liver over the fire. After a moment, Tharma joined him. The savory smell of roast meat drove the thought of magic from the Fox's mind. The meat wasn't well roasted; both foundling monsters had accepted the notion that meat needed cooking before being eaten, but they'd accepted it reluctantly, and ate even roast meat bloodier than was to Gerin's taste.

They were also halfhearted about any notions of manners. With their teeth, they hardly needed to cut bites from a slab of meat so they could chew them. They just bit down, and a juicy gobbet disappeared forever every time they did.

Van handed Gerin a kidney on a stick. He cooked it a good deal longer than the monsters had their pieces of liver. "I wish we had some herbs, or even a bit of salt," he said, but that was almost ritualistic complaint. The strong, fresh flavor of the kidneys—which went stale so quickly after you killed an animal—didn't need enhancement.

Van roasted the deer's other kidney for himself. When he lifted it away from the flames, he took a bite and then swore: "Might as well be right out of your five hells, Fox: I just burned my mouth."

"I've done that," Gerin said. "We've all done that. We ought to bring the rest of the carcass back to the keep."

The outlander checked the sun through the forest's leafy canopy. "We still have some daylight left. I don't feel like going back yet. Suppose I do the heart in four parts and we cook that, too?"

"Do that!" Geroge said, and Tharma nodded. Any excuse to eat more meat was a good one for them.

"Go ahead," Gerin said after he too gauged the sun. "The cooks will jeer at us for stealing the best bits ourselves, but that's all right. They didn't catch the beast, and we did."

Before slicing up the heart, Van kicked the pile of guts away from the fire. He frowned a little. "Not so many flies on 'em as I'd've thought."

"It's been a cool spring. That has something to do with it," Gerin said. Then he too frowned. Sometimes the most innocent remark, when you took it the wrong way—or maybe the right one—led to fresh ideas . . . and fresh worries. "Is it a cool spring because that's how it happens to be, or is it a cool spring because the gods of the Gradi are getting a toehold here and want it to be cool?"

"You have a cheerful way of looking at things, don't you, Fox?" Van handed him a piece of the meat he'd just cut. "Here, get some fresh heart in you."

Gerin snorted. "You have been at Fox Keep a goodish while, haven't you? When you first got here, you never would have made a joke like that."

"See how you've corrupted me?" the outlander said. "Bad jokes, staying in one place for years at a time, having brats and knowing it—I probably sired some out on the road, but I never stayed in one place long enough to find out. It's a strange life settled folk live."

"All what you're used to," Gerin said, "and by now you've been here long enough to be used to this."

He glanced over to Geroge and Tharma. Sometimes the two of them—especially Geroge—would closely follow human conversation. Humans were all they knew, and they wanted to fit in as best they could. Today, though, both of them seemed more intent on the roasting quarters of heart than on what Gerin was saying. He didn't let that bother him as much as he would have a few years before. He'd done a better job of making them into more or less human beings than he'd ever expected.

No. He'd made them into more or less human children.

He still had no proof their true essence would stay hidden as they matured. He still had no idea what to do with them as they did mature, either. The just thing would be to let them grow up as if they were people, and to treat them as such unless and until they gave him some reason to do otherwise. The safe thing would be to put them out of the way before he had to do it.

He took his piece of roasted heart off the fire, blew on it, and took a bite. The meat was tough and chewy, and he lacked the teeth to slice effortlessly through it as Geroge and Tharma had. He sighed. The safest thing would have been to put them out of the way as soon as they came into his hands. He hadn't done that then, fearing the hands of the gods, not his own, had true control over their fate. He still feared that now. He'd do nothing—except worry.

Van's teeth were merely human, but he made short work of his chunk of deer heart. He licked his fingers and wiped them clean on the grass, then dug around with a fingernail to rout out a piece of meat stuck somewhere in the back of his mouth. "That hit the spot," he said. "Enough to make my belly happy, not so much that I won't be able to enjoy myself come supper."

"The way you eat, the only thing that amazes me is that you're not as wide as you are tall," Gerin said.

Van looked down at himself. "I am thicker through the middle than I used to be, I think. If I get too much thicker, I won't be able to fit into my corselet, and then what will I do?"

"Save it for Kor," Gerin answered, "unless Maeva takes it before he has the chance."

"You had that thought run through your head too, eh?" Van started to laugh, but quickly swallowed his mirth. "It could happen, I suppose. There's not a boy her age can match her, and she's wild for weapons, too. Whether that'll still be so once she sprouts breasts and hips—the gods may know, but I don't. She'll not be one of the common herd of women any which way; so much I'll say already."

"No," the Fox agreed. In musing tones, he went on, "I wonder, now: is there any such thing as 'the common herd of women,' once you come to know 'em? Selatre wouldn't fit there, nor Fand, the gods know" —he and Van both chuckled, each a little nervously— "nor Elise, either, thinking back."

"You seldom speak of her," Van said. He scratched at his beard. "To a shepherd, I suppose, each of his sheep is special, even if they're nothing but bleating balls of wool to the likes of you or me."

"I know that's so," Gerin said, warming to the discussion. "I've seen it with my own eyes. It makes you wonder, doesn't it? The better you know the members of a class, the less typical of the class they seem. Does that mean there really isn't any such thing as 'the common herd of women'?"

"Don't know if I'd go so far," Van answered. "Next thing, you'll be saying there's no such thing as a common grain of sand or a common stalk of wheat, when any fool can see there is."

"A lot of times, the things any fool can see are the things only a fool would believe," Gerin said. "If you looked hard enough, I daresay you could find differences between grains of sand or stalks of wheat."

"Oh, you could, maybe," Van allowed, "but why would you bother?"

A question like that, intended to dismiss a subject, often started Gerin thinking harder. So here; he said, "I can't tell you why you might want to know one grain of sand from another, but if you could tell which stalk of wheat would yield twice as much as the others, wouldn't you want to do that?"

"You have me, Fox," his friend said. "If I could do that, I would. I can't, not by looking. Can you?"

"No, though I wish I could." Gerin paused. "I wonder if I could make a magic to see that. Maybe with barley, not wheat: Baivers god of barley knows I've never scanted him, and he might lend me aid. That would be a sorcery worth taking risks for, if I could bring it off."

He wondered if he knew enough, or could learn enough here in the northlands, even to plan such a spell. Or rather, he started to wonder; Geroge's formidable yawn distracted him. The monster said, "I'm bored, sitting around here. Can we go back to the keep now?"

"Aye, we can." Gerin climbed to his feet. "In fact, we'd better, so we're there before sunset. With the deer, we have enough for a decent offering for the ghosts, but you don't want to use such things if you don't have to."

They tied the carcass to a sapling, which they took turns shouldering by pairs as they carried it to the chariot waiting at the edge of the woods. The car had been crowded for four, and was all the more crowded for four plus a gutted deer, but Fox Keep wasn't far.

When they got back, a stranger waited in the courtyard. No, not quite a stranger; after a moment, Gerin identified him: "You're Authari Broken-Tooth, aren't you? One of Ricolf the Red's vassals?"

"Your memory is good, lord prince," the newcomer said, bowing. "I am Authari." When he opened his mouth to speak, you could see the front tooth that gave him his sobriquet. "But I am not Ricolf the Red's vassal. I came here to tell you, Ricolf has died."

IV

"But he can't have done that," Gerin exclaimed: looking back on it, surely one of the more foolish things he'd ever said. Authari was polite enough not to point that out; Authari, whatever else he was, was usually polite. Gerin recovered his wits and went on, "I am in your debt for bringing me the news. You will, of course, stay the night and sup with me."

"I will, lord prince, and thank you," Authari said, bowing again. "It happened four days ago now. He was drinking a cup of ale when he said he had a headache. The cup fell out of his hand and he slid off the bench. He never woke up again, and half a day later he was dead."

"Worse ways to go," the Fox remarked, and Authari nodded. Like most men, both of them had seen a great many worse ways. But that was not the point of this visit, and Gerin knew it. "The succession to his barony—"

Authari coughed. "Just so, lord prince: the succession to his barony. Several of Ricolf's vassals banded together and bade me tell you—"

"Tell me what?" Gerin said, his voice deceptively mild. "What have you and your fellow vassals of Ricolf's to tell me? In law, his heir is surely my son Duren, as he has no sons of his own living."

"Were you still wed to his daughter Elise, lord prince, no one would contest Duren's right of succession," Authari replied. The Fox did not believe that for an instant, but waited for the minor noble to go on. After a moment, Authari did: "By her own actions, though, if tales be true, Elise severed her connection with you. And Duren has been raised here, not in the holding of Ricolf the Red. But for the thin tie of blood, we keepholders have no reason to feel any special loyalty toward your son, and would sooner see one of our own number installed in Ricolf's place."

"Of course you would," Gerin said, mildly still. "That way, when, a year and a half down the line, the rest of you decide you don't care for whichever of your number you've chosen, you can go to war against him with a clear conscience and make his holding as much a mess as Bevon's ever was."

"You misunderstand," Authari said in hurt tones. "That is not our concern at all. Our fear is having foisted upon us a youth who does not know the holding."

Gerin felt his patience leaking away like grains of sand—whether individually identifiable or not—between his fingers. "Your concern is, if Duren takes over Ricolf's holding, you'll all have to become my vassals as well as his. There—now it's out in the open."

"So it is." Authari sounded relieved—he hadn't had to come right out and say it himself. "No one denies you're a good man, lord prince, but we who served Ricolf value our freedom, as true men must."

"You value freedom even more than law, seems to me," Gerin replied, "and when you use the one to flout the other, soon you have neither."

"As may be." Authari drew himself up to his full height. "If you seek to install Duren by force of arms, I must tell you we shall fight."

At most times, that threat, if it could be so dignified, would have made Gerin laugh. Lands where the barons did acknowledge his suzerainty surrounded the holding of Ricolf the Red. The main reason Ricolf had never sworn fealty to him was that he'd been too embarrassed to ask it of the older man after Elise ran away with the horseleech. He could easily have summoned up the force to quash Ricolf's restive vassals . . . were he not facing war with Adiatunnus and a bigger war against the Gradi. He did not need distractions, not now.

And then Authari said, "If you seek to interfere with our freedom, I must tell you we have friends to the south."

"You'd call on Aragis the Archer, would you?" Gerin said. Authari nodded defiantly. "I ought to let you do it," the Fox told him. "It would serve you right. If you think you wouldn't fancy being my vassals, you deserve to be his. First time anyone stepped out of line, he'd crucify the fool. That would make the rest of you think—if anything could, which I doubt."

Authari's angry scowl showed the stump of his front tooth. He shook a finger in Gerin's face. "Now that's just the kind of thing we don't want in an overlord—showing off how much better than us he thinks he is. Aragis would respect us and respect our rights."

"Only goes to show how much you don't know about Aragis," Gerin answered with a derisive snort. But then he checked himself. The more he antagonized Authari, the more the loon and his fellow fools were liable to summon Aragis to their aid. Since the Archer's forces would have to pass through areas under Gerin's control, that would touch off the long-threatened war between them . . . at the worst possible time for the northlands as a whole.

"We may not know about Aragis, by Dyaus, but we know about you," Authari said. "And what we know, we don't trust."

"If you know me, you know my word is good," the Fox said. "Has anyone ever denied that, Authari? Answer yes or no." Reluctantly, Authari shook his head. When he did, Gerin went on, "Then maybe you'll hear out the proposal I put to you."

"I'll hear it," Authari said, "but I fear it may be another of your tricksy schemes."

Gerin thought seriously about taking Authari up onto the palisade and dropping him headfirst into the ditch around Fox Keep. But his head was so hard, the treatment probably would neither harm him nor knock in any sense.

And so the Fox said, "Suppose we ask the Sibyl at Ikos who the rightful heir to Ricolf the Red is? If the oracle says it should be one of you people, I won't fight that. But if Duren should succeed his grandfather, you accept him without any quarrels. Is that just?"

"Maybe it is and maybe it's not," Authari answered. "The god speaks in mysterious ways. We're liable to get an answer that will just keep us squabbling."

"Some truth to that," Gerin said, not wanting to yield any points to Ricolf's vassal but unable to avoid it. "And, of course, people of bad will can deny the meaning of even the plainest verses. Will you and your fellows swear a binding oath by the gods that you'll do no such thing? I will—and I trust Biton's judgment, however he sees the future."

Authari gnawed at his underlip. "You're so cursed glib, lord prince. You always have a plan ready, and you don't give a man time to think about it."

As far as the Fox was concerned, planning came as naturally as breathing. If Authari hadn't thought he might suggest the Sibyl as a means of resolving their dispute, Authari hadn't looked very far ahead. Silently, Gerin sighed. People seldom did.

At last, much more slowly than he should have, Authari said, "I'll take that back to my fellows. It's worth thinking on, if nothing else."

"Don't spend too much time thinking about it," Gerin said in peremptory tones. "If I have to, I can ravage your countryside and maybe take several of your keeps before Aragis could hope to get far enough north to do you any good." With luck, Authari had no idea how reluctant he was to launch such a campaign. Still sharply, he went on, "You'll ride out tomorrow. Ten days after that, I'll follow, and meet you at Ricolf's keep to hear your answer. Don't think to waylay me, for I'll have plenty of men along to start the war on the spot if that's what you people decide you want."

He waited. Authari had the look of a man who'd just discovered his lady friend not only had a husband but that the fellow was twice his size and bad tempered to boot. He licked his lips, then said, "I'll take your word back with me, lord prince. Since you put it so, I expect we'll let the Sibyl and the god decide it, if that's their will."

"I hoped you'd see it that way," Gerin said, with irony that sailed past Authari. He sighed again. "Sup, drink, stay the night. I have to find my son and let him know what's happened."

"Grandfather dead?" Duren's face twisted in surprise. That startlement was all the more complete because, when Gerin tracked him down in a corridor back of the kitchen, death had been the last thing on his mind; exactly what he'd been about to do with a serving girl wasn't obvious, but that he'd been about to do something was.

"That's what I said," Gerin answered, and summarized what Authari had told him, finishing, "He lived a long life, and a pretty good one, taken all in all, and he died easy, as those things go. A man could do worse."

Duren nodded. Once over his initial surprise, he starting thinking soon enough to please his father. "I wish I'd known him better," he said.

"I always thought the same," Gerin said, "but he was never one to travel much, and I—I've had an active time, most of these years. And—" He hesitated, then brought it out: "And the matter of your mother clouded things between us."

He watched Duren's face fall into a set, still mask. That happened whenever the youth had to think of Elise, who'd given him birth and then abandoned him along with Gerin. He didn't remember her at all—for as long as his memory reached, Selatre had been his mother—but he knew of his past, and it pained him.

Then he made the mental connection he had to make: "With Grandfather dead, with my mother—gone—that leaves me heir to the holding."

"So it does," Gerin said. "What do you think about that?"

"I don't know what to think yet," Duren answered. "I hadn't thought to leave Fox Keep so soon." After a moment, he added, "I hadn't thought to leave Fox Keep at all."

"I always knew this was one of the things that might happen," his father said. "That it chose now to happen—complicates my life."

"It complicates my life, too," Duren exclaimed with justifiable indignation. "If I go down there—do you really think I can give orders to men so much older and stronger than I am?"

"You won't be a youth forever. You won't even be a youth for long, though I know it doesn't seem that way to you," the Fox said. "By the time you're eighteen at latest, you'll have a man's full strength. And take a look at Widin Simrin's son. He wasn't any older than you when he took over his vassal barony, and he's done a fine job of running it ever since."

"But he's your vassal," Duren said. "I wouldn't be. I'd be on my own." His eyes widened as he thought that through. "I'd have as much rank as you, Father, near enough. I wouldn't call myself prince or anything like that, but—"

Gerin nodded. "I understand what you're saying. You'd owe no one allegiance, not unless you wanted to. That's right. You could go to war with me if you chose to, and you'd break no oaths doing it."

"I wouldn't, Father!" Duren said. Then, proving he was indeed the Fox's son, he added, "Or rather, I don't see any reason to now."

"I didn't expect you to call out the chariots the moment you become a baron," Gerin said, chuckling. "I'd hope you wouldn't. And, even though you wouldn't be my vassal as Ricolf's heir, you're still my son, and Ricolf's chief vassals know that. It's one of the things that bother them: if they don't answer to you, they'll have to answer to me, and not in ways they fancy. That will help you for a while, and by then, Dyaus willing, they'll have the habit of obeying you."

"I can't lean on you forever," Duren said. "Sooner or later, likely sooner, I'll have to lead on my own."

"That's true." Duren's being able to see it made Gerin want to burst with pride. "When the time comes—and it'll come sooner than you think; it always does—I expect you'll be able to do it."

"What if—" Duren paused, then went on: "What if the Sibyl at Ikos says I'm not to rule Grandfather's holding?"

"Then you're not," Gerin answered. "That's all there is

to it. You can try to twist a god's will, you can try to trick a god, but if you try to go dead against what a god says, you'll fail. If the Sibyl says Ricolf's holding is not for you, you know you have a place here."

"I don't even know that I want to try to run that holding," Duren muttered, perhaps more to himself than to his father.

"If you don't think you want it, if you don't think you're ready, I won't set on you a burden you can't bear," the Fox assured him. "That's what we'll tell Authari, and he'll ride south and tell it to the rest of Ricolf's vassals."

"And the holding will be lost to us," Duren said. It didn't sound like a question, as it easily might have. It came out flat and harsh.

"Things aren't always lost forever," Gerin said. "My guess here is that once the vassals fought among themselves for a while, they'd welcome an overlord who wasn't a jumped-up equal but someone they could all follow without any jealousy."

Duren looked at him in blank incomprehension. Gerin smiled and put a hand on his son's shoulder. For Duren, half a year felt like a long time, and waiting a few years to let things sort themselves out was beyond his mental reach. Gerin didn't blame him. He'd been the same himself at the same age, as had everyone else who made it to and then past fourteen.

"I do want it," Duren declared. "If Biton says I have the right to rule that holding, I'll do the best I can there. One day, maybe—"

He didn't go on. He set his jaw, as if to say Gerin could not make him go on. Gerin didn't try. He could make a pretty good guess as to what was in his son's mind: one day he would die, too, and then Duren would inherit his broad holdings as well as Ricolf's single barony.

His son was right. That was what would happen. If the Gradi got their way, it was liable to happen before the year was out. Of course, if the Gradi got their way, Duren would be in no position to inherit anything but a grave.

Selatre said, "I wish I were coming with you." That wasn't serious complaint; if she'd made serious complaint about riding south with Gerin and Van and Duren, she would have gone. Wistfully, she went on, "I'd like to see how Biton restored his shrine after the earthquake laid it low."

"From all we've heard, it's just the same as it used to be," Gerin said, which was both true and in large measure beside the point: when it took divine intervention to bring back what had been destroyed, the restoration was on the face of it worth seeing.

"And it would be so interesting to go into the underground chamber of prophecy just as a person, not as a Sibyl—to see the prophetic trance from the outside instead of being a part of it."

"It's because you were the Sibyl that I want you to stay here," Gerin told her. "My vassals are more likely to listen to you because the god once spoke through you than they are to any of their own number. And a good thing, too, if you ask me, for you're more clever than any of them."

"More clever than Rihwin?" Selatre asked, mischief in her voice. Her gaze flicked out to the hallway beyond the library chamber where they sat quietly talking: there of all places in Fox Keep they were least likely to be disturbed. But Rihwin, formidably educated himself, was one who might come in to look at a scroll or codex.

Gerin glanced outside, too, before replying, "Much more clever than Rihwin, for you have the sense to know when cleverness for its own sake isn't the answer, and he's never yet figured that out."

"For which I thank you," his wife said. "I'd have been angry if you told me anything else, but I do thank you for what you did tell me."

"Van would say something like 'Honh!' about now," Gerin said.

"So he would," Selatre agreed. "He'll probably say it several times on the trip down to Ikos. He'll probably do several other things on the way down to Ikos, too, things where he'd be better off if Fand never heard of them."

"She won't hear about them from me, or from Van, either, I hope," Gerin said. "Only trouble is, that won't matter. Whether he'll tell her about them or not, she'll know what he's been doing, and they'll have a row when we get home. Or maybe she'll do something to keep herself amused—or to make him furious—while he's gone. Do you suppose you could keep her from trying something like that?"

"Me?" Selatre stared at him in horrified disbelief, then clutched his hand as if she were drowning in the Niffet and he a floating log. "Take me with you to Ikos after all, oh, please! Anything but trying to keep Fand from what she sets her mind on doing!" She laughed, and so did Gerin, but he knew she wasn't altogether joking. She went on, quite seriously, "If anyone can restrain Fand, it's Van, and the other way around. But neither has much hope of that out of the other's sight."

"Too true," Gerin said, and then again, "Too true. I've given up on it, for both of them."

"And you expect me to manage with her?" Selatre said. "I like that!"

Dagref poked his head into the library. "Manage what, Mama? And with who?"

"What I need to manage, and with the person I was talking about," she said.

"Why won't you tell me?" Dagref demanded. Any child would have let out that eternal complaint, but he went on, "Why shouldn't I know? Would I tell someone? Would it make that person angry?" He brightened. His string of questions had led him to an answer. "I'll bet it has something to do with Aunt Fand! She gets angry faster than anyone else I know. Why didn't you want to tell me that? I wouldn't tell your secret, whatever it is. It must have something to do with Uncle Van going away. Is that right?"

Gerin and Selatre looked at each other. It wasn't the first time Dagref had done that to them. His relentless pursuit of precision would take him a long way—unless he failed to notice it leading him into trouble. *He's nine now,* Gerin thought uneasily. *What will he be like as a man grown?* Only one answer occurred to him: *as he is now, only more so.* It was a vaguely—or perhaps not so vaguely—alarming notion.

He said, "No, son, we were talking about one of the

cows down in the village, and what your mother should do if it has chickens."

"Cows don't have chickens," Dagref said indignantly. Then his face cleared. "Oh. You're making a joke." He sounded like Gerin letting off some serf after a minor offense, and warning the wretch of how much trouble he'd be in if he ever did such a thing again.

"Yes, a joke," the Fox agreed. "Now go on out of here and let us finish talking about whatever it was." Knowing secrecy was a losing battle, he fought it anyhow.

Dagref left without any more disputation. That surprised Gerin for a moment. Then he realized his son, having won the argument, didn't need to stay and fight it through a second time. He rolled his eyes. "What are we going to do with that one?"

"Hope experience lends him sense to go with his wits," Selatre answered. "It often does, you know."

"Yes, leaving Rihwin out of the bargain." Gerin glanced warily toward the door, half expecting Dagref to reappear and ask, *Out of what bargain?*

Selatre's gaze had gone in the same direction, and probably for the same reason. When her eyes met Gerin's, they both started to laugh. But she sobered quickly. "If the Gradi or Adiatunnus attack us, I can't lead the men into battle," she said. "Who commands then?"

Gerin wished he hadn't just made his joke, because that question had only one answer. "Can't be anyone but Rihwin," he said. "He's the best of all of them here, especially if he has someone to check his enthusiasm. That's what you'll do, up till the fighting starts. Once it does . . . Well, when the fighting starts, everyone's plans, good and foolish alike, have a way of breaking down."

"I'll miss you," Selatre said. "I always worry when you're away from Fox Keep."

"Sometimes I have to go, that's all," Gerin said. "But I'll tell you this: with you here, I have all the reason I need and then some to want to come back again."

"Good," Selatre said.

The Fox rode south with a force of twenty chariots at his back. That wouldn't be as many as all of Ricolf's vassals could gather, but it was plenty to make him dangerous in a fight. Besides, if Ricolf's vassals didn't have factional squabbles of their own, that would be a miracle about which the minstrels would sing for years to come.

Instead of Raffo, Duren was driving the chariot in which Gerin and Van rode. He handled the reins with confidence but without undue arrogance; unlike some a good deal older than himself, he'd come to understand the importance of convincing the horses to do what he wanted rather than treating them like rowboats or other brainless tools.

As Fox Keep disappeared behind trees when the road jogged, Van let out a long, happy sigh. "Does my nose good to get away from the castle stink!" he said. "Yours is cleaner than most, Fox, but that only goes so far, especially with all the extra warriors packed in."

"I know," Gerin answered. "My nose is happier away from the keep, too. But if we keep rattling along like this, my kidneys are liable to fall out."

"Pity you can't keep the Elabon Way repaired up to the way it used to be," Van said, "but I suppose I should be grateful there's any road at all."

Gerin shrugged. "I haven't the masons to keep it the way it was, or the artisans to build the deep strong bed that holds up to traffic and weather both. Cobbles and gravel keep it open in the rain and mud, even if they are hard on a man's insides and a horse's hooves."

"To say nothing of the wheels," Van added as they jounced over a couple of particularly large, particularly rough cobbles. "Good thing we have spare axle poles and some extra spokes in case we break 'em."

"This isn't even a particularly bad stretch," Gerin said. "Those places farther south where Balamung wrecked the roadway, those are the ones that haven't been the same since in spite of all the effort I've had the peasants put into them."

"You'd expect wizardry to smash a road worse—or faster, anyway—than ordinary wear and tear," Van said. A glint came into his eyes as he went on, "I wonder if you could set it right by wizardry, too."

"Maybe you could." The Fox refused to rise to the bait. "The gods know I wouldn't be madman enough to try."

His little army halted by a peasant village to spend the night. As the sun set, the serfs sacrificed several chickens, letting their blood run down into a small trench they'd dug in the dirt. The offering of blood, the torches flickering outside their huts, and the great bonfire the warriors made were enough to keep the keening of the night ghosts down to a level a man could bear.

Up in the sky, pale Nothos was a fat waxing crescent; Gerin was surprised to realize it had almost completed one of its slow cycles since he'd made his ruling on the rightful ownership of Swifty the hound. A lot had been crowded into that time.

Quick-moving Tiwaz, also a waxing crescent, hung a little to the east of Nothos. Ruddy Elleb, a nail-paring of a moon, soon followed the sun into the west. Golden Math would not rise till after midnight.

Inside the borders of his own holding, he posted only a couple of sentries for the night. Not all his men went straight to sleep, anyhow. Some of them tried their luck with the women, unattached and otherwise, of the village. Some of that luck was good, and some of it was bad. One thing Gerin's subjects had learned during the generation he ruled them: they did not have to give in for no better reason than that a warrior demanded it of them. He'd outlawed fighting men who forced women. His men knew what he expected of them, too, and by and large lived up to it.

When Duren made as if to go after a pretty girl who looked a couple of years older than he was, the Fox said, "Go ahead, but don't tell her who your father is."

"Why not?" Duren asked. "What quicker way to get her to say yes?"

"But will she have said it because you're you or because you're my son?" Gerin asked. He wondered if Duren cared, so long as the answer turned out to be the one he wanted. Probably not; he remembered how little he'd cared at the same age. "Try it," he urged his son. "See what happens."

"Maybe I will," Duren said. And maybe he did, but the Fox didn't find out one way or the other. Feeling no urge to chase after any of the peasant women, he lay down, wrapped himself in a blanket, and slept till the sun woke him the next morning.

The ride down to Ricolf's keep was more peaceful than the journey had been when he'd made it in his younger days. Now all the barons between his own holding and Ricolf's acknowledged him as their overlord, and had, for the most part, given up squabbling among themselves. Even what had been Bevon's barony—now held by his son Bevander, since his other sons had backed Adiatunnus against Gerin in their last clash—seemed to be producing more crops than brigands. *Progress*, he thought.

Because Ricolf had always formally remained free of Gerin's suzerainty, he had kept up the post between his land and Bevon's. His border guards saluted when the Fox and his fighting tail drew near. "Pass through," one of them said, standing aside with a spearshaft he had held across the road. "Authari said you would be coming after him."

"And so we are." Gerin set a hand on his son's shoulder. "And here is Duren, Ricolf's grandson, who, if Biton the farseeing agrees, will become your lord now that Ricolf—a brave man and a good one, if ever such there was—no longer lives in the world of men."

The border guards looked curiously at Duren. Nodding to them, he said, "If I can rule this holding half so well as Ricolf did, I will be pleased. I hope you will be pleased with me, too, and teach me what I need to learn."

Gerin hadn't told him what to say on first meeting Ricolf's men. He wanted to see how his son fared on his own. He would be on his own if he succeeded to the barony. The guardsmen seemed happy enough with what he'd said. One of them asked, "If you take the holding, will it be as vassal to the Fox here?" He pointed at Gerin.

Duren shook his head. "He hasn't asked that of me. Why would he? I'm his son. What kind of oath could I give to bind me to him tighter than that?"

"Well said," one of the border guards answered. He waved southward, deeper into the territory Ricolf had ruled. "Ride on, then, and may the gods make it all turn out for the best."

Once they'd passed beyond the border station, Gerin

said, "You did fine there. You can give Authari and the rest of the petty barons the same answer. I don't see how they can fault you on it, either."

"Good," Duren answered over his shoulder. "I've been thinking about these things ever since Authari came to Fox Keep. I want to do them as best I can."

"You will, with that way of looking at them," Gerin told him. He studied his son's back as the chariot rattled along. Duren was starting to do his own thinking, not coming to the Fox for every answer. *He's becoming a man*, Gerin thought, bemused, but he took it for a good sign.

They came to the keep that had for so many years been Ricolf's as the sun was sliding down the western sky. Elleb had grown to a plump waxing crescent, while Nothos, at first quarter, hung like half a coin a little east of south. Tiwaz had swelled in the past three days to halfway between quarter and full, and was climbing toward the southeastern part of the sky.

"Who comes to this castle?" the watchman called, and Gerin felt a jar inside him at hearing Ricolf's name omitted from the challenge. Approaching Ricolf's keep gave him an odd feeling these days anyhow: old memories twisted and stirred and muttered in his ear like the night spirits, fighting to be understood once more in the world of the living. Here he had met Elise, here he had spirited her away south of the High Kirs, here on returning he had bedded her, here after beating Balamung he had returned and claimed her for his wife.

And she was gone now, and had been gone for most of the time since then, and taken a piece of his spirit with her when she went. And so, for all the happiness he'd found since with Selatre, coming here was like poking at a scar that, while it had healed on the surface, remained sore down below. It probably would be, so long as he lived.

But change came along with memory. He answered the watchman: "I am Gerin, called the Fox, come with my son Duren who is also the grandson of Ricolf the Red to discuss the succession to this holding with Authari Broken-Tooth and whichever of Ricolf's vassal barons he may have summoned hither."

"You are welcome here, lord Gerin," the sentry said. He could hardly have failed to know who the Fox was, but the forms had to be observed. With a rattle of chains, the drawbridge lowered so Gerin and his companions could cross over the moat and enter the keep. Unlike Gerin's, Ricolf's ditch had water in it, making it a better ward for the castle.

Ricolf's men stared down from the walls at Gerin and the small chariot army he'd brought with him. In the failing light, he had trouble reading their faces. Did they think him ally or usurper? Even if he could not tell now, he'd find out soon enough.

Authari came out of the great hall along with several other men who wore authority like a cloak. Authari bowed, well-mannered as usual. "I greet you, lord prince." His eyes swung to Duren. "And you as well, grandson of the lord who held my homage and fealty."

He conceded Duren nothing. Gerin had expected as much. Duren said, "Dyaus and the other gods grant you give me vassalage as good as my grandfather got from you."

Gerin admired his son's self-possession. It seemed to startle Authari, but he quickly rallied, saying, "That is what we have gathered here to decide." He gave his attention back to Gerin. "Lord prince, I present to you Hilmic Barrelstaves, Wacho Fidus' son, and Ratkis Bronzecaster, who with me are—were—Ricolf's chiefest vassals."

Hilmic Barrelstaves was short and stocky, with bowed legs that had probably given him his ekename. A streak of white ran through his black hair, almost like a horse's blaze. The end of a scar that must have seamed his scalp just showed on his forehead. Gerin had seen cases like that before, where hair grew in pale along the length of a healed wound.

Wacho, by contrast, could have been a Trokmê from his looks; he was tall and blond and ruddy, with pale eyes above knobby cheekbones and a long, thin nose. Ratkis seemed an ordinary Elabonian till you noticed his hands, which were callused and scarred, probably from the craft from which he derived his sobriquet.

As with Authari, Gerin knew them, but not well. They

greeted him as equal to equal, which was technically correct—till Ricolf had a successor they acknowledged, they were their own men—but struck the Fox as arrogant all the same. He let it go. Power still lay with him.

"Shall we start the wrangle now, or wait till after supper?" Authari asked once the greetings were done.

"No wrangle," Gerin answered. "Two things can happen. First, you can accept Duren as your baron straightaway—"

"We won't," Wacho said, and Hilmic nodded emphatic agreement. Neither Authari nor Ratkis backed Wacho by word or gesture. That disconcerted him; he choked down whatever he might have been about to add and instead asked, "What's the other thing?"

"We wait to see what the Sibyl at Ikos says," Gerin told him. "If Biton says Duren is to rule here, rule he will, and nothing you try to do about it will change things a bit. And if the god says he's not meant to be your baron, he'll go back to Fox Keep with me. Where's the wrangle in any of that? Or don't you agree to the terms Authari and I settled on?" Without changing his voice in any easily describable way, he let Wacho know disagreeing with those terms would not be a good idea.

Ratkis spoke for the first time: "The terms are fair, lord prince. More than fair: you could have brought a real army with you, not a guard, and installed the lad in this keep by force. But sometimes, when Biton speaks through the Sibyl, what he means isn't clear till long afterwards. Life's not always simple. What do we do if it's complicated here?"

Gerin almost grabbed him by the hand and swore friendship with him for life for nothing more than recognizing that ambiguity could exist. To most men in the northlands, something was either good, in which case it was perfection, or bad, in which case it was abomination. The Fox supposed that made keeping track of things simple, but simplicity was not always a virtue.

"Here's what I have in mind," he said. "If anyone thinks the Sibyl's verse can have more than one meaning, even if interpreted with all possible goodwill, then we put it to the four of you on the one hand and Duren, Van, the lady Selatre, and me on the other. Whoever has the most backers among those eight will see his view prevail."

"And if the eight of us divide evenly?" Authari asked.

"The four of you against the four of us, you mean?" Gerin said.

"That seems likeliest," Authari answered.

The Fox was about to reply, but Duren spoke first, his voice for once man-deep, not cracking at all: "Then we go to war, and edged bronze will tell who has the better right."

"I was about to say the same thing," Gerin said, "but my son—Ricolf's grandson, I remind you once more—put it better than I could hope to do." He didn't add that he wanted a war with Ricolf's vassals about as much as he wanted an outbreak of pestilence in the village by Fox Keep.

"If we go to war, Aragis the Archer will—" Wacho began.

"No, Aragis the Archer won't," Gerin interrupted. "Oh, Aragis may choose to fight me over Ricolf's holding here, but he won't be doing it for you and he won't do you any good. I'll have beaten you before his men get this far north, I promise you that. A bear and a longtooth may quarrel over the carcass of a deer, but it doesn't matter to the deer any more, because it's already dead."

Hilmic Barrelstaves scowled at him. "I knew it was going to be like this. You come down here and threaten us—"

"By all the gods, I've gone out of my way *not* to threaten you," Gerin shouted, clapping a hand to his forehead. When he lost his temper, he usually did it for effect. Now he was perilously close to losing it in truth. "We could overrun this holding: Ratkis said as much. You know it, I know it, any half-witted one-eyed dog sniffing through rubbish down by the shore of the Orynian Ocean knows it, too. Instead of that, I proposed letting Biton decide. If that didn't satisfy you, I proposed a way to solve the difficulty. And if you won't heed the god and you won't heed men, sirrah, you deserve to have your thick head knocked in."

A silence rather like the one just after the crash of a thunderbolt filled the courtyard to Ricolf's castle. Authari chuckled nervously. "Well, if the god is kind, he'll give us a response that tells us what we want to know. Then we won't have to worry about any of the rest of this."

Gerin pounced on that. "So you do agree—all four of you do agree—to let Biton speak on this matter?"

One after another, Ricolf's vassals nodded, Authari first, Hilmic last, looking as if he hated to be moving his head up and down. Ratkis Bronzecaster said, "Aye, we agree. We'll take any oath you set to bind us to it, and you'll take ours to do the same."

"Let it be so," Gerin said at once. Of the four of them, Ratkis impressed him as a man of sense. Hilmic and Wacho spoke before they thought, if they thought at all. He wasn't sure what to make of Authari, which probably meant Authari would play both ends against the middle if he thought he saw a chance.

"Let it be so," Authari said now, "and let us sup. Perhaps this will look better after meat and bread."

"Almost anything looks better after meat and bread," Gerin said agreeably.

Ricolf had always set a good table, if not a fancy one, and his cooks carried on after his passing: along with beef and roast fowl, they set out plates of boiled crayfish, fried trout, and turtles baked in their shells. There was plenty of good chewy bread to eat along with the meat and soak up the juices, and scallions and cloves of fragrant garlic to spice up the food. For the hundredth, maybe the thousandth, time, Gerin missed pepper, though he could find no complaint with what was set before him.

His men and those who owed allegiance to Ricolf—or rather, to his chief vassals—crowded the hall. They got on well enough, even after the servants had refilled their drinking jacks a good many times. Some of Gerin's retainers and some of Ricolf's had fought side by side in old wars, after the werenight and against the monsters and in the four-cornered struggle that had wracked Bevon's barony for so long. If they had to battle one another, it would not be with any great enthusiasm.

That didn't mean they wouldn't battle one another. Parol Chickpea said, "If the lord prince gives the order, we'll squash you lads underfoot like a nest of cockroaches. I won't much care for that, but what can you do?"

"You can get beaten back to your own land where you belong," said the fellow sitting beside him: one of Ricolf's troopers, and one who, by his look and bearing, a man of sense would not annoy.

Parol was a lot of things, but seldom sensible. A monster had bitten off a large chunk of one of his buttocks; Gerin wondered if sitting lopsided for years had unbalanced his brain. Probably not, the Fox judged. Parol hadn't been bright before he developed a list.

"No one in this hall wants to go to war with anyone else here," Gerin said loudly, wishing Parol would keep his mouth shut. "If we wanted to go to war, we would have done it already. I always reckoned Ricolf a friend and his men allies. Father Dyaus grant that my men and those of this holding always stay friends and allies."

"Truth there," Ratkis Bronzecaster said, and raised his drinking jack in salute. Gerin was pleased to drink with him.

A buxom young serving girl did everything she could to attract Duren's notice but plop herself down in his lap. Duren did notice her, too. His eyes stuck to her the way little scraps of cloth would stick to amber after you rubbed it. But he did not get up and follow her, despite the glances she kept throwing over her shoulder.

"Good for you," Gerin told him. "If you're going to rule this holding, you don't want to get a reputation as a man who thinks with his spear first and his head later. You're a likely-looking lad; finding willing women shouldn't be any trouble for you. But this wench—who knows what she's after, making up so soon to the fellow who's likely to be her overlord?"

"That's what I was thinking," Duren answered. What else he was thinking, though, was also obvious from the way he kept watching the girl.

Wacho Fidus' son breathed ale fumes into Gerin's face. "So you will be going on to Ikos, eh, lord prince?"

"A man with a gift for the obvious," Gerin observed, which, as he'd expected, made Wacho stare at him in beery incomprehension. Sighing, he went on, "As a matter of fact, what point in going on to Ikos if you retainers of Ricolf's try to ignore what the god tells you if it's not to your liking? I don't want to do it, mind you, but we might as well just fight the war. You'd have no doubt of what you were supposed to do then, anyhow."

Wacho understood that well enough, and looked appalled. He said, "No such thing, lord prince. We were just talking about what to do if the Sibyl's verse turned out to be obsc—ob—hard to make head or tail of, that's all. If it's plain, we have no quarrel."

"By everything you and your three comrades have said and done, you'd do anything to show the Sibyl's verse was obscure, regardless of whether that's really so," Gerin said. "I don't know why I'm wasting my time with you."

He knew perfectly well why he was wasting his time with them: he didn't want to get into a little war down here, not when two bigger ones were building in the west and Aragis the Archer loomed, watching and waiting, in the south. But if he could push Ricolf's vassals into forgetting that, he'd do it without hesitation or compunction.

Still looking horrified, Wacho went off and collared Authari, Ratkis, and Hilmic. The four of them put their heads together, then came back over to the Fox. "See here," Authari said, his voice full of nervous bluster. "I thought we had a bargain to abide by what the Sibyl at Ikos said."

"So did I," Gerin answered. "But when I got down here, what I found you people meaning was that you would interpret Biton's words they way they suited you, no matter what he said."

"We never said any such thing," Hilmic Barrelstaves said indignantly.

"I didn't say you said it. I said you meant it," Gerin told him. " 'What do we do if we don't agree? What do we do if we don't agree?' You might as well have been crickets, all chirping the same note." He got up as if to stamp out of the great hall, as if to stamp out of Ricolf's keep altogether, in spite of the ghosts that turned the night to terror.

"Give us an oath," Ratkis said. "Give us an oath we can swear and we will swear it. Authari was talking about that with you, I know, and I said as much earlier myself. We want—I want—fair dealing here."

Him Gerin believed. He was less sure about the other three. But a strong enough oath would attract the notice of even the rather lackadaisical Elabonian gods if it was violated. "All right. Will you swear by Father Dyaus and farseeing Biton to accept the words of the Sibyl on their face if there is any possible way to do so. Will you also swear that, should you violate your oath, you pray you will have only sorrow and misfortune in this world and that your soul will not even wander the world by night, but will rest forever in the hottest of the five hells?"

Ricolf's four vassals looked at each other, then went off to put their heads together again. When they came back, Authari Broken-Tooth said, "That's a strong oath you require of us."

"That's the idea," Gerin said, exhaling through his nose. "What point to an oath you don't fear breaking?"

"Will *you* swear the same oath?" Wacho demanded.

By his tone, he expected the Fox to recoil in dismay from the very idea. But Gerin said, "Of course I will. I don't fear what Biton says. If Duren isn't fated to rule this holding, the god will make that plain. And if he is so fated, Biton will tell us that, too. So I will swear that oath. I'll swear it now, this instant. Join me?"

They went off once more. Gerin sipped his ale and watched them argue. It seemed to be Authari and Ratkis on one side, Wacho and Hilmic on the other. He couldn't hear them, but he would have been willing to guess which men were on which side.

At last, rather glumly, the barons returned. Speaking for them, Authari said, "Very well, lord prince. We will swear the oath with you. If we disagree in spite of it, we will settle the disagreements as you proposed. In short, we agree with all your proposals, straight down the line."

"No, we don't agree with them," Hilmic Barrelstaves said angrily. "But we'll go along with them. It's either that or fight you, and our chances there don't look good to us, not even if Aragis comes in on our side."

"You're right," Gerin said. "Your chances wouldn't have been good. Shall we swear now, before our men?"

Wacho and Hilmic looked as if they would have delayed if they could have found any good reason for doing so. But Ratkis Bronzecaster said, "It would be best so. That way, our retainers can have no doubt about what the agreement is."

"Exactly my thought," Gerin said. *It also makes it harder for you to go about breaking the oath later: your own men will call you on it if you do.*

When the two hesitant barons nodded at last, Duren said, "I will swear this oath, also. If this is to be my holding, it will be *mine*, so I should speak for myself in matters that touch on it."

"Good enough," Gerin said heartily, and Ricolf's vassals also made approving noises. Down deep, Gerin wondered how good it really was. Would his son, if he became lord here, suddenly start ignoring everything he said? Duren was of about the right age to do something like that. And his mother, from whom he drew half his blood, had always been one to follow her impulses to the hilt, whether it was running away with Gerin or running away from him a few years later. Was Elise's blood showing itself in Duren? And if it was, what could the Fox do about it?

He quickly answered that one: *nothing*. Forcing the issue by bringing Duren here had been his idea. Now he would have to face the consequences, whatever those turned out to be.

He got to his feet. So did Duren, and so, a moment later, did Ricolf's four leading vassals. Gerin looked at them, hoping one of their number—maybe Authari, who liked to hear himself talk—would announce to the expectantly waiting warriors his approval of what they had agreed upon. That would make it look as if the oath had been in large measure their idea, not his.

But Authari and his comrades stood mute, leaving it up to the Fox. He made the best of it he could: "We now seal by this oath we are about to swear to abide by the far-seeing god's choice as to whether Duren should rule this holding, the oath setting out what we hope will happen to us in this world and the next if we go against any of its provisions. I will say the terms, and Ricolf's vassals and my son will repeat them after me, all of us committing ourselves to this course."

He waited for any objection from his men or from those who owed allegiance to Ricolf's vassals. When none came, he said, "I begin." He turned to Duren and to Ricolf's lordlets: "Say each phrase of the oath after me: 'By Dyaus All-Father and farseeing Biton I swear—' "

" 'By Dyaus All-Father and farseeing Biton I swear—' " Authari and Ratkis, Wacho and Hilmic, and Duren all echoed him. He listened carefully to make sure they did. If not everyone swore the same oath, people would be able to question its validity. That was the last thing he wanted.

He made the oath as comprehensive and strict as he could, so much so that Wacho and Hilmic and even Authari looked at him sidelong as provision after stern provision rolled off his tongue. Duren took the oath without hesitation. So did Ratkis Bronzecaster. The Fox thought Ratkis honest. If he wasn't, he was so shameless as to be deadly dangerous.

At last he could think of nothing more to bind Ricolf's vassals to their promises. "So may it be," he finished, and, with evident relief, they repeated the words after him: "So may it be." The oath had done what it could do. The rest would be up to the men who had followed Ricolf so long—and to the farseeing god.

Eight chariots rattled down the narrow track through the strange and haunted wood that grew around the little valley housing the hamlet of Ikos and Biton's shrine nearby. Gerin, Duren, and Van rode in one; their retainers filled three more; and Authari, Wacho, Ratkis, and Hilmic each headed one crew.

"I've never been to see the Sibyl, not in all my days," Hilmic Barrelstaves said, his voice unwontedly quiet as he peered this way and that into the wood. "Did I see a—? No, I couldn't have." He shook his head, denying the idea, whatever it had been, even to himself.

Gerin had been through that curious wood a good many times, but he was wary there, too. You were never quite sure what you saw or heard—or what saw and heard you. Sometimes you got the strong feeling you were better off not knowing.

Even Van spoke softly, as if not wanting to rouse whatever powers rested in uneasy sleep. "I think we'll make it to the town before sundown," he said. "Hard to be sure, when the leaves block the sunlight so—and when you're in this place any which way. Time feels—loose—here, so it's hard to judge how long you've really been traveling."

"This forest is as old as the world, I think," Gerin answered, "and now, it's a little, mm, disconnected from the rest of the world. It puts up with this road through it, but only just barely."

Duren drove on in silence. The horses were nervous, but he controlled them. Like Hilmic, he was making his first visit to Ikos, and he was as busy as Ricolf's vassal trying to look in every direction at once, and as wide-eyed at the things he was—and the things he wasn't—seeing.

To Gerin's relief, Van proved right: they emerged from the wood with some daylight left. The idea of having to camp in among those trees chilled the Fox. Who could say what kind of ghosts lived in this place? He did not want to find out, and was glad he would not have to.

"Rein in," he told his son, and Duren obediently brought the chariot to a stop. Gerin stared down into the valley at the white-marble splendor of Biton's shrine and the almost equally splendid wall of marble blocks surrounding its compound. "Will you look at that?" he said softly.

"Amazing," Van agreed, nodding. They'd both seen that shrine and that wall overthrown in the earthquake that had released the monsters from their age-long underground captivity and loosed them on the upper world. Van went on, "It looks the same as it always did."

"That it does," Gerin said. It would have been impossible for any men in the northlands to restore that temple, built as it was with the full resources of the Empire of Elabon in its glory days and all the talented artists and artisans the Empire provided. But Biton had rebuilt the shrine, and in an instant. Because of that, Gerin had wondered if it would be even more magnificent than it had been before. But no—at least from a distance, it merely seemed the same.

Ikos—the town, as opposed to the shrine—was different from what it had been. Biton had not restored the overthrown hostels and eateries as he had his own temple. There were fewer of them now than there had been before the quake; some then had been just hanging on, for traffic to the Sibyl's underground chamber had shrunk since the Empire of Elabon cut itself off from the northlands. The ones who had been suffering, evidently, had not rebuilt. By the quiet streets that wound between the surviving shelters, more would have been superfluous.

When the innkeepers saw eight cars bearing down on them at once, they fell with glad cries on the warriors those cars carried. Gerin remembered the outrageous prices he'd paid to rest his head in the days before the werenight. He and his companions got bigger rooms, with meals thrown in as part of the bargain, for less than half as much. Any business, these days, was better than none to the townsfolk.

"How do these people live when the inns are empty, the way they look to be most of the time?" Van asked in the taproom later that evening.

"They get rich, taking in one another's laundry," Gerin answered, deadpan.

Van started to nod, then stared sharply and let out a snort. "You want to watch that tongue of yours, Fox. One fine day you'll cut yourself with it." Gerin stuck out the member in question and stared down at it, cross-eyed. Van made as if to drench him with a jack of ale, but didn't do it. That relieved the Fox; his friend started tavern brawls for the sport of it.

Gerin and Duren shared a chamber. Van took the one next to theirs, and didn't want any of the rest of the Fox's followers in there with him. Even with the bargain rates they were getting, Gerin, who made money last till it wore out, fretted at the extra expense. But it quickly became obvious Van did not intend to sleep alone. He made advances to both serving girls who were bringing food from the kitchens, and soon had one of them sitting on his lap, giggling at the way his beard tickled while he nuzzled her neck.

The Fox sighed. One way or another, word of what Van was doing would get back to Fand, and that would start another of their fights. Gerin was sick of fights. How were you supposed to live your life in the middle of chaos? But some people reveled in such disorder.

Van was one of them. "I know what you're thinking,

Captain," he said. "Your face gives you away. And do you know what? I don't care."

"That's what Rihwin said, when he danced his wife away," Gerin answered. Van wasn't listening to him. Van wasn't listening to anything save his drinking jack and the stiff lance he had in his breeches.

Duren looked hungrily at the serving girl. But then he took a long look around the taproom. A couple of other wenches were serving there, true. But all the men they were serving were both older and far more prominent than he. He took a sip from his jack of ale and then said, "My chances aren't good here tonight, are they?"

The Fox set a hand on his shoulder. "You're my son, sure enough," he said. "There're men twice your age—Dyaus, there're men four times your age—who'd never make that calculation, and who'd sulk or rage for days because they didn't have some doe-eyed girl helping 'em pull their breeches down."

Duren snorted. "That's foolish."

"Aye, so it is," Gerin answered. "Doesn't stop it from happening all the time—and women aren't immune to it, either, not even a little bit. People *are* foolish, son—haven't you noticed that yet?"

"Oh, maybe once or twice," Duren said, as dryly as the Fox might have. Gerin stared at him, then started to laugh. If Duren did take over at what had been the holding of Ricolf the Red, Wacho, Hilmic, and Authari would never know what hit them. Ratkis Bronzecaster might, but the Fox had the feeling he'd be on Duren's side.

After a while, Gerin tipped his drinking jack over on its side and went upstairs carrying a candle, Duren trailing along behind him. Van and the serving maid had already gone up there; the noises from behind the outlander's door told without any possible doubt what they were doing. The amatory racket came through the wall, too. As Gerin used the candle to light a couple of lamps, Duren said, "How are we supposed to sleep with *that* going on?"

"I expect we'll manage," Gerin said. A moment later, a moan from the other side of the wall contradicted him. He thought about rapping on the timbers, but forbore; as any man was liable to do, Van grew testy if interrupted, and a testy Van was not something to contemplate without trepidation. "We'll manage," the Fox repeated, this time as much to convince himself as his son.

When the shutters were closed, they made the bedroom dark and hot and stuffy. Leaving them open let in fresh air, but also bugs and, come morning, daylight, which woke Gerin earlier than he would have liked.

He sat up and rubbed his eyes with something less than enthusiasm. He hadn't slept as well as he would have liked, and he had had a little more ale than he should have—not enough for a true hangover, but plenty to give him the edge of a headache behind his eyes and to make his mouth taste like something scraped off the dung heap.

To improve his mood yet further, a rhythmic pounding started in the chamber next door. That was enough to wake Duren, who stared at the wall. "I *was* asleep," he said, as if not quite believing it. He lowered his voice. "Is he at it still, Father?"

"Not still, the gods be thanked. Only again." Gerin raised an eyebrow. "If he's not down by breakfast, we'll rap on the door. Of course, if he's not down by breakfast, the serving girl won't be, either, so breakfast may be late."

Van did come down for breakfast, looking mightily contented with the world. After bread and honey and ale, he and Gerin and Duren, along with Ricolf's four leading vassals, walked down to Biton's shrine, a little south of the hamlet of Ikos.

At close range as from a distance, the shrine and its grounds seemed identical to the way they had been before the earthquake tumbled them and loosed the monsters on the northlands. There within the marble wall was the statue of the dying Trokmê; there not far away stood the twin gold-and-ivory statues of Ros the Fierce, conqueror of the northlands, and Oren the Builder, who had erected the temple to Biton in half-Sithonian, half-Elabonian style.

Both Ros and Oren seemed perfect and complete. Gerin scratched his head at that. After the temblor, he'd taken away the jewel-encrusted golden head of Oren when it rolled outside the bounds of Biton's sacred precinct, within which it was death to steal. The precious metal and gems had helped him greatly in the years since, and yet here they were, restored as they had been. The Fox shrugged. The ways and abilities of gods were beyond those of men.

Yet not even Biton, it seemed, had been able to bring back to life the guardsmen and eunuch priests who had served him. All those here now looked young (though more and more of the world looked young to Gerin these days), and no faces were familiar. The ritual, however, remained the same: before a suppliant went down below the temple to put a question to the Sibyl, money changed hands. Because Gerin was prince of the north, his offering was larger than any ordinary baron's would have been. That irked him, but he paid. You tried to constrain the gods, or their priests, at your peril.

When the plump leather sack he handed to a eunuch had been judged and found adequate, the priest said, "Enter lord Biton's shrine and pray for wisdom and enlightenment."

"Remember when you used to have to queue up even to get into the temple?" Van said to Gerin. "Not like that any more."

"But perhaps it shall be again one day," the eunuch said before Gerin could reply. "The fame of Biton's restored temple has spread widely through the northlands, but times are so unsettled, few make the journey despite its reputation: travel is less safe than it might be."

"I know," Gerin answered. "I've done everything I could do to make it safer in the lands whose overlord I am, but it's not all it could be. That hurts trade, and costs money, too."

He and his companions followed the eunuch into Biton's shrine. As always on entering there, the ancient image of the farseeing god caught and held the Fox's eye, more than all the architectural splendor Oren had lavished on the building surrounding it. Given a choice, Oren surely would have discarded the image and replaced it with a modern piece from one of his stable of sculptors. That he hadn't discarded it suggested someone, whether a priest of Biton, the Sibyl at the time, or the god himself, had given the Elabonian Emperor no choice.

The statue, if it could be dignified by that word, was a pillar of black basalt, almost plain. The only marks suggesting it was more than a simple stele were an erect phallus jutting from its midsection and a pair of eyes scratched into the stone a hand's breadth or two below the top. Gerin studied those eyes. Just for an instant, they seemed brown and alive and human—or rather, divine. He blinked, and they were scratches on stone once more.

Along with his son, his friend, and Ricolf's vassals, he sat in the front pews of the temple and, peering down at the tiny tesserae of the floor mosaic, prayed that the farseeing god would give him the guidance he sought. When he raised his eyes, the eunuch priest said, "I shall conduct you to the Sibyl's chamber. If you will come with me—"

A black slit in the ground led to the countless caverns below Biton's shrine. Duren's eyes were large as, side by side with Gerin, he set foot on the stone steps that eased the suppliant's way on the beginning of the journey. Gerin's heart pounded, though he had been this way several times before. Behind him, Wacho and Hilmic muttered nervously.

He wondered whom Biton's priests had found for a Sibyl to replace Selatre. When the farseeing god restored his temple compound, he'd wanted to restore Selatre to her place as well. Gerin would not have—indeed, how could he have?—hindered that, but Selatre had begged Biton to let her stay in the new life she'd found, and the god, to the Fox's relief and joy, had done as she asked. Now Biton spoke through someone new.

The air in the caverns was fresh and cool and moist, with a hint of a breeze. Gerin, with his itch to learn, wished he knew how it circulated rather than merely that it did. The priest carried a torch, and others burned at intervals along the rock wall. The flickering light did strange, sometimes frightening things to the shadows the travelers along that ancient way cast.

Yet it also picked out sparkling bits of rock crystal set into the rough walls of the passage, some white, some orange, some red as blood. And, now and again, the torchlight showed ways branching off from the main track, some open, some walled up with brick and further warded by potent cantrips.

Gerin pointed to one of those walled-off passages. "Do the monsters still lurk back there, behind the spells that hold them at bay?"

"We believe so," the priest answered, his sexless voice quiet and troubled. "Those wards are, however, as the lord Biton made them. None of us has been past them to be certain—nor, I might add, have the monsters made any effort to return to the world of light."

"Those horrible things." Ratkis Bronzecaster made a hand sign to avert ill-luck. "They gave us no end of trouble when they were loose." *And do I get any credit for tricking the gods into taking them off the surface of the world?* Gerin thought. *Not likely*. But then Ratkis went on with a thought that hadn't occurred to him before: "I wonder if they have gods of their own down here."

Now Gerin's fingers twisted in the avert-evil sign. Some of the monsters—not all—might well be smart enough to conceive of gods, or to have whatever gods who already dwelt in these caves take notice of them: philosophers argued endlessly about how the link between gods and men (or even between gods and not-quite-men) came into being. The Fox was certain of one thing—he didn't want to meet whatever gods might dwell down here in this endless gloom.

"I wonder what Geroge and Tharma would think if we ever brought them down here," Duren said as he walked along the fairly smooth path uncounted generations of feet had worn in the stone.

"That's another good question," Gerin agreed. He started to add that he didn't want to answer it, but stopped and held his peace. If the monsters at Fox Keep did prove troublesome as they matured, he might have no choices left but to slay them or send them down here with their fellows.

The passage wound down and down through the living rock. Most times, that was just a semipoetic phrase to the

Fox. Down in the midst of it, though, the rock of the cave walls did seem alive, as if it were dimly conscious not only of his presence but also of separating him from the monsters in the deeper, walled-off galleries.

And it would have twitched and writhed like a living thing in the earthquake that had freed the monsters. Gerin wondered what being underground here when the quake struck would have been like. He was glad he hadn't found out; he and Van had spoken with Selatre (whose name, of course, he had not then known) less than a day before the temblor shook the whole northlands.

A pool of brighter light ahead marked the entrance to the Sibyl's chamber. The priest asked, "Would you like me to withdraw so you can put your question to Biton's voice on earth in private?" Having him withdraw would have involved paying him more. When no one seemed ready to do that, he shrugged and led the suppliants into the chamber.

Torchlight shimmered from the Sibyl's throne, which looked as if it was carved from a single, impossibly immense black pearl. Clad in a simple white linen shift, the girl on the throne was plainly of the old northlands stock whose blood still ran strong around Ikos; by her looks, she might have been cousin to Selatre.

"What would you ask my lord Biton?" she asked. Her voice, a rich contralto, made Gerin move her age up a few years: though maid-slim, she was probably on his side of twenty, not the other one.

He asked the question in exactly the words upon which he and Ricolf's vassals had agreed: "Should my son Duren succeed his grandfather Ricolf the Red as baron of the holding over which Ricolf held suzerainty till he died?"

The Sibyl listened intently—as well she might, for she was listening for her divine master as well as herself. The mantic fit hit her hard, as it had the predecessors of hers whom Gerin had seen on that black-pearl throne: Selatre, and before her an ancient crone who had been Biton's voice on earth for three generations of suppliants.

Eyes rolled back in her head to show only white, the Sibyl writhed and twitched. Her arms jerked and flailed, seemingly at random. Then she stiffened. Her lips parted.

She spoke, not with her own voice, but with the firm, confident baritone Biton always used:

"The young man shall hold all the castles
And all within shall be his vassals.
But peril lurks, like dark in caves
And missteps here fill many graves.
Aye! Danger lurks in many shapes,
O'ershadowing you like bunchèd grapes."

Ricolf's vassals were being difficult. Gerin had been sure they would be difficult, from the instant the eunuch priest led him, his son, Van, and them out of the Sibyl's chamber. Now, back at the hostel in the village of Ikos, they, or at least three of them, openly bickered with the Fox.

"Didn't mean a thing," Wacho Fidus' son declared, thumping his balled fist down onto the table. "Not one single, solitary thing."

" 'The young man shall hold all the castles/ And all within shall be his vassals'?" Gerin quoted. "That means nothing to you. Are you deaf and blind as well as—" He broke off; he'd been about to say *stupid*. "We asked about Ricolf's holdings, and the god said he'd rule all the castles. What more do you want?" *A good dose of brains wouldn't hurt. You could take them by enema, so they'd be close to what you use for thinking now.*

"The god said 'all *the* castles,' " Authari Broken-Tooth declared. "The god said nothing about *Ricolf's* castles. Duren here is your heir, too. When you die, he stands to inherit your lands and the keeps on them."

Gerin exhaled through his nose. "That's clever, I must admit," he said tightly. "Are you sure you didn't study

Sithonian hair-splitting—excuse me, philosophy—south of the High Kirs? The only problem is, the question wasn't about the keeps I control. It asked specifically about the holding of Ricolf the Red. When you take the question and the answer together, there's only one conclusion you can reach."

"We seem to have found another one," Hilmic Barrelstaves said, tipping back his drinking jack and pouring the last swallow's worth of ale down his throat. He waved the jack around to show he wanted a refill.

"Aye, you've found another one," Gerin answered. "Is it one that will let you keep the oath you swore to Dyaus and Biton and Baivers" —he pointed to Hilmic's drinking jack— "and all the other gods?"

Wacho, Hilmic, and Authari appeared to take no notice of that. But Ratkis Bronzecaster, who'd said little, looked even more thoughtful than he already had. *Oathbreaker* wasn't a name anyone wanted to get for himself. It hurt you in this world and was liable to hurt you worse in the next.

Duren said, "From all I've heard and read of Biton's prophetic verse, the god never names names straight out."

"What do you know, lad?" Wacho said with a sneer.

"I know insolence when I hear it," Duren snapped. Physically, he was not a match for the bigger, older man, but his voice made Wacho sit up and take notice. Duren went on, "I know my letters, too, so I can learn things I don't see with my own eyes and hear with my own ears. Can you say the same?"

Before Wacho answered, Gerin put in, "I've been to the Sibyl several times now, over the years, and the next name I hear in one of those verses will be the first." Van nodded agreement.

Ratkis broke his silence: "That is so, or it has been for me, at any rate. It gives me one thing more to think about."

"You're not going to turn against us, are you?" Hilmic Barrelstaves demanded. "You'd be sorry for that—three against one would—"

"It wouldn't be three against one for long," Gerin broke in. Hilmic glared at him. He glared back, partly from anger, partly for effect. Then, musingly, he went on, "If your neighbors outside Ricolf's barony hear how you'd seek to go back on your sworn word, they might hit you from behind while you were fighting Ratkis, too, for fear you'd treat them the same way after you'd beaten him. And that doesn't begin to take into account what I'd do."

He carefully avoided saying exactly what he would do. Absent other troubles, he would have descended on Ricolf's holding with everything he had, to make sure it would be in Duren's hands before Aragis the Archer could so much as think of responding. Absent other troubles— He laughed bitterly. Other troubles were anything but absent.

Then Ratkis said, "I expect I can hold my own. If the Trokmê tide didn't swamp me, I don't suppose my neighbors will." He looked from Hilmic to Wacho to Authari Broken-Tooth. "They know I don't go out looking for mischief. Aye, they know that, so they do. And they know that if mischief comes looking for me, I mostly give it a set of lumps and send it on its way."

By the sour expressions on the faces of his fellow vassal barons, they did know that. Authari said, "Do you want to see us dragged into doing whatever Gerin the Fox here orders us to do?"

"Not so you'd notice," Ratkis answered. "But I can't say I'm dead keen on going against what a god says, either, and looks to me as if that's what the three of you have in mind."

Wacho Fidus' son and Hilmic shook their heads with vehemence that struck Gerin as overwrought. Smoothly, Authari said, "Not a bit of it, Ratkis—nothing of the sort. But we do have to be certain what the lord Biton means, don't we?"

"I think we're all of us clear enough on that," Van rumbled, and then drained his drinking jack. "If we weren't, some people wouldn't be trying so hard to get around the plain words."

"I resent that," Authari said, his versatile voice now hot with anger.

Van got to his feet and stared down at Authari. "You do, eh?" He set a hand on the hilt of his sword. "How much d'you resent it? Care to step onto the street and show me how much you resent it? What d'you suppose'll happen after that? D'you suppose your successor, whoever he is, will resent it, too?"

The taproom got very quiet. The warriors who'd accompanied Ricolf's vassals eyed those who'd come to Ikos with Gerin, and were eyed in return. And everyone waited to hear and see what Authari Broken-Tooth would do.

Gerin did not think Authari a coward; he'd never heard nor seen anything to give him that idea. But he did not blame Authari for licking his lips and keeping silent while he thought: Van was two hands' breadth taller, and likely weighed half again as much as he did.

"Well?" the outlander demanded. "Are you coming out?"

"I find—I find—I am not so angry as I was a moment before," Authari said. "Sometimes a man's temper can make him say things he wishes he had kept to himself."

To Gerin's relief, Van accepted that, and sat back down at once. "Well, you're right there, and no mistake," he said. "Even the Fox has done it, and he's more careful with his tongue than any man I've ever known."

Much of what Van called being careful was simply knowing when to keep his mouth shut. But Gerin knew not to say that, too. What he did say was, "Since you're not out of temper now, Authari, can you take a calmer look at the verses the god spoke through the Sibyl and admit the lines that talk about my son can have only one meaning?"

Authari looked resentful again, but carefully did not claim he was. Gerin's intellectual challenge was as hard for him to withstand as Van's physical challenge had been. At last, very much against his will, Ricolf's vassal admitted, "There may be some truth in what you say."

That made Hilmic and Wacho let out indignant bleats. "You've sold us, you traitor!" Wacho shouted, quickly red in the face with fury. "I ought to cut your heart out for this, or worse if I could think of it."

"I'd face *you* any day," Authari retorted. "I'd face the Fox, too. I don't fear him in the field, not when he has so many concerns besides me. But Biton? Who can fight against a god and hope to win? Since the farseeing one knows my heart, he knows I thought to oppose his will. But thought is not deed."

"You speak truth there," Gerin agreed. "Now, though, you will recognize Duren as your rightful overlord?"

"So I will," Authari said sourly, "when he is permanently installed in Ricolf's keep, and not a day sooner."

"That is fair," Gerin said.

"This was all your idea, and now you're running away from it?" Wacho bellowed. Hilmic Barrelstaves set a hand on his arm and whispered in his ear. Wacho calmed down, or seemed to. All the same, Gerin wouldn't have cared to be Authari right then. By himself, Authari was more powerful than either Wacho or Hilmic. Was he more powerful than both of them put together? Ratkis had said he could hold out against all three of Ricolf's other leading vassals, so presumably Authari could hold out against two of them. But that didn't mean he'd enjoy doing it.

And then Duren said, quietly but firmly, "When I succeed my grandfather, my vassals will not fight private wars against one another. Anyone who starts that kind of war will face me along with his foe."

Gerin had imposed that rule on his own vassals. For that matter, Ricolf had enforced it while he lived. A strong overlord could. All of Ricolf's leading vassals had assumed Duren, at least apart from Gerin, would not be a strong overlord. But Duren hadn't said anything about asking help from his father, nor had he sounded as if he thought he'd need it. By the looks on their faces, Authari, Hilmic, and Wacho were all having second thoughts.

So was Gerin. He'd done his best to train Duren up to be a leader one day. He hadn't realized he'd succeeded so well, or so fast. A boy turned into a man when he could fill a man's sandals. By that reckoning—his games among the serving women at Fox Keep to one side—Duren was a man now. Scratching his head, Gerin wondered exactly when that had happened, and why he hadn't noticed.

Ratkis Bronzecaster noticed. Speaking to Duren rather than Gerin, he asked, "When do you expect to take up the lordship of the holding that had been your grandfather's?"

"Not this season," Duren answered at once. "After my father has beaten Adiatunnus and the Gradi and no longer needs me by his side."

"Your father is lucky to have you for a son," Ratkis observed, with no irony Gerin could hear.

Duren shrugged. "What I am, he made me."

In some ways, that was true. In those ways, it might have been more true of Duren than of a good many youths, for, with his mother gone, Gerin had had more of his raising than he would have otherwise. But in other ways, as the Fox had just realized, Duren had outstripped his hopes. And so he said, "A father can only shape what's already in a son."

Ratkis nodded at that. "You're not wrong, lord prince. If a lad is a donkey, you can't make him into a horse you'd want pulling your chariot. But if he's already a horse, you can show him how to run." He turned to Duren. "When that time comes, you'll have no trouble from me, not unless you show you deserve it, which I don't think you will. And I say that to you for your sake, not on account of who your father is."

"I will try to be a lord who deserves good vassalage," Duren answered.

Ratkis nodded again, saying, "I think you may well do that." After a moment, Authari Broken-Tooth nodded, too. Hilmic and Wacho sat silent and unhappy. They'd been as difficult and obstructive as they could and, by all the signs, had nothing to show for it.

If only all my foes were so easy to handle, the Fox thought.

The drive back from the Sibyl's shrine to the Elabon Way showed the damage the monsters had done in their brief time above ground. The peasant villages that lay beyond the old, half-haunted wood west of Ikos were shadows of what they had been. In a way, that made the journey back to the main highway easier, for the peasants, who were their own masters, owing no overlord allegiance, had been apt to demonstrate their freedom by preying on passing travelers.

"Serves 'em right," Van said as they rode past another village where most of the huts were falling to ruin and a handful of frightened folk stared at the chariots with wide, hungry eyes. "They'd have knocked us over the head for our weapons and armor, so many good-byes to 'em."

"Land needs to be farmed," Gerin said, upset at the sight of saplings springing up in what had been wheatfields. "It shouldn't rest idle."

The state of the land was not the only worry on his mind, for he very much hoped he would find that his warriors had rested idle while he was consulting the Sibyl. Ricolf's vassals had men enough to crush his small force if they set their minds to it, and to seize or kill him as he returned to their holding, too. He vowed to take Wacho and Hilmic—and Authari, for luck—down to the underworld with him if their followers turned traitor.

But when he came upon those of his troopers he'd left behind, they and the men who had served Ricolf were getting on well. When they recognized him and his companions, they hurried toward them, loudly calling for news.

"We don't know what we're going to do," Wacho said, still unready to resign himself to recognizing Duren as his suzerain.

"No, that isn't so," Ratkis Bronzecaster said before Gerin—or Duren—could scream at Wacho. "Sounds like the god thinks the lad should come after his grandfather. But he won't take over Ricolf's keep quite yet."

"Why aren't we fighting the Fox, then?" one of the soldiers demanded. "His kin have no call taking over our holding."

"Biton thinks otherwise," Ratkis said; having made up his mind, he followed his decision to the hilt. With a nod to one of his comrades, he added, "Isn't that right, Authari?"

Authari Broken-Tooth looked as if he hated the other baron for putting him on the spot. "Aye," he answered, more slowly than he should have. He could hardly have been less enthusiastic had he been discussing his own imminent funeral obsequies.

But that *aye*, however reluctant, produced both acclamations for Duren and loud arguments. Gerin glanced toward Hilmic Barrelstaves and Wacho Fidus' son. Hilmic, sensibly, was keeping quiet. Wacho looked as if he had no intention of doing anything of the sort.

Gerin caught his eye. Wacho glared truculent defiance at him. He'd seen it done better. He shook his head, a single tightly controlled movement. Wacho glared even more fiercely. The Fox didn't glare back. Instead, he looked away, a gesture of cool contempt that said Wacho wasn't worth noticing and had better not make himself worth noticing.

Had Wacho shouted, Gerin's men might have found themselves in a bloody broil with the troopers who followed Ricolf's vassals. But Wacho didn't shout. He was big and full of bluster, but the Fox had managed to get across a warning he could not mistake.

Gerin said, "Hear the words of farseeing Biton, as spoken through his Sibyl at Ikos." He repeated the prophetic verse just as the Sibyl had given it to him, then went on, "Can any of you doubt that in this verse the god shows Duren to be the rightful successor to Ricolf the Red?"

His own men clapped and cheered; they were ready to believe his interpretation. Three out of four of Ricolf's leading vassals, though, had disputed it. What would the common soldiers from Ricolf's holding do? They owed Gerin no allegiance, but they did not stand to lose so much as Authari and his colleagues, either: who the overlord of the holding was mattered less to men who had to take orders regardless of that overlord's name.

And, by ones and twos, they began to nod, accepting that the verse meant what he said it did. They showed no great enthusiasm, but they had no reason to show great enthusiasm: Duren was an untried youth. But they seemed willing to give him his chance.

Ricolf's vassal barons saw that, too. Ratkis took it in stride. Whatever Authari thought, he kept to himself. Wacho and Hilmic tried with indifferent success to hide dismay.

"I thank you," Duren said to the soldiers, doing his best to pitch his voice man-deep. "May we be at peace whenever we can, and may we win whenever we must go to war."

Van stuck an elbow in Gerin's ribs. "Have to be careful with that one," he said under his breath, pointing to the Fox's son. "Whatever he wants, he's liable to go out and grab it."

"Aye," Gerin said, also looking at Duren with some bemusement. His own nature was to wait and look around before acting, then strike hard. Duren was moving faster and, by the way things seemed, able to be gentler because of that.

For Ricolf's troopers were nodding at his words, accepting them more readily than they had Gerin's interpretation of the oracular response. Before the Fox could say anything, Duren went on, "I will not take up this holding from my grandfather now, for my father still has need of me. But when that need has passed, I will return here and accept the homage of my vassals."

Gerin wondered how the troopers would take that; it reminded them of Duren's link to him. By their anxious expressions, Hilmic and Wacho were wondering the same thing, and hoping the reminder would turn the warriors against Duren. It didn't. If anything, it made them think better of him. One comment rising above the general murmur of approval was, "If he looks out for his kinsfolk, he'll look out for us, too."

The Fox didn't know who'd said that, altogether without being asked. He would gladly have paid good gold to get one of Ricolf's men to come out with such a sentiment; getting it for free, and sincerely, was all the better.

Ratkis looked satisfied. Authari Broken-Tooth's expression could have meant anything, though if it betokened delight, Gerin would have been very much surprised. What Hilmic's and Wacho's faces showed was at best dyspepsia, at worst stark dismay. The Fox knew they—and probably Authari, too—would be haranguing their retainers every day till Gerin got back to Ricolf's holding. How much good that haranguing would do them remained to be seen.

Then Ratkis got down from his chariot and went to one knee on the stone slabs of the road close by the car Duren was driving. Looking up at Duren, he said, "Lord, in token of your return, I will gladly give you homage and fealty now." He pressed the palms of his hands together and held them out before him.

At last, after seeing so much maturity from his son, Gerin found Duren at a loss. He tapped the youth on the shoulder and hissed, "Accept, quick!"

That got Duren moving. He'd seen Gerin accept new vassals often enough to know the ritual. Scrambling down from the chariot, he hurried over to stand in front of Ratkis Bronzecaster and set his hands on those of the older man.

Ratkis said, "I own myself to be your vassal, Duren son of Gerin the Fox, grandson of Ricolf the Red, and give you the whole of my faith against all men who might live or die."

"I, Duren, son of Gerin the Fox, grandson of Ricolf the Red, accept your homage, Ratkis Bronzecaster," Duren replied solemnly, "and pledge in my turn always to use you justly. In token of which, I raise you up now." He helped Ratkis to his feet and kissed him on the cheek.

"By Dyaus the father of all and Biton the farseeing one, I swear my fealty to you, lord Duren," Ratkis said, his voice loud and proud.

"By Dyaus and Biton," Duren said, "I accept your oath and swear in turn to reward your loyalty with my own." He looked to Ricolf's other leading vassals. "Who else will give me this sign of good faith now?"

Authari Broken-Tooth went to one knee more smoothly than Ratkis had. He too gave Duren homage and then fealty. So far as Gerin could see, the ceremony was flawless in every regard, with no error of form to let Authari claim it was invalid. He was glad Authari had subordinated himself, but trusted the vassal baron no more on account of that.

Everyone looked at Hilmic and Wacho. Wacho's fair face turned red. "I'm not pledging anything to a lord who isn't here to give back what he pledges to me," he said loudly. Turning to Gerin, he went on, "I don't reject him out of hand, lord prince; don't take me wrong. But I won't give homage and swear fealty till he comes back here to stay, if I do it then. I'll have to see what he looks like when he's here for good." Hilmic Barrelstaves, perhaps encouraged that Wacho had spoken, nodded emphatic agreement.

Again, Duren handled matters before Gerin could speak: "That is your right. But when I do return, I'll bear in mind everything you've done since the day my grandfather died."

Neither Hilmic nor Wacho answered that. Several of Ricolf's men spoke up in approval, though, and even Wacho's driver looked back over his shoulder to say something quiet to him. Whatever it was, it made the vassal baron go redder yet and growl something pungent by way of reply.

Gerin caught Duren's eye and nodded for him to get back into the chariot. He didn't want to give his son orders now, not when the boy—no, the young man—had so impressed Ricolf's followers with his independence. Duren had impressed the Fox, too, a great deal. You never really knew whether someone could swim till he found himself in water over his head.

Duren jumped up into the car and took the reins from Van, who'd been holding them, saying, "When my duties farther north are done, I'll come back here. The gods willing, we'll have many years together." He flicked the reins. The horses trotted forward. The rest of Gerin's little army followed.

The Fox looked back over his shoulder. There in the roadway stood Authari Broken-Tooth, Ratkis Bronzecaster, Wacho Fidus' son, and Hilmic Barrelstaves. They were arguing furiously, their men crowding around them to support one or the other. Gerin liked that fine.

Half a day south of Fox Keep, Gerin spied a chariot heading his way. At first he thought it belonged to a messenger, heading down toward Ricolf's holding with news so urgent, it couldn't wait for his return. The only sort of news that urgent was bad news.

Then the driver of the car held up a shield painted in white and green stripes: a shield of truce. "Those are Trokmoi!" the Fox exclaimed. A few years earlier, he wouldn't have been able to recognize them as such at so long a distance, but his sight was lengthening as he got older. That made reading hard. He wondered if there was a magic to counter the flaw.

He had little time for such idle thoughts: a moment later, he recognized one of the Trokmoi in the car. So did Van, who named the fellow first: "That's Diviciacus, Adiatunnus' right hand."

"His right hand, aye, and maybe the thumb of the left," Gerin agreed. "Something's gone wrong for him, or he'd not have sent Diviciacus out to try to make it better—and probably to diddle me in the process, if he sees a chance."

The Trokmoi made out who Gerin was at about the same time as he recognized Diviciacus. They waved and approached. Duren stopped the team. The rest of Gerin's men halted their chariots behind him.

"What can we be doing for you, now?" Gerin called in the Trokmê tongue.

"Will you just hear the sweet way he's after using our speech?" Diviciacus said, also in his language. He quickly switched to Elabonian: "Though I'd best be using yours for the business ahead to be sure there's not misunderstandings, the which wouldn't be good at all, at all." Even in Elabonian, he kept a woodsrunner's lilt in his voice.

"The years haven't treated you too badly," Gerin remarked as Diviciacus got out of his chariot. The Trokmê was thicker through the middle than he had been when he was younger, and white frosted his mustache and the red hair at his temples. He still looked like a dangerous man in a brawl, though—and in a duel of words.

"I'll say the same to your own self," he answered, and then astonished Gerin by dropping to one knee in the roadway, as Ratkis Bronzecaster had done for Duren. As the Trokmê clasped his hands together in front of him, he said, "Adiatunnus is fain to be after renewing vassalage to your honor, lord prince, that he is."

"By the gods," Gerin muttered. He stared at Diviciacus. "It took the gods to get me his allegiance the last time he gave it. I always thought—I always said—I'd need them again to get him to renew it. Before I accept it, I want to know what I'm getting . . . and why."

Still on that one knee, Diviciacus replied, "Himself said you'd say that, sure and he did." His shoulders moved back and then forward as he sighed. "He'd not do it, I tell you true, did he not find worse in these lands south o' the Niffet than you'd be giving him."

"Ah, the Gradi," Gerin said. "A light begins to dawn. He wants my help against them, and reckons the only way he'll get it is to pretend to be a good little boy for as long as he needs to, and then to go back to his old ways."

Diviciacus assumed a hurt expression. He did it very well—but then, he'd had practice. "That's not a kind thing to be saying, not even a bit of it."

"Too bloody bad," Gerin told him. "The only debt I owe your chief is that I had my retainers gathered against him at Fox Keep when the Gradi raided us, and so I was able to throw them back without too much trouble."

"Would that we could say the same," Diviciacus answered gloomily. "They lit into us, that they did. I gather you're after hearing about their raid on us by boat, and that they did it in the aftermath of striking you."

"Yes, I heard of that," Gerin answered. "If they hadn't hit us and you, Adiatunnus and I would be at war now, I suppose, and you wouldn't have to come to me and swallow his pride for him."

Diviciacus winced. "Sure and you've an evil tongue in the head o' you, Fox. They say that in the olden times a bard could kill a man by no more than singing rude songs about him. I never would have believed it at all till I met you." He held up a hand; a gold bracelet glittered on his wrist. "Don't thank me, now. You've not yet heard what I'm about to tell you."

"Go on," Gerin said, concealing his amusement; he had been about to thank the Trokmê for noting the bite of his sarcasm. "What haven't I heard that you're about to tell me?"

"That the black-hearted omadhauns struck us again ten days ago, this time coming by land, and that they beat us again, too." Diviciacus bared his teeth in an agony of frustration. "And so, for fear of worse from them, Adiatunnus will fight alongside you, will fight under you, will fight however you choose, for the sake of having your men and your cars in the line with us. Whatever should befall after that, even if it's you turning into our master, it's bound to be better nor the Gradi ruling over us."

He shivered in almost superstitious dread. The Trokmoi who'd come in the chariot with him gestured to avert evil. The Gradi whom Gerin had captured took beating the woodsrunners for granted. Evidently the Trokmoi felt the same way about it. That worried Gerin. What sort of allies would the Trokmoi make if they broke and fled at the mere sight of their foes?

He asked Diviciacus that very question. "We fight bravely enough," the Trokmê insisted. "It's just that—summat always goes wrong, and curse me if I know why. Must not be so with you southrons, not if you beat the Gradi the once. With you along, we'll do better, too—I hope."

"So do I," Gerin told him. He mulled things over for a bit, then went on, "Come back to Fox Keep with me. This is too important to decide on the spur of the moment."

"However you like it, lord prince," Diviciacus answered. "Only the gods grant you don't take too long deciding, else it'll be too late for having the mind of you made up to matter."

When they started north up the Elabon Way toward Fox Keep, Gerin told Duren to steer his chariot up alongside the one in which Diviciacus rode. Over squeals and rattles, the Fox asked, "What will Adiatunnus say if my whole army comes into the land he holds as his own?"

"Belike he'll say, 'Och, the gods be praised!—them of Elabonians and Trokmoi both,' " Diviciacus answered. "More than half measures we need, for true."

"And what will he say—and what will your warriors say—when I tell them to fight alongside my men and take orders from my barons?" the Fox pressed.

"Order 'em about just as you wish," Diviciacus said. "If there's even a one of 'em as says aught else but, 'Aye, lord Gerin,' take the head of the stupid spalpeen and be after hanging it over your gate."

"We don't do that," Gerin said absently. But that wasn't the point. Diviciacus knew perfectly well that Elabonians weren't in the habit of taking heads for trophies. What he meant was that Adiatunnus and his men were desperate enough to obey the Fox no matter what he said. Given Adiatunnus' pride in the strength he'd had till the Gradi struck him, that was desperate indeed. Unless . . . "What oath will you give that this isn't a trap, to lead me to a place where Adiatunnus can try to take me unawares?"

"The same frickful aith I gave your lady wife when she put me the same question," Diviciacus said: "By Taranis,

Teutates, and Esus I swear, lord Gerin, lord prince, I've told you nobbut the truth."

If swearing by his three chief gods would not bind a Trokmê to the truth, nothing would. Gerin smiled a little when he heard Selatre had asked the same guarantee of Diviciacus: Biton didn't speak through her these days, but she saw plenty clear on her own. "Good enough," the Fox said.

"I pray it is; I pray you're right," Diviciacus told him. "The priests, they've been edgy of late, indeed and they have. It's as if, with the gods o' the Gradi so near 'em and all, our own gods have taken fear, if you know what I'm saying."

"I think perhaps I do," Gerin said after a moment's pause. The Gradi prisoners had also boasted of how much stronger their gods were than those of the woodsrunners, and again seemed to know whereof they spoke.

Diviciacus sent Gerin a keen look. "You know more of this whole business than you let on, I'm thinking." When Gerin didn't answer, the Trokmê went on, "Well, that was ever the way of you. Adiatunnus, he swears you stand behind him and listen when he's haranguing his men."

"With the way Adiatunnus bellows, I wouldn't need to be that close to overhear him," Gerin said. Diviciacus chuckled and nodded, acknowledging the hit. Gerin was careful not to deny possible occult means of knowledge. The more people thought he knew, the more cautious they'd be around him.

The one thing he wished as the chariot clattered northward was that he really knew half as much as friends and foes credited him with knowing.

"Are we ready?" Gerin looked back at the throng of chariots drawn up behind him on the meadow by Fox Keep. The question was purely rhetorical; they were as ready as they'd ever be. He waved his arm forward, tapping Duren on the shoulder as he did so. "Let's go!"

They hadn't gone far before Diviciacus' chariot came up beside Gerin's. "It's a fine thing you do here, Fox, indeed and it is," the Trokmê said. Then his face clouded. "Still and all, I'd be happier, that I would, were you bringing the whole of your host with you and not leaving a part of 'em behind at Castle Fox."

"I'm not doing this to make you happy," Gerin answered. "I'm not doing it to make Adiatunnus happier, either. I'm doing it to protect myself. If I leave Fox Keep bare and the Gradi come up the Niffet again" —he waved back toward the river— "the keep falls. I don't really want that to happen."

"And if your men and Adiatunnus' together aren't enough to be beating the Gradi, won't you feel the fool, now?" Diviciacus retorted.

"Those are the risks I weigh, and that's the chance I take," Gerin said. "If I could bring my whole army, and Adiatunnus', too, down the Niffet against the Gradi, I'd do that. I can't, though. The Gradi control the river, because they have boats beside which ours might as well be toys. And as long as that's true, I have to guard against their taking advantage of what they have. If you don't care for that, too bad."

"Och, I'd not like to live inside your head, indeed and I wouldn't," Diviciacus said. "You're after having eyes like a crayfish—on the end of stalks, peering every which way at once—and a mind like a balance scale, weighing this against that and that against this till you're after knowing everything or ever it has the chance to happen."

Gerin shook his head. "Only farseeing Biton has that kind of power. I wish I did, but I know I don't. Seeing ahead's not easy, even for a god."

"And how would you know that?" Diviciacus said.

"Because I watched Biton trying to pick out the thread of *the* future from among a host of might-bes," Gerin answered, which made the Trokmê shut up with a snap. Diviciacus knew that Gerin had made the monsters vanish from the face of the earth, but not how he'd done it or what had happened in the aftermath of the miracle.

They soon left the Elabon Way and rolled southwest down lesser roads. Serfs in the fields alongside the dirt tracks stood up from their endless labor to watch the army pass. One or two of them, every now and then, would wave. Whenever that happened, Gerin waved back.

Diviciacus stared at the serfs. "Are they daft?" he burst

out after a while. "Are they stupid? Why aren't they running for the woods, aye, and taking the livestock with 'em, too?"

"Because they know my men won't plunder them," the Fox answered. "They know they can rely on that."

"Daft," Diviciacus repeated. "I'll not tell Adiatunnus, for himself wouldna credit it. He'd call me drunk or ensorceled, so he would."

"I had trouble making sense of it when I first came here, too," Van said sympathetically. "It still strikes me strange, but after a while you get used to it."

"For which ringing endorsement of my ideas I thank you very much," Gerin said, his voice dry as the dust the horses' hooves and chariot wheels raised from the road.

"Think nothing of it," Van said, dipping his head.

"Just what I do think of it, and not a bit more," Gerin said.

Both old friends laughed. Diviciacus listened and watched as if he couldn't believe what he was hearing and seeing. "If any of our Trokmoi, now, bespoke Adiatunnus so," he said, "the fool'd be eating from a new mouth slit in his throat, certain sure he would, soon as the words were out of his old one."

"Killing people who tell you you're a fool isn't always the best idea in the world," Gerin observed. "Every so often, they turn out to be right." Diviciacus rolled his eyes. That wasn't the way his chieftain handled matters, so, as far as he was concerned, it had to be wrong.

They came to the keep of Widin Simrin's son late the next day. Widin and Diviciacus greeted each other like old neighbors, which they were, and old friends, which they weren't. "Better you southrons for friends nor the Gradi," Diviciacus told him, and that seemed to suffice.

Widin had a good-sized garrison quartered at his keep: had Adiatunnus begun the war against Gerin rather than the other way round, those troopers would have done their best to slow the Trokmê advance and buy the Fox time to move down and deal with the woodsrunners. "So we'll really be on the same side as the Trokmoi?" Widin said to Gerin. "Who would have believed that at the start of the year?"

"Not I, I tell you for a fact, but yes, we will," Gerin replied. "The Trokmoi would rather work with us than with the Gradi, and from what I've seen of the Gradi, I'd rather work with the Trokmoi than with them, too."

"I haven't seen anything of them, lord prince," Widin said, "but if they're rugged enough to make the Trokmoi cozy up to us like this, they must be pretty nasty customers." He grinned wryly. "I won't be sorry to move out against the Gradi myself, I tell you that much. You go feeding a good-sized crew of warriors for a while and you start wondering whether anything'll be left for you to eat come winter."

"You don't sing me that song, Widin," Gerin told him. "I sing it to you." His vassal baron grinned and nodded, yielding the point. The Fox had been feeding a lot more warriors for a lot longer than Widin. The Fox had also made the most thoroughgoing preparations for feeding and housing a lot of warriors of any man in the northlands, save perhaps Aragis the Archer—and he would have bet against Aragis, too.

Ruefully, Widin said, "And now, of course, the whole army guests off me, even if it is for only the one night."

"I don't see you starving," Gerin observed, his voice mild.

"Oh, not now," Widin answered. "The apples are harvested, and the pears, and the plums. The animals are getting fat on the good grass. But come the later part of next winter, we'll wish we had what your gluttons will gobble up tonight."

"Well, I understand that," Gerin said. "The end of winter is a hard time of year for everyone. And Father Dyaus knows I'm happy to see you thinking ahead instead of just living in the now, the way so many do. But if we don't beat the Gradi, how much you have in your storerooms won't matter to anyone but them."

"Oh, I understand all that, lord prince," Widin assured him. "But since you take so much enjoyment complaining about every little thing, I wouldn't think you'd begrudge me the chance to do the same."

"Since I what?" The Fox glowered at his vassal, much as if he were serious. "I expect to hear that from Van or Rihwin, not from you."

"Can't trust anyone these days, can you?" Widin said, now doing a wicked impression of Gerin himself. The Fox threw his hands in the air and stalked off, conceding defeat.

By the extravagant way Widin fed the army that had descended on his castle, his plea of hunger to come had been a case of averting an evil omen, nothing more. As if to extract some sort of revenge on the lesser baron, Gerin ate until he could hardly waddle off to his blanket. He committed gluttony again the next morning, this time because he knew what sort of country lay ahead.

The land between Widin's holding and Adiatunnus' territory belonged to no one, even if it was formally under Gerin's suzerainty. The Fox and the Trokmê chieftain had been probing for advantage down there for years; even after giving Gerin homage and swearing fealty, Adiatunnus conducted himself like an independent lord.

Caught between two strong rivals, most of the peasants who had farmed that land in the days before the werenight were dead or fled now. Fields were going back to meadows, meadows to brush, and brush to saplings. Looking at some pines as tall as he was, Gerin thought, *This is how civilization dies*. When his army—or Adiatunnus'—wasn't crossing this country (on dirt roads also vanishing from disuse), it belonged more to wild beasts than to men. And it bordered his own holding. That was a profoundly depressing thought.

Adiatunnus had pushed his border station north and east, toward the edges of Gerin's land. More than once, Gerin had moved against the Trokmoi with an army, routing his enemy's guards and overturning the prevaricating boundary stones they would set up to support their claims. When he and his army came upon the Trokmê guards now, the red-mustachioed barbarians cheered and waved their long bronze swords in the air.

Laughter rumbled from Van. Turning to Gerin, he said, "There's something you've never seen before, I'll wager."

"Woodsrunners cheering me?" The Fox shook his head. "The only time I ever thought the Trokmoi would cheer me was after I died."

Diviciacus rode near enough to hear that. "We tried to

arrange it, Fox dear, time and again we did," he said, "and we'd have cheered like madmen if we'd done it. But things being as they are—"

"Yes, things being as they are," Gerin agreed. Without the Trokmoi, he wouldn't have become baron of Fox Keep, wouldn't have set forth on the path that had made him prince of the north. The woodsrunners had ambushed his father and older brother, putting an end to his hopes of passing his days as student and scholar.

And, on returning from the City of Elabon to take up the barony, he'd sworn never to stop taking revenge on the barbarians for what they'd done to him and his. Over the years, he'd taken that revenge many times and in many ways. And now he found himself allied to the Trokmoi against a danger he and they both recognized as worse than either was to the other. Did that leave him forsworn?

He didn't think so. He hoped not. He hoped the spirits of his father and brother understood why he was doing what he was doing. He thought his brother would. Of his father, he was less certain. The Dagref after whom he'd named his first son by Selatre had not been the most flexible of men.

The Fox shrugged. Regardless of what his father would have thought, he'd chosen this course and would have to see it through. What came afterwards, he'd sort out afterwards.

He knew the way to the keep Adiatunnus had held as his own since the Trokmê invasion after the werenight. He'd been that way before, with soldiers at his back every time. He'd had to fight his way through Adiatunnus' holding then. The Trokmoi welcomed him and his men now.

Trokmoi were not the only folk still living on the land, of course. A good many Elabonian peasants remained, serfs toiling for tall, fair overlords now, not for barons of their own race. Whenever he rode past one of their villages, Gerin wondered how much that bothered them. He suspected they cared only how much of their crops their overlords, whoever those overlords were, exacted from them and how much those overlords interfered in the day-to-day routine of their lives.

He passed a couple of strongpoints he'd burned out in

his last serious campaign against Adiatunnus, more than a decade before. One had been rebuilt, the other was still in ruins. Here and there in his holding, ruins remained from the werenight, well before that. The Trokmoi were moving at a pace not too far from his own.

When night fell, the Elabonians stopped at a village dominated by a stockaded building too large and strong to be a house, too small to be a castle. Several Trokmê warriors dwelt there with their wives and children, plainly to lord it over the Elabonian serfs who lived in the usual huts of wattle and daub. Had Gerin extended his dominions to the forests of the Trokmoi north of the River Niffet, he might have used a similar system, save with Elabonians controlling woodsrunners.

Golden Math, just past first quarter, floated high in the south when the sun set. Pale, slow-moving Nothos, full or a day past, rose in the east during evening twilight. Elleb, approaching third quarter, would not come up till nearly midnight, while Tiwaz was too close to the sun to be seen.

"I wonder what the Gradi call the moons," Gerin said, staring up at Math from his seat close to a fire outside the village.

"That I can't tell you, Captain," Van answered. He paused to use a thumbnail to pry at a piece of mutton stuck between two back teeth, then resumed: "I'm amazed at how much of their speech has come back to me, now that I've had to try using it again, but I never was much interested in finding out about the moons. Maybe if some Gradi lass had looked up at 'em while I was on top of her—but she'd have been thinking about other things, or I hope she would."

"You are impossible," Gerin said, "or at least bloody improbable."

"Thank you, Fox," his friend answered. Gerin gave up and wrapped himself in his blanket. He had plenty of sentries out. Even in the worst of times, the Trokmoi weren't likely to brave the ghosts for a night attack, and his men and theirs were supposed to be allies. Nevertheless, he hadn't got as old as he had by taking needless chances. Knowing he'd taken none here, he slept sound.

✧ ✧ ✧

Warriors Gerin led had—once—reached the village around the keep Adiatunnus had taken for his own. They'd fought their way in among the houses there, but never had managed to force their way into the keep. With both Trokmoi—men and women—and monsters opposing them, they'd lost men too fast to make the assault worthwhile even if it did succeed.

And now here they were, more than ten years later, coming up to Adiatunnus' fastness once more. This time, no monsters fought them; the monsters, all save Geroge and Tharma, were back in the trackless caverns under Biton's temple at Ikos. The Trokmoi—men and women—stood in the narrow, rutted streets of the village, shouting for the Elabonians till their voices grew raw and hoarse. The drawbridge to the keep was down, and Adiatunnus rode out from it to greet the Fox. The last time Gerin had come this far, the two of them had done their best to kill each other, and they'd both nearly succeeded.

"Rein in," Gerin told Duren. The Fox also held up a hand to halt the rest of his chariots. His son pulled back on the reins. The horses obediently came to a stop.

Adiatunnus halted his own car perhaps twenty feet from Gerin's. He got out of it and walked half the distance before going down on one knee in the roadway. The watching Trokmoi sighed.

Gerin jumped down from his chariot and hurried over to Adiatunnus. The Trokmê chieftain clasped his hands together, Gerin covered them with his own, and they went through the same rituals of homage and fealty in person as they had by proxy through Diviciacus.

Speaking the Trokmê tongue so his folk could follow, Adiatunnus said, "I want no misunderstanding, now. You are my lord, and I own it's so. What you're after ordering me and mine to do against the Gradi, that we'll do, and promptly, too. You'll find us no more trouble than any of your other vassals."

The Fox noted Adiatunnus' reservation—he would take orders against the Gradi, but hadn't said anything about other orders. Gerin decided not to make an issue of it. Maybe the alliance against the new invaders would lead to better things later, maybe it wouldn't. For now, he wouldn't argue that it was necessary.

Also speaking the woodsrunners' language, he said, "Glad we are to have your valiant warriors with us in the fight. We'll teach the Gradi they chose the wrong foes when they decided to trifle with us."

The Trokmoi yelled and cheered; Gerin doubted they'd ever given any Elabonian a greeting like the one he was getting. Most of his own men understood the Trokmê speech well enough to have followed what he was saying. They cheered, too.

Some of them, he saw, had their eyes on Trokmê women, many of whom were strikingly pretty and who had a reputation among the Elabonians for easiness. Gerin knew that reputation was not altogether deserved; it was just that Trokmê women, like their menfolk, said and acted on what they thought more readily than most Elabonians. But, as Fand had taught him, you tried going too far with them at your peril. He hoped no trouble would spring from that.

Adiatunnus waved back toward his keep, whose drawbridge remained down. "Come in, Fox, come in, and the men of you, too. I'll feast the lot of you till you're too full to futter, that I will." Maybe he'd been watching Gerin's troopers eyeing the Trokmê women, too.

"For my men, I thank you," Gerin said. Save for insults on the battlefield, this was the first time he'd exchanged words with Adiatunnus. The Trokmê chief was close to his own age, a couple of digits taller and a good deal thicker through the shoulders and through the belly, with a balding crown and long, drooping fair mustaches now going gray. He wore a linen tunic and baggy woolen trousers, both dyed in checks of bright and, to Gerin's eye, clashing colors.

He was studying the Fox with the same wary care Gerin gave him. Seeing Gerin's eye on him, he chuckled self-consciously and said, "I've always been after thinking you're so high" —he reached up as far as he could— "with fangs in your mouth and covered all over with fur or a viper's scales, I never could decide which. And here, to look at you, you're nobbut a man."

"And you likewise," Gerin answered. "You've given me enough trouble for any other ten I could name, though; I tell you that."

"For which I thank you," Adiatunnus said, preening a little. His eyes were an odd shade, halfway between gray and green, and quite sharp. Looking intently at Gerin, he went on, "Ah, but if one o' them ten you could name was Aragis the Archer, now, would you still be telling me the truth?"

"Not altogether," the Fox admitted, and Adiatunnus preened again, this time admiring his own cleverness. Gerin said, "If you won't let me flatter you now, how am I supposed to fool you later?"

Adiatunnus stared at him, then started to laugh. "Och, what a wonder y'are, Fox. I've been glad to have you for a neighbor betimes, that I have, for you've taught me more than a dozen duller men could have done."

"For which I suppose I thank you," Gerin said, at which Adiatunnus laughed again. The Trokmê was telling the truth there. Over the years, Gerin had noted, Adiatunnus, more than any other Trokmê chieftain, had learned from the Elabonians among whom he'd settled. He played far more sophisticated—and far more dangerous—political games than his fellow woodsrunners, most of whom still seemed hardly better than bandits after all these years.

The game he was playing now was designed to make him seem a good fellow to the Fox and his warriors, and to make them forget they were more likely to be his foes than his friends. When he wanted to use it, he had a huge voice. He used it now, bellowing in Elabonian, "Into the keep, the lot of you. The meat and bread want eating, the beer wants drinking, aye, and maybe the lasses want pinching, though you'll have to find that out your own selves."

Gerin tried to shout just as loudly: "Any man of mine who drinks so much today that he's not fit to travel tomorrow will answer to me, and I'll make him sorrier than his hangover ever did." That might also keep his men from getting so drunk they started fights, and from being too drunk to defend themselves if the Trokmoi did.

"The same goes for my warriors," Adiatunnus said in his

speech and in Elabonian, "save only that they answer to me first and then the Fox, and they'll care for neither, indeed and they won't."

Roast meat was roast meat, though the Trokmoi cooked mutton with mint, not garlic. Some of the bread the serving women set before the warriors struck Gerin as odd: thick and chewy and studded with berries. It wasn't what he ate at home, but it was good. He wasn't so sure about the beer. It wasn't ale, nor anything like what he and other Elabonians brewed, coming almost black from the dipper and tasting thick and smoky in his mouth.

Adiatunnus drank it with every sign of enjoyment, so it evidently was as it was supposed to be. "Aye, we make the pale brew, too," the Trokmê chieftain said when Gerin asked him about it, "but I thought you might be interested in summat new, you having the name for that and all. You roast the malted barley a good deal longer here, you see, so it's nearly burnt, before you make it into the mash."

"I'll bet the first fellow who brewed this did it by accident, or because he was careless with his roasting," Gerin said. He took another pull and smacked his lips thoughtfully. "After you get used to it, it's—interesting, isn't it? A new way of doing things, as you say."

"When all this is done, I'll send a brewer to Fox Keep to show you the making of it," Adiatunnus promised.

"When all this is done, if you're able to send him and I'm able to receive him, I'll be glad to do that." Gerin drained his mug of beer. Getting up to fill it with another dipper of that dark brew seemed the most natural thing in the world, so he did.

Van had other ideas about what the most natural thing in the world might be. If he got any friendlier with that serving woman—a lively redhead who, Gerin thought, looked a lot like Fand—they'd be consummating their friendship on top of the table, or maybe down in the rushes on the floor.

Gerin peered around for Duren but didn't see him. He wondered whether his son had found a girl for himself or was just off visiting the latrine. When Duren didn't come back right away, the first guess seemed more likely.

"A fine-looking lad y'have there," Adiatunnus said, which made the Fox start a little; he wasn't used to anyone save Selatre or sometimes Van thinking along with him. Adiatunnus went on, "Am I after hearing the grandfather of him is a dead corp, the which puts him in line for that barony?"

"That's so," Gerin agreed. He eyed the Trokmê with genuine respect. "You have your ear to the ground, to have got the news so soon."

"The more you know, the more you can do summat about," Adiatunnus answered, a saying that might have come straight from the Fox's lips.

Gerin peered down into the black and apparently bottomless mug of beer. When he looked up again, Duren was coming back into the great hall, a smug look on his face. That eased Gerin's mind; after the boy had been kidnapped when he was small, the Fox wasn't easy about letting him out of his sight.

Turning to Adiatunnus, Gerin said, "It will be strange, riding alongside you instead of at you."

"It will that." Adiatunnus knocked back the black beer in his mug at a single gulp, then sat there slowly shaking his head. "Strange, aye. But you southrons, now, you've no fear of the Gradi, have you?"

"No more than I do of you," Gerin answered. "By the fight they made with us, they're brave and they're strong, but so are you Trokmoi—and so are we."

"I canna tell you what it is, Fox," Adiatunnus said, his features sagging in dismay, "but when we face 'em, summat always goes wrong for us. And when you get to the point where you expect to have a thing happen, why, happen it will."

"Yes, I've seen that," Gerin said. He remembered Kapich, his Gradi prisoner, sneering at the Trokmê gods. Whether that had anything to do with the woodsrunners' bad luck against the Gradi, he couldn't have said, but the notion wouldn't have surprised him.

Adiatunnus said, "When we go against the Gradi, now, how will you work it? Will you mix our men together like peas and beans in the soup pot, or do you aim to keep 'em apart, one group from the other?"

"I've been chewing on that very thing," Gerin said, noting with some relief that Adiatunnus really did seem to accept his command. "I'm leaning toward mixing: that way, it's less likely your warriors or mine will think the other bunch has run off and left 'em in the lurch. How do you feel about it?"

He asked for more than politeness' sake; Adiatunnus had proved himself no fool. The Trokmê said, "Strikes me as the better notion, too. If we're to have an army, it should *be* an army now, if you ken what I'm saying."

"I do." Gerin nodded. "My chief worry is that your men won't follow my commands as quickly as they might, either because they think I'm trying to put them in more danger or just out of Trokmê cussedness."

"As for the first, I trust it won't be so, else I'd never have bent the knee to you," Adiatunnus said. "You fight hard, Fox, but you fight fair. As for t'other, well, there are times when I wonder you Elabonians don't bore yourselves to death, so dull you seem to us."

"I've heard other Trokmoi say as much," Gerin admitted, "but, of course, they're wrong." He brought that out deadpan, to see what Adiatunnus would do with it.

The chieftain frowned, but then started to laugh. "Try as you will, lord prince—I should be saying that now, eh? being your vassal and all, I mean—you'll not get my goat so easy."

"Good," Gerin said. "So. You're flighty to us, and we're dull to you. What of the Gradi? You know them better than we do."

"Belike, and how I'm wishing we didna." This time, Adiatunnus' frown stayed, making his whole face seem longer. "They're—how do I say it?—they're serious about what they do, that they are. It's not your fault you're in their way, mind you, but y'are, and so they'll rob you or kill you or whatever they like. And if you have the gall to be offended, mind, then they'll get angry at you for trying to keep what's always been yours."

"Yes, that fits in with what I've seen," Gerin agreed. "They're very sure of themselves, too: they don't think we can stop them. That goddess of theirs, that Voldar—"

Adiatunnus twisted both hands into an apotropaic sign.

"Dinna be saying that name in this place. A wicked she-devil, no mistake." He shivered, though the inside of the great hall was smoky and hot. "Wicked, aye, but strong—strong. And the others—" His fingers writhed again.

You fear her, eh? Gerin started to ask that aloud, but held his tongue. Dabbling in magic had taught him how much power lay in words; saying something could make it real. Voldar undoubtedly knew—or could find out—Adiatunnus' feelings about her, but putting words in the air made it more likely the Trokmê chief would draw her notice.

"Father Dyaus will prosper our enterprise," Gerin said, and hoped the chief Elabonian god was paying as much attention to him as Adiatunnus feared the chief Gradi goddess was paying to *him*. Dyaus usually seemed content to reign over those who worshiped him without doing much to rule them. Gerin had always taken that for granted. Only in facing the Gradi had he come to realize it had drawbacks as well as advantages.

He was distracted from such musings when a very pretty Trokmê girl less than half Adiatunnus' age sat down on the chieftain's lap. Adiatunnus was holding a mug of black beer in one hand. The other closed over her breast through her tunic. The public display of what Gerin would have kept private didn't disturb her; indeed, she seemed proud Adiatunnus acknowledged she'd captured his affection, or at least his lust.

"And can I be finding you summat lively in the line of women?" the Trokmê chieftain asked. His hand opened and squeezed, opened and squeezed. "I'd not want you to think me lacking in hospitality, now."

"I don't," Gerin assured him. "Good food and good drink are plenty for me, and you've given me those. As for the other, I'm happy enough with my wife not to care to look anywhere else, though I thank you all the same."

"And what a daft notion that is," Adiatunnus exclaimed. "Not that you're happy, the which is as may be, but that your being happy back there would keep you from poking a wench here. What has the one to do with t'other? A friendly futter is worth the having, eh, no matter where you find it."

The Fox shrugged. "If that's how you want to live, I'm not going to say you shouldn't. It's your affair—and you can take that however you like. And since I'm happy enough to let other people do as they please, I'm even happier when they let me do the same."

"You're happy to drive a lesson home like a man splitting logs with an axe, too," Adiatunnus retorted. "But all right, have it as you will, since you're bound to, anyhow. And if you're not fain to have yourself a good time, I'll not be after making you do it. So there."

Gerin laughed out loud and raised his own mug in salute. Not many men could puncture him at arguments of that sort, but Adiatunnus had just done it. That said something about how sharp the Trokmê's wits were, not that Gerin hadn't already had a good notion of that. It also said Adiatunnus would make a useful ally—provided Gerin kept an eye on him.

The Trokmê's leman found something interesting to do with her hand, too. Gerin wondered with abstract curiosity whether Adiatunnus would suddenly need to change his trousers. Before that happened, the woodsrunner got up and slung the girl over his shoulder—no small display of strength—and carried her upstairs while she laughed.

Gerin turned to Duren and said, "I daresay you're learning some things here that you wouldn't see at Fox Keep."

"Oh, I don't know," his son answered, sounding very much like him. "Van and Fand do things like that sometimes."

"Mm, so they do," the Fox admitted. He thumped Duren on the shoulder and started to laugh, then got to his feet. "Well, now you're going to see something you *have* seen before: I'm going to bed." Also laughing, his son went up with him.

Van scratched his head, then, in fashion most ungentlemanly, reached inside his breeches and scratched there, too. He squashed something between his thumbnails, look at it, wiped it on his trouser leg, and let out a long sigh. "I'm going to have to go over myself for nits," he said, and dug in the pouch at his belt for a fine-toothed wooden comb. As he started raking it through his beard and hissing as the thick, curly hairs got stuck, he shook a thick forefinger at Gerin. "And don't you twit me about these cursed lice and where I got 'em. I know where I got 'em, and I had fun doing it, too."

"Fine," Gerin said. "You can have fun explaining to Fand where you got 'em, too."

But Van refused to let that sally faze him. "There's too many ways to—ouch!—pick up lice for anybody to be sure which one I found."

That was true. Gerin, for his part, had fresh bedbug bites, courtesy of no one more intimate than whoever'd last slept in the bed Adiatunnus had given him and Duren. But he also knew that Fand, given a hundred possibilities, would always choose the one likely to lead to the wildest fight—and, this time, she'd be right.

The Fox didn't waste a lot of time brooding over it, though he did spend a moment hoping he wouldn't come down with lice himself. As he got grayer, the vermin and their eggs got harder to spot in his hair.

Getting the army ready to move soon made all such insectile worries seem of insectile size and importance. His own men were quickly ready to ride, whether on horseback or in their chariots. He'd never before watched the Trokmoi getting ready to move out on campaign—most of the campaigns on which they'd moved in these parts had been aimed at him. Now that he was watching them, he concluded they had to start days earlier than he would have to set out at the same time.

They bickered. They bungled. They got drunk instead of eating breakfast. They went off for a fast poke with a serving girl instead of eating breakfast. An Elabonian captain would have killed a couple of his men on the spot before he put up with insubordination the Trokmê leaders ignored.

When the woodsrunners had finally fought, they'd always done well against the Fox's troopers. He had to hope the same would hold now. The longer he watched them—and he had a good long while to watch them—the more forlorn that hope seemed.

Adiatunnus was everywhere at once, shouting, blustering, cursing, cajoling. The chieftain did get his fair measure of respect, but, as far as Gerin could see, matters moved no faster because of the racket he made. Gerin had to hope Adiatunnus wasn't making things slower, another hope that faded as the morning wore on.

Van muttered, "We'd have done better if the woods-runners lined up with the Gradi, I'm thinking."

"I wouldn't argue," Gerin said mournfully, watching two Trokmoi draw swords and scream at each other before their friends pulled them apart.

The closest Adiatunnus came to acknowledging anything was wrong came when he said, "Och, you're ready a bit before us, looks like," and gave a breezy shrug to show how little that mattered to him. The Fox, ignoring the way his stomach churned, managed to nod.

At last, with the sun a little to the west of south, not even the Trokmoi could delay any more. Their women calling last farewells, they rode west from Adiatunnus' keep along with Gerin's men. The Fox murmured a prayer to Dyaus that the campaign would end better than it had begun.

VI

Early omens were less than good. The army crossed the Venien River, which flowed into the Niffet, not far from where the Gradi had come down in their galleys and beaten the Trokmoi. Though the woodsrunners had burned the bodies of their comrades who had fallen, they still muttered among themselves as they passed the battlefield.

On the west side of the river—land that had been still in Elabonian hands, not under Adiatunnus' control—the hair prickled up on Gerin's arms for no reason he could see or feel. He kept quiet about it, doubting his own judgment, but after a while Van said, "The air feels—uncanny."

"That's it!" Gerin exclaimed, so vehemently that Duren started and the horses snorted indignantly. "Aye, that's it. Feels like the air in the old haunted woods around Ikos."

"So it does." Van frowned. "We've been out this way a time or two, and it never did before. What's toward, Fox? Your usual Elabonian gods, they don't make a habit of letting folk know they're around like this."

"You're right; they don't, and they certainly never have around here—you're right about that, too." Gerin scowled.

What followed from his words did so as logically as the steps in a geometric proof from Sithonia. "I don't think we're feeling the power of Elabonian gods."

"Whose, then?" Van glanced around to make sure no Trokmoi could overhear him. "The woodsrunners' gods are too busy brawling amongst themselves to pay much heed to impressing people."

"I know," Gerin said. "Folk get the gods they deserve, don't they? So who's left? Not us, not the Trokmoi, not . . ." He let that hang in the air.

Van had been many places in his travels, but never to Sithonia. Yet he needed to be no logician to see what Gerin meant. "The Gradi," he said, his voice as sour as week-old milk.

"Can't think of anyone else it could be," the Fox said unhappily. He waved, trying to put into words what he felt. "We're heading toward high summer now, but doesn't the air taste more the way it would at the start of spring, when winter's just loosed its grip? And the sun." He pointed up to it. "The light's . . . watery somehow. It shouldn't be, not at this season of the year."

"That it shouldn't," Van said. "I've lived here long enough to know you're right as can be, Captain." He shook his fist toward the west, toward the Orynian Ocean. "Those cursed Gradi gods are settling in here, making themselves at home, growing like toadstools after a rain."

"My thought exactly," Gerin said. "Voldar and the rest of them, they must be strong to do . . . whatever they're doing. Dyaus and the Elabonian pantheon, they wouldn't interfere with the sun." He didn't say, *They couldn't interfere with the sun*, though that was in his mind, too. He didn't know whether it was so or not. The Elabonian gods were so lax about manifesting themselves in the material world, he honestly didn't know the full range of their power.

He didn't know the full range of Voldar's power, either, or the powers of the other Gradi gods and goddesses. He had the ominous feeling he was going to find out. This would have been a fine mild day, had it come a little before the vernal equinox. Drawing near the summer solstice, though . . .

Over his shoulder, Duren said, "I wish we could find out what the weather's like back on the east side of the Venien. That would tell us more about whether what we're worrying about is real or we're shying at shadows."

Gerin smiled. "There are times when I wish I could send Dagref down to the City of Elabon to learn all the things he can't learn here in the northlands. Maybe you should go, too, for that's reasoned like a scholar."

"Aye, so it is," Van rumbled, "but there's more going on here than scholarship or whatever you call it. It's not just the weather, lad. It's what I feel in the hair on the nape of my neck, and I'm not talking about lice." He set a hand on the flared neckpiece of his helmet.

"What do we do about it?" Duren said, yielding the point.

"Fight it," Van declared. As usual, the world looked simple to him.

Gerin wished the world looked simple to him, too. Here, though, he saw no better answer than the one his friend had proposed.

By the time they camped, that first night west of the Venien, the Trokmoi were all edgy, looking over their shoulders and muttering to themselves over anything or nothing. The presence of the more stolid Elabonians seemed to steady them, as Gerin—and Adiatunnus—had hoped it would.

They were still in land under Gerin's suzerainty, but not land where his control was as firm as it was closer to Fox Keep. The serfs hereabouts had not seen enough of him and his armies to have any confidence in their goodwill. They probably had seen enough of Trokmê raiders to have no confidence in them whatever. At first sight of a large force heading their way, they fled into the woods.

The warriors took—even Gerin did not like to think of it as stealing—enough chickens and sheep to sacrifice to keep the night ghosts quiet. Other than that, they did not harm the villages or the fields around them. They built great bonfires not only to hold the ghosts at bay but also to give themselves warning if the Gradi were close enough to dare a night attack.

To reduce the risk of that as much as he could, Gerin set scouts out all around the campsite, each small group with a fowl to offer so the ghosts would not trouble them in spite of their being away from the fires. Adiatunnus watched that with interest and attention; the Fox got the idea the Trokmê was storing the notion to use against him one of these years.

Swift-moving Tiwaz had come round close to first quarter. Math was almost full, while Nothos, though four days past, still had only a bit of his eastern edge abraded by darkness. Out where the light of the bonfires grew dim, men had three separate shadows, each pointing in a different direction.

Except to go out to stand sentry or to answer calls of nature, though, few men, either Elabonians or Trokmoi, strayed far from the fireside. The warriors either rolled up in their blankets or sat around talking, often with folk not of their own kin. Most of them understood and could speak at least some of the language of their hereditary foes, and most relished the chance to swap tales with the men they usually met with weapons, not words.

Drungo Drago's son turned to Van and said, "Give us a tale, why don't you?"

Instantly, all the Elabonians began clamoring for a tale from the outlander, too. He'd seen and done things none of them, Gerin included, could match, and he told a good story, too. Seeing how enthusiastic the Elabonians were to hear him, the Trokmoi started shouting, too.

"Well, all right," Van said at last. "I thought I'd sooner sleep, and I thought a lot of you would sooner sleep, too, but who knows? Maybe I'll put you to sleep and then get some myself. You'd like that, hey?"

Somebody threw a hard-baked biscuit at him. He caught it out of the air and went on without missing a beat: "Well, I've yarned a good deal about creatures of one kind or another I've seen, and those tales haven't had too many people flinging their suppers my way, so maybe I'll give you one of them just to stay safe. How does that sound?"

No one said no. Several warriors said yes, loudly and enthusiastically. Van nodded. "All right, then," he said.

"South and east of the City of Elabon, way south of the High Kirs, the coast of the Bay of Parvela runs southeast between Kizzuwatna, which is far away from here and hot as you please, to Mabalal, which is even farther, even hotter, and muggy to boot." He looked around. The night, like the day, was cooler than it should have been. "Feels good to think about something hot right now, doesn't it?"

His listeners nodded. Gerin wished he could put into a jar whatever his friend used to draw an audience into a story. Even if it wasn't sorcery, it was magic of a sort.

Van went on, "Some of you, now, some of you may have heard I had to get out of Mabalal in a kind of a hurry once upon a time." He got more nods, from a few of the Trokmoi and a lot of the Elabonians. He grinned; his teeth flashed white in the firelight. "By the gods, some of you have heard a whole raft of different reasons why I had to get out of Mabalal in a hurry. Now does that mean I get into a pack of trouble or I tell a pack of lies?"

"Both, most likely," Drungo said. He wasn't a match for Van in size or strength or speed, but he was a large, strong man, and confident of his prowess. Even so, he made sure he was grinning, too.

The outlander, busy shaping his story, didn't take it for a challenge, as he might have in his younger days. He just said, "Well, I was there, and I'm the only one here who was, so nobody'll prove anything on me, and that's a fact. Anyway, there I was, sailing away from Mabalal up toward Kizzuwatna, getting away from whatever I was getting away from, and we put in at this miserable little port called Sirte.

"There's only two reasons anybody would ever put in at Sirte. One is, you can fill your waterskins there. The water you get is harsh, and it can give you a flux of the bowels if you're not used to it, but the spring never fails. And the other is that, a ways inland, there's a grove of myrrh trees in a valley that some more springs water. If you can get the myrrh, which is a sticky resin that grows on the trees, you'll sell it for a goodly price."

"It's one of the incenses they burn at Ikos, isn't it?" Gerin put in.

"That it is, Fox." Van nodded. "When we got to Sirte,

maybe half of dozen of us—ne'er-do-wells every one, you'd say—we decided to see if we couldn't get hold of some of this myrrh for our own selves, and strike out inland to see what we could do with it. I don't know about the others, but me, I was sick of being cooped up on a ship.

"The folk at Sirte spoke some of the language of Mabalal, and so did we. When they got the drift of what we wanted to do, they told us to watch out for snakes on the way to the myrrh trees. We'd just come out of Mabalal, now, so we thought we knew something of snakes—I've told stories about the serpents there, I expect."

"I liked the yarn about the snake with the stone in its head that was supposed to make you turn invisible, but didn't," Parol Chickpea said.

"For which I do thank you, friend," Van said. "Aye, we thought we knew something of snakes, that we did, so when the folk of Sirte warned us of the kinds they had out there in their desert—the chersidos and the cenchris and the seps and the prester and the dipsas and the scytale and I don't know what all other sorts they named—we just nodded our heads and said 'Yes, yes' when they told us about the different kinds of venom the serpents had. We figured they were spinning tales to frighten us and make us stay away from the myrrh."

The outlander shook his head. The firelight deepened the lines that carved his face and exaggerated his expression of rue. "Only goes to show what we knew, or rather, what we didn't. We bought waterskins and filled 'em and trudged out into the desert toward the myrrh trees, which were about a day and a half's travel inland from Sirte. The local folk shook their heads watching us go, as if they didn't expect to see us ever again, which, truth to tell, they probably didn't. To this day, if they remember us, they probably think we all perished in the desert. Lucky we are that we didn't—or some of us didn't, too."

"I suppose the people of Sirte went back and forth to the myrrh trees every so often," Gerin said. "If they looked for the snakes to get you, wouldn't they have expected to find your bodies along whatever trail there was?"

"That's a good question, Captain, and before I trod that trail I would have thought the same thing," Van said, "that is, if I'd believed them about the snakes, which I can't say I did. Like I told you, my notion was that they were just trying to scare us and keep us from going after the myrrh. I mean . . . well, hear me out and you'll see.

"We'd been walking along for a bit when all of a sudden something reared up out of the sand and gravel and hit me a lick right here." The outlander tapped his left greave, not far below the knee. "If I hadn't been wearing it, there's an awful lot of stories I wouldn't have told since, and that's the truth.

"I took a whack at the snake with my sword, and off flew its head. But we'd stirred up more than one, it turned out. Maybe the second was mate to the first. I won't ever know that. I killed it, too, but not till after it bit one of my friends.

"It wasn't a very big snake, and we hoped it wasn't any of the kinds the locals had warned us about, but it turned out to be a seps, and oh" —Van covered his eyes with a hand— "how I wish it hadn't been."

"How do you know it was, if it was only a little snake you killed?" someone asked.

"By the action of the venom," Van answered. "The seps bit my friend—well, actually, he was a robber and a thief, but we were traveling together—just above the ankle. Half an hour later, the gods beshrew me if I lie, there was nothing left of him but a little puddle of greenish fluid."

"What?" that same somebody exclaimed. "A snakebite doesn't do that."

"I thought the same thing," Van said, "but I was wrong. The natives at Sirte had told us the seps' venom made you disappear, and they knew what they were talking about. The fellow's flesh got clear around the bite, so you could see the bone through it, and then it just melted away, and the bone with it." He shuddered dramatically. "I never saw a man dissolve before and, if the gods are kind, I'll never see it again. How he screamed as he watched himself vanish—till he couldn't scream any more, of course. The rest of us, we pushed on in a hurry, let me tell you, and by the time we got out of there, like I say, he was nothing more than a little, stinking puddle the hot sun was already drying up.

"You can't blame us for not sticking around the spot where anything that horrible happened, but running away so fast turned out to be a mistake, too, for we didn't watch where we were putting our feet as carefully as we should have, and one of us stepped right on a prester.

"The thing looked like the vipers they have here, more or less, but when it came writhing out of the sand, it was the color of melted copper. It sank its teeth into poor Nasid—that was his name; it comes back to me even after all these years—then dove back into the sandbank and disappeared before anybody could do anything to it.

"And poor Nasid! Instead of melting, he started to swell, like rising bread dough but a hundred times as fast. His skin turned as fiery red as the prester's. He looked like there was a storm inside him, puffing him out every which way at once.

"Here's how fast he blew out: he was wearing trousers and a tunic with buttons, almost Trokmê-style, and the buttons flew right off the tunic, so hard that the one that hit me gave me this little scar over my eye, right here." The outlander pointed to a mark on his much-battered hide.

Gerin admired that touch. If Van's stories weren't true, they should have been, for he adorned them with a wealth of circumstantial detail. "What happened then?" the Fox asked.

"What do you mean?" Van returned. "To Nasid? He exploded, and there was no more left of him than of the other poor devil. To the rest of us? We ran. We probably should have run back to Sirte, but we went on toward the myrrh instead, and actually got to it with nobody else dying on the way. Then we headed up toward the Shanda country, but my other three friends—friends? ha!—tried to kill me for my share of the myrrh, and I left them as dead as anybody a snake bit."

"And what would the moral o' the tale be?" Adiatunnus asked. "A fine one it is, but it should have a moral."

"You want a moral, eh?" Van said. "I'll give you one. What this story shows is, some things are more trouble than they're worth."

The Trokmê chieftain laughed and nodded. "It does that.

And a truth worth remembering it is, too." He glanced up at the moons. "And if you'd gone on much longer, the story'd have been more trouble nor it was worth, with us having to get up in the morning and all. But you didna, for which I thank you." He laid a blanket on the ground and wrapped himself in it.

Gerin couldn't resist a parting shot: "Even if you do get up in the morning, will you be moving before afternoon?" Adiatunnus made a point of ignoring him. Chuckling, the Fox also swaddled himself in a blanket and was soon asleep.

Maybe sleeping in the open was what the Trokmoi needed. Maybe they were starting to remember what being on campaign was all about. Whatever the reason, they moved reasonably fast when the sun came up the next morning. Gerin had been looking forward to screaming at them to hurry. Disappointed, he gnawed dry sausage and made sure he was ready to get going so they couldn't twit him.

The farther west they traveled, the more heavily the unnatural coolth lay on the land. Gerin eyed the fields with curiosity and concern mixed. "They'll not have much of a crop this year," he observed.

"Aye, the wheat's well behind where it ought to be," Van agreed. "They look like they had to plant late to start with, and they won't make up for lost time, not with weather like this they won't." His shiver held only a little exaggeration for dramatic effect.

"Pity you couldn't have brought one of those prester snakes along with you from Sirte—is that the name of the place?" Gerin said. Van nodded. The Fox went on, "Sounds like just what we'd need to heat up . . . a certain goddess I'd be better off not naming."

Van chuckled and nodded. "Aye, a prester would heat her up if anything would. The thing of it is, would anything?"

"I don't know and I don't care," Gerin answered. "If we beat the Gradi and drive them away, it doesn't matter, anyhow. Without men and women to worship her, that goddess won't gain a foothold here."

He didn't know whether not naming Voldar would do

any good. But he'd been of the opinion that Adiatunnus knew more about the Gradi than he did, and the Trokmê chief had given him no reason to change his mind. If Adiatunnus thought saying Voldar's name would draw her notice, the Fox was willing to refrain.

He wished, though, that he could draw the notice of the local barons by speaking their names. Many of them seemed to have abandoned their keeps, though the Gradi didn't seem to be garrisoning those keeps, either. Some of the serf villages looked deserted, too. Again, Gerin saw the delicate fabric of civilization tearing.

He sent scouts out farther ahead and to either side than he was used to doing. He also maintained a substantial rearguard: the Gradi, with their ability to travel down rivers, were liable to try to set troops behind him and pin him between two forces. He would have thought about doing that had he been in their place, anyhow.

As his army advanced through country that lay ever deeper in the frigid embrace of the Gradi gods, he wished he could come to grips with the Gradi themselves. He began to worry when he encountered none of them, and started complaining shortly thereafter.

When he did, Van fixed him with a gaze that might have belonged on a battlefield itself and said, "We'll come across them soon enough, and when we do, you'll be wishing just as loud you'd never set eyes on them." Since that was undoubtedly true, the Fox maintained what he thought was a prudent silence. Van's snicker said it might have been less prudent than he'd hoped.

And then, a couple of days later, the army did come upon a troop of Gradi; the invaders were happily plundering a peasant village. They'd killed a couple of men, and a line of them were having sport with a woman they'd caught. They seemed utterly astonished to find foes so far into territory they obviously thought of as theirs. As some of them were literally caught with their breeches down, they put up a fight less ferocious than they might have otherwise, and several made no effort to slay themselves rather than submitting to capture.

Gerin ordered the men who'd been holding down the peasant woman and the one who'd been on top of her bound and handed over to the surviving serfs. "Do as you like with them," he said. "I'm sure you'll think of something interesting."

The peasants' eyes glowed. "Let's get a fire going," one of them said.

"Aye, and we'll boil some water over it," another added enthusiastically.

"Will we want sharp knives—or dull ones?" somebody asked.

"Both," said the woman who'd been raped. "I claim first cut, and I know just where I'm going to make it, too." She stared at the crotch of one of the Gradi with an interest anything but lewd. Gerin couldn't tell whether any of the bound Gradi understood Elabonian. They might not know what was in store for them. He shrugged. If they didn't, they'd find out soon enough.

One of the other northerners did speak the language of the land they'd invaded. "I not tell you anything," he said when Gerin started to question him.

"Fine," the Fox said. He turned to the warriors holding the captives. "Take him where he can watch the serfs at work. If he doesn't come back talkier after that, we'll give him to them, too."

"Come on, you," one of the Elabonians said. They frogmarched the Gradi away. Before long, the Fox heard hoarse screams rising up from inside the village. When the guards brought the Gradi back, his face was paler than it had been. The guards looked grim, too.

"Hello again," Gerin said briskly. He looked thoughtful, a look he'd had occasion to practice over the years. "Do you suppose your goddess would be interested in keeping you around for the afterlife if you end up dead with some interesting parts missing? Do you suppose you'd enjoy the afterlife as much if you didn't have them? Do you want to find out the answers to those questions right away?"

The Gradi licked his lips. He didn't answer right away; maybe he was taking stock of his own spirit. Dying in battle, even slaying yourself to avoid capture, seemed easy if you measured them against mutilation that would be long agony in this world and might ruin you for the next.

Gerin smiled. "Are you more in the mood to talk now than you were a little while ago? For your sake, you'd better be."

"How I know I talk, then you do things to me anyway?" the Gradi asked.

"How do you know you can trust me, you mean? That's simple—you don't. Nothing complicated there, eh? But I tell you now that I won't do all those interesting things to you if you do talk. You can believe me or not, as you choose."

The Gradi sighed. "I talk. What you want?"

"For starters, tell me your name," Gerin said.

"I am Eistr."

"Eistr." Gerin found a stick and wrote the name in Elabonian characters in the soft ground at his feet. "Now that I know it and have captured it here, I can work magic against it—and against you—if I find out you lie."

Eistr looked appalled. Gerin had hoped he would. Nothing the Fox had seen made him think the Gradi knew the use of writing. Literacy was thin enough among Elabonians, and almost nonexistent among the Trokmoi, who, when they did write, used the characters of their southern neighbors. Ignorance added to Eistr's fear. And the truth was that Gerin, if sufficiently ired, might even have been able to use name magic against him, though it wasn't anything the Fox really wanted to try.

"You ask. I tell," the Gradi said. "I tell true, swear by Voldar's breasts."

Gerin had no idea how strong an oath that was, but decided not to press it. He said, "Where did your band come from? How many more of you are back there?"

Eistr pointed back toward the west. "Is keep, two days' walk from here. Is by a river. We have maybe ten tens when I there. Is maybe more now. Is maybe not more, too."

The Fox thought that over. It struck him as a likely way to get his army to walk into a trap without leaving Eistr forsworn. Gerin said, "Why don't you know how many men of yours are likely to be in this keep now?"

"We use for—how you say?—for middle place. Some go out to fight, some come in to fight, some stay to mind thralls," Eistr said. "Is now many, is now not."

"Ah." That did make a certain amount of sense. "Is your band supposed to be back at this base at any set time, or do you come and go as you please?"

"As we please. We are Gradi. We are free. The goddess Voldar rules us, no man." Pride rang in Eistr's voice.

"You may be surprised," the Fox said dryly. Eistr's cold, gray eyes stared at him without comprehension. Gerin turned to the guards. "Take him away. We'll find out what some of the others can tell us."

He got pretty much the same story from the rest of the Gradi who spoke Elabonian. Then he had to figure out what to do with them. Killing them out of hand would have meant having the same thing happen to any of his men the Gradi captured. Holding them prisoner would have made him detach men from his own force to guard them, which he didn't think he could afford to do. In the end, he decided to strip them naked and turn them loose.

"But these thralls, they catch us, they kill us," Eistr protested, he being the most articulate of the Gradi. He glanced nervously toward the peasant village.

"You know, maybe you should have thought about that before you started robbing and raping and killing them," Gerin said.

"But they *ours*. We do with them how we like," Eistr answered. "Voldar has said, so must be true." The other Gradi who followed Elabonian nodded agreement to that.

"Voldar isn't the only goddess—or god—in this land, and people here have more sway on their own than you're used to," the Fox said. As if to add emphasis to his words, another scream came from one of the raiders he'd given over to the serfs. He blinked in surprise; he'd thought those Gradi surely dead by now. The peasants had more patience and ingenuity than he'd given them credit for. He finished, "Now you're going to find out what it's like being rabbits instead of wolves. If you live, you'll learn something from it."

"And if you don't live, you'll learn summat from that, too," Van added with ghoulish glee.

When ordered to strip bare, one of the captured Gradi, though weaponless, threw himself at Elabonians and Trokmoi and fought so fiercely, he made them kill him.

The rest looked much less fearsome without jerkins and helms and heavy leather boots. They ran for the woods, white buttocks flashing in the sun.

"They have no tools for making fire," Gerin observed, "nor weapons to hunt beasts for sacrifices to the night ghosts. They'll have a thin time of it when the sun goes down." He smiled unpleasantly. "Good."

He gave the helms and shields and axes he'd taken from the Gradi to the men of the peasant village. He didn't know how much good they would do folk untrained to war, but was certain they couldn't hurt. Some of the villagers were still busy with the captive Gradi. He did his best not to look at what was left of the arrogant raiders.

He did say, "When you're done there, find someplace to be rid of the bodies so the Gradi never find them. For that matter, if you get word we've lost, you probably ought to think about running for your lives."

"You won't lose, lord prince," one of the serfs exclaimed. "You *can't*."

Gerin wished he shared the fellow's touching optimism.

The Fox pushed the pace as his force of chariotry approached the keep the Gradi were holding. He didn't want any of the men he'd released deciding to act heroic and getting there ahead of his warriors to warn the garrison. Taking a keep was hard enough without having the foe alerted in advance.

One thing: the Gradi seemed to have no idea he and his troopers were anywhere nearby. To make sure they didn't, on his approach he sent out dismounted scouts, who, if they were seen, were likely to be taken for either Gradi or for Elabonian peasants. The scouts came back with word that, sure enough, the Gradi did hold the keep, but that they had the drawbridge down and were keeping no watch worth mentioning.

"Why don't we just march up on foot and tramp right in, then?" the Fox said. "With luck, they won't notice we aren't who we're supposed to be till it's too late to raise the drawbridge against us."

"What, and leave the cars behind?" Adiatunnus demanded.

"We can't fight with them inside the keep anyhow, can

we?" Gerin said. The Trokmê chieftain scratched his head, then shrugged, plainly not having looked at it that way. Gerin said, "They've got us here faster than we could have come on foot, and we're not worn out from walking, either. They've served their purpose, but you can't use the same tool for every job."

"Ah, well," Adiatunnus said. "I told you I'd follow against the Gradi where you led, and if you'll be after leading with the feet of you, I'll walk in your footsteps, that I will." His eyes, though, said something more like, *And if this goes wrong, I'll blame you for it, that I will.*

That was the chance you took in any battle, though: if you lost, you got the blame, assuming you lived. Actually, you could get the blame if you died, too, but then you had other things to worry about.

The Fox told off approximately equal numbers of Elabonians and Trokmoi to stay behind with the horses. As for the rest, he put those who in looks and equipment most closely resembled the Gradi at the head of the column, to confuse the warriors in the keep for as long as he could. Being dark haired himself, with gear of the plainest, he marched along at the fore.

Van, who with his blond hair and fancy cuirass resembled almost anything in the world more than a Gradi, was relegated to the rear, to his loud disgust. He complained so long and so bitterly, Gerin finally snapped, "I'm getting better obedience out of the Trokmoi than I am from you."

"Oh, I'll do it, Fox," the outlander said with a mournful sigh, "but you can drop me into the hottest of your five hells if you think you'll make me like it."

"So long as it gets done," Gerin said. He wished he'd been able to find an excuse to hold Duren back at the rear. If both of them fell, all his hopes would fall, too—not, again, that he'd be in a position to do anything about it.

He led the column of warriors on a looping track to bring them up to the keep from the south, figuring the Gradi were less likely to take alarm if he and his men didn't come into view from straight out of the east. "We'll get as close to the keep as we can," he said, "and then charge home. If enough of us can get inside, they'll be very unhappy."

"And if not enough can," somebody—he didn't see who—said, "we will." Since that was undoubtedly true, he wasted no time arguing about it.

His first view of the keep confirmed the scouts' reports and his own hopes. The Gradi had only a handful of men up on the walls. Several more were passing time outside, a couple going at each other with axe and shield, three or four more standing around watching.

When the Gradi caught sight of the oncoming column, the first thing they did was raise a loud, wordless cheer. "Yell back!" the Fox hissed to his own men, who did. A shout was a shout in any language.

One of the Gradi perfecting his axework was the first to notice that Gerin and his followers were not what they appeared to be. By then, though, they were less than a hundred yards from the drawbridge. The sharp-eyed Gradi let out a shout that, though still without words, was of altogether different tone from those his countrymen had been exchanging with Gerin's masquerading warriors. He rushed at the Elabonians and Trokmoi, the sun glinting off the bronze head of his axe.

Several archers shot him. He fell before he got close to the attackers. "Run!" Gerin shouted, giving up the pretense. "We seize the gateway, we get inside, and we clean them out."

Yelling for all they were worth, his men and Adiatunnus' dashed for the drawbridge. The Fox wasn't the first man onto it—some of the young bravos ran faster—but he wasn't far behind. He wondered if the Gradi were going to raise it with warriors on it and inside the keep.

They didn't, as they hadn't tried raising it before their enemies reached it. When he stormed into the keep, Gerin realized the raiders from the north hadn't kept any sort of gate crew on the winches that would have moved the bridge up or down. Maybe they hadn't seen the need. Maybe castles in their own cold homeland had gates that worked differently. Whatever the reason, they made his work easier for him.

As soon as he and his men got inside the keep's outer wall, the fight was as good as won. The Gradi would have done better to throw down their axes and beg for mercy.

Not all of them even had axes, or helms, or leather jerkins. They'd been expecting no attack. Had they yielded, they would have lived.

With few exceptions, they would not yield. Instead, they hurled themselves at the Elabonians and Trokmoi with loud cries of "Voldar!" As had a couple of their warriors back at the peasant village, many of them, armed with nothing more than belt knives and stools and whatever they could snatch up, fought so fiercely, they made their foes slay them.

And they slew their foes, too. Outnumbered, outmatched, they still did a lot of damage. One of them, swinging a bench from the great hall, leveled a whole row of Elabonians, as if he were scything down wheat. A couple of the warriors who went down didn't get up again, either: he'd managed to split their skulls.

His next flailing swipe with the bench almost took Gerin out with it. The Fox had to skip back in a hurry to keep from getting his ribs stove in. But a bench was an unhandy thing with which to make a backhand stroke. Gerin stepped forward, thrust his sword into the Gradi's belly, twisted to make sure the stroke killed, and jerked the blade free. The Gradi toppled, clutching himself and howling.

Adiatunnus shouted in his own language: "Into the castle, now! We'll not be letting 'em use it for refuge against us!"

Had the Gradi thought to do that, they might have given Gerin's army a hard fight. Many of them tried to get into the great hall to lay hold of their weapons and then return to the fight out in the courtyard. When Elabonians and Trokmoi got in with them, the chance of using the castle as a citadel disappeared.

And when the fighting raged in the great hall as well as outside, the servants in the kitchen—Elabonians all—joined Gerin's warriors, throwing themselves at the Gradi with kitchen knives and cleavers and spits and two-tined serving forks. They had no armor, they had no skill at fighting, some of them were women, but they had hatred and to spare. In the tight quarters, in the chaos, that let them bring down more than one of the men who had oppressed them, though more of their number fell making the effort.

After the great hall of the castle was forced, the battle became a hunt for any Gradi who still lived. The tall, pale, dark-haired men would find shelter and then spring out, selling their lives dear as they could. Before the sun went down, almost all of them were dead.

The castle servants helped there. They knew every hiding place in the keep, and led Gerin's men to them one by one. The Gradi, deprived of surprise, wreaked a smaller toll than they might have otherwise.

"We won," Adiatunnus said, looking around at the carnage with dazed, almost disbelieving eyes. "Who'd have thought we could lay into those omadhauns and beat 'em, the way they've pounded us like drums?"

"They're only men," Gerin said. From inside the castle, screams rose. The kitchen servants were having their revenge on some of the Gradi who yet lived. The air was thick with the smell of roasting meat. Gerin decided he didn't want to know what sort of meat was being roasted.

He went to do what he could to help the wounded, sewing up gashes and setting broken bones. A physician down in the City of Elabon would no doubt have laughed at his efforts. Here in the northlands, he came as close to being a physician as anyone, and closer than most.

A skinny young woman came up to him with bread and beef ribs and ale. He took some, but said, "Here, you eat the rest. You look as if you need it more than I do." The very idea of a scrawny kitchen helper struck him as strange.

So did the amazed way the woman stared. She started to cry. "The Gradi, they'd beat us or worse if we ate of what we made for them." She didn't talk for a while after that, instead cramming her mouth full of bread and beef. Then she asked, "Do you want me? I don't have anything else I can give you for setting us free."

"No, that's all right," Gerin answered. The young woman—young enough, easily, to be his daughter—didn't look as if it was all right. She looked as if she wanted to punch him in the eye. *So much for gratitude*, he thought, a thought that frequently crossed his mind when he was dealing with human beings. The woman went off and approached a Trokmê. Gerin thought it likely that, if she wanted to thank him that particular way, he'd let her.

He was about to send a runner to order the chariots up to spend the night with the rest of the army when they came up without orders, a driver sometimes leading another team or two behind the car in which he stood. "Figured we wouldn't break surprise now, and you might be able to use us," said Utreiz Embron's son, the warrior he'd left in charge of the chariotry.

"Nicely reasoned," Gerin said with an approving nod. He'd thought well of Utreiz for years. The man thought straight and kept his eyes on what was important all the time. He was no swashbuckler, but he got the job done, and done well. He was, in fact, rather like a small-scale model of the Fox.

"I expected you'd have things well in hand," he said now. "If they'd gone wrong, you'd have been yelling for us a long time ago."

"That's likely so," Gerin agreed. He went on in a thoughtful tone of voice: "You know, Utreiz, this land is going to need reordering if we ever drive the Gradi out of it. I think you'd be a good man to install as a vassal baron."

"Thank you, lord prince," Utreiz said. "I'd be lying if I said I didn't hope you'd tell me something like that." Gerin wondered if he ought to be annoyed Utreiz had anticipated him. He shook his head: no, not when he'd thought for years that the fellow's mind worked like his.

He looked around to make sure his men up on the wall of the captured keep were more alert than the Gradi had been. He didn't know how close their next large band was, and didn't want to throw away the victory he'd won over them.

The harried Elabonian servitors at the keep assumed the Fox would want to sleep in the room the Gradi commander had used, and led him up to it when he said he was tired. One whiff inside convinced him he didn't want to do that. Even by the loose standards of the Elabonian northlands, the Gradi were not outstandingly clean of person. He wondered whether that came from living in such a cold climate.

No matter where it came from, it made him go on down into the great hall and roll himself in a blanket there with his men. The racket in the hall was still loud, as warriors drank and refought the battle over and over again. The Fox didn't care. After he'd learned to fall asleep with newborn infants in the same room, nothing his men could do fazed him.

He was not a man who dreamed much or often remembered the dreams he had. When he found himself walking along a snowy path through a white-draped forest of pines, he thought at first he was awake. Then he realized he wasn't cold and decided it had to be a dream, even though he hardly ever remembered having such a clear one. When he understood he was dreaming, he expected to wake up at once, as often happens when a dream is seen for what it is.

But he stayed asleep and kept walking down the path. He tried to force himself awake, but discovered he couldn't. Fear trickled through him then. Once, years before, the Trokmê wizard Balamung had seized his spirit and made it see what the wizard would have it see. He hadn't been able to fight his way from that dream till Balamung released him. Now—

Now, suddenly, the pines gave way. The path opened out into a snow-covered clearing dazzlingly white even under a leaden sky. And in the middle of that clearing stood a comely naked woman with long dark hair, twice as tall as the Fox, who held in her right hand an axe of Gradi style.

"Voldar," Gerin whispered. In the silence of his mind, he thanked his own gods that the Gradi goddess had chosen to meet him in a dream rather than manifesting herself in the material world. He was in enough danger here in this place that was not a true place.

She looked at him—through him—with eyes pale as ice, eyes in which cold fire flickered. And he, abruptly, *was* cold, chilled in the heart, chilled from the inside out. Her lips moved. "You meddle in what does not concern you," she said. He did not think the words were Elabonian, but he understood them anyhow. That left him awed but unsurprised. Gods—and, he supposed, goddesses—had their own ways in such matters.

"The northlands are my land, the land of my people, the land of my gods," he answered, bold as he dared. "Of course what happens here concerns me."

That divinely chilling gaze pierced him again. Voldar tossed her head in fine contempt. Her hair whipped out behind her, flying back as if in a breeze—but there was no breeze, or none Gerin could sense. In face and form, the Gradi goddess was stunningly beautiful, more perfect than any being the Fox had imagined, but even had she been his size, he would have known no stir of desire for her. Whatever her purpose, love had nothing to do with it.

She said, "Obey me now and you may yet survive. Give over your vain resistance and you will be able to live out your full span most honored among all those not lucky enough to be born of the blood of my folk."

Did that mean the people who worshiped her or the people she'd invented? Gerin had never thought he'd have the chance to ask a god that philosophical riddle, and, with the moment here, discovered having the chance and having the nerve were two different things.

He said, "I'll take my chances. I may end up dead, but that strikes me as better than living under your people—and under you. Or I may end up alive and free. Till the time comes, you never know—and we Elabonians have gods, too."

Voldar tossed her head again. "Are you sure? If you do, where are they? Drunk? Asleep? Dead? I have hardly noticed them, I tell you that. The Trokmoi have gods—aye, gods who flee before me. But you folk here? Who would know? I think you pray to emptiness."

Gerin knew he could not afford to give full heed to anything she told him. She had her own interest, and fooling him and dismaying him were to her advantage. But what she said about the Trokmê gods paralleled all too well what had happened in the material world for him to dismiss it out of hand. And what she said about Dyaus and the rest of the Elabonian pantheon put him in mind of his own thoughts . . . and his own worries. He wondered how much of the dream he would remember when he woke.

"I'll take the chance," he said. "The Trokmoi brought their gods south of the Niffet when they crossed over it some years back, and those gods do live in this land now, but they haven't run off the gods we Elabonians follow. The Trokmoi haven't conquered us, either, you'll notice, as they surely would have if our gods were as weak as you say."

"As I also told you, it's the Trokmê gods who are weak," Voldar answered. But she did not sound so grimly self-assured as she had before; maybe he'd given her a response she hadn't expected. She gathered herself before resuming, "In any case, my people and I are not puny and foolish, as are the Trokmoi and their gods. We do not come here to visit or to share. We come to *take*."

As far as Gerin was concerned, the Trokmoi had come for the same reason. But the Gradi and Voldar and the rest of their gods were much more serious, much more methodical about it than the woodsrunners.

Voldar went on, "I tell you this: if you stand against us, you and your line shall surely fail, and it will be as if you had never been. Be warned, and choose accordingly."

For a moment, Gerin knew stark despair. Voldar had struck keenly at his deepest secret fear. Almost, he was tempted to give in. But then he remembered Biton's verses promising Ricolf's barony to Duren. Had the farseeing god been lying to him? He had trouble believing that. He wondered if Voldar had so much as sensed Biton's presence in the land, the Sibyl's shrine being far from anywhere the Gradi had reached and Biton himself being only superficially Elabonian. He did not ask. The more ignorant the Gradi and their gods remained of the northlands, the better off their opponents would be.

He also wondered whether Voldar had yet encountered whatever older, utterly un-Elabonian powers dwelt *under* the Sibyl's shrine, the powers controlling the monsters. Then he wondered if there were any such powers. So much he didn't know, even after a busy lifetime in the world.

"What is your answer?" Voldar demanded when he did not speak.

"Who can say whether what you tell me is the same as what will be?" he replied. "I guess I'll take my chances fighting on."

"Fool!" Voldar screamed. She stabbed out a finger at him. Cold smote, sharp and harsh as any spear thrust. He clutched at his chest, as if pierced—and woke up, panting, his heart pounding with fear, in the great hall of the keep he and his army had just seized.

Adiatunnus was lying a few feet away. No sooner had Gerin's eyes flown open in the gloom of guttering torches than the Trokmê chieftain gave a great cry—"The hag! The horrible hag!"—in his own language and sat bolt upright, his pale eyes wide and staring.

Several warriors muttered and stirred. A couple of men woke up at Adiatunnus' shout and complained before rolling over and going back to sleep. Adiatunnus gaped wildly, now this way, now that, as if he did not know where he was.

"Did you just visit a certain goddess in your dreams?" Gerin called quietly. He still didn't know whether mentioning Voldar by name would help make her notice him, but, after what he'd just seen, he didn't want to find out, either.

"Och, I did that," Adiatunnus answered, his voice shaky. He needed a moment to realize why Gerin was likely to be asking the question, a telling measure of how shaken he was. His gaze sharpened, showing his wits beginning to work once more. "And you, Fox? The same?"

"The same," Gerin agreed. "She—whoever she was" —no, he'd take no chances— "tried to frighten me out of going on with the campaign. What happened to you?"

"Just the look of her turned the marrow in me to ice for fair," Adiatunnus said, shivering. "Humliest wench I'm ever after seeing, and that's nobbut the truth. And the blood running from the jaws of her, it came from some good Trokmê god, I'm thinking, puir fellow."

"Ugly? Blood? That's not how she showed herself to me," Gerin said, more intrigued than surprised. Gods were gods, after all; of course they could manifest themselves in more than one way. "She was beautiful but terrible, fear and cold and awe all mixed together. What I thought was, *No wonder she's chief among all the Gradi gods*."

"We saw her different, that we did," Adiatunnus said with another shudder. "I wonder which was her true seeming, or if either one was. We'll never ken, I'm thinking. However you saw her, though, what did the two of you have to say to each other?"

As best he could, Gerin recounted his conversation with the Gradi goddess, finishing, "When I told her I wouldn't give up, she—I don't know—flung a freeze at me. I thought my heart and all my blood would turn to ice, but before that happened, I woke up. What befell you?"

"You said her nay?" Adiatunnus asked in wondering tones. "You said her nay, and she didn't destroy you?"

"Of course she destroyed me," Gerin answered irritably. "Look—here you are, talking with my blasted corpse."

Adiatunnus stared, then frowned, then, after a long moment, started to laugh. "Fox, it's many a time and oft I've wished to see the dead corp of you, blasted or any way you choose. The now, though, I'll own to being glad you're still here to give me more in the line of troubles."

"I thank you for that in the same spirit you meant it," Gerin said, squeezing another chuckle out of Adiatunnus. The Fox went on, "What did . . . she . . . say or do to make you wake up with such a howl?"

"Why, she showed me the ruin of everything I'd labored for all these years, if I was to go on with the war against her people," the Trokmê answered.

"And you believed her?" Gerin said. "Just like that?"

"So I did," Adiatunnus said with yet another chuckle. "What I want to know is, why you didna."

"Because I assumed she was lying to me, to put me in fear and make me lose heart," Gerin said. "If I were a Gradi god, it's what I'd do. You Trokmoi are a tricksy folk—have you no trickster gods?"

"Aye, we do that," Adiatunnus admitted. "But the goddess in my dream, now, she's not that sort, not from all the tales of her I ken, any road. And the Gradi, they're not that sort, either. They come and they take and they kill and they go, with hardly even a smile to say they're enjoying the work."

That last phrase drew a snort from the Fox, who said, "Well, from what I've seen, you're right about the Gradi. You may even be right about . . . that goddess. Maybe she wouldn't lie for the sport of it, the way a woodsrunner would." He relished Adiatunnus' glare, a sign the chieftain's spirit was recovering. "But would she lie to help her own folk? Of course she would. This side of Biton, can you think of a god who wouldn't?"

Adiatunnus pondered that. Slowly, he nodded. "Summat to what you say, lord prince." He used Gerin's title in a tone half grudging, half admiring. "You've got sand in you, that you do. You aim just to keep on after the Gradi as if you'd never dreamt your dream, do you now?"

"We've beaten them once, you and I together," Gerin said. "I've beaten them another time, all by my lonesome. Till they show me they can beat me, why should I pull back?"

"Sure and you have a way to make it all sound so simple, so easy," Adiatunnus said. "But they're after beating us a whole raft o' times—us Trokmoi, I mean. When that happens" —he sighed— "the only thing you can think of is that it'll happen again, try as you will to stop it."

"Which is why you made common cause with us," Gerin observed.

"Truth there," Adiatunnus said.

"Then let me take the lead, since you gave it to me, and don't trouble your head with dreams, even dreams with goddesses in them," the Fox said.

"Dinna fash yoursel'. Dinna fash yoursel'." Adiatunnus made his voice high and squeaky, as if he were a mother shouting at a little boy. "Easy to say. Not so easy to do, not when you're in the middle o' the dream."

There was truth in that, too. But Gerin asked, "Are you dreaming now?"

"No," the Trokmê chieftain said at once. But then he looked around the dim-lit great hall. "Or no is what I think, the now. But how can you be sure?"

"Good question," Gerin said. "If I had a good answer, I'd give it to you. I'll tell you this much: I don't think I'm dreaming, either." He pulled his blanket up around him; the rough wool scratched at his neck. "With any luck, though, I will be soon." He closed his eyes. He heard Adiatunnus laugh softly and, a little later, heard his snores join those filling the hall. A little later than that, he stopped hearing anything.

When the Fox's army rode west from the captured keep the next morning, they rode toward dark gray clouds piled high on the horizon and scudding rapidly toward them on a startlingly nippy breeze. "Wouldn't know we were at the summer season, would you?" Gerin said, shivering a little as that wind slid under his armor and chilled his hide.

Duren looked back over his shoulder at his father. "If I didn't know what season it was, I'd guess those clouds held snow in them, not rain."

"I wish they did," Van said, peering ahead with a frown. "Snow'd leave the road hard. Rain like the rain those clouds look to have in 'em'll turn these dirt tracks into hub-deep soup." He turned from Duren to Gerin. "Your Elabonian Emperors were no fools when they made their fine highways. Hard on a horse's hooves, aye, but you can move along 'em and bite the thumb at the worst of the weather."

"I won't say you're wrong, because I think you're right." Gerin studied those fast-moving clouds and shook his head. "I've never seen weather so ugly this late in the year."

Even as he spoke, the wind freshened further. It smelled of rain, of damp dust somewhere not far away. A moment later, the first drop hit him in the face. More rain followed, the wind blowing it almost horizontally through the air. Rain in summer should have been pleasant, breaking the humidity and leaving the air mild and sweet when it was gone. This rain, once arrived, chilled to the marrow and gave no sign it would ever leave.

A few of the warriors had brought rain capes with them, of oiled cloth or leather. For once, Gerin found himself imperfectly forethoughtful and getting ever more perfectly wet. The horses splashed through the thickening ooze of the roadway and began to kick up muck instead of dust.

The chariot wheels churned up a muddy wake as the car rolled west.

Gerin's world contracted; the rain brought down dim curtains that hid the middle distance and even the near. He could see the couple of teams and chariots closest to him, no more. Every Gradi in the world might have been gathered a bowshot and a half off to one side of the road, and he would never have known it. After a while, he stopped worrying; had the Gradi been there, they wouldn't have known about him, either.

Water dripped from Van's eyebrows and trickled through his beard. "This is no natural storm, Fox," he boomed, raising his voice to make himself heard through wailing wind and drumming drops.

"I fear you're right," Gerin said. "It puts me in mind of the one Balamung the wizard raised against us before he led the Trokmoi across the Niffet." He remembered the gleaming, sorcerous bridge over the river as if it had been yesterday, though more than a third of his life had passed since then.

Van nodded. The motion shook more water from his beard. "And if a wizard could do what Balamung did, how hard a grip can gods take on the weather?"

"A good question," Gerin answered, and then said no more for some time. A lot of people had been coming up with good questions lately. At last, he added, "It's such a good one, I wish you hadn't asked it."

As if to give point to what the outlander had said, a lightning bolt crashed down and smashed a tree somewhere not far away. Gerin saw the blue-purple glare and heard the crash, but could not see the tree through the driving rain.

As the rain went on, the army traveled more and more slowly. The Fox had trouble being sure they were still traveling west. He had trouble being sure they were still on the road; the only way to tell it from the fields through which it went was that the mud seemed deeper and more clinging in the roadway.

Days were long at this season of the year, but the clouds were so thick and black, they disguised the coming of night almost till true darkness arrived. The army, caught away from a keep and even away from a peasant village, made a hasty, miserable camp. The only offering they could give the ghosts was blood sausage from their rations. Starting fires was out of the question. So was hunting.

Gerin set his jaw against the discontented, disappointed wails of the night spirits and did his best to ignore them, as he would have tried to ignore the first twinges of a tooth beginning to rot in his head. He squelched around the unhappy encampment. There were tents enough for only about a third of his men. He shouted and cajoled troopers into packing those tents as tight as serfs stuffed barley into storage jars. That helped, but it wasn't enough. Nothing would have been enough, not in that rain.

He got the men who could not be stuffed into tents to rig what shelters they could with blankets and with the chariots they'd been riding. Such would have done against the usual warm summer rain. Against this— "Half of us will be down with chest fever in a couple of days," he said, shivering. "I wouldn't be surprised if we got sleet."

"I'd sooner fight the Gradi than the weather, any day," Van said. "Against the Gradi, you can hit back." Glumly, Gerin nodded.

Adiatunnus called, "Fox, where are you the now? With the murk so thick and all, I'm liable to fall in a puddle and drown myself or ever I find you."

"Here," Gerin answered through the hiss of the rain. He spoke again a moment later, to guide the Trokmê chieftain to the blanket under which he huddled. Adiatunnus sat down beside him with a series of soft splashes.

"Lord prince, can we go on in—and against—this?" the woodsrunner asked.

"I aim to try," Gerin answered.

"But what's the use?" Adiatunnus wailed. "If we go on, we'll drown for fair, unless you're after reckoning death from sinking in the muck a different thing nor drowning."

"There's a question over which I suspect the philosophers have never vexed themselves," Gerin said, thereby amusing himself but not the Trokmê. He went on, "And what if we give up and the sun comes out before noon tomorrow? This is a bad storm, aye, but not so bad as all that." That he'd been saying just the opposite to Van a little while before fazed him not at all; he wanted to keep Adiatunnus' spirits as high as he could.

That proved not to be very high. With a sigh, the chieftain said, "One way or another, they'll overmaster us. If they canna be doing it by force of arms, that goddess and the rest will manage. We're better for having you here, Fox, but is better good enough? I doubt it, that I do."

Gerin fell back to the last ditch: "Do you remember your oath?"

"Och, that I do." Adiatunnus sighed again. "While you go on, lord prince, I'll go with you, indeed and I will. So I swore. But whether I think 'twill do any good—there's another story." He splashed away, leaving Gerin without any good reply.

Spurred largely by the Fox's shouts and curses, the Elabonians and Trokmoi did fare west again after dark gave way to a grudging, halfhearted morning twilight. Riding straight into the teeth of the rain only made things worse. So did the miserable breakfasts the troopers choked down, the slow pace the mud forced, and the out-of-season cold of the rain.

Toward midmorning, little bits of ice began to sting the soldiers' faces. "Not so bad as all that, you say?" Adiatunnus shouted through the slush after his chariot plowed forward to come up level with Gerin's. Again, the Fox found none of his usual sharp comebacks.

A little later, the army came up to a peasant village. The serfs were frantic. "The crops will die in the fields!" they screamed, as if Gerin could do something about that. "We'll starve come winter if we don't drown first—or freeze to death. Ice in summer!"

"Everything will be all right," Gerin said. He wondered if even the most naive serf would believe him.

As he and his men slogged on, he looked back enviously at the thatch-roofed huts in which the peasants huddled. They would undoubtedly keep drier than his army. Had the village been large rather than small, he would have been tempted to turn the serfs out of their homes and appropriate the shelters for his men. He was glad he didn't have to worry about that.

The farther west he and his troopers went, the worse the weather got. Somewhere, the Gradi were waiting. He hoped they were as wet and miserable as his own men.

Duren said, "At this rate, we could drive straight into the Orynian Ocean and we'd never know it. I don't see how we could get any wetter than we are now."

"Oceans taste of salt, lad," Van said. "I've been on 'em and in 'em, so I know. Past that, though, you're right. I keep expecting to see fish swim by me. Haven't yet, so maybe this is still land."

Whatever it was, it was dreadful going. Some small streams had climbed out of their banks, their water pouring in brown sheets across fields already sodden from the downpour. As had that first lot across which the army had come, serfs huddled in their villages, looking out with glum astonishment on the ruin of the year's crops. Gerin shuddered to think what winter would be like. The peasants were liable to end up eating grass and bark and one another. Uprisings started after years like this, among men who had nothing left to lose.

Toward evening (or so the Fox thought; by then, he seemed to have been traveling forever), the army did come across some Gradi: a double handful of the invaders were trudging, or rather squelching, across a field, oiled-leather rain capes over their heads. "There they are!" Gerin shouted. "The men whose gods are making this campaign so horrid. What do you say we pay those gods back for the grief they've given us?"

Afterwards, he didn't know whether to be glad or sorry he'd put it that way. The Gradi, spying his forces coming out of the rain at about the same time as he saw them, started running clumsily toward some trees bordering the edge of the field. The ground was mucky, but not quite so impossible as some he'd been through. That meant chariots could outdistance men afoot. His troopers cut the Gradi off from escape, then jumped down and slaughtered them, one after another. The water standing in the field was puddled here and there with red till the rain eventually diluted it and washed it away.

The fight itself wasn't what disturbed Gerin. But the savage glee both Elabonians and Trokmoi had taken in massacring the Gradi gave him pause, even though—and perhaps especially because—he'd encouraged them to do just that. Putting the best face he could on it, he told Adiatunnus, "There—you see? Every time we come on them, we beat them."

"Truth that," Adiatunnus said. "The warriors, we can beat them, sure and we can." He didn't sound happy about it, continuing, "And what good does that do us, I ask you? When the gods and goddesses are all after pissing out of the heavens down onto us, what good does killing men do?"

"If we hadn't shown we could do that, the Gradi gods and goddesses wouldn't have joined the fight against us," Gerin said.

"Are you saying that'd be better, now, or worse?" Adiatunnus asked, and splashed off before the Fox could reply.

The ghosts did not trouble the army that night, not with the fallen Gradi nearby to give them their boon of blood. But rain and sleet kept pelting down, which made the encampment as wretched as it had been the night before. Gerin wondered if Voldar would appear to him when he slept (if he slept, wet and cold as he was), but he remembered nothing after finally dropping off.

Dawn was the same misnomer it had been since the storm began. The Fox got the army moving more by refusing to believe it would not move than any other way. Exhausted, dripping men hitched exhausted, dripping horses to chariots and did their best to keep moving west against the Gradi.

Gerin would have relished a big fight that day. It would have been a focus for the anger that filled his men. But how could you fight back against a gray sky that kept pouring rain and ice on your head? You couldn't, which was precisely the problem.

"You won't make 'em go tomorrow," Van said as they slowly slogged on. "Damn me to the five hells if I know how you made 'em go today."

"They're more afraid of me than of the Gradi gods and

goddesses right now," the Fox said. "They know what I can do, and they still aren't sure about them."

But by the next day it wasn't just streams out of their banks, it was rivers. And rain and sleet turned to hail and then to snow. Gerin shook a fist at the heavens, wishing he had a bow that could reach beyond them. Wishing was futile, as usual.

Shivering, teeth chattering, he gave in. "We go back," he said.

VII

Back on the eastern side of the Venien River, in territory Adiatunnus controlled, the weather was cool and rainy. No one there seemed willing to believe the tales the returning warriors told of what they had endured trying to penetrate to the heart of the Gradi power.

"Only thing I can think of," Gerin said, standing close to the fire roaring in the hearth at Adiatunnus' great hall, "is that Voldar and the rest don't hold full sway this far east. Not yet, anyhow."

Adiatunnus' long face grew even more dolorous than it had been of late when he heard the Fox name the Gradi goddess. Gerin didn't care. Defiance burned like fever in him. Maybe it was making him delirious, as fever sometimes did. He didn't care about that, either. He wanted to hit back at the Gradi any way he could, and at their deities, too.

"How will you keep 'em from stretching their sway, though?" Adiatunnus demanded. He too stood close by the fire, as if he couldn't get warm enough. The Fox understood that, for he felt the same way. "You're nobbut a man, lord prince, and a man who fights a god—or even a goddess—he loses afore he begins."

"Of course he does," Gerin answered, "if he's stupid

enough to make the fight straight on. Gods are stronger than men, and they see farther than men, too. That doesn't mean they're smarter than men, though."

"And how smart d'you need to be to step on a cockroach, now?" Adiatunnus returned. "That's what you are to the gods, Fox: lord Gerin the Bug, prince of cockroaches."

"No doubt," Gerin said, annoying Adiatunnus by refusing to be annoyed himself. "But if I can get other gods angry at the ones the Gradi follow, and if I can steer them in the right direction—" Listening to himself, he could gauge how desperate he was. Playing with vipers—even the ones Van had described—was a safer business than getting involved with the gods. But if he didn't get divine aid of his own, the Gradi and their grim deities would swallow up the whole of the northlands. He felt it in his bones.

"And which gods will you summon, now?" Adiatunnus sounded both anxious and worried. "Our own, now, they willna face the ones the Gradi follow. So we've seen, to our sorrow. Is it any different with your Elabonian powers?"

"I don't know," Gerin said. That wasn't all he didn't know: he was wondering if he could make Father Dyaus pay any real attention to the affairs of the material world at all. The head of the Elabonian pantheon had swallowed up the savor of any number of fat-wrapped thighbones over the years; could he now give value for value? Gerin had taken his power for granted till he saw how Voldar supported the Gradi. Ever since, and especially since the storm, he'd wondered . . . and worried.

" 'I don't know' isn't much to rest the hopes o' the land on," Adiatunnus said.

"If I thought you were wrong, I would say so," Gerin answered. "As a matter of fact, I don't intend to summon an Elabonian god to deal with the goddess and the gods the Gradi follow. There's a foreign god with whom I've dealt before . . ."

He stopped. Adiatunnus noticed him stopping. "Tell me more," the Trokmê urged. "What foreign spirit is it, now? What powers has he got?"

"Mavrix is the Sithonian god of wine and poetry and

fertility and beauty," the Fox answered. "Along with Biton, he's also the god who drove the monsters back underground after the earthquake."

"A mighty god indeed," Adiatunnus said, looking impressed. "I was talking with one of those monsters, that I was, figuring ways to smash you to powder, Fox, when he softly and silently vanished away, leaving nobbut the rank smell of him behind to show he'd been no dream."

"So Diviciacus told me," Gerin said. "That was when you swore vassalage to me the first time." Adiatunnus nodded, not a bit abashed. He'd been frightened into swearing submission then, just as he had now because of the Gradi. If the danger went away, he was liable to try to reclaim his freedom of action once more, as he had a decade earlier.

What the Fox didn't tell him was that he faced the prospect of summoning Mavrix to his aid with the same enthusiasm he would have given the notion of having an arrowhead cut out of his shoulder: both were painful necessities, with the emphasis on *painful*. Mavrix and he had never got on well. He hadn't persuaded the Sithonian god to get rid of the monsters so much as he'd tricked him into doing it. Mavrix would just as soon have got rid of him instead—maybe sooner.

He'd survived Mavrix once, he'd tricked him once. Could he do it again? He'd said a man could be more clever than a god. Now he was going to have his chance to prove it . . . if he could.

Adiatunnus found another interesting question to ask: "Is your Sithonian god truly strong enough to beat back . . . that goddess?" He wouldn't name Voldar. "She's no mere monster, monster though she seems."

"I don't know that, either," Gerin told him. "All I can do is try to find out." He held up a hand. "And I know what your next question is going to be: what will we do if Mavrix turns out not to be strong enough?"

He didn't answer the question. He made a production out of not answering it. Finally, Adiatunnus prodded him: "Well, what will we do then?"

"Jump off a cliff, I suppose," the Fox said. "I haven't got any better ideas right now. Have you?"

To his surprise, the Trokmê chieftain spoke up, asking, "Will you be taking all your southrons back to your own holding the now?"

"I hadn't thought about doing anything else with them," Gerin admitted. "I didn't think you'd want them on your land—they are Elabonians, after all—and I didn't think you'd want to keep feeding them any longer than you had to. Why? Am I wrong?"

Adiatunnus hesitated, but at last, looking shamefaced, said, "I wouldn't mind your leaving a couple of hundred behind for the sake of watching the line of the Venien and fighting alongside us should the Gradi be after trying to force it. Indeed, I ask that, Fox, as your vassal I do."

"You mean it," Gerin said in slow wonder. His expression unhappier than ever, Adiatunnus nodded. The Fox scratched his head. "Why, after spending so many years trying to kill every Elabonian you could find?"

"Because if it's us by our lonesome and the Gradi coming over the river and all, we'll lose," Adiatunnus answered bleakly. "Summat'll go wrong, same as it always does when the shindy's 'twixt us and the Gradi. You southrons, though, you can stand up to 'em. With my own eyes I saw it. And so—"

Gerin slapped him on the shoulder. "For that, I'll leave men behind. A lord protects his vassals, or else he doesn't stay their lord long—or deserve to. Would it suit you if I left Widin Simrin's son to command my men?"

"We're all your men now, Fox—however little we like it," Adiatunnus said with a wry grin. "Aye, Widin pleases to lead the Elabonians. I know his worth—I should, the trouble he's given me. But will he follow my lead when it's a matter of southrons and Trokmoi together?"

"Without me here?" Gerin rubbed his chin. "That seems fair. There'll be more of your men here than mine." He wondered if Adiatunnus really wanted him to leave a good chunk of his army behind so the woodsrunners could fall on it. He didn't believe that, though, not after their aborted campaign against the Gradi. Any man who feared him more than Voldar was a fool, and Adiatunnus didn't qualify there.

The Trokmê said, "I hope your foreign god knows too little of these Gradi to be in fear of 'em."

Mavrix was, or could be, a great coward. The Fox didn't tell that to Adiatunnus.

"There it is." Gerin breathed a great sigh of relief. Fox Keep still stood; the land around it hadn't been disturbed since the last Gradi raid. He thought he would have heard of any catastrophe as he traveled through his own holding, but you could never be sure. Sometimes the only way you found news was by stumbling over it.

The lookout in the watchtower was alert. Gerin heard, thin in the distance, the horn call he blew to alert the garrison to the approach of the army. Armed men popped up on the palisade with commendable speed.

"Ride out ahead," the Fox said, tapping Duren on the shoulder. "We'll let them know we came through in one piece." He'd hoped to be coming back in triumph. That hadn't happened. He'd feared coming back in defeat, perhaps with a force of fierce Gradi in pursuit. That hadn't happened, either. Had he won, then, or had he lost? If he didn't know himself, how was he supposed to tell anybody else?

Someone up on the wall shouted, "It's the Fox!" The warriors cheered. They didn't know what he'd done, any more than he knew what had gone on here. As he had been after the earthquake that toppled Biton's shrine, he was on the outermost ripple of spreading news.

"All well, lord prince?" Rihwin the Fox called down to him.

"All well—enough," Gerin answered. "And you? And the keep? And the holding? How has the weather been?"

"You go off to war and you ask about the weather?" Rihwin demanded. When Gerin only nodded, the southern noble who'd chosen to come to the northlands spread his hands in confusion. At last, pierced by his overlord's stare, he answered, "Weather's not been bad. On the cool side, and more rain than I remember most summers, but not bad. Why? How was the weather farther west?"

"Well, let's see—how do I put it?" Gerin mused. "If it weren't for the sleet's getting me prepared, I would have liked the hail even less than I did." That drew all the incredulous comments he'd thought it would. He waved impatiently. "Let down the drawbridge and we'll tell you what went on."

The drawbridge lowered. Duren drove the chariot into the keep. The rest of the force followed. Questions rained down on them: "Did we beat the Gradi?" "Did the Gradi beat us?" "Is Adiatunnus ally or traitor?" "Will we go back out on campaign again this season?"

Gerin answered abstractedly, for Selatre was waiting for him in the courtyard with their children. Seeing her and them reminded Gerin he had indeed come home. Seeing her also reminded him she'd been the intimate of a god, even if Biton was in many ways Mavrix's opposite. He wanted to talk with her before summoning—or trying to summon; you never could tell with gods—the Sithonian deity.

Before he could talk with his wife, though, he had to keep on answering questions and to deal with what seemed like everything that had happened at Fox Keep while he was away on campaign. Not for the first time, he wondered how anything important ever got done when people had to wade through so many trivia first.

At last, those who'd stayed behind stopped asking questions, at least of him. He'd settled arguments, handed down judgments, put off handing down others till he found out more, confirmed almost everything Rihwin and Selatre had done in his name while he was gone, and, somewhere along the way, acquired a couple of juicy beef ribs and a jack of ale. He ate gratefully: having your mouth full was a good excuse for not saying anything for a while.

When he finally did get the chance to speak of what he intended to do, Selatre nodded gravely. "A risky course, but one I think we have to take if the danger from the Gradi and their gods is as great as you say," was her verdict.

"Exactly what I thought," the Fox said, which was pleasing but not surprising; over the past eleven years, he'd come to see that his mind and Selatre's worked in ways very much alike—and ways that, as time went on, grew more alike as they went on living and planning together.

Rihwin the Fox was all excitement. "A chance to work with gods!" he burbled. "A chance to match wits with the immortals, to manipulate forces far stronger than we even dream of being, to—"

"—Get killed in nasty ways or have other unpleasant things happen to us," Gerin finished for him. "Or don't you remember why you can't work magic any more? You were trying to manipulate Mavrix then, too, as I recall."

Rihwin had the integrity to look embarrassed. All he'd done—a small thing, really—was ask Mavrix to turn some wine that had soured into vinegar back into something worth drinking once more. But the Sithonian god, already piqued at Gerin for reasons of his own, had not only not fixed the wine but had robbed Rihwin of his sorcerous talent to keep from being bothered by him any more in the future. If you went through rapids in a canoe and came out the other side alive and unhurt, you hadn't manipulated them, you'd just survived. You forgot the difference at your peril.

"Why should Mavrix concern himself with Voldar and the other Gradi gods?" Selatre asked. "What are they doing that he'll particularly loathe?"

"For one thing, they're making the part of the northlands the Gradi have seized as cold and bleak as the Gradi homeland," Gerin answered, glad to marshal arguments for his wife so he'd have them ready when he had to give them to the god. "For another, they'll kill or torment those who don't bow down to them. Sithonians and their gods are fond of freedom; one of the things they don't like about us Elabonians is that we give our rulers too loose a rein."

"Voldar doesn't sound as if she likes the idea of wine," Rihwin remarked.

"Yes, I think you're right about that," Gerin said. "It would be more useful, though, if we could get wine in the northlands these days. The winters are too hard to let the vines live even now. If the Gradi and their gods settle down to stay, even the summers will be too cold." He shivered, remembering the unnatural freezing storm through which he'd tried to lead his army.

Rihwin's mobile features assumed a comically exaggerated expression of longing. "How I miss the sweet grape!" he cried, sighing long and deep like a minstrel with a song of unrequited love.

"You miss finding a great deal of trouble because you miss the sweet grape," Selatre pointed out.

Now Rihwin looked indignant, an expression perhaps not altogether assumed. "My lady," he said with a low bow, "I regret to have to offer the opinion that your judgments have been clouded by overlong association with that lout there." He pointed to his fellow Fox.

"Heh," Gerin said. "She's right, Rihwin, and you know it bloody well. Oh, you can drink yourself stupid with ale as easily as you can with wine, but you never got Baivers' dander up at you. Whenever you touch wine, you seem to bump up against Mavrix, and when you bump up against the lord of the sweet grape, horrible things happen."

"They aren't *always* horrible," Rihwin insisted. "Without Mavrix, we might never have been rid of the monsters."

"True," Gerin admitted, "but *getting* rid of them wasn't your doing, and the odds were all too good we'd end up getting rid of ourselves instead." He paused. "And speaking of monsters, how have Geroge and Tharma been?"

"Except for eating as much apiece as any three people I could name, they've been fine," Rihwin answered, and Selatre nodded agreement. "If your vassals and your serfs gave as little trouble, your holding would be easier to run."

"Back to Mavrix," Selatre said firmly. Even more than Gerin, she had a knack for holding to the essential.

"Aye, back to Mavrix," Rihwin said. "How, lord prince, do you purpose summoning him without wine?"

"Books, grain, seed, fruits—a naked peasant girl, if that's what it takes," Gerin replied. "I'll aim at his aspects as patron of the arts and fertility god, not the ones that pertain to wine." He shrugged. "Wine would probably be a stronger summons, but we do what we can with what we have." He took that for granted; he'd been making do, improvising, ever since he became baron of Fox Keep. He knew he couldn't keep juggling forever, but he hadn't dropped too many important things, not yet, anyhow.

Rihwin pursed his lips and looked thoughtful. Mavrix hadn't robbed him of his magical knowledge, merely the ability to use it. "You may well encounter success by this means," he said. "It may even be that the aspect of Mavrix you summon thus will be less flighty by nature than that which has to do with the grape. Or, of course, it may not." The last sentence and the shrug with which he accompanied it said he'd been associating with Gerin for a long time, too.

"When will you summon the god?" Selatre asked.

"As soon as may be," Gerin told her. "The Gradi and their gods are pushing hard. If we don't do something to push them back soon, I worry about what they—and Voldar—will do to us next."

"Surely your blow against them gained something," Rihwin said.

"A little, no doubt," Gerin said. "A fortress and a few villages cleared of them—but we couldn't keep those. And when we tried to press on, the storms I have to think their deities raised stopped us cold—literally. Much as I wish I could, I can't claim a victory there."

"And so you shall bring to bear the power of the god," Rihwin declared.

"So I shall," Gerin agreed. "The next intriguing question is whether I'll bring it to bear against the Gradi . . . or against me."

Had the world wagged exactly as the Fox wanted, he would have undertaken the conjuration that afternoon. But more than the minutiae of running his holding made him wait for a couple of days. Much as he liked to deal with problems by attacking them head-on, he also knew that attacking them without full understanding was liable to be worse than ignoring them altogether. And so he spent most of those next two days closeted in the library above the great hall, reading every scrap about Mavrix he had in his book-hoard.

He had less than he would have wanted. That was true of his store on every subject where he had any scrolls or codices at all. Books were too rare and precious for any man, even with an insatiable itch to know and the resources first of a barony and then of a principality behind him, to have as many as he would have liked.

In her time at Fox Keep, Selatre had made the library as much her domain as it was his. She had once enjoyed a knowledge of a different sort from that contained in books, knowledge that came to her direct from Biton. Since she'd lost that, she'd made up for it in every other way she could. She helped Gerin in his studies, finding even the most obscure mentions of Mavrix and passing them to him.

The more he read, the more he hoped: the Sithonian god's hatred of ugliness was one of his most salient characteristics. That had been one of the hooks the Fox had used to get Mavrix to drive the monsters back into their dark caverns, but the more he read, the more he worried, too. Mavrix was among the flightiest of gods. He would do whatever he did and then go off and do something else altogether. One thing Voldar seemed to have was implacable purpose.

Gerin rolled up the last scroll. "I don't know if this is going to work," he told Selatre, "but then, I don't know what choice I have, either. A man will pick a bad course when all the others look worse."

"It will be all right," Selatre said.

He shrugged by way of reply. She didn't know that, and had no rational basis for believing it. Neither did he. After a moment, though, he admitted to himself that hearing it from her made him feel better.

As was his way, Gerin carefully assembled everything he thought he would need and everything he thought he might need before he tried to summon Mavrix. He sent Rihwin to the peasant village to bring back a girl who would be enticing enough naked to tempt the fertility god if that proved necessary. Rihwin's experience with the peasant women was wider than his own. Moreover, by having his friend pick the girl, he made sure he would not have Selatre asking how he knew what she looked like without clothes.

Though the woman, whose name was Fulda, wore a long, woad-dyed linen tunic when Rihwin led her up to the keep, Gerin had to admit she did look likely to shape well in the role if required. By the half-amused, half-tart sniff Selatre let out, she thought the same.

The little shack where Gerin tried magic when he got up the nerve to try magic was set well away from Castle

Fox. It was also set well away from the palisade, the stables, and everything else in Fox Keep. If something went wrong—and Gerin's conjurations, like those of any half-trained mage, had a way of going wrong—he wanted the destruction to be as limited as possible.

When he, Rihwin, Selatre, and Fulda went out to the shack, the rest of the people packing Fox Keep made a point of keeping their distance, and of not looking at the ramshackle building, either. Nothing had gone too hideously wrong over the years, but everyone got the idea that meddling with Gerin while he worked at his magic—or, for that matter, meddling with him when he worked at anything—was less than a good idea.

He began to chant from the Sithonian epic of Lekapenos. He'd had the verses literally beaten into him by his teachers, and so did not need the scroll he held to be sure he had the words right. He held it nonetheless, to remind Mavrix of another reason he was being summoned.

On a rickety table, he set out wheat (not barley; Mavrix had nothing but scorn for Baivers), ripe and candied fruit, and several eggs from the castle henhouse. "Do you want me to strip off now, lord prince?" Fulda asked, reaching up to the neck of her tunic.

"Let's wait and see if we can bring the god here some other way first," Gerin answered, to Rihwin's evident disappointment. One of Selatre's eyebrows rose for a moment. Gerin didn't know exactly what that meant. He didn't much want to find out, either.

He used his rusty Sithonian for as much of the invocation as he could, wanting to make Mavrix feel as much at home as he could in the northlands. Despite repeated beseechings, though, the god declined to appear. Gerin wondered if that wasn't just as well, but went on anyhow.

"Fulda," Selatre said, and nodded.

The peasant woman pulled the tunic off over her head. One glance told Gerin she was as lushly made as he'd guessed. Past that one glance, he didn't look at her. If he made a mistake with his invocation, whether her body was beautiful or not wouldn't matter. Rihwin's eyes lit up. Gerin suspected he would try to see Fulda naked under other circumstances as soon as he could. That thought appeared in his mind, but vanished a moment later: Mavrix still showed no sign of coming forth.

Gerin wondered if the Sithonian god now refused to have anything to do with him at all. He also wondered whether he should have brought a pretty boy into the shack instead of Fulda. Mavrix's tastes sometimes veered in that direction.

Stubbornly, he kept on working as many variants of the spell as he could imagine. A man without his perseverance—or a man in less desperate straits—would have quit a long time before. The Fox realized he wouldn't be able to go on much longer, either, not without making an error that would at least invalidate everything he'd already done and at most . . . he didn't want to think about all the unpleasant things that might happen then.

As he was about to give up, the inside of the shack seemed all at once to grow vastly larger, though its exterior dimensions had not changed in any way. Gerin had felt that happen before. The hair prickled up on the back of his neck. Here was Mavrix, so now he had what he'd thought he wanted. How much would he regret seeing his prayers granted?

"You are the noisiest little man," the god said, his deep, honeyed voice sounding somewhere in the middle of Gerin's head rather than in his ears. The Fox was not sure whether Mavrix spoke Sithonian or Elabonian; he took meaning directly, at a level more basic than words.

Gerin spoke Sithonian, in the hope of making Mavrix better inclined toward him. "I thank you, lord of the sweet grape, lord of fertility, lord of wisdom and wit, for deigning to hear me."

"Deigning to hear you?" Mavrix's eyebrows rose almost all the way to his hairline. His handsome features, had they been human, would have been impossibly mobile. But he was not human, even if his rosebud mouth would have made any boy-lover quiver with lascivious delight. His eyes were all black, fathomless, deep beyond deep, warning of power and terror far beyond any to which a mere human could aspire. "Deigning to hear you?" he repeated. "You were doing your best to deafen me, not so?"

"I would not have troubled you were I not deep in

trouble myself," Gerin answered, which was no less than truth: even as he spoke, he wondered whether his proposed cure was worse than the Gradi disease.

"And why should I care a fig for your troubles, lord Gerin, prince of the north?" In Mavrix's mouth, the Fox's titles were poisonously sweet. "Why should I not rejoice, in fact?"

"Because I did not make them, for one," Gerin answered. "And, for another, because the gods who did make them now purpose turning the northlands into a cold and dreary country where next to nothing will grow, and where for months at a time all will be covered by ice and snow." Hearing his own accidental rhyme, he wished he'd thought to include metre as well; Mavrix appreciated such artful touches.

"That sounds—distasteful," the Sithonian god admitted. "But, I ask you again, why should I care? These barbarous northlands are scarcely part of my normal purview, you know. You Elabonians are quite bad enough" —the fringes on his fawnskin tunic fluttered as he shivered to show what he thought of Elabonians— "and the woodsrunning savages now infesting the land worse. If something dreadful befalls the lot of you—so what?"

"The Gradi are worse, and so are their gods," Gerin said, stubborn still. "You may not think much of Dyaus, and I have no notion what you think of Taranis, Teutatis, and Esus, but you have your place and they have theirs, and you don't try to drive them off, nor they you."

He didn't mention Baivers, some of whose aspects were close enough to those of Mavrix to make them compete with rather than complementing each other. He especially didn't mention Biton, whose quarrel with Mavrix had led to banishing the monsters infesting the northlands back to their gloomy caverns. If the god remembered those quarrels, he would remind Gerin of them. If he didn't, Gerin wasn't going to remind him.

Mavrix sniffed. "I have never impinged upon these Gradi gods, nor they on me. For all I know, you lie for your own reasons. Humans are like that." He sniffed again, in fine contempt.

But he wasn't so smart as he thought he was, because,

while suspicious of Gerin's arguments, he didn't notice the logical flaws and omissions in them. If you were sly enough and quick enough and lucky enough, you could guide him like a man leading a barely broken horse. You'd never be sure he'd go in the direction you wanted him to take, but if you made all the other choices look worse, you had a chance.

Mavrix, though, was no horse, but a god, with a god's abilities and strength. Gerin said, "If you doubt me, look into my mind. See for yourself my dealings with the Gradi and with Voldar. With your divine wisdom, you will know whether I lie or not."

"I do not need your permission, little man; I can do that any time I choose," Mavrix said. A moment later, he added, "I do think better of you—a bit better—for the invitation."

And then, all at once, Gerin's world turned inside out. It did not feel as if Mavrix entered his mind, but more as if his mind suddenly became a small fragment of the god's. He'd expected Mavrix to grub for facts like a man opening drawers in a cabinet. Instead, the power of the god's intellect simply poured through him, as if he were air and Mavrix rain. The search was far quicker, far more thorough, and far more awesome than he'd expected.

When Mavrix spoke to him again, it was almost as if he listened to, almost as if he were a part of, the god's thoughts, which echoed all through his own mind: "What you say is true. These Gradi are indeed nasty and vicious men, and their gods nasty and vicious deities. That they should infest their own homeland is quite bad enough, that they should seek to spread to this relatively temperate and tolerant district intolerable. And, being intolerable, it shall not be tolerated. I commence."

Mavrix set out on a journey across the plane the gods customarily inhabited, a plane that impinged on the mundane world of men and crops and weather but was not really a part of it. He had not released the Fox's mind from its place, if that was the right word, as part of his own, and so Gerin, willy-nilly, accompanied him on his travels.

Afterwards, Gerin was never quite sure how far to trust his sensory impressions. Eyes and ears and skin were not made to take in the essence of the divine plane, nor was he really along in the flesh, but only as a sort of flea-bite, or at most a wart, on Mavrix's psyche. Did the god truly drink his way through an ocean of wine? Did he really fornicate his way through . . . ? If he did, why on earth—or not on earth—would Fulda have drawn the least part of his notice? Even the dim part-understanding of what might have just happened left the Fox's sensorium spinning.

Then the going got more difficult (*not harder*, Gerin thought, being unable at the moment to imagine anything harder than . . .). Gerin felt Mavrix's surprise, discomfort, and displeasure as if they were his own. They were, in fact, his own, and more than his own.

Pettishly, Mavrix snapped, "I should never have let you entice me into this predicament." The Sithonian god did not take well to discomfort of any sort, that being a negation of everything he stood for. In the little mental cyst inside Mavrix' mind that remained his own, Gerin had all he could do to keep from bursting into laughter that would surely anger the god. Enticing Mavrix was just what he'd hoped to do. And Mavrix would have to endure more unpleasantness if he reversed his metaphysical route . . . wouldn't he?

Gerin wondered about that. For all he knew, Mavrix could break free of where he was and be somewhere else without bothering to traverse the space in between. And even if he couldn't do that, the combination of overwhelming wine and even more overwhelming satiety might be plenty to counteract whatever lack of pleasure the god knew now.

And then, without warning, Mavrix found himself in a place, or a sort of a place, Gerin recognized from his dreams: the chilly forest to which Voldar had summoned him during his dream. "How bleak," Mavrix murmured, moving along a track in it.

This is the domain of the Gradi gods, Gerin thought, not knowing whether Mavrix was paying any attention to his small separate fragment of consciousness.

"Really?" the god replied as he came to a snow-filled clearing. "And here all the while I thought I was back in my native Sithonia. The grapes and olives are looking particularly fine this time of year, aren't they?"

Had Gerin been there corporeally, he would have turned red. Having Mavrix flay him with sarcasm wasn't what he'd had in mind when he summoned the god. Of course, when you did summon a god, what you got wasn't always what you had in mind, for gods had minds of their own.

He tried to pitch his thoughts so they would carry to Mavrix, forming them as much like speech as he could: "Voldar summoned me to this place in a dream."

"A nightmare, it must have been," the Sithonian god replied. Maybe he shuddered, maybe he didn't: Gerin's view of this plane shook back and forth. Mavrix went on, "Why any self-respecting deity would choose to inhabit—or I might better say, infest—such a place when so many better are there for the taking must remain eternally beyond me."

"We like it here."

Had that actually been a voice, it would have been deep and rumbling, like an outsized version of Van's. Gerin didn't truly hear it; it was more as if an earthquake with meanings attached had shaken the center of his mind. A great form reared up out of the snow. Gerin sensed it as being half man, half great white bear, now the one predominating, now the other.

"This ugly thing cannot possibly be Voldar," Mavrix said with a distinct sniff in his voice. Sniff or not, Gerin thought he was right: the Gradi god, whether in human or ursine form, was emphatically male. Mavrix directed his attention toward the god rather than the Fox. "Who or what are you, ugly thing?"

Given a choice, Gerin would not have antagonized anything as ferocious looking as that white, looming apparition. He was not given a choice; that was one of the risks you took in dealing with gods. The half-bear, half-man shape roared and bellowed out its reply: "I am Lavtrig, mighty hunter. Who are you, little mincing, puling wretch, to come spreading the stink of perfume over this, the home of the grand gods?"

"Grand compared to what?" Mavrix said. He waved his

left hand, the one in which he carried his thyrsus, an ivy-tipped wand more powerful than any spear would have been in the hands of a mere man. "Stand aside, before I rid the plane of the gods of an odious presence. I have no quarrel with underlings, not unless they seek to trouble their betters. Since, in your case, anything this side of a horse turd would be an improvement, I suggest you leave off the business of troubling altogether."

Lavtrig roared with rage and rushed forward. He had more claws and teeth and thews than Gerin cared to contemplate. The Fox had hoped Mavrix would fight the Gradi gods. He hadn't intended to get stuck, absolutely helpless, in the middle of such a fight. Mavrix didn't care what he intended.

Wand notwithstanding, the Sithonian god's semblance was as nothing when measured against Lavtrig's fearsome aspect. But, as Gerin should have realized, appearances among gods were apt to be even more deceiving than among mankind. When Lavtrig's hideous jaws closed, they closed on nothingness. But when Mavrix tapped the Gradi god with his thyrsus, the howl of pain he evoked might have been heard in distant Mabalal, by the deities there if not by the men.

"Run along now, noisy thing," Mavrix said. "If you force me to become truly vexed, the barbarians who worship you will have to invent something else more hideous than themselves, for you will be gone for good."

Lavtrig bellowed again, this time more with rage than with pain, and tried to keep fighting. He scratched, he clawed, he snapped—all to no effect. Sighing, Mavrix lashed out with a sandal-shod foot. Lavtrig spun through the air—if the gods' plane had air—and crashed against a pine. Its burden of snow fell on him. He writhed once or twice, feebly, but did not get up to resume the struggle.

Mavrix let him lie and strode on. "Could you really have destroyed him?" Gerin asked.

"Oh, are you still here?" the Sithonian god said, as if he'd forgotten all about the Fox. "A god can do anything he imagines he can do." The answer did not strike Gerin as altogether responsive, but he could hardly have been in a worse position to demand more detail from Mavrix.

The god he had summoned to his aid strode down a path through more snow-covered trees. If Mavrix was cold, he did not show it. Once, as if to amuse himself, he pointed his thyrsus at one of the pines. Clumps of bright flowers sprang into being at the base of its trunk. Gerin wondered if they continued to exist after Mavrix stopped paying attention to them.

Golden-eyed wolves stared out of the woods at Mavrix: wolves as big as bears, as big as horses, divine wolves, the primeval savage essence of wolf concentrated in their bodies as a cook might concentrate a sauce by boiling away all excess. When Gerin felt their terrible eyes on him, he wanted to quail and run, even though he knew he was not there in body. Wolves like that could—would—gulp down his very soul.

Mavrix pulled out a set of reed pipes and blew music such as had never been heard in the grim realm of the Gradi gods, not in all the ages since they shaped the place to their own satisfaction. It was the music of summer and joy and love, the music of wine and hot nights and desire. Had he been able to, Gerin would have wept with the sorrow of knowing that, try as he might, he would never be fully able to remember or reproduce what he heard.

And the wolves! All at once, utterly without warning, they lost their ferocity and came rushing through the snow at Mavrix, not to rend him but to frisk at his heels like so many friendly puppies. They yipped. They leaped. They played foolish games with one another. They paired off and mated. They did everything but guard the road, as the Gradi gods had plainly intended them to do.

Amusement seeped from Mavrix's mind to Gerin's. "Perhaps we should throw cold water on some of them," the Sithonian god said. "Plenty of cold water here."

"Oh, I don't know," Gerin replied. "Why not let them enjoy themselves? I have the feeling this is the first time they've ever been able to."

"That is nothing less than the truth," Mavrix said, and then, "I own that I responded to your summons with resentment, but now I am glad I did. These Gradi gods need to be dealt with. They have no notion of fun." He spoke as the Fox did when passing sentence on some particularly vicious robber.

Gerin wondered if the Sithonian god could instill levity into whatever Voldar used for a heart. If he could, that would be a bigger miracle than any he had yet worked.

But Mavrix had not yet won through to confront the chief goddess of the Gradi. When he stepped out into a clearing, Gerin wondered if Voldar would await him there. But it was not Voldar. It was not anything anthropomorphic at all, but a whirling column of rain and mist and ice and snow, stretching up as far as the eye could see.

From the middle of the column, a voice spoke: "Get you gone. This is not your place. Get you gone."

At Mavrix's feet, the wolves whined and whimpered, as if realizing they'd betrayed themselves with a stranger and were going to be made to regret it by the powers that were their proper masters. Mavrix, however, spoke lightly, mockingly, as was his way. "What have we here? The divine washtub for this miserable place? Or is it but the chamber pot?"

"I am Stribog," the voice declared. "I say you shall not pass. Take your jests and japes somewhere we do not yet touch, then await us there, for one day, rest assured, we shall overwhelm it and quench them."

"Ah—right the second time," Mavrix said cheerfully, perhaps to Gerin, perhaps to Stribog. "It is the chamber pot."

He moved out into the clearing. Stribog did not attack as Lavtrig had. Instead, the Gradi god hurled all the vile weather he had inside him straight at Mavrix. Gerin's soul felt frozen. Here, he saw, was the god who had raised the summer storms against him and his army. Those, though, had been storms of the world, even if divinely raised. This was the very stuff of the gods, used by one to fight another.

And Mavrix noticed this onslaught, where he had been impervious to Lavtrig's. The chill and wet Stribog raised struck at his spirit. He grunted and said, "Now see—someone's gone and spilled it. We'll just have to set it to rights once more."

The wolves fled back to their gloomy haunts. With

Mavrix's attention not on them, they forgot the dimmest notion of happiness. Too, they were soaked to their metaphysical skins. Stribog had indeed poured a bucket of cold water on them, a bucket big as the world.

Mavrix lashed out with his wand, as he had against Lavtrig. It must have hurt, too, for Stribog bellowed in pain and rage. But the Gradi god was a more diffuse entity than Lavtrig; he had no central place to strike that would do him lasting damage. And his rain and ice, his winds and lightnings, hurt Mavrix, too. The Sithonian god's anguish washed through Gerin, who knew that, had his spirit been there alone, he would swiftly have been destroyed.

When Mavrix tried to go forward against the storm that was Stribog, he found himself unable. The Gradi god's laughter boomed like thunder. "Here you will perish, you who try to trouble Gradihome!" he cried. "Here you will drown; here you will rest forevermore."

"Oh, be still, arrogant windbag," Mavrix said irritably, and for a moment Stribog *was* still, the storm silent. Even as it resumed, Mavrix went on, "Not just an arrogant windbag, but a stupid one, too. If you water a fertility god, you promote—"

"Growth!" Gerin's mind exclaimed.

"There, you see?" Mavrix told him. "You have more wit to you than this blowhard. Not much of a compliment, I fear, but you may have it if you want it."

And with that, he began to grow, to soak up all the stormstuff Stribog flung at him and make it his own instead of letting it remain a weapon belonging to the Gradi god. The pain he felt at Stribog's attacks vanished, or rather was transmuted into a satisfaction somewhere between that of a good meal and that which follows the act of love.

Stribog realized too late that he was no longer doing Mavrix any harm. He boomed like thunder again, but this time in alarm. Where before he had reached as high as the eye—or whatever sense passed for vision here—could see and Mavrix seemed small beside him, their relative sizes reversed with startling speed. Now, from his place in the Sithonian god's consciousness, Gerin peered down on a small, furious, futile whirlwind that churned up the snow around Mavrix's ankles.

Mavrix stooped and seized the whirlwind. He flung it away: whither, the Fox had no idea. Maybe Mavrix didn't, either, for he said, "I hope the alepot tempest lands among the Kizzuwatnan gods or some others who properly appreciate heat."

He was, without warning, the apparent size he had been before his fight with Stribog began. He reached up and adjusted the wreath of grape leaves around his forehead to the proper jaunty angle. The landscape of Gradihome seemed undisturbed by the divine tempest that had lashed it; Gerin wished the land of the material world recovered from rain so readily.

"Onward," Mavrix said, and onward they went. But the Sithonian god, despite his triumph, seemed wearier and less sure of himself than he had been. If defeating Lavtrig was like climbing a flight of stairs, besting Stribog had been more like climbing a mountain. If the next challenge proved correspondingly harder still . . . Gerin did his best not to think about that, for fear Mavrix would sense it and be moved either to anger or to despair.

The god came to a clearing in the snowy woods. Gerin waited to see what sort of Gradi god would confront Mavrix there, but the clearing seemed empty. More snow-covered pines stood at the far edge of the open space, perhaps a bowshot away, perhaps a bit more.

"Well," Mavrix said brightly, "variety in the landscape after all. Who would have thought it?" He brought his pipes to his lips and began to play a cheerful tune as he strolled across the rolling ground.

Had Gerin had his normal, physical eyes, he would have blinked. Something strange had happened, but he wasn't sure what. The god came to a clearing in the snowy woods. Gerin waited to see what sort of Gradi god would confront Mavrix there, but the clearing seemed empty. More snow-covered pines stood at the far edge of the open space, perhaps a bowshot away, perhaps a bit more.

"Well," Mavrix said brightly, "variety in the landscape after all. Who would have thought it?" He brought his pipes to his lips and began to play a cheerful tune as he strolled across the rolling ground.

That sensation of needing to blink repeated itself in the Fox's mind. There was the clearing . . . the same clearing. When Gerin realized that, he recovered at least a part of what he and Mavrix had just been through.

"Well," Mavrix said brightly, "variety in the landscape after all. Who would have thought it?" He brought his pipes to his lips.

Before he could begin to play, Gerin said, "Wait!"

"What do you mean, wait?" the Sithonian god demanded irritably. "I aim to celebrate coming across something different for a change." And then Mavrix, as Gerin had before him, hesitated and went back over what had gone on. "Have I—done this before?" he asked, now sounding hesitant rather than irritable.

"I—think so," Gerin answered, still far from sure himself.

"I am in your debt, little man," Mavrix said. "I wonder how many times I would have done that before I twigged to it myself. I wonder if I would ever have twigged to it myself if I didn't have you riding along like a flea on my bum. It would have been a beastly boring way to spend eternity, I can tell you that."

Gerin wondered if the only reason he hadn't been completely caught in the trap was its being set for gods, not mere men. He had spoken before of mankind's occasional advantages in dealing with vastly more powerful beings, but hadn't expected his littleness to become one: he'd slipped through the spaces in a net intended to catch bigger fish.

In tones more cautious than Mavrix usually used, he asked, "Who is out there in the clearing?"

Nothing answered: "I am Nothing," it said, voice utterly without color or emotion.

"Trust these stupid Gradi to worship Nothing," Mavrix muttered.

"Why not?" Nothing returned. "Soon or late, all fails. In the end, everything fails. I am what is left. I deserve worship, for I am most powerful of all."

"You're not even the most powerful god in your pantheon," Gerin jeered, trying to ruffle that uncanny calm. "Voldar rules the Gradi, not you."

"For now," Nothing said imperturbably.

"Stand aside, Nothing, or know nothingness," Mavrix said. From caution, he had swung back to anger.

"Wait," Gerin said again. If finding a way to hurt Stribog had been hard, how could the Sithonian god harm Nothing? Hoping he was pitching his thoughts in such a way as to let Mavrix but not Nothing hear them, he suggested, "Don't fight—distract. You're a fertility god—you can make all sorts of interesting . . . somethings, can't you?"

Mavrix's mirth filled him, as strong sweet wine might have had he been there in the flesh. "Somethings," the god said, and then, changing the timbre of his thoughts so he addressed not the Fox but the thing—or the no-thing—in the clearing: "Nothing!"

"Aye?" the Gradi god said, polite but perfectly indifferent.

Mavrix held out his hands. He breathed on them, and a flock of bright-colored singing birds appeared, one after another. "Do you see these?" he asked as he waved his hands and the birds began to fly around the clearing.

"I see them," Nothing replied. "In a little while, in a littlest while, they will cease to be. Then they will be mine."

"That's so," Mavrix agreed, "but they're mine now. And so is this." He sent a deer bounding across the open space. Gerin hoped the wolves of Gradihome wouldn't notice it. "And so are these." Flowers sprang up in the clearing, made with a purpose now instead of merely for a game. "And so is this." An amphora of wine appeared. "And so are these." Four preternaturally beautiful women and a like number of handsome and well-endowed men sprang into being. They enjoyed the wine and then began to enjoy one another. They had no more inhibitions than they did clothes.

Gerin wondered if they were figments of the Sithonian god's imagination or if Mavrix had plucked them from some warmer, more hospitable clime. He didn't ask, not wanting to bump the god's metaphysical elbow.

"They're all mine!" Mavrix shouted. "They're all doing things, right there before you."

"For now," Nothing said.

"Yes, for now," Mavrix said. "And the things they do now will cause other things to be done and to be born, and those will cause still others, and the ripples that spread from those will—"

"Eventually come to Nothing," Nothing said, but with—perhaps?—the slightest hesitation as Mavrix's creations cavorted in the clearing.

Speaking in a sort of mental whisper, Mavrix said to Gerin, "If it's not distracted now, it never will be. I am going into the clearing. If I end up here again and that space before us is empty—we are apt to be here . . . indefinitely."

Gerin's small sensorium, carried pickaback on the god's vastly larger one, crossed the clearing in a hurry. He could even look back as Mavrix regained the path that led ever deeper into Gradihome. All at once, the Sithonian god's creations vanished as if they had never been.

"That was petty of old Nothing," Mavrix said, a chuckle in his voice. "As it told us, they would have been its sooner or later. Ah, well—some deities simply have no patience." Then Mavrix suddenly seemed less sure of himself. "Or do you think Nothing will pursue me through this frigid wilderness?"

"If I had to guess, I'd say no," Gerin answered. "The Gradi gods seem to be testing you, each in his own place. Lavtrig and Stribog stayed behind once you'd bested them. I think Nothing will, too."

"You had better be right," Mavrix said. "And if I have to test and best every single puerile godlet the Gradi own—or the other way round—I shall grow quite testy myself, Fox. Bear that in mind."

"Oh, I shall," Gerin assured him. "I shall." Mavrix was more powerful than he; he knew that full well. But he had seen the progression in the actions of the Gradi gods where Mavrix was uncertain about it. Did that prove him divinely clever? If it did, he was clever enough to know he shouldn't let himself get carried away by the idea.

He did not think Mavrix had stepped up the pace, but the next clearing appeared very quickly. Mavrix went out into it with almost defiant stride, as if expecting Nothing to sow confusion in his mind once more.

But the god—or rather, goddess—standing in the open space had a definite physical aspect. "Gerin the Fox, the

Elabonian," Voldar said. "You have proved more troublesome than I reckoned on, and your ally stronger." Her smile struck the Fox as imperfectly inviting. "Whether he is strong enough remains to be seen."

Her aspect was not quite as Gerin had seen her in the dream she'd induced him to have. She seemed partway toward the hag image with which she'd so horrified Adiatunnus—now and again, by starts and flickers, her hair would gray, her skin wrinkle, her teeth grow broken and crooked, her breasts lose their eternally youthful firmness and sag downward against her chest and the top of her belly. Sometimes her whole body seemed squat, slightly misshapen—and sometimes not. Gerin had no idea what her true seeming was, or if indeed she had but one true seeming.

Mavrix spoke with some indignation: "Well! I like that: a goddess greeting a mortal before a god. But I'm not surprised, not with what I've seen of manners here in Gradihome. Go ahead—ignore me."

"Nothing tried that," Voldar said. "It failed. That means I must deal with you—and when I have, you'll wish you'd been ignored. But I spoke to the mortal first because, without him, you would not be here—and would not have caused so much damage to the lesser gods around me."

"I greeted them in the spirit with which they greeted me," Mavrix replied. "Is it my fault if their spirits could not bear up under the force of my greeting?"

"Yes," Voldar said in the deadly cold voice Gerin remembered from his dream. "You should have been driven from Gradihome wailing, or been swallowed by Nothing for all eternity."

"I'd be delighted to leave this cold, ugly place," the Sithonian god said, "and I will, in an instant, once you vow you'll make no more of the material world into as close a copy of it as you can engender. God may not lie to god in such vows: so it has been, so it is, so shall it be."

"I could lie to you," Voldar said, "but I shall not. Gradihome in the world grows. So it is, so shall it be."

"No," Mavrix said. "It shall not be. There is too much cold and ugliness and sterility in the material world as it is now. I shall not permit you to increase their grip on it."

"You cannot stop it," Voldar said. "You have not the power for that, nor have you the roots in the land of which you speak that would let you draw upon its strength, as we even now are beginning to do."

"It is not your land, either," Mavrix said. "And if I have not the strength, how do I come to stand before you now?"

"You come before me, as I said before, on account of the guile of the mortal whose consciousness you carry with you," Voldar answered, "and I should not be surprised if his cunning helped you pass and overcome my fellows."

"Well! I like that!" Mavrix drew himself up straight, the picture of affronted dignity. "First speak to the mortal ahead of me, then count him as more clever. I shall take vengeance for the slight."

Gerin felt rather like a mouse that had the misfortune to find itself in the middle of a clearing where a bear and a longtooth clashed. Whichever won might not even matter to him, because they were liable to crush him without so much as knowing he was there.

And yet the fight did not begin at once. Voldar was plainly given pause because Mavrix had managed to reach her, and Mavrix in turn seemed thoughtful at facing the goddess who lorded it over the formidable foes he had already beaten.

Suddenly, his voice grew sweet, persuasive, tempting: "Why do we have to quarrel at all, Gradi goddess? You can be pleasing to the eye when it suits you; I sense as much. Why not lie with me in love? Once you know what proper pleasure is, you'll feel less attracted toward death and doom and ice." He began to play on his pipes, a tune a shepherd might have used to lure a goose girl to a secluded meadow on a warm summer evening.

But Voldar was no goose girl, and Gradihome knew nothing of warmth. "You cannot seduce me from my purpose, foreign god. May your lust curdle and freeze; may your ardor wither."

"I *am* ardor," Mavrix said, "nothing else but, and I kindle it in others. I would try even in you, to teach you somewhat of the ways of existence about which, it would seem, you now know nothing."

"I told you, I am not your receptacle." Voldar's voice grew sharp. "Leave Gradihome now and you will suffer nothing further. If you stay, you will learn the consequences of your folly."

"I *am* folly," Mavrix said, in the same tone of voice he had used to declare himself ardor. Gerin thought he meant the one as much as the other. Ardor, to his way of thinking, certainly engendered folly. Maybe that was what the god had had in mind.

"You are a fool, that certainly." Voldar spoke as Gerin might have while chiding a vassal for something stupid he'd done. "Very well. If you will be a fool, you will pay for it." Raising her great axe, she advanced on Mavrix.

All the Sithonian tales of the fertility god named him an arrant coward. The Fox had seen some of that himself. He more than half expected Mavrix to run away from that determined, menacing advance. Instead, though, Mavrix jeered, "Are you truly a battleaxe, Voldar, or just after my spear?" That part of him leaped, leaving Voldar in no possible doubt of his meaning.

She snarled something Gerin didn't understand, which was probably just as well. Then she swung the axe with a stroke any of the warriors who worshiped her would have been proud to claim as his own. Gerin wondered what would have happened had that blow landed as she intended. His best guess was that the Sithonian pantheon would have wanted a new deity.

But the blow did not land. Mavrix's phallus was not all that had leaped. He used his wand to bat the axehead aside. The thyrsus looked as if it would break at such usage, but looks, when it came to gods and their implements, were apt to be deceiving.

Voldar evidently had been deceived. She shouted in fury at finding herself thwarted. "There, there," Mavrix said in syrupy, soothing tones, and reach out to pat her—not at all consolingly—on her bare backside. Gerin couldn't tell whether his arm had got long to let him do that, or whether he'd shifted his position in some way allowed to gods but not men and then returned in an instant to where he had been.

However he'd done it, it made Voldar even angrier than

she had been already. Her next cut with that axe would have left Mavrix metaphorically spearless. Again, he used the wand to turn aside the stroke, though Gerin, perched there on the edge of his consciousness, felt the effort that had required. Mavrix was not a god of war, where Voldar seemed to exist for no other purpose than conquest and subjugation.

"Are you going to be able to hold out against her?" he asked the Sithonian god. The question had immediate practical import for him. If Voldar beat Mavrix, would his own spirit be trapped here in Gradihome? He was hard-pressed to imagine a gloomier fate.

"We'll find out, won't we?" Mavrix answered, not the most reassuring reply the Fox could have got.

He quickly became convinced Mavrix was overmatched. The Sithonian god was indeed no killer; he sought to provoke Voldar, to infuriate her, to drive her to distraction. She, by contrast, was grimly intent on harming him—on destroying him, if she could.

The longer they struggled, the more Gerin grew concerned she could do exactly as she intended. This was not a struggle of the same sort as Mavrix had had with the other Gradi gods. It put the Fox more in mind of some of the desperate fights he'd had on the battlefield, ferocious brawls with anything past the notion of bare survival forgotten. Voldar and Mavrix hammered and pounded and cursed each other, the curses landing as heavily and painfully as kicks and buffets.

When Mavrix squeezed her, Voldar would for a moment weaken and lean toward him as if intending an embrace: the struggle was, in some ways, a spectacularly violent attempt at a seduction. But Voldar never really came close to yielding, however much Gerin wished and hoped she would. She had her own purposes, which were not those of Mavrix.

And when she gained the upper hand for the time being, the Fox felt Mavrix's nature changing into something harder and colder than seemed fitting for the Sithonian god. Voldar, he realized, was trying to bend Mavrix to her will no less than he her to his. Those stretches came more and more often as the battle progressed. Gerin wondered if

Mavrix realized as much himself, and if he should warn the god.

Suddenly Mavrix gave a great cry—not of pain but of rejection—and broke away from Voldar. The disengagement was not like that between two struggling humans. One instant, he was locked in the fight with the Gradi goddess, the next he stood at the edge of the clearing in which she had awaited him.

"No," he said hoarsely. "You shall not make me into something you can rule." He understood the stakes, then. "I will not allow it. I do not allow it."

"If you stay here, I shall," Voldar said. "This is Gradihome, and Gradihome is mine." She strode toward the Sithonian fertility god, implacable purpose on her face and in every line of her body.

Mavrix broke and fled. Voldar's harsh, mocking laughter rang in his ears as he dashed away, snow flying up under his sandal-clad feet. "Be careful," Gerin shouted in his metaphysical ear. "Don't fall into Nothing's lair again."

Mavrix swerved aside, off the path. The fierce wolves of the home of the Gradi gods came coursing after him, but fawned like friendly pups once more when they drew near: so much of his power, at least, he still retained. And then he was on the path again, and running faster than ever. "I thank you for reminding me of the trap," he said, "though I do not thank you for involving me in this misadventure in the first place."

"I was trying to save what was mine," Gerin answered. *And I've failed*, he thought, wondering if he could keep that from Mavrix. *That means I have to try something else, and I don't know what.*

"I am not rooted in your northern land well enough to be as effective as I might have been fighting for Sithonia if the Gradi gods were coming there, which the power above all deities prevent," Mavrix said. "You would do better seeking out the powers in and under your own soil, those who have most to lose if enslaved or expelled by Voldar and her vicious crew."

He had been vicious himself; neither Stribog nor Lavtrig cared to try conclusions with him a second time. Soon he was out of the realm of the Gradi gods. Gerin, meanwhile, wondered which Elabonian deities Mavrix meant. Biton, perhaps, but anyone else? He put the question to the god who carried his spirit.

"No, not that wretched farseeing twit," Mavrix said scornfully. "He'll be useless to you here, I guarantee it. Voldar would chew him up and spit him out while he was still looking every which way. He and Nothing might get on well, though; with luck, they'd bore each other out of existence."

He sounded very sure of himself, which alarmed Gerin. If Biton was not the answer against the Gradi gods, who was? "Who in the northlands can hope to stand against them?" the Fox persisted.

"I've told you everything I know, and more than you deserve," Mavrix answered, petulant now. "This is not my country. I keep saying as much: this is not my land. I don't keep track of every fribbling, stodgy godlet infesting it, nor would I want to. Since you were foolish enough to choose to be born here, I leave all that up to you."

"But—" Gerin began.

"Oh, be still till you have flesh to make noise with," Mavrix said, and Gerin perforce *was* still. The god went on, "Here we are, returned to this dank, chilly, unpleasant hovel you inhabit. If only you knew the sunshine of Sithonia, the wine, the sea (not all gray and frigid like the nasty ocean splashing your soil, but blue and bright and beautiful), the gleam of polished marble and sandstone yellow as butter, as gold— But you do not, poor deprived thing, and maybe for the best, for you might slay yourself in despair at your lack. Since you are trapped here, I return you now to the really quite ordinary body from which I abstracted you."

All at once, Gerin was seeing with his own eyes, hearing with his own ears, moving his head, his hands, his legs. There before him stood Mavrix. There too stood Selatre and Rihwin and Fulda, who remained lushly nude. "How long were we gone?" the Fox asked. As Mavrix had said, in his own flesh he could speak again.

"Gone?" Selatre and Rihwin spoke the word together. "You've been here all along," Gerin's wife went on. "Where did you go? What did you do?" She turned to Mavrix. "Lord of the sweet grape, are the Gradi gods vanquished?"

"No," Mavrix said. The simple denial brought a gasp of dismay from Rihwin. Mavrix continued, "I did what I could. It was not enough. I can do no more, and so I depart this unpleasant clime." Like mist under the sun, he began to fade.

Gerin had been with him, and knew he had been beaten. Selatre and Rihwin recognized he meant what he said. But Fulda, like so many people Gerin knew, had unquestioned and unquestioning faith in those above her. Hearing a god admit failure was more than she could bear. She cried, "Do you leave us with nothing, then?"

Mavrix resolidified. You could not tell which way his uniformly dark eyes were turned, but, by the direction in which his head pointed, he was probably looking at her. "So you want me to leave you with something, do you?" he said, and laughed. "Very well. I shall."

Fulda gasped. At first Gerin thought it was surprise, but after a moment he realized it was something else entirely. Fulda's eyes closed. Her back arched. Her nipples went stiff and erect. She gasped again, and shuddered all over.

"There," Mavrix said, sounding smug and self-satisfied, or possibly just satisfied: despite what he'd done on the plane of the gods, he hadn't disdained Fulda after all. On the contrary, for he continued, "I've left you something. In three fourths of a year, you'll find out exactly what, and that, I have no doubt, will prove interesting for all concerned. But now . . ." He faded again, this time till he disappeared. The shack in which Gerin attempted to perpetrate magic abruptly seemed to resume its normal cramped dimensions, which convinced the Fox Mavrix was truly gone.

Fulda opened her eyes, but she wasn't looking at the inside of the shack. "Oh," she said, shivering once more. Then she too realized Mavrix had vanished. "Oh," she repeated, this time in disappointment. She reached for her tunic and put it back on. Selatre being there, Gerin made a point of not watching her.

He looked instead to his wife and to Rihwin. They plainly shared his thought. "The god didn't—" Rihwin said.

"The god wouldn't—" Selatre echoed.

"Didn't what?" Fulda asked. "Wouldn't what?"

"Unless we're all daft, you're going to have a baby," Gerin told her. "Quite a baby." She yelped. No, she hadn't understood. The Fox sighed. "One more thing to worry about," he said.

VIII

Selatre shook her head. "I fear the lord of the sweet grape was right in what he told you," she said to Gerin. "Biton is principally concerned with the valley that holds his shrine and the enchanted wood beyond it. The chief reason he involved himself in the broader affairs of the northlands when the monsters burst out is that they sprang from his valley, or from below it."

"Oh, a pestilence!" the Fox said. "You're supposed to tell me what I want to hear, not what you think is true."

Selatre stared at him. Then, warily, she started to laugh. "You are joking, aren't you?" Only when he nodded did she relax, a little.

"When you start telling me things for no better reason than you think they'll please me—" Gerin stopped. "I don't need to go on with that, because you know better, the gods be praised." The phrase tasted sour in his mouth. "The gods who are awake and listening to me, anyhow."

"I don't know whether Mavrix is listening to you, but no one could doubt he's awake," Selatre answered. "I went into the village yesterday. Fulda's courses should have started. They haven't. She says she hasn't lain with any of the men there since her last flowing. I believe her. That leaves—"

"Divine ecstasy?" Gerin suggested, not quite so sardonically as he would have liked.

But Selatre's face was serious as she nodded. "Just so. We were talking about that. It was, I think, different from the ecstasy Biton gave me . . . but then, he and Mavrix are very different gods. And when next spring comes—"

"We'll have a little demigod on our hands," Gerin said. "If, of course, the Gradi haven't overrun us by then. If they have, they'll be the ones worrying about a little demigod. It would almost be worthwhile losing, just to find out what they do about that. Almost, I say."

"We still don't know how to keep that from happening," Selatre said.

"Don't remind me," Gerin told her. "For all I can tell, what Mavrix was really saying was to give up, because none of the gods on or under the ground of the northlands whom I know are likely to have the power to stop the Gradi gods, or even to care about doing it."

"No, I don't think so," Selatre said. "You're letting yourself be too gloomy. After all the trouble you've had with Mavrix, if you had no hope he'd come right out and say as much. He'd probably gloat about it, as a matter of fact."

Gerin chewed on that and found himself nodding. "Yes, that's just what he'd do. He doesn't love the Gradi gods or what they stand for, so he was willing to go against them, but he doesn't love me, either. I've seen that over the years, and no mistake about it."

Downstairs, in the great hall, a hideous commotion erupted. Selatre raised an eyebrow. "I've heard a lot of strange noises down there, but hardly anything like this. Who's killing whom, and why are they torturing them before they finally let them die?"

That was an exaggeration of the quality of the racket, but not a large one. "I'll go down there and tell whoever it is to stuff a pair of drawers in his gob," Gerin said. "If I have to, I'll smash a couple of heads together. That generally shuts people up."

Down he went, left hand on the hilt of his sword. He didn't know what he'd find when he got downstairs—an argument just this side of a brawl was his best guess. What he did discover was in a way more reassuring, in another way more alarming: Van and Geroge and Tharma sitting around beside an enormous jar of ale that had probably been full when they started it and now was certainly almost empty.

What Gerin and Selatre and probably everyone else in Fox Keep had mistaken for strife was the outlander and the two monsters trying to sing. The result sounded more nearly catastrophic than musical. But that was not what made Gerin snap, "What do you think you're doing?" at Van.

"Oh, hullo, Fox," Van said with a broad, foolish grin. "Trying to see if I can hold more ale than these walking fur rugs here. I thought so when I started, but I'm not so sure any more."

"Lord prince," Geroge rumbled. He grinned, too, displaying his formidable teeth. The Fox didn't doubt the grin was meant as friendly, but it raised his hackles all the same. Geroge was at least as strong as Van. He usually behaved himself very well, but who could say how he'd act with a bellyful of ale sloshing around inside him? More to the point, if he decided to behave monstrously, how much damage would he do before he could be controlled or killed?

Like everyone else at Fox Keep, he and Tharma drank ale every day, with their meals and when they were thirsty. But they didn't drink—or they hadn't drunk—for the sake of getting drunk, not till now they hadn't. It was not a habit Gerin wanted to encourage in them.

He glared at Van, wishing his friend had shown better sense. As usual for such wishes, this one came too late. With what he thought was commendable restraint, he said, "Looking into the bottom of a jack of ale is one thing. Looking into the bottom of a jar of ale is something else again. You'll be clearer on the difference come morning," he added with malice aforethought.

"Likely tell you're right." Van scowled. "And likely tell I'll have Fand screeching at me, too, making me wish my poor aching head would fall off." He held his poor, not yet aching head in his hands.

If the prospect of hangovers daunted Geroge and

Tharma, they didn't show it. "Oh, I bless lord Baivers, yes I do, for making me feel so fine," Geroge howled. He spilled what he probably intended as a little ale on the table for a libation. He wasn't moving so smoothly as he had been, though, and ended up emptying most of his jack of ale. He didn't care about the mess; he cared about the missing ale. He got up, went over to the jar, and dug with the dipper. He didn't get much back for his effort. Peering down into the jar, he howled again, this time in desolation. When words came back to him, he said, "It's all gone! How did that happen?"

Van laughed then, morose though he'd been a moment before. So did Tharma; she laughed so hard, she fell off her bench and rolled in the rushes before slowly climbing back to her feet. And Gerin said, "Do you think you might have had something to do with it?"

"Who, me?" Geroge's narrow little eyes went as wide as they could when that idea worked its way into his fuddled wits: it plainly hadn't occurred to him. "Well, maybe I did."

He laughed, too, in big, snarling chuckles that would have sent any sensible watchdog running for its life, tail between its legs. Like Tharma, he was turning out to be a good-natured drunk, for which Gerin thanked not only Baivers but every god he could think of this side of Voldar. A nasty, sullen drunken monster was about the last thing Gerin wanted to contemplate. If Geroge rampaged out of control, how was anyone supposed to stop him without spearing him or filling him full of arrows?

The Fox stuck two fingers in the puddle of ale Geroge had spilled on the table. He sucked the brew off one of them, then flicked a golden drop from the other in a libation of his own. "I bless you, Baivers," he said out loud, and silently appended, *because your bounty turns monsters friendly and foolish, not vicious and savage.* Considering what they were, that was no small boon from the god.

Van with a hangover was a shuddering horror. But Van had had a great many hangovers in his time. He drank a tiny bit more ale come morning, nibbled at a heel of bread, and did his best to stay away from bright sunlight and loud noises (though Fand didn't make that latter easy) until his poor abused body had the chance to recover.

Geroge and Tharma felt every bit as bad, if not worse, and had no idea what to do about it. Some forms of virginity were more enjoyable to lose than others. They moaned they were dying, and flinched from the harsh din of their own voices. Gerin did very little to make them more comfortable. The less they enjoyed the aftermath of their debauch, the less likely they were to repeat it.

Having been moderate the day before, he didn't flinch from leaving the shade of the great hall for the bright sunlight that streamed down into the courtyard. As soon as he went out there, he began to sweat; it was a fine, hot summer's day.

He wondered if that meant Stribog hadn't recovered from the drubbing Mavrix gave him. He also wondered what the weather was like west of the Venien, in lands where the Gradi held sway. If Stribog really was out of commission, the peasants might bring in some kind of crop even there. *Have to try to find out*, he thought. The more he learned about what the Gradi and their gods could do, the better his own chances of figuring out what to do about them.

He climbed up onto the palisade. Everything looked normal enough, as far as the eye could see: the trouble was, the eye couldn't see far enough. But here, peasants labored in the fields, cattle and sheep grazed on the meadows, pigs foraged for whatever they could find. In the peasant village near the keep, smoke came out the smoke holes in a couple of roofs as women simmered soup or stew for the evening meal.

What was Fulda doing there? Cooking? Weaving? Brewing? Weeding? Whatever she was doing, her courses hadn't come. She was pregnant, sure enough, and without a human partner. Why had Mavrix chosen to spawn a demigod in the northlands? What sort of demigod would the child be?

Time would answer those questions, provided Gerin remained alive to see the answers. Actually, time would answer those questions whether he remained alive or not, but he preferred not to dwell on that.

He didn't have to dwell on it for long. The lookout in the watchtower above the castle winded his horn and cried, "A chariot approaching, lord prince, out of the west!" Gerin peered southwest, in the direction of Adiatunnus' lands. For years, that was the direction from which trouble had come, out of the west. Then the lookout amplified his earlier words: "A chariot along the path by the Niffet."

Gerin whirled. When he thought about the Niffet these days, he thought of war galleys full of Gradi with axes, every one of the raiders bellowing Voldar's name. Much to his relief, he saw no galleys. For a little while, he saw no chariot, either. His watchtower was the tallest around, precisely to afford the sentries up there the widest possible view.

No, there it was, coming out from behind a grove of plum trees. The horsemen were trotting along at a pace that, while not the quickest, covered the most ground if you held it for a long time. Somebody up on the palisade next to Gerin said, "From out of Schild Stoutstaff's holding, maybe."

"That would be my guess," Gerin agreed. "Now we have to find out what sort of news he's bringing."

When the chariot came up to the keep, the fellow in the car named himself Aripert Aribert's son, one of Schild's vassal barons, though not a man the Fox knew well. Since there was only the one car, Gerin's warriors did not hesitate to lower the drawbridge and let him into the keep.

Once in the courtyard, he jumped down from the car and looked all around, calling, "The Fox! Where is the Fox?" He didn't know Gerin by sight, either. He was about thirty-five, stocky, with sharp features and a quick, jerky way of moving.

"I'm the Fox." Gerin had made his way down from the palisade. "What's gone so wrong in Schild's barony that you had to rush here and tell me about it?"

"You have the right of it, lord prince," Aripert said, pacing back and forth. He evidently couldn't stand to hold still more than a few breaths at a time. He cracked his knuckles, one after another, till they all popped, and hardly seemed aware he was doing it. "The wild men from out of the west, the Gradi, ships full of them landed in Schild's holding. His keep held against them, and those of his vassals, too, but they burned villages and killed serfs and trampled crops and stole livestock and we're all going to be hungry this winter on account of it." He stared at Gerin, as if convinced it was the Fox's fault.

"We haven't been sitting idle, Aripert," Gerin said. Aripert gnawed dead skin at the edge of his thumbnail. Gerin wondered if he had a wife. Living with such constant fidgeting would have driven him mad. But that was not what mattered at the moment. He went on, "Your own overlord has fought against the Gradi at my side."

"So what?" Aripert said, swatting at something that might have been a gnat and might have been a figment of his imagination. "It didn't do me any good. It didn't do Schild's holding any good."

"That's not so," Gerin said. "It might have been worse for you—it might have been much worse—if we hadn't. If you don't believe me, send a messenger down to Adiatunnus and ask him."

Aripert scratched his head, tugged at his ear, and plucked a hair out of his beard. Spinning it between thumb and forefinger, he answered, "All right, maybe it would have been worse. I don't know. It was cursed bad, I tell you." He started pacing again. "How are you going to keep those bastards off the Niffet? That's what I want to know." He yanked out his knife and cleaned his nails with it.

Just watching him made Gerin tired. "I don't know how we can keep the Gradi off the Niffet," he said. "They make better ships than we do. Best we can hope for is to beat them once they get off their ships to fight. But they can pick the spots where they do that."

"Not good enough." Aripert stuck one of his newly clean fingernails deep into his ear, stared with interest at what he dug out, and wiped his hand on his breeches. "Not good enough, not even close. We have to keep them from doing that."

"Fine," Gerin said, which surprised the newcomer into

several heartbeats of immobility. The Fox fixed him with a sour stare. "How?"

Aripert opened his mouth, closed it, licked his lips, noisily sucked in air, licked his lips again, and finally said, "You're the prince of the north. I'm not. You're supposed to tell that to me."

Gerin laughed. Aripert glared. Gerin glared back, and kept on laughing. "If I had a cow for everyone who's said that to me since spring," he said, "I'd eat beef the rest of my life."

That left Aripert unimpressed. "If the prince of the north doesn't have the answers, who does?" he demanded.

"Maybe no one," Gerin said, which made the vassal baron's eyes open very wide. As Aripert was scuffing the ground with one foot, the Fox thought, *Maybe Voldar*. He wouldn't say that out loud, and wished it hadn't crossed his mind. What he did say was, "You'll have to put more watchers along the river, to keep an eye out for Gradi galleys and give the alarm when they spot them. Then you can decide whether you want to show yourself in force enough to keep them from wanting to land or hole up in your keep."

Aripert started pacing again, then hopped up in the air suddenly enough to startle the Fox. Even before his feet hit the ground again, he was talking: "Well, that's something, lord prince, so it is. If these cursed Gradi come and go on the Niffet as they please, the way you say, we will have to keep a tighter watch for 'em, do those kinds of things."

"If they land, try to burn their boats," Gerin said. "They guard them, but it would be worth doing if you could. If they're stranded in our country, we can hunt them down the way we would any dangerous wild beasts."

"Aye, lord prince—sense in your words." Aripert's jaws worked, as if literally chewing up and swallowing Gerin's advice.

"Had you done any of these things before the Gradi raided you?" Gerin asked. Aripert shook his head. He gnawed some more at the skin of his thumb, looking contrite. Now the Fox glared in good earnest. "Why not?" he shouted. "You know what the Gradi did to us here this spring. By the five hells, why did you think you were immune?"

"It wasn't that so much, lord prince," Aripert said, shifting from foot to foot and twisting his body back and forth as if he were dancing. "We didn't know what to do, so we didn't do anything much. If they come back, we'll give them a better fight for your wise words."

"How much wisdom does it take to see this?" Gerin held a hand out in front of his face. "How much wisdom does it take to feel this?" He wanted to hit Aripert over the head with a rock, with luck letting in some light and fresh air, but contented himself with squeezing the minor baron's arm. "You don't need to go to the Sibyl's shrine at Ikos for advice like what I've given you. You don't need to come to me, either. All you need to do is sit down on your fundament and ask yourself a few simple questions. *Are the Gradi likely to come here? If they do, how will they come? If that's what they do, how can I best pour sand in their soup? How will they try to stop me? How can I keep them from doing that?* It's not hard, Aripert. Any man can do it, if he will." He knew he sounded as if he were pleading. He couldn't help it. He *was* pleading.

Aripert Aribert's son scratched his head. He sighed, long and deep. "What am I supposed to say, lord prince?"

"You're not supposed to say any one thing," Gerin answered, quietly now. "You're not supposed to do any one thing. You're just supposed to think for yourself."

Aripert scratched his head again. He scratched his neck. He scratched his forearm, and the back of his hand. Watching him made Gerin itch. He started scratching his own head. Aripert said, "When a serf asks me something, I don't tell him to figure it out for himself. I give him an order, and I make certain sure he follows it."

"Sometimes that works fine." Gerin was always ready to talk about the art—or maybe *magic* was a better word—of ruling. "Sometimes it keeps him from getting a different idea, one as good as yours or maybe better. And sometimes, unless you're a god—maybe even if you're a god—you're going to be flat-out wrong. If the serf blindly goes ahead and does what you tell him, you've done him wrong. Of course, sometimes he'll know you're wrong and go ahead and do what you tell him anyhow, for spite or anger or to show you up for a fool. That's why I give fewer orders like that than I used to."

"By the way you talk, you want every man doing so much for himself, there'd be no need for barons—or for a prince," Aripert added pointedly.

"If every man were as smart as every other man and if everybody got along with everyone else, that would be fine," Gerin said. "But some men can't think, and, worse, some who can won't. And some people are quarrelsome and some want what their neighbors have but don't want to work the way the neighbors did. I don't think lords will disappear from the landscape tomorrow, nor even the day after."

"Heh," Aripert said. He sketched a salute. "All right, lord prince, I'll try not to be one of those people who can think but won't. Thinking about watchers along the river is a good place to start. Beacon fires, maybe." He plucked at his beard, then tugged at an earlobe.

"A string of beacon fires would be a good thing to have," the Fox agreed. "If you do set 'em up, I'll put a watcher next to Schild's land to relay news here to Fox Keep."

"Well, that's fine, lord prince. One thing I can't do for myself is make men out of thin air. Can you spare me some soldiers to come leap on the Gradi if they do land again?"

"Not a one," Gerin answered firmly. "But if you want to arm your serfs against them, I won't say a word. Peasants don't usually make the best soldiers—the gods know that's so—but if they have weapons, they'll do the Gradi some damage, anyhow."

"But if they learn to fight, they'll do us nobles damage down the road, too," Aripert protested.

"Which has the greater weight, what may happen down the road if you do arm them or what's almost sure to happen now if you don't?" Gerin asked. Aripert bit his lip, stamped his foot, and finally nodded. He was thinking, even if he didn't like the answers he was getting; Gerin gave him credit for it. The Fox said, "Here, spend the night with us. We'll feed you; you can drink some ale with us, if any turns out to be left in the cellar."

"Uh, thank you, lord prince." Aripert sounded a little unsure of himself, as if he couldn't decide whether Gerin was joking. Since Gerin couldn't decide, either, no reason for Aripert to be able to.

Geroge came out of the great hall, braving the vicious sunlight for a chance to breathe fresh air instead of the smoke inside the castle. The Fox's men, knowing the monster's delicate condition, prudently left him alone. He might have been good-natured most of the time, but anyone feeling the aftereffects from a day's binge was liable to be on the testy side. If you were huge, hairy, and armed with teeth like a wolf's, no one wanted to find out whether you were feeling testy or not.

"Father Dyaus!" Aripert yelled, grabbing for his sword. "It's one of those horrible things! I thought they were all gone."

Gerin seized Aripert's arm and kept him from getting the length of edged bronze out of the scabbard. Geroge swung his intimidating gaze toward Aripert. "Well!" he said, with almost as much condescension as Mavrix could have loaded into the word. "Some people don't insult strangers just for the fun of it, or so the Fox tells me, anyhow." His long, narrow nostrils were ideally suited to sniffing.

For once, Aripert stood completely motionless. He stared at the monster. By the look on his face, he would have sooner expected one of the logs on the palisade to say something to him than Geroge. "If you'll look closely, you'll notice he is wearing breeches," Gerin said. "We're friends."

"Friends," Aripert repeated through frozen lips. "You have some . . . unusual friends, lord prince."

Gerin set a hand on his shoulder. "Oh, I don't know. You're not so unusual as all that, are you?"

Geroge got the point of the gibe before Aripert did. The monster started to throw back his head and roar laughter. One or the other or both of those must have hurt, for he stopped with a grimace that showed off his formidable dental equipment. Aripert started to draw his sword again, but checked himself before Gerin had to stop him.

The Fox introduced the monster to the vassal baron, then explained for Aripert's benefit: "He was deep in the ale pot yesterday, the very first time, and he's feeling it now."

"Oh." Aripert stuck out a finger at Gerin. "Now I understand why you were wondering if you had any ale left. Must take up a bit to fill up one his size."

"Not one," Geroge said. "Three: me, Tharma, and Van of the Strong Arm."

Aripert didn't know who Tharma was, but he knew about Van. He let out an awed whistle. Gerin said, "There, you see? You can think, after all."

"What I think is, I'd like to have seen that," Aripert said. "From a safe distance, I mean. When you see a Gradi galley out on the Niffet, it's pretty, too, but you don't want it getting any closer."

"A good deal of truth there," Gerin said. "If we weather the storm, we'll have to see about making galleys of our own. But that's for later, in the great by-and-by. For now, come into the hall and we'll start feeding you. And you can watch Geroge and Tharma be very moderate tonight, unless I miss my guess." He turned to the monster. "How about it, Geroge? Feel like having your head pound like a drum again tomorrow morning?"

Geroge held up both hands in a gesture of genuine horror. "Oh, no, lord prince! Doing that once was plenty for me."

"He's not stupid," Aripert said, hopping into the air in surprise. He belied his own words, speaking as if Geroge wasn't there or couldn't understand even when giving a compliment. But then he went on, "Plenty of ordinary men who don't think getting drunk once is enough. Plenty of ordinary men who don't think getting drunk once in a day is enough, come to that."

"Aye," the Fox agreed mournfully. "We both know too many like that. Everyone knows too many like that. Well, come on. We'll see if we can make you happy without having you sleep in the rushes under the table when you're done."

✧ ✧ ✧

Aripert Aribert's son rode out of Fox Keep the next morning, every bit as fidgety as he had been when he rode in. Gerin dared hope he would put some of that restless energy to work watching for the Gradi and resisting them if they struck Schild's holding again.

A few days later, he got word from a trader who had come out of the forests north of the Niffet with a load of fine beeswax and amber that the Gradi had also raided that side of the river. The trader, a lean, weathered, balding man named Cedoal the Honest (a sobriquet the Fox would have bet he'd invented himself), said, "I didn't see the bastards my own self, lord prince; you got to understand that. But I did see the woodsrunners who were running from 'em. They like to swamp the village where I was at, and every one of 'em had worse tales to tell than the next."

That was logically impossible, but Gerin didn't press the merchant about it. Instead, he tried to figure out exactly when the raid had taken place. He wished he had Aripert back, to nail down the exact day. As best he could tell, though, both raids had probably been by the same band. Figuring out where Cedoal had been in relation to Schild's holding wasn't easy, either. The Fox thought the Gradi had hit Schild first and then raided the Trokmoi on the way west, but knew he couldn't be sure.

And then, a few days after that, Gradi galleys came rowing up the Niffet toward Fox Keep. Fires from Schild's holding warned of them, so Aripert had not only thought but also acted. "We'll smash them, Father!" Duren cried as he drove the chariot with Gerin and Van out toward the river. The Fox had decided to meet the raiders on the bank, not wanting them to ravage fields and assail the peasant village again.

But the Gradi did not land. Instead, sails taking advantage of the wind from the west and oars working with drilled precision, they propelled their galleys past Fox Keep and on up the Niffet. Gerin and a good many Elabonians shot arrows at them, but most of the shafts fell short: the Niffet was a broad stream, and a ship closer to the northern bank than the southern all but immune to archery.

Van normally disdained the bow in war. Seeing that the Gradi were not going to stop and fight, though, he grabbed the strongest bow any of Gerin's comrades carried: it belonged to Drungo Drago's son. Drungo had put a couple of arrows close to the galley. He growled when Van took the bow from him, but stared, slack-jawed, as the outlander bent it till the wood creaked and threatened to snap, then let fly.

One of the Gradi who weren't rowing—by that, a captain of some sort—went down. The Elabonians raised a cheer. Drungo bowed to Van. "I thought I put everything into that bow it would take," he said. "I was wrong."

"Not bad for a lucky shot, was it?" Van said, laughing. He proceeded to empty Drungo's quiver at the galleys, and made a couple of more hits. Neither was as spectacular as that first had been. Whatever Van did, he had a flair for the dramatic.

Gerin watched in some consternation as the Gradi kept sailing east up the Niffet. "What are they doing?" he demanded, perhaps of the Elabonian gods—who, as usual, did not answer. "I thought they meant to close with me and find out once for all who would rule the northlands."

"What else could they want?" Duren demanded. "Till they've beaten you, they haven't really accomplished anything."

"Oh, I don't know, lad." As he often did, Van had a ruthlessly pragmatic way of looking at things. "If they plunder other people, they bring home loot and slaves with less risk and cost to themselves. And we won't be able to rest easy, not with them farther up the river than we are. For all we know, they may try and hit us on their way back toward the ocean."

"Let's make life difficult for them," Gerin said. He hadn't thought of setting up a chain of watchfires east of Fox Keep, not imagining the Gradi would go on past his holding. But that didn't mean he couldn't send riders east to warn the petty barons along the banks of the Niffet the raiders were coming.

Watching the cars rattle off down the road, Van said, "I wonder if they'll get there ahead of the galleys. Horses tire out same as men do, and the Gradi have the wind working for them, though they are rowing against the current, and that's not easy."

"It's in the hands of the gods," Gerin said, and then wished he hadn't: the Gradi gods were too greedy by half to suit him. More consolingly, he added, "I've done everything I can."

"I wish we could move the whole army after them," Duren said.

"That we can't do," Gerin answered. "If we did, they'd let us stay with them for a while, and then they'd turn around right in the middle of the Niffet, take down their sails, and use oars and current to rush back here. They'd swoop down on the keep before we could get here, and that," he added with what he thought of as praiseworthy understatement, "would be very bad."

"Aye, you're right, Fox," Van said. "I'm all for charging straight ahead most times, but not now. If we run away from what's most important to us, we end up losing it, sure as sure."

"Well, we haven't lost it this time, the gods be praised." Gerin didn't know whether that was irony in his voice or the hope that, if the Elabonian gods repeatedly heard themselves addressed, they would pay more attention to this corner of the world.

He waved. The army rode back from the banks of the Niffet toward Fox Keep. The men on the palisade raised a cheer. So did the serfs who lived in the village near the keep. Some of them came out of the fields and huts to congratulate the warriors on keeping the Gradi from landing. Gerin didn't know whether those congratulations were truly in order, or whether the Gradi had intended to bypass his holding from the beginning. If the peasants were so eager to approve of him, though, he was willing to let them.

Among the serfs came Fulda. Her fellows regarded her with more than a little awe. So did a good many of the warriors; she hadn't been shy about spreading the story of what had happened inside the shack that served as Gerin's magical laboratory. The proof of how the other peasants in the village felt was that they'd been doing a lot of her work for her since her encounter with Mavrix.

The Fox had never doubted she was pregnant by the Sithonian god, and, if he had, those doubts would have perished. Not only had her courses failed to come, but she glowed in a way that was similar to the glow other pregnant women got, but so magnified that Gerin would almost have taken oath she didn't need a lamp by night.

That wasn't so; incurably curious, he'd gone over to the peasant village one night to find out. But he did note that the night ghosts, perhaps sensing the demigod in her belly, stayed far away from the village, and that even those whose wails could be heard at a distance seemed less cold and fierce than was their wont.

"Lord prince," Fulda said now. She still treated him with respect, perhaps from lifelong habit, perhaps because he was married to Selatre, who had also known intimacy with a god, even if intimacy of a different sort from hers.

"How are you feeling today?" he asked her. He knew he sounded cautious. How else could he sound when, though she was still one of his serfs, the god who had impregnated her might be listening?

"I'm well, thank you," she said. Her smile, like everything else about her, was radiant. One of the advantages of having a god for the father of her child, it seemed, was immunity to morning sickness.

"Good," Gerin said. "That's good." No, he hadn't figured out how to react to Fulda. She was a good-looking young woman, certainly, but not very bright. And yet Mavrix had chosen to sire a child on her. The Fox shrugged. A fertility god no doubt cared for beauty more than wit. After all, that had been the point in having her there in the first place.

Rihwin the Fox, mounted on a horse, came up to Fulda. Gerin suspected Rihwin would sooner have mounted her. She smiled up at him in a way that suggested she might have been interested in the same thing.

"Rihwin, are you trying to make Mavrix angry at you again?" Gerin asked.

"Who, me?" his fellow Fox asked, looking innocent so convincingly as to be altogether unconvincing. "Why should Mavrix be angry at me for conversing with this charming lady when I, in a manner of speaking, introduced the two of them? And why, furthermore, should he be angry with me if I do rather more than converse with her? He could never doubt the paternity of the child to be born, and I would raise it as one of my own. He might even be grateful to me."

Rihwin, as far as Gerin could see, was thinking with his lance, not his head. Gerin sighed. Rihwin would do whatever he would do, and would probably end up paying the penalty for it. He did pay those penalties without complaint; Gerin gave him that much. As far as Gerin was concerned, not putting yourself in a position where you would have to pay them would have been wiser yet, but he'd learned Rihwin, like a lot of people, didn't think that way.

"Be careful," he said to Rihwin. Rihwin nodded, almost as if he would heed. Gerin sighed again.

"Lord prince?" Carlun Vepin's son still spoke hesitantly whenever he needed to address Gerin. The Fox might have made him steward, but he had the ingrained habits of a serf—and knowing he thrived by Gerin's sufferance couldn't have made matters any easier. But, hesitantly or not, he went on, "Lord prince, I do need to speak to you for a moment."

"Here I am," Gerin said, agreeably enough. "What's troubling you?"

Carlun looked around the great hall. Several warriors sat here and there along the benches, some drinking ale, one gnawing the roasted leg of a fowl, three or four more rolling dice. Lowering his voice, Carlun said, "Lord prince, may I speak with you in private?"

"I suppose so," Gerin said. "Shall we walk down toward the village, then? That should do the job."

Carlun agreed at once. Whenever he got out of Fox Keep these days, he seemed a flower spreading itself in the bright sunshine. And the sunshine remained bright and hot. The drubbing Mavrix had given Stribog did keep the Gradi god from meddling with the weather.

"Here we are," Gerin said. "I asked you once, so I'll ask you twice: what's troubling you?"

"Lord prince, how long will Fox Keep be full of warriors?" Carlun asked. "How much longer will they stay here?"

"How long?" The Fox frowned. "Till we've beaten the Gradi, or till they've beaten us, whichever happens first. Why?"

"Because, lord prince, they are eating us—eating you—out of house and home," Carlun answered. "If you hadn't been so prudent about storing up food, your larder would long since have been bare. As things are, this will be a hungry, thirsty winter even without your vassals here."

"What do you suggest I do, then?" Gerin asked. "Shall I send everyone home, with the Gradi still on the Niffet east of here? Shall I surrender to the Gradi? Is that better than letting them make me poor instead of prosperous?"

Carlun licked his lips. "That's not, uh, what I had in mind, lord prince. But you do need to know that even the supplies you have stored up won't last forever."

"Oh, I know that all too well," Gerin said. "Every time I go down into the cellars and see another storage jar opened or another jar gone, it gives me something new to worry about, and I have plenty of things already, thanks."

"Every time you go down into the cellars—" Carlun repeated. He stared at the Fox. "Lord prince, I didn't know you did that. As far as I could see, lords know only about taking, not about saving and watching."

"That's because you've looked at things with the eyes of a serf," Gerin answered. *It's also because I look further ahead than most lords*, he thought, but he didn't say that out loud. What he did say was, "I have to manage this entire holding the way you ran first your house and then the village. Here, I'll tell you what I have left down there—" He started reeling off jars of ale, of wheat, of barley, of rye, of beans, of peas, of salted beef and mutton, of smoked pork, so many hams, so many sausages, so many hung joints of beef, and on and on till Carlun's eyes all but popped from his head.

"Lord prince," the peasant-turned-steward whispered when the Fox was finally through, "I couldn't have done that without checking the latest records, nor come close to it, but I think from what I do remember of those records, your memory is as near perfect as makes no difference."

"I would have made a splendid scholar," Gerin said, "since I have a jackdaw's memory for useless bits of this and that. Every now and again, it comes in handy in the world where I find myself."

"Lord prince, if you remember all these things, why did you put me in the place where you put me?" Carlun asked. "Not that I'm not grateful mind, when I think what you could have done, but you don't need me. You could do the job yourself."

"Of course I could," Gerin said, with confidence so automatic he didn't notice it himself. "But with you doing it, I don't have to. And so I don't, not really. If we do run low, you're the one who's going to make sure we lay in more supplies from . . . somewhere. And if you do a bad job at it, I'll throw you out on your ear."

"Oh, I've known that all along, lord prince," Carlun said. Both men smiled, although they both knew Gerin hadn't been joking: he expected no less from those around him than he did from himself. Carlun's smile faded first. He asked, "How am I to pay for whatever I have to bring in?"

"You have my leave to spend my gold and silver," Gerin answered. "I wouldn't have brought you here if I didn't intend to let you do that. I do expect you to spend as little of it as you can."

Carlun bowed his head. "I wouldn't think of doing anything else." He grinned wryly. "I wouldn't dare do anything else."

"No, eh?" Gerin hadn't said one word about checking on Carlun. He didn't intend to say one word about checking on Carlun. He did, however, intend to check on him. If Carlun couldn't figure that out for himself, the Fox had made a mistake in promoting him rather than sending him off to some other village. And if Carlun tried cheating, he'd find he'd made a mistake himself.

They were almost out to the village where he had been headman not long before. Abruptly, he spun on his heel and started walking back toward Fox Keep again, much faster than he'd left it. "I don't want to go back to the hut that used to be mine," he said. "I don't even want to see it, not up close. Do you understand that, lord prince?"

"Maybe I do," the Fox said. "Is it that you don't want to be reminded of how you started out—and of how you could end up?"

Carlun jerked as if Gerin had stuck him with the pin from a fibula. "Did you work magic to see that, lord prince?"

"No," Gerin answered, and immediately wished he'd said *yes*—if Carlun thought his magic better than it was, he might be more tempted to walk the straight and narrow. But, having answered honestly, he went on, "Seeing that one wasn't hard. When you were headman, you had to know what the rest of the people in the village were thinking, didn't you?" When Carlun nodded, the Fox finished, "I've had to do that for my holding, and for much longer than you needed to do it. I've seen a lot, I've remembered a lot, and I can put all that together. Do you follow me?"

A lot of men—some of them his vassal barons—wouldn't have. They remembered little and learned less, going through life, or so it seemed to Gerin, more than half-blind. But Carlun, whether honest and reliable or not, was anything but stupid. "You may not be casting a spell," he said, "but that doesn't mean it isn't magic."

Since Gerin had had the same thought about the craft of ruling men as recently as Aripert's arrival at Fox Keep, he glanced toward Carlun with considerable respect. As they came back to the keep, he said, "I have your gracious permission to keep the garrison here a while longer, eh?"

"Of course, lord prince," Carlun said, sounding on the lordly side himself. When Gerin gave him a sharp look, his burst of bravado collapsed and he added, "Not that you need it, mind you."

"There is that," Gerin agreed, happy Carlun knew his place after all.

Dagref, Clotild, and Blestar were playing with Maeva and Kor. Gerin watched the game with faint bemusement. Dagref was not only oldest but sharpest witted. A lot of the time, he couldn't be bothered playing with his sibs; his mind, though not his body or spirit, was nearly that of an adult. When he did join them and Van's children, the role he saw for himself was halfway between overseer and god: he invented not just rules but a whole imaginary world, and put himself and them through their paces in it.

"No, Maeva!" he shouted. "I told you. Don't you remember? The bark of that tree" —a stick— "is poisonous."

"No, it's not," Maeva said. To prove her point, she picked up the stick and whacked Dagref with it. "There. You see?" But for the high pitch of her voice, that self-satisfied directness might have come straight from Van. "Didn't hurt me a bit."

"You're not playing right," Dagref said angrily: by his tone, he could imagine no felony more heinous.

"Be careful, son," Gerin muttered under his breath. Dagref was older, but Maeva, girl or no girl, was both stronger and more agile. If Dagref forced a confrontation, he'd lose. If he wanted to get his way here, he'd have to figure out how to do it without getting into a fight.

Just then, Geroge and Tharma came out of the great hall. All the children greeted them with glad cries. The brewing quarrel between Dagref and Maeva was forgotten. The two monsters, though now approaching adulthood, had always been part of the children's games at Fox Keep. They were bigger and stronger than any of the others, which more than balanced their also being duller. Had they been bad-tempered, their strength would have made them terrors. Since they weren't, they became companions all the more desirable.

"What game are you playing?" Tharma asked Dagref.

"Well," he said importantly, "Clotild here is a wizard, and she's turned Kor into a longtooth" —a role well suited for one of Kor's fierce, blustery temper— "and we're all seeking ways to get him back his own shape. Maeva seems to be immune to poisons, and so—" He went on laying out the framework of the world that existed only inside his own head. Gerin noted he'd incorporated Maeva's recalcitrance into the structure of the game.

Geroge laughed, loud and boisterously—so loud and boisterously, Gerin's ears quivered in suspicion. Geroge sounded as if he'd been dipping deep into the ale jar again, in spite of earlier promises. He said, "That's a *good* game!"

His voice quivered with enthusiasm. "Let's make the longtooth fly and see what happens then."

He picked up Kor and threw him high in the air—so high, he had time to circle under the little boy before he came down. The circling was wobbly—yes, he'd been drinking more than he should have.

Gerin started toward him on the dead run, but Geroge plucked Kor out of the air neat as you please. Tharma grabbed Blestar and threw him even higher. Even more than it had when Kor soared, Gerin's heart leaped into his mouth. He breathed out a harsh sigh of relief as his little son came down safe.

He and Kor both squealed with glee at their flights. The Fox was less amused. "This game is over," he said in a voice filled with as much doom as he could manage.

That evidently wasn't enough. Barons and Trokmê chieftains quailed before him. His own children, along with Van's and with Geroge and Tharma, protested loudly and bitterly. He held his ground. "We were fine," Clotild said, stamping her foot. "I wanted to go next. No one got hurt."

"No, not this time. But you were lucky, because someone might have," Gerin answered. He'd long since found out that arguments based on *might have* were for all practical purposes useless with children. So it proved here. But when he got a whiff of Geroge's breath, he had another, better argument. "Baivers and barley!" he exclaimed, wrinkling his nose. "You didn't just dive into the ale jar, you went swimming around in there."

Geroge looked as shamefaced as a tiddly monster could. The result would have made anyone who didn't know him flee in terror, but Gerin recognized the display of fangs as placatory, not hostile. "I'm sorry," Geroge said with a growl that also sounded more fearsome than it was. "I don't know what came over me. But I feel so good with the ale inside." He punctuated that with an enormous belch. Gerin's children and Van's dissolved in gales of laughter.

The Fox felt like laughing, too, but didn't let his face show it. He rounded on Tharma. "I thought you had better sense than he did," he said accusingly.

"I'm sorry," she answered, hanging her homely head. "But he started drinking the ale, and I—"

"If he decided to jump off the palisade and break his fool neck, would you do it, too, just because he did it?" Gerin had trotted that one out so many times for his own children, it sprang forth of its own accord now.

He'd used it on Geroge and Tharma a few times, too, generally to good effect. Today, though, Tharma looked back at him. "It wasn't like that," she protested. "It was like, like . . . something was pushing at us to drink the ale."

"Probably the same sort of thing that pushes at me when I feel like getting into the candied fruit or the honey cakes," Dagref said, sounding far more dubious than someone his age had any business doing. *What will he be like when he grows up?* Gerin thought uneasily. His eldest by Selatre would be a man to reckon with . . . if nobody murdered him young.

"It wasn't like that," Tharma said. "It really was . . . I could almost feel something pushing me toward the jar." Geroge's big head jerked up and down, up and down as he nodded agreement.

Gerin started to shout at both of them for being not just liars but stubborn liars to boot. He stopped, though, before the words passed his lips. Mavrix had used Rihwin as an instrument in a way much like this, prodding him to get drunk on wine and afford the Sithonian god an easy conduit into the northlands. But this wasn't Mavrix, who had nothing to do with ale. It was . . .

"Baivers." Gerin's mouth shaped the name of the god in silent astonishment. Baivers was as Elabonian a deity as any. And, up till now, the Elabonian gods had been uniformly quiet, even when Voldar and her Gradi cohorts added their weight to the invaders' power.

Up till now . . . Gerin wondered if he was a drowning man grabbing at straws as he tried to stay afloat. The affection Geroge and Tharma suddenly felt for ale might have nothing whatever to do with Baivers, might, in fact, have nothing to do with anything save an increasingly well-developed thirst, of the sort that turned ordinary men into drunks with no divine intervention whatever.

"Well," the Fox said, more to himself than to the

monsters, much more to himself than to the still-disappointed children, "if you're going to grab at straws, by Dyaus—and by Baivers—*grab* at them. Don't let them slip through your hands."

"What *are* you talking about, Father?" Dagref, as usual, sounded highly insulted when Gerin said something he didn't follow.

"Never mind," Gerin said absently, which insulted his son all the more. To compound his crime, he took no notice of Dagref's annoyance. Instead, he seized Geroge's arm in one hand and Tharma's in the other. "Come back to the great hall with me, you two. You're going to drink some more ale."

Geroge greeted that pronouncement with a roar of delight. Tharma said, "You're not going to make us drink till we hurt the next day, are you?" That made Geroge thoughtful; the memory of his first hangover was after all still painfully vivid in him, too.

Had Gerin been able to get away with not answering that, he would have done it. He didn't think he could, and the prospect of enraging two monsters, each bigger and stronger than he, was disquieting at best. He said, "I don't know. I want to find out why you like ale so much lately. I want to see if a god is meddling with your fate."

He wished Baivers' meddling weren't so subtle he had trouble telling if it was even there. Till the Gradi came, he had enjoyed being free from interference at the hands of the Elabonian gods. Now, just when he really would have relished interference, he wasn't sure whether he had any or not.

In the great hall, Carlun Vepin's son sat at a corner table, well away from the four or five warriors in the chamber. The steward was quietly nursing a mug of ale. When Gerin called for another jar to be brought up from the cellar, Carlun's face expressed ostentatious disapproval. Gerin was just as ostentatious about ignoring him.

Geroge smacked his lips as he guzzled ale. The Fox studied him in the same way he might have studied some curious new beast that had wandered in from the forest. "How do I find out why you've got so fond of ale?" he murmured.

"Because it tastes good? Because it makes me feel good?" Geroge suggested.

"But you've been drinking it since you were tiny," the Fox said. Imagining Geroge as tiny wasn't easy now. Gerin persisted nonetheless: "It made you feel good then, too, didn't it?"

"Not as good as I feel now," the monster said enthusiastically. Beside him, Tharma nodded, also with great vigor. She drained her jack of ale, then filled it again. Carlun tried to catch Gerin's eye. Gerin didn't let him.

"Does it feel better because you're drinking more now," Gerin asked, "or is there something over and above that, too?"

Both monsters gave the question serious consideration. Gerin admired them for that, the more so considering how much ale they'd already drunk. A lot of ordinary people he knew wouldn't have looked so hard for an answer. At last, Tharma said, "I think it's made us feel better than we did since the time we drank and drank with Van."

"Didn't feel so good afterwards, though," Geroge said, making a horrible face at the memory. As if to help himself forget, he drank deep.

Gerin, meanwhile, called down curses on his friend's head. But that wasn't fair, either; a god might have been nudging Van into getting the monsters drunk that day. For that matter, Gerin thought he was acting as a free agent now, but he was honest enough to admit he didn't know for certain whether he really was one. How much did being prince of fleas mean when a dog started scratching?

That thought led nowhere, though. Whether he was truly his own man or nothing more than a tool of the gods, he had to act as if he were free and independent. Not even a god could restore to you an opportunity you'd missed yesterday.

He studied Geroge and Tharma. They weren't paying much attention to him, or to anything but their ale. When he was down below Biton's shrine at Ikos, he'd wondered whether the monsters had gods of their own. Now that thought came back to him. If they had gods, what did those gods think of two of their number's being left aboveground when Biton and Mavrix had returned all the others to their gloomy haunts? Even more to the point, what did they think about the Gradi?

He shook his head. Here he was, building castles in the air—or rather, castles under the ground. He didn't know for a fact that the monsters had any gods at all. Geroge and Tharma gave the Elabonian deities the same absent-minded reverence he did himself. Why not? That was what they'd learned from him.

How was he supposed to find out if they had gods of their own? Asking them didn't seem likely to give him his answer. Whom to ask, then? Biton would probably know, but, even if he did, he'd cloak whatever reply he gave to the Fox in such ambiguity, it wouldn't come clear till it was too late to do him any good.

Who else might know? He thought of Mavrix, and wished he hadn't. Disaster felt very close whenever he dealt with the Sithonian fertility god—and Mavrix had already shown he despised the monsters, which meant he was certain to despise their gods, too.

Then he realized Baivers might know. The god of barley and brewing was intimately connected to the earth, and so were the monsters. If Gerin invoked him, Baivers would be a logical deity to ask. *If* Gerin invoked him—if he *could* invoke him—the Elabonian gods seemed so uninterested in the world, though, that it might not be possible.

The Fox had resolved to try when the lookout in the watchtower winded his horn and cried, "The Gradi! The Gradi are coming down the river!"

Baivers forgotten, Gerin rushed out of the great hall. Men on the palisade were pointing east. The sentry had got it right, then: these were the Gradi who had gone up the Niffet to see what damage they could do beyond Gerin's holding, not a new band coming to join them. That was something, if not much.

"We'll greet them as we did before: on the riverbank," the Fox ordered. "If they want to try to land here in the face of that, let them, and may they have joy of it."

Ahead of the rest, he sent out Rihwin the Fox and the other adventurous sorts who rode horses. They had their animals ready for action faster than teams could be hitched to chariots. He also sent out a fair number of men on foot: the more resistance the Gradi faced at the water's edge, the less likely they were to try to land.

By the time Van, Duren, and he were rattling across the meadow toward the Niffet, the raiders' war galleys were already passing Fox Keep. The Gradi shouted unintelligible insults across the water, but stayed near the Trokmê bank of the river and showed no desire to clash with foes so obviously ready to receive them.

"Cowards!" Gerin's men yelled. "Spineless dogs! Eunuchs! White-livered wretches!" The Gradi probably could make no more sense of their pleasantries than they could of those coming from the raiders.

Duren said, "The gods be praised, we frightened them away."

"Here, for now, yes," Gerin said. "But what did they do, farther upstream? Whatever it is, they've come faster than the news of it." When he was younger, fits of gloom had threatened to overwhelm him. They came on him less often these days, but he felt the edge of one now. "They can do as they like, and we have to respond to it. With them controlling the river, they can pick and choose where to make their fights. Where we seem strong, they leave us alone. Where we're weak, they strike. And when we try to hit back over land, their gods make even moving against them the next thing to impossible."

"Have to light our beacons, to warn Aripert and the rest of Schild's vassals still in his holding," Van said.

"Right," Gerin answered, with a grateful glance at his friend. The outlander had shown him something simple and practical he could do that would help his cause. He shouted orders. A couple of Rihwin's riders went galloping back to the keep for torches with which to light the watchfires.

Before long, the first fire was blazing, glowing red and sending a great pillar of smoke into the sky. Gerin peered west. His own watchers quickly spotted the warning fire and started another to pass the word into Schild's holding. And, soon enough, another column of smoke rose, this one small and thin in the distance. The Fox nodded somber approval. Either Aripert Aribert's son or another of Schild's vassals—but someone, at any rate—was alert. The Gradi might land again in Schild's holding, but he did not think they would be delighted with their reception.

"We've done something worthwhile there," he said, and both Van and Duren nodded.

Hagop son of Hovan was a man who put Gerin in mind of Widin Simrin's son: a baron who'd taken over his holding as a youngster but who had matured into a good enough overlord for it. He acknowledged the Fox his suzerain, paid him his feudal dues, and sent men to fight on his behalf. Had all Gerin's vassals been so tractable, he would have had an easier time of it by far.

Now, though, he was a man in despair. "Lord prince," he cried as he got down from his chariot, "the Gradi dealt me a heavy blow, and it fell on me all the harder because so many came here to fight the raiders along with you. I never dreamed they could sail up the Niffet and strike my holding." His swarthy, big-nosed face was still haggard with shock.

"I didn't dream of it, either," Gerin answered. "That's the only excuse I can make for not setting up watchfires running east from here. Using oars and sails both, the Gradi outran the news of their coming. I did send out riders to try to warn you and the others upstream. I'm sorry they didn't get there in time."

"So am I," Hagop said bitterly. "They got there half a day after the Gradi did. I give them credit; they fought at my side, and a couple of them were wounded. They're still back at my keep. But the damage is done, lord prince, and we'll be a long time getting over it."

What he meant was, *You are my lord, and your duty is to keep such things from happening to me. You failed me.* That he was too polite to come out and scream what he meant, as so many of Gerin's vassals would have done, made the Fox feel worse, not better.

Gerin said, "They're bad enemies, worse than the Trokmoi and" —he looked around to make sure Geroge and Tharma were out of earshot— "worse than the monsters, too. I have a couple of things I intend to try to see if I can't get the upper hand on them, but it hasn't happened yet. I'm sorry."

Hagop's dour countenance immediately became more confident. "If you think you can overcome them, lord prince, I am sure it will be so in the end."

I wish I were, Gerin thought. Explaining exactly how worried he was, though, struck him as less than wise. The more you seemed to believe in yourself, the more your vassals would believe in you . . . till you let them down. Hagop, luckily, didn't seem to think he'd been let down for good—not yet, anyhow.

Hagop asked, "How long do you intend keeping my vassals under your direct command, lord prince? I tell you true, I would not be sorry to see them back in my holding to stand off the Gradi, should the raiders come again."

"I aim to hold them here through the summer, while we can move against the Gradi," Gerin answered. To his great relief, Hagop accepted that with no more than another frown. If Gerin's leading vassals started pulling *their* vassals out from under him, he wouldn't be able to accomplish anything against the invaders.

In short order, he realized, he wouldn't be prince of the north any more, either. He'd be one petty baron among many, with no more power and no more reach than any of the rest. And the Gradi would eat up the northlands a barony or two at a time, and after a while a new, cold, dismal Gradihome would arise here. Voldar would be very happy, no doubt. So would the Gradi. The Elabonians, even the Trokmoi, would have less reason to rejoice.

"Not that I want to jog your elbow—" Hagop began, an opening almost invariably a lie. So it proved here, for he continued, "—but whatever you're going to set in motion against the Gradi, the gods grant you start it soon. The busier they are answering us, the less chance they'll have to make us answer them."

That was inarguably true. It also marched with Gerin's own thoughts. He said, "I intend to start as soon as I can. I still have some more sorcerous research to undertake before I can begin, though."

As he'd hoped, mentioning magic impressed Hagop. His vassal said, "Lord prince, if you know a spell for turning the lot of those buggers into toads, that would be a great thing."

"So it would," Gerin agreed. He didn't say anything past that. If Hagop wanted to conclude he did have such a spell, that was Hagop's concern. By the awestruck look on Hagop's face, he wanted to conclude just that.

"I hope your spell succeeds," he breathed.

"So do I," the Fox replied. He still hadn't said that the spell was one for the batrachifaction of the Gradi. He always hoped his spells succeeded, and knew such hope was always urgently necessary. Repeatedly finding himself in deep trouble had made him try spells a half-trained, lightly talented wizard had no business undertaking. Here he was in deep trouble again, and about to go into sorcery over his head once more, too.

"How soon can you do the—what did you call it?—the research, that was the word you used?" Hagop asked.

"I have to go through the volumes in my library. It will be a couple of days," Gerin told him. "I don't care for much companionship when I incant, but if you'd like to stay and see the results of the magic, you're more than welcome."

Most of his vassals would have accepted at once. Hagop shook his head. "I thank you, lord prince, but no. I shall go back to my holding after tonight. My people need me there. They need more than me, but I am willing to believe—for now—you need my vassals more. I trust you will use them wisely."

"I hope so." Gerin bowed to Hagop. "I'm lucky to have you for a vassal; your serfs are lucky to have you for a lord."

"They do not think so right now," Hagop answered. "If your research and your spell go as you would have them go, that may yet prove so, though. The gods grant you do it well, and that you do it soon." He plainly meant, *What are you waiting for?*

Gerin went up to the library. He had the feeling Hagop was right—every moment he delayed invited disaster. But if he was going to summon Baivers, to dicker with the god to aid him against the Gradi and Voldar, he wanted to learn everything he could about him before he started.

When you'd worshiped a god all your life, you took him for granted. Gerin poured Baivers a libation whenever he drank ale, as did every other Elabonian in the northlands and down in whatever was left of the Empire of Elabon south of the High Kirs. In return, Baivers made the barley flourish and made it ferment into ale. He was very reliable about that. Beyond it, he wasn't often a pushy god, of the sort who frequently stuck his nose into human affairs.

What the Fox wanted to find out from his scrolls and codices was how to make Baivers pushy, how to make him want to intervene in the northlands. As he began working the handles of a scroll, he shook his head. What he really wanted to find was whether there was any way to make Baivers pushy. If Baivers was resolutely confined to his one power, what point in summoning him?

Baivers was the son of Father Dyaus and a daughter of the earth goddess. Gerin knew that, of course, as he knew most of the other bits and pieces of lore he dug out about the god of barley. But they weren't things he commonly thought about; reading of them was a quicker way to call them to mind than rummaging through his memory, good though that was.

Selatre came in, saw what he was doing, and pulled out another two scrolls and a codex for him. "These talk about the god, too," she said, and then, cautiously, "Have you found anything that will help you?"

"Not as much as I'd like," he said, his voice edgy with discontent. "By most of this, and by most of everything I've seen, once barley turns to ale, Baivers is content." He paced back and forth. "I don't want him content. I want him angry. I want him furious. He's a power of the earth, and Mavrix half told me a power of the earth was my best hope against Voldar and the Gradi gods."

"Is he the right one?" Selatre asked. "Many powers rest in the earth."

"I know. But Mavrix wouldn't have been shy about naming most of them. He despises Baivers. He wouldn't come out and say, 'I failed, but this god I detest might succeed.' He wouldn't *say* it, but I think it's what he meant."

After considering that, Selatre gravely nodded. "Yes, that rings true. Mavrix reminds me of a child who can't admit he isn't always the best at something and, even when it's plain he isn't, won't give the one who really is his due."

"The trouble is, you can't take a god, turn him over your knee, and spank that kind of foolishness out of him." Gerin let out a long, weary sigh. "But oh, Father Dyaus, how I wish you could."

IX

Geroge and Tharma stared fearfully at the interior of the shack where Gerin worked—or tried to work—magic. As he had with his own children and Van's, the Fox had warned them of the dire consequences they would suffer if they ever so much as set a toe inside. The monsters had taken him more seriously than the children had; he'd never had to punish either of them.

"It's all right," he said now, for about the fourth time. "You're here with me, so that's different." Constant repetition eventually eased the monsters' worries. Gerin wondered if it should have. The mischief they might have raised coming in by themselves was as nothing next to the disaster of a spell gone awry.

"What do we need to do?" Geroge asked.

"Well, for starters, you get to drink some ale," Gerin answered. That made both monsters visibly cheerier. Gerin used a knife to cut the pitch sealing the stopper of a fresh jar. He dipped out large jacks for Geroge and Tharma, and half a jack's worth for himself. Normally, he would no sooner have tried magic after drinking ale than he would have tried leaping off the palisade headfirst, but when the god whose aid he sought was also the deity who turned malted barley to ale, what he would normally do took second place to that special concern.

He filled the monsters' jacks after they emptied them, thanking all the gods—Baivers in particular—they didn't grow rowdy or fierce as they took on ale. He sipped at his own jack, too. He wanted to feel the ale ever so slightly, but not so much that it interfered with the passes and chants he would have to make.

Selatre spread seed barley and unthreshed ears of the grain on the worktable in the shack. She stayed sober. If the conjuration went very wrong, she would try to set it right. Gerin did not think that would be the problem. Getting Baivers to respond at all would be the hard part.

"We begin," the Fox said. Selatre stood quiet, watchfully waiting. Geroge and Tharma watched, too, their deep-set eyes wide with wonder as Gerin began to chant, begging the boon of Baivers' presence. He praised the god for barley, not just transformed as ale, but also as porridge and even as bread, though barley flour refused to rise as high as that ground from wheat: *a little hypocrisy in a good cause never hurt anyone*, he thought.

When he began his song in praise of ale, he made sure he set it to the tune of a drinking song he knew Van had taught to Geroge and Tharma. He gestured, and the monsters, quick on the uptake for their kind, began to sing. Their voices were unlovely, but he hoped that would not matter: unlike Mavrix, Baivers was not a snob in such matters.

Once started, the monsters didn't stop singing. That suited Gerin fine. If they didn't attract the god's attention, nothing would. That nothing would, however, remained dismayingly possible. As he generally did when dismayed, the Fox carried on as if success were assured.

He discovered that changing from the chant in the tune of the drinking song to a new one was harder than he'd expected, because having Geroge and Tharma braying out the one tune made him struggle to keep the other. Some of the ancillary spells he was using required quick and difficult passes from the right hand, too. For most wizards, that would have made matters simpler. The left-handed Fox found it a nuisance.

"Come forth!" he cried at last. "Come forth, great Baivers, lord of barley, lord of ale! Come forth, come forth, come forth!"

Nothing happened. He turned away from the barley on the worktable, convinced he had failed. What was the point to trying to summon the Elabonian gods? They might have all gone off on holiday, leaving their portion of the world to look after itself. But now other gods were looking—hungrily—at that portion of the world. Did they know? Did they care? Evidently not.

And then, as he was about to tell—to shout at—Geroge and Tharma to cease their wretched din, the inside of the shack seemed to . . . enlarge. The monsters fell silent, quite of their own accord. "It is the god," Selatre said quietly: she, of all people, recognized the presence of the divine when she felt it.

Gerin bowed very low. "Lord Baivers," he said. "You honor me by hearing my summons."

"You have summoned others before me, not least that wine-bibbing mountebank from Sithonia," Baivers answered. As with Mavrix, Gerin heard the god's voice in his mind, not with his ears. The rustic accent came through anyhow.

"Lord Baivers, who comes first is less important than who comes last, for that says where help was truly found," Gerin said.

"Aye, likely tell," Baivers said, like a sour old farmer who hadn't believed anyone's tales about anything since his wife told him she was going out to gather herbs in the woods and he found her in bed with the village headman. Grudgingly, though, he nodded to the Fox. "Well, I'm here. Say your say."

"Thank you." Gerin knew he sounded more sincere than most people giving thanks. Most people, though, didn't get the chance to thank gods, not in person.

Baivers nodded again. If a god could look like an old farmer, he did. His hair wasn't hair, but ears of ripe barley, a pale yellow. His craggy face was tired and weathered, as if, like the crop whose lord he was, he spent his whole lifetime in the sun and open air. Only when you looked in his eyes, which were the color of fresh new green barley shoots poking up out of the ground after the first rains of spring, did you get the sense of divine vitality still strong under that unprepossessing semblance.

What he looked like, Gerin thought, was a part of the land. That raised hope in the Fox: not only did it hold echoes of what Mavrix had said to him, but it also made him think Baivers truly belonged in the northlands, that the long Elabonian presence here had made him as much a god of this terrain as he was around the City of Elabon, as much a god here as one longer established like Biton.

With that in mind, Gerin asked, "Do you want the Gradi and their gods seizing this land that has been Elabonian for so long, that has given you so much barley and so many libations—so much reverence, not to put too fine a point on it?"

"Do I want that?" Baivers spoke in mild surprise, as if the question had not occurred to him in such a form. "Do I want it? No, I don't want it. The Gradi and their gods feed on blood and oats." He spoke with somber scorn. "Their land is too poor, too cold, their souls too meager, too cold, for my grain."

Geroge and Tharma had stopped singing their hymn when Baivers appeared. They'd stared in awe at the god. Now Geroge burst out, "If you don't want these nasty Gradi around, why haven't you done anything about them and their gods?"

"Why haven't I done anything?" Again, the question seemed to startle Baivers. With some bitterness, Gerin found that unsurprising: the idea of actually doing anything appeared to be one that was alien to the entire Elabonian pantheon. Baivers turned his green, green gaze on Geroge. "A voice from below the roots," he murmured, more to himself than to any of the mortals with him. "There are powers below the roots."

"What are you talking about?" Geroge demanded. "I don't understand what you're saying."

Gerin had often heard that complaint from Dagref. When he and Selatre would talk about adult matters, the oldest child they'd had together would listen, following as far as his own experience let him, and would keep on trying to follow past that point, trying to make his parents slow down and let him know what they meant.

Baivers' murmurs perplexed the Fox, too, but he thought he had some notion of what was in the god's mind. Groping for words, he asked, "Lord Baivers, are the powers below the roots connected to those who make a habit of living down there?" To show what he meant, he pointed to Geroge and Tharma.

"Of course," Baivers answered, once more sounding surprised. "Where there are no folk there are no powers."

"Ah," Gerin said. That answered one question he'd long had: at least in the eyes of the god, the monsters were people. From the day they'd emerged from the caverns below Biton's shrine, Gerin had wondered. He'd phrased his question carefully, to avoid both saying they were and saying they weren't. He found another question: "Will that power—?"

"Those powers," Baivers corrected, sounding finicky and precise.

"Those powers, then. Will they fight for us against the Gradi?"

Still finicky, the god replied, "They will fight. It is why they exist: to fight. Against the Gradi? Who can say for certain. For us?" Those sprout-green eyes swung to Gerin. "Why do you think you and I are 'we'?"

"Why?" Gerin said in some alarm. "You just said you didn't like the Gradi or their gods. If they take the northlands, you get no more libations here, no more worship. I'm only a mortal, lord Baivers, I know that, but as mortals go, I'm strong. If you can help me fend off the Gradi gods, I think I can beat the Gradi themselves."

"Could be so," Baivers said. "Could be nonsense, too. But what I think and what I do, they're not the same. My power is over growing and brewing—you know that. I'm not a god of blood, a god of war."

"But you can fight—I know you can." Gerin came up with one of the bits of lore he'd culled from the scrolls up in his library: "When that demon sent the barley blight, you didn't just fight him and beat him, you made him swallow his own tail and eat himself up."

Selatre silently clapped her hands.

"Well, of course I did," Baivers said. "He was causing my crop all kinds of trouble. He had it coming, he did, and I gave it to him." For a moment, he seemed a formidable deity indeed.

"The Gradi are the same," Gerin insisted. "If they win here, there won't be any barley, because they'll make the northlands too cold for it to grow. Do you want that to happen?"

"Do I want it to happen? Of course I don't want it to happen. It would sadden me," Baivers answered. "But if the grain won't grow, then it won't and that's all there is to it. It's not the same, it's not close to the same, as murdering it in the shoot, the way that demon did. He'll never find his way back to this world, never once."

The distinction Baivers drew was so fine it meant nothing to the Fox, but it plainly did to the god. Gerin kicked at the dirt floor of the shack. He'd feared that, even if Baivers did appear for him, the god would keep on doing what the gods of the Elabonian pantheon did most of the time: nothing. He'd needed an angry Baivers, a furious Baivers, and what he found was a regretful but resigned Baivers, which did him no good.

How to find a furious Baivers? Even as the question formed in his mind, so did an answer. He tried to find another, because he didn't like that one. But nothing else occurred to him. And, when he was about to enrage a god, he didn't think prayer would do him any good.

His laugh was loud and scornful. George and Tharma stared at him. So did Selatre, in dismay: she knew more about gods, or about gods more directly, than Gerin. And so did Baivers. "Don't like your tone, young fellow," he said sharply.

"Why should I care?" Gerin retorted. "I've spilled a lot of ale to you over the years, and what has it got me? Not bloody much, that's plain. I should have paid more heed to Mavrix. He has a long memory for foes, but he has a long memory for friends, too, and that's more than I can say about you. He was right about what he told me—he certainly was."

"The Sithonian?" Baivers snorted. "The next time he's right'll be the first."

"Oh, no!" Jeering at a god was something of which Gerin would never have dreamt were his need less great. If he overdid it, he was liable to be destroyed by a deity he might have brought to his side. But if he didn't do it, he was all too sure he *would* be destroyed by the Gradi and their gods. And so jeer he did: "Mavrix said you were useless, said you'd always been useless, said you'd always be useless, too. And he's right, looks as if to me."

"Useless? Mavrix talks about useless?" Baivers threw back his head and laughed; his barley hair rustled. "The Sithonian, who can't play the pipes, who manures himself whenever he's in trouble" —that wasn't fair or true, but Gerin had long since noted gods were no more fair and probably less truthful than human beings— "who buggers pretty boys and calls himself a fertility god? He thinks *I'm* useless? I'll show him!"

As the Fox knew, buggering pretty boys was not all Mavrix did to amuse himself. He feared Baivers' tirade would draw the notice of the Sithonian god. He'd wanted Biton and Mavrix together; they'd spurred each other on against the monsters. He didn't want Baivers and Mavrix together, lest they go after each other instead of the Gradi.

But he had to keep Baivers roused. And so he kept on jeering: "You might as well be from the law courts of the City of Elabon, not the fields where the barley grows. All you care about is the detail of the law" —he was being unfair himself; that charge applied more justly to his son Dagref than to Baivers— "if you'd fight that demon but not the Gradi gods. The barley is gone, whether killed in the shoot or never planted. Yes, Mavrix was right—useless is the word."

For a moment, he glanced over to Selatre. Her face was white as milk; she knew, probably better than he, all the different risks he was running. *If I get through this, I'll never traffic with gods again*, he told himself, though he knew that was a lie. If he got through this, he'd have to try to find some way to enlist whatever gods the monsters had against the Gradi. That was likely to make dealing with Baivers seem a stroll on the meadow by comparison.

Then Tharma spoke to the god of barley and brewing:

"Please don't let the barley go away from here. We like your ale."

"Call me useless?" Baivers said to Gerin. "Mavrix said it and so you believe it? I'll show you useless, I will. Powers of the earth, powers under the earth, we're stronger than you think, little man. Loose us against the invaders and—" The Fox had hoped he'd prophesy victory. He didn't, instead finishing, "—and we'll give 'em all the fight in us."

Gerin wished he knew how much that was. Relieved he hadn't been turned into an insect pest or something else small and obnoxious, he dared one more question, no longer mocking: "Lord Baivers, can you bring Father Dyaus into the fight, too?"

Baivers looked astonished, then sad. "I wish I could," he said. "We'd win certain sure then. But Dyaus, he's—gone round to the far side of the hill, you might say, and I don't know what it'd take to call him back."

"You know, lord Baivers—or maybe you don't know, if I don't say it—we Elabonians have the feeling sometimes that all our gods have gone round to the far side of the hill," Gerin said.

"We're pleased enough with the way things are here, or we have been, anyhow," Baivers answered. "When a thing is to your liking, you don't need to meddle with it, and you don't want to, either, for fear you'll make it worse." Gerin nodded at that, for he thought the same way himself. Baivers suddenly grunted, a most ungodlike sound. "Could be that's why Elabonians latch onto Sithonian gods sometimes, I suppose. They're born meddlers, every one of them. And Mavrix worse than the others," he added with a growl.

He was angry, all right. Now Gerin could but hope he would stay angry till the monsters' gods joined the cause—if they joined it. The Fox asked, "Once I go down under Ikos, how will I summon you back to the world?"

"You found a way once," Baivers said. "Likely tell you can find a way twice." And with that, he vanished as abruptly as Mavrix had, but without—Gerin devoutly hoped—leaving any progeny behind.

As they did whenever a god departed, the walls of the

shack seemed to close in around Gerin. He sighed, long and deep, then turned to Geroge and Tharma. "I thank you both. You did very well there."

"You're going down to Ikos," Selatre said: statement, not question. Gerin nodded to her in the same sort of agreement he'd given Baivers not long before. His wife went on, "And you're going to take Geroge and Tharma with you."

After a good many years together with Selatre, the Fox knew how well she thought along with him. "Aye, I am," he said. "I see no other choice. If I'm going to treat with the powers under the ground, I can't think of better intermediaries than the two of them. Can you?"

"No," Selatre answered. "And you're going to take someone else along, too."

"Duren, do you mean?" Gerin said. "That's a good notion. We'll pass through the holding that was Ricolf's and will be his. Might as well let the barons there have another look at him."

"Take Duren if you like, but I didn't mean him," Selatre said. "I meant me."

Dagref and Clotild had at last given up their nightly struggle against sleep. Blestar had drifted off some time before; he fought sleep, too, but had fewer resources than his older sister and brother. Gerin and Selatre generally relished the time when their children were asleep, for it gave them their best chance to make love. Now it gave them the chance to argue without having to explain everything to Dagref as they went along.

Gerin's argument was simple: "I need you here," he said.

"You'll need me more there," Selatre said, almost as if she were still the Sibyl at Ikos. "How will you manage to get down to the underground passage that leads to the monsters' caves? You won't be going down there to ask farseeing Biton any question, which is the only reason for those who aren't priests—or the Sibyl—to enter that passage."

"Carlun hasn't told me the whole treasury is empty," Gerin answered, "so I expect I can bribe my way down there if I can't talk the priests into letting me go.

Eunuchs love gold. Why shouldn't they? It's all they *can* love."

"Yes, I suppose you may be able to talk your way or pay your way down there—if you go by yourself," Selatre said. "But you're going with Geroge and Tharma. Do you think the priests and temple guards will be glad to see monsters after it took a miracle from the god to restore his shrine?"

"All right, the bribe will have to be bigger," Gerin said. He had seldom been wrong in counting on the greed of his fellow man.

But Selatre shook her head. "That won't work," she said positively. "Oh, you may be able to spread enough gold around to let you take the monsters down under the temple. If anyone else were trying, I'd say no, but you've shown you have a gift for such things." She set a hand on his arm to let him know she didn't disapprove. But then she went on, "All right, now you have Geroge and Tharma under the temple. You want to meet the rest of the monsters and their gods. What do you do then?"

"What I have to do," the Fox replied. "I break through the wall—"

"You break through the charms and spells that keep the monsters from breaking through in the other direction," Selatre interrupted.

"Well, yes, I would have to, because . . ." Gerin's voice trailed away. He saw, all too clearly, the point Selatre was making.

She drove it home anyhow: "There isn't enough gold in all the northlands—there isn't enough gold in all the world—to pay the bribes you'd need for the priests to let you do that. You know it as well as I do." Her voice brooked no denial; she understood him too well to believe for an instant that he didn't know it as well as she did.

He used the only weapon he had left: "Why would your being there make the priests see things any different?"

"Because Biton spoke through me," she said. "I'm Sibyl no more, and by my own choice, and glad of it" —she shifted in the bed, getting up on one elbow so she could look at their sleeping children— "but the god has spoken through me, and the priests cannot help but know it. If I tell them this must be done, they are far more likely to listen to me than they are to you."

Gerin mulled that over. "You're very annoying when you make good sense," he said at last.

"Oh? Why is that?" Selatre asked.

"Because it means you're right and I'm wrong, and I'm going to have to change my plans," he told her. "I don't usually have to do that, but I will this time."

"A lot of people won't change their plans even when they're wrong," Selatre said. "I'm glad you're not one of them."

"A lot of people are fools," Gerin said. "If they weren't, how do you think I'd have done as well as I have for as long as I have? Of course" —he took Selatre in his arms— "it doesn't hurt to find other people who aren't fools."

"Who, me?" she said, just before he kissed her.

Gerin looked back over his shoulder as Fox Keep disappeared when the road jogged behind a stand of trees. "I haven't felt so nervous about leaving the place behind since I went south to the City of Elabon," he said. "That's a long time ago now."

Beside him on the seat in the wagon, Selatre nodded. "I didn't think then that I would be the one to replace Biton's Sibyl when at last the god called her to himself. And I certainly never imagined everything that would happen afterward." For a moment, fondly, she let the palm of her hand rest on his leg, a little above the knee.

The wagon was not the only unusual part of the procession of chariots making the journey south along the Elabon Way. In the chariot Duren drove stood Geroge and Tharma, exclaiming at every new thing they saw. Their travels hadn't taken them far from Fox Keep till now. They would be going a good ways now—farther from home than most serfs traveled in all their lives. But for them, this was in a way a return to the very root of their race.

With Gerin driving the wagon and Duren sharing a chariot with the monsters who had been his friends since childhood, Van rode with Raffo Redblade as his driver and Drungo Drago's son his companion in the car. The three of them probably made a fighting team more to be feared than Van, Gerin, and Duren: Raffo was in the prime of life, and Drungo the only warrior among the Fox's followers who came close to Van for strength.

Another dozen chariots rode with those two. That gave Gerin enough of a fighting tail to overawe bandits and make petty barons think twice about trying to end his career prematurely. If Ricolf's former vassals joined together and fell on him, his force would not be enough to withstand them, but he thought Ratkis Bronzecaster would be an ally there. In any case, he had to go through the holding that had belonged to Ricolf, for the path to Ikos branched off the Elabon Way not far south of it.

Selatre enjoyed the unwinding countryside as much as did Geroge and Tharma, and for the same reason. She'd not traveled far from Fox Keep since Gerin and Van saved her from the monsters and brought her there more than a decade earlier. Before then, her only journey had been from the village where she grew up to Ikos to become Biton's voice on earth. Everything she saw seemed fresh and new to her.

"You have no idea how lucky you are, being a man," she told Gerin. "If you want to go somewhere, you up and go, and you don't have to worry about it. How long has it been since I've been farther from the keep than the village close by?"

"I don't know," the Fox answered, "but the reason I leave the keep most often is that unfriendly strangers—or unfriendly neighbors—are trying to take what's mine, and so I have the great privilege of giving them the chance to ventilate my carcass in ways the gods didn't intend. That may be luck, but I'm not nearly sure it's good luck."

Had he said that to Elise, she would have got angry at him. Had Van said it to Fand, she not only would have got angry, she might have tried ventilating the outlander's carcass in ways the gods didn't intend. Selatre said, "I hadn't thought of it that way." A little later, she added, "The balance may be more nearly fair than it seemed when I've stayed behind. Not that it is, mind you—but more nearly."

"I love you," Gerin said, which left her looking puzzled but pleased.

When they camped that night, the ghosts were quieter

than the Fox was used to, although the offering he and his men had given them—the blood of a couple of chickens bought from a roadside village—wasn't much for as many men as they had.

"It was like this when we were bringing your lady from Ikos up to Castle Fox, too," Van said to Gerin. "I remember. She calms the night spirits, that she does."

"That's true," Gerin said. "It was like this then." He scratched his head. On the earlier journey, Selatre was still a maiden, and barely removed from serving as Biton's voice on earth, her only debarment being that the Fox had had to touch her to save her from the monsters unleashed in the earthquake. That was a long time ago now, and four children ago, too, though only three still lived. If Selatre still had the effect on the ghosts that she'd had then, it meant . . . what? That Biton still spoke through her? If he did, he'd given no sign of it, not in all those years. That he still paid attention to her?

When Gerin wondered about that out loud, Selatre shook her head. "If the farseeing one still watched over me, I would know," she said. But then her face clouded—or perhaps it was just a trick of the light, the fires blending with golden Math's nearly round disk, a couple of days from full, pale Nothos' smaller gibbous fragment of a circle east of it, and Elleb's slim young crescent. "I think I would know it."

"When you were Sibyl, could you feel the god's presence?" Gerin asked.

"I took it so much for granted, I never needed to feel it," she answered, and then looked thoughtful. "Am I taking his absence so much for granted now, I'm not feeling it, either?" She laughed. "You've started me wondering."

"We'll find out," the Fox said, and Selatre nodded. She had come along because of how useful she might be at Ikos, and she could be more useful than she'd dreamt if Biton did still pay attention to her and to what she did. Gerin hoped the god was paying attention. As he'd said, he'd find out before long.

The guards at the border between Bevander's holding and the one that had been Ricolf's looked to their weapons when Gerin and his companions bore down on them. Not so long before, they would have had those weapons ready to hand, for years of civil war among Bevander, his three brothers, and his father had wracked the holding north of them. Bevander had won with the Fox's help, and brought quiet to a stretch of land that had known only turmoil for too long.

"Who seeks to enter this holding?" the chief guard called, which kept him from having to worry about whether to name it *the former holding of Ricolf the Red* or *the holding of Duren Gerin's son* or to give it some other name altogether. Gerin approved of playing safe when you had the chance.

He named himself and Duren. That made the guards stir. Before they could say anything, he went on, "We make no claims on this holding now. All we are doing here today is passing through on the way to Ikos."

"But, lord prince," the leader of the guards said, "no one at the castle of—once of—Ricolf the Red will be ready to receive you. We had no word you were planning to come south."

That had not been accidental. "It's all right," the Fox answered easily. "As I said, we're only passing through. No need for anyone to go to any special pains over us." He knew that would fluster the guards more than anything else he could say, but no help for it.

One of the troopers spotted Geroge and Tharma. "Those things!" he exclaimed. "I thought we were rid of those things for good."

The monsters had drawn horrified looks ever since they left the vicinity of Fox Keep, where people were used to them. Gerin had warned them that would happen, in case the reactions of strangers coming to the keep hadn't been warning enough. Now Geroge said, "I am not a thing. Are you a thing?" The guard stared at him. The last thing he'd expect was for Geroge to talk.

Gerin didn't feel like discussing the monsters—or anything else—with the guards. Looking down his nose at their leader, he said, "Do we have your generous permission to pass through?"

They would pass through with or without the border

guard's generous permission, and his face said he knew it. Ignoring Gerin's sardonic tone, he replied, "Aye, pass through in peace, and may you learn what you need at Ikos."

Duren spoke up: "Thank you. Give me your name, for I value good vassalage."

That pulled the guard up straighter. "Young lord, I'm Orbrin Darvan's son, and pleased to make your acquaintance." Now he waved the chariots and wagon through with a flourish.

At Van's order, Raffo steered his chariot up near Gerin's wagon. Van said, "I like that. The vassal barons will have a hard time raising any strife against your son if their men feel the way those guards do."

"You're right," the Fox replied, "and Duren handled him just right, too. I don't think we'll have any trouble on the way south, as a matter of fact—not least because Authari and the other leading vassals won't find out we've been here till we're already gone. What worries me is the trip back from Ikos. They'll have had time by then to ready whatever they aim to try."

"Aye, likely so," the outlander said. "Well, we deal with that when we come to it. Can't do anything else." Gerin could only nod; he'd been thinking the same thing himself.

Seeing the keep of Ricolf the Red, as he did late that afternoon, always made him feel strange, what with all the memories it brought to the surface. Seeing that keep with Selatre by his side felt stranger still. When he'd brought her up from Ikos, Ricolf had seen more between them than he had; he'd put the older man's remarks down to the short temper of a former father-in-law. But now Selatre was his wife of many years, and Ricolf gone from men. Things changed.

He found out how much they had changed when a lookout called the challenge: "Who comes to the castle to be Duren Gerin's son's?"

Gerin had been going to answer that challenge. When he heard how it was framed, he waved to his son instead. Duren said, "Duren Gerin's son comes to his own castle, not yet to live in it, but for a night's shelter."

That brought the drawbridge down in a hurry. The warriors who'd lowered it looked much less happy when they saw Geroge and Tharma in the chariot with Duren, but by then it was too late. Between them, Duren and Gerin managed to convince the soldiers the monsters were, if not harmless, at least unlikely to run wild unless provoked. A good look at their teeth gave an incentive against provoking them.

A lame old fellow name Ricrod Gondal's son was serving as steward for the castle in the absence of a lord in residence. He settled Gerin and his comrades in the great hall and fed them barley porridge, roast duck, and ale. When Gerin poured a libation, he wondered if Baivers would manifest himself in the hall. The god did nothing, though, as Elabonian gods were all too wont to do.

Ghosts crowded the hall for Gerin—not the night spirits, pacified by blood and held at a distance by fire, but ghosts from his own past: Rihwin, drunk and dancing obscenely; Wolfar of the Axe, an Elabonian as savage as any Gradi; Ricolf the Red himself, solid, steady, reliable; and Elise, of whom he still could not think without pangs of regret.

He glanced over to Selatre. She had no ghosts here, and could not sense his. She was the present, the reality, and better than he'd known in days gone by. He understood that. Understanding it, though, did not make his ghosts vanish. They would be with him till he died.

"Lord," Ricrod said, "what brings you back to this keep, your business in the north being unfinished?"

Gerin started to answer, but realized Ricrod had not directed the question at him. The steward had not said *lord prince*, and the Fox was not lord here. Duren was. He replied, "I'm bound for Ikos, with my father and my companions. If the gods are kind, it will help end the business in the north."

The gods Gerin sought under the Sibyl's shrine were unlikely to be kind. The less kind they were, in fact, the more likely they were to be useful to his cause. Ricrod, though, nodded and said, "I hope farseeing Biton gives you an answer you can unriddle fast enough for it to do you some good."

"I hope we can use what we learn, too," Duren said. He had not said a word about Biton. He'd let Ricrod draw his own conclusions, then encouraged him to believe they were right, all without telling a lie as he did it. Gerin was impressed. He couldn't have handled it any more neatly himself.

Selatre had seen the same thing. That night, in the chamber the steward had given them, she said to Gerin, "He'll do well here. He handles himself like a man: more so here, away from Fox Keep, where he's your son first. He's ready to rule."

"Yes, I think so, too," Gerin answered, "and so do . . . some of the vassal barons here. If we win, if Duren comes down here to take up his grandfather's barony, it will feel very strange at Fox Keep, not having him around. I'll have to start training up Dagref, see how he shapes."

Selatre laughed quietly. "It won't be a matter of his not knowing enough to lead men. The question will be whether they want to follow him or to wring his neck."

"That is one of the questions," the Fox agreed, laughing. Then he fell into a thoughtful silence. If Dagref did shape as a leader of men, was Gerin to leave his title to his son by Selatre and have Duren, as baron of one small holding, overshadowed by his younger half brother? Or was he to name Duren his heir in all matters and leave Dagref frustrated and resentful? Either path could lead to war between them.

Best way to solve the problem, Gerin thought, *is not to die*. The gray spreading in his beard warned him that solution, however desirable, wasn't practical—and that didn't consider unfriendly weapons at all. *Plenty of trouble around already*, the Fox reminded himself. *No need to borrow more*. No telling how Dagref would shape. If he couldn't lead and Duren could, nothing Gerin did for him would matter after the Fox was gone.

Selatre stirred on the rather lumpy bed. She'd always cared for Duren as if he were one of her own, and she'd never yet pushed for her children at his expense. But she couldn't be blind to the ties of blood, either. One of these days, she and Gerin would have to hash it out. This was not going to be the day, though. Like Gerin, she recognized that waiting sometimes solved problems better than arguing about them.

"We'll see," Selatre said at last, and then, as if fearing even that might have been too much, she added, "It's not that we don't have plenty of other things to see about first."

"Oh, is that why we're here and on our way to Ikos?" Gerin said. "And all the time I thought we were traveling for the fun of it." Selatre snorted and poked him in the ribs. Before long, lumpy mattress or no, they both fell asleep.

Gerin almost missed the standing stone carved with the winged eye that marked the track leading from the Elabon Way east to the town of Ikos and the shrine of Biton it served. He cursed under his breath; every time he wanted to go to the shrine, he had to worry about getting lost along the way.

As before, the country between the highway and the forest surrounding the valley of Ikos left him dismayed. People would be a long time making up for the devastation first from the earthquake and then the monsters. The survivors who still struggled to make a go of farming were sadly overworked; he would have had more sympathy yet for them had they not been in the habit of sometimes robbing travelers before misfortune had smote. When they saw Geroge and Tharma, they fled for the shelter of the woods by their fields. They knew all they cared to of monsters.

One of the things Gerin had not thought about was how the enchanted forest around Ikos would react to the presence of the monsters. The Fox rarely missed important details, which made his discomfiture when he did all the more acute. Geroge and Tharma stared about with interest when, along with Gerin and Selatre and their companions, they plunged into the cool greenness of the track through that forest and under the leafy canopies of its trees.

The forest seemed to stare, too, and then to exclaim in outrage. Ten years before, the monsters must have worked outrages untold under those trees. And the trees seemed to remember, as did all the other strange creatures living in the forest, creatures a traveler who stayed on the path never saw but whose presence he often sensed, like a prickling at the back of his neck. Gerin felt more than a prickling now. He felt as if the whole forest full of all of those mysterious creatures, whatever they were, were about to fall on him and his companions—and that, when they were done, nothing whatever would be left to show he'd been rash enough to come this way.

Beside him, Selatre quivered. He wondered what she was feeling. Before he could ask—saying anything, here and now, took a distinct effort of will—she spoke, and loudly: "By farseeing Biton, I swear we all" —she stressed the last word— "come in peace, meaning no harm to this wood or to any in it."

Her words were not swallowed among the thick gray-brown boles of the trees, as others had been before them. Instead, they seemed to echo and reecho, somehow spreading farther from the path than they had any natural business doing. After that, the feeling of menace vanished, far more suddenly than it had grown.

"Thank you for winning the argument about whether you should come," Gerin said.

Selatre seemed as pleased and surprised as he was. "That worked—very well, didn't it?" she said in a small voice. Unlike the words of her oath, the reply did not ripple outward from the wagon.

When the Fox and his companions emerged from the strange and ancient wood, Geroge and Tharma both sighed with relief. "I didn't like that place," Geroge said, "not after the first little bit. It made me feel all funny inside."

"That place makes everyone feel funny inside," Gerin said. Then he glanced over to Selatre. "Almost everyone."

"And you wonder why Dagref has a way of pitching a fit if everything isn't exactly right," she said. The Fox maintained a dignified silence, knowing any other response would only leave him vulnerable to more truths from his wife. But Selatre was looking down into the valley of Ikos from the high ground on which they had paused. "The shrine, I see, looks as it always did—the god promised it would, so of course it must—but how sad and shrunken the town seems."

"I thought that when I came here to ask you what had become of Duren, all these years ago," Gerin answered. "Ikos started to wither when it couldn't draw questioners from south of the High Kirs. The earthquake and the fires it started made things worse, though; I wouldn't argue with that."

As they had earlier in the year, the innkeepers of Ikos greeted Gerin and his comrades with joy pure and unalloyed, save perhaps by greed. When it seemed as if that greed were about to keep their rates altogether extortionate, Van scowled at them and said, "We could just camp out in the open. We've got hard bread and smoked sausage, and in the god's valley fires should be enough to hold the ghosts at bay." Reason suddenly reentered the conversation, and Gerin got his men settled and horses stabled for about what he'd expected to pay, or perhaps even a bit less.

"So strange," Selatre said, over and over. "When you come back to a place you knew well, you expect it to be as it was when you left it. Seeing Ikos like this . . ." She shook her head.

A temple guardsman, a grizzled veteran, sat drinking ale in the taproom of the inn Gerin had chosen for himself and Selatre, and for Duren and Van, Geroge and Tharma. When the fellow saw the monsters, he coughed and choked and grabbed for his sword. Gerin had just managed to calm him down when he took a longer look at Selatre. Instead of choking again, he went white. "Lady," he blurted, "you're dead! Farseeing Biton has a new voice now."

"Farseeing Biton has a new voice," Selatre agreed. "As for the other, Clell, I thought you were dead, too, and glad I am to be wrong."

"Some few of us did live," Clell answered. "When we saw how many monsters came boiling up out from under the shrine, we went up into the woods, and skulked there like bandits, you might say, till the day all the monsters disappeared. Almost all the monsters," he amended, casting a dubious eye toward Geroge and Tharma.

"You went up into *those* woods?" Gerin pointed back at the haunted forest through which he'd just passed. He leaned forward, intense curiosity on his face. "You couldn't have stayed on—you couldn't have stayed near—the road that runs through them. What is it like, in there away from the road?"

"It's not *like* anything." The temple guard shivered. His eyes went wide and faraway. "I never would have done it—none of us would have done it—if it hadn't been a choice between that and the monsters. We lived, most of us, so I guess we did right, but . . ." His voice trailed off.

Gerin would have probed harder at him, but Selatre had another question: "Did you chance to see the temple restored when Biton worked his miracle and undid the damage from the earthquake?"

"Lady, I did," Clell replied, and his eyes went wider yet. "I was at the edge of the wood, hunting a—well, one of the creatures that dwells in it: a bird, you might say, for lack of a better word. As I drew my bow to shoot at it, it fluttered away. I glanced down, sadly, toward the ruins of the great shrine—"

"I never saw that, for which I thank the farseeing god," Selatre broke in. "When the earthquake hit, I was in a faint after the last oracle he gave me."

"I remember, lady." Clell paused to drink ale. "But anyhow, there I was, figuring I'd go hungry a while longer, and all of a sudden, the air started to quiver. I was afraid it was another earthquake, or the start of one, even though the ground wasn't shaking. And I looked down at the wreck of what had been the temple, and it was quivering, too. It was like it was coming alive. And then, in the blink of an eye, it was back, exactly the way it had been before. The monsters were gone, too, though we needed longer to be sure of that. But I haven't seen one since, till now."

"I'd have paid gold—a lot of gold—to see that with my own eyes," Gerin said. But, since he'd caused Biton to help Mavrix get rid of the monsters and the god had rebuilt the temple in that same sequence of events, he supposed he was entitled to some small part of the credit for it.

Clell said, "Most amazing thing I've seen in all my born days . . . except maybe some of the creatures and trees in the woods. I wondered if I dared try killing them, but when your belly drives you, you take the chance. And some were good eating, and some weren't, but I managed not to starve to death till farseeing Biton stretched out his hand."

"Good," Gerin said. "I'm as surprised—and as glad—as my wife to learn any of the old guards lived after the monsters came up from under the shrine."

"As your—wife, lord prince?" Clell stared, first at Gerin, then at Selatre. "We had heard somewhat of this—at Ikos, we hear a deal of news, though not so much as in the old days—but hearing and crediting are two different things. When you think what the god requires of his Sibyls—"

"I am Sibyl no more, as you must know," Selatre told him. "And I am now mother of three living children, all begot in the regular way. And it is by my choice; Biton would have taken me back when he restored the shrine, but I asked him if I might stay where I was, and he allowed it."

"Not all this news ever reached Ikos," Clell said, and Gerin believed him, for Selatre seldom spoke of what had passed between her and Biton after the monsters were banished back to their gloomy underground haunts. The guardsman took another pull at his ale, then said, "If my asking does not offend, what question will you put to the farseeing god when you go below the shrine to meet his Sibyl? The Sibyl he has now, I should say."

"We're not here to ask farseeing Biton anything," Gerin replied. Clell was no priest, but was a servant of Biton's all the same. Gauging his reactions would give the Fox an idea of how the priests would respond. "We're here to treat with whatever gods or powers the monsters reverence. The monsters aren't gone, you know—they're just back where they were before the earthquake."

"You're joking," Clell said. Gerin and Selatre both shook their heads. The guardsman delivered another snap judgment: "You're mad."

"We don't think so," Selatre said.

She who had been the Sibyl at Ikos spoke with a certainty close to that which she had used when Biton spoke through her. Gerin had noted that several times since he'd decided to come here and to bring her with him. He did not know what it meant. He did not know for certain it meant anything. He did not even know whether to be awed or frightened or both at once.

Selatre's tone inspired respect in Clell, but no agreement. "They'll never let you do that," he said, sounding very certain himself. "They have the monsters walled and warded off so they can never break free again, and if you think I'm sorry about that, you're bloody daft."

"The wards are to keep the monsters from getting out," Gerin countered. "They aren't intended to stop anyone from going in to them."

"Of course they aren't," Clell said. "Nobody in his right mind would want to do such an idiot thing. Why d'you want to do such an idiot thing, anyhow?"

"Because Baivers lord of barley has told me their gods, with him, offer the northlands the best hope against the Gradi and their gods," the Fox answered. "I don't know whether that best hope is a good one, but I have to find out."

He wondered whether Clell had even heard of the Gradi incursion. As the guard had said, Ikos wasn't the center for news it had been in years gone by. Clell did turn out to know; he said, "If that's true, lord prince, it may change things, but I wouldn't bet anything I didn't care to lose on it."

"I'm betting everything I have on it," Gerin answered: "my holding, my family, my life. The way things are now, I don't think I have any other choice. Do you?"

Clell didn't answer, not directly. What he did say was, "You poor bastard." After a moment's reflection, Gerin decided that fit the situation well enough.

Van rode with Gerin and Selatre in the wagon as they approached Biton's shrine. Beside them came Duren, Geroge, and Tharma in the chariot Gerin's son drove. The rest of the warriors stayed back in the town of Ikos. Gerin had not brought enough men to fight his way into the temple precinct. If Biton opposed him, he did not think he could have brought enough men to fight his way into the temple precinct.

"It all looks just as I remember it," Selatre said, "but then it would, wouldn't it? I thank the farseeing god for not letting me see it all tumbled into ruin."

No one else waited ahead of them to hear what the Sibyl would say. Selatre was used to that, her term as Biton's voice having begun after the Empire of Elabon blocked the last remaining pass through the High Kirs into the northlands. To Gerin, it still felt strange, unnatural. He remembered Ikos full to bursting, with folk from all over the Empire—and from beyond it as well—coming to consult the oracle.

The temple guardsmen stared in horror and what looked like a good deal of fear at the two monsters who rode with Duren. But the guards did not attack; Gerin's guess was that word of Geroge and Tharma had already reached them, most likely from Clell but also, perhaps, from the innkeeper who ran the hostel where they'd stayed or from anyone who worked with or for him.

"We do come in peace," the Fox called, holding up his right hand to show it was empty. The two monsters imitated the gesture.

"You had better," said a soldier whose gilded helmet proclaimed him a captain. "You'll be sorry if you don't. If we don't take care of that, the farseeing god will."

Gerin didn't mention that he hadn't come down to the shrine to talk to Biton, but to the powers that dwelt below it. He did say, "I'd like to speak with one of Biton's priests, to talk over what we need to do on our visit."

"All right," the guard captain said. He pointed to Geroge and Tharma. "You want to take them underground, you're going to have to see one of the priests first. Unless you do, it won't happen, and that's flat." He hadn't called the monsters *things*, though, which Gerin took for a better sign than most he'd had lately. One of the guards in a helmet not only ungilded but also unpolished hurried off to find a priest.

He returned a little later with one of Biton's eunuch servants. The plump, beardless priest bowed and said, "You may call me Lamissio. How may I, serving Biton, also serve you?"

The Fox nodded at that; Lamissio made his priorities plain. Gerin also approved of his taking no outward notice of Geroge and Tharma, who, by his bearing, might have been a couple of troopers rather than a couple of monsters.

Thus encouraged, Gerin explained to the priest exactly what he had in mind.

Lamissio heard him out, which raised his hopes further. But then the eunuch shook his head, the soft, flabby flesh of his jowls wobbling as he did so. "This cannot be," he said. "Item: those not affiliated with the temple are not allowed below it, save only to consult with the Sibyl in her subterranean chamber."

"But—" Gerin began.

"I heard you out in full, lord prince," Lamissio said. "Have the courtesy to extend me the same privilege." Challenged so, Gerin had no choice but to bow his head in acquiescence. The eunuch ticked off successive points on his stubby fingers: "Item: creatures of the kind of these two" —he pointed to Geroge and Tharma— "are not permitted within the holy precinct for any reason whatsoever."

"We're no more 'creatures' than you are," Tharma said.

If her speaking surprised Lamissio, he did not show it. "That is true," he said gravely, "but you are no less creatures than I am, either." While Tharma pondered that, Lamissio went on, "Item: any meddling with the wards restraining creatures of the kind of these two is forbidden on pain of death, even were the other two difficulties abated."

By that, Gerin concluded, he meant he might have been bribed into letting the monsters into the temple precinct and even into the underground passages below the shrine, but that he would not let the Fox try to meet with their kin no matter what. "Are you sure you won't be reasonable?" he asked. "The temple would benefit from this—"

"The temple would be endangered," Lamissio countered. "That is unacceptable. We were lucky enough when far-seeing Biton restored the shrine with one miracle; we may not rely on his giving us two."

He had a point. But Gerin had a point of his own: "If we don't treat with the powers that may dwell with the monsters down below Biton's shrine, all the northlands will need a miracle to restore them."

"This grieves me," the eunuch said. "What happens beyond the shrine, though, and especially what happens beyond this valley, is not my concern. I have to look to my own first."

"Look to your own long enough and you'll soon be looking at Gradi swarming out of the woods," Gerin said.

"I doubt that," Lamissio replied with great confidence: confidence that, considering those woods, might well have been justified.

Gerin corrected himself: "Swarming down the path, I should say. And, before too long, swarming up from the south where the woods don't protect you."

"I do not think this likely," Lamissio said. Did he sound smug? Yes, he did, the Fox decided.

"Why not?" Van demanded. "Did they take your brains along with your balls?"

"You will speak to the servant of farseeing Biton with the respect his position deserves," Lamissio said, his voice cold as a winter night in Gradihome.

"I'm not speaking to your position," Van retorted. "I'm speaking to *you*. If you talk like an idiot, I'm going to let you know it."

Lamissio gestured to the temple guards. They hefted their weapons and made as if to surround Gerin and his comrades.

"Stop that." The command came not from the Fox, not from the outlander, but from Selatre. It was not loud, but most authoritative. And the temple guards stopped.

"What is the meaning of this?" Lamissio demanded. "Who are you, woman, to—" He checked himself, looking cautious. "Wait. You are she who was once the voice of Biton on earth."

"That's right," Selatre said, and added, with a certain relish, "I trust you will treat me with the respect my position deserves."

That was probably a mistake. Gerin knew he wouldn't have said it, at any rate. Flicking a priest on his dignity was only likely to make him angry. And, angrily, Lamissio said, "And what position is that, you who have polluted yourself by contact with a whole man?"

"Be careful with your mouth, priest," Gerin warned.

But Selatre held up her hand. "I will tell you what my position is. When Biton remade this shrine after the earthquake cast it down, he purposed restoring me to the Sibyl's throne. That is simple truth. If you like, you may inquire of the Sibyl that is. Through her, the farseeing god will tell you the same. If Biton was satisfied enough to want to retain me as his instrument, though I was then no longer untouched, no longer even maiden, who are you, priest, to question me?"

Lamissio licked his lips. "But you are not Sibyl now," he said: more a question than a contradiction, for it was obvious Selatre intended to permit no contradiction.

"No, I am not Sibyl now," she agreed. "But by my choice I am not Sibyl, not by Biton's, though the farseeing god was generous enough not to force me back into a place I had outgrown."

"If you are not Sibyl, and it is by your own choice, why should we pay you any heed?" the priest asked.

"Because even though I am Sibyl no more, the god spoke truth through me," Selatre answered. "Has the god spoken through you, Lamissio?"

The eunuch priest did not answer. The temple guardsmen muttered among themselves. They made no further move to surround the chariot and wagon. A couple of them, in fact, stepped back toward where they had been.

Gerin said, "Can we talk about this like a couple of reasonable men?"

Only after the words left his mouth did he realize the answer could be something other than *yes, of course.* Himself reasonable to the core, he had come to see over the years how unreasonable so many people were, though their lack of reason struck him as being unreasonable in and of itself. And priests, by the very nature of their calling, were more apt to incline toward what they saw as following their god's dictates than toward thinking out what was best for them to do.

And how am I different? he asked himself while waiting for Lamissio's reply. *Why am I here, if not at the advice of a god, to recruit other gods to oppose still other gods?* But there was a difference; Lamissio not only accepted that Biton was more powerful than he, but made that fact the cornerstone of his being. Gerin accepted the gods' superior strength—he could scarcely have done otherwise—

but did everything he could to exploit their rivalries and blind spots to build as much freedom for himself as he could.

Slowly, Lamissio said, "I shall do this, lord prince, not for your sake—for you are a mere man—but for the sake of the lady to whom you are wed, through whose lips the words of the god once sounded."

"Thank you," the Fox answered, and said no more. The priest's reasons were his own. So long as they gave Gerin what he wanted, or a chance to get what he wanted, he would not make an issue of them.

Selatre accepted Lamissio's acquiescence as no more than her due. She also accepted it without the slightest hint of I-told-you-so aimed at Gerin. The Fox took that for granted till Van whispered behind his hand, "If Fand ever got me out of a scrape like that, d'you think she'd let me forget it? Not bloody likely!"

No doubt the outlander was right. Fand came first with Fand, first, last, and always. Selatre put the good of the principality ahead of her own self-importance without a second thought. *I'm lucky*, Gerin thought, not for the first time.

Hoping to benefit his own cause, he asked Lamissio, "Shall we move the discussion to the forecourt of the temple?" He pointed to the opening in the marble wall surrounding the temple precinct.

But the eunuch priest shook his head. "As I told you, it is not permitted that creatures of their kind" —he pointed once more to Geroge and Tharma— "enter the holy grounds."

"That's foolish," Geroge said. "If what we've heard is true, there are lots of creatures like Tharma and me right under your silly temple. How are you keeping them out? And if you can't keep them out, why fuss over us?"

Lamissio opened his mouth, then shut it again without saying anything. Geroge might not have been reasonable, but a lifetime lived with Gerin had shown him how to reason. For a monster, he was clever; even for a human being, he wouldn't have been stupid. And he had a child's directness to him.

"I had not thought of it like that," the priest admitted,

winning Gerin's respect as he did so. "We do not think—we do not like to think—of the monsters still under Biton's shrine. We have walled them away with bricks and with magic charms, and we have walled them away with forgetfulness, too."

"Letting these two come onto the temple grounds would be a way of remembering, then," Gerin said. "And if it displeases Biton, the god has ways of making that known without going through priests or guards."

The Fox knew that was true; Biton smote with a loathsome and fatal curse those who tried to steal his treasures from within the sacred precinct. Asking Geroge and Tharma to pass inside that marble wall put them in some danger, but Gerin could not believe Biton would reckon them a worse threat to the northlands than the Gradi and their gods.

"You would have made a formidable priest, lord prince," Lamissio said.

"Maybe," Gerin said, though he aimed to profit himself first and the gods only afterwards and as he had to. He also contemplated with something less than eager enthusiasm the mutilation Lamissio had suffered so he could serve Biton and the Sibyl.

Selatre said, "Will you let us—will you let all of us—enter the temple precinct, Lamissio? No one will seek to harm or steal anything inside."

"Very well," the priest said, which made several of the guardsmen give him surprised stares. He went on, "As you say, and as I find impossible to deny, Biton has the power to punish these monsters, should that prove his will."

"Of course he does," Gerin said reassuringly. "He banished them underground, didn't he?" What he said was true. What he didn't say was that banishing the monsters back to haunts in which they'd dwelt for ages was different from destroying a couple of them. If Lamissio couldn't figure that out for himself, that was his lookout.

A couple of temple guards came up to take charge of the wagon and the chariot in which Gerin and his companions had approached the shrine of the farseeing god. Lamissio led Gerin and Selatre, Van and Duren, and

Geroge and Tharma inside the gleaming white wall delimiting the temple precinct.

No hideous blight fell on the two monsters. Gerin breathed a silent sigh of relief at that. Selatre breathed something, too: "All the same. It's all the same." Unlike Gerin and Van, she had no memory of its ever being different.

Like them, and like Duren, too, she had seen the treasures displayed outside the temple. Past a glance to make sure they were the same, too, she concentrated on the business at hand. To Geroge and Tharma, though, the statues of painted marble and of gold and ivory, the bronze pots on golden tripods, the stacked ingots of gold, were all new and marvelous.

"Pretty," Tharma said in a voice halfway between a growl and a croon. For the first time, a couple of the temple guards smiled at her.

Having talked Lamissio into letting the monsters into the temple precinct, Gerin hoped for further success. "The sooner we can go down under the shrine, the sooner we'll be able to start driving the Gradi and their gods out of the northlands," he said, a sentence with enough unexamined assumptions in it to give a Sithonian logician a bad case of dyspepsia.

It made Lamissio dyspeptic, too. "This cannot be," he declared. "I said as much before; were you not listening? We do not allow visitors below the shrine, save on their journey to the Sibyl, and we most of all do not allow the wards holding the monsters at bay to be tampered with, lest those monsters flood out into the world at large, as they did a decade ago."

"Aye, that's a risk," Van rumbled, "but the cursed Gradi are already loose in the world at large. They may not have sharp teeth like Geroge and Tharma here, but I don't want 'em for neighbors."

"I know nothing of the Gradi, and care to learn nothing," the priest replied. "I know the monsters required Biton's personal intervention to be bundled back into their caves once more. And I know the destruction they worked here and in the town and all through this valley, and I will not see its like repeated." As far as he was concerned, the temple, the town of Ikos, and the valley in which they lay might have been the whole world. If they stayed safe, he cared nothing for what happened in the rest of the northlands.

Duren saw that as plainly as Gerin. "Think past the valley!" he told Lamissio. A glance at the eunuch's face told Gerin the plea was in vain. Lamissio's mental horizon had no stretch in it.

What to do, then? The Fox couldn't take Lamissio aside and try to bribe him into cooperation, though he had planned to do just that. The temple guardsmen were obviously as leery as the priest about loosing the monsters once more. And, for all Gerin knew, their fear was liable to be justified. He was far from sure of his own course, despite Baivers' urging. All he knew for certain was that, so long as he could find a blow to strike against the Gradi and Voldar, he would try with everything in him to strike it, and would worry later about what came afterwards.

But he could not storm the temple, not if Biton did not care to permit it. If Lamissio remained inflexible, he was thwarted. And Lamissio could have been no more inflexible had he been carved from basalt like Biton's ancient image in the temple.

Dejected, the Fox turned to go, to try to figure out what other ploys he could find against the Gradi. "Wait," Selatre said suddenly, in a voice not quite her own. Gerin turned toward her. Her eyes were wide and staring, and looked straight through him. When she spoke again, it was in the powerful baritone Gerin had heard before, the voice Biton used in speaking through his Sibyls:

> *"Let the travelers go below*
> *That they may learn what powers show.*
> *The land is wide, the powers deep—*
> *Shall they now a bargain keep?*
> *Through Sibyl past I speak out now*
> *To say to learn this I allow."*

X

When the god abandoned possession of Selatre, she staggered as if stunned. Gerin put an arm around her, steadying her and keeping her from falling. She looked around in surprise. "Did I say something?" she asked. "What did I say?"

"That was the farseeing god," one of the temple guardsmen said, his voice clotted with awe. "No one else—the lord Biton."

"Biton?" Selatre's eyes opened very wide. "Did the lord Biton speak through me?" She seemed to be taking mental stock. "It might be so. I feel the way I did when—after—" She stopped in confusion. "But he couldn't have."

"He did," Gerin said. He let his hand tighten for a moment. "We all heard it." His companions and the guards nodded. He repeated the verses that had come from her mouth, adding, "Not much doubt about what they mean, either."

He was looking straight at Lamissio. Of all those present when the mantic fit hit Selatre, only Biton's priest doubted it was genuine. "How could the farseeing god speak through a vessel he himself discarded?" Lamissio said. "How could he speak through a woman not a maiden?"

But the guard who had first acknowledged that Biton

was speaking through Selatre answered. "Gods make rules, and gods break rules, too. That's what makes them gods. And the prince of the north has the right of it here, too. No way to mistake the meaning of the oracular response."

Not all the response was clear. Gerin saw that, even if no one else did. Biton had given him leave to go down under the shrine and bargain with whatever powers were associated with the monsters. He had not said those powers would keep any bargain once made.

Van took a step toward Lamissio, plainly intending to force his cooperation if he could get it no other way. Gerin started to step away from Selatre to block the outlander. Before he could, Duren did. Their eyes met for a moment. The Fox knew he and his son were seeing the same thing: that if even the guardsmen recognized that Biton had, rules or no rules, filled Selatre for a moment, the priest could not help but give way.

And so it proved. Muttering something ungracious under his breath, Lamissio said, "Very well, it shall be as you say—and pray the farseeing god will permit no disasters to spring from it." Then his dour front tottered and collapsed, as the temple behind him had during the earthquake a decade before. "The god has expanded my notion of the possible," he murmured, which struck Gerin as far from the worst way to phrase it.

Van had let Duren hold him away from Lamissio, but he hadn't been happy about it. Now he growled, "You expand my notion of time wasting. Take us down there, and quit dawdling about it."

"It shall be as you say," Lamissio answered. "In the face of the words of the god I serve, how could it be otherwise? But there shall be one more brief delay." Van growled again, this time dangerously. Lamissio held up a plump hand. "The Sibyl has already taken her place in the chamber below the shrine. I shall send one of my colleagues down there to bring her forth. Should the worst befall and the monsters break loose once more, would you have her trapped in that chamber, with them between her and safety?"

That left Van with nothing to say. His gesture might have meant, *Get on with it*. The priest went into the shrine.

Gerin, meanwhile, turned to the temple guardsmen. "You'd better be ready at the mouth of the underground opening. If we don't come up and the monsters do, your best bet is to try to hold them below ground. If they spread over the land again—" He didn't go on. He didn't need to go on.

Time seemed to crawl by very slowly. How long did a priest need to go down to the Sibyl and come back with her? At last, after what seemed much too long a time, a eunuch came out with the maid who had given Gerin and Duren the oracular response earlier in the year.

She and Selatre stared at each other. Gerin saw the shock of recognition run through both of them as each knew the other for what she was. The Sibyl nodded to Selatre, then let the eunuch lead her away. Lamissio came out of Biton's shrine and beckoned the Fox and his companions forward.

As she walked up to the temple, Selatre said, more to herself than to anyone else, "I never dreamt I would come here. And oh!—I never dreamt the god would speak to me, speak through me, again. Amazing." Her face glowed, as if a lamp had been lighted inside her.

Walking along with her, Gerin quietly worried. She had forsaken the god for him, but now that Biton had returned to her, would she still care about the merely human? The only way to find out was to wait and see. That would not be easy. Any other choice, though, looked worse.

Geroge and Tharma exclaimed in wonder at the magnificent ornamentation within Biton's shrine. Lamissio stood waiting near the black basalt cult statue with the jutting phallus, and near the rift in the ground through which supplicants descended to the Sibyl's cave—or, as now, to a journey and a fate apt to be blacker than any found there.

"I think our usual rituals no longer apply," the eunuch priest said. "We are not going into the depths of the earth to see the Sibyl, nor even to treat with the farseeing god in any way. All we can pray for now is our own safety."

"You don't have to come with us, Lamissio," Gerin said. "You're liable to be safer if you don't, in fact."

But the priest shook his head. "I am in my place. The god has permitted this. I leave my fate with him."

Gerin bowed, honoring his courage. "Come, then," he said.

As he strode toward the rift in the ground opening onto the hidden ways that ran deep underground, he glanced at the cult statue of Biton. For a moment, the eyes scratched into the living rock came alive: the god, he thought, was looking out at him. Then, as they had before on other visits to the shrine, Biton's eyes faded back into the hard, black stone.

Or they faced into the stone for him, at any rate. Selatre murmured, "Thank you, farseeing one," as she drew near the image, and seemed to speak more intimately than she would have to basalt alone.

Lamissio picked up a torch and lighted it at one of those near the entrance to the caves. Then, long robe flapping about his ankles, he walked down the stone steps that led into the cavern. Gerin took a deep breath and followed.

Sunlight vanished quickly, at the first turn of the path. After that, the torch Lamissio carried and those stuck in sconces set into the wall gave the only light. Geroge and Tharma whooped with glee at the way their shadows swooped and fluttered in the moving, flickering light.

"Keep an eye on them," Van muttered to Gerin.

"I am," the Fox answered, also under his breath. Caves and the underground were the monsters' native haunts, or at least the haunts of their kind. If their blood called to them, this was where they were liable to revert to the bloodthirsty ways of which the aboveground world had seen all too much eleven years before. For now, they showed no sign of any such reversion, only fascination with a place whose like they'd never seen.

Some passages in the tunnel that led to the Sibyl's cave were walled off because they held more treasures than Biton's priests displayed outside the shrine. Some were walled off because they held the monsters at bay. Magical wards set before them reinforced brick and mortar.

One of those walls was made of bricks in the shape of loaves of bread, a marker of very ancient brickwork indeed. Actually, the Fox reminded himself, the wall was no older than any other part of the shrine and underground caverns, having been restored by Biton after the earthquake. But, so far as he could tell, the farseeing god's restoration had been as perfect here as elsewhere, so the wall might as well have been—in effect, was—as ancient as it looked.

"Wait," he called to Lamissio, who had gone a few steps down toward the Sibyl's chamber. His voice echoed oddly along the winding corridor. The priest came back. The torch he carried gave the only light, as those in the brackets ahead of the wall and beyond it had burned out. With a deep breath like the one he had drawn when he entered the caverns, Gerin said, "I think this is the place."

"Very well: this is the place," Lamissio said. His round, pale face was far and away the brightest thing visible. "What now?"

"I don't quite know," Gerin answered. Some of the magical wards lay on the stone floor in front of the wall. Others hung from cords or lengths of sinew set into the rock above it. Methodically, the Fox kicked away the ones on the floor and knocked down those hanging in front of the wall.

The wall itself remained, solid and strong despite the oddly shaped bricks. "What now?" Van asked, as Lamissio had. He hefted his spear. The bronze-shod butt would make a fair prybar, but was not really the right tool with which to go knocking down a wall. "Shall we shout up to the guardsmen for some picks?"

"I don't know," Gerin said again.

"I don't think we'll need to do that," Selatre said in a small, strained voice.

Lamissio gasped. The torchlight showed his face even paler than it had been. All at once, Gerin realized they would not have to break down the wall. What waited on the other side knew the wards were down, and was coming to see what had happened, and what it could make of what had happened.

The torch Lamissio held flared and then went out, plunging the corridor into perfect darkness.

Because he was effectively blinded, Gerin was never sure afterwards how much of what followed took place down below Biton's shrine and how much in the peculiar space the gods could travel but mortals most often could not. Wherever the place was, it didn't strike him as pleasant.

He felt himself weighed, measured, tested in the silent black. After what might have been a moment and might have been some much longer time, the monsters' powers—he got the idea more than one of them was communicating with him—inserted a question into his mind. It was a simple question, one he himself might have asked under the same circumstances: "What are you doing here?"

"Seeking aid against the gods of the Gradi," he answered.

Another pause followed. "What are the Gradi? Who are their gods?"

Marshaling his thoughts in the midst of this blackness was hard. It was as if he had trouble remembering what vision meant, how it was used. As best he could, though, he pictured everything he knew not only about the Gradi but also about Voldar and the rest of their gods.

"They are only another band of you dirt-walking things," some of the powers that dwelt in darkness said scornfully. But now the Fox heard other voices, too, these saying, "For dirtwalkers, they seem strong and fierce."

"They are warlike," Gerin said. "They will even kill themselves to keep from being captured."

"Captured? What is captured?" The monsters' powers did not understand that. The monsters did not fight for booty or for slaves. What they were after was prey. When the Fox mentally explained as best he could, they seemed partly amused, partly horrified. The voices in the dark spoke all together now: "These Gradi are right. You kill or you are killed. Otherwise, you do not fight."

"Not everyone up on the surface would agree with you," Gerin said. "Like everything else, enmity has degrees."

"No!" The voices of the unseen powers dinned in his head, shrieking out their denial. They must have dinned in everyone else's head, too, for with his ears rather than his mind he heard Lamissio whimpering in fright. Frightened as he was himself, he could hardly blame Biton's servant.

But he kept up a bold front, saying, "I speak the truth. If I did not speak the truth, I would have slain Geroge and Tharma here when they came into my hands, for their kind was and had been the enemy of my people."

That made the voices divide again. Some of them said, "You should have slain them," while others said, "Good you left them alive." After that division, the voices snarled at one another. Gerin could not understand all or even much of that; he got the idea they were disagreeing among themselves. He hoped they were. Getting help from even some of them would be better than nothing.

Some of the voices seemed to fall silent after a while. Others said, in ragged chorus, "This he and she you have with you, they are a strangeness, not all of our kind, not all of yours. Yes, a strangeness."

"Proving we don't have to be foes, your kind and mine," Gerin said. He didn't know if it proved any such thing. Raising Geroge and Tharma, he'd had every possible advantage on his side. He'd got them as infants; they were clever as monsters went, which let them perform more like human beings than many of their fellows could have done; and there had been no other monsters around to distract them and perhaps lead them away from mankind.

"Why should we join you and your god of dirt-plants against the Gradi things?" the voices demanded.

The answer Gerin had braced himself to give—*to keep yourselves from being overrun*—did not seem good enough to offer here. He stood silent for a dangerously long time, trying to come up with a response that might satisfy these ferocious powers. He felt them gathering around him, ready to snuff out his life as they had snuffed out Lamissio's torch.

And then Van said, "Why? I'll tell you why, you bloodthirsty things! The Gradi and their gods are just about as nasty as you are, that's why. That's what the Fox has been telling you all along, if only you'd listen. Where else are you going to find such good fighting?"

A spell of silence followed. Gerin wondered whether Van should have kept quiet. If the monsters' powers joined forces with the Gradi gods, they could easily wrest control of the northlands from the Elabonians and Trokmoi and their deities. He'd never thought he would reckon the Trokmoi as standing on the side of civilization, but he had new standards of comparison these days.

At last, the voices spoke again: "This is so. Foes worth fighting are a boon worth having. We will bargain for the chance to measure ourselves against them, for the chance to meet them with teeth and claws."

"A bargain," Duren murmured. Gerin was pleased, too, but less than he might have been. It was a bargain, aye, but one Biton had not promised these subterranean powers would keep. The monsters loosed on the northlands once more would be a problem as bad as the Gradi.

But the Gradi were a certainty—they were loose in the northlands now. The monsters were only a possibility. Gerin said, "Very well. Here are the terms of the bargain I propose: we will leave this breach in the wards open until I return to Fox Keep and summon Baivers once more. Then you and he will fight the Gradi gods, doing your best to defeat them."

He waited for the monsters' powers to demand access to the surface in exchange for their help. With the breach in the wards down, they could hardly be deprived of it—not by him, at any rate, although Biton might have something to say in that regard. If the powers dwelling down here were on good terms with him, though, he dared hope the monsters might not prove so vicious as they had on their first eruption from the caves.

None of those sometimes agreeing, sometimes arguing voices said anything about that. Instead, speaking all together, they rumbled, "It is a bargain."

Gerin stared, though in complete darkness that had no point. Maybe Van had had the right of it after all, and the powers here wanted nothing more than a good brawl. Still, with Biton's verses fresh in his memory, he asked, "How shall we seal this bargain, so we know both sides can be sure it is good?"

That brought on more silence, the silence, Gerin judged, of surprise. When the monsters' gods answered, it was again in chorus: "Bargains have only one seal, the seal of blood and bone."

"Now wait a minute," Gerin said in some alarm. If he agreed to that without defining its limits, the underground powers were free to seize and rend him or any and all of his companions.

But he was too late. Somewhere in the darkness close by, a harsh, hoarse scream rang out. "The seal of blood and bone," the powers repeated. "What we agreed, we will do. It is sealed."

"My tooth!" someone groaned: Geroge, the Fox realized after a moment. "They tore out my tooth."

"Blood and bone," the subterranean gods said yet again. "That one is blood of our blood, but he is bone of your bone, for you raised him and his sister. That we take from him is fitting. And while we take, we also give."

Something was pressed into Gerin's hand, which closed around it. All at once, Lamissio's torch began to burn once more. The Fox looked down. He discovered he was holding the last two joints of a hairy, clawed finger, the blood from which stained his own hand. He almost threw the severed digit away with a cry of disgust, but in the end tucked it into a pouch on his belt instead, as security that the underground gods would live up to the bargain they had made.

That done, he went to see Geroge, who had both hands clutched to his muzzle. The monster's blood ran between his fingers and dripped to the floor. "Let me look at you," Gerin told him, and gently separated Geroge's hands. "Come on, open your mouth."

Moaning, Geroge obeyed. Sure enough, only a bloody socket showed where his right top fang had been. "It hurts," he said—almost unintelligibly, because he kept his mouth wide open all the time so the Fox could see.

"I'm sure it does," Gerin said, patting him on the shoulder. "When we get back to the inn, you can have all the ale you like. That will help dull the pain. And after we get back to Fox Keep and you're healed, I'll get you a new fang, all of gold, and have it fixed with wires to the teeth on either side. It won't be as good as the one you gave to the gods here, but it should be better than nothing."

"A gold tooth?" Tharma said, plainly trying to picture that in her mind. She nodded approval. "You'll look fine with a gold tooth, Geroge. You'll look splendid."

"Do you think so?" he asked. He was trying to adjust to the idea, too. Suddenly, absurdly, he began to preen. "Well, maybe I will."

Gerin turned to Lamissio. "Take us up now. We're done here." He pointed to the magical wards he'd disturbed. "And leave those down. You may be able to trap the monsters' gods down below if you restore them, but I know the northlands will have bad luck if you do, and I don't think the shrine and the valley would long be better for it, either."

"Lord prince, there I think you have nothing but reason," the eunuch priest answered. "It shall be as you say, I promise. And now, again as you say, let us return to the realm of light." He propelled his bulky frame up the path at a better pace than the Fox had thought he had in him.

Temple guards crowded Biton's shrine. They peered down anxiously into the rift in the earth leading down into the caves. When Lamissio called to them, their exclamations of relief were loud and voluble. "No monsters at your heels?" the captain in the gilded helm asked.

"Only the two who accompanied us," the priest replied. "The underground gods tore a tooth from one, which he bore bravely." It was, so far as Gerin could remember, the first good thing he'd had to say about Geroge and Tharma.

"Let us by, if you please," Gerin said, and the guards did step aside, though they kept watching the cave's mouth as if fearing surprise attack. The Fox did not suppose he could blame them for that.

More guards—and a bewildered suppliant—crowded the precinct outside the shrine itself. Lamissio asked, "Lord prince, with the wards down, do you think it safe for the Sibyl to return to her chamber and deliver the words of the god to those who come seeking them?"

Gerin shrugged. "Ask Biton. If he doesn't know, what point in worshipping him?"

"A point," Lamissio said. "A distinct point." He stopped at the entranceway set into the white marble fence around the temple precinct. "One of the more . . . unusual mornings in my years of service to the god."

" 'Unusual.' That's a word as good as any, and better than most. I do thank you for your help there," Gerin said, politely failing to mention that Lamissio had needed to have his god order him to help before he got moving and did it.

On the way back to the village, Selatre said, "Biton spoke through me again—he spoke through me." She said it several times, as if trying to convince herself. Gerin kept quiet. If Biton had spoken through her once now, would he do it again . . . and again? If he did, would Selatre decide she preferred him to the Fox? And if she did that, what could he do about it? Nothing, as he knew perfectly well. If you fought a god straight out, you lost.

Why are you worrying? he asked himself, but here, for once, he knew the answer. *When a woman you've loved runs off with a horseleech, you're less inclined to take the world on trust than you used to be.*

Alongside having Biton speak through her, Selatre had a gift for fathoming Gerin's silences. After a while, she said, "You don't need to fear for me on account of Biton. I know where I want to be, and why," and set a hand on his arm. He set his own hand on hers for a moment, then walked on.

When he and his companions got back into the town of Ikos, the warriors he'd brought with him crowded round, wanting to know every detail of their visit to the Sibyl's shrine. They made much of Geroge and the courage with which he bore the loss of his fang. "Wouldn't want one of my teeth yanked out like that," Drungo Drago's son declared, "and they aren't near as big as yours."

As Gerin had promised, he let the monster have all the ale he could drink. Geroge grew boisterous in a friendly sort of way, made hideous attempts at singing, and eventually fell asleep at the table. Van and Drungo, who had also both had a good deal of ale, carried him upstairs to bed.

When Gerin and Selatre went up to their own chambers a little later, she barred the door, something he usually did. Then, quickly and with obvious determination, she got out of her clothes. "Come to bed," she said, and come to bed he did. Most times, making love solved nothing; it just meant you didn't think about things for a while. Drifting toward sleep afterwards, Gerin was glad to have found an exception to the rule.

✧ ✧ ✧

The Fox and his comrades entered with imperfect enthusiasm the holding that had belonged to Ricolf. Gerin would have been happiest scooting through that holding, seeing no one, and getting back to lands where he was suzerain. As he had discovered a good many times in life—Selatre being the splendid exception—what made him happiest was not commonly what he got.

A good-sized force of chariotry, quite a bit larger than his own, waited for him not far south of Ricolf's keep. At its head was Authari Broken-Tooth. Gerin nodded, unsurprised. "We have no quarrel with you and yours, Authari," he called when he recognized the baron who had been Ricolf's leading vassal. "Get out of our way and let us pass."

"I think not," Authari answered.

"Don't be foolish," the Fox told him. "Remember the oath you and your fellow barons swore."

"Like chicken or fish, oaths go stale quickly," Authari said.

What with the indolence of the Elabonian gods, Authari had a point, however much Gerin wished he didn't. But the Elabonian gods weren't the only ones loose in the land these days. Gerin pointed to the west, where thick gray clouds, nothing like those usually seen in summer, were building up. He feared Stribog had at last recovered from what Mavrix had done to him. "If you get rid of me, the only ones who will thank you are the Gradi and their gods."

"I'll take that chance, too," Authari said easily. "With you out of the way, I can afford to worry about them next."

"No," Duren said, not to that last comment, but to everything Authari had said: one comprehensive word of rejection. "Even if your men win a fight here, you will not follow my grandfather as baron to this holding."

"Oh? Why is that, pup?" Authari asked, still with mild amusement.

"Because all the men here will make straight for *your* car, Authari," Duren answered. "Your men may win, as I say, but you will not live to enjoy it."

The mild smile slipped from Authari's face. He did not have enough warriors with him to make it certain that

Gerin's men could not live up to the threat. He could not hang back from the fighting, either, not unless he wanted his own soldiers to turn on him as soon as it was over.

"Stand aside and let us go," Gerin told him. At the same time, he sent his son an admiring glance. He couldn't have come up with—and hadn't come up with—a better way to throw Authari off-balance.

Off-balance the baron certainly was. Had he ordered a hard charge the moment he spotted Gerin's little force, he could have crushed them before they'd hit on that way of fighting back. But he'd hesitated, as he had the earlier time when the Fox and Duren entered his territory. Now he licked his lips, trying to make a choice that would have come naturally to a more ruthless man.

Van pointed to the west, too, but not to the building clouds. "Whose friends are those, I wonder?" he said: chariots were heading cross-country toward the Elabon Way, and toward the brewing trouble on it.

"Wacho has his holding in that direction," Gerin said. "So does Ratkis Bronzecaster, I think." He smiled over at Authari. "Isn't that interesting?"

Authari didn't answer. He didn't smile, either. He set his jaw and looked grim—but, again, not grim enough to order combat before the newcomers, whoever they were, arrived. If they were Wacho's men, he'd roll over Gerin's small band all the more easily. If they weren't . . .

They weren't. Heading up enough chariots to counterbalance Authari's force, Ratkis approached the standoff. He waved to Gerin. "I didn't hear from Ricrod you'd passed through till day before yesterday," he said. "I thought it would be good to see you on your way back."

"I think it's good to see you," Gerin said. He smiled again at Authari. "Don't you think it's good to see him, too?"

"I can think of people I'd rather have seen," Authari growled. He clapped his driver on the shoulder. The fellow flicked the reins. The horses strode a couple of paces forward. Gerin grabbed for his bow. Then the driver swung the team into a turn. They started rolling away. Authari shouted angrily to his men. They followed.

"Hello, there," Gerin said to Ratkis. "If you'd turned out to be Wacho, I'd have been very embarrassed."

Ratkis shook his head. "I doubt it, lord prince. Hard to embarrass a dead man."

"A point. A distinct point," Gerin said, as Lamissio had earlier. He looked westward, wondering if he would see Wacho and his warriors riding up—*like Wacho to be late*, he thought. No new army was coming. But the clouds piled there were getting thicker and darker and spreading over more of the sky. That probably did mean Stribog was feeling chipper again, and probably also meant the Gradi and their gods were ready for another push against the Trokmoi and the Elabonians.

Ratkis said, "An oath is an oath. Once you've sworn it, you can't go forgetting it." He held up a hand. "No, I take that back. You can, but you'd better not. The gods don't like it."

He had more faith in the gods than Gerin did, which probably meant he had less knowledge about their present condition. The more fervent believers the Elabonian gods had, the likelier they were to take a more active part in the world. A year earlier, Gerin would have thought that a disaster. At the moment, it looked distinctly attractive.

Ratkis said, "Shall we ride with you a little ways?"

"I wouldn't mind that," Gerin allowed. Together, the two groups passed by the keep that had been Ricolf's without stopping. Not fully trusting Ricrod any more, Gerin preferred to shelter in a peasant village for the night.

The sun was sinking into that thick bank of building clouds when the Fox spotted a fair-sized force of chariotry approaching the Elabon Way from the east. Whoever was leading that force—Hildic was a good bet, he thought—saw the size of his contingent, too, and turned around and rode back in the direction from which he'd come.

"Another scavenger out to see what dead meat he could find," Ratkis remarked, and leaned out over the rail of his chariot to spit down onto the paving stone of the Elabon Way.

"You're probably right," Gerin said. "No, you're certainly right. We've gone past Wacho's keep, and he doesn't live east of the road, anyhow. Besides, I didn't get the idea that Wacho picked up news in a hurry, or was likely to figure out what to do about it if he did hear something."

"Right on both counts, lord prince," Ratkis said with a chuckle. He rode on in silence for a little while, then asked, "Why are you watching me out of the corner of your eye?"

Gerin's cheeks heated. "You weren't supposed to notice," he muttered. That wasn't answer enough, though, and he knew it. He sighed. "You have more men here than I do, Ratkis. I want to make sure you're not going to try to get me all cozy and then jump on me like a starving longtooth."

"I thought that was it," Ratkis answered. "But, like I said, I swore an oath to your son, so you've got nothing to worry about there."

"Duren will be lucky to have you for a vassal," Gerin said. He did not tell Ricolf's former vassal that he always worried, whether he seemed to need to or not. If Ratkis got to know him better, he'd find that out for himself.

Here, though, for once, he did not need to worry. By the time they made camp, he was close to lands that recognized his suzerainty. And all Ratkis' men did that night was drink ale along with his and leer at the good-looking young women of the peasant village where they lay over. After fear going down below the shrine at Ikos to call on the underground powers, after more fear on the road earlier in the day, with still more fear ahead, the Fox treasured that small stretch of peace of mind. He wondered when—or if—he would find another.

Cold rain drummed down on the canvas cover of the wagon and soaked Gerin as he drove up to Fox Keep. The wind out of the west had a bite. It wasn't the blizzard Stribog and the other Gradi gods had blown up against the army he and Adiatunnus led against them, but it didn't feel like an ordinary summer storm, either. He scowled. Some rain now was fine, normal. Too much rain and he'd have a disaster on his hands even if the Gradi stayed at home.

He and his comrades had to come close to the keep and shout up to the men on the walls so those warriors could recognize their voices before the drawbridge came down with a wet, squelching slap. "Welcome back, lord prince," Rihwin the Fox called as Gerin came in. "Sorry we were so slow, but we couldn't be sure you weren't Gradi trying a sneak in the rain."

"I'm not angry," Gerin said. "The opposite, in fact." Any small bits of caution Rihwin showed were to be encouraged, nurtured, praised, in the hope they would grow. The longer Gerin knew Rihwin, the less likely that was: he knew as much, but had never been a man to give up easily.

"What luck had you, lord prince?" Rihwin asked.

"Geroge and Tharma's kind have gods," Gerin answered, which produced startled exclamations from several men who heard him. "They say they'll fight alongside Baivers and us. We'll know more tomorrow."

"Why tomorrow?" Rihwin said.

"Because that's when I intend to get magicking again," Gerin said. Rihwin gaped at him. He ignored that, continuing, "I'd do it today, but after we get the horses stabled, I'm going to have to spend the rest of the day readying what I'll need and studying the spells I intend to try." Rihwin was still gaping. Gerin condescended to notice him: "Aye, Rihwin, for once I'm as headlong as you. This storm tells me we have no time to waste. It's too much like what we saw west of the Venien. The Gradi are all too likely to use it as a cloak to hide whatever they intend to do till they're set to do it."

"Whatever you say, lord prince," Rihwin assured him, though his fellow Fox still looked somewhat dazed. Gerin had no time to worry about that, either. He jumped down from the wagon, then had to grab at it when he slipped in the mud. Once his own footing was secure, he handed Selatre down.

Their children came running out of the keep to greet them. Gerin hugged Dagref, Clotild, and Blestar in turn. So did Selatre, but then she said, "Now get back indoors this instant, before you catch cold." That led to noisy protests from all three children, and what looked suspiciously like deliberate falls in the mud by Dagref and Blestar. Dagref declared his innocence before the world when Selatre shouted at him; Blestar, as yet unpracticed in deceit, merely got up and ran, dripping, into the castle.

Shaking his head, Gerin went into the castle, too. He'd been wet for a good long while already, and enjoyed changing into a dry tunic and trousers. He knew the spell that had brought Baivers to him, but reviewed it in the library all the same. A mistake might mean the god's failure to appear, which might mean the northlands' going under.

Selatre poked her head into the library, saw him busy, and slipped away. When she came back, she set sausage, bread, and a jack of ale at his elbow. He'd eaten the food and almost emptied the jack before he noticed they were there and thought back on how they'd arrived. When he studied, he studied hard.

As far as Baivers was concerned, he was ready. Bringing forth the monsters' gods was a different business altogether. He had no invocation specifically intended to do that; whatever dealings with those powers mankind had had till now were designed to keep them under control and far away, not to bring them forth. Considering his meeting with them, he understood that down to the ground—and down under it, too.

Desperation, though, drove him to turn the usual way of doing things on its head. He got parchment and quill and ink and began adapting the spells of repulsion into ones that would draw the monsters. The spells he was crafting had not been refined by trial and error—others' error, corrected by mages who had observed . . . and survived . . . their colleagues' failure. That increased his risk in another way, and he knew it: if his own creations had flaws, the only way he would find out about it was the hardest way possible.

He looked up at the timbers of the ceiling. "If I had a choice, I wouldn't be doing this," he told them. They didn't answer. He suspected that was because they already knew.

Along with Selatre and Duren, Van, and Geroge and Tharma, Gerin squelched through the mud of the courtyard toward the shack that doubled as his sorcerous laboratory. Cold rain still fell, stubbornly, steadily, out of a leaden sky, as if it had looked around, decided it liked the country, and settled in to stay.

Gerin patted his chest. He was carrying inside his undertunic the spells he'd written, to make sure—or as sure as he could—the rain didn't land on them and soak them into illegibility. The roof of the shack leaked. Normally, he didn't worry about such things. Today, they were liable to matter.

He'd been out there before, getting everything ready for the conjurations he would attempt: barley, ale, and porridge for summoning Baivers, and other things for summoning the monsters' gods. One of the other things, a billy goat, bleated as he and his comrades came in. He'd tied it to a post, with a rope so short it couldn't chew itself free. Its gaze was fixed on the barley on the worktable, which it could see and smell but could not reach.

"Sorry, old fellow," he told the goat. It bleated again, indignantly. He ignored it, pouring ale for himself and for Geroge and Tharma. After they'd drunk it, he got to work summoning Baivers. "Come forth!" he called when the spell was done. "Come forth, lord Baivers, come forth, come forth, come forth!"

For a moment, he wondered if he would have the same difficulty making the god notice him as he'd known the time before. But then the shack seemed to get bigger inside without enlarging on the outside: the sure mark of a god's presence. "I am here," Baivers said, and the stalks of barley that did duty for his hair rustled softly. His green, green eyes took in the interior of the shack. They rested on the billy goat: none too kindly, Gerin thought, for a goat could wreak havoc in the fields. "You have all in readiness to summon the other powers, the powers from under the ground?"

"Lord Baivers, I hope I do," Gerin answered, a statement true on several different levels.

"Begin, then," Baivers said. "We have little time to lose. The Gradi gods are reaching out, greedy as grasshoppers. Can you feel them?"

"Yes," Gerin said. He reached under his tunic and drew out the spells he had hastily devised. He started to shield the parchment from drips from the roof with his hand, then realized it hadn't leaked since Baivers came forth: an unexpected advantage of the god's presence.

Now he wished he'd drunk no ale. A slip in the spells summoning Baivers might well not have been fatal. A slip in the spells he was trying now surely would be. Geroge and Tharma watched him, their deep-set eyes wide, as he incanted. What were they thinking? They'd said little on the way up from Ikos by which he could judge how they'd taken their first meeting with the gods who ruled their own kind.

He shook his head, though the motion had nothing to do with the magic he was working. Even the monsters' gods had said Geroge and Tharma were neither fully of their kind nor of mankind. He wondered how those gods would have responded to his overtures had he slain the two monsters as cubs, as he'd been sorely tempted to do. He was glad he didn't have to find out.

Maybe that relief helped steady him. Whatever the reason, he managed to get through the chants and intricate passes of the spells unscathed. Nothing in those hastily adapted chants had either loosed the monsters' gods on the northlands or provoked them to eat them up. He reckoned that a triumph. The powers, though, still remained unsummoned.

"Let the blood bring them hither," he said, at the same time thinking, *Now we find out what sort of fool I am, meddling with things beyond my power*. He knelt beside the billy goat. Up till his last trip out to the shack, he'd intended to slit its throat with a bronze knife. Since then, he'd had what he hoped was a better idea. From a pouch on his belt, he drew the severed finger of the monster the powers had given him in exchange for taking Geroge's fang. The finger had not decayed to any discernible extent, which made him think some power still lingered in it.

He used the claw to tear the goat's flesh. Though it did not feel unusually sharp to him, it might have been the keenest dagger he'd ever handled. Blood fountained from the goat's throat and drowned the animal's terrified, anguished bleat. "Let the blood bring them hither!" Gerin cried again, as it made a great red steaming pool that slowly began to sink into the ground.

The interior of the shack seemed to . . . expand again. For a moment, it seemed to go dark, too. Gerin wondered if the monsters' gods could stand the light of day. But then that light returned, and for the first time he saw the gods he had summoned.

As mankind's gods mostly partook of and modified the

manlike shape, so the monsters' powers resembled the mortal creatures whose patrons they were. They too modified the basic pattern. One of them glowed. One had eyes bigger and rounder than an owl's, another great, batlike ears. One seemed nothing but muscle and fur and fangs and talons: if he didn't do duty as a war god, the Fox would have been mightily surprised.

"Blood brings us," they said all together, their voices dinning in his mind. "We have kept the bargain. Now it is for you to keep it as well. Show us the way to battle and slaughter."

"I'll do that," Gerin told them. Fighting *was* all they wanted, he realized; had he set them against Biton or against the Elabonian gods, they would have entered that fray with as much ferocity as this one. He shivered. If this fight should be won, he'd do what he could either to restore those wards under Biton's shrine or to form some arrangement between the monsters' gods and those who lived on the surface of the earth.

This is the way to the Gradi gods: he cast his thought toward Baivers. As Mavrix had, the Elabonian god picked up his mind and carried it along with his own over a plane of being no mortal could reach without divine aid. From his place as a small cyst on Baivers' vaster consciousness, the Fox sensed the underground powers following where the god of ale and barley led.

The route felt different this time: no sea of wine, no equally turbulent sea of sensuality. Gerin wondered if he was perceiving the same "places" through a different god's sensorium, or if Baivers had simply chosen a different path. Amber waves of grain were certainly more sedate than wine and polymorphous fornication.

Whatever the truth, whatever the route, in the end they reached the snow-covered forest of conifers to which Mavrix had brought him. "Too bleak for barley," Baivers said, in a tone of condemnation and abhorrence. "This is what they want to make my land into, is it?" The monsters' gods said nothing at all. They stared, hungrily, every which way at once, as if looking for rivals to massacre.

A path led through the woods, as it had before. Baivers started down it, the underground powers at his heels. The wolves of the divine Gradihome stared out from the trees at the strange gods who dared walk it. A couple of monsters sprang at the wolves. Maybe that was blood on the snow when they were done, maybe ichor. It looked like blood to Gerin.

"Who comes to Gradihome?" As he had during Gerin's visit with Mavrix, the fierce god named Lavtrig stood in a clearing as Voldar's first sentinel against attack.

Baivers pointed a finger. Through the snow under Lavtrig's feet burst shoots of green. The Gradi god stared at them in something like horror. Mavrix had joked by setting flowers blooming in this grim land. Baivers used fertility as a weapon.

Lavtrig thundered toward him, stamping the shoots flat as he came. He raised a great club, plainly intending to smash the Elabonian god out of existence. Baivers pointed at the club. It turned into leaves and blew away on a sudden warm breeze. Lavtrig roared with rage. He drew from a sheath a bronze sword with a gleaming edge. Over metal Baivers had no power.

The monsters' god that was all thews and claws and teeth sprang out from the pack and onto Lavtrig. Lavtrig smote him. He smote back. "Good battle!" he shouted joyously.

Gerin sent a thought toward Baivers: "Shall the rest of us go on? He seems to have found what he wanted."

Go on they did; Lavtrig, though not defeated, was far too busy to block their path. More wolves stared out at Baivers and the underground powers as they pushed along the path. The wolves, though, no longer stayed to fight, but fled through the pine woods, wailing the alarm in all directions.

"They summon the rest of the Gradi gods," Baivers said.

He sounded worried to Gerin. If the monsters' gods shared his concern, they gave no sign of it. "We want those gods," they said in ragged chorus. "We will chew their flesh; we will gnaw their bones."

When they reached the next clearing, there stood Stribog, the father of all storms. He shouted in what might have been wrath and might have been fear at having his place in Gradihome assailed once more. Giving his foes no chance to enter the clearing, he flung a blast of chilly rain into their faces.

Baivers spread his arms wide. "I thank you for your gift of water," he told the Gradi god, "and shall turn it into blessed barley."

Stribog shouted again, this time in obvious fury. "Go back!" he roared wetly. "You and your band are doomed. Flee while you may." The rain changed to sleet, then to hail that pounded the unwelcome visitors like bullets from a sling.

The monsters' god who glowed stepped forward from among his fellows. That glow had been pale and wan; Gerin had associated it with the pallid gleam of fireflies and molds and certain mushrooms. All at once, though, its nature changed. It grew red as fire, red as the vents through which lava spilled out of some mountains and over the land. The glow grew hot as fire, too.

"Light," the other underground powers crooned. "Precious light!" To them, Gerin realized, any source of illumination, whether from decay or an underground vent for molten rock, was precious and potent.

Their light-bearing god sent a blast of fiery heat back at Stribog, melting hail, sizzling sleet into steam, sending the snow under the weather god's liquid feet boiling up as steam. Stribog roared in anger and pain and fought back with whips of winter. He rushed forward to bluster at the monsters' god, making steam rise up from his shining skin as snow and ice threatened to douse his flame. The underground power in turn redoubled his own effort.

Again, Gerin said, "The rest of us can push on, I think," and again Baivers and the monsters' gods did push ahead through the clearing. Like Lavtrig before him, Stribog was far too busy to prevent their passage. As they found the next path, the Fox warned, "Up ahead is the clearing where Nothing dwells. Watch out for him—he's dangerous."

Baivers, sensibly, stopped at the edge of the next clearing. Gerin let out a tiny mental sigh. He didn't know if he would be able to tell whether Nothing had been playing his tricks this time. He'd managed when Mavrix came this way, but who could guess whether the Gradi god was able to learn new tricks?

His old ones were quite bad enough. A couple of the underground powers, maybe filled with contempt for Baivers' cowardice, maybe just looking for a fight wherever they could find one, sprang out into the clearing with ferocious roars, staring all about them in search of a foe.

They sprang out, they roared . . . and they were gone.

It was not merely that they vanished. It was as if they had never been. Gerin needed a distinct mental effort to recall that they had been part of the ravening pack of gods accompanying Baivers here.

As for Baivers, he said, "You were right, mortal. This power is not to be despised."

"Mavrix didn't beat him," Gerin answered. "He managed to distract him, and that proved enough to get him by."

"Mavrix is full of distractions," Baivers answered. "Distraction is all he's good for. Sometimes I think distraction is all he is."

Behind the Elabonian deity, the monsters' gods were milling around and muttering among themselves. After a moment, one of them, in the shape of a monster but perfectly, light-drinkingly black, stepped past Baivers and out to the very edge of the clearing. "Nothing!" he called in a voice that sounded as if it was echoing and reechoing down the corridors of a cave.

"I am here," Nothing answered, his own voice quiet and flat. "I am everywhere, but I am here most of all."

"Give me back my comrades," the monsters' god said.

"It cannot be," Nothing said.

"Give them back, or you shall not be," the monsters' god warned.

"It cannot be," Nothing repeated.

"It can," the underground power answered, "for I am Darkness." He raised his hands, and the clearing was plunged into blackness as absolute as that Gerin had known when the monsters' gods met his summons below Biton's shrine. Darkness went on, "No one will know whether you are here or not, Nothing. No one will care. When you cannot be found, no one will miss you."

"Or you," Nothing returned, and for a moment black shifted to gray, or rather to the shade of complete and utter neutrality for which gray is the closest earthly approximation.

"I think we'd best move on, while they're busy figuring out which of them is less than the other," Gerin said.

"That's the right way, sure enough," Baivers said, and the rough chorus of the monsters' gods muttered agreement. They advanced into the clearing in which their comrades had ceased to be—into it and through it. As best Gerin could tell with his limited senses, Baivers did not need light to know where he was going.

On the far side of the clearing, light returned. Baivers seemed to glance through Gerin's mind. "Only this Voldar to go, eh?" the god of barley asked.

"I think so," the Fox answered. "After Mavrix got past Nothing, she was the last deity he met. She beat him, but we have more strength with us now."

"We will devour her and gnaw her bones," the monsters' gods chorused. Gerin remembered some of the things the monsters had done while they roamed above ground. If their gods did things like that here . . . he would, he supposed, be glad. And then he would worry about how to make sure the monsters didn't come boiling up onto the surface of the world once more . *If I can make sure of that*, he thought.

Whatever the answer was, he could worry about it later. The fight with Voldar was the immediate concern: immediate indeed, for the path opened out just then into the clearing where the queen of the Gradi gods stood waiting.

That clearing, Gerin thought, was larger than it had been when Voldar summoned him in the dream, larger than when he had come here with Mavrix. That jolted him far less than it would have back in the merely material world; the stuff of the gods had change as part of its very nature.

And it needed to be changeable, for Voldar did not stand alone here: the clearing had grown to accommodate what looked to be the rest of the Gradi pantheon. Most of the gods looked, not surprisingly, like Gradi—tall, fair, gray-eyed, with dark hair and grim expressions. Voldar led them, taller than any, grimmer than any, beauty and terror and rage all commingled.

She started to shout something to the divinities she

headed. Before she could, though, Baivers outshouted her: "You frosters! You freezemakers! You bloodspillers! You blighters!" In the little encysted space in Baivers' mind where Gerin sheltered, he had all he could do not to giggle. Down in the City of Elabon, a few languid, affected young men had used *blighters* as a name for those of whom they did not approve. Imagining Baivers in their company was deliciously absurd. The god of barley, though, meant his insult literally.

Voldar did shout then, a belling contralto that sent shivers up and down the spine from which the Fox was divorced at that moment: "It's the local grass god, all puffed up with himself. And he's brought the kennel with him. We whip them back home, and then we go on about our business."

"Blighters!" Baivers bellowed again, and rushed forward. Voldar loped toward him, as deadly graceful as a longtooth. He picked her up; she let out a most ungodlike squawk of startlement as he slammed her down to the snowy ground. Inside Baivers, Gerin was cheering wildly. He'd wanted the god of barley angry, and now he'd got what he wanted. Not at his finest had Mavrix given Voldar such an overthrow.

But she was on her feet in an instant—feet around which little shoots of barley began to show, pushing their way up through the eternal snow of the divine Gradihome. Voldar hewed at those shoots with her axe. Each one she cut bled real blood, and at each stroke Baivers groaned as if she were cutting him down.

"Forward!" Voldar shouted to her divine companions. "Let's get them, and get them now. We'll—"

She got no further than that. Her cropping the growing barley had hurt Baivers, but had not quenched his determination—very much the reverse. He grabbed the axe handle. Voldar screeched in rage. Gerin felt a harsh tingling run up Baivers' arms, as if he'd grabbed hold of a lightning bolt. Baivers wrestled the axe from Voldar and threw it far—maybe infinitely far—away.

Gerin had hoped a good part of Voldar's power dwelt in that axe, and that without it she would be diminished. If she was, she gave no outward sign of it. She dealt Baivers a buffet that would have caved in the skull of an ordinary mortal.

The only ordinary mortal in that clearing, though, was Gerin, and he wasn't there in the flesh. A lot of flesh was flying, and fur, and divine ichor, from both the underground powers and the Gradi gods. The Fox couldn't help thinking Sithonian deities would have handled the battle with more elegance and panache. Any elegance or panache would have been more than was on display at the moment. Neither the monsters' gods nor those of the Gradi had much in the way of subtlety. They found the nearest foe and went at him, much as monsters and Gradi would have done had they collided in the northlands.

One of the Gradi gods burst into flame. The underground power he was fighting screeched. Another of the monsters' gods, though, tackled the Gradi god and rolled with him in the snow, after which his fire was extinguished for a while. And the subterranean god who had been burned healed with supernatural speed.

An underground power sprang on Voldar, claw raking cuts along her haunch. She screamed in mingled pain and fury and kicked out behind her like an angry horse. The monsters' god flew through the air and smashed headfirst into the trunk of a fir. He did not get up right away. He did not get up at all. Gerin wondered if he would ever get up again.

A Gradi god to whom the Fox had not been introduced tried to freeze Baivers where he stood, blowing an icy blast at him as if from the side of some snow-covered northern mountain. However hostile his intent, his power did not measure up to it. In response, Baivers pointed a finger at him. All the hair on his arms, on his face, on his head, turned to growing barley. He wailed and clawed at himself, but remained green and growing.

"How *dare* you interfere with our plans?" Voldar demanded of Baivers.

"Who's interfering in whose part of the world?" the god of barley retorted. "You leave my earth alone, maybe I'll think of leaving you alone. And maybe not, too. You deserve what you're getting, all the trouble you've caused there 'twixt the Niffet and the Kirs."

"Not half so much as we *will* cause," Voldar snarled. "We'll take revenge for eons, see if we don't."

She broke off then, with a howl of outrage, for one of the monsters' gods, one who beside her was like a small dog beside a man, bit her in the ankle. Gerin admired the courage of the underground power, and wished he'd had the chance to meet more of the monsters' gods in anything but the most perfunctory way before leading them into this fight.

The monsters' god was small, but held power not to be despised. Voldar's leg did not work as it should have after he sank his teeth into her. She beat on him with all her strength, but he would not let go his hold. "What are you, you savage worm?" she cried.

Speaking mind to mind, the underground power did not have to leave off biting her to reply, "I am Death."

Excitement rippled through Gerin when he caught that answer. Even Voldar might have trouble against such a foe. Were gods truly immortal? Would he find out now? Something that might have been alarm in her voice, Voldar shrilly cried, "Smerts! To me!"

Seeing Smerts, the Fox realized he—no, she, for the emaciated frame carried shrunken breasts—was Death's Gradi equivalent. Where Voldar had been unable to free herself from the underground power's onslaught, Smerts tore the fierce little god away from the queen of the Gradi pantheon. "You are mine," Smerts crooned in a fierce, hungry whisper.

"No," the monsters' Death said, just as hungrily, "you are mine." And he bit the hand that held him. Smerts squeezed him with her other hand. Gerin wondered what would happen if they slew each other. Would that bring immortality into the world?

Whether or not Voldar was immortal, she was imbued with enormous vitality. As soon as Smerts had plucked Death from her, she regained full use of that leg, and used it to smash in the ribs of an underground power who had torn a Gradi god almost in two.

The kicked power stumbled backward, groaning, and knocked Death out of Smerts' hands. Smerts seized the new underground power, while Death clamped his teeth into the first Gradi god he could reach. Gerin wished he had a body with which to groan. Mortality's power in the world would continue to hold sway.

He risked a question of Baivers: "Are we winning?"

"Don't know," the Elabonian god replied. He looked around the field, which meant Gerin perforce looked around the field, too. What he saw was what he'd seen since the brawl began: chaos loosed in the divine Gradihome. "Don't know if we're winning," Baivers repeated, "but I don't reckon we're losing, neither."

That was as much as Gerin had hoped for when he led the underground powers here. It seemed to be plenty to satisfy the monsters' gods, too. Some of the Gradi gods knocked down or uprooted trees with their bare hands and swung them, like enormous spearshafts, at their foes. That distressed the monsters' gods, who were unused to trees in all ways, and especially as weapons.

But Baivers knew about trees. Some of the power he used to make barley spring to life also worked on them. Their branches and roots turned unnaturally lively, grappling with the Gradi gods who tried to wield the trunks. And while the trees discommoded the Gradi gods, the underground powers sprang on them, rending and tearing.

Before the monsters' gods reached the divine Gradihome, their grim and savage intensity, their bloodthirsty devotion to slaughter, had alarmed the Fox, who wondered whether they weren't apt to be a worse bargain for the northlands than Voldar and her companions. He had thought the underground powers would only have grown more ferocious once they joined battle with the Gradi gods.

So far as he could tell, that wasn't happening. The clearing was filled not just with quasiphysical screams and shouts and groans, but also with the thoughts and feelings of the battling gods, sometimes as weapons, sometimes merely there. Gerin did not catch the same rage now from the monsters' gods as he'd felt when they were coming toward this fight. What he did get from them was so surprising, he had to pause and consider before he was willing to admit, even to himself, that he fully grasped it.

"They're enjoying themselves!" he told Baivers, almost indignantly. "They're like a serf village on a holiday, when they've got a couple of pigs roasting over the fire and plenty of your good ale and no work to do. They're having the time of their lives."

"They wanted battle," Baivers answered. "You've given 'em what they wanted, and then some. Bet they'll like you real well when this here is done."

Gerin didn't know whether that prospect was more appealing—if the underground powers felt well disposed toward him, they might be inclined to control the monsters' depredations—or appalling. What he did know was that the Gradi gods were not enjoying themselves. He had the feeling from previous encounters with them that they seldom enjoyed themselves, at least by any standards with which he was familiar.

What they felt now was anger, of a peculiar sort: the anger of those who see plans they had reckoned certain of success suddenly falling to pieces all around them. In his little space inside Baivers' sensorium, the Fox exulted. The Gradi and their gods had reckoned the northlands ripe for conquest and transformation. Now they were finding it wasn't so, and not caring for the discovery.

Here came Smerts, looking more deathly than ever. She seized Baivers as she had seized the death god among the underground powers. As she had with him, she crooned, "You are mine."

Baivers groaned. Dwelling inside him—dwelling, in effect, as part of him—Gerin felt vitality flowing out of him and into Smerts. It was like watching ale leak out of a cracked jar—the level went down, down, down, steadily, inexorably. That gave the Fox an idea. "Feed Smerts more life than she can hold all at once," he thought at Baivers. "You're a god of growing things—make her grow lively if you can."

"If I can," Baivers said doubtfully. He seemed to quiver, gathering himself. Then—it was as if a lightning bolt passed from him to Smerts.

The Gradi goddess gasped. Her eyes opened very wide. The stringy white stood out straight on her skull. Was it the Fox's imagination, or did she all at once look less skeletal than she had?

"You can't do that," she gasped at Baivers. "You can't."

But her voice was not the harsh croak it had been a moment before. It was smoother, richer: almost the voice of a being concerned with something other than extinction.

Gerin still wondered if he was more hopeful than he should have been, if he was letting that hope color what his senses (always unreliable on this plane anyhow) told him. No: Baivers sensed Smerts' weakness, too. "Yes I can," he said, fresh confidence in his own voice.

Watching Smerts, Gerin watched years peel away and emaciation flesh out. Contemplating his own middle-aged carcass back in the merely material world, he wished Baivers would put him through a similar course. It soon proved too much for the Gradi goddess. She broke free of Baivers and fled. At each stride, she seemed to age a few years, and was soon back to what she had been, but she did not challenge the god of barley again.

"I thank you," Baivers said to Gerin. "That was right sly. Worst thing for a lot of folks is too much of what they tell you they want." He strode toward Voldar, shouting to her, "You, there! We weren't done, the two of us!"

She whirled to face him. "No, we weren't," she said. Gerin wondered about the wisdom of confronting the queen of the Gradi pantheon so directly. Before he could more than begin to frame that thought, though, Voldar's pale gaze pierced the encystment within Baivers where his own small spirit sheltered. "You!" she cried, and she was not speaking to the Elabonian god.

"Yes, me," Gerin answered, as steadfastly as he could. "I told you that you weren't welcome in the northlands, and that I'd do everything I could to stop you."

Voldar's eyes flashed pale fire. "I never dreamt one mortal could cause so much trouble." Her wave encompassed the chaos all around, chaos with no resolution anywhere near at hand. Then she stabbed out a finger at the Fox. "And I say you may not come to the Gradihome of the gods." Her voice rose to a shrill shriek: "Begone!"

Darkness.

Gerin opened his eyes. He was in the shack again. "Did we win?" Van asked.

XI

Gerin cast a wary eye up to the sky. The day was hot and fair; the sun blazed down like a ball of molten bronze in the middle of a blue enamel bowl. The cold, nasty rain that had plagued the last part of the ride up from Ikos was gone, vanished more suddenly than a natural storm had any business disappearing.

Wiping his forehead with a sleeve, he said, "Unless I miss my guess, Stribog is either still fighting one of the monsters' gods or else laid up from having fought him."

"Been four days now since you and Baivers and all the underground powers went to fight Voldar and her chums," Van said. "Still no notion of how the fight turned out?"

"Not even the slightest," Gerin answered. "Every day since, I've tried to summon Baivers, I've tried to summon the monsters' gods, but I get no answer. Maybe they've been destroyed, but I don't think so. If they had been, the Gradi would be swarming up the Niffet in their war galleys, and we haven't seen a single fire beacon. The weather's too fine to make me think the Gradi gods won, too."

"What then?" Van asked.

"My best guess is that they're still fighting up there, out there, on that plane where the gods can go and we mostly can't," the Fox said. "Neither side looked to have any sort of edge when Voldar booted me off my perch on Baivers' shoulder, you might say."

"A fight that doesn't stop." Van sighed wistfully. "Must be a fine thing to be a god, to never need to eat or sleep, to heal up as fast as you're hurt, to war for as long as you like, for years on end, maybe." He let out a snort of laughter. "But then, I know a bit about warring for years on end. I ought to, married to Fand like I am."

He looked indignant when Gerin didn't chuckle at that. "Warring for years on end," Gerin said. He nodded, more to himself than to Van. "It could be so." He hoped it was so. If the Gradi were locked in battle with the underground powers and with Baivers for years, they'd have neither the time nor the ability to help their human followers. He smacked one fist into the other palm. "We have to hit the Gradi while their gods are busy—can't waste a moment. The more we drive those cursed raiders back, the harder the time they'll have recovering, even if their gods do end up beating the ones I turned loose on them."

Van stared at him. "You sound like you're heading out on campaign this very day."

"Tomorrow will have to do, I think," the Fox said reluctantly. "But I'm going to send out a messenger this instant to let Adiatunnus know we're on our way. We're going across the Venien again, and this time we're not coming back till we've beaten the Gradi."

"You've said that before," Van answered. "It didn't work out."

"I wish you hadn't reminded me," Gerin said, which made the outlander chuckle and bow as if he'd just been thanked for doing a favor. Slowly, Gerin went on, "If we can't beat them on the land they've stolen while their gods are busy, though . . . I don't think we'll be able to beat them at all. What we'll have to do in that case is not go after them any more, but hunker down in our keeps, fight them as hard as we can for as long as we can when they come to us, and probably end by going down fighting."

"There are worse ways to end," Van said. "I don't think I'd want to get old and creaky and have a fit so one side of my body doesn't want to work and spend my last days gumming gruel on account of I can't chew and I can hardly swallow. Next to that, an axe that splits my skull is kind."

"I wasn't thinking so much of my end," Gerin said. "I don't want to watch everything I've spent my life building fall to pieces, though, and see my children made into serfs for the Gradi."

"If the Gradi win, you won't see any of that, for they'll surely kill you," Van said, and the Fox could hardly disagree. "Still and all, I follow what you're saying," the outlander continued. "I tell you true, there are times I'm glad I don't try to look so far ahead as you do."

"We're all different," Gerin said with a shrug, "and we're all still free. Now we'll find out how long we get to stay that way."

In times gone by, the guards at the eastern border of Adiatunnus' holding would have fled at the approach of the Elabonian army Gerin led—either fled or, with mad Trokmê courage, tried to sell their lives dear. Now, instead, they let out whoops of delight. Their voices broke as they cried out: they had hardly more than Duren's years, with only light down on their faces.

"What word from the Venien?" Gerin called to them in their own language.

" 'Twas said the Gradi were after moving men up toward that stream," one of the youths replied. "How any man could be sure, though, with the bad weather we've been having and all, is past me, indeed and it is."

"What's the weather like on the other side of the river these days?" the Fox asked, remembering the summer blizzard that had done more to defeat him than the axes of the Gradi.

Both the young sentries shrugged. "Been warmer here o' late," said the one who hadn't spoken before. "And you're only a day and a little bit behind the chariot you sent out, the which, I've no doubt, our chief will be right glad to see."

"And even gladder to see the whole lot of you," the other youngster added. "Adiatunnus is after gathering all the men he may, to hold the Gradi back, that being the reason the two of us get to do a soldier's job so soon."

"Do well. Do as well as you can," Gerin told them. "But we don't aim to hold back the Gradi. We aim to go after 'em and beat 'em." The Trokmê sentries cheered again. So did his own men.

On into Adiatunnus' holding rode the Elabonian army. The Elabonian serfs in the fields, seeing soldiers, mostly fled into the woods regardless of whether they spoke the same language. Soldiers were soldiers, and all too liable to be dangerous. "We might as well be Gradi or Trokmoi ourselves, as far as they're concerned," Duren said, watching them run.

"Remember that," Gerin told him. "My serfs don't think of my warriors that way, and yours shouldn't, either, once you've taken over at the holding your grandfather ruled."

Mischief in his voice, Van said, "But these are your serfs, too, Fox, for isn't Adiatunnus your vassal?"

"When he feels like it," Gerin answered dryly, which made his son and his friend laugh. Gerin drummed his fingers on the chariot rail. "If we win against the Gradi, he may have to decide whether he's my vassal or my foe—I may make him decide that, I should say. Till then, I'm just glad he hasn't sided with them instead of with me."

They passed that night camped by a keep that had held an Elabonian petty baron in the days before the Trokmoi swarmed south over the Niffet and was now home to woodsrunners who lorded it over the serfs at a nearby village. A lot of the men were gone from the keep, summoned by Adiatunnus to protect his western border. The Trokmê women, bolder in their habits than Elabonians would have been, wasted little time in getting friendly—or more than friendly—with the newcomers.

The night was made for such games, being unusually dark in its early states: all four moons were past full, the first of them, Nothos, not rising till almost halfway between sunset and midnight. Gerin was anything but surprised to see Van heading upstairs with a brash Trokmê woman who put him in mind of Fand. He had no doubt Fand would guess, one of these days before too long, what the outlander was up to. His ears rang in anticipation.

He sighed. He couldn't do anything about that. He wasn't Van's nursemaid. If the outlander didn't get so drunk as to make himself too hung over to stay in the chariot come tomorrow, the Fox had no call to upbraid him.

"But it's—untidy, that's what it is," he said to no one in particular. Finding exactly the right phrase satisfied him in a way even shouting at Van couldn't have done. He wrapped himself in a blanket and went to sleep.

Outriding the news of its coming, the Elabonian army descended on Adiatunnus' keep and the village—almost the town—close by it. "If I'd done as well as this when I was the Trokmê's enemy, he'd have feared me more," Gerin said.

As he'd been doing all along, he looked up into the sky. The weather remained hot and dry. He and his men were close to the Venien now. If Stribog interfered with the normal run of things, they would know it sooner and more surely than back at Fox Keep. He saw no sign of any such thing, and was relieved.

Adiatunnus rode out from his castle to greet Gerin and the men with him. "The fellow you sent ahead, he said you're after thinking of fighting the Gradi on their own ground again," he said, sounding anything but delighted at the prospect.

"It's not their ground," the Fox answered. "Some of it, in point of fact, is mine. I intend to take it back, and to drive them off it."

"You intended the same earlier in the year, and had nobbut bad cess," Adiatunnus said. "Why d'you think your luck'll be better on a second go?"

"I'll tell you why," Gerin said, and did. He finished, "I don't know whether Baivers and the monsters' gods have beaten Voldar and the Gradi crew, but I'd say they haven't lost. If they had, the weather would be worse."

Adiatunnus tugged at one side of his drooping mustaches. "It could be so," he said at last, after some thought. "Not long ago, the cold storms came rolling over the Venien one after t'other, you might say, and the Gradi looked to be gathering for a push right at us." He scowled. "Shamed as I am to own it, we'd have broken and run without your Widin. On our own, we canna stand against the Gradi. But he said he'd fight 'em with us or without us, and so I called up all the men, to give him what help we could."

Making himself stand against a foe who had trounced his folk time after time had taken courage, and courage of an unusual sort. "Widin's not the only man here with spirit," the Fox said, acknowledging that. "What happened then? I haven't heard of the Gradi crossing the Venien."

"They didna," Adiatunnus said. "Not so many days ago, the storms stopped and it was summer again, as fine a summer as any I've seen. And the Gradi drew back a ways from the Venien. We slipped a few o' Widin's men and mine over the river to see if they could find out what was toward, and they tell me the reivers seem all in an uproar, like as if summat they'd expected hadna happened after all."

"Maybe, just maybe, I kept it from happening," Gerin replied. "And if I did, the best thing we can do now is hit them as hard a blow as we can, give them something else they aren't expecting."

"Can we do it?" Adiatunnus asked.

"Of course we can," Gerin said heartily, though he did not think the Trokmê chieftain had in fact aimed the question at him. Adiatunnus sounded more as if he were putting it to his own gods, the gods whom Voldar and the Gradi had beaten and terrified. What sort of answer would he find, whether from them or in his own heart?

After a long pause, Adiatunnus said, "Well, we'd best have a go. If we dinna go to them, they'll come to us, sure as sure, and no good will spring from that."

The endorsement, while anything but ringing, was an endorsement. "We'll move against them tomorrow, your men and mine together," Gerin said. Adiatunnus stared at him. Now the Fox glared, playing to the hilt the role of outraged feudal overlord. "Tomorrow I said and tomorrow I meant. And I mean in the morning, too, even if I have to boot every one of you lazy, sleepy woodsrunners in the arse to make it happen."

"Lazy!" Adiatunnus clapped a hand to his forehead. "Sleepy? We'll show you, you black-hearted spalpeen!"

"I hope you do," Gerin said. "But if you don't" —he waved back at his army— "I've brought enough Elabonians along to get you moving."

"Elabonians? Foosh!" Adiatunnus said. "We make no special shivers for Elabonians. It's not as if you were so many Gradi, now."

"To the crows with you," Gerin exclaimed. Both men laughed. They'd tried to kill each other before; they might well try to kill each other again one day. Meanwhile, though, they saw they had more urgent things to worry about than their old animosity. That in itself eased Gerin's mind. He had been far from sure Adiatunnus would be able to look to what might lie ahead rather than remembering the past. For that matter, he'd been far from sure he'd be able to do that himself.

"If you're right, Fox, and we beat the Gradi . . ." The Trokmê chieftain's voice trailed away, as if he had trouble believing such a thing possible. After a moment, he started up again: "If we do that, 'twill be a braw thing you've managed: aye, a braw thing indeed."

"We'll see what happens, that's all," the Fox said. "I've always tried to take the fight to the other fellow when I stood any chance of doing it."

"That I ken," Adiatunnus said, "for you've done it to me more times nor I care to recall. May we have the same luck against the Gradi."

"Sounds like a toast to me," Van said, "and only a fool would make a toast without washing it down." It was not a subtle hint, but Van was not a subtle man: in that he matched the Trokmoi more closely than the Elabonians among whom he lived. As Adiatunnus had taken on more Elabonian ways than most of the woodsrunners south of the Niffet, he might have found Van's approach imperfectly polished. If he did, he was too polished himself to show it. Smiling, he waved Gerin, Van, and the rest of the Elabonian warriors toward his keep.

Gerin looked back at the Venien River. It wasn't a great stream like the Niffet into which it flowed; it seemed hardly enough to serve as the boundary between not just two peoples but almost between two worlds. But back there on the eastern side, Gerin had been prince of the north, overlord of all he surveyed. If he claimed to rule here, he would have to make that claim good against the Gradi.

As he had even in his own holding, he kept a weather eye on the sky. Storm clouds building in the west might give warning the Gradi gods had won their war. He saw none; the day remained fine. What he did see was Adiatunnus, also nervously eyeing the western horizon.

Catching his glance, the Trokmê looked briefly shamefaced. "It's only that I'm after remembering the last time we tried coming this way," he said. "Another summer blizzard like that—" He broke off, plainly not wanting to think of it. Gerin didn't want to, either, but couldn't help himself.

A car holding Widin Simrin's son rolled up alongside Gerin's. Widin pointed ahead. "Gradi up that way, lord prince, based at what was a peasant village." He spoke with authority; the scouts, Elabonian and Trokmê both, who had been slipping off over the Venien to spy out the raiders' doings reported to him when they returned—if they returned.

The Fox waved half the chariots off to the left and the other half to the right, wanting to hit the Gradi from two directions at once. He led the left-hand column himself. At his father's order, Duren urged the horses up into a gallop. "Speed and surprise will get us more here than stealth," Gerin judged.

Surprised the Gradi certainly were. When they spied the chariots rushing toward them they let out loud bellows of alarm. Some of them dashed back into the peasant huts they'd appropriated and then came back out with axes and a few bows. And a handful did something Gerin had never before seen Gradi do: they turned tail and ran for their lives.

Even as he nocked his first arrow, the Fox pointed to them and called, "I want some of those men taken alive. We may be able to learn a lot from them." A handful of chariots peeled off after the fleeing Gradi.

The fight with the ones who hadn't fled was as fierce as usual, but did not last long: between them, the Elabonians and Trokmoi had their foes badly outnumbered, and the arrival of the second column moments after the first threw the Gradi into confusion, for a good many of them could not decide which group of opponents to resist.

When they saw they had no hope of winning the fight, the Gradi began slaying one another to keep from being taken prisoner. Rather more of them than usual, though, did let themselves be captured. That piqued Gerin's curiosity in the same way as the earlier spectacle of running Gradi had done.

After helping see to his own men, he went to question the warriors who'd fled or been captured. They sat glumly on the ground, hands bound behind them with leather thongs. "Who speaks Elabonian?" Gerin demanded.

Several Gradi stirred. "I speak it, somely," one of them said, proving his own point.

Gerin wasted no time with ancillary questions. "Why did some of you run? Why did some of you give up?"

The Gradi looked at one another, then down at the ground. The Fox knew shame when he saw it. The prisoner who had spoken before answered, "It is not what the chiefs tell us. It is not what the gods tell us." A couple of others who understood Elabonian exclaimed, trying to silence him, but he went on, "It is so. We were to strike, not to be striked. The gods do not do what they say they do. They trickfool us. Why we do for them?"

"How did your gods fool you?" Gerin did his best to make the question sound casual. He had to work not to lean forward and throw it out like a man casting a baited line into a pond.

And that Gradi seized the bait. "They say they help us," he answered. "They say you not can backfight. They say they chase your pisspot gods, eat them, throw dead of them on dunghill. They trickfool us."

His gray eyes were full of angry indignation. For a little while, Gerin had trouble understanding that. Then he realized he was used to living in a part of the world where the gods seldom played an active role. That was not true of Voldar and the rest of the Gradi pantheon. Now the raiders were having to do things for themselves, without their gods to help them. If this first taste of how they performed under such circumstances meant anything, they were going to have some trouble adjusting.

Gerin hoped they had a lot of trouble adjusting. Turning to Adiatunnus, he said, "You see? We're fighting just them now, not their goddess." Here across the Venien, he didn't feel like naming her, even if she was otherwise occupied.

Adiatunnus noticed that. He said, "You started well before, Fox, and then it all went sour. Finish well, now, and you'll show yourself right."

"Fair enough." The Fox spoke to the warriors guarding the Gradi prisoners: "Send them back over the Venien. The work we get out of them as slaves will pay back a little of what they've done to us."

He watched the prisoners closely as he spoke. Some of them admitted to understanding Elabonian. He saw no tries for escape, no tries for suicide, among those men or any others. The likeliest explanation was that they were cast into confusion because their gods were less with them than those gods usually were.

He very much wanted the likeliest explanation to be true. Because he so much wanted it to be true, he distrusted it all the more.

"Only one way to find out," he said. Adiatunnus gave him a curious look. He pretended not to see it.

Whether or not the Gradi had been readying themselves to cross the Venien a few days before, they were not ready to defend against a strike from the eastern side of the river. Each group of them, gathered in villages or encamped in the woods, fought Gerin's army with an effort individually often heroic but invariably futile: those groups were crushed, one after another.

"Why don't they come together, Father?" Duren asked as the army made camp after one such little battle. "They'd be tougher meat if they did."

"I'm still not sure," Gerin answered, wiping sweat from his forehead with his sleeve. He'd earned that sweat fighting the Gradi, but it had come easy: the day was a muggy scorcher. "But I'm beginning to think they're so used to talking with their gods, and to listening to them, that they have trouble figuring out what to do when they're on their own."

"Enjoy it while it lasts," Van said. "My guess is, that won't be long. Sooner or later, they'll come out of their fog and remember they're men, not gods' toys. Life gets harder after that."

"I'm the one who's supposed to come up with cheery thoughts like that," Gerin said. "Your job is to say, 'No, no, Fox, everything will be fine. We'll whip these Gradi right out of their furs.' " He deepened his voice and gave it a slight guttural rasp, doing his best to imitate the outlander.

His friend grunted laughter. "Nobody can always see what he's going to do himself, let alone what the fool standing next to him is liable to come up with. When you threw Baivers and the underground powers at the Gradi gods, you surprised even them, I think."

"As long as they keep on being surprised." Gerin looked at the sky so often these days, he hardly noticed himself doing it. So long as the clouds stayed away, so long as the hot weather held, he would assume the monsters' gods and Baivers still kept Voldar and the other Gradi gods too busy to make trouble down on the merely mortal plane of being.

He knew how rough a gauge that was. Voldar and her crew might overcome the invaders before Stribog recovered from the supernatural wounds he'd received in his fight. If that happened, the first the Fox would know of it was running headlong into the angry Gradi gods. He did not look forward to that sort of confrontation.

Best way to keep it from happening, he told himself, *is to beat the Gradi so badly, their gods won't have much of a place to roost in the northlands*. He'd known all along what needed doing. Knowing how to do it was another matter, worse luck.

An Elabonian spy brought him news the next day that the Gradi had regarrisoned the tumbledown keep in which he'd defeated them in his earlier foray into the country they held. "They don't have much in the way of imagination, do they?" the Fox said.

When he sent scouts out to approach the place, he

discovered how little imagination the Gradi were showing: their sentries seemed no more alert to attack than on his previous incursion. It was as if the idea that their enemies could bring the war to them rather than the other way round had never occurred to them. Gerin aimed both to exploit their naïveté and, having exploited it, to fill the gap in their education.

"Shall we dismount again and trick them?" Duren asked.

"They'd never fall for the same trick twice," Van protested. Gerin got the feeling the protest sprang more from his inability to look like a Gradi than from any consideration of grand strategy: the outlander felt cheated out of a good fight. No wonder he'd been able to fathom the minds of the monsters' gods—his own worked the same way. Could he have been projected up into the plane of the gods, he would have had a splendid time battling Voldar and her companions.

In the end, the Fox decided to try the same plan again, taking advantage of the confusion the Gradi seemed to feel without their gods leading them by the noses. These were, after all, not the same men in the keep as the ones his force had overwhelmed before. He led the band of foot soldiers who approached the keep. Many of them were wearing captured Gradi helmets and carrying captured Gradi axes in place of their own weapons, doing their best to make the ruse convincing.

When the band of men on foot approached, the drawbridge to the keep was up. He cursed on seeing that. A Gradi up on the wall shouted something at him and his men. A couple of the Trokmoi spoke a little of the Gradi tongue. One of them shouted back, presumably saying something like, *It's all right—let us in.*

And the drawbridge came down. "We *are* lucky," Duren breathed.

"We certainly are," Gerin said. "We're lucky enough to run in there and see how many of us are going to get killed. Aren't you glad to have luck like that?" Duren nodded eagerly. Gerin cursed—that wasn't the answer his son would give when he had a little more sense.

But then, if he'd been sensible himself, he wouldn't have attacked this keep in the first place. He yanked his sword out of the scabbard and ran for the drawbridge. His men followed, their shouts making the morning hideous. The drawbridge started to rise, but it could come down faster than it went up.

Gerin got over the bridge and into the courtyard. He ran into the gatehouse with half a dozen men at his heels. They quickly slew the pair of Gradi who had been working the big capstan around which the drawbridge chain was wound. With another shout, the Fox let the capstan spin in the opposite direction. The drawbridge thumped all the way down again, and this time stayed down.

In swarmed the warriors who had approached on foot. Gerin knew the rest of his army would soon join them: a runner would report initial success to the chariotry hanging back just out of sight. Meanwhile, how many Gradi were in the keep and how ferociously would they fight?

A good many of them fought as ferociously as they ever had. One snarling knot of men near the entrance to the great hall of the castle did not come undone till the last Gradi fighting there had fallen. But fewer Gradi manned the keep than had been here before, and not all of them chose to fight to the death. When Elabonians and Trokmoi began leaping out of chariots and running to join the fight, a startling number of the raiders still on their feet threw down their axes and gave up.

"Where is great Voldar? Where is Lavtrig? Where is Smerts?" one of the prisoners said in fair Elabonian. "How can we beat you thralls without our gods? It is not fair."

Gerin found the Gradi's notion of fairness curious, but did not try to persuade him it needed changing. Instead, he allowed himself the luxury of a sigh of relief that the Gradi gods were still preoccupied, and the even greater luxury of hope that they would keep on being preoccupied.

After he'd pressed west from the keep on his earlier incursion into territory the Gradi held, the weather had gone bad on him. When he woke now to find the sun rising in a cloudless sky, he smiled and murmured, "Thank you, lord Baivers." Every day the god of barley and the underground powers bought for him was another day in which to strike the Gradi.

The wind did blow out of the west, but it was a natural

wind, a warm wind. And, toward the end of the day, it brought a fresh scent with it, a tang he had known before but couldn't name at once. Duren noticed it, too, and asked, "What's that smell?" —for him, it was unfamiliar.

Van identified it before the Fox could. "That's the smell of the ocean, lad. We're closer to it now than back at Fox Keep, and no rain washing it out of the air before your nose can find it."

"You're right!" Gerin snapped his fingers in annoyance at himself. "When the wind swung round and blew out of the east, off the Greater Inner Sea, the air in the City of Elabon would smell like this."

"And when the wind didn't swing round, the air in the City of Elabon would smell like all the privies and stables in the world, same as it does in every other city," Van said.

"That's so," Gerin said. "When I lived there—back before you were born, Duren—I didn't notice the city stink, but by the gods I did when I first came into it. After a while, you get used to things."

Later that day, the army he led came upon a group of Gradi in a peasant village who behaved more in the manner the raiders had done before their gods made the acquaintance of Baivers and the subterranean powers. They went down to defeat, but the large majority of them fought until killed, and several of those who didn't also did not surrender, but broke away into the woods to the west.

Gerin sent men into those woods after them, but they got away. "I don't care for that," he said when his warriors brought back the news of their failure. "They didn't look like men running for their lives. They looked more like men who wanted to take warning to their friends."

"Why do you say that, Father?" Duren asked.

"Because they all went off in the same direction," Gerin replied. "If they'd been panicked, they'd have run every which way—woods just as near these huts to the north and south as to the west. But that's the direction they went."

Adiatunnus walked up in time to hear that last. "You're after thinking it'll be harder now, Fox?"

"I wish I could say no, but I have to say yes," Gerin told him. He tried to keep the Trokmê's spirits up, adding,

"Have you noticed how well your warriors have fought against the Gradi this time out? I certainly have."

"That I have, and I thank you for seeing it, too," Adiatunnus said. "It's as if a great burthen o' fear's fallen off our backs, for the which I suppose you're the man I should be thanking."

"I've taken the Gradi gods out of play," Gerin said. "Now it's you Trokmoi against them, not you against them and their gods, who had already put your gods in fear."

As soon as the words were out of his mouth, he wished he had them back. He did not want to insult Adiatunnus by calling Esus, Teutates, Taranis, and the rest of the Trokmê gods cowards. But the woodsrunners' chieftain only nodded. "Truth that—I've owned it myself. We do the best we can, is all—who can do more?" He stopped and thought about what he'd just said, then clapped a hand to his forehead. "The gods forfend, Fox, I'm after starting to sound like you."

"We've lived next to each other too long," Gerin answered. "This wouldn't be happening if one of us had managed to kill the other somewhere back down the line."

"And that's truth, too," Adiatunnus said. "We're both after having worse neighbors the now, though, the which makes me think I may be glad after all I didna overfall you. You never know till the end how these things turn out sometimes, do you?"

"No, you don't," Gerin said shortly. "If you like, Adiatunnus, and if we come out the other side of these hard times, I'll teach you your letters. They'll make your world seem wider, and you'll profit for that."

"I'll think on it, indeed and I will," Adiatunnus said. Gerin scratched his head. For years, he'd tried to preserve civilization in the northlands not least by driving the Trokmoi over the Niffet. For the first time, he wondered if, having failed to do that, he might civilize them instead. The idea made him laugh. *If they invade my country, that's what they get*, he thought.

Before he thought about civilizing the Trokmoi (and before he had time to do more than briefly wonder whether a literate Adiatunnus might prove a more dangerous

Adiatunnus), he had to worry about the Gradi. The farther west he got, the bigger a worry they became. They fought harder and more cleverly than they had. He was no longer taking them by surprise, either: they knew he and his men were coming after them.

The weather worried him, too. The breeze that smelled of the Orynian Ocean was cool and moist, which made him wonder whether Stribog was no longer busy battling the underground power who had taken him on. Only when local peasants assured him summers close by the sea were generally of that sort did the worry recede—a little.

He kept scouting parties close by the Niffet, to make sure the Gradi could not use their war galleys to land a large band of soldiers behind him by surprise. That precaution paid for itself a couple of days later, when his men spotted two galleys full of Gradi going up the river. When some of the scouts brought that news back, he reversed the course of his army: two galleys' worth of warriors was not a force large enough to do much in the way of raiding upriver, and seemed likelier to be aimed at him.

Had he guessed wrong there, he might have lost the momentum that had kept his troopers surging forward. But he guessed right: his men swept down on the Gradi close by the riverside, and apparently not long after they had left their ships. The fight that followed, on flat, open ground with the Niffet against which to pin the raiders, was more nearly slaughter than anything deserving the name of battle.

Foot soldiers armed mostly with axes, the Gradi here found themselves at the mercy of Gerin's chariot-riding archers. The Gradi could neither close with them nor escape, and had no weapons able to strike their foes from a distance. One by one, they fell, until, seeing the end rapidly approaching, they began killing one another to keep from being captured.

After the fight was over, the Fox sent a party east along the Niffet to find the galleys from which the Gradi had come. Two pillars of smoke rising into the sky said they'd not only found but fired them.

"I wish they hadn't done that," Gerin said, pointing back toward the smoke.

"And why ever not?" Adiatunnus demanded. "With the boats found and all, they should be getting rid of them, eh?"

"Most times, I'd say yes," Gerin answered. "But people will see that smoke a long way. I'm afraid the Gradi army in the west just beyond our farthest advance yet will spot it and know we've smashed their friends."

"What army are you talking about?" Adiatunnus said, and then, "It's daft y'are, I'm thinking, when all we've seen is dribs and drabs of Gradi, no proper armies to 'em at all. Not that I'm sorry for it, mind you now."

"Think it through," the Fox told him. "Why would the Gradi have landed a force of that size behind us? Those men couldn't have caught us, not on foot, and they couldn't fight all of us by themselves if they did catch us. Am I right so far?"

"Aye, belike," the Trokmê chieftain said. "What of it, and what has it got to do with a whole great whacking Gradi army up ahead?"

Gerin too seldom got the chance to play games with logic. When he did, he used it to the hilt. "Think it through," he repeated. "These Gradi couldn't have caught us or fought us, not alone. What does that leave for them to do? The only thing I can think of is that they were meant to be a blocking force, to slow us down while we're retreating and let whoever we're retreating from catch up with us. We wouldn't be retreating from dribs and drabs of Gradi. The only thing that could make us retreat is an army. And so . . . does that make sense to you?"

Adiatunnus' long, bony face was intent as he followed the Fox's reasoning. At last, he said, "You may be after having the right of it. What a tricksy wight y'are, to see that army or ever you set eyes on it. Have you been watching me the same way, all these years?"

"As best I could," Gerin told him.

"I hold myself lucky, then, for still being here for you to keep an eye on," Adiatunnus said, "though you'll likely tell me you'd be as pleased if I weren't."

"More pleased," the Fox said, deadpan. Adiatunnus gave him a glare as heartfelt as he could have desired. Then both men started to laugh. Gerin went on, "Now let's go see what we can do to flush that army my mind's eye sees—or find out that I'm full of eyewash."

"Indeed and I'll be surprised if it turns out y'are," Adiatunnus told him. "The way you laid out your thoughts, so neat and all, there I was, following along behind like you were lighting up a dark path with a torch."

"You do need to learn to read," Gerin told him. "I'll make a philosopher out of you yet, see if I don't."

"Och," Adiatunnus exclaimed, "maybe I should let the Gradi kill me instead." The Fox glared at him, only to realize the Trokmê had just taken his revenge.

Every so often, Gerin's instinct and his logic let him down with a splat. As he led his army westward, he began to wonder if this was going to be one of those times. He had scouts out well ahead of the main body of his force. They and then he passed a couple of spots where he would have judged the Gradi likely to stand and fight.

Then a scout came back from the southwest with a frightened-looking peasant clinging to the rail of his chariot. "This fellow says he knows where the Gradi are," he called.

"Good." Gerin waved, bringing his army to a halt. The scout came on at a slightly less intrepid pace, which made the elderly peasant seem happier, or at least less unhappy. "Who are you and what do you know?" Gerin asked him.

"Lord, my name is Osar Pozel's son," he answered, though Gerin wondered if he'd heard the name aright. He might have felt happier speaking to Osar through an interpreter, for the serf had a western accent that would have made him hard to understand at best, and also spoke mushily because he was missing most of his teeth.

"Well, Osar, what do you know?" Gerin repeated.

The peasant pointed back in the direction from which the scout had brought him. "Lord, there's Gradi back there, lots of Gradi. Over by Bidgosh Pond, they are. Wish somebody could do something about 'em."

"Why do you think I'm here?" the Fox said. "For my amusement? For the scenery, maybe?"

"Who knows what lords do, or why?" Osar returned. "Anyone who's smart, he stays outen the way of lords."

That saddened Gerin, but did not surprise him. "Where is this Bidgosh Pond?" he asked.

"Where is it? What do you mean, where is it? How can you not know where Bidgosh Pond is?" Osar had, no doubt, lived in his village all his life. Everything in the neighborhood—this pond, wherever it was; a hill; a forest—would be as familiar to him as his own fingers, and would no more need locating than those fingers at the far end of his hand. He'd have trouble imagining someone who'd never seen Bidgosh Pond, as he'd also have trouble imagining the terrain more than a day's walk from his village, terrain he'd probably never seen.

"Never mind," Gerin said, sighing. "Here, come up into my chariot. You tell me which way I have to go to get to the pond. If a fight starts, I'll let you jump out beforehand. Does that suit you?"

"What choice have I got?" Osar asked, the peasant's age-old bitter question. He got up into the Fox's chariot and said, "All right, back the way I came from, back toward the fields I know."

"Think what a hero you'll be to the other people in your village," Gerin said. "Now you've ridden in a chariot—two chariots, in fact—and you're going to help get rid of the Gradi so they don't trouble you any more."

"I'm going to have all these fancy chariot things churning up the fields so we all go hungry," Osar Pozel's son said. He shook his head. "Wouldn't've had much crops anyways, not with the weather so bad till just lately."

As soon as he found ground he recognized, he went from being nearly useless to being altogether authoritative, telling Gerin much more than he wanted to know about every crop, every herd, that had been on that ground for as far back as he remembered, which was about as long as Gerin had been alive. In his little corner of the world, he remembered *everything*: chuckling, he said, "Had my first girl back o' those trees, not that they was so tall in them days. Pretty little thing she was, too, and a pair on her that'd make you cry—"

After a while, Gerin cut off the flow of amatory reminiscences by asking, "How much farther to this pond?"

Osar gave him a dirty look. The Fox had trouble blaming

him; remembered lovemaking was surely more enjoyable than thinking about battle. After a moment, though, the peasant pointed. "Just past that stand o' trees there."

Sure enough, through the trees came the glint of sun off water. Also through the trees came shadowy glimpses of moving figures. "Rein in," Gerin told Duren. When his son obeyed, the Fox told Osar, "You'd better get out here. Those aren't the people from your village, are they?"

"Not likely," the peasant answered, and jumped down. He scurried away from the chariots behind the Fox's, surprisingly spry. Given the fight that loomed ahead, Gerin would have been spry in his shoes, too (not that Osar was wearing shoes).

Pointing ahead, Van said, "There's a whole great whacking lot of Gradi in amongst those trees."

"There certainly are," Gerin said. "The next interesting question is, how in the names of all the Elabonian gods are we going to get them to come out into the fields and fight us on our own ground?"

Van grunted thoughtfully in response to that, but made no more definite answer. Gerin pondered the problem. Out on open land, his men in their chariots could ride rings around the Gradi and fill them full of arrows without exposing themselves to much danger. Under the trees, everything changed. The horses would have to pick their way, and the men in the cars would be hideously vulnerable to enemies leaping out of the bushes or from behind tree trunks and not seen till too late.

Gerin touched his son on the shoulder. "Ride up close to the woods," he said. "There's something I want to try." Duren did as he asked. Raising his voice to a great shout, the Fox called, "If the lot of you aren't sniveling cowards, come out and fight us!"

Against Trokmoi, the ploy probably would have worked: the woodsrunners made a point of proving how brave they were. It might have worked against Elabonians; his own people, Gerin thought, were by no means free of brave blockheads. But from out of the forest came an answering shout in pretty good Elabonian: "If you are such a great fighter, you come make us!"

It was exactly the reply Gerin would have given. Getting it thrown in his face didn't make him any happier. Neither did the cheers that rose from the throats of the Gradi who had understood their leader's answer. Only a man with a strong hold over the warriors he led could have so forcefully rejected the most openly courageous course of action. The Fox turned to Van. "You were right, worse luck. I think they've found a captain."

"And what do we do about that?" the outlander asked.

"What I'd like to do is set the forest afire and flush them out that way." Gerin bit his lip. "The only trouble being, I don't think it would work, not with no wind and not with the trees all wet and full of sap from the rains that have poured down on this place."

Van nodded. "Aye, a fire'd be slow going. They might head out away from us, toward the pond, instead of at us, too. But what does that leave?"

Gerin looked back at the chariots full of Trokmoi and Elabonians. He looked ahead to the woods full of Gradi. The Gradi captain had rejected the obvious choice Gerin offered him. He, in turn, had offered Gerin a choice just as obvious—and just as fraught with peril.

Sighing, the Fox said, "If they don't come to us, we could go in after them."

He had hoped Van would try to talk him out of it. Instead, the outlander whooped and grinned and slapped him on the back, almost hard enough to pitch him out of the chariot. "Every now and then, Fox, I like the way you think," he said.

"I don't," Gerin said.

When the Fox shouted orders for his men to dismount from their cars and fight the Gradi on foot, Adiatunnus had his driver bring his chariot alongside and said, "Are you daft, to go fighting them under the trees? 'Tis the very thing they want you to do!"

"We'll see how much they want it once they have it," the Fox replied. "I am not wild to do this: I plainly own as much. But this is our land by rights. If we can't beat the Gradi with their gods out of the picture, we might as well leave and hand them the whole countryside."

"But they're Gradi!" Adiatunnus exclaimed—a fear-filled

sentence freighted with the memories of long years of losses. "Fighting 'em in chariots, aye, or in the keep, but here—"

"If you won't, then go back across the Venien," Gerin said harshly. If Adiatunnus and the Trokmoi did go back across the Venien, the fight was doomed. His heart felt packed with jagged ice. Doomed or not, he would go after the Gradi: a sentiment the raiders might well have understood. To Adiatunnus, he added, "If I win this battle with you, well and good. If I win it after you turn oathbreaker, your turn comes next."

He meant it. Adiatunnus could see he meant it. The Trokmê chieftain bit his lip. Gerin coldly stared his way, trying to make Adiatunnus more afraid of him than of the Gradi. After a long moment, Adiatunnus said, "I am no oathbreaker. We fight beside you."

"Prove it," Gerin said, and jumped down out of his chariot. Van thudded to the ground beside him. A moment later, so did Duren, who tethered the horses to a bush that wouldn't hold them more than a moment if they seriously decided to try breaking free.

"To the crows with you, lord prince!" Adiatunnus said, and jumped down, too.

Seeing their foes descend to the ground, the Gradi began shouting, "Voldar! Voldar!" The goddess' name rang in Gerin's ears. But however loud the Gradi yelled, the Fox felt no hum of power in the air, no sign that Voldar was near. He would not have to fight against an angry goddess, merely against her angry followers, who were apt to be quite bad enough.

He turned to his own men. "Our cry is 'Baivers!' " He didn't think the Elabonian god any more likely to take part in the fighting than Voldar, but, for one thing, he might have been wrong, and, for another, maybe those cries would reach and aid Baivers up in the divine Gradihome. After a moment, he went on, "If we win this fight, I think we win the war. We've pushed them a long way back. Now we can make sure what we've done doesn't slip out of our hands. What do you say, lads?"

"Baivers!" The war cry drowned out the shouts of the Gradi and also seemed to startle the raiders, who might still have been unused to the idea that anyone or any god could presume to stand against them or their pantheon. *Too bad for them*, Gerin though. *Life is full of surprises*. He waved his arm. Elabonians and Trokmoi trotted toward the trees.

When the Gradi saw their foes on foot, some of them came out into the field to fight there. Several Elabonians and Trokmoi snatched bows from their chariots and started shooting at their enemies. After two or three Gradi went down, the rest retreated back into the woods.

Two or three we won't have to fight in there, Gerin thought. He tried to stay in front of Duren. This, whatever else it turned out to be, was going to be an ugly fight. His son had a man's courage without a man's full strength or a man's full caution. If the Fox could shield him from danger in the forest, he would. Rationally, he knew worrying about two persons' safety at the same time made it less likely either one of them would stay safe. *To the crows with being rational*, he thought.

A Gradi sprang out from behind the trunk of an oak. Shouting Voldar's name, he swung his axe in a deadly arc. Gerin batted it aside with his shield. He had to be careful not to let the axehead hit the shield square, lest it bite through thin bronze facing, through leather, through wood, and perhaps into his arm.

He cut at the Gradi. The fellow parried with his axe, beating Gerin's blade to one side. He backed up a pace, his eyes intent, wary: he wasn't used to facing a left-handed swordsman, while Gerin had had a lifetime of struggle against right-handed foes.

The Gradi chopped again. This time, Gerin used his sword to turn the axe. He rushed in close, pushing at the Gradi with his shield till the big man from the north tripped over a root and went down. Gerin used his sword as if it were a dagger, stabbing the Gradi in the throat. The man let out a bubbling scream that quickly cut off as he choked on his own blood.

Gerin scrambled to his feet. He looked around. He couldn't see Duren, and cursed foully. The one plan he'd had in this fight was to watch over the youth, and it hadn't lasted past his own first encounter with the Gradi. The only thing left to do, then, was sweep through the woods till there were no more Gradi left to encounter.

He'd never been in a battle like this. He had scant control over it. He couldn't see more than a few feet in any direction, nor could any of the other warriors, on his side or among the Gradi. He ran from one nasty little fight to the next, helping Elabonians and Trokmoi and doing his best to stretch Gradi dead on the ground.

He was used to maneuvering scores, even hundreds of chariots as if they were war galleys out on the sea, all of them moving in accordance with his will. Not now. This was two Gradi leaping out from behind trees set close together and hacking down an Elabonian, or three Elabonians and a Trokmê slashing and stabbing at two Gradi fighting back to back till one of them fell and then swarming over the other. The woods were full of shouts and screams, full of the outhouse stink of pierced guts and the metallic odor of fresh-spilled blood.

Whenever he saw his men, he sent them toward the last band of Gradi he had spotted. Whenever he saw Gradi, he shouted for his men to come and fight them. He soon noted that he saw very few wounded men down on the ground. He didn't need long to realize each side was finishing off the other's injured men it found. He bit his lips. Fights among Elabonians, even fights between Elabonians and Trokmoi, weren't commonly so savage.

His heart jumped. There up ahead strode Duren, sword in one hand, shield on the other arm, prowling forward, his head going back and forth as he picked his way west through the woods. When the youth heard Gerin coming up behind him, he whirled around, ready to fight.

"I'm not the enemy," Gerin said, although, to a boy first sprouting his beard, any older relative, and especially his father, was liable to look like a foe a lot of the time.

Here, though, Duren understood him as he'd intended. He asked the same question as had been in Gerin's mind: "Are we winning?"

"Drop me into the hottest of the five hells if I know," the Fox answered: quietly, so as not to draw the attention of the Gradi. That might have been excess caution, for the woods rang with cries of every description. Still, caution did no harm if exercised when not needed, while needing it and not exercising it often led straight to disaster. "I don't know," he repeated. "But we're well into the woods, and they haven't thrown us back, so I'd say we're not losing."

When the words were spoken, he remembered Baivers' telling him much the same thing in the middle of the fight against Voldar and the Gradi gods. No, he though, it probably wasn't the middle of the fight, but only the beginning—by all the signs, that fight was still going on. It might go on for days more, or, for all Gerin knew, for years more. Gods didn't need to eat or sleep in any ordinary senses of the words, and they were a lot harder to kill than mere men.

He reached out and tapped Duren's shield with his sword. "Come on," he said. "Let's see what sort of lovely company we have waiting for us."

They hadn't gone far before they came to a screen of bushes around the edge of a small clearing. Again, the scene eerily reminded Gerin of the clearings in the divine Gradihome. The battle going on in the clearing was hardly less confused and no less savage than the one from which Voldar had expelled him.

"Baivers!" Duren shouted, and ran for the fighting. Gerin, had he had his way, would have gone into the fight without shouting first, and might have cut down a Gradi or two before the enemy knew he was there.

Well, no help for it now. "Baivers!" he cried, and sprinted after his son.

One Gradi who turned to meet Duren's onslaught died a moment later, the victim of the Trokmê from whom he'd been distracted. Maybe outrageous openness was as good at inducing surprise as stealth. Gerin reminded himself to think that one over if he ever found a moment when no one was trying to slaughter him.

If he did find such a moment, it wouldn't be any time soon. Here in the clearing, his men and the Gradi could find and fight one another. That was just what they were doing, with sword and spear and knife and axe, with stones grubbed from the ground with their hands, and with those broken-nailed hands themselves.

"Voldar!" the Gradi cried, over and over again. Gerin had heard that shout more often than he'd ever wanted, and had gauged the different ways the Gradi used it. What he heard now gave him hope: the Gradi sounded imploring, as if they hadn't heard from their goddess for a long time and desperately wished they would.

"Voldar is dead!" he yelled at the raiders. Some of them understood enough Elabonian to recoil in horror from that claim. The Fox knew perfectly well it was a lie. He didn't care. If the Gradi couldn't prove him wrong—and their reaction suggested they couldn't—he might as well have been right. Voldar too preoccupied with her battle on the gods' plane to come to the aid of the men she had intended to rule the northlands might as well have been Voldar dead.

But the Gradi remained fierce opponents even without Voldar tilting the natural order of things in their favor. One of them, shouting incomprehensible things that Gerin did not think were compliments, swung his axe at the Fox. His shield turned the stroke so that the flat of the axehead rather than the edge slammed against his helmet, but that was plenty to send him staggering. The Gradi rushed after him. He raised his sword to block the next vicious stroke, but it sent the blade flying from his hand.

Bellowing in triumph, the raider brought back the axe to finish him off. Gerin seized the fellow's wrist and twisted. The Gradi bellowed again, this time in pain and alarm. Gerin gave him another twist, spinning his foe over his hip and slamming him down to the ground. The Fox was still one of the best wrestlers in the northlands, and the Gradi, as far as he could tell, knew nothing whatever of the art.

The fall knocked the axe loose. The Gradi scrambled after it. Gerin kicked him in the ribs, then in the face. He grabbed the axe himself—it was closer than his sword. He swung it up, then down. Blood sprayed out from the wound it made. The Gradi's limbs convulsed. Gerin hit him again. He let out a snoring cough and died.

"Baivers!" shouted someone from behind the Fox. The shout was so fierce, he glanced back over his shoulder—and leaped aside just in time as Drungo Drago's son swung a sword at him.

"Drungo, you idiot, I'm your overlord!" Gerin screamed.

Drungo stared. "Oh, it is you, lord prince," he said in what sounded like sincere apology. "I saw the axe and I figured you were a Gradi. I didn't think one of us might have taken it off one of them."

Gerin sighed. Drungo wasn't much good at thinking. Drago the Bear, his father, hadn't been, either. Both of them, though, were handy men to have in a brawl.

More Elabonians and Trokmoi stormed into the clearing. More Gradi came in, too, but not so many more. After a while, no more Gradi were left on their feet in the open space. The ground was strewn with Gradi down and moaning, and with Gradi down and forever silent. A good many of their enemies lay there with them. Gerin's followers who were still upright stalked across the red-splashed grass, finishing off the wounded Gradi who still lived.

"Come on," Gerin said when that grim task was done. He pointed into the woods. "We've still got plenty of the whoresons to deal with in there."

Some of his men, even those who had fought bravely in the clearing, hesitated before leaving it for the forest. He couldn't blame them. Fighting in the open was what they knew. Sneaking among the trees was more like hunting, except that here the quarry was also hunting them.

Somewhere west in the woods, a Gradi was shouting to his comrades. Gerin couldn't understand a word he was saying, but he recognized the voice: that was the captain who'd spoken Elabonian, marshaling his troops. The Fox stopped and cocked his head and listened to the fighting. It got fiercer off to his left. He sent men of his own in that direction. Unlike the Gradi, he didn't roar and bellow while he was doing it.

Then he started moving toward that great voice. "Van was right all along," he remarked to Duren. "They've found themselves a leader who's trying to whip them into shape, Voldar or no Voldar. If we kill him, my bet is they start falling to pieces."

With their chieftain alive, the Gradi showed no signs of falling to pieces. Gerin had to fight several times as he approached the roaring Gradi leader. He was getting close when a big man emerged from behind a tree that didn't look to have been wide enough to conceal his bulk. As Drungo had, he started to attack the Fox; unlike Drungo, he checked himself without Gerin's having to scream at him.

Gerin halted what would have been his own attack. He nodded to Van, hardly more surprised than if he'd met him walking out of the great hall back at Fox Keep. "Good to see they haven't let the air out of you."

"And you," the outlander answered. "You heading over to put paid to that fellow giving orders at the top of his lungs?"

"Just what I'm doing," Gerin agreed. "Killing one man and breaking their backbone is a cheaper way of beating them than having to make the fight on his terms."

"I thought the same," Van said. "That's why I was going for him, too."

"We'll all go for him," Duren said. "Who does it doesn't matter, as long as someone does."

Van slapped Gerin on the back. "Well, Fox, you've trained up the sapling to grow the same way as the tree. And since the tree grows straight, that's a good way for the sapling to follow. Which is a fancy way of saying that the lad is right. Come on." He glided forward, amazingly light and quiet on his feet for so large a man.

Gerin and Duren followed. The Gradi chieftain kept on bawling orders to his men. He wasn't hard to find, any more than a roaring longtooth would have been. The Fox suspected he would have been about as glad to stumble over a longtooth as over the chief.

Van stretched out his arm, palm facing the Fox. Gerin obediently halted. Van didn't even point. That he'd stopped was enough. Gerin peered through the screen of bushes. A Gradi came running up to one of his fellows who stood there. He gasped out something. The other man listened, then turned to one side and shouted. This was the enemy's leader, sure enough.

"We'll all dash out together," Gerin whispered, wishing he had his bow—killing the big, fierce raider from a distance would have been safe and convenient. "One, two—"

As he said "three," another Gradi runner burst into the

clearing. The Fox grabbed at his friend and son, trying to hold them back, but too late—they'd already launched themselves at the Gradi chieftain. He burst out of the woods, too, half a step behind them.

Half a dozen strides and they were on the three Gradi. That was, unfortunately, just enough time to let the raiders break free from their momentary shock, raise their axes, and fight back. The two lesser Gradi sprang in front of their chief. One of them engaged Van, the other Duren: the first two foes they found. That left the leader for Gerin.

He would willingly have forgone the honor. The Gradi was bigger than he was, and younger than he was, too. The Gradi also knew more about using an axe than did Gerin, who still held the weapon he'd snatched from his fallen foe. The only advantage Gerin had . . . Try as he would, he couldn't think of any.

"Voldar!" the Gradi shouted, and cut at his head. He ducked—and almost fell victim to a backhand cut: the Gradi was as strong as he looked, and as quick, too. Gerin made a cut of his own, a tentative one, which the enemy leader easily evaded. The Gradi chopped at him again. He took this blow on the shield, and felt it all the way up his arm to his shoulder. His best hope, he thought, was for Van and Duren to beat their men and help him. He didn't see any way he was likely to beat the Gradi chief on his own.

By the fierce sneer the Gradi wore, he didn't see any way Gerin was likely to beat him, either. He feinted once, feinted twice, then chopped again. Gerin once more managed to get his shield in front of the blow—but it hit square and true, the axehead smashing through his protection.

The very corner of the sharp edge of the axe kissed his arm with fire. He held on to his grip on the shield, though—the wound was not severe. And, when the Gradi captain tried to pull the axe free so he could strike again, he found he could not. It had twisted, and would not go back through the narrow hole it had made. He shouted in fury and alarm.

Gerin did not give him the chance to clear the axe from the shield. Instead of backing away, he moved close to the

Gradi, so the fellow had no room in which to draw back his arm. The Gradi didn't like that. His lips skinned back from his teeth in a horrible grin.

He should have let go of the axe and run. Instead, he kept trying to jerk it loose, and to fend off Gerin's own left-handed blows. Since his left arm and the Fox's were on opposite sides, and since his right hand clutched the useless axe handle, he could not do it. After Gerin's second stroke got home, the Gradi groaned and his grip faltered.

The Fox hit him again, this time in the side of the neck. The Gradi let out a startled grunt. His eyes went very wide. He let go of the axe. His mouth shaped a word. Gerin thought it was "Voldar," but it had no breath behind it. The Gradi swayed, toppled, fell.

Gerin whirled to help Van and Duren. Van had his own man down, and was yanking his spear out of the Gradi's belly. A loop of gray-pink gut came with it. Duren was fighting a defensive battle against his foe. When Van and Gerin both rushed to his aid, the Gradi who opposed him turned to flee. He did not get far.

Another Gradi burst into the clearing, staring in shocked dismay at what he found there. He did escape before Gerin and his comrades could pursue.

"Come on," the Fox said. "This isn't the whole job. We can't just beat them here—we have to break them."

If he lived, he knew he'd want to sleep three days, and would wake up stiff and sore in every joint even if he did. He plunged into the woods nonetheless.

There was more hard fighting as the day wore along, but something seemed to have gone out of the Gradi when their chieftain fell. The sun was only a little more than halfway down toward the west when Gerin emerged from the woods and saw a few, a very few, Gradi running off toward the west past Bidgosh Pond. Behind him, the sounds of battle were ebbing. Such shouts and cries as he could hear were almost all in either Elabonian or the Trokmê tongue.

Half a bowshot north of him, someone else came out from among the trees: a Trokmê. He looked toward the Fox and waved. Gerin waved back. "Adiatunnus!" he called.

Slowly, Adiatunnus came toward him. The woodsrunner looked as tired as Gerin felt. "Diviciacus went down, puir wight," he said. "My own right hand he was, all these years. A rare sad thing. But—" He straightened. "Lord prince, we've beaten the buggers, and in a way I don't think they'll be over soon. From here, we can clear the northlands of 'em, right out to the edge o' the sea."

"I think that may be so," Gerin answered. More men, Elabonians and Trokmoi both, came out of the woods and gathered around their two leaders. Hardly daring to believe what he'd just said, Gerin repeated it: "I think that may be so."

"It is that, lord prince," Adiatunnus said positively. Then he paused, perhaps to weigh his own words. "Aye, it is so, lord prince, and 'twas you who made it real. I couldna ha' done it: I own as much. No man but your own self could ha' done it, lord prince." He shook his head. "Nay. That isna right."

"Who says it's not?" Van boomed angrily.

"I do," Adiatunnus answered. He sighed, then went, not to one knee, but to both. "No man but your own self could ha' done it . . . lord king."

XII

From a hillock not far away, Gerin stared at the Orynian Ocean. It was not like the Greater Inner Sea, save in being a large body of water. The blue Inner Sea was calm, peaceful. The gray ocean rolled and pulsed and smashed against rocks, sending spray high into the air. It was, in its way, as barbarous and as vigorous as the Gradi who rode it.

A strong stone keep sat by the ocean, not far south of the Niffet. The Fox had driven the Gradi from most of the northlands. Their remnant lingered here. He did not think he could storm this keep. He could not properly besiege it, either, not with its back to the Orynian Ocean: the Gradi from the north could keep it supplied by a road he did not control.

Duren climbed to the top of the hillock. He looked out at the ocean for a while; he found it endlessly fascinating. Then he pointed toward the keep the Gradi still held. "What will you do about them, Father?" he asked, confident the Fox would come up with something even if he couldn't see for himself what it was.

Gerin gave him the only answer he could: "This year, nothing. We've done all we could. We've done more than I ever expected. As long as the Gradi gods are at war on their own plane, the Gradi themselves we can beat, or at least meet on even terms, which is good enough."

"What if they sally after we go away, though?" Duren said.

"I'll leave men behind—my vassals, Elabonians and Trokmoi both. The Gradi killed most of the local lords; their claims have lapsed. We'll restore some keeps, maybe build some new ones, and make this a harder land for them to overrun than it used to be. Before, all the lords were rivals to all the others. Now, they'll be able to call on one another against the Gradi—and on me, too."

"Aye," Duren said. "They can call on their king."

On his own, Gerin would not have claimed the title. Aragis the Archer, who styled himself grand duke, had stayed quiet this summer, probably hoping Gerin and the Gradi would wreck each other, leaving him to pick up the pieces—and the rank that went with picking up the pieces. What he would do when he found out Gerin was wearing the rank . . . remained to be seen.

But Adiatunnus had been a rival almost as dangerous as Aragis, and Adiatunnus had been the one to call him king. "Almost makes me think there is such a thing as gratitude," Gerin murmured.

"Father?" Duren asked.

"Never mind," the Fox answered. The Trokmoi had been as willing as his own men to acknowledge his kingship. How long that willingness would last also remained to be seen.

While it did, he would make the most of it. You could push people further if you moved them in the direction they were already going. And fear of a Gradi revival would make them want to pay attention to the man who had stopped the raiders the first time.

"We have to have ships of our own," he said. He knew he'd said that before. Without ships of his own, the Gradi would be able to rebuild their strength and assail the northlands again at a time of their choosing.

Duren had another thought: "What do we do if the Gradi gods end up overcoming Baivers and the underground powers?"

Gerin set a hand on his son's shoulder. "I'm less worried

about that now than I was before I saw how potent Baivers could be when he chose. Even if Voldar beats him, she won't rout him. If she could do that, she would have done it already. And if she does beat him, well, we may be able to stir up other sleepy Elabonian gods against her and her friends. Baivers will let them know the fight is one they need to make."

"That will put the gods more in the world, if you know what I mean, than they have been since time out of mind," Duren said.

"I've thought the same thing," the Fox agreed. "I don't like the notion—in the face of the gods' powers, the ones we have look pretty small. But if that's what happens, then it is, that's all. We'll have to make the best of it we can. One way or another, I expect we'll manage."

"You will," Duren said. Remembering himself at the age when his beard had begun to sprout, Gerin knew how rare and precious his son's unalloyed approval was. Duren went on, "You always find a way."

Is that how I want to be remembered? Gerin wondered. He tasted the words in his mind. *He always found a way.* It wasn't the sort of memorial a hero in a minstrel's song would have chosen for himself. Or was it? Gerin was himself the hero of more than one song cycle, though the Fox of whom the minstrels sang bore scant resemblance to the one who dwelt inside Gerin's body. *He always found a way.* Aye, you could do worse than that.

"When we get back to Fox Keep, my mother will be so proud," Duren said.

He was, without a doubt, right. He meant Selatre, of course. He knew she hadn't given him birth, but he hardly ever seemed to think about that; as best Gerin could tell, he didn't remember Elise any more. The Fox did. He wondered if she was still alive. If she was, he wondered what she would think, to hear him called king of the north. His mouth twisted. No point to thinking about it. He'd never know.

Knowing he'd never know, he forced his thoughts toward more immediate concerns, saying, "I'm not much worried about what Selatre will think of me. She's fond of me whether people call me king or not. When we get back to Adiatunnus' holding, though, I do want to see how the rest of the Trokmoi take to the title."

"What will you do if they reject it?" Duren asked.

"I don't know." Gerin looked sidelong at his son. "Maybe we'll have a war."

"I've seen enough of war for a while," Duren burst out.

"You're learning, lad," Gerin told him. "You're learning."

"You leave everything to me, now," Adiatunnus said as they were about to go back east over the Venien River.

Gerin laughed out loud. "I didn't get this old by leaving everything to anybody—except me."

"I named you king once now," the Trokmê chief said in some exasperation. "Am I likely to go back on that naming with your own southron warriors all around me, the ugly kerns?"

"Truth to tell, I don't know what you're likely to do," Gerin answered. As he'd hoped, Adiatunnus took that for a compliment, a tribute to his deviousness. The woodsrunner slapped his driver on the back. The driver urged the team ahead. They splashed through the Venien's ford at a gallop, their hooves and the chariot's wheels kicking up spray that sparkled in the sun.

"You don't want to let him get too far ahead, or who knows which way his mouth is liable to start running?" Van said. Even before he'd spoken, though, Duren had sped up, crossing the Venien right behind Adiatunnus and in the same style. Van rumbled approval, down deep in his chest. "That's a fine lad you have there."

"I'd noticed," Gerin remarked, which made the outlander laugh and Duren, standing there in front of both of them, fidget noticeably.

Trokmoi working in the fields called questions to the returning warriors. The shouts of victory they got back started them whooping in turn. Adiatunnus added, whenever he got the chance, "Come back to the keep, now, and I'll give you summat even more worth the hearing of it."

He didn't actually go into the keep, but gathered with his own people and the returned Elabonian warriors in the square of the large village in front of the castle. With the sense of drama any good chief had, he waited for the crowd to build—and to buzz. Serving women brought ale out of the keep and poured out dippersful to whoever looked thirsty.

When the Trokmê judged the moment right, he clambered up onto a big stump and shouted, "The Gradi are ruined for fair, sure and they are, their nasty gods still locked in a shindy and themselves pushed all the way back to the ocean." That unleashed an ocean in the village, an ocean of cheers. Adiatunnus reached down and hauled Gerin up onto the stump with him. He went on, "The southron here, he had summat to do with it—a wee bit, you might say."

Gerin was used to both the excesses and understatements of Trokmê oratory. So were Adiatunnus' listeners, who cheered the Fox. Adiatunnus warmed to his theme: "And I'll have you know I'm vassal no more to the prince of the north." That brought cheers, too, but cheers of a different sort—the cheers of Trokmoi bayingly eager to break free of any feudal obligations. The Fox wondered if Adiatunnus was about to betray him after all. Then the Trokmê shouted, "Nay, for now I'm vassal to Gerin the Fox, king o' the north, and so named out of my very own mouth."

Silence slammed down for a moment as the Trokmoi took that in and worked out what it meant. Then they and Gerin's Elabonian retainers all cheered louder than ever. Adiatunnus gave the Fox an elbow in the ribs. Taking half a step forward—any more and he would have fallen off the stump—Gerin said, "I'll try to be a good king, a fair king, for everyone, Elabonian or Trokmê. And if anyone, Elabonian or Trokmê, tries to take advantage of me, he'll think a tree trunk fell on him. Is it a bargain?"

"Aye!" they roared. He suspected they were cheering deliverance from the Gradi more than they were cheering him, but he didn't mind that. Without him, they wouldn't have had the deliverance. He was glad they had sense enough to realize that—for a little while.

He hopped down off the stump. A very pretty Trokmê girl with red-gold hair handed him a dipper of ale. He poured it down. When he gave the dipper back, he noticed how bright a blue her eyes were, what moist, inviting lips she had, just how snugly her linen tunic fit over firm young breasts. He was meant to notice; in what seemed more a purr than a voice, she said, "A king, is it? What might it be like, to sleep with a king?"

"If you ever come to Fox Keep, you can ask my wife," he told her. She stared at him. Those blue, blue eyes went hard as stone, cold as ice. She flounced off. He counted himself lucky she hadn't crowned him with the dipper.

"You're a wasteful man, Fox," Van said. "The gods don't make 'em that good-looking every day."

"I'll survive," Gerin said, "and I won't have any crockery thrown at me when I get home, which is more than I can say for you."

"You mean Fand?" Van said. Gerin nodded. The outlander rolled his eyes. "She'd throw things at me whether I futtered other women on the road or not, so the way I see it is, I might as well."

That sort of reasoning would have sent a Sithonian sophist running for cover. It sent Gerin looking for another dipper of ale, with luck one from a serving girl not quite so anxious to try him on for size just because he was wearing a fancy new title. He sighed, a little. Van was right: she had been very pretty.

A sentry up on the palisade peered out at the approaching force of chariotry. "Who comes to Fox Keep?" he called.

He knew the answer to that question. Gerin had sent messengers ahead with news of what he'd done. Nevertheless, he answered, loudly and proudly: "Gerin the Fox, king of the north."

"Enter your keep, lord king!" the sentry shouted. The rest of the men on the palisade erupted in cheers, cheers that soon echoed from within the keep as well. The drawbridge thudded down. Gerin tapped Duren on the shoulder. His son drove him over the drawbridge and into the courtyard.

He hopped out of the chariot then, and embraced Selatre. She said, "I hoped this would happen one day. I'm so glad it has, and so proud of you."

"I thought it might happen one day," Gerin answered, "though I never expected Adiatunnus to be the one to proclaim my rank. Up until the Gradi grew to be serious trouble, I thought killing him would likely be what made folk style me king."

Rihwin the Fox came over and set his hands on his hips. "For your information," he said loftily, "I find this ever-swelling titulature of yours in questionable taste." Then, grinning, he clasped Gerin's hand.

"You're impossible," Gerin told his fellow Fox. Rihwin's mouth opened. Gerin beat him to the punch line: "Bloody implausible, anyhow."

"The king!" Geroge shouted. The monster, still short a fang, held up a jack of ale in salute. "The king!"

One more feast, Gerin thought. *One more big feast and I can send my vassals back to their own keeps and let them eat their own food*. The fields past which he'd ridden on the way back to Fox Keep looked to have good crops coming in. He hoped they would; that would let him begin to rebuild his stores, which were painfully low. If his vassals had good harvests, too, they might even be able to send grain west to the lands across the Venien, which had had such a dose of Gradi-style weather that their fields were unlikely to yield much this year.

Then the Fox stopped worrying so much about the fields and the harvest. Dagref, Clotild, and Blestar came rushing out of the great hall and swarmed over him and Duren. "I want to hear everything that happened after you left," Dagref said. "I want you to tell it to me now, in order, so I don't get anything mixed up."

"I'm sure you want that," Gerin said, hugging his eldest by Selatre. He was also sure that, having heard everything once, Dagref would be able to correct him on details for years afterwards. And the boy would be right, too, almost every time: Dagref could be quite alarming. Gerin went on, "I'll tell you everything soon, maybe even tomorrow. Right now I want to—I need to—spend time with my vassals."

"It's not fair," Dagref protested. "You'll start to forget things."

"It'll be all right," Clotild told him. "Papa has a pretty good memory—most of the time," she added with a small sniff.

"Papa!" Blestar said happily. "Papa!" Gerin hugged him, too. He wasn't finding fault with his father: probably, though, for no better reason than that he was too young.

Selatre gave Gerin a jack of ale. He poured a small libation down onto the ground and said, "Thank you, lord Baivers." As with the battle cries there in the woods not far from the ocean, he had no idea whether the god of barley and brewing heard or was still too busy fighting the Gradi gods to pay any attention to mere mortals. He didn't care. He was grateful, and willing—no, eager—to show it.

He went through the keep—into the great hall, back out to the courtyard—several times, drinking, eating, clapping his vassals and their vassals on the back and telling them how splendidly they had fought, something which, in most cases, had the virtue of being true. They were doing much the same thing themselves, though less systematic in their mingling. He got called "lord king" often enough to begin to get used to the new title, even if he still wondered what Aragis the Archer would do in response to his wearing it.

Night fell. So many torches burned, people hardly seemed to notice. And then, here and there—on benches in the great hall, in quiet corners of the courtyard—the warriors who had returned to Fox Keep with him began falling asleep. Gerin remembered wishing he could sleep for three days after that fight in the woods. He was still far, far behind, and likely would be for . . . oh, the next twenty years, if he lived so long.

Not far away from him, Fand demanded of Van, "And how many wenches were you after sleeping with this time?" She sounded half-drunk and more than half-dangerous.

To Gerin's horror, Van, who had drunk a good deal himself, began counting on his fingers to make sure he got things right. "Seven, it was," he announced at last, as proud of his precision as Dagref might have been.

"It's an old man you're turning into," Fand told him. "You said a dozen the last time." Her voice rose to a screech: "Keep your breeches on, curse you!" She dashed her jack of ale into his face. Dripping and sputtering, he roared at her. She roared back, even louder.

Gerin's head started to ache. He looked around for his children. The younger ones, along with Van's son and daughter, were curled up on the rushes not far from the doorway to the great hall, but well away from the path people used to go in and out. Someone had spread a couple of wool blankets over them. They were fine where they were; he saw no point to waking them up and taking them to their bed. They might not fall asleep again for half the night.

He didn't see Duren at all. That probably meant his eldest was finding a way to celebrate his return that would have made his wife shout as Fand was shouting at Van. Since he didn't have a wife, though . . .

The Fox did see Selatre. With Dagref, Clotild, and Blestar conveniently asleep, he also saw an opportunity. He caught her eye, then glanced toward the stairway that led up to their bedchamber. She smiled and nodded.

With only the two of them in it, the bed seemed uncommonly large, uncommonly luxurious. Making love without having to hurry or to worry about the children waking up at an inconvenient moment seemed uncommonly luxurious, too.

Afterwards, Gerin thought of the pretty Trokmê girl who hadn't managed to tempt him into imitating Van. Chuckling, he told Selatre the story, then asked her, "What might it be like, to sleep with a king?"

"I," she said, "like it."

Geroge looked dubious as Gerin walked up to him carrying a small bowl filled with fine, moist clay. The monster's thin lips skinned back from his teeth. Those teeth looked so extremely formidable, Gerin wondered whether he wanted to go through with what he had planned.

He decided he did. "Open your mouth," he told the monster.

"You're going to have me eat clay?" Geroge protested. "You didn't tell me I'd have to eat clay."

"You don't have to eat it," Gerin told him. "You just have to let me press it up against your teeth so I can get the shape of the fang you have left. I'll use the mold you're giving me to make a gold tooth like it to put on the other side, to take the place of the one the gods under Ikos took."

"It'll taste horrible," Geroge said. "I don't think I want to do it."

"It's only dirt," Gerin said. "It's not even very dirty dirt, if you know what I mean: it's the fine clay they use for baking pots." When Geroge still shook his massive head, the Fox sighed and said, "When we're done, I'll give you a jack of ale to wash away whatever taste there is."

"Oh, all right." Geroge still sounded reluctant even after Gerin's promise, which showed how unwilling he had been before.

"Open your mouth," Gerin said again.

Eyes rolling, Gerin did. The Fox brought the lump of clay up to it with more than a little trepidation: if Geroge chose to bite down now, he'd spend the rest of his days one-handed. Geroge grunted as Gerin made the impression of his fang and the teeth near it. He went from grunt to growl, but held still.

"Splendid," Gerin said, gently freeing the clay. "If you'd wiggled there, I would have had to do this all over again." *Oh, what a liar I'm getting to be*, he thought. Doing it once had been hard. Doing it twice . . . He didn't care to contemplate doing it twice.

Geroge peered down with interest at the marks his teeth had made in the clay. "They're big, aren't they?" he remarked. "I didn't know they were that big. I thought they were more like yours."

"Did you?" Gerin said. *That's what comes of living among humans all your life—we're your touchstone, your standard of comparison*. That probably made Geroge and Tharma a lot safer to be near than they might have been otherwise.

He took the bowl with the impression to the oven the potter used in his trade and fired it, as the potter would have fired a platter or a storage jar. When it came out and had cooled, he took it to the shack where he worked his magic. He had no intention of doing anything magical to it, but had a small furnace of his own there. In it in another small bowl he put some armlets and rings from his treasury: loot taken from the Trokmoi. He stoked the little furnace and used goatskin bellows to make the fire burn hotter yet.

He'd carved his tongs himself, of wood, and faced them with bronze so they wouldn't char so fast or even catch fire at an inopportune moment. With them, he lifted the bowl and poured molten gold into the mold he prepared for it. The mold took almost all the metal he had melted; Geroge did indeed have big teeth.

When the metal had cooled, he broke the mold. He used a bronze chisel to cut away the gold that filled the impressions of other teeth near the fang, then polished the fang by shaking it in a hide bag full of fine sand. After he'd attached a couple of thin wires to the base, he took the gold tooth to Geroge.

This time, the monster opened his mouth willingly enough. Gerin put the gold tooth in the gap the monsters' gods had left when they ripped the real fang from Geroge's mouth. He used the wires to anchor the artificial fang to the genuine teeth on either side of it. "What do you think?" he asked Geroge.

The monster explored with his tongue the change in his mouth. "It feels all right," he said. Then he opened his mouth in an enormous smile. "What does it look like?"

"Your other fang, except it's gold," Gerin answered.

That was literal truth, but it wasn't what Geroge wanted to hear. He waved to Tharma, who was walking across the courtyard, and pointed to Gerin's dentistry. "How do I look?"

Like a monster with a gold tooth, Gerin thought, but held his tongue, waiting to see what Tharma would say. "I think you look very handsome," she replied after grave contemplation. Geroge preened and swaggered. Gerin didn't know whether the answer, and Geroge's response to it, pleased or worried him more.

Chariot wheels rumbled on the paving blocks of the Elabon Way. Along with the chariots, Gerin led a good-sized force of men riding horses. The army he headed was smaller than the one he had taken west over the Venien against the Gradi, but more than large enough to be formidable. Like the force that had traveled west, it included both Elabonians and Trokmoi, Adiatunnus having sent a contingent of woodsrunners at Gerin's request.

Van looked back and chuckled. "If this doesn't have 'em ready to piss their breeches, nothing ever will."

"That's the idea," Gerin answered. "Anything worth doing is worth doing properly—or worth overdoing, if you'd rather think of it like that."

"Aye, that suits me pretty well," the outlander said. Considering his excesses whenever he got out of Fand's sight, Gerin had to agree with him.

Duren pointed ahead. "There's the border post between Bevander's holding and Ricolf's."

"No, that's not right," his father told him. "There's the border post between Bevander's holding and yours. And if anyone has any doubts about that, well, I expect we can convince him to change his mind." He waved back over his shoulder to show what he meant.

The guards on Ricolf's side of the border stared in popeyed wonder at the army bearing down on them. Gerin started to tell Duren to stop and parley with them, then decided to hold his tongue: Duren was going to be the baron here, not himself. Duren did stop. In a shaken voice, one of the border guards asked, "Who, ah, who comes to the holding formerly of Ricolf the Red?" He sounded as if he couldn't decide whether to sell his life dear or flee for the nearest woods.

His companion at the border crossing added, "Not just who—why?" He was gawping at the Trokmoi, as if wondering if they'd decided to settle down in the neighborhood.

"I am Duren Gerin's son, grandson to Ricolf the Red and heir to this holding through my mother, Ricolf's daughter Elise," Duren answered. "Having completed the service I owed my father, I have come to take my rightful place as baron here. From this day forth, I stay in this holding."

"Brought a few, ah, friends along, have you, lord?" the first guard asked. He was looking at the Trokmoi, too.

"He has my support, as you might have guessed he would," Gerin put in.

Both border guards nodded. "Oh, yes, lord prince," they chorused.

Gerin, Van, and Duren grinned at one another. Being at the forefront of news was always enjoyable. To the guards, Duren said, "Allow me to present you to my father, Gerin the Fox, king of the north, so proclaimed first by Adiatunnus the Trokmê after we all vanquished the Gradi together."

In a way, Gerin thought, it was too bad the two guards had already been staring. Their eyes couldn't get much wider; they jaws couldn't drop much farther. The first one, the one with the slight hitch to his speech, said, "I would, uh, be glad to have more of that, uh, tale, lord."

"And I would be glad to give it—another time," Duren answered. "Now I want to settle myself in the keep that is mine." He flicked the reins. The horses began to trot. Because he was driving the lead chariot in the army, that was the best signal he could give for the rest of the cars to enter the holding that was now becoming his.

On the way down to the keep that had been Ricolf's, peasants who saw Duren's army fled for their lives. "I don't like that any better than you do, Father," Duren said, pointing to serfs running for the shelter of the woods.

"I worry about it less here than I would otherwise," Gerin answered. "For one thing, this is a good-sized force, and all the more frightening on account of that. And for another, remember, we've got Trokmoi with us. The woodsrunners haven't been seen in these parts since just a little while after they flooded over the Niffet."

"Aye, that's so," Van agreed. "And the reason they haven't been seen in these parts for so long is that you've held them away from these parts—not that anybody around here will want to give you credit for it."

"I didn't do it to get the credit for it," the Fox said. "I did it because it needed doing." He chuckled. "Besides, the only thing a baron in one holding is liable to give his neighbor credit for is catching unpleasant diseases from his sheep." Van snorted. So did Duren, although he, unlike the outlander, tried to pretend he hadn't.

Lying by the Elabon Way, the keep that had been Ricolf's was well positioned for its holder to keep an eye on north- and southbound travelers. The frantic stir and bustle on the walls said nobody there had seen anything like the approaching army for a long time. The cry of "Who comes to this castle?" betokened not just curiosity but genuine alarm.

Duren needed no prompting from Gerin to answer as he had at the border: "Duren Gerin's son, come to claim the lordship here, which passes to me from Ricolf the Red through his daughter Elise, my mother." Then he added, "Let down the drawbridge this instant, Ricrod." He did not say *or suffer the consequences afterwards*, but his meaning was plain to Gerin.

It was evidently plain to Ricrod, too, for the drawbridge came down in short order. Duren drove over it into the courtyard of the keep, followed by so many other cars that resistance from the men already inside quickly became hopeless. As he snapped orders, some of Gerin's men took charge of the doors into the great hall of the castle, to make sure they could not be slammed shut against the newcomers. Gerin approved: he would have taken charge of the keep the same way.

But instead of a host of armed men, only Ricrod the steward came out of the great hall. He looked round in amazement at the force that had come to install Duren as baron. The size of that force drove from his head whatever objection he might have had. "Welcome, lord," he said to Duren, and then, to Gerin, "And welcome to you as well, lord prince."

"My father's style these days, with the Gradi beaten, is 'lord king,'" Duren said.

That made Ricrod stare and several soldiers exclaim. In the holding that had been Ricolf's the Gradi had never been more than a name; as he had with the Trokmoi, Gerin had shielded the lands belonging to his former father-in-law from the onslaughts of the invaders. But if only a name, the Gradi were a potent name to the men here, and the importance of the name only grew if beating them had been enough to let Gerin assume a royal title.

After the tale had been briefly told, Duren said, "Ricrod, send messengers at once to Authari and Hilmic, Wacho and Ratkis. Order them to report here to my keep at once, that they may give me homage and fealty." The look he gave the steward was less than warm. "I know you can get messages to them quickly."

"Er—yes," Ricrod said. To Gerin, he sounded nervous. In Ricrod's boots, the Fox would have been nervous, too.

The messages he'd sent the last time Duren had been through this holding had almost ended up getting its rightful overlord killed. Ricrod coughed a couple of times, then bowed low. "It shall be as you say, lord, in all things. With dawn tomorrow, the messengers go forth."

"That will do," Duren said grudgingly. He still stared through the steward. "Did you wait till the next morning to send them out when I left this keep on the way to Ikos?"

"Lord, I did," Ricrod said. He nodded toward the altar that smoked close by the hearth. "In Dyaus All-father's name I swear it."

"Very well," Duren said, mollified by the answer. Gerin thought his acceptance wise unless he planned to remove Ricrod, in which case it didn't matter. But if he was going to keep the steward and work with him, he needed to show he trusted him. Otherwise, even if Ricrod hadn't been inclined toward plots, he was liable to acquire that inclination in a hurry.

The Fox's eyes went to the altar dedicated to Dyaus. He wondered if the head of the Elabonian pantheon noticed when someone swore an oath in his name. From what Baivers had said, Dyaus was even further removed from the material plane than the rest of the Elabonian gods. Voldar, now— Gerin didn't want to think what the Gradi goddess might have done to one of her people who falsely swore by her (except, perhaps, one who swore falsely to gain advantage over her foes). But Dyaus seemed to ignore such transgressions. Would Ricrod know that, or feel it somehow? Gerin studied the steward. He had trouble deciding.

He shook his head. It wasn't properly his concern, or wouldn't be for long. This was Duren's holding. Duren would choose whom to believe here, whom to doubt. If he chose wrong, he'd pay for it.

To Duren, Ricrod said, "Er, lord, with the lord prince your father now become the lord king your father, do you hold this keep as a free and independent baron, or as his vassal?"

Gerin's respect for Ricrod's wit, till then low, rose sharply. That was a good question, and one whose answer every petty baron in the holding would want.

"I am my own man here," Duren answered. "I have sworn vassalage to no one for this keep, nor has anyone asked me to swear it. If you think I will deny I am my father's son, though, you are making a mistake."

He'd said much the same thing here shortly after his grandfather's death. It had seemed theoretical then. Now it mattered, and mattered a great deal. Ricrod smacked his lips, tasting the reply. "I could not ask you to speak fairer, lord," he said at last, and sounded as if he meant it.

Several of the soldiers at the keep also nodded. "Well said," came from one of them. Gerin grinned to himself. Duren was starting off here as well as anyone could hope. What would happen after Authari and the other leading vassals arrived was liable to be a different story, though.

Up on the wall of Duren's keep, Ricrod looked away toward the southwest. "Why don't they come?" he muttered fretfully, glancing over to Gerin, who stood beside him. "They should have begun appearing a couple of days ago."

"If they don't come soon—Authari Broken-Tooth especially—I'll go pay them a visit, and we'll see how they like that," Gerin said.

"It would keep your men from eating this keep out of food," Ricrod muttered. Gerin didn't think he was supposed to hear that, so he politely pretended he hadn't.

The first of Ricolf's leading vassals came in that afternoon. Gerin would have bet on Ratkis Bronzecaster's arriving before any of the others, and would have won that bet had he made it with anyone. Ratkis wasted no time in going to one knee before Duren and saying, "Good to have a lord again in this holding."

"Good to be here," Duren said. "I'm sure I still have a lot to learn. Some of that, I expect, I'll learn from you."

Ratkis got to his feet and turned to Gerin. "He's already learned a good deal from you, sounds like." He raised an eyebrow. "And did the messenger have it right that you're calling yourself king these days?"

"He had it right," Gerin answered, and waited to see how Ricolf's vassal—now Duren's vassal—would respond to that.

"I hope you get away with it, lord king," was all Ratkis said. Considering that Gerin hoped he would get away with it, too, he didn't see how he could complain about Ratkis' answer.

Authari Broken-Tooth, Wacho Fidus' son, and Hilmic Barrelstaves all arrived within a couple of hours of one another on the following day. Each of them came with a large force of chariotry, no doubt as large as he could muster; in his mind's eye, Gerin saw messengers hurrying from one keep to another. The sum of their three little armies, though, was about half the size of his, as they were crestfallen to discover.

"Got their line nibbled by a bigger fish than they expected," Van said gleefully. "Instead of pulling him up onto the bank, they find that they're going out into the creek."

"So they do," Gerin said. "And do you know what? I'm not the least bit sorry for them. Maybe now, seeing what I can do if I like, they'll realize they aren't big enough to quarrel with me, and they'll settle down and be good—or at least not impossible—vassals for my son."

If that was what the three vassal barons had in mind, they didn't show it right away. Authari stomped up to Ricrod and, all politesse forgotten, demanded, "Has your messenger gone daft? What's this nonsense about kings he was babbling?"

Glancing nervously toward Gerin, the steward cleared his throat and answered, "Ah, lord Authari, no nonsense to it. There stands the king of the north."

Authari clapped a hand to his forehead. "You haven't had enough of lording it over men who are by rights your peers?" he snapped at Gerin. "Who named you king, anyhow? Did you do it yourself?"

As the Fox had more than once already, he took considerable pleasure in answering, "No, the first man to use the title was my vassal, Adiatunnus the Trokmê."

Authari's jaw dropped. Hilmic and Wacho both gaped at Gerin. All three of them must have known how much trouble Adiatunnus had given him over the years, and had probably hoped to match his thorny independence. Authari found his voice first: "What did he go and do that for?" He sounded not just disbelieving but outraged.

"For driving the Gradi back to the edge of the ocean

and for embroiling their gods with others so we could pin 'em back there," Gerin answered calmly.

"If you'll think back," Van added, "you'll recall the Fox here was the one who put paid to the monsters a few years back, and to the wizard Balamung a few years before that. So he's done a thing or three to deserve being called a king. What in the five hells have *you* done to deserve to say he doesn't?"

Several of Authari's men nodded when they heard that, which made Gerin work hard to keep a stiff face. He said, "What I've done doesn't matter, not here, not now. This trip isn't about me. It's about my son here, and about the oaths you swore after you heard what the Sibyl had to say about him."

"I said I had to serve my father before I came and ruled this barony on my own," Duren put in. "Now I've done that, and now I'm ready to take up my rule here. Does any man in this keep say I have not the right?"

There it was, a challenge set out with more blunt force, perhaps, than Gerin would have used, but with undeniable power. The crowded great hall in the castle that had been Ricolf's and was now passing to his grandson grew very still. Men leaned forward to hear if any of Ricolf's vassals would challenge that succession.

Always a temporizer, Authari asked, as Ricrod had before him, whether Duren intended to hold the barony as his father's vassal. As Duren had before, he denied it. "It doesn't matter," Authari said then, gloomily. "We're still going to be in the middle of this kingdom, whether we're a part of it in name or not. Bah!"

Gerin thought he was right about that. Everyone outside Duren's barony with whom he would deal would be one of the Fox's vassals . . . unless he tried dealing with Aragis the Archer, in which case Gerin would make him regret it faster than he'd ever imagined.

Authari, still looking for a way to play ends against middle, hadn't noticed all the implications of what he'd said. Wacho, for a wonder, did. "Give it up," he said. "We're fighting somebody too big for us now."

"You say that?" Authari demanded angrily, his suave manner eroding with his hopes.

But Wacho nodded, and so did Hilmic, who said, "Look around you. He's got too many men for us to fight, he's got Adiatunnus' Trokmoi backing him instead of making his life a misery—"

"And how did you manage that?" Authari snapped at Gerin. "Aren't you the one who was always prating about what a pack of savages the Trokmoi were and how we Elabonians shouldn't do anything with 'em except drive 'em back over the Niffet?"

Since Gerin had done a good deal of prating on exactly that theme, he answered carefully: "When you've seen the Gradi, it's amazing what a bunch of good fellows the Trokmoi seem alongside 'em." He looked down his nose at Authari. "Not that you've ever seen a Gradi, of course."

Authari's scowl was a joy to behold till the Fox remembered he was trying to get the petty baron to accept his son's overlordship, not to make an enemy for life of him. Scowling still, Authari said, "Had they come here, we'd have beaten them back."

"Maybe we would, Authari," Wacho said, "but the point is that they didn't come here, and the reason they didn't come here is that the lord prince—uh, the lord king—beat 'em back before they could."

Gerin studied Wacho in some bemusement; he was showing more in the way of common sense than he'd given any hint of having till now. Hit a man over the head with an idea often enough and he sometimes got it.

Authari Broken-Tooth was getting it, too, but not caring for it once he had it. He set a hand on the hilt of his sword as he glared at Ratkis Bronzecaster. "If you hadn't shown up at the wrong time, we'd all still be free," he snarled.

"What, there on the Elabon Way when the Fox here was coming back from Ikos the second time?" Ratkis asked. Authari nodded. Ratkis, by contrast, shook his head. "I heard about what happened there. You could have squashed him, but you funked the job. And you've got no one to blame for that but yourself." Under his breath, he added, "Not that you will."

And, sure enough, Authari snapped, "That's a lie." But it wasn't a lie. Gerin knew it, and Authari probably knew it, too, down in his heart of hearts: he lacked the gambler's nerve that would have spelled the difference between a petty baron and something more prominent. He looked around the great hall, out toward the courtyard, and out toward the encampment some of Gerin's men had made beyond it. The Fox could gauge the moment when he accepted that he could not change what he saw. "Bah!" Authari said. "We might as well get this over with." He looked around again, this time for Duren.

Ratkis Bronzecaster did more than look. He waved, and got Duren's attention. Gerin waved, too: if Authari was going to give homage and fealty, the opportunity had to be seized, not wasted.

Duren hurried over. Gerin used elbows to help clear a space in the crowd where Authari and his fellows could kneel. Ratkis Bronzecaster had already sworn loyalty to Duren, but had no objection to doing it again. On the contrary: when he gave his new overlord homage and fealty, he obviously meant what he said, which exerted extra pressure on the other three men who had formerly been Ricolf's vassals to mean what they said, too.

After they had given Duren homage and fealty, he said in a loud voice, "Now we see how the prophecy Biton delivered through his Sibyl at Ikos is fulfilled. May the omen prove good!"

Gerin's men cheered raucously. So did a good many of the ordinary troopers Hilmic, Wacho, and Authari had brought with them. That in turn cheered the Fox. If ordinary soldiers favored his son, their leaders would have a harder time making trouble for Duren. And reminding the folk here of the oracular response also struck Gerin as clever. Duren could claim—and claim truthfully—he took the barony with the support of the gods.

The Fox made his way over to his son. "It's yours now. Use it the best way you know how. If you have trouble, you know you can call on me."

"Yes, I know that." Duren nodded. "I shouldn't do it save in direst need, though, or people will think I can't handle my own troubles."

"That's the answer a man gives." Gerin thumped his son on the shoulder.

Duren might have sounded like a man, but he didn't look like one, not in that moment. He looked about the way Gerin would have expected a youth leaving the only home he'd ever known to look: worried and a little afraid. "I'll have to make my place here," he said. "I won't have it on account of who you are."

"That's so," Gerin said, choosing to misunderstand him a little: "Your place here comes from your grandfather . . . and your mother." He wondered again what Elise would think if she learned her son had taken over her father's barony. He wondered again if she was still alive. Then he wondered what he'd think, what he'd feel, if he found out she was alive. All things considered, he hoped he'd end his days content just to wonder.

"My place here will spring from *me*, from what I do and what I don't do," Duren persisted. "If I'm right, if I'm clever, I'll do well. And if I'm not, I'll have no one to blame but myself."

"You're my son, all right," Gerin said. Duren looked puzzled. Gerin explained: "Most men—aye, and most women, too—will blame anything and anybody but themselves for everything that goes wrong in their lives. If you know better, that puts you ahead of the game from the start."

"I know better." Duren dropped his voice. "I'm not Authari, to try to blame Ratkis because he didn't strike hard when he had the chance."

"If Authari were as bold in truth as he dreams of being, you'd have more trouble with him, sure enough. With him as he is, though" —Gerin also spoke quietly— "the most you'll have to fret about is poison in your soup. Unless I miss my guess, he'll never try to fight you straight up."

"If you do miss your guess, I expect you'll avenge me," Duren said.

"Bite your tongue—hard." Gerin gestured to turn aside the evil omen. "I've tasted revenge too many times already, and it's a dish I'd sooner not eat of again."

"As you say, Father." Duren matched the Fox's gesture.

Gerin set a hand on his shoulder. "You'll do fine, lad," he said. "The men jump when you talk to them, and that's a gift straight from the gods: if it isn't there, you can't bring it out. And you have a head on your shoulders, even if it's a head without much beard on it right now. Don't take too much for granted, don't fall head over heels in love with the first pretty girl you find down here—or even the third pretty girl—and try to learn from your mistakes. Do that and you'll make a fine baron."

"Good advice," Duren said. Maybe he would turn out to be the one young man in a hundred who actually took good advice. More likely, he'd have to do a lot of learning from his mistakes. *So long as he doesn't make one that kills him*, Gerin thought. *Hardly anybody learns much after that*.

A servant came by carrying a pitcher of ale. Gerin held out his drinking jack. The servant filled it. He drank. As far as he could tell, he badly needed more ale in him if his mind filled with such gloomy thoughts in the aftermath of a good-sized triumph.

The ale didn't make him stop worrying. Maybe he would do that when they flipped earth onto his shrouded body. On the other hand, he was liable to be thinking they weren't doing a proper job of burying him. That was a morbid thought, too. It made him laugh anyhow.

Authari, Wacho, and Hilmic took their men back to their castles the day after they acknowledged Duren as their overlord. Ratkis Bronzecaster, who was on better terms with his new suzerain, stayed a day longer. Then he too departed, leading his retainers off to the southwest. Ricrod looked visibly distressed when Gerin didn't leave the next morning.

"You think they're liable to come charging back as soon as they decide we've upped and gone?" Van asked.

"I don't know," Gerin answered. "I'm not what you call dead keen about finding out the hard way, either. And if the steward here wants to grumble about us eating the storerooms empty, let him." He lowered his voice so only Van could hear: "If I'm not crazy, I'd say Duren picks himself a new steward as soon as he has his feet on the ground."

"You are crazy, Fox, but nobody ever said you were stupid," Van answered. "Nobody ever said that about Duren, either, which means you're almost sure to be right."

None of the reluctant vassals tried anything untoward, so Gerin and his army rode north three days later. Duren stood on the wall of the keep now his, waving till a bend in the road took his father out of sight. The Fox was waving, too. When high ground hid Duren, he felt it had robbed him of a piece of himself, too. He wondered how long he would take to get over the feeling. He wondered if he ever would.

Up in the watchtower of Fox Keep, the sentry winded his trumpet. "A chariot approaches from the south, lord prince!" A moment later, sounding embarrassed, he corrected himself: "Lord king, I should say."

Still not being altogether used to his own royal title, Gerin did not take offense when those around him had trouble remembering it. He hurried up onto the palisade to see who had traveled almost to the Niffet to pay him a visit. A couple of the men up there shouted out a challenge to the newcomer.

From his chariot, he shouted back, at formidable volume: "I am Marlanz Raw-Meat, sent to treat with Gerin the Fox by my overlord, the grand duke Aragis the Archer."

That got complete and attentive silence from the men up on the wall, Gerin included. He'd been sure he would hear from Aragis about his assumption of the kingship. He hadn't expected to hear so soon. He called, "Marlanz, you're my guest-friend from ten years ago. Use my keep as your own for as long as you choose to stay here." Hearing that, the men at the gatehouse lowered the drawbridge so Marlanz could ride over the ditch and into the keep.

Aragis' envoy was much as the Fox remembered him: a big, strong, muscular fellow, smarter than he looked and now a bit thicker through the middle than he had been ten years earlier. Gerin also remembered he had a streak of wereblood in him, but the moons had not come full together in clumps of late, and so Marlanz remained wholly human in form.

He clasped Gerin's hand in a grip few warriors could have matched. "Good to see you again, Fox," he said. "It's been a long time. You look well."

"I was thinking the same of you," Gerin answered.

"That was your son heading up what was old Ricolf's holding?" Marlanz asked. "Word came down Ricolf had passed on."

"It's true, I'm sorry to say." Gerin looked sharply at Marlanz. Maybe he hadn't come about the title after all. "Has the Archer a quarrel with that? Unless I were going to claim Ricolf's barony for my own, which I've never wanted to do, it has no other heir but Duren. If you doubt me, go speak to the Sibyl at Ikos."

Aragis' envoy spread his hands and shook his head. "You haven't meddled in the grand duke's part of the northlands, so he has no business meddling up here. And, so far as he knows, what you say about your son's claim is true. But—"

Gerin realized his first guess had been right after all. "Go on," he said.

Marlanz Raw-Meat coughed, as if to advertise he spoke hesitantly. He'd gained in subtlety since his previous trip north. But the point of the visit could not be delayed: "Is it true, Fox, what the grand duke has heard, that you've taken the title of king for yourself?"

"Actually, I had it given to me," Gerin answered. "By Adiatunnus the Trokmê, of all people."

"We heard that, too, but had trouble crediting it," Marlanz said. "If you say it's so, though, I'll believe you. The question grand duke Aragis would have me put is this: what do you mean by it?"

"When Adiatunnus offered it to me, I kept it, because I think I've earned it," Gerin answered. "If Aragis disapproves—"

Marlanz broke in to repeat, "What do you mean by it? When you style yourself king of the north, do you lay claim to the whole of the northlands? Do you claim to be overlord to the grand duke? If you do, I am to tell you he rejects out of hand any such claim."

"Oh," Gerin said, and then, "Oh," again, because that let him make noise without obliging him to make sense. It also gave him a chance to think, and think he did. He felt as he had when light returned under the shrine of Ikos after he and the monsters' gods finished their strange parley: no longer altogether in the dark. "I see what troubles Aragis.

Tell him no, Marlanz. In my own lands, my style is now king, not prince. But I do not claim any lands I did not claim before simply because of my new style. As far as I'm concerned, the grand duke Aragis is lord of his own lands, and is not obliged to me in any way for them."

"That is the question I was asking, yes," Marlanz said gratefully. "The grand duke will be pleased at the news I bring him. You and he have lived side by side with each other for a long time now. He may not be your closest friend, but he respects you."

"And I him," Gerin said truthfully. He was glad he had earned Aragis' respect. Aragis, from all he had seen, either respected you or fell on you like a landslide and crushed you. He was a man with no middle ground in him.

"He has always thought so, Fox," Marlanz replied. He did not call Gerin *lord king*, possibly because Aragis had told him not to. Gerin gave a mental shrug. He was not about to fret over trifles. Marlanz looked thoughtful, then went on, "You said you claimed no new lands because of your new style. Do you claim new lands for some other reason?"

Gerin eyed him with considerable respect. A decade earlier, he wouldn't have noticed such a subtle point. The Fox would have been just as well pleased if he hadn't noticed it now. But, since he had noticed it, he had to be answered: "Aye, I do. Most of the land between my former western border and the Orynian Ocean has passed into my hands by right of conquest over the Gradi."

"We've heard somewhat of this down in the south, but the tales are new and sound confused," Marlanz said. "What really happened?"

That was a dangerous question to ask a man who'd studied historical philosophy down in the City of Elabon. It was a particularly dangerous question to ask in this case, where the quarrels of the gods, which mortals could at best only partly understand, clouded (or, with Stribog's discomfiture, unclouded) the picture. But Gerin knew Marlanz didn't want the truth, or not all of it. What he wanted was a story: the truth set into an interesting framework. That the Fox could give him.

"Come into the great hall and drink a jack or two of ale with me," he said easily. "I'll tell you what happened."

In the hall sat Geroge and Tharma. Marlanz reached for his sword, then checked himself. "These are the two of whom I've heard, not so?"

"Yes," Gerin said. Marlanz Raw-Meat, when his were streak came out, hadn't looked much different from Geroge. The Fox decided mentioning that would be imperfectly tactful, and so kept quiet. He introduced the monsters and Marlanz to one another.

"Pleased to make your acquaintance," Geroge said politely, speaking as he usually did for the two of them.

"Uh, pleased to make your acquaintance as well," Marlanz answered, perhaps taken aback by the spectacle of a well-mannered monster but doing his best not to show it. His best was good enough to satisfy Geroge and Tharma, who were less than exacting critics. They both smiled at him, which left him taken aback again. Warily, he said, "I hope you don't mind my asking, but is that tooth made of gold?"

"Real gold," Geroge agreed. "Lord Gerin made it for me, to make up for the one the gods under Ikos tore out of my head. It's not as good as a real tooth, but it's better than a hole in my head."

"Yes, I can see how it would be," Marlanz said. Turning to Gerin, he asked in a low voice, "This is what you spoke of earlier? By the gods under Ikos, he means the gods of his own kind?"

"This is what I spoke of earlier, aye," the Fox said. "As for the other, he does mean the monsters' gods, but he never calls them the gods of his kind or anything like that. He may well be right not to call them that, too, for he and Tharma are of the monsters' blood, but they don't act like them."

"I would not presume to quarrel with my host," Marlanz replied, by which he meant he thought Gerin was spouting nonsense. Then Gerin remembered the hunt on which he'd joined the monsters earlier in the year, and Geroge's excitement—in every sense of the word—after he'd killed. *Maybe I am spouting nonsense*, the Fox thought. *I expect I'll find out*.

Instead of pursuing that, he changed the subject: "I brought you in here for ale, but we've been standing around talking instead."

"Don't let it worry you," Marlanz told him. "Ale I can get anywhere, even the meanest peasant village. Here at Fox Keep, I have many things to see and to talk about that I think I would find nowhere else in all the northlands."

Despite that, Gerin did get him a jack of ale. Only after he'd handed it to Marlanz did he pause to wonder about the propriety of pouring ale for someone else now that he was a king. Since Marlanz accepted it without comment, he decided not to make an issue of it himself. "Is it all that different at Aragis' keep?" he asked, half slyly, half from genuine curiosity.

"It is," Marlanz answered. "The grand duke is, you will forgive me, of steadier and more orderly temper than yourself." Yes, he had learned the arts of diplomacy in the years since Gerin had last seen him. The Fox, who knew Aragis, had no trouble extracting the reality from the bland phrasing: anyone who made Aragis unhappy once was quickly disposed of so he never got the chance to do it twice.

Gerin knew that could happen to him. The best way to keep it from happening was to be—or at least to seem—too strong for the grand duke to attack with any hope of success, but not so strong as to put Aragis in fear of him. The balance between those two was delicate. Picking his words with care, the Fox asked, "How will Aragis respond to my taking the kingship once you've made it plain I intend him no harm?"

"That depends," Marlanz said. "If he believes me when I tell him—if he believes you for what you've told me—all should be well. If he decides not to believe me, or rather, you . . ." He let Gerin draw his own pictures.

None of the pictures his fertile imagination conjured up filled him with delight. Aragis the Archer was a long way from the best of rulers. Obedience through fear worked, but not well. But as a soldier, Aragis was not only as direct and aggressive as a Trokmê, but also more cunning than any woodsrunner, even Adiatunnus. Going to war against him, even with superior force, carried distinct risks.

The Fox said, "I hope you'll be convincing, Marlanz, for your sake and the grand duke's." *And mine*. But that was one more thing he would not say to Aragis' envoy.

He wondered if Marlanz would cast about for some

incentive to be convincing. The bluff young warrior he'd known a decade before would never have thought of such a thing. But this Marlanz was subtler, smoother; Aragis had felt no need to send an older, more polished man with him, as he'd done the last time he'd used him as ambassador.

Marlanz took a long pull at his ale. Gerin eyed him narrowly. That sort of thoughtful pause was exactly what a man looking for a bribe would give in an effort to demonstrate that the notion had only just now occurred to him. The Fox wondered how much in the way of gold and silver he had left after a summer spent campaigning with his warriors and feeding them when they weren't in the field. Carlun Vepin's son would know—or, if he didn't, Gerin would either have to train up a new steward or go back to doing the job himself.

But all Marlanz said was, "I think I will be, Fox. Will you give me your oath by Father Dyaus that what you've told me is true?" He held up a hasty hand. "Not that I doubt you, mind: I mean no offense. But if I can tell the grand duke you've sworn it—"

"I understand," Gerin replied, and gave him the oath. Even as he said the words, his eyes traveled to the altar to Dyaus that stood close by the hearth. He wondered once more if the All-father paid any attention to oaths offered in his name. From what Baivers had said, he had his doubts. But you didn't want to be wrong about something like that. Best to go on as if Dyaus were as immanent in the material world as Voldar had been before Baivers and the monsters' gods distracted her.

He wondered what would happen if one day Voldar won her fight up in the divine Gradihome. He'd told Duren he could deal with her, and still thought he was right, but, again, he didn't want to have to find out.

"Do you know," he said to Marlanz, "sometimes the most you can hope for is to stay ignorant."

"I'm ignorant of what you mean," Marlanz answered, smiling.

"Good," Gerin said, and slapped him on the back.

The Fox began reckoning achievements in negatives: Voldar did *not* come down to the material world against him, and Aragis the Archer did *not* go to war. The monsters did *not* burst out of the caves under Biton's temple at Ikos, one more worry he'd had, and Authari, Hilmic, and Wacho did *not* join together to overthrow or slay his son.

As the days flowed past, one after another, he began to believe those negatives might hold together for a time. That let him savor the positives: a good harvest and peace among his vassals, even including Adiatunnus. The best surprise of all came from Carlun. Once the harvest had been gathered and payments in kind brought into Fox Keep, the steward came up to Gerin with parchments in his hand and a surprised look on his face.

He thrust the parchments at the Fox, saying, "Lord king, if I've reckoned rightly, we have enough here to get through the winter. I never would have believed it, not with all those gobbling warriors trying to eat the keep empty."

He still thought like a serf. "If it weren't for those gobbling warriors," Gerin reminded him, "you'd be explaining how this keep is set for supplies to some Gradi chieftain—if you were lucky. More likely, you'd be dead."

"I suppose so," Carlun admitted, "but it seems—wasteful." He made the ordinary word into a curse.

"Why fix a roof in summer, when the weather's fine and looks like staying fine for a long time?" Gerin asked. "The same reason you have men trained in war: sooner or later, you know trouble's going to come. Being ready ahead of time is a better idea than trying to fix things at the same time as they're falling apart."

Carlun chewed on that for a while, then reluctantly nodded. Gerin, meanwhile, checked the steward's figures with meticulous care. As far as he could tell, everything gibed. That meant Carlun was either a very clever cheater or too afraid of him to take any chances. He suspected the latter. That suited him fine.

Winter was the quiet time of the year, serfs and lords alike living on what they'd stored up in summer and fall. When they hadn't stored enough, what they got was famine, which, all too often, brought peasant uprisings in its wake. To try to head them off, Gerin did send what grain he could west of the Venien, to the lands where unnatural summer weather, courtesy of the Gradi gods, had ruined the crops. He scored another negative success: the serfs there did *not* revolt.

"In a horrid sort of way, I understand why things are quiet there," he said to Selatre one day. "They don't have much food, but there aren't many of them left, either, not after living under the Gradi for a while and then after the war. What little they've got, along with what little we could give them, is somewhere close enough to get them by."

His wife nodded. "Life for farmers is never easy." Having grown up a peasant's daughter, she knew whereof she spoke. After a moment, she added, "You've done everything you could, and more than most lords would have dreamt of trying."

"It sounds like an epitaph," Gerin said, laughing. A moment later, as with Duren, his hand and Selatre's twisted in a sign to avert the evil omen. That done, he let out a long sigh. "We got through it."

Selatre nodded again. "So we did. And after what we got through, it has to get better, because how could it get worse?"

"That's why we go on living," he answered: "to find out how it could get worse." Selatre poked him in the ribs, and he had to admit (though he didn't have to admit out loud) he deserved it.

As winters went, this one was mild, again to Gerin's relief: he'd feared the Gradi gods, if they got free at that season of the year, would do their best to freeze the northlands solid. Nothing of the sort happened, though, and in due course winter gave way to spring. Leaves came out on the formerly bare branches of oaks and maples, apples and plums; fresh grass sprouted on the meadows, pushing up through the yellow-brown dead growth of the year before. The peasants yoked their oxen to the plow and planted wheat and rye, oats and barley. Gerin blessed Baivers, and hoped the god heard him.

He had one more worry in the middle of spring: Elleb, Math, and Tiwaz came to fullness on successive nights. No reports of werebeasts ravaging flocks or peasants reached him, though. He hoped Marlanz Raw-Meat hadn't given way to his lycanthropic tendencies during the run of full moons.

And then, when for once he saw no trouble on the horizon at all, the midwife came rushing up from the peasant village near Fox Keep to let him know Fulda had been delivered of a baby boy. He thumped his forehead with the heel of his hand, angry at himself for letting the imminence of the event slip his mind. "What's Mavrix's bastard like?" he asked.

"Lord king, you'd better come see for yourself," said the midwife, a sturdy, middle-aged woman named Radwalda.

And so the Fox followed her down to the village. She pointed the way to Fulda's hut, but showed no eagerness to go into it herself. Shrugging, Gerin stepped through the low entrance, ducking his head as he went.

His eyes needed a moment to adjust to the gloom. When they did, he saw Fulda sitting up on the bed. She didn't look nearly so worn as other women he'd seen just after childbirth: one more advantage of divine parentage, he supposed.

Smiling, she held up the newborn baby. "Isn't he beautiful, lord king? I'm going to call him Ferdulf."

"Hello, Ferdulf," Gerin said.

Ferdulf's eyes, which had been closed, came open. "Hello yourself," the infant demigod said in a distinctly unbabylike baritone.

Gerin looked at Fulda. She nodded. "Oh, dear," the Fox said.

Fox & Empire

I

Up in the watchtower, the lookout winded his horn: a long, unmelodious blast. "Two chariots approach from the south, lord king!" he bellowed.

From the courtyard far below, Gerin the Fox, king of the north, cupped a hand to his mouth and replied: "Thanks, Andiver. We'll see who they are when they get here."

"Aren't you going to go up on the palisade and have a look?" the sentry demanded indignantly.

"In a word, no," Gerin answered. "If two chariots' worth of warriors can conquer Fox Keep, either they're gods, in which case looking at them won't do me any good, or else we're all such cowards that the men who are on the palisade now would be running away, and that's not happening, either. So I'll wait for them down here, thanks very much."

Andiver said something the height of his perch kept Gerin from understanding. The Fox decided it was probably just as well.

His son Dagref smiled at him. "That was very logical," he said. Dagref, at fourteen, was as remorselessly logical as the most terrifying Sithonian philosopher who'd ever made a living lecturing in the Elabonian Empire. Up until twenty years before, Gerin's kingdom, as well as the rest of the land north from the High Kirs to the River Niffet, had been a frontier province of the Empire. Elabon, though, had abandoned the land north of the mountains in the face of the devastating werenight caused by all four moons' coming full at the same time and, almost incidentally, the barbarous Trokmoi swarming south over the Niffet.

"It was indeed," Gerin said. "So what?"

Dagref stared at him. Man and youth shared a long face, long nose, and swarthy complexion. Dagref, though, had only fine down on his cheeks and chin, and his hair was a brown almost black. Gerin's neat beard and his hair were gray, and getting grayer by the year: he was past fifty now, and often knew it by the creaking in his bones.

"Logic is the greatest tool, the greatest weapon, in the world," Dagref declared.

"That depends on what you're doing," Gerin replied. "If you're in the middle of a brawl, you can't slay a Gradi or a Trokmê or one of Aragis the Archer's jolly henchmen with a well-aimed syllogism. That's why we carry these things every now and then."

He hefted his sword. The sun glinted, red as blood, from the polished edge of the bronze blade. Dagref held a sword, too. He enjoyed fencing with it much less than fencing with his wits. He was very dangerous with the latter, only somewhat so with the former.

"Come on." Gerin made as if to attack him. "If some big ugly lug carves chunks off you, it doesn't matter that he's never heard of the law of the excluded middle. You won't be around to instruct him afterwards."

Dagref parried the slash. His answering cut made Gerin give back a pace. They did not work against each other as often as Gerin would have done had he not been left-handed: learning how to fight him went only so far in teaching Dagref how to fight others. His son was left-handed, too, which gave Gerin the rare chance to see what others faced when they met him.

"Keep the blade up!" the Fox cautioned. "You don't keep the blade up, I can do something like this—" He snapped a cut at Dagref's head, so quick and sharp that his son had to stagger back. "Or even this." The Fox feinted another head cut; if he hadn't stopped his thrust, he would have put it into Dagref's chest.

"Yes, I see." Dagref nodded. And he did see, too. He had the makings of a good swordsman; he had long arms and quick feet and didn't do the same thing wrong over and over again. But he didn't automatically do the right thing, either, and, when he did do it, he didn't do it fast enough. Only years of patient practice would give him the speed he needed. Intellectually, he realized that (he was very good at realizing things intellectually). "Let's try it again, Father."

Those were the words Gerin wanted to hear. Before he could go through the passage again, though, one of his men up on the palisade called a challenge to the approaching chariots: "Who comes to Castle Fox?"

The answer made Gerin forget about swordplay and hurry up onto the palisade after all: "I am Marlanz Raw-Meat, emissary of King Aragis the Archer, come to have speech with King Gerin."

"Hello, Marlanz," Gerin called once he reached the walkway and could peer over the tops of the palisade timbers. "Come in and be welcome. I'll listen to whatever Aragis has to say, though I don't promise I'll do anything about it."

At his command, the gate crew let down the drawbridge over the ditch around the palisade. Marlanz's chariot rattled into Fox Keep. King Aragis' representative was a big, burly man in his late thirties; from previous encounters with him, Gerin knew he was smarter than he looked. "Hello, lord king," Marlanz said as the Fox came down to greet him.

When Gerin clasped hands with him, Marlanz's big paw (a word that came naturally to Gerin's mind, as Marlanz had a were streak in him) almost engulfed his own. "What brings you north this time?" the Fox asked, though he had the bad feeling he already knew.

And sure enough, Marlanz said, "Lord king, Aragis bids me tell you that he is not going to stand idly by if Balser Debo's son swears homage and fealty to you. He warns you not to pursue that further."

The Fox looked down his nose at Aragis' ambassador, no mean feat since Marlanz was three or four digits' width taller than he. "Aragis has no business telling either Balser or me what sort of relationship we can have. Balser was never Aragis' vassal, nor was his father before him. Balser styles himself baron, nothing more, but he's as free a man and as independent a lord as I am—or as Aragis is."

"Yes, and Aragis intends that he remain free, and not come under your influence," Marlanz said.

"If, of his own free will, he wants to declare himself my vassal, Aragis has not the right to forbid it."

Marlanz Raw-Meat folded thick arms across his broad chest. "Lord king, King Aragis is strong enough to enforce his will on Balser—and on you."

In the end, it came down to strength, Gerin thought. Adiatunnus the Trokmê, a rival now a vassal, had first declared the Fox king of the north after he'd beaten the Gradi pirates back to a single keep on the edge of the Orynian Ocean. Aragis had started calling himself king a little later, his claim springing from his being the only noble left in the northlands with strength enough to stand against Gerin.

"If Aragis tries that, he will get the war he's been saying he doesn't want ever since the days right after the werenight," Gerin answered. "Tell him that, Marlanz. Make sure he understands it. And tell him that, if he does try it, I believe he'll end up being the sorriest man ever born."

Marlanz scowled. He'd known Gerin long enough to know the Fox did not casually make such boasts. In Marlanz's younger days, he'd been more a bruiser than a diplomat. He'd gained skill with years. These days, Aragis probably trusted him further than anyone else—not that Aragis trusted anyone very far. Trying to strike a conciliatory tone, Marlanz said, "You have to see how things are, lord king. Balser's holding points like a knife straight at the heart of the lands that acknowledge King Aragis' suzerainty. If it comes under your control, you're halfway to invading his domain right there."

Gerin scowled back. In Aragis' sandals, his acquisition *would* look that way. "I don't want to use the holding as a knife. I want to use it as a shield against Aragis," the Fox said. "It's hardly less dangerous to me in his hands than it is to him in mine. You might remind him that he was the one who paraded chariots past Balser's border to frighten him into yielding. I can't help it if Balser started talking to me instead."

"It might be best if we could keep Balser neutral between you and Aragis, inclining neither to the one nor the other," Marlanz said.

"That would have been fine," Gerin said. "It *was* fine, while it lasted. I wasn't the one who changed it. Now Balser doesn't think he can trust Aragis to keep his hands where they belong. Am I supposed to tell him, 'No, I'm sorry, I won't protect you from your neighbor, even if you want me to'?"

Marlanz looked unhappy. "I knew that was foolish," he muttered; Gerin didn't think he was supposed to hear. Aragis' envoy gathered himself. "Lord king, I'm sorry, but I don't have a lot of room to wiggle here. King Aragis has told me to tell you that, if Balser becomes your vassal, it will mean war between the two of you."

"Then it will be war." Gerin slapped Marlanz on the back and waved him toward Castle Fox. "We don't have to start killing each other quite yet, I don't think. Why don't you come into the great hall and drink some ale with me, eat some bread, and we'll see what else we can scare up for you."

"I'll do that right gladly," Marlanz said. "You brewed a fine ale the last time I was here, lord king, and you're not the sort to let something like that slip. And you have a name all through the northlands for feeding your guest-friends well."

"I probably earned it when I managed to get you out of my keep before you ate the larder empty—just before," Gerin said. Marlanz laughed, although, like most of Gerin's jokes, that one had a hard core of truth. "Come on," the Fox urged, and they walked into the great hall side by side.

Van of the Strong Arm, Rihwin the Fox, and Carlun Vepin's son sat at a table near the hearth, and near the altar to Dyaus Allfather in front of it. A tarred-leather jack of ale sat in front of each of them. Van was also gnawing a roast rib of mutton. As Gerin and Marlanz walked in, the big outlander tossed it into the rushes on the floor to watch a couple of dogs squabble over it.

"By all the gods, it's Marlanz Raw-Meat," Van rumbled, recognizing Aragis' envoy. He rose from the bench and strode up to clasp Marlanz's hand. As they did whenever they met, the two big men studied each other. Gerin studied them both. The golden-haired outlander was taller and broader through the shoulders, but he was also older, being within a year or two either way of the Fox's age. At his peak, he'd been stronger than Marlanz—he'd been stronger than anyone Gerin had ever known. But Marlanz, a decade younger, was closer to his own peak, which had also been formidable. If the two of them fought . . . Gerin didn't know what would happen. That was strange. In the more than twenty years since Van had come to Fox Keep, he'd always been sure his friend could best anyone merely human. Now—

Now we're getting old, Gerin thought. *Strength goes*. He smiled to himself. *Guile, though, guile endures*. Aloud, he said, "Marlanz says Aragis will go to war with us if Balser gives me homage and fealty."

"He's welcome to try it," Van said. "I don't think he'll be so happy afterwards, though." A few years earlier, he would have whooped with glee at the prospect of a fight. He still didn't shrink from it—Gerin couldn't imagine him shrinking from a fight—but he no longer rushed toward it like a man rushing toward his beloved.

"My king is not happy about it now," Marlanz answered, "but he will not shrink from it, not if that means seeing his own rights overthrown."

That made Rihwin the Fox speak up: "In good sooth, King Aragis has no right pertaining to the holding of Balser Debo's son, it never having been a fief of his."

"I said the same thing," Gerin told him, "but not half so prettily."

"You have not the advantages of a noble upbringing south of the High Kirs," Rihwin replied, as if forgiving his fellow Fox for flaws beyond his control. After two decades in the northlands, Rihwin still clung to the elaborate phrasing he'd learned at the heart of the Elabonian Empire, and to the gold hoop he wore in his left ear, an affectation to which the rest of Gerin's vassals had never quite accommodated themselves.

Marlanz looked from Rihwin to Gerin and back again. "As I have noted before, he has the right to keep a stronger neighbor from taking advantage of a weaker one."

"As *I* noted before," Gerin said pointedly, "if Aragis weren't a strong neighbor liable to take advantage of a weaker one, Balser wouldn't be interested in having me as his lord."

"If you told him as much out there," Van said, "did you bring him in here to tell it to him over again?"

"As a matter of fact, I brought him in here for some ale and some bread and whatever we can pry out of the kitchen in the way of meat," Gerin said. He slapped Aragis' vassal on the shoulder again. "Sit you down, Marlanz. If Aragis and I have to fight, we'll fight. Meanwhile, you're my guest-friend."

Servants brought Marlanz a drinking jack, a round of flatbread, and some ribs like the one Van had been gnawing. Carlun Vepin's son, Gerin's steward, looked as if he was calculating the cost of everything. And so, no doubt, he was: the Fox wouldn't have wanted him for the job if he didn't keep track of every jar of ale, sack of beans, and barrel of salt pork.

Whatever Carlun thought, he kept it to himself while warriors other than Gerin were around. He was no fighting man. He'd been the headman of the serf village close by Fox Keep till Gerin caught him cheating on the records there, trying to hold back produce from his overlord's notice. That had earned him both a promotion and a warning about what would happen if the Fox ever caught him cheating again. Either he hadn't cheated since or he'd done it too well for Gerin to have noticed. The Fox didn't think Carlun was clever enough to get away with that; he almost but not quite hoped he was wrong.

Marlanz made eyes at one of the serving women. Gerin happened to know she was newly married, and happy with her husband. She kept on serving Aragis' envoy, but did nothing to encourage him, and twisted away before he had the chance to pull her down onto his lap.

He glanced over to Gerin. "You always did give your serfs a lot of say in what they should do to keep your guests happy."

"I haven't changed," the Fox answered. "Far as I can see, forcing them to bed men they don't want only causes trouble. If she's interested in you, Marlanz, that's fine. If she's not, maybe you can find someone else who is."

Marlanz didn't make an issue of it. Gerin remembered how he'd been inclined to do just that, the first time he came up to Fox Keep. Yes, he'd learned a thing or two over the intervening fifteen years. And, of course, since he was fifteen years older himself, he didn't burn so hot as he had then, either.

"I passed the night at your son's holding on my way up to your keep here, lord king," Marlanz remarked, changing the subject with a smoothness he hadn't had as a younger man. "He seems to be shaping into a fine baron in his own right."

"For which I thank you," Gerin said. "Aye, I think Duren's a splendid lad. Of course, being his father, I'd think that even if it weren't so."

"Well, it is," Marlanz said. "And I didn't see any signs that his vassal barons are anything but what they ought to be, either. You had some trouble with that, as I recall."

"A bit," the Fox admitted. Duren held his holding as grandson to the previous baron, Ricolf the Red, not as Gerin's son. Ricolf's petty barons had been anything but enthusiastic about accepting him, partly because they feared Gerin's influence and partly because, with Ricolf gone, they'd had hopes of escaping vassalage altogether and setting up on their own. As far as Gerin could see, the hope had obviously been foolish, but that hadn't kept them from having it. A lot of the hopes men had were obviously foolish to everyone but them.

"Aye, Duren's a fine young fellow." Marlanz cocked his head to one side. "Is he the heir to your kingdom, or is that Dagref whom I saw out in the courtyard with you?"

"Yes," Gerin answered, and let Marlanz make whatever he would of it. Duren was his son by Elise, Ricolf's daughter. He hadn't seen her since Duren was a toddler; she'd run away with a traveling horse doctor. Dagref, his sister

Clotild, and his brother Blestar were his by Selatre, the former Sibyl at the farseeing god Biton's shrine down at Ikos. The Fox sighed. Life was never so simple as you wished it would be.

"Yes to which?" Marlanz demanded: he was, Gerin knew, persistent. The Fox just smiled at him. After a bit, Aragis' vassal figured out he wouldn't get a straight answer. He smiled back, shrugged, and emptied his jack of ale. A serving woman—not the one he'd tried to paw—refilled it for him.

Gerin took a pull at his own ale. He wondered where Dagref had gone. His eldest child by Selatre had a curiosity as fierce and ruthless as a longtooth: he should have been besieging Marlanz with every sort of question. The Fox wondered what he'd found more interesting than the arrival of a near-stranger.

Had it been Duren at the same age, Gerin would have guessed he was off with a girl. But Dagref's curiosity was, as yet, more of the intellect than of the body. One day soon, the Fox suspected, a serving girl would kick his feet out from under him. What happened after that would be interesting.

No sooner had Gerin thought of his son than Dagref, as if summoned, came running into the great hall. He spared Marlanz Raw-Meat no more than a hasty glance. "Father, come quick, out back by the stables," he exclaimed. "It's Ferdulf again."

"Oh, by the gods," Gerin said, which, where Ferdulf was concerned, had alarmingly literal implications. The Fox sprang to his feet. Dagref, the message delivered, was already dashing away. Gerin pounded after him, aware with every step that he wasn't as fast as he had been.

Behind him, he heard Van and Rihwin exclaiming, too. A moment later, they followed the Fox. And Marlanz came right on their heels. He hadn't a clue about what was going on, but he wanted to find out.

Dagref sprinted around Castle Fox, then pointed with a dramatic forefinger. "There!" he said.

There were Clotild and Blestar. There too were Maeva and Kor, Van's children. Maeva, though a year younger than Dagref, was already blossoming into ripe womanhood—but womanhood of heroic proportions. Van's blood told in her temperament as well as her size and strength; she wanted to be a warrior, and Gerin, rather to his own alarm, thought she would make a good one. Kor was even more alarming. He also had his father's build, but took his incendiary temper straight from Fand, the Trokmê woman with whom Van lived in something less than wedded bliss.

And there were Geroge and Tharma. The two monsters towered over all their companions, even Maeva. They were large and hairy and remarkably ugly, with clawed hands and feet, low foreheads, little eyes under beetling brow ridges, and long jaws full of big teeth (though Geroge's right upper canine was of gold rather than being a natural fang). They both waved to Gerin, who had raised them from . . . he supposed *cubs* was the best word.

He didn't see Ferdulf. And then, just before Dagref said "There!" again, he did. The preternaturally beautiful four-year-old had doffed his tunic and was walking around in the air about twenty feet off the ground.

"Magic?" Marlanz asked from behind Gerin with what was, under the circumstances, commendable calm.

The Fox shook his head. "Not exactly." He raised his voice to Ferdulf: "Come down from there this instant, before you—" He stopped. *Before you hurt yourself* didn't work, as it had with his own children. Ferdulf wasn't going to hurt himself. Gerin wasn't sure Ferdulf could hurt himself. He tried a different tack: "—before you drive everybody down here crazy."

"What do I care?" Ferdulf stood on his head, supported by exactly nothing. His voice was not a four-year-old's, but the same rude, rich baritone he'd had since he was a newborn babe.

Marlanz said, "Lord king, will you please tell me what's going on here?" He took Geroge and Tharma in stride; he'd met them before. Ferdulf, however, was new to him. Like most men in the northlands, he viewed the new with suspicion.

Gerin didn't, in most cases. With Ferdulf, he made an exception. Trying to sound casual, he answered, "That's Mavrix's son by Fulda, a peasant woman here. Now do you understand?"

For a moment, Marlanz didn't. Then he did, and his eyes got wide. "Mavrix?" He tried his best to imitate Gerin's flat, unemphatic tones, but didn't have much luck. "The Sithonian god of wine?" Calm crumbled into astonishment: "You've got a god's get here, lord king?"

"Yes, the little bastard," Gerin said, which, in dealing—or trying to deal—with Ferdulf, had proved true in any number of ways.

Dagref plucked at his father's sleeve. "I brought you out here so you could do something about him," he said pointedly. "The last time he started going around up in the air this way, he piddled on all of us, and I wanted to see if we could keep that from happening again." The glare he gave the Fox said his father's reliability had just come down a peg for him.

"What exactly do you want me to do?" Gerin asked in some exasperation. "I can't lean a ladder against the air, the way I would against the palisade." He cast a cautious eye up toward Ferdulf's little pecker. Mavrix's get had divine powers and a four-year-old's sense of humor; the Fox was hard pressed to imagine a more terrifying combination.

Dagref took a deep breath. "If you don't come down from there this instant," he told Ferdulf, "none of the rest of us is going to play with you for a long time." His voice broke in the middle of the threat, so he didn't sound so fierce as he might have, but he did sound as if he meant what he said. He always sounded as if he meant what he said. He gestured to his comrades. Clotild and Blestar nodded. So did Maeva and Kor. And, a beat late, so did Geroge and Tharma.

"Oh, all right," Ferdulf said sulkily, sounding very much like his own father, who raised petulance to an art. He came floating down and put his tunic back on.

"That was bravely done," Maeva said. She eyed Dagref with a thoughtful interest to which he as yet remained in large measure blind.

"That *was* bravely done," Gerin agreed; telling Ferdulf what to do took nerve. Well, his son had never lacked for that. Sense, possibly, but not nerve. The Fox went on, "But why did you call me when you could handle it by yourself?"

"I didn't know if that would work," Dagref answered,

"and I thought you would have a better idea. When you didn't—" He raised one eyebrow, as Gerin might have done. *You* should *have had a better idea*, he said without words.

In a much more cautious voice than he'd used till now, Marlanz Raw-Meat asked, "What all can the little godlet do besides fly?"

"What all?" Gerin clapped a hand to his head, as if it ached. When he thought about Ferdulf, it soon did ache. "Who knows? I'll tell you this much: I went to see him as soon as I got word he'd been born, and he said hello to me in that same voice you heard him use now. Life hasn't been dull since, believe me."

"Is his mother a goddess, too, or a demon, or—?" Marlanz fell silent, seeming to guess how little he could guess.

Gerin's smile was ironic. "I told you, his mother's name is Fulda. She still lives down in the village close to the keep here. She has a pretty face and a ripe body, which is why I used her when I was summoning Mavrix against the Gradi—which, in case you're wondering, was a good idea that didn't work. Ferdulf listens to her when he feels like it and ignores her the rest of the time, which is about what he does for everybody else."

"You told me you'd summoned Mavrix the last time I came up here," Marlanz said, remembering. "You didn't tell me he'd got a woman with child."

"Ferdulf hadn't been born then," the Fox answered. "I didn't know then what I'd get. For that matter, I still don't know what I have. Why don't we go back to the great hall and have another jack of ale, and we can talk some more about it?"

"Good enough, lord king." Marlanz hurried back to the hall, as if he feared Ferdulf and was trying to conceal it from everyone, especially from himself.

Selatre had been working in the kingdom's library—an overstatement of what one upstairs room of Castle Fox held, but an overstatement Gerin had been making ever since he'd succeeded his father as local baron, more than twenty years before. She came down for supper.

When she did, Marlanz bowed before her. "Lady, seeing

as you were Sibyl at Ikos, and seeing as the farseeing god spoke through you there," he said, getting around to his question a clause at a time, like a lawyer south of the High Kirs, "does that mean this Ferdulf you've got here pays any special heed to what you say?" He spoke of Mavrix's son as he might have of a dangerous wild beast, which struck Gerin as fitting enough.

Selatre gave the question grave consideration, almost as if she expected Biton to speak through her here and now. After scratching the side of her pointed chin for close to a minute, she delivered a short answer: "Not very often."

Marlanz stared, then started to laugh. "Well, that's straight, and no mistake," he said, his last couple of words blurring into an enormous yawn. He turned back to Gerin. "If you'll be kind enough to have somebody show me up to my bedchamber, I'll thank you for it. I've spent a good many days on the road, coming up from Aragis' keep."

"I can do that," Gerin said, and waved for a servant, who led Aragis' envoy away. The warriors who had accompanied Marlanz would sleep in the great hall; the Fox had made sure they had plenty of blankets to stay comfortable. No one at Fox Keep had to fear night ghosts, for he made a point of giving them the blood they needed to keep from molesting mortals.

Once Marlanz was gone, Selatre put on that thoughtful expression again. "Do you suppose we *could* find a way to use Ferdulf?" she said in a low voice.

"Against Aragis, you mean?" Gerin asked, as quietly. His wife nodded. He said, "I never thought about it before. I never imagined Ferdulf doing anything but whatever he wants." He looked around. None of the men who'd come to Fox Keep with Marlanz seemed to be listening, and a couple of them were already asleep, but Gerin had not grown as old as he had—*older than I ever thought I'd be*—by taking unnecessary chances. The necessary ones were quite bad enough. "Let's talk about it upstairs."

"All right." Selatre rose from the bench in one smooth motion. She and Gerin walked up the wooden stairway hand in hand.

In the chamber nearest the top of the stairs, Van and Fand were arguing. The outlander and the Trokmê woman looked on quarrels as most folk looked on meat and drink. Gerin met Selatre's eye. Wryly, he shook his head. After Elise had left him, before he'd met Selatre, he'd shared Fand's affection—and her temper—with Van for a while. No wonder he did his best to keep his even-tempered wife that way. He had standards of comparison.

He and Selatre shared the next bedchamber with their children. Since he didn't feel like explaining everything to Dagref (however much his son thought himself entitled to explanations), and since Clotild might well also still be awake, he led Selatre past that door, too. She nodded, understanding his reasons without his having to spell them out. *One more reason to love her*, he thought.

Rihwin had the chamber on the other side of the Fox's. Since Rihwin could no more keep secrets than Fand could keep calm, Gerin walked by his room. The next bedchamber held Marlanz. Across from it was the library, to which Gerin and Selatre were both drawn like feathers gliding toward rubbed amber.

Few in the northlands knew their letters. Selatre hadn't, not till Gerin taught them to her after bringing her to Fox Keep. He'd thought to give her a useful place here, not knowing he would fall in love with her in short order—and she with him, too, which struck him as stranger and more marvelous. She'd also fallen in love with books. That, unlike falling in love with him, he understood completely. He'd done it himself.

He opened the door, then gestured for her to go in ahead of him. She did—and started to laugh. When he followed her into the chamber, he laughed, too. There sat Dagref in front of a lamp, his nose in a scroll.

Gerin glanced over at Selatre. "Anyone would think he was our child," he said.

Dagref looked up at his parents. "Of course I'm your child," he said testily, "and I'm sure you came in here so you could talk about something you think is none of my business."

"You're right," Selatre told him.

"It isn't fair," he said. "How am I supposed to learn what I need to know if you won't let me find out about it?" He started to stalk off, then stopped under Gerin's glare. When he went back, rolled up the scroll, and replaced it in its proper pigeonhole, his father stopped glaring.

"That was good," Selatre said with a smile after her son did depart. "He figured out why you were unhappy."

"Something, anyway," Gerin agreed. "Tell him the same thing four hundred times in a row and he will start to listen—if it suits him. If it doesn't . . ." His scowl said what happened then. After a moment, he went on, "And yet, if it's something he *wants* to learn, he'll soak it up the way dry ground soaks up the first rain of the year."

Selatre gazed at him with amused fondness. "Anyone would think he had you for a father," she murmured.

The Fox tried to glare again, but ended up laughing instead. "You know me too well—and you have altogether too little respect for your king." That made Selatre laugh, too. But Gerin quickly sobered. "*Can* we use Ferdulf as a weapon against Aragis if we do go to war?"

"I would be happier trying it if he were the son of any other god than Mavrix," Selatre said.

"Why do you say that? Because Mavrix is about the least predictable god in anyone's pantheon, or because he's shown he isn't fond of me in particular?"

"Yes," Selatre said, as Gerin had with Marlanz. He made a face at her. Despite her joke, though, both halves of the question could legitimately be answered *yes*. Mavrix was the Sithonian god of wine, beauty, fertility, creativity . . . and of the chaos accompanying all those. He did not know, from one moment to another, what he would do next, nor did he care. And his encounters with the Fox over the years had mostly ended up alarming both the god, who was a coward at heart, and the man, who was anything but.

Gerin said, "For once, I'd like to use a weapon against my foes that isn't stronger than I am, so I won't have to spend so much time worrying whether it will turn in my hand and end up being worse than simply losing whatever fight I happen to be making."

"The question, then, it seems to me, is, if we go to war with Aragis, whether we can beat him without resorting to . . . extraordinary means," Selatre said.

Gerin paused a moment to admire the precise phrasing of that. He tried to answer with similar precision: "We can—if everything goes right. If Adiatunnus chooses to remember he's my vassal, and doesn't take the fight as an excuse to throw off his allegiance and set up on his own, for instance."

"He'd better not," Selatre said with no small anger, "not when he's the one who first proclaimed you king."

"He's been a good enough vassal since, too," Gerin admitted, "but he's a Trokmê, which means he's almost as fickle as Mavrix. If he sees the two greatest Elabonian lords in the northlands going at each other, the temptation may be too much for him to stand. And there are the Gradi, too."

The seafaring invaders from the chilly lands north of the Trokmê forests had tried to establish themselves and their grim gods in the northlands a few years before. Fear of them was what had made Adiatunnus remember he was Gerin's vassal. Fighting together instead of against each other, Elabonians and Trokmoi had pinned the northerners against the Orynian Ocean. More than that they could not do, not when Gradi galleys controlled the sea.

Because Voldar, the chief Gradi goddess, and the rest of the northerners' gods contemplated making the northlands into a frigid copy of the home from which they'd come, a land too cold for even barley to grow there, Gerin had managed to persuade Baivers, the Elabonian god of barley, beer, and brewing, to join with the ferocious powers of Geroge and Tharma's kind and battle those Gradi gods. He didn't know whether that battle on the spiritual plane had been won or lost. His best guess was that it still went on, five years after its beginning: time, for the gods, was not as it was for men. What he did know was that, without help from their gods, the Gradi hadn't been able to stand against him. That was the only thing that mattered.

No, not quite the only thing. "If Voldar and the other Gradi powers ever manage to pull loose from the battle I found for them, they won't be very happy with me."

"They haven't done it yet, and it's been a long time now." Selatre spoke with her usual brisk practicality. "And, if they do, you'll come up with something."

That wasn't practicality; it was, as far as Gerin could see, madness. "Everyone else expects me to have all the answers and pull them out of my beltpouch whenever I need them," he growled. "I thought you knew better."

She looked steadily back at him. "You forget, I've been living by your side these past fifteen or sixteen years. I know what you can do. Everyone else just guesses." When that drew nothing more than a sardonic snort from the Fox, Selatre went on, "You *would* come up with something. I know you too well to doubt it. Maybe, with Ferdulf here, you could use him to call on Mavrix, and—"

"That would be wonderful, wouldn't it?" Gerin said. "Mavrix likes me about as well as Voldar does. Trying to use one god who can't stand me to head off another one who can't stand me, either . . . I think I'd be better off jumping out of the watchtower and hoping I broke my neck when I hit. Besides, Voldar's stronger than Mavrix. I found that out."

"Well, you'd do something else, then." Selatre still sounded confident. "I thought of Mavrix because we were talking about Ferdulf."

"So we were," Gerin said. "The best thing I can think of to do with him is to hope that his being here frightens Aragis, and to hope Aragis never finds out how much his being here frightens me."

"You're the king of the north." Amusement glinted in his wife's eyes. "Nothing is supposed to frighten you."

She was poking him in the ribs to make him jump. He knew as much, but answered seriously: "No, that's Aragis. As far as I've ever seen, nothing does frighten him—and that frightens me. He's very simple, like a hunting hawk. He goes straight for what he wants, knocks it down, and kills it. The only reason he's never gone after me is that I've always looked too big to knock down. Maybe I don't, not any more. I don't think Marlanz is bluffing."

"No. Aragis doesn't want you becoming Balser's overlord," Selatre agreed. She cocked her head to one side and studied him. "Wouldn't you say that means he's afraid of you?"

Gerin started to say something, then stopped. What he did say, in tones of appreciation, was, "I think I've just been outargued."

Selatre was still studying him, but now in rather a

different manner. "And what do you propose to do about that?" she inquired.

He got up, walked over to the door, and barred it. He'd had a serf skilled in carpentry install the bar and the brackets that held it a couple of years before. At about the same time, he'd taken to storing a bolt of thick woolen cloth in one corner of the library. That had perplexed Dagref, who'd noted, pointedly and accurately, that nothing else but books ever got stored in that room. "It's not doing any particular harm there, so let it alone," Gerin had told him. That was also true. Dagref had grumbled about it for a while, but then, as is the way of such things, he'd got used to it. He probably didn't even notice it was there any more.

The other thing he didn't notice, however alert he was to connections between events around him, was that that bar and the roll of cloth had appeared in the library at about the same time he and Clotild grew to the point where they didn't sleep much more than Gerin and Selatre did. The Fox's bedchamber had only one large bed in it. Private moments there got harder and harder to find.

"What *are* you doing?" Selatre asked now, though her tone of voice suggested she knew perfectly well what he was doing—and that she might have done it herself if he hadn't.

"Who, me?" Gerin unrolled the cloth on the floor. When he'd doubled it over onto itself, it was a little longer than a woman, or even a man, might be, lying at full length.

Selatre came over and stood beside him. As if altogether of its own accord, his arm slid around her waist. She moved closer. Her voice, though, was thoughtful as she said, "It's really not quite so soft as the bed, is it? And you don't always remember to keep your weight on your elbows instead of on me." She let out a small sigh that might have proclaimed she was resigned to his iniquities.

Some pleasant little while later, Gerin murmured, "There. You can't say I'm squashing you now." Selatre, astride him, nodded agreement altogether too solemn for the moment. Both of them started to laugh—quietly. Gerin slid his hands along her smooth, warm length. "Is this better, then?"

"Better?" Her shrug was delightful. Even then, though, the answer she gave was carefully considered: "I don't know. It's not the same, and you're not squashing me. That's enough." She began to move, and the answers she and Gerin found were not expressed in words.

Once he'd put on his linen tunic and wool trousers, Gerin rolled up the bolt of cloth and slung it back in its corner. In the light of the single lamp still burning in the library, it looked altogether mundane: just one more thing for which there hadn't been room anywhere else in the crowded castle.

Suddenly, Selatre started to giggle. The Fox raised an interrogative eyebrow. She said, "I wonder what Ferdulf would have thought if he'd been walking in the air outside the window just then."

There was an aspect of Ferdulf's unusual abilities Gerin hadn't contemplated till then. "Maybe he would have learned something," he said, which made Selatre laugh again. He went on, "Considering which god he's the son of, maybe he wouldn't have, too." He and Selatre both laughed at that. Were they a little nervous? If they were, they both kept quiet about it. He unbarred the door. Selatre blew out the lamp. They went off to bed.

Marlanz Raw-Meat looked as if he'd bitten into something sour. "It's still no, is it?" he said, and swigged at the ale which, with bread and honey, made up his breakfast.

"It's still no," Gerin said firmly. "If Balser Debo's son acknowledges that he is my vassal—and I expect he will—I'll protect him from all his neighbors, including Aragis the Archer."

"I'm sorry to hear that, lord king," Marlanz said. "I'll take your words down to King Aragis. After that, I expect I'll see you in the field." He put down the loaf on which he'd been gnawing and made cut-and-thrust motions. "Guest-friends don't slay each other, of course, but that doesn't hold for your men."

"I know," Gerin said. "Tell Aragis also that I have no quarrel with him if he has no quarrel with me. Tell him I don't aim to use Balser's land against him. Tell him he and I have managed to keep from going to war with each other up till now even though we've been the two strongest men in the northlands for most of the past twenty years. I'm in no great hurry to change that."

"I'll tell him everything you say, lord king." Marlanz upended his jack, then looked into it as if amazed it held no more ale. "I'll tell him, but his mind's made up. If Balser claims you for his overlord, Aragis will go to war. When he says something like that, it's as sure as the sun coming up tomorrow."

From everything Gerin had gleaned by intently watching his rival over the years, Marlanz was telling the truth. When Aragis said he would do something, he *would* do it, no matter how appalling it might be. He was not a man who deviated from his declared purposes. That made him more dangerous than someone who might be intimidated, but also made him more vulnerable because he was more predictable.

But the lands he controlled and those acknowledging the Fox's overlordship already marched over a long stretch of the northlands. If he went to war with Gerin, he could pick the spot for the first assault. "Tell Aragis one thing more from me," the Fox said, and Marlanz Raw-Meat nodded attentively. "Tell him that if he starts this war, I will finish it, and he won't care for that."

By Marlanz's expression, he didn't care for it, either. "I will take your words to him just as you say them, lord king," he promised. His face got longer yet. "I don't think it will help, but I'll do it."

"All right. I'll tell you one thing, too, Marlanz," Gerin said: "I don't hold this against you personally. You're doing as a good vassal should, following the orders of your suzerain. I think you'll be sorry for doing it even so."

"That's in the hands of the gods," Marlanz said, and then looked as if he wished he could have the words back. They must have made him think of Ferdulf, and from Ferdulf go on to Mavrix. He wouldn't know Mavrix was none too well disposed toward Gerin. Aragis did know that—or had known it some years before. But Aragis had also seen Gerin cozen Mavrix into doing what the Fox wanted him to do. He might well reckon that meant man and god had patched things up. With luck, the prospect—even if it wasn't a true prospect—of facing an irate god would give even the Archer pause.

The prospect of facing an irate god had given Gerin pause several times. That didn't mean he hadn't done it. It didn't mean he hadn't got away with it, either. He had no reason to assume Aragis couldn't get away with it, too. He wished he did have such a reason.

"Try to make Aragis see that I don't want this war, will you?" the Fox persisted. "If I did want it, I'd hold you here, and the first thing Aragis would know was that my men were coming over the border at him."

"As I say, lord king, I'll pass on everything you say to me," Marlanz replied. "I don't think it will do much good, as I told you before. King Aragis will answer that it only means you don't want war now, right this minute, not that you don't want war at all." He sat a little straighter, a little more defiantly. "Can you tell me my king would be wrong?"

"Yes," Gerin said. "If I'd wanted war, I could have had it whenever I chose, and I've never chosen war with Aragis, not down through these past twenty years." He sighed; he was blessed—or perhaps cursed—with the ability to see the other fellow's point of view. "And he'll say the only reason I didn't do it was because I wasn't ready all this time, and now I finally am." He felt tired. "Go on home, Marlanz. Pretty soon Aragis and I can try killing each other, and then we'll find out who's better at that."

The warriors who had accompanied Aragis' envoy up to Fox Keep had their chariots ready for the return journey. Gerin's resignation to the prospect of war ahead seemed to reach Marlanz where his earlier denials had been brushed aside. As Marlanz stepped up into his car, he spoke urgently: "I'll urge him to hold the peace—by Father Dyaus, I swear it. Whether he listens to me . . ."

"If he doesn't listen to you, maybe he'll listen to edged bronze." Gerin waved to the gate crew. "Let down the drawbridge." The men in the gatehouse turned the capstan. Bronze chain rattled out, a link at a time. Down went the bridge. The Fox waved again, this time to Marlanz Raw-Meat.

Marlanz looked to be on the point of saying something more. Instead, he bowed stiffly and tapped his driver on the shoulder. The fellow flicked the reins. The horses got moving. The chariot's axle squeaked as it began to roll. The other car, the one with a crew of warriors, followed. Horses' hooves thundered and wheels boomed on the drawbridge. Marlanz was still peering back over his shoulder at the Fox when his driver swung south and took the car out of the narrow line of sight the gate offered.

Gerin could have mounted to the palisade and watched Marlanz till he was out of sight, but what point to that? He went back into the great hall and called for ale instead. Carlun Vepin's son sat in there, cutting a length of sausage into identical bite-sized chunks before he ate them. He looked up from that fussily precise task and said, "There will be war then, lord king?"

"I'm afraid there will," Gerin answered. "I don't see how I can turn Balser down. Evidently Aragis doesn't see how he can let me accept Balser's vassalage. If that's not a recipe for war, I don't know what is."

Carlun stabbed one of those chunks of sausage with the knife he'd used to cut it. He brought it up to his mouth, chewed, swallowed. Only then did he deliver his verdict: "It will be expensive."

"Thanks so much—I hadn't realized that," Gerin snapped. The steward choked on another bite of sausage; he'd always been vulnerable to sarcasm. Gerin slapped him on the back. "Steady there—expensive, yes; fatal, no."

"I suppose not, lord king," Carlun said. "Nothing else you've undertaken has been fatal—though the gods can drop me in the hottest of the five hells if I understand why not." He cocked his head to one side. "Maybe it's magic."

Gerin turned his most enigmatic stare on the steward. "Maybe it is," he answered, which made Carlun look nervous. Gerin had studied sorcery down in the City of Elabon before the Elabonian Empire severed itself from its fractious northern province. He'd had to return to the northlands with his magical studies, like all the rest, incomplete: the Trokmoi had slain his father and brother, leaving him baron, a job he'd wanted about as much as a longtooth wanted an aching fang.

Despite insatiable curiosity, he hadn't intended to practice much sorcery after coming back to the north. The only thing more dangerous, commonly to himself, than a half-trained mage was . . . The Fox backed up and started that thought again, because he couldn't think of anything more dangerous than a half-trained mage.

That didn't mean he hadn't practiced magic every now and again. *Amazing what desperation will do*, he thought. When faced with a Trokmê wizard bent on destroying him for a fancied slight, or with the eruption of the monsters from under Biton's temple down at Ikos, or with the invasion of the Gradi and their ferocious gods, the risks of sorcery suddenly seemed smaller.

He hadn't killed himself yet. That was the most he could say for his sorcery. After a moment, he shook his head, rejecting false modesty. In hair-raising fashion, the magic had done what he'd wanted it to do. Balamung the Trokmê mage was destroyed, the monsters—except Geroge and Tharma—were made to return to their gloomy caverns, the Gradi were pinned back to a single castle at the edge of the ocean.

And because Gerin hadn't killed himself once—*though not for lack of effort*, he thought—both his friends and his foes had conceived the notion that he really was a formidable wizard in his own right. So long as he didn't conceive the same foolish notion and try to act on it, he figured he'd be fine. Thinking he had a true sorcerous talent also made people think twice about crossing him.

As now: Carlun said, "Then I will prepare for war sure everything will turn out right, even if I don't see how."

That went too far. Gerin shook his head again. "Prepare as if you think everything will go wrong. In your mind, make things look as black as you can. Figure out how we'd come through that. Then, when something works out better than you expect—if anything works out better than you expect," he added from the depths of a deeply pessimistic nature, "you can take it as a bonus."

"I understand, lord king." Carlun hesitated, then said, "Forgive me, lord king, but in a lot of ways you think more like a serf than how I thought a noble would think. I always thought nobles had so much, they never needed to worry about what to do when things go wrong."

"Only goes to show you were born a serf and not a

noble," Gerin answered. "The only people without worries are the dead ones and the ones who haven't been born yet. Nobles don't worry about their overlords' taking too much of the harvest away and making them starve, they worry about their neighbors' taking their lands away and killing them. Comes out about the same in the end, I'd say."

"Maybe so," Carlun said, "but nobles press on peasants all the time, and on their neighbors only now and again."

"Nobles in my domain had better not press on peasants all the time, or on their neighbors, either," Gerin said. But he understood what Carlun meant: that was how things commonly worked in the northlands, and how they had worked for generations. He wondered if he ought to despair when his own steward seemed to think the changes he was making were anomalies that wouldn't last.

He got no time to contemplate that gloomy notion, which might have been just as well: Herris Bigfoot, the headman of the peasant village close by Fox Keep, came running into the great hall, crying, "Lord king! Lord king! Come quick, lord king! Ferdulf's at it again."

"Hullo, Herris," said Carlun, who was the headman's brother-in-law.

"Hullo." Herris grudged his kinsman by marriage the one word, but then gave his attention back to the Fox. "Will you come, lord king?"

Gerin had already risen to his feet. "I'm coming, Herris, though by all the gods I'm not certain what I can do to rein in Ferdulf that you couldn't manage for yourself."

"But, lord king, that's your job," Herris said.

The Fox sighed. It *was* his job, which didn't mean he relished it. How was he supposed to impose his will on a four-year-old demigod? Rather more to the point, how was he supposed to do it without regretting it afterwards? In weary resignation, he asked, "What's he gone and done this time?"

"Uh, lord king, you'd better come see for yourself," the headman answered.

People had been saying that about Ferdulf since the day he was born. He'd spoken to the midwife while she was cutting the cord that had linked him to his mother. He'd greeted Gerin when the Fox came down to the village to see what Mavrix had begotten on Fulda. And he'd only become more alarming since, as his power had grown with his body.

Out of Fox Keep and over the drawbridge strode Herris and Gerin. The village was only a short walk south of the keep. The peasants lived in thatch-roofed huts of wattle and daub. Smoke issued from the holes in the center of several of those roofs: women cooking, no doubt. Other women were working in the vegetable gardens by the huts or feeding the chickens that ran around as if they thought the place belonged to them, not to the Fox.

Most of the men were away from the village, either tending to cattle and sheep or weeding in the fields of growing wheat and barley. Gerin didn't notice any signs of unusual chaos, which wasn't always the case when Ferdulf got into mischief. He noticed as much, with something approaching hope in his voice.

"You'll find out, lord king," Herris Bigfoot said.

He led the Fox toward Fulda's hut. Before they got there, Fulda came outside. She might well have been the best-looking young woman in the village; the long tunic she wore lessened but could not hide the impact of her figure. Rihwin the Fox had chosen her at Gerin's urging, to help attract Mavrix to Fox Keep to fight the Gradi gods; after failing in that fight, Mavrix himself had chosen to impregnate her.

"Lord king," she said now, "I'm sure he didn't mean it."

When that phrase got stuck to the mischief of an ordinary small boy, it meant said mischief was worse than it had any business being. When it was applied to the mischief of a small demigod . . . "What's he gone and done now?" Gerin asked, not sure he wanted to find out. No, that wasn't true. He did want to find out. He wished he didn't have to find out.

"You'd better see for yourself," Herris and Fulda said in the same breath. They looked at each other and laughed. The headman's eyes lingered on Fulda. Any man's eyes had a way of lingering on Fulda. Seeing that, Gerin thought it was liable to cause trouble one of these days. It would, however, be trouble of an ordinary sort, trouble he'd seen many times before, trouble he knew how to handle. The kind of trouble Ferdulf caused was something else again.

"What's he gone and done?" the Fox repeated.

"He was playing in the mud by the pond, and he—" Fulda began. She gave up. Her shrug was magnificent.

"You'd better see for yourself," Herris said again.

Gerin loudly exhaled through his nose. Spinning on his heel, he stalked off toward the pond close by the village. Herris and Fulda hurried after him, both expostulating. None of the expostulations made much sense. That didn't surprise him; had things made sense to the villagers, they wouldn't have needed him to straighten them out.

He strode past the last hut. There was the pond: not much of a pond, perhaps, to a connoisseur of such, but enough. Ducks swam in it. In the mud by its edge, the village pigs wallowed. Their happy grunting filled the Fox's ears, much as the gabble from Herris and Fulda had done not long before. But not all of that grunting came from the edge of the pond, nor were all the quacks that punctuated it from ducks on the water.

After a second, more careful, look at the peaceful scene ahead, Gerin turned back to the village headman and the demigod's mother. "I owe you an apology," he said, not a common admission for a lord to make to a couple of serfs.

"What are we going to do, lord king?" Herris Bigfoot demanded.

"I—don't—know." Gerin stared out at the pond. Most of the ducks there were of the ordinary sort, the males with shiny green heads, the females drab and brown all over. A couple of them, though . . .

A couple of them, Gerin's eyes confirmed, were ducks only from the neck down. From the neck up, they were pigs. Because their heads were smaller than they had any natural business being, the grunts those heads admitted sounded strange, but they were undoubtedly piggy grunts.

And, sure enough, one of the piggy bodies by the pond sported an outsized green head with a flat bill, and another a head similar but brown. *Neither pork nor fowl*, the Fox thought dazedly.

"What are we going to do?" It seemed to be the sort of day where everyone repeated himself: Herris' turn again.

"I don't know." Gerin was echoing his own words, too. Then he found something new to add: "Hope they breed true, maybe."

Herris and Fulda both stared at him. He'd succeeded in startling them, anyhow. Well, they—and Ferdulf—had succeeded in startling him, too. Suddenly, the village headman started to laugh. "I wonder if they'll lay eggs or have live young," he said.

Fulda voiced a more immediately pragmatic consideration: "I wonder what they'd taste like."

Gerin tried to imagine a flavor halfway between duck and pork. His stomach rumbled; he didn't know whether his imagination was accurate, but it was vivid enough to make him hungry. He said, "If you find out what they taste like now, you won't find out later whether they lay eggs or not."

"You're right, lord king." Fulda didn't seem to have thought so far ahead.

But Herris Bigfoot said, "Lord king, what will you do to Ferdulf on account of this? Even if he is a god's son, he's got no business changing things around so. What if he starts putting the wrong heads on people next?"

"A lot of people are wrongheaded enough without getting switched around," Gerin said. But that was a quip, not an answer. Knowing it was necessary, the Fox went on, "I'll have a word with him." *And what if he decides to put the wrong head on* me? There was a thought the Fox wished he hadn't had. Pretending—most of all to himself—it had never crossed his mind, he turned to Fulda. "Is he back at your house?"

"Yes, lord king," she said. She hesitated, torn between a mother's love for her child and the certain knowledge the child she had borne to Mavrix was not of the ordinary sort. "Whatever you do, lord king, be careful."

That was good advice. It was such good advice, in fact, that Gerin wished his career had given him more chances to take it. As things had worked out for him, though, had he been careful, he probably would have been dead several times over.

He started back toward the hut where Fulda lived. She and Herris trailed after him. He discovered Ferdulf had come out while he was staring at the pigducks in the pond and the duckpigs by it. Ferdulf was whacking at something in the grass with a stick, for all the world like any other four-year-old. But he was not any other four-year-old. He looked up at Gerin and spoke in his mellow baritone: "I wonder how *you'd* look with a big green duck's head." He frowned in concentration.

Nothing happened, for which the Fox was duly grateful. "Probably pretty silly," he replied after considering. He refused to let Ferdulf put him in fear—or rather, he refused to let Ferdulf see he put him in fear. In the same mild, thoughtful tones he'd just used, he went on, "I wonder how you'd look with your backside all red and sore."

"You wouldn't dare," Ferdulf said. "You know whose son I am."

Gerin did know, only too well. "I've spanked you before, when you earned it," he answered, which was also true. He didn't tell Ferdulf he'd gone back to Fox Keep and got drunk afterwards, to celebrate surviving the experience.

Ferdulf frowned. "I was littler then. I didn't know all the things I could do."

"Just because you *can* do something doesn't mean you *should* do it," Gerin said. If Ferdulf thought he was coming into his full powers at four, what would he be like at fourteen? At thirty-four? The Fox did his best not to think about that. He also did his best not to think about how unlikely it was for Mavrix's get to understand what restraint meant.

"Why not?" Ferdulf asked with what sounded like genuine curiosity. Sure enough, he didn't understand Gerin's point.

Patiently, Gerin explained, "Because some of the things you can do either frighten people or make them unhappy."

"So what?" Yes, Ferdulf was Mavrix's son, all right.

"How do you like it when someone frightens you or makes you unhappy?" Gerin asked.

"You're about the only one who ever tries to do anything like that," Ferdulf answered. He looked thoughtful. "I wonder if I could stop you."

The Fox felt fingers prying in his mind: that was how he recalled the sensation later, at any rate. It showed him that Ferdulf, however strong he was by merely mortal standards, was weak by those of the gods—Mavrix had rummaged through Gerin's thoughts and memories like a man going through a beltpouch in search of a pin.

"Stop that!" the Fox said, and tightened his mental muscles. He wasn't sure that would do any good, but had no intention of yielding to the little demigod without first putting up whatever fight he could.

Ferdulf looked astonished, as he usually did when things failed to go as he'd thought they would. "How are you doing that?" he demanded. "You're supposed to be thinking about what *I* want you to think about, not what you want to think about." By his tone, that latter wasn't worth contemplating.

Those probing mental fingers groped harder. Gerin grunted. Ferdulf had told him his resistance had some success (something an older, wiser foe would have known better than to do), so he kept on resisting, as the palisade to Fox Keep had withstood a Trokmê siege.

He got the feeling resistance wasn't enough, not by itself. "Here," he said. "You're going to think about what I want *you* to think about." He couldn't reach out and touch Ferdulf's mind, not directly. But there were other ways of gaining the demigod's attention. Gerin grabbed Ferdulf and flipped him over his knee.

Ferdulf let out a squeal of pure outrage. "I said you wouldn't dare!" he cried. The probing fingers vanished from Gerin's mind. If nothing else, the Fox had managed to distract him.

"Just because you said it doesn't make it so." Not without a certain amount of trepidation, Gerin brought down the hand that wasn't restraining Ferdulf.

The demigod's howl was quite satisfactory. Ferdulf tried to rise straight up into the air, as he had while playing at Fox Keep. He did rise, too, but not very far, not with the Fox holding onto him.

"Have I got your attention yet?" Gerin asked. Even with his feet off the ground, he retained enough presence of mind to administer another dose of the medicine he had chosen. "Why don't you put us both down, and we can talk about it some more instead of fighting?"

"Oh, very well." Ferdulf's petulant tones were an echo of those Mavrix used when, as did happen once in a while, the Sithonian god was compelled to change his ways.

"Thank you," Gerin said, most sincerely, when his feet touched the ground again.

"You're welcome," Ferdulf answered, an unexpected bit of politeness he must have acquired from his mother. He gave the Fox a dirty look. "Why are you so much harder to change than pigs and ducks?"

As the implications of that sank in, Herris Bigfoot and Fulda gasped. Gerin gulped. Ferdulf *had* been trying to give him a duck's head, then. "I don't know why," he said. "I'm just glad I am. And I want you to remember I am. The next time you try to change me—or anything else—you're going to be in trouble. Have you got that?"

"Yes, I've got it." Ferdulf didn't look happy about it, either, which was a long way from breaking Gerin's heart. The little demigod glared up at him. "How come you get to tell me what to do, when you're only a mortal?"

"Why?" The Fox considered that. "I can think of a couple of reasons. One is, I may be just a mortal, but I've been around a lot longer than you have. I know more about the world than you do."

The first of those statements was undoubtedly true. The second would undoubtedly have been true were Ferdulf an ordinary four-year old. Were Ferdulf an ordinary four-year-old, though, he wouldn't have tried flying off with the Fox, and he wouldn't have tried decorating him with a mallard's head, either.

Whatever else Ferdulf was, he wasn't trained to catch logical flaws. He accepted what the Fox told him more readily than Gerin would have. "That's one," he said. "What's two?"

"Two is very simple," Gerin answered. "I just showed you I'm strong enough to do it, didn't I?"

Besides being Aragis' argument over Balser's allegiance, that also had its logical flaws. How long would Gerin go on being stronger than Ferdulf? What would happen when he wasn't stronger any more? Gerin didn't know the answers to those questions. He could think of things liable to be more pleasant than discovering what those answers were.

But Ferdulf, though a demigod, was a four-year-old demigod. As with any other four-year-old, things as they were now seemed close to the way they would be forever. "Yes, you're stronger," he said, angry resignation in his voice. "But not everybody is."

If that aside didn't want to make Herris, and maybe Fulda, too, run somewhere far, far away, maybe it should have. Gerin carefully chose a different issue. "I'm not the only one who's stronger than you, Ferdulf. What about Selatre, my wife?" Despite her disclaimer to Marlanz, Ferdulf had been known to heed what she said.

"That's not fair!" he exclaimed now. "The god she knows still keeps an eye on her, and my father won't pay any attention to me."

"You can tell that farseeing Biton still holds Selatre in his mind?" Gerin asked.

"Of course," Ferdulf said. "Can't you?"

He didn't altogether grasp how limited the ordinary human sensorium was. He'd also said something else interesting, though he probably didn't know it. So Mavrix was less than attentive to his offspring, was he? That didn't surprise Gerin, though he hadn't known it before. A god of unbridled fertility didn't strike the Fox as likely to make the most devoted parent for any one child.

"Will you behave yourself?" he demanded of the little demigod.

"I suppose so," Ferdulf answered.

"No more pigducks or duckpigs?" Gerin said. Having Dagref in his household, he'd learned better than to leave loopholes open: "And no more mixing any other creatures—or people—together, all right?"

"All right," Ferdulf said, not too much sulk in his voice. Gerin didn't trust his promise very far, but didn't altogether discount it, either. From what he'd seen of Ferdulf, the promise was worth about as much—and as little—as that of any other child of the same age. Sooner or later, the demigod would forget he'd made it and do something else appalling. That was how children behaved, even children of large powers. But the Fox didn't think Ferdulf would go out and deliberately break his word.

"Fair enough," he said. "We have a bargain, then."

Ferdulf nodded and went off to play. Gerin didn't think he walked a couple of feet off the ground intending to intimidate. More likely, he just wasn't thinking about what he was doing.

Herris Bigfoot, by now, took such minor impossibilities in stride. He said, "Thank you, lord king. We are grateful to you, believe me, for keeping him under what control you do."

Gerin looked him straight in the eye. "Quack," he answered seriously. "Quack, quack, quack." Herris looked horrified. Fulda gasped in dismay. Gerin let both of them stew for a moment, then started to laugh.

"That wasn't nice, lord king," Fulda said, sounding more sorrowful than angry.

He thought about it. When Ferdulf terrorized the villagers, he didn't know any better. Gerin did. "You're right, of course," he told Fulda. "I shouldn't have done it. I'm sorry."

If anything, the apology—the second in the space of a few minutes—disconcerted her more than the quacks had. "You're the king," she blurted. "You don't have to say you're sorry to the likes of me."

He shook his head. "No, you're wrong. It's Aragis who never needs to say he's sorry. That's the difference between us, right there." Fulda didn't understand. He hadn't expected she would.

II

"Who comes to Fox Keep?" called the sentry up on the palisade.

"I am Balser Debo's son," came the reply from the chariot outside the keep. "I am here to give homage and fealty to Gerin the Fox, the king of the north, to acknowledge him as my suzerain and overlord of my barony."

The sentry whirled to see where Gerin was. As it happened, he was standing in the courtyard not far away. "Did you hear that, lord king?" he exclaimed, his voice going high and shrill with excitement. "Did you hear that?"

"I heard it," the Fox answered. He'd been waiting for this moment for some time, waiting for it and at the same time half hoping—maybe more than half hoping—it would not come. Now that it was here, though, he would have to make the most of it. He raised his voice: "Balser Debo's son is welcome at Fox Keep. Let him enter!"

Bronze chain clattered as the gate crew lowered the drawbridge. Balser's chariot rolled into the courtyard. The driver reined in the fine two-horse team. Balser got down from the car and walked over to the Fox. He was a young man, dark, slim, not very tall but well put together, who wore his beard in the forked style that had long been out of date but was suddenly all the rage again.

Like the first stone sliding down a mountain to start an avalanche (Gerin remembered how the Elabonian Empire had blocked the last pass through the High Kirs with just such an avalanche, leaving the northlands to their own devices when the Trokmoi invaded), Balser was going to cause a lot more trouble than he ever could have accounted for by himself. His coming here, in fact, was no doubt the beginning of the rockslide.

Well, no help for it. Gerin hurried to meet him halfway. The two men clasped hands. "I greet you, Balser Debo's son," the Fox said as his men gathered to watch the drama unfold. "Use my keep as your own as long as you are here."

"I thank you, lord king," Balser replied. "If you should ever come south, my keep is likewise yours."

Gerin nodded. He was glad to make a new guest-friend. Webs of host and guest, guest and host, each bound by the sacred ties of friendship to do no harm to the other, stretched across the northlands. Without them, feuds among barons would have been even worse than they were.

But Balser had not traveled here to become a guest-friend, however pleasing that might have been for the southern baron. "You're certain you want to become my vassal?" Gerin said. "You don't care to stay your own lord, as your father and grandfather were before you?"

"My father and grandfather never had to worry about Aragis the Archer." Balser sent Gerin a curious look. "Is it that you don't want my vassalage, lord king? That's not what you gave me to understand before."

"No. It isn't that. Aragis has threatened you. Aragis has tried to scare you out of your breeches, as a matter of fact." The breeches in question were dyed in bright checks of maroon and yellow, a Trokmê mode that had grown fashionable among men of Elabonian blood, too. Scaring Balser out of them would, in Gerin's opinion, have improved his wardrobe. That, however, was not of the essence. "I don't blame you for wanting me to protect you from him, and I'll do just that."

"The gods be praised—and you, too, lord king, for your generosity," Balser said. "That's exactly what I want. I'm not strong enough to hold him off on my own—he's shown me that. You let your vassals remember they're men; I'd sooner go with you than have him swallow me down."

"For which I thank you." The Fox didn't want to thank Balser, not really. He wanted to kick him. He wanted to kick Aragis, too, for frightening Balser into his own arms. He wanted to kick Aragis for being too arrogant to blame himself for frightening Balser, too. Had Aragis shown only a little more restraint, Balser would have stayed neutral.

But the only man in all the northlands who had ever made the Archer show restraint was Gerin. Precisely because Gerin worried him, he could not bear to have the Fox ruling Balser's barony, which lay close to his own. Another round of war was the last thing Gerin wanted, but that had nothing to do with anything. War had come up to Fox Keep, riding in Balser's chariot.

Balser's name had brought Van and Rihwin out of Castle Fox—and Selatre, too, a few paces behind them. Gerin didn't know where Dagref materialized from: one moment, he wasn't anywhere to be seen, but he stood at his father's elbow the next. Van's daughter Maeva had a quiver on her back and a bow in her hand; she must have been practicing her shooting. Unlike Dagref, she hung back a little from her elders. But Balser's name drew her, too—she knew it meant fighting, and that was what she wanted.

As the crowd grew, Balser said, "I'll do it here and now if you like, lord king. We seem to have enough witnesses."

"Oh, indeed," the Fox said. "It's getting anything done without witnesses that's hard around here." Geroge and Tharma came ambling around the corner of the castle. Gerin didn't think Balser's name had attracted them. But, when they saw people gathering, they hurried up to find out what was going on. They were people, too—or they were convinced they were.

Balser didn't look so sure. "Lord king, I'd heard you kept a couple of those monsters at your keep, but I hadn't believed it."

"You may as well, because it's true. I'm quite fond of them, as a matter of fact." Gerin offered no compromise there whatever. If Balser didn't like it, he could go back to his barony. That would disappoint Maeva, who wanted a war, but not the Fox, who didn't.

But Balser showed no signs of packing up and leaving. "Are they your vassals, too?" he asked. "I do like to know the company I'm keeping."

One of Gerin's eyebrows rose at that display of sangfroid. "Stepchildren, more like," he answered, and had the satisfaction of startling Balser in return.

"Why is everybody standing here?" Geroge asked. He pointed at Balser with a clawed index finger. "And who is this strange gentleman?"

Hearing him speak and make good sense startled Balser again. The baron could have remarked on Geroge's being a strange gentleman himself. Gerin gave him points because he didn't. Instead, he answered the question seriously: "I am Balser Debo's son, and I have come to give homage and fealty to your . . . stepfather."

Geroge and Tharma both clapped their large, hairy hands together. "Oh, good!" they said.

Seeing that everyone who dwelt at Fox Keep took the monsters for granted helped Balser do the same. He turned back to Gerin, saying, "Where were we, lord king?" He answered his own question by going to one knee before the Fox.

Rihwin coughed and said, "Meaning no offense, son of Debo, but the ritual of offering submission to the king, he being of rank superior to that enjoyed by other sorts of overlords, requires the vassal to rest both knees on the ground."

Gerin hadn't intended to make an issue of it. As far as he was concerned, one knee would have been as binding as two. Balser, fortunately, didn't seem inclined to make an issue of it, either. "Very well," he said, and went from one knee to two, at the same time offering his hands to Gerin, palms pressed together. The Fox enclosed Balser's hands with his own. Balser gave him homage: "I, Balser Debo's son, own myself to be your vassal, Gerin the Fox, King of the North, and give you the whole of my faith against all men who might live or die."

"I, Gerin, King of the North, accept your homage, Balser Debo's son, and pledge in my turn always to use you justly.

In token of which, I raise you up now." The Fox pulled Balser to his feet and kissed him on the cheek, sealing the ceremony of homage.

"By Dyaus the father of all and the other gods of Elabon, I swear my fealty to you, lord king," Balser said with a bow.

Gerin bowed to him in turn. "By Dyaus the father of all and the other gods of Elabon, I accept your oath and swear to reward your loyalty with my own."

"I am your man, lord king," Balser said: not a formal part of the ceremony, but a truth nonetheless.

"So you are," Gerin said. "We'll feast tonight to celebrate"—not that he felt much like celebrating—"and then tomorrow I'll send out messengers to some of my other vassals, telling them your lands need protecting against Aragis. I want warriors down there as fast as may be."

Balser looked less than delighted at that prospect, but in the end nodded. He seemed to be realizing for the first time what all having an overlord entailed. Gerin's men were going to be overrunning his holding, and he couldn't do anything about it. They wouldn't burn and loot and kill, as Aragis' men would have done (at least not to anywhere near the same degree), but they would be there, and the holding would no longer be his in the sense it had been for so long.

And, of course, the presence of the Fox's men in Balser's holding was liable to bring Aragis' army over the border, in which case the Archer's men would do the burning and looting and killing Balser had come to Gerin to prevent. The Fox thought he saw the moment in which Balser figured that out, too. His new vassal wasn't so good as he might have been at holding his face straight.

"Second thoughts?" Gerin asked him.

"Some," Balser answered, which bespoke a certain basic honesty. "I couldn't go it alone any more, and I couldn't stomach bending the knee—bending both knees—to Aragis. That left bending the knee—the knees—to you."

"For which ringing endorsement I thank you," Gerin said. Balser's worried expression made him hold up a hand. "Don't fret. You haven't offended me. You knew what you were doing and why you were doing it. That's more than a lot of people ever manage. Now come on." He waved Balser toward Castle Fox. "We'll enjoy ourselves for the time being, and then—"

Van broke in from the crowd of onlookers: "—And then we'll go off and fight ourselves one bloody big war." He didn't sound so eager as he would have in his younger days, but he did sound very sure. No one who heard him claimed he was wrong, either.

Gerin shouted for ale, and ordered an ox slain. Carlun Vepin's son grimaced at that. Gerin took no notice of him, telling the cooks, "Lay the fat-wrapped thighbones on Dyaus' altar and set them afire, so the smoke will rise up to heaven and the Allfather will favor what Balser and I have done today." Actually, by everything he'd seen, by everything other gods had told him, Dyaus hardly bothered noticing what went on in the material world. Gerin shrugged. He still had to make the effort.

Fand came downstairs to see what the commotion in the great hall was about: a big, rawboned Trokmê woman, still more than handsome though gray streaked her once-fiery hair. She carried a couple of pieces of cloth she'd been sewing into a tunic and a long bone needle.

She'd heard Van's last remark. "Go off and fight a war, will you now?" she said, advancing on him. "Leave me behind, will you now?"

The outlander scowled. "I will," he rumbled, and pointed to the needle. "There's a weapon for piercing cloth, not flesh."

Fand scowled right back at him. "You've got a weapon in your breeches for piercing flesh," she jeered, "and better nor half the reason you're so wild for going off to battle is that along the way you find some pretty young things to stick it into, girls who aren't after hearing your lies a thousand times, the way I have."

"Better than half the reason I'm wild to go off to battle is that you aren't carping and cawing at me while I'm away," Van retorted.

Fand shouted at him again. He shouted back. Each one's opening shot had made the other angrier, no doubt because both contained a painful amount of truth. Gerin eyed with some concern the needle Fand was holding. She'd stabbed a Trokmê lover before she turned up at Fox Keep. She and Van occasionally quarreled with more than words, but neither of them had ever seriously damaged the other. The Fox wanted that to stay true.

Balser glanced over at him. "They must care for each other," Gerin's new vassal remarked, "else they'd try and kill each other over some of the things they're saying."

That marched very well with Gerin's own thoughts. "Some people enjoy quarreling," he said. "I've never seen the sport in it myself."

In the midst of her own tirade, Fand heard his quiet comment. She spun away from Van and toward him. "Sure and I'm not quarreling for nobbut the sport of it, lord king Gerin the Fox." She loaded his title and name with the familiar scorn that could only have come from a former lover. Pointing at Van, she went on, "I'm quarreling for that he willna keep his trousers on the instant he's out of my sight."

"Am I the only one?" Van shouted. "By the gods, it's hardly better than luck my children look like me."

Instead of coming to blows, they went upstairs a few minutes later. Gerin breathed a silent sigh of relief. He'd seen them do that a good many times before, too. They found being angry added spice to their lovemaking. That bemused the Fox, too. It wasn't the way he worked.

Rihwin the Fox said, "As a calm descends over the battlefield . . ." He winked.

"If you had a wife, she'd be after you the same way," Gerin said.

"Without a doubt, you have reason, lord king." Rihwin gave a bow that was only slightly mocking. "Therefore I was wise enough never to wed."

"Therefore you've got bastards in half the peasant villages in my domain," Gerin said, which was also true.

"I am not a eunuch," Rihwin said with dignity, "and I do all I can for my byblows." Gerin had to nod. Rihwin was erratic and extravagant, but not badhearted.

"Never a dull moment around these parts, is there?" Balser Debo's son was looking a trifle walleyed, as if he hadn't expected anything like the turbulent stir of personalities he'd found at Fox Keep. Maybe he was having more second thoughts about becoming Gerin's vassal. Too late now.

In all seriousness, Gerin replied, "I do keep trying for them, but I haven't had much luck." Balser laughed, wrongly thinking he'd made a joke.

Riders went out of Fox Keep the next morning to summon Gerin's vassals to bring their retainers to his holding for the likely campaign against Aragis. "So many men climbing up on horses' backs," Balser said, as bemused by the show of equitation as by what had gone on in the great hall the night before (which, to the Fox's way of thinking, had been on the mild side). "Always something new here, eh, lord king?"

"I hope so," Gerin answered. That, he saw, startled Balser anew. He went on, "Don't you think life would get dull if we kept doing the same things the same old way forever, the more so as a lot of those old ways don't work as well as they might?"

Balser plainly hadn't thought about it at all. As plainly, he would have been quite happy to go on not thinking about it at all, and to see the same old ways go on forever if he could. Most people were like that, as Gerin had discovered to his continued disappointment.

"About this business of horseriding," Balser said, "we don't hardly see it down in my part of the northlands."

He'd steered clear of openly arguing with his new overlord, and was turning the conversation back toward the comment he'd made first: not a bad performance, Gerin thought. Aloud, he said, "It's been more than twenty years now since one of my vassals, Duin the Bold, came up with those footmounts—*stirrups*, we call 'em—that let a man stay mounted while he uses both hands for archery, and let him charge home with a spear without having to worry about going back over the horse's tail the instant he strikes home. We had good luck using mounted men against the Gradi; I think the chariot is on the way out."

"For traveling, I can see that it might be," Balser said. "Easier to ride than to harness up a car every day, and you don't have to worry about your axle or your wheels breaking, either." Suddenly seeming to realize what he'd said, he scratched his head. "I've just spoken well of the new, haven't I?"

"I'll not tell if you don't," Gerin said solemnly.

"That's a bargain." Balser laughed, but then held up a hand. "I don't speak well of everything new, mind you. Are you saying riders will take the place of chariots in war, too? I have trouble believing that. A man on horseback isn't nearly so frightening to his foes as a chariot thundering down on them."

"Maybe not," Gerin said, "but riders can go places chariots can't, and can fight on ground that would have chariots tipping over. And with chariots, remember, your driver has to tend to the horses. He can't do much fighting. With men on horseback, you're not wasting one in three."

"But every rider has to tend to his horse," Balser returned. "I don't see that the gain's worth it."

"One way or the other, we'll find out," Gerin said. "There will be a lot of chariotry in the force I bring down to defend your land—there'll have to be, because a lot of my vassals don't like the idea of riding any better than you do. I'll have a good many horsemen along, too, though, and we'll see how they fare against Aragis' chariots. They gave the Gradi plenty of trouble, as I've said, but the Gradi fight on foot. This will be a different test."

"A . . . test?" Balser Debo's son tasted the words: a fitting comparison, for he went on, "You sound as if you're trying out different ways of brewing ale."

"As a matter of fact, Adiatunnus the Trokmê gave me one, not so long ago," Gerin answered. "His people have taken to roasting the barley malt almost to the point where it's burnt. I'd lay long odds they did it by accident the first time, but it makes a pretty good brew: black as rich earth and full of flavor."

Balser threw his hands in the air. "I might have known you'd have something of the sort to tell me," he exclaimed, and then looked at the Fox from under lowered eyelids. "You haven't given me any of this funny black ale."

"I don't like to spring it on people as a surprise," Gerin said. "It does take a bit of getting used to, or so most folk find. But if you're game for something new, I have a few jars down in the cellar."

Balser was more willing to contemplate novelty in ale than he was in ways of fighting. After he'd downed a jack of the Trokmê-style brew, he smacked his lips a couple of times and said, "That's not too bad. I don't think I'd care to drink it all the time, but for now and again it'd be fine. It'd go right well with blood sausage, I'd say."

"Now that you mention it, it does," Gerin said, and called for some to prove the point. While they were eating, he went on, "You ask me, the more choices you have in anything, the better. If you're bedding a woman, for instance, you don't want to just climb on top and pound away all the time."

Balser looked as astonished as he had at the idea of fighting from horseback rather than in a chariot. "What other way is there?" he demanded.

Gerin spent a moment silently pitying his new vassal's wife, if Balser had one. But then, the Fox, while a student down in the City of Elabon, had become acquainted with a scroll that got copied and recopied as it passed from hand to hand and from generation to generation. The text had been educational, the illustrations even more so.

He didn't go into great detail. The more he talked, though, the wider Balser's eyes got. Balser could see possibilities if you pointed them out to him. "Lord king," he burst out, "I'd've become your vassal for this all by its lonesome—to the five hells with anything else."

"I never thought of getting vassals like *that*," the Fox said with a laugh. "More flies end up stuck in honey than in vinegar, though, don't they? I wonder if Adiatunnus would have given me less trouble over the years if he'd spent more time figuring out all the different postures he could bend the Trokmê girls into."

Balser ran his tongue over his lips. "I'm from far enough south that I haven't had much dealing with the Trokmoi—or their women. Are the wenches as loose as I hear?"

"Well, no," Gerin answered, and Balser looked disappointed. The Fox went on, "Their ways are freer than ours. You'll never find a Trokmê who's shy about telling you what he—or she, very much *or she*—thinks. If they like you, you'll know about it. And if they don't like you, you'll know about that, too."

"Ah," Balser said. "Well, that's not too bad, I suppose." He was young enough, and of rank high enough, to assume that women *would* like him. Maybe he was even right. On the other hand, given how much he'd shown he didn't know, maybe he wasn't.

On the other hand . . . Gerin sighed. "On the other hand," he said, "there's Adiatunnus. He's as good at hiding what he thinks as any Elabonian ever born. He's learned from us, too, since he brought his band of woodsrunners south over the Niffet. If he hadn't had me for a neighbor, he might be the one styling himself king of the north these days."

"He sounds like trouble," Balser said. "You should have killed him."

"He is trouble," Gerin answered. "He *was* trouble, anyhow. I did try to kill him. It didn't work. If it hadn't been for the Gradi, I'd have tried again, and that probably wouldn't have worked, either. The past five years, he's been as good a vassal as a man could want. He even came to Fox Keep so I could teach him his letters."

"A woodsrunner?" Both Balser's eyebrows shot up. "Why on earth did he want to do that? I never felt the need myself."

"He's always thought we Elabonians were more civilized than his people, and so aped us, though he'd never own as much out loud," Gerin said. "I'll teach anyone who wants to learn. I don't mind having serfs able to read and write. For one thing, it makes keeping track of what they have and what they owe easier. For another, some of them are sharp—my steward used to be a serf, for instance."

"I've heard some things about that." Balser didn't say whether he thought those things good or bad.

Gerin didn't much care, one way or the other. He also wasn't quite ready to change the subject. "But I was talking about Adiatunnus. Trokmê or not, he never shows ahead of time how he'll jump. He's my biggest worry in going to war against Aragis, as a matter of fact."

"How's that, lord king?" Balser asked. "Afraid he'll jump you from behind?"

"That's just what I'm afraid of." The Fox looked at Balser with somber approval. The baron from the south might not think much of reading, but he was not a fool. "And that's why I'll be waiting and watching to see what he does now that I've asked him for men. If he gives me all I've asked for, well and good. If he comes himself at their head, better than well and good. If he sends me excuses instead of men . . . in that case, I have to leave more men behind myself."

"But then you won't be able to do a proper job of defending me!" Balser exclaimed.

"I won't be able to do a proper job of defending you if I'm fighting a big war up here, either," Gerin pointed out. He held out his hands as if they were the pans of a scale and moved them slowly up and down. "It's not a matter of doing all one thing or all the other. It's finding a proper balance between them."

Balser didn't say anything. The noise he made in the back of his throat, though, did not sound like agreement.

"Of course, we may be fretting over shadows," Gerin said. "It depends on Adiatunnus."

Balser made the same noise, rather louder.

By dribs and drabs, vassals started coming into Fox Keep. They slept in the rushes of the great hall, they slept in the courtyard, and, as the army grew, they began setting up tents on the meadow near the keep and sleeping there. Every time a new contingent arrived, Gerin would look delighted and Carlun Vepin's son appalled. The Fox thought of them as fighting men; to his steward, they were but extra mouths to be fed.

"I'll tell you what they are," Van said one day after a dozen or so warriors led by a young baron named Laufram the Lean stared in wonder at the nondescript keep of their overlord, and at the swelling host. "They're peculiar, that's what."

"How do you mean?" Gerin asked.

"I don't quite know," the outlander confessed. "But they're different from the way they used to be when I first came to Fox Keep."

"*We're* different from the way we used to be when you

first came to Fox Keep," Gerin said. "We were young men ourselves then, or near enough."

Van shook his head. With some impatience, he answered, "I know that. It's not what I mean. I've taken it into account, or I think I have."

"All right." Gerin spread his hands. "But if that isn't what you mean, and you can't tell me what you mean, how am I supposed to make sense of it?"

Van shrugged a massive shrug and walked off muttering into his beard. A little while later, though, he came up to Gerin at a pounding trot. "I have it, Captain!" he said; he'd never called his friend *lord* or *lord prince* or *lord king*. "By all the gods, I have it!"

The Fox raised an eyebrow. "Do you suppose taking a physic will cure you of it?" When Van made as if to hit him, he laughed and said, "All right, you have it. Now that you have it, what is it?"

"It's this," the outlander said importantly: "Back in the old days, your vassal barons would just as soon spit in your eye as look at you. Is that so, or isn't it?"

"Oh, it's so, all right," Gerin agreed. "A lot of them had been used to dealing with my father. To them, I was nothing but a puppy sitting in the big dog's place. I had to prove I belonged there every day." The smile he wore was slightly twisted. Some of his memories of the early days after he took over the barony were fond ones, others anything but.

"That's right." Van's head bobbed up and down. "That's exactly right. But these troopers coming in now, and the barons leading them, too—what do they treat you like? To the five hells with me if they don't treat you like a king."

Gerin thought about it. Then he too slowly nodded. "Maybe they do," he said. "The ones who are lordlets now are the sons and grandsons, most of them, of the lords who held those keeps back twenty-odd years ago. You and I, Van, we've outlived most of the men who started with us."

"We haven't outlived Aragis," Van said. "Not yet, anyway." His big fist folded around the hilt of his sword in grim anticipation.

"No, nor Adiatunnus, either." Gerin plucked at his beard. Outlasting the competition wasn't a very dramatic way of gaining the upper hand, but it worked. How many young men died long before they were able to show all they could do? How many times had he nearly died himself? More than he cared to think of, that was certain.

"Ah, Adiatunnus." Van spoke with a certain fond ferocity. Gerin often heard the same note in his own voice when he talked about the Trokmê chieftain. The outlander went on, "And what will you do if himself himself"—he put on a Trokmê lilt for a moment—"doesn't care to come when he's called, as a good vassal should?"

"Worry," the Fox answered, which made Van laugh. "It's not funny," Gerin insisted. "I was talking about this with Balser, too, and fretting over it before I talked with him. If Adiatunnus waits till I'm all tied up with Aragis and then rises against me . . . I don't think I'd enjoy that much."

"Neither would he, after you were through with him," Van said. Gerin thought that even his friends got the idea he could do more than he knew to be humanly possible. Van continued, "If he betrays you, you could loose the Gradi against him."

"Oh, now there's a fine notion!" Gerin exclaimed. "If you have a sore toe, take an axe and whack off your foot."

"Well, you could make him think you were going to do it," Van said.

And that, when you got down to it, wasn't the worst idea in the world. Ferocious as they were, the Trokmoi feared the Gradi, who had often beaten them in battle and whose gods had trounced their own. If they hadn't feared the Gradi so much, Adiatunnus would have gone to war against Gerin years before, instead of asking him for aid. Nevertheless—

"I hope I don't have to think about it," Gerin said. "I hope he shows up here with a whole great whacking unruly lot of Trokmoi in chariots." He laughed at himself. "And if I'd said anything like that a few years back, everyone would have been sure I was out of my mind."

"Don't you fret about it, Captain," Van reassured him. "Everyone was sure you were out of your mind anyhow."

"It's such ringing endorsements that have made me what I am today," the Fox said, "which is bloody fed up with people who use friendship as an excuse to insult me."

He did not intend to be taken seriously, and Van obliged him. "Don't fret about that, either. I'd insult you even if we weren't friends." Both men laughed.

Gerin laughed even more four days later, when Adiatunnus and a whole great whacking unruly lot of Trokmoi in chariots did show up at Fox Keep. He had all the relief off his face by the time the Trokmê chief swaggered over the drawbridge and into the courtyard.

Or so he thought, at any rate. After the bows and the handclasps were over, Adiatunnus tilted his head back to look down his long, thin nose at the Fox. He blew out a long breath through his luxuriant, drooping mustachios and said, "Sure and I'll wager you're not sorry to set eyes on me at all, at all."

"Well, if you're bright enough to see that, you're bright enough to see I'd be lying if I said anything else," Gerin answered. "You're not the sort of man I can take for granted, you know."

Adiatunnus preened. Like a lot of Trokmoi, he was vulnerable to flattery. But Gerin hadn't been lying, either. He would much sooner have had the woodsrunner under his eye than behind his back.

"So you're finally going after Aragis the Archer, are you now, lord king?" Adiatunnus said. "About time, says I. Past time, says I." His pale eyes gleamed in his knobby-cheekboned face. "For years I waited for the shindy 'twixt the two of you to start, so I could put paid to you once for all." He shook his big fist at Gerin in anger not altogether assumed. "And you, you kern—you wouldna fight him!"

"You were one of the reasons I never did," Gerin said, again truthfully. "I knew you'd land on my back if I got into it with Aragis—till you and I made peace with each other, that is." He said not a word about any worries he'd had on summoning Adiatunnus as a vassal this time. If the Trokmê chief didn't already have ideas in his head, the Fox had no intention of putting them there.

Adiatunnus, as it happened, already had them. "Oh, aye: I thought on doing it the now, but I held myself back, indeed and I did."

"That's . . . interesting." Gerin felt a drop of sweat slide down his back. "Why, if you don't mind my asking?"

"Not a bit," Adiatunnus answered. "Two reasons, in all. The first is, you came to my aid against the Gradi when you were right on the point o' going to war against me instead. What a blackhearted spalpeen I'd be to forget it."

"Well, by the gods!" the Fox exclaimed. "Gratitude's not dead after all." He bowed to Adiatunnus. "Now you've put me in your debt. But go on. Two reasons, you said, and you gave only one. What's the other?"

The Trokmê scuffed his foot against the ground, more like an abashed boy than a man who'd ably led his clan for more than twenty years. "Sure and I'm shamed to own it, but I'm shamed to lie, too. Here it is, Fox, and to the crows with you if you brag of it: I was after fearing that, did I hit you whilst you looked the other way, you'd still somehow or other make me sorry I ever was born. *I* say that, mind, and I reckon myself not the least tricksy man living these days, nor the weakest, either."

Gerin considered. "Mm, I don't know whether I could have or not. I tell you this, though: I would have tried."

He doubted he could have done much to Adiatunnus, not if he was embroiled against a foe as formidable as Aragis at the same time. Again, he did not mention his doubts to the Trokmê. Ideas about how dangerous he was were ones he wanted Adiatunnus to have.

"When do we move against Aragis?" Adiatunnus asked. "Whenever it is, my warriors will be ready."

"Likely tell!" Gerin gave him a saucy grin. "I'll set the day for you two days before the one I tell my Elabonians, so we can all set out at the same time."

Adiatunnus glared. "Is that a tongue you carry in your mouth, or a woodworker's rasp? We're not so slow as all that, indeed and we're not, for you'd fret over less an we were."

"Fair enough," Gerin said. "Come drink some ale with me now, and your warriors and mine can get drunk together and tell lies about all the different times they tried to kill each other."

"And some of the tales they tell won't be lies at all, Fox darling," Adiatunnus said. "Widin Simrin's son would be here, for instance, I'm thinking? He wasna in his own keep when I passed it by on the way hither."

"Yes, he's here," Gerin answered. "Remember, he and you are both my vassals now. You can't go having your own little wars for the fun of it."

"Indeed and I'd never think such a thing!" The sparkle in Adiatunnus' eyes said he didn't expect Gerin to believe a word of it. "But I do recall the days when we went after each other, and not a doubt have I got that they're in his memory as well. Hashing them out over some ale will be safer nor going through them ever was."

"Truth that," Gerin agreed, falling into the Trokmê tongue for a couple of words. Like a lot of Elabonians who'd grown up on the border, he used it almost as readily as his own language.

Adiatunnus held up a forefinger. "One more question, before I drink deep and forget I meant to ask it: have you had more of your books copied out, that I might buy them of you?"

"Yes," Gerin answered: "a chronicle and a poem."

"Ah, that's fine, that's fine indeed," the Trokmê chieftain said. "When you told me you'd teach me the art of reading, I bethought myself I'd learn it as I learned to use a tool or a weapon. The more such things you know, the better, after all. But, you omadhaun, you, why did you not tell me beforehand it'd be near as much fun as futtering?"

"Why?" Gerin's eyes were wide and innocent. "If I had told you that—beforehand, mind you—would you have believed me?"

"Nay, I wouldna," Adiatunnus admitted. He gave the Fox a sudden, suspicious stare. "Don't go thinking you're civilizing me the now, or whatever you're after calling it. A Trokmê I am and I remain, and proud of it."

"Of course," Gerin said, more innocently still.

"Lord king, I beg you, put the army in motion soon," Carlun Vepin's son said. "You have no idea how fast they're going through the stores you've built up over the years."

"I have a very good idea how fast they're doing it," Gerin returned. "I ought to. And the reason you build up stores in the first place, Carlun, is to be able to use them at times like these."

Normally, that sort of answer would have silenced the steward. Now, though, he shook his head and said, "Truly, lord king, you must see this for yourself. Come down into the storerooms under the castle. Look at the empty shelves. Look at the empty chambers, by the gods! See what this campaign is doing to Fox Keep."

The Fox sighed. The trouble with Carlun, as with any good steward, he supposed, was that accumulating got to be an end in itself for him, not a means to an end. Shouting at the former serf had produced no lasting relief. Humoring him might buy Gerin a longer quiet stretch. "All right, let's go have a look," he said, and rose from the bench in the great hall he and Carlun had been sharing.

After exclaiming in glad surprise, Carlun rose, too. Pausing in the kitchen only to light two clay lamps at a cookfire, the steward handed Gerin one of them and then led him down into the cellars below Castle Fox. The air was cool and damp down there, full of the yeasty smell of ale and a greener odor suggesting that, somewhere back among those corridors, a crock of gherkins had gone over.

Carlun pointed to a bare wall. "Look, lord king! We had jars of ale set there not so long ago."

"I know that," Gerin said patiently. "If we all started drinking river water, the first thing it would do is make all my vassals and all *their* vassals and all *their* retainers hopping mad at me. The second thing it would do is give about half of them a flux of the bowels. That's not really what you want if you expect to fight a war sometime soon."

"And here," Carlun said dramatically, paying no attention whatsoever to him. He held the lamp close to another row of jars, so the Fox could see they had the lids off and were empty. "These were full of wheat, and these over here were full of barley, and these—"

"And you, Carlun, you're full of beans." Gerin's patience was breaking now; when it broke, it left sharp edges. "If I don't feed my soldiers, that will get me talked about worse than not giving them ale."

The steward still was not listening. The steward was determined not to listen. In the darkness all around, the flickering lamplight gleamed off his pale, set face. Gerin had seen less battle-ready faces coming at him over shields. Carlun pointed toward a corridor down which they'd not yet gone. "And the peas, lord king! When you think what's happening to our peas . . ."

What Gerin was thinking was that this wasn't working as he'd hoped. No matter what he did, Carlun wasn't going to stop nagging him about how much the warriors were eating. Wearily, he said, "All right, show me the peas, Carlun, and then we'll go back upstairs. The men aren't eating any more than I thought they would, and the stores don't look to be in any worse shape than I thought they were."

Carlun rounded the corner. Gerin followed close behind him. With a gasp, the steward stopped in his tracks. Gerin had to stop in a hurry, too, lest he walk up Carlun's back and perhaps set the steward's tunic on fire. Then the Fox's hand flew to the hilt of his sword, for he heard two other gasps from farther up the corridor.

He took his hand away from his sword as fast as it had gone there. He started to laugh. Down here, two gasps didn't mean thieves. They meant two people surprised when they wanted privacy. He had fond memories of some of the corridors in the cellar, not this one in particular but some nearby. He knew his son Duren had amused himself down here, too.

"Sorry to disturb you," he called into the gloom at the end of the passage, wondering if he'd interrupted Dagref at a moment in his education he couldn't possibly have acquired from a book.

From out of that gloom came a deep voice: "You startled us, lord king. We didn't think anyone would be down here."

Gerin clapped a hand to his forehead. He knew that voice. It wasn't Dagref's. "Carlun and I will go up to the great hall now," he said. "When the two of you have put yourselves back together, I want you to come up there, too. We have some talking to do, I'm afraid."

"Aye, lord king," came the answer from the darkness.

"Come on," Gerin said to Carlun, who was still staring down the passageway. "Let's go."

The steward looked back toward him as if he'd gone

mad. "But, lord king, we're not nearly through the vegetables, and we haven't even begun on the smoked meats and, er, sausages."

"To the five hells with the vegetables and the smoked meats." Gerin didn't mention the sausages. If he didn't think about them, maybe he wouldn't think about . . . On the other hand, maybe he would. He grabbed Carlun by the arm. "Come on, curse you. Do you want to annoy them, hanging about down here?"

That got Carlun moving, as the Fox had thought it would. It got Carlun moving so fast, he tripped on the stairs going up to the kitchens not once but twice. Once up in the kitchens, he hurried out through them. Gerin followed more slowly. He wondered if Carlun would wait in the great hall to discuss beans and radishes and smoked pig's knuckles. When Carlun chose to find something else to do out in the courtyard, the Fox nodded without any particular surprise. He hadn't hired his steward to be a hero.

He sat down at the bench where he and Carlun had been talking. A couple of troopers started to come into the great hall. The Fox waved them out again. A serving girl walked over to him with a pitcher of ale. He waved her away, too, wanting both a clear head and no audience for the discussion he knew he was going to have.

A couple of minutes later, Geroge walked out of the kitchens, looking as nonchalant as he could. Gerin nodded and slapped the bench beside himself. Some of the monster's nonchalance evaporated as he came over and sat down.

Gerin nodded again. He didn't say anything, not until Tharma came out of the kitchens, too. She didn't even try for nonchalance. Worry twisted her face as she joined Geroge and the Fox. "Well, well," Gerin said, then, as mildly as he could. "How long has this been going on?"

Geroge and Tharma were too hairy for him to tell whether they blushed. By the way they wiggled on the benches, he thought they did. "Not long, lord king," Geroge answered. He did more talking than Tharma.

The Fox glanced over to the female monster. "You're not with child, are you?"

"Oh, no, lord king!" she said quickly. "I would know."

"That's good," he said, and wondered where to go from there. Geroge and Tharma had been raised as brother and sister. He thought they *were* brother and sister; the peasant who'd found them as cubs and brought them to him said they'd been together. But discussions of incest seemed out of place when they were the only two of their kind above ground in the northlands. He'd actually thought this moment would come sooner than it had.

"Are you angry at us, lord king?" Geroge asked. Reading his expression and tone of voice weren't easy, but he seemed more worried about the Fox's anger than one of his own children would have been. Gerin shook his head. If that wasn't irony, he didn't know what was.

With a sigh, he answered, "No, I'm not angry. You're the only two like yourselves in these parts, and you're . . . a man and a woman." He knew no better way to put it. "What else are you going to do?"

"Oh, good," Tharma said. "I hope I do get to be with child before too long."

Gerin coughed. "I'm not so sure that's a good idea," he said, one of the better understatements he remembered making in some time.

"Why not?" Tharma asked. "You could marry us the way you or the headman does for the serfs, and then the children wouldn't be bastards."

"We wouldn't want that, lord king," Geroge added seriously.

The Fox was tempted to pound his head against the top of the table at which he was sitting. All things considered, he was more proud of himself than not over how he'd raised them. They earnestly wanted to do everything the right way, the proper way. The only trouble was, they didn't see enough of the picture, a failing anything but unique to their kind.

He explained as gently as he could: "You know how people who don't know you get upset when they first see you, because you remind them of the trouble that happened around the time when you were born?" He couldn't come up with a politer way of putting that. The monsters had done their horrific best to overrun the northlands, and that best had nearly proved good enough.

"Oh, yes, we know about that," Geroge answered, nodding his large, fearsome head. "But once people get to know us, they see we're all right, even if we don't look just like them."

Part of the reason people saw that—a big part—was that the two monsters were under Gerin's protection. Another part, the Fox admitted to himself, was that, as monsters went—even as people went—Geroge and Tharma were good people. And another big part of the reason they got such tolerance as they did was that they were the *only* two monsters above ground.

"I don't know how happy regular people would be if you started raising a family," Gerin said carefully. "They might worry that the things that happened when you were born would start happening again."

"That's foolish!" Tharma bared her prominent teeth in indignation. "We know how to behave. We should. You taught us yourself. And we'd teach our little ones the same way."

"I'm sure you would." Gerin was absurdly touched at the faith they put in his teachings. No, his own children didn't pay nearly so much attention to them. "Even so, though, people would worry, and they might get nasty. I don't want that to happen."

"You're the king," Geroge said. "You could tell them to stop it, and they'd have to listen."

That was how the monsters had lived to grow up in the first place. Gerin didn't know if he could stretch it to a family of them. He didn't really want to find out. He'd contemplated getting rid of Geroge and Tharma when they reached the age where they could reproduce their kind. He hadn't done it. The reason he hadn't done it, he now discovered, was that he couldn't do it. He'd raised them as his stepchildren, and they *were* in essence his stepchildren.

"By all the gods, be careful," he told them. He might have told Dagref the same thing. One of these days soon, he *would* be telling Dagref the same thing. He gestured sharply. Geroge and Tharma hastily rose from their seats and went out into the courtyard.

Gerin stared after them. He bunched his right hand into a fist and brought it down hard on the tabletop. He'd known this day was coming. He was a man who prided himself on acting with decision. Now the day had come and gone, and all he had to show for it was ambiguity.

He looked down at his fist and willed it to unfold. When it did, he started to laugh. It was not amusement, or not amusement with anything but the human condition: the part of it that had to do with the difference between the way men thought things would work and the way they actually turned out, and with making the best of that difference.

"Twenty years ago," he muttered under his breath, "twenty years ago, I thought I was going to slaughter every Trokmê on the face of the earth." He'd had good reason to think that, too. What better reason than the woods-runners' killing his father and older brother and making him leave the City of Elabon to return to the northlands he'd learned to despise? He'd taken vengeance as great as any man could have done, and now . . .

And now Adiatunnus walked into the great hall, waved, walked over and sat down beside him, and clapped him on the back while shouting for ale. And the Fox was genuinely glad to have the Trokmê with him. He was too honest to try to pretend otherwise to himself.

"Life," he observed with a profound lack of originality, "is a much stranger and more complicated thing than we think when we first set out on it."

"Truth there," Adiatunnus agreed, "or would I be after calling a cursed southron like your own self a friend and meaning it?" That so closely mirrored Gerin's own thought, he blinked in startlement. Adiatunnus went on, "But not a chance at all have we of making the pups believe it. I've given up, I have. They think everything's simple, sure and they do. A grave, now, a grave's a simple thing. What comes before—nay."

"You should have gone down to the City of Elabon, to study philosophy," Gerin said. "You'd have made the Sithonian lecturers work for a living, I think."

"Philosophy? We're getting old, you and I. Is that philosophy?"

"It will do, till something better comes along." Gerin called for ale himself.

✧ ✧ ✧

Carlun Vepin's son stood beaming from ear to ear. The army Gerin had assembled was leaving Fox Keep. The soldiers wouldn't stop eating and drinking, of course. But they would stop eating and drinking where the steward could see them doing it, and where he could see the results of their depredations. To Carlun, nothing else mattered.

Dagref drove Gerin's chariot. Concentration turned the youngster's face masklike. This was his first campaign, and he was determined to make no mistakes. He would, of course, despite all his determination. Gerin wondered how he would deal with that. The only way to find out was to let him have the chance and see what happened.

Van had another thought. Setting a hand on Dagref's shoulder, he said, "I rode to war with your brother at the reins not so long ago."

"Yes, I know," Dagref answered. "Duren is older than I am, so of course he got to do all these things first."

"Of course," Van echoed, and winked at Gerin. The Fox nodded. That qualification was Dagref to the core: not only precise but also just a little slighting to anyone who dared presume he wasn't precise.

Gerin said, "When we get down to Duren's holding in a few days, he'll be surprised how much you've grown."

"Yes," Dagref said, and fell silent again. Five years earlier, Dagref had wanted to be like Duren in every way he could. Now he was his own person, and increasingly insistent that everyone acknowledge him as such.

No doubt he also thought about Duren in a different way these days. One of them would succeed the Fox. Duren was Gerin's firstborn, but Dagref was his firstborn by Selatre. Duren already ruled in his own right the barony that had been his grandfather's. Dagref, as yet, ruled nothing and nobody. In another five years, though, or ten . . .

Since Gerin had yet to decide who would succeed him, he didn't blame Dagref for having the question a good deal in his mind, too. He wished he could send the lad down to the City of Elabon. Even more than himself, perhaps, Dagref was made for the scholar's life. The Fox sighed. He hadn't been able to stay a scholar, and there was no guarantee Dagref would, either. Life, as Gerin had learned, did not come with a guarantee.

That was a lesson serfs sucked in with their mothers' milk. Most serfs, seeing an army on the move, whether made up of the enemy or of their overlord's warriors, ran for the woods and swamps with whatever they could carry. Women ran faster than men—and had better reason to run.

The serfs who labored in the Fox's holding, though, watched the chariots come forth from the keep without fear. A few of them even waved from the fields and vegetable plots where they labored. Slowly, over the years, they'd let Gerin convince them his soldiers were likelier to mean protection than rapine and rape.

As Dagref drove past the village, a small figure came out of one of the huts there and trotted after his chariot. No child should have had any business gaining on a two-horse chariot. This one did so with effortless ease. "Father," Dagref asked in a small, tight voice, "did you intend for Ferdulf to campaign with us?"

"Of course not," Gerin answered. He waved to the little demigod. "Go back to your mother!"

"No," Ferdulf answered in his utterly unchildlike tones. "The village is boring. And with you and all your soldiers gone from the keep, it'll be boring there, too. I'll go with you. Maybe you won't be boring." He sounded as if, with some reluctance, he was giving the Fox the benefit of the doubt.

Gerin's reaction was that life with Ferdulf wasn't likely to be boring, either, but that didn't mean it would be more enjoyable. "Go back to your mother," the Fox repeated.

"No," Ferdulf said, in his stubbornness not only child-like but godlike, a point in common between the two aspects of his nature Gerin had noticed before. Ferdulf stuck out his tongue. Like Mavrix, he could stick it out improbably far when he wanted to. "You can't make me, either."

As if to emphasize that, he leaped into the air and flew along ten or fifteen feet above Gerin's head, jeering all the while. "If the little bugger doesn't knock that off," Van muttered behind his hand, "he's liable to find out just how close to immortal he is when he comes in for a landing."

"I know what you mean," Gerin said. He didn't expect Van to try wringing Ferdulf's neck, or to succeed if he did try. He understood—he understood down to the ground—the reasons the outlander had for contemplating semideicide.

Glaring up at Ferdulf, the Fox declared, "If you don't come down from there this minute, I'll tell your father on you."

"Go ahead," Ferdulf answered. "He doesn't like you, either."

"That's true," Gerin said calmly, "but he wouldn't pick such foolish ways of showing it." He thought he was even telling the truth. Whatever else could be said about him—and a great deal else could have been said about him—Mavrix had style.

Ferdulf did hesitate. In his hesitation, he fell a few feet—almost low enough for Gerin to reach up and try plucking him out of the air. At the last minute, he thought better of it. He'd laid hold of Ferdulf on the ground, and had got away with it there. Doing the same thing from a moving chariot struck him as imperfectly provident.

Dagref spoke over his shoulder: "Aren't you going to make him go back to the village?"

"I'm open to suggestions," Gerin snarled. "Right now, I'd be satisfied with making him shut up."

"Oh, I can do that," Dagref said. "I thought you wanted what you said you wanted in the first place."

"One of these days, you'll learn the difference between what you want and what you'll settle for," Gerin said, to which his son responded with only a scornful toss of his head. Nettled, the Fox snapped, "What forfeit will you pay if you don't make the little bastard shut up?"

"Why, whatever you like, of course," Dagref replied.

Van whistled softly. "He's asking for it, Fox. You ought to give it to him."

"So I should." Gerin tapped Dagref on the shoulder. "Go ahead. Do it. Now."

"All right," Dagref said. "What forfeit will *you* pay if I do?"

"Whatever you like, of course." Gerin spoke in mocking imitation of his son.

"Hmm." Dagref looked up to Ferdulf, who was still flying along making a hideous racket. "You know, right now you'd annoy my father much more by keeping quiet than you do with all that noise."

Silence.

After a minute or so, Van broke that silence with a thunderous guffaw. Gerin glared up at Ferdulf, who flew along, still silent, but made a horrible face back at him. Merely human features could never have accommodated that sneer. Of course, a merely human being wouldn't have been flying along above the chariot, either.

"Have I won, Father?" Dagref asked.

"Aye, you've won," Gerin admitted, more than a little apprehensively. "What will you ask of me?"

He'd promised too much. He knew he'd promised too much. Now he had to deliver. If Dagref said something like *Declare me your successor on the spot*, he didn't see how he could do anything else—unless he could talk his son out of it. Talking Dagref out of anything was no easy task.

He couldn't see his son's face; Dagref was concentrating on driving the chariot. More silence stretched. Gerin knew what that meant. Dagref was thinking things over. One thing he seldom did was speak too soon. In that he was very like his father. Gerin had broken his own rule, and now he would have to pay for it.

"I don't know right now," Dagref answered after that pause for thought. "When I decide, I'll tell you."

"All right," Gerin said. "You'll know best. Whatever it turns out to be, make sure it's what you really want now and what you really want years from now, too."

"Ah." Dagref rode on for another little while, then said, "You're not going to tell me you were only joking and you didn't really mean it?"

Had he and Dagref been having a purely private argument, Gerin might have tried telling him just that. With a demigod as witness, he thought the consequences of granting whatever Dagref asked for would be less than those of trying to break his word. "No, I'm not going to tell you that," he said. "I'm going to count on your good sense."

Van poked him in the ribs. He grimaced. The outlander's face bore an unseemly smirk. The Fox knew what he was thinking: at Dagref's age, good sense was hard to come by. With anyone of that age but his contemplative son, he would have had little hope himself. As things were, he had . . . some.

Dagref said, "All right, Father." His chuckle was eerily like the one Gerin would have used under the same circumstances. "I'm not likely to get another promise like that out of you, am I?"

"You weren't likely to get the first one," Gerin answered. "That was a sneaky bit of business you used, playing Ferdulf off against me."

"I learned it from you," Dagref said. "You've been playing foes off one against another for years now. Sometimes they even notice you're doing it, but never till too late."

He spoke matter-of-factly. He knew what he knew. That Gerin's foes—all of them men grown—had failed to see it till too late was their misfortune, not his. In his own rather withdrawn way, he was formidable.

Rihwin and a squadron of his riders came up and surrounded the chariot just then. Gerin was glad to watch them for a while. They took his mind off both Dagref and Ferdulf. The horseriders were staring up at Ferdulf and exclaiming; not all of them had paid the little demigod much heed till now. Ferdulf responded with a series of aerial maneuvers that would have left an eagle dizzy. The riders clapped and cheered. Ferdulf's face bore a smug grin. Like Mavrix, he was vain.

Dagref, having used Ferdulf to score his point against his father, paid no more attention to him. He watched the riders, too. Gerin understood that: most of them were young men, a good number hardly older than Dagref. Gerin hadn't seen so many nearly smooth cheeks and chins since his days in the City of Elabon, where shaving was the custom.

Even the riders who had raised beards looked absurdly young to the Fox. One of them, though very fuzzy, made Gerin wonder if he had even Dagref's years. The Fox shook his head. He'd been thinking more and more lately that the whole world was looking too bloody young.

But then he saw Dagref eyeing that very young-looking horseman too, and decided his eyes and wits hadn't been playing tricks on him after all. He said, "Son, I can tell that riding horses is the coming thing. You won't have to spend all your time driving a chariot. You can learn what you need to know."

Dagref looked away from the rider. "Umm—" he said, rather foolishly, as if his mind had been somewhere else. That was unlike him. Then he gave his usual serious notice to what Gerin had said. "Oh, it's all right," he said. "I can ride a horse now—Rihwin's been teaching Maeva and me and some of his own bastards when they come to Fox Keep. I haven't done any fighting from horseback yet, but not a lot of men have."

"You're right," the Fox said. "I don't think it will go on being so much longer, though. If we fight Aragis now, everybody in the northlands will know what horsemen can do. And if they do what I think they will, everybody in the northlands will want to have his own riders by this time next year."

"Now there's an interesting question, Father," Dagref said. "You could profit by sending out men to teach your neighbors how to fight from horseback, but that would also be teaching them to fight better against you. Would it be worthwhile, do you suppose?"

"Yes, that *is* interesting," Gerin said. "Do I sell a man the axe he wants to use to chop off my head? I suppose I'd have to decide one case at a time instead of laying down a blanket rule beforehand. Some I'd think I could trust, some of the ones I couldn't trust I'd be sure I could beat, and some I wouldn't want to help any which way."

"Ah." Dagref considered that, then nodded. "You're saying that making a rule is like making a promise: once you've made it, you have to stick by it, whether that looks like a good idea or not." He coughed a couple of times, then added, "I wish you'd have said that more often when I was smaller."

Straight-faced, Gerin answered, "I haven't the faintest idea what you're talking about." Dagref turned to give him an irate stare. After a moment, they both started to laugh.

When evening came, the army was still on land that had been in the Fox's family for generations. Peasants who lived near the roadway came up to the army with sheep and pigs and chickens to sell. Adiatunnus watched the dickering with no small astonishment. "They run toward you, not away," he said to Gerin. "It's not that they stay in their fields, the which is strange enough, but they run *toward* you." By the way he spoke, the peasants might have practiced some unnatural vice.

"They've seen me lead armies south on campaign a good many times," the Fox answered. "They know we won't rob them or take any woman who doesn't want to be taken."

"Doesna seem right," the Trokmê chieftain said. "If they dinna fear you, how can you rule them?"

"Oh, they fear me—if they get out of line, they know I'll make them sorry for it," Gerin said. "But they don't fear that we'll steal or rape for the amusement of it. The idea is to make them feel safer with me over them than with anyone else they might think of." Adiatunnus walked off shaking his head.

As the sun neared the horizon, Tiwaz's waxing gibbous disk, halfway between first quarter and full, grew brighter. Golden Math, a day before full, crawled over the eastern horizon. Ruddy Elleb and pale Nothos were not in the sky; both a little past third quarter, they would rise not long after midnight.

Just before sunset, Gerin's men dug several short, narrow trenches on the outskirts of their encampment. They wrung off the chickens' heads and cut the throats of the other animals they'd got from the peasants, letting the blood spill into the trenches: an offering for the night ghosts that might otherwise have driven them mad.

The ghosts came forth as soon as the sun disappeared from the sky. Gerin had been trying all his life to grasp their shape, trying and failing. Nor could he understand their cries, which dinned in his mind. Grateful for the boon of blood, they tried to give him good advice, but he perceived it only as wind and noise.

"I've heard 'em howl worse," Van remarked.

"I was thinking the same thing," Gerin said. "We've fed 'em well, and we've got good-sized fires going to hold 'em away from us a bit, but I've heard 'em a lot louder and more frightening than they are now. I know what part of the answer is, or I think I do."

Van grunted. "I've seen it myself, around your keep and in the village close by. It's that Ferdulf, isn't it?"

"I think so," Gerin said with a sigh. "The ghosts are just ghosts—spirits that never found their way into the five hells. They're stronger than we are—stronger in the nighttime, anyhow—because they haven't got any bodies to worry about. But stack them up against a demigod, and they know they'd better walk—uh, flitter—small."

"Belike you're right." Van made a fist and smacked it into his open palm. "But I tell you this, Captain: there's been plenty of times I wanted to slaughter the nasty little bugger, no matter whose son he is."

"Heh," Gerin said, and then, "You know I don't set much stock in being king, not among friends I don't. This time, though, I'm going to claim my rank. If anybody tries killing him, it'll be me first."

"Wait till after we've fought Aragis," Van said.

"Well, yes, that thought crossed my mind, too," the Fox admitted. "I do wonder why Ferdulf decided to come along, though. What worries me is that he *is* half a god—"

"The wrong half," Van put in. "The wrong god, too, come to that."

"Maybe. But what does he know that I don't, and how does he know it?"

The outlander's jaw worked, as if he truly were chewing that over. And, as if he didn't like the taste of the answer he got, he spat on the grass. "Bah!" he said. "Best I can tell you is, we're all liable to be better off if we never find out."

"Can't argue with you there," Gerin said. "But my guess is, we're *going* to find out, one way or the other. I dare hope Ferdulf is here so that, if we do need some strange sort of help against Aragis, he'll be able to give it to us."

"Aye," Van said. "I hope that, too. And if we're wrong,

and he's along to let Aragis have some help against us, he'll give it to us then, too, right up the—"

"Yes, I know. I understand that," Gerin broke in hastily. "It's the chance we take, that's all. I've taken a lot of chances, these past twenty years and more. What's another?"

"The one that kills you, could be," Van said.

"Well, yes." The Fox shrugged. "There is that."

III

Every time a chariot came up the Elabon Way from the south, Gerin tensed, wondering whether this would be the one that brought him word Aragis had swarmed over the border into Balser's holding—or whether Aragis had swarmed over the border in some other place altogether, in which case he would have to change his line of march in a hurry.

But no such news came. On the fifth day after setting out from Fox Keep, the army reached the castle from which Gerin's son Duren ruled his holding. The pace was slower than the Fox would have liked, but an army on the march, of necessity, moved no faster than its slowest parts.

Holding the keep by descent from his grandfather, as Duren did, he maintained full formal independence from Gerin. Gerin had asked his eldest son's leave before entering his barony at the head of a fighting force. He would have been astonished and dismayed had Duren refused him that leave, but Duren did nothing of the sort. The border guards he still maintained at the frontier between his holding and the lands over which the Fox was suzerain stood aside as the warriors came past them. Their eyes got wide when they saw how many men Gerin had with him.

Gerin could not see the eyes of the sentry on the wall of Duren's keep, but he would have bet they were wide, too. The fellow's voice sounded more than a little awestruck as he hallooed: "Who comes to the castle of Duren Ricolf's grandson?"

He knew perfectly well who came, but the forms had to be observed. A great many men, Gerin had seen over the years, got very upset when jolted out of the smooth routine of their everyday lives. And so, as if he were an unexpected arrival, he answered, "I am Gerin the Fox, king of the north, come to guest with my son, Duren Ricolf's grandson." He didn't blame Duren for using Ricolf's name after his own: on the contrary. He found it a clever touch.

"Enter, lord king, and be welcome as lord Duren's guest-friend, and as his father," the sentry replied. The drawbridge to the keep was already down; with his holding altogether surrounded by the Fox's lands, Duren feared no sudden assault. Gerin tapped Dagref on the shoulder. Duren's half brother drove the chariot across the drawbridge, over the moat, and into the keep.

Duren was waiting in the courtyard, as Gerin had been sure he would be. Coming into this keep, Gerin saw ghosts that had nothing to do with the ones that came forth when the sun went down: Ricolf the Red and Elise and his own younger self. He saw Duren's younger self, too, coming here at about the age Dagref had now to claim this barony and make it his own. That, over these past five years, Duren had done.

He was nineteen now, and looked enough like a young version of the Fox to make Gerin wonder for a crazy instant if he hadn't somehow slipped back across the years to his own early days. Oh, Duren was a little fairer, a little stockier, but the biggest difference between him now and his father at the same age was that his face held not the slightest trace of dreaminess. Gerin had been a second son, able to afford such luxuries as thinking about whatever he chose. With five years as a baron already under his belt, Duren worried about essentials first and everything else afterwards.

That did not mean he wasn't smiling. "Good to see you, Father, by Dyaus and all the gods!" he said, his voice deeper than Gerin's. He folded the Fox into a bear hug when Gerin got down from the car. Then he nodded to Dagref, who still held the reins. "You've got him learning the trade, I see, same as you did with me at the same age. How does it feel, Dagref?"

His half brother weighed that with deliberation he'd probably got from Selatre. "Too much to do, not enough time to do it in," he answered. "Probably would be more if I were better at what I did."

"You will be," Duren told him, then turned back to Gerin. "He's shaping well, seems like." He spoke thoughtfully, in a way Gerin hadn't heard from him before. The Fox knew what that meant: the succession was in his mind. Well, he would have been a fool if it weren't. The awkward moment passed quickly. Duren went on, "Mother's well, I trust?"

He meant Selatre. He knew she hadn't birthed him, of course, but she was the only mother he remembered; he hadn't been weaned long when Elise ran off with the horseleech. "Yes, she's fine," the Fox said, nodding. "Clotild and Blestar, too."

"And my pair as well," said Van, who had got down to stand beside Gerin and beam at the young man who was as near his nephew as made no difference. "You've grown up, that you have. Beard's thicker than mine was at the same age, I'd say."

"It's darker," Duren said judiciously, "so it will look thicker than a yellow one like yours. Come into the great hall. Drink some ale with me. So you're finally going to war with Aragis, are you, Father?"

"No," Gerin said. "He's going to war with me, or he says he is. Marlanz Raw-Meat told me he'd stopped here, so you'll have heard Aragis' side of the story. He frightened Balser into going over to me, and now he'll try to punish Balser and me both. He's welcome to try."

"Coming back from your keep, Marlanz didn't seem very happy," Duren said.

"Good," Gerin said. "He shouldn't be happy. Neither should Aragis. The Archer is strong and tough and dangerous. He can pick his time and his spot to start the war. And once he's done that, I aim to lick him."

"I'm sure you will," Duren said—as usual, more confident than the Fox himself. "What help do you want with me?"

"If your vassals will send a few chariots south with the rest of the army, that would be fine," Gerin answered. "If they don't want to do that, though, I'm not going to lose any sleep over it. They don't love me, some of them, and they can say it's not their fight."

"Do you want me to go myself?" Duren asked.

"As I say, I won't turn you down, but I don't see any great need for it, either," Gerin said. He nodded toward Dagref. "You said it yourself: it's your brother's turn to learn the trade. You already know."

"Yes." Duren didn't say anything more. His eyes narrowed. Gerin's mouth tightened. Things would never be the same for Duren and Dagref. They'd be watching each other—and watching him—till the day he died. After that, regardless of the provisions he'd made, they were liable to square off against each other. For that matter, if Gerin lived long enough, Blestar was liable to square off against both of them.

Duren said, "I'll feast your leaders tonight. Will you be swinging off the Elabon Way and heading over to Ikos to find out what Biton has to say about the fight against Aragis?"

"I hadn't planned to, no," Gerin said. "When the Sibyl speaks the prophetic verses, they usually stay obscure until after the fact. And even when they aren't obscure, some people will try to make them so. You ought to know that for yourself."

"Oh, I do," Duren said. "My loving vassals, doing everything they could to keep from admitting the god had said I was meant to be baron of this holding after all." He snorted. "They've got used to the idea by now—or if they haven't, they keep quiet about it."

"That will do," Gerin said. "It will have to do. You can't control how they think, only what they do—and only so much of that." He raised an eyebrow. "A feast, eh? What does your steward have to say about that?"

"He says it will cost too much," Duren answered. "As best I can tell, that's what stewards always say." The Fox laughed and nodded.

He ate bread and honey and smoking beef ribs and berry tarts in the great hall a little later, and washed them down with ale. As he ate and drank, he thought of other, long-ago feasts he'd had in this place. Rihwin the Fox sat across the table from him. He'd feasted here, too, when he was courting Elise. With a mischievous grin, he asked, "Shall I dance for you, lord king?"

"Go howl!" Gerin exclaimed. If Rihwin hadn't got drunk and danced an obscene dance, Ricolf the Red would have wed Elise to him, and then . . . Gerin didn't know *and then what*. The world would have been vastly different for him. He did know that.

The chamber Duren gave him for the night was only a couple of doors down from the one in which he'd slept twenty-one years before, the one in which Elise had begged him to help her escape from a marriage to Wolfar of the Axe, a marriage that, most sensibly, she did not want. Before too long, she'd been wed to the Fox, which also turned out to be a marriage she did not want. Duren couldn't have known where his father had stayed on that earlier visit. Gerin had no intention of ever telling him.

Van had been in the next room then. He was in the next room now. He'd brought a serving girl in there then. He'd brought a serving girl in there now. (The walls were thin; Gerin had no doubts.) He'd been unattached then. He was married to Fand now. Gerin hoped he wouldn't bring her back an itemized list of his infidelities on campaign, as he'd been known to do. Life was hard enough already.

The outlander didn't have the stamina he'd enjoyed two decades before. Quiet returned now sooner than it had then. Gerin took advantage of the quiet to go to sleep. He woke up in the middle of the night. In the next room, Van was snoring. So was the girl. They kept Gerin awake almost effectively as they would have, making love. After a while, he did drift off again.

He woke the next morning with a headache that wasn't quite a hangover. A jack of ale and some bread and honey made it retreat if not disappear. Van washed raw cabbage down with his ale, suggesting he had more morning pain than Gerin did. Seeing the Fox watching him, he grinned and said, "I keep reminding myself what a good time I had last night."

"Last night, I kept reminding myself how miserable I'd be today if I let myself drink too deep." The Fox felt smugly virtuous for feeling as good as he did.

"There's the difference between us, all right," Van said. "I had the good time, and I'll take the bad that goes with it. You miss the bad, aye, but you miss the good, too, sometimes."

"Some people like mountains and valleys," Gerin replied. "Some people like flatlands better. Me, I'm one of them. Besides, I don't really want any woman but Selatre—mm, not enough to do anything about it, anyhow. And," he added with considerable dignity, "I don't snore."

"Honh!" Van said. "That's what *you* think."

When Adiatunnus didn't come out for breakfast as soon as Gerin thought he should, the Fox asked Duren to send a servant to pound on his door. Adiatunnus duly emerged, looking much worse for wear than Van did. "You see, son?" Gerin said to Duren. "He was slow getting up when we campaigned against the Gradi, and he still is."

"I'm not slow, Fox darling," the Trokmê said, in the cautious tones of a man who does not want to hear himself talk too loud. "What I am is dead. Be after having some respect for the corp of me."

He shuddered at the first taste of ale, but looked more lifelike after he'd downed a couple of jacks. "Since you may not have to bury him in the courtyard after all," Gerin said to his son, drawing a glare from Adiatunnus, "we'll be off soon."

"I don't know, Fox," Van said. "Remember, the rest of the woodsrunners are liable to be as sleepy as this one is. We may not be out of here for two or three days."

"And to the corbies with you as well," Adiatunnus said. "Remind me once more we're allies, so I don't go cutting your throat from the sheer high spirits of it."

"You and which army?" Van returned politely.

They were just warming to the debate, and still on this side of sword and axe and mace and spear, when Gerin said, "Slaughter each other some other time, if you must, but remember for now that we have to take on Aragis first."

"Sure and it's all the fun out of life you're stealing," Adiatunnus said, and Van rumbled agreement. The two of them united, quite happily, in complaining about the Fox till the army left Duren's keep and headed off to the south.

Balser Debo's son's driver brought his chariot up alongside the Fox's. "Now we're getting close to my lands," Balser said. "Better country, if you'll forgive my saying so, than what you've got up around your own keep."

"Maybe," Gerin answered. "The timber's a little different—you've got more elms and beeches and such down here, not so many pines. And your peasants can plant a few days earlier in spring and won't have to worry about frost quite so soon in the fall."

"Better country, as I said." Balser sounded smug.

"Maybe," Gerin said. "Or better some ways, might be a truer way to put it. You'll grow a few things we don't. But the Elabon Way here has gone back to gravel, because peasants and local lords plundered the stone paving when there was nobody around to tell 'em they couldn't or shouldn't." As if to prove his point, gravel kicked up from one of the wheels to Balser's chariot and hit him in the hand. He grunted. "Wasn't even gravel here when this land first came under my suzerainty."

Balser coughed. "Well, lord king, the way that works is, you do what you think you have to do for the moment, and let later on take care of itself."

Gerin knew what that meant. It meant Balser and his vassals—and his serfs, too, if they thought they could get away with it—had been plundering the Elabon Way in his holding for building stone whenever they needed it. He wouldn't do anything about that, not when it had happened before Balser was his subject. He did say, "No more pulling up paving stone. That's all over now. If the road weren't here, Balser, we wouldn't be able to get to your holding fast enough to do you any good about Aragis."

"I suppose not." Balser, plainly, hadn't looked at it in that light before. Just as plainly, he didn't care, either.

"I mean it," the Fox said. "This is part of what you bought when you gave me homage and fealty. The Elabon

Way is the one good thing the Empire left behind when it pulled back from the northern lands. I've done everything I could to keep it in good shape. It's turning into the backbone for my own kingdom."

"Well, yes, I have seen that you care about it," Balser admitted. "It's only a road, though, after all." He and Gerin looked at each other with complete mutual incomprehension.

"You'll have to get used to some new ways of doing things, now that you are my vassal," Gerin said, and let it go at that.

"Yes, lord king." Balser didn't sound dutiful. He sounded resigned. The Fox had no doubt about what he was thinking: something on the order of, *How many of those new ways of doing things will I really have to get used to, and how many will I be able to ignore?* Every one of his new vassals had thoughts like that. After a while, they—or most of them, anyhow—got the idea that the new ways—or most of them, anyhow—worked pretty well.

When Gerin had come by this road years before, on his way down to the City of Elabon with Elise and Van, he'd thought the barons here well away from the River Niffet were soft. They hadn't trimmed the brush back from the road as well as they should, they hadn't kept their castles in good repair, they'd half forgotten they were supposed to be fighting men.

The past twenty years and more had changed that. The Trokmê invasion, the eruption of the monsters from under Biton's shrine, and endless rounds of strife among the Elabonians themselves meant barons who weren't alert didn't live long. The ones who did live made sure no one ever got the chance to take them by surprise.

"*Still* no move from Aragis," Gerin said when they made camp that evening. "That's not like him. He's never been one to bluff and then back down. If he says he'll do something, he does it. He's a bastard, but a reliable bastard."

Not far away, an Elabonian fell on his face, as if he'd tripped over a stone in the grass. But there were no stones in the grass; the meadow was as smooth as an ornamental lawn in front of a high functionary's residence in the City of Elabon. Ferdulf giggled.

Gerin scowled. "Van said it—he does tempt you to find out just how nearly immortal he really is."

"Compose yourself, lord king," Rihwin said. "Could it not be that, by mere rumor of his presence, the demigod intimidates and inhibits Aragis the Archer from trying conclusions with you?"

Remembering how thoughtful Ferdulf had made Marlanz Raw-Meat, Gerin had to nod. "Ferdulf certainly intimidates and inhibits me," he said. "It would be nice if he did it to everyone else."

Van looked around to see if Balser Debo's son was in earshot. Not spotting him, the outlander chuckled and said, "Balser's going to be mighty unhappy if you bring this army down to his holding, eat every storeroom he has empty, lay tight hold on the land that was his, and then don't even have to do any fighting."

"Myself, I wouldn't mind that a bit," Gerin replied. "Fighting is wasteful. But you're right. Balser became my vassal so I could protect him. If he doesn't need protecting—"

"But, had he not come to you for protection, Aragis could have swallowed him at his leisure," Rihwin pointed out.

"That's so," Van agreed, "but he won't think about it. He'll think he never should have come to the Fox at all."

"If wheat and barley were as thin on the ground as thankfulness, we'd all go hungry most of the time, and that's a fact," Gerin said. "Still and all, the crop does grow. Adiatunnus told me one of the reasons he set out on this campaign with me instead of revolting—"

"Being a Trokmê, he's revolting almost by definition," Rihwin broke in.

"You keep quiet," Gerin told him, which, aimed at Rihwin, was good advice almost by definition. "As I was saying, or trying to say, one of the reasons he set out on this campaign was that he was grateful I'd gone to his aid against the Gradi five years ago."

"Aye, that was one," Van said. "The other, if I recall, was a nasty hunch you'd turn around and kick him in the ballocks if he tried stabbing you in the back."

"I never claimed gratitude was the only reason he chose

to bring his men along with ours, just that it was *a* reason," Gerin said. He started to elaborate, but both his old friends were laughing too hard to pay any attention to him. After a moment, he gave up and started laughing himself.

They reached Balser's keep the next morning, eight days after setting out from Fox Keep. Math and Tiwaz floated in the sun-pale sky, the one at the third quarter, the other a waning crescent not far from the sun's skirts. Seeing the keep still undisturbed, Balser, who was riding at the head of the army with Gerin, let out a sigh of relief. "We won't have to try to take it back from Aragis, the gods be praised," he said.

"I hadn't thought we would," Gerin said. "The countryside, maybe, but not the keep. He hasn't had anywhere near the time he'd need to starve it out, and storming a castle is expensive even if you win. If you lose, trying it is likely to ruin you."

He looked east, then west. If Aragis the Archer hadn't come charging straight into Balser's holding, he'd probably gone and hit the Fox somewhere else along their border, with the news not having reached him yet. Try as he would, Gerin couldn't make himself believe Aragis really would stay quiet after giving such a blunt warning that he would go to war if Gerin accepted Balser's vassalage.

A look at Balser's keep suggested why Aragis might have thought it wise to launch his attack somewhere else. The keep perched atop of knob of high ground that the baron had scrupulously swept clear of all undergrowth above ankle high. A kitten would have had trouble approaching unseen. No man could have, not even afoot.

"Strong place," the Fox observed.

"Your strong place now, lord king," Balser said, "and you didn't even have to win it at war." Was that bitterness? It might have been. In Balser's shoes, Gerin, seeing peace and tranquillity in the holding, would have been wondering whether he could have gone on playing his two bigger rivals off against each other instead of finally yielding to one of them.

Balser had alert men in his keep. They were on the walls

and ready long before the army came into archery range. Nor did they assume it was friendly for no better reason than its coming from the north. With Aragis for a neighbor, Gerin would have been alert, too.

The men on the wall raised a cheer when they recognized their overlord. They raised another cheer when he told them Gerin's warriors had come to protect them from anything Aragis might try to do. The second cheer was not so lusty as the first; perhaps they hadn't looked to be quite so thoroughly protected. But, at Balser's shouted command, they lowered the drawbridge and let the Fox's forces into the keep. As far as Gerin was concerned, that finally proved Balser's good faith.

"I am your vassal, lord king," Balser said, thinking along with him. "What is mine is yours, and you have handsomely met your obligations to me."

Gerin had no doubt met those obligations altogether too handsomely to suit Balser, whose holding now lay in his hands. "I'll send some men down toward your frontier with Aragis," he said. "Most of the army will camp outside here. We won't pack the keep too full, and we'll try not to eat up everything you own. This is the business of the whole kingdom now, not just of the lands you rule. The whole kingdom's resources will help support it."

"Thank you, lord king." Balser bowed. "That you say such a thing is why I would sooner be your vassal than Aragis'."

Balser's men came out to help the Fox's warriors deal with their horses and chariots. They exclaimed to see so many men on horseback. Rihwin's troop galloped over the flatlands and drew more exclamations and applause at the way they handled their animals. Afterwards, Gerin and Van started to head up into Balser's keep. The Fox looked around for Dagref, to bring him along, too.

He spotted his son talking with one of the improbably young, implausibly fuzzy riders: the one he'd noticed early in the marches as being both younger and fuzzier than anyone had any real business being. Dagref seemed to sense Gerin's eye on him. He made a hasty farewell and hurried up to the Fox.

In the great hall, Balser served up stewed trout and apple tarts and ale flavored with honey. He introduced to the Fox his wife, a plump young woman named Brinta. "She'll be glad of what I've learned from you, too, lord king," he said.

"I do hope so," Gerin answered, resolutely keeping his face straight. No, Balser hadn't forgotten their talk on different ways of doing things.

Just at that moment, the dogs in the great hall, who had been happy enough to root around in the rushes for scraps, all seemed to decide at once that soldiers' legs were the long-lost objects of their affection. The soldiers, for some reason, did not share that opinion. A great racket of shouts and yelps erupted. "What on earth—?" Brinta said with a giggle.

Gerin looked this way and that till he spotted Ferdulf. The little demigod was giggling, too, nastily. Catching his eye, Gerin shook his head. Ferdulf stuck out his tongue. The Fox sighed. Ferdulf had already worked his mischief; nothing to be done about it.

A serving maid was sitting on Van's lap. Gerin suspected she'd be sitting on the outlander's lap again, or in some other posture, as soon as the two of them found some privacy.

And another serving girl was hovering over Dagref, and doing it so obviously that he couldn't help but notice. She was older than he, but not by a great deal, and looked more friendly than calculating. Dagref himself looked . . . interested, and surprised at himself for being interested.

Yes, your body will surprise you, Gerin thought, watching while seeming not to watch. If Dagref was going to discover just what his flesh could do, Gerin was as well pleased that he should do it away from Fox Keep, with a woman he probably wouldn't see again. She wouldn't want so much to put on airs for being his first, and he'd be less inclined to imagine himself in love with her for no better reason than discovering what she hid between her legs.

"Oh, by the gods," Gerin murmured, "when I make calculations like that, I know I've been a ruler a long time. Too bloody long, maybe."

"I'm sorry, lord king?" Balser said. "I didn't quite hear that."

"It wasn't anything, really," the Fox answered turning toward him. "Only the fuzz that gathers if you don't dust your brains every now and then."

Brinta laughed a little; she understood what he was saying. A frown slowly spread over Balser's face—he didn't. And then, a moment later, he did, and enlightenment slowly replaced confusion. He had, by then, drunk enough ale to keep him from doing anything in a hurry. "That's well put, lord king," he said.

"I thank you," Gerin answered. Courtesy of any sort, he'd found, was uncommon enough to deserve encouragement.

"Well put," Balser repeated. His breath was enough to get a man drunk. "Reminds me of a story that—" The story, as he told it, had not much point and went on for so long, Gerin wished he hadn't encouraged it.

When at last it ended, he looked around the hall again. Van and his new friend had disappeared. Gerin had expected nothing less. He wondered what Fand was doing back in Fox Keep, and with whom. When this campaign was over, he'd probably find out in alarming detail.

And Dagref and the young serving girl were gone, too. Gerin stared down at the table. His son would be different when the sun rose tomorrow, in ways he didn't yet suspect. Being Dagref, he was liable to be different in ways Gerin didn't yet suspect, too.

He still hadn't said what he wanted from Gerin as a forfeit for making Ferdulf keep quiet. With some people, the Fox might have taken that to mean he'd forgotten about it. As far as he could tell, though, Dagref never forgot about anything.

Gerin realized he'd been woolgathering when he looked up again and discovered Balser and Brinta had gone off to bed without his noticing. He poured down the ale left in his drinking jack. The woman who refilled it said, "Lord king, if you're weary, I'll take you up to your bedchamber now."

Maybe he'd been doing more than woolgathering there. Maybe he'd been dozing. He picked up the jack and said, "Maybe that's a good idea."

"Lord Balser has put you in the chamber next to his own," she said. "Up these stairs here . . . down this hall"—as she spoke, she guided him—". . . and it's this door right here." She worked the latch. A lamp was already burning on a stool set by the bed. She hesitated, then asked, "Lord king, do you want me to go in with you?"

"What?" Gerin said, and then felt foolish. The young woman had made *what* perfectly plain. The Fox smiled a lopsided smile. "My thanks. That's kind of you, but no. I don't forget I have a wife when I'm away from home."

He waited to see how she would take that. He'd had such offers a good many times. When he said no, as he habitually did, about half the time he ended up offending the woman whose company he'd declined. Some people fondly imagined they were irresistible, and that their beauty could move even a king. Had he been half his age, a lot of them probably would have been right.

This time, though, the serving girl just shrugged and nodded. "However you like, lord king. Sleep well, then." She went back toward the stairway, not even waggling her rump to show him what he'd be missing.

He went into the bedchamber, took off his sandals, and stripped down to his undertunic and drawers. After he'd used the chamber pot, he lay down on the bed and blew out the lamp. He didn't go to sleep right away; the walls here were no thicker than those at Duren's keep, and the noises from the chamber next door distracting. By the sound of things, Balser was intent on trying out every variation on an ancient theme about which he'd learned in Fox Keep. And, by the sound of things, Brinta also found the experiments . . . interesting.

For a little while, listening to them amused the Fox. After that, he just wished they'd shut up so he could doze off. He tried not to listen to them, which was like trying not to think about the color red: the more he tried, the more he failed. Finally, about the time when he should have got thoroughly annoyed, he fell asleep instead.

His first thought on waking up to early morning sunshine was to wonder if Balser and Brinta would be at it again: his new vassal was a young man. But things next door were quiet. Either Balser had worn himself out, or he'd already gone downstairs. The Fox splashed water from a basin onto his face, got into his clothes, and went downstairs himself.

Balser was sitting in the great hall, drinking ale and looking absurdly pleased with himself. A couple of tables over sat Van, who was also drinking ale and looking absurdly pleased with himself. And a couple of tables over from him sat Dagref, who was drinking ale and looking thoughtful—but a long way from displeased with himself.

Gerin started to go over to him, then decided that wasn't the best idea he'd ever had. If Dagref thought he was prying, he not only wouldn't get anywhere, his son would also be more inclined to hide things later. So the Fox remembered from his own youth, anyhow.

He called for ale and he called for a couple of apple tarts and he made a point of not looking in Dagref's direction while he ate and drank. After a little while, Dagref got up and came over to him. "Good morning, son," the Fox said, concealing the pride he took in the success of his restraint.

"Good morning, Father," Dagref answered, and seemed at a loss how to go on from there. Gerin hadn't asked if he'd slept well, against which he could have reacted—one way or another. After a moment, the youth brightened. "Could you break me off half of that tart, please?"

"Certainly," Gerin said, and did. He kept on eating his own breakfast. When he spoke again, it was of business: "We'll probably pass today here, too. Tomorrow, I'll send men down along Balser's border with Aragis, to show the Archer we are here and we do intend to protect this holding."

"That sounds good enough." Dagref had no trouble talking about things that would happen away from the keep. "It's not as if we've tricked Aragis in any way. We let him know what we were going to do before we did it. He has no proper cause for complaint I can see."

"Ha," the Fox said. "Just because you can't see it doesn't mean Aragis can't see it."

"But in justice—" Dagref began in his most didactic tones. Then his tongue clove to the roof of his mouth. That startled his father, who had seen him in a great many states, but confusion seldom among them. Gerin's gaze followed Dagref's, and all grew clear. Coming out of the kitchen was the serving girl who'd stayed close by Dagref the night before. Exactly how close by him she'd stayed, Gerin suspected he was about to find out.

The girl looked as if she hadn't had a whole lot of sleep, but she was also of an age where she could get through a day without much sleep. She also looked tousled and happy, a look often harder to counterfeit than passion at the moment itself.

She came over to Dagref and stood behind him. Of itself, his hand found hers. He sent Gerin an alarmed look, as if realizing he'd given away the game. He didn't realize he'd given it away sometime earlier. A little more slowly than he should have, he also figured out he needed to say something. "Father," he announced, "this is Rowitha."

"Hello, Rowitha," the Fox said gravely.

"Hello, lord king," she answered. Her hand tightened on Dagref's; she found the moment almost as awkward as he did. At last, she managed, "Your son, he's . . . very nice."

Dagref's face went as hot and red as the fire in the hearth. "I think so," Gerin said, grave still. "I'm glad you do, too. I'd also say" —he nodded to Dagref— "he thinks you're very nice."

"Yes!" Dagref agreed with great fervor. Now he squeezed Rowitha's hand. Gerin hoped he wasn't going to decide he was in love with her. Dagref clung to his opinions as tenaciously as fresh-water mussels clung to rocks. That was fine, when those opinions had some rational basis. Gerin didn't reckon bedding a woman for the first time any such rational basis. Convincing Dagref it wasn't, however, was unlikely to be easy.

Then he stopped worrying about how to deal with the beginnings of his son's love life, for one of Balser's men dashed into the great hall from the courtyard beyond, crying, "Lord king! Lord king! Aragis! Aragis the Archer!"

Gerin sprang to his feet with an oath. "Aragis has crossed over the border?" he demanded.

"Aye, lord king," Balser's man replied. Balser and Van were on their feet, too, and so was Dagref, Rowitha for the moment forgotten. "He's here, lord king."

"What, with his army?" Gerin said. "By the gods, is there

fighting out there? How did he get here, with no word beforehand?" He looked around for his armor, which hung on the wall not far from the fireplace.

And Balser's man stunned him again, saying, "No, lord king. As far as anyone on the wall can tell, he's here by his lonesome."

Down went the drawbridge. As soon as it had thumped onto dry land on the other side of the moat, Aragis' driver crossed over it and into Balser's keep. *No hesitation*, Gerin thought, standing there in the courtyard with Balser and Dagref and Van and some of his leading vassals. But then, Aragis the Archer seldom showed hesitation about anything, which was one reason the Fox wondered why they weren't already at war.

Without waiting for the chariot to stop, Aragis hopped out of it and strode briskly over to Gerin. He was a slim, hawk-faced man of about the Fox's age who leaned slightly forward as he walked, as if he were a hunting dog following an exciting scent.

Abruptly, he stuck out a hand. "I greet you, lord king," he said. As an obvious afterthought, he nodded to Balser. "Baron."

"I greet you, lord king," Gerin said, accepting the clasp. Aragis' grip was firm and hard, as it had been for as long as the Fox had known him. "You don't mind my asking, why aren't we trying to kill each other right now?"

"Don't worry, I thought we'd be doing just that by this time, too." Aragis bared his teeth in what was as much snarl as smile. "I think I'd have won, too. But something more important's come up."

"More important than which of us ends up ruling the northlands?" Gerin said incredulously. Aragis' head jerked up and down in a sharp, emphatic nod. Gerin whistled softly under his breath. A few times in his life, he'd been at the very edge of spreading news, the outermost boundary between those who knew and those who didn't. Aragis, plainly, was such an outer ripple now. The Fox said, "You'd better tell me, then, hadn't you?"

Aragis nodded again. "It's not a question of which of us ends up ruling the northlands any more," he said. "It's a question of whether we can keep our heads on our shoulders."

"By your five Elabonian hells, what are you talking about?" Van boomed.

"The Empire's come back to the northlands," Aragis answered.

For a few heartbeats, that didn't mean anything to the Fox. Save for memories of his student days down in the capital, he hadn't thought much about the Elabonian Empire in the more than twenty years since it had closed itself off from its former northern province. He'd thought about it as little as he could get away with in the days before it had done so, too; he hadn't paid the tribute required of him because he hadn't got the protection the tribute was supposed to earn.

But if the Empire had returned . . . "Father Dyaus," he whispered.

"That's the way of it, all right," Aragis the Archer agreed. "They've cleared two of the passes through the High Kirs, and they're sending soldiers through 'em. I don't know what all's been happening down there these past years, but it surely looks as though they've got a lot of soldiers to send."

"Father Dyaus," Gerin said again. He'd worried about Aragis. He'd worried about Adiatunnus and the Trokmoi. He'd worried about the monsters from the caverns under Biton's shrine at Ikos. He'd worried about the Gradi. He'd worried about Ferdulf. Worrying about the Empire of Elabon, long vanished from the northlands, had never crossed his mind.

Dagref spoke with his usual precision and accuracy: "Something might perhaps be done against the Empire if you two kings joined forces."

Aragis turned his clear, cold-eyed gaze on Dagref, but spoke to his father, saying, "No fools in your family, are there, Fox? This wouldn't be the lad who was kidnapped, would it, the one I got back for you from that cursed minstrel?"

"No, that's Duren, his older half brother," Gerin answered. "This is Dagref, whom I present to you with the warning that you'd better not ever be wrong in his presence, or you *will* hear about it."

"Ah, one of those," Aragis said, and then paused, the small grin he'd put on slowly fading. He gave Dagref another long look. "Mm, no, maybe not. Most of that kind think they know it all and turn out not to know a thing. If this one says something, he'll have a good notion of what he's talking about. You'd have been the same way before your beard sprouted, eh?"

"Oh, yes," Gerin answered, putting an arm around his son, who looked as if he could have done without the attention. "I was always sure in those days. I wasn't always right, mind you, but I always thought I was."

Dagref squirmed under the Fox's arm. "Let me be," he said indignantly. "The only other way either one of you could come through this mess would be to ally with the Empire against the other, and how far do you suppose you could trust the imperials? They'd use you and then sweep you aside."

Both Gerin and Aragis stared at him then. Gerin was pretty sure he eventually would have reached that same conclusion himself, but not with his son's effortless ease and ruthless clarity. Aragis made a sharp, short bow to Dagref. He said, "I came here to propose alliance to your father. You help me see I chose right. I am in your debt."

"Don't let it worry you," Dagref said tranquilly. "My father's in my debt, too. You didn't lose a bet to get there."

Aragis turned a speculative eye on Gerin. "Don't ask me about that now," the Fox said. "More important things to think about."

"As you say." Aragis the Archer managed a thin smile. "Still, anyone who gets the better of you at anything needs careful watching. Shall we speak, then, of what needs doing against the Empire?"

Balser Debo's son said, "Use my great hall as your own, lord kings." Of all the people in the courtyard, he was the only one who sounded delighted at the news Aragis had brought. Gerin had no trouble figuring out why: it meant Aragis and he wouldn't be fighting their war through Balser's holding. The noble might not even have to feed his new overlord's large, expensive army very long. If the warriors headed south to fight against the Elabonian Empire, they'd end up on Aragis' lands.

"They want the land back," Aragis said after he'd sat down and had a jack of ale pressed into his hand. "As far as they're concerned, it's as if they've never been away. The one who came to my keep said I could stay on—as baron, mind you, not as king—if I paid twenty-one years' worth of back tribute."

"Dyaus Allfather!" Gerin exclaimed. "Did you let him live?"

"I'm afraid I did." The Archer sounded faintly embarrassed at the admission. "I wasn't ready to fight in the south then—I had all my strength shifted north to go to war with you." He spoke as if Gerin should have expected nothing else. Since the Fox *had* expected nothing else, he only nodded. Aragis went on, "I just sent him out of my lands naked, to let the Empire have a clue as to how much it could ever expect to take away from me."

"Well done!" Van boomed. Adiatunnus clapped his hands. Gerin admired Aragis' gesture, too, but probably would have handled the imperial envoy rather differently himself.

Before he could decide whether to say as much, Dagref did it for him: "Being less abrupt with the fellow might have proved more prudent." Dagref was still at the age where, if something seemed obviously true to him, he let the world know about it without troubling his head about things like tact.

"I thought about that later," Aragis said. After pausing to down his ale and hold out the jack for a refill, he went on, "At the time, all I thought about was that the arrogant bastard had angered me, and so I was going to anger him right back, by the gods."

"Are you fighting with the imperials down on the southern border of your kingdom, then?" Gerin asked.

Aragis shook his head. "They're holding some of the territory that's rightfully mine, the whoresons. I don't know whether you know it or not, but these days I rule almost down to the foothills of the High Kirs." Again, his smile was one that a wolf might have offered. "Easier pushing south against the odds and sods there than coming north against you, Fox."

"Good." Gerin gave back that same display of teeth.

Aragis' concern about him was the only thing that had kept them from clashing years before. "So you want my help against the Empire, do you?"

"It's your neck, too," Aragis answered steadily. "If they beat me by myself, do you think they'll stop at the northern border to my realm? And if they look like beating me, do you think I wouldn't go over to them, as your boy says, and save what I can by helping them smash you flat?"

"No and no, respectively," the Fox admitted. Aragis gave him that fierce smile again. He sighed. "Equal allies, as we were against the monsters fifteen years ago?" Aragis nodded, as if that went without saying. From his perspective, no doubt it did. Gerin might have tried extorting more from him, since he was the one more threatened, but didn't bother. Aragis had a notoriously long memory for slights. Thinking as much, Gerin realized that, while he intimidated Aragis, Aragis also intimidated him.

Adiatunnus realized the same thing at the same time. "You're giving him better terms than ever you offered me," the Trokmê said indignantly.

"You've been my vassal the past fifteen years, and of your own free will, too," Gerin retorted. "Of course, you spent a lot of that time forgetting it of your own free will, but that doesn't make it any less so." Adiatunnus didn't look any less aggrieved, either. *Too bad for him*, the Fox thought.

Aragis the Archer coughed. "There's one thing more," he said.

Gerin didn't care for his tone. Of course, Gerin hadn't care for his tone since he'd come into the courtyard, or for any of the news he'd delivered. Wondering what he was saving for last, the Fox asked, "And that is?"

"They've got wizards with 'em," Aragis answered glumly. "Real wizards, I mean, trained in that Sorcerers' Whatchamacallit of theirs, down in the City of Elabon."

"Collegium," Gerin said, and Aragis nodded; he'd forgotten the unfamiliar term. "Well, isn't that jolly?" Gerin went on. "I don't think there's a single sorcerer like that in all the northlands. And they'll have more than one along, sure as sure. Thank you, my friend. I didn't think I could feel any worse. Now I find I'm wrong. They'll know what they're doing, too—really *know*." Every spell he'd tried, he'd tried knowing he was liable to make a horrid botch of it.

He needed a couple of heartbeats to recognize the expression on Aragis' face. For one thing, it didn't sit well there; Aragis had for years molded his features to project harsh certainty and very little else. For another, he hadn't thought the Archer granted him so much respect in this particular area. But Aragis said, "Another reason I want you with me, Fox, is the skill *you've* shown as a mage since the days of the werenight."

"You haven't got any idea what you're talking about," Gerin said, his voice not far from a groan.

Aragis went on as if he hadn't spoken: "And when Marlanz Raw-Meat came back from your keep, he told me you had a god's son living in the village close by. If we have a god's son with us, even those cursed imperials will have to sit up and take notice." The Archer grew eager. "Did this—Fergulf, was that his name?—come south with you to campaign against me? Can we use him against the Empire?"

"Ferdulf," Gerin corrected absently. "Yes, he came along. He didn't come to campaign against you so much, I don't think. He said he came because Fox Keep would be boring once the army left." Aragis looked blank. Gerin sighed. Looking around Balser's great hall, he didn't see Mavrix's annoying son. He turned to Dagref. "Go track down Ferdulf, would you please? My fellow king here had better get a good idea of what he's pinning his hopes on."

Dagref took a deep breath, as if about to argue: he didn't want to miss a single word of what passed between his father and Aragis the Archer. Seeing Gerin's face, though, he sensibly decided arguing here wouldn't do him any good and would land him in trouble. He got up with no more than a small grimace and hurried out into the courtyard.

He came back soon enough, Ferdulf at his side—and, for a wonder, walking on the ground. Ferdulf, as the Fox had seen to his own discomfiture, got on with Dagref better than he did with almost anyone else. Gerin wasn't sure what that said about his son's character, and wasn't sure he wanted to find out, either.

Dagref pointed Aragis out to Ferdulf. The demigod strode up to him, inspected him, and shook his head. "This is supposed to be another king?" he said. Aragis' eyes widened when he heard the deep voice coming out of the small body. Ferdulf sniffed. "Doesn't seem so much of a much to me." His gaze swung toward Gerin. "Of course, you're not so much of a much, either."

"I'm so glad I have your respect," Gerin said.

Aragis stared from one of them to the other. Gerin already knew the Archer tolerated much less in the way of back talk and disrespect from subjects than he did himself. And now, despite having heard about Ferdulf, despite having heard for himself that Ferdulf was not the ordinary four-year-old his body made him out to be, he made the mistake of treating him as if he were: "You, boy!" he said, as he might have to any serf. "Who was your father again?"

Gerin could have told the Archer he'd just done something foolish. Before he got the chance, Ferdulf demonstrated it. As usual, showing proved more effective than telling. Ferdulf walked over to Aragis. Then he walked up Aragis' legs, treating their vertical as a horizontal. Then he walked across Aragis' lap. And then he walked up Aragis' chest, treating that in the same fashion as he had the Archer's legs. Planting his feet on Aragis' collarbones, he looked across—effectively, down—at his startled face. "My father, *man*, was the god Mavrix of Sithonia. Who was yours, or didn't your mother know, either?"

Aragis had courage. Not even his worst enemy would ever have denied that. So, now, he heard only the insult, and forgot a demigod had delivered it. Grabbing Ferdulf by the ankles, he tried to throw him away. That didn't work; Ferdulf refused to be budged. Snarling an oath, Aragis sprang to his feet and grabbed for his sword.

Everyone who was anywhere near him snatched at his arm to keep him from drawing the bronze blade. "Enough!" Gerin said sharply. "My judgment is that dishonors are even here."

"What gives you the right to judge?" Aragis and Ferdulf said the same thing at the same time, then glared at each other for having done so.

"Aragis, I've put up with you since just after the were-night, and you, Ferdulf, I've put up with you for as long as you've been around—it only seems like forever," Gerin said. "If I haven't got the right to judge, who does?"

"No one." Again, demigod and king spoke together. Again, they glared at each other. Neither was fond of the Fox. Each was fonder of him than of the other.

"Get off King Aragis, Ferdulf," Dagref urged. "Standing on him like that won't do any good."

"It does me plenty of good," Ferdulf said, but he took a step off Aragis' chest into midair, then drifted to the ground like a chunk of thistledown. Aragis rubbed at his collarbones; he must have felt the weight of the demigod on him.

"Ferdulf, you haven't got much use for Elabonians, have you?" Gerin asked, a question whose answer seemed obvious.

"Would you, were you I?" Ferdulf returned, rolling his eyes.

"Oh, I don't know." Gerin spoke musingly now. "After all, you're half Elabonian yourself."

"All the more reason to despise that half," the demigod said. "Without it, I'd be altogether divine."

Without it, you wouldn't be here at all, Gerin thought. But he didn't bother mentioning that. Instead, he said, "Well, from what King Aragis here tells me, the Empire of Elabon is coming. The Emperor wants to make this part of the world do as he says when he's down in the City of Elabon. He wants to make this part of the world obey him the same way that Sithonia has to obey him."

Even after more than four years, he didn't know just how much instruction Mavrix had given Ferdulf about Sithonia, or how much knowledge of his father's homeland Ferdulf had inherited, or whatever the process was by which Ferdulf knew what he knew. He did know Ferdulf knew enormously more than any purely human four-year-old had any business knowing. Would that be enough? He could but hope.

Ferdulf had disappointed his hopes a good many times, and blasted them a few more. This time, he lived up to them. "The Elabonian Empire will never do to this land what its overmuscled morons have done in and with and to fair Sithonia," the little demigod cried, his big voice echoing back from the roof beams of the great hall. "It shall not come to pass. I shall not permit it."

Aragis started to say something. Gerin caught the Archer's eye and shook his head ever so slightly. For a wonder, Aragis listened to someone other than himself. He kept quiet.

"I shall destroy the Elabonians, root and branch! I shall smite them, hip and thigh!" Ferdulf thundered. Some of Balser's men broke into applause. Aragis the Archer looked as if he was about to join them.

Gerin caught his eye once more. The Fox shook his head again, a gesture even smaller than the first one. As slightly, Aragis' ever so erect shoulders slumped. Gerin was glad Ferdulf wanted to take on the forces of the Elabonian Empire. He didn't think Mavrix's son would be able to beat them singlehanded. Elabon had ruled Sithonia for hundreds of years, no matter how much the Sithonians looked down their noses at their overlords. Divided into quarreling city-states, the Sithonians also looked down their noses at one another. Their gods squabbled among themselves. If all their men and all their gods hadn't been able to keep the Elabonians out of Sithonia, one bad-tempered little demigod wasn't going to keep the Empire out of the northlands, not by himself he wasn't.

As long as he despised the Elabonian Empire more than he despised either Gerin or Aragis, though, having him along wouldn't hurt.

"What are we waiting for?" Ferdulf demanded. "The sooner we strike these bronze-bound blockheads, the sooner we send them scurrying back into the south! When we fight, let us give no quarter."

Every once in a while, when trying to work magic, the Fox had a spell succeed too well. He hadn't worked magic here, not in the strict sense of the word, but got something of that feeling nonetheless. What would happen if and when Ferdulf discovered he couldn't beat the Empire by himself? Would all his joy in trying disappear? Would he turn on Gerin and Aragis instead?

This once, Gerin wished he weren't quite so good at

coming up with unpleasant questions long before he had any answers for them.

Aragis said, "Are we allies against the Empire, then, you and I and Ferdulf here?"

"You and I are," Gerin said. "I already told you that. Having the Empire on my border I like even less than having you on my border." Aragis showed his teeth again in that snarling smile. The Fox went on, "As for Ferdulf—" He turned to the demigod. "Will you join with us against the Elabonian Empire?"

"*I* am against the Elabonian Empire," Ferdulf said. "If you want to stand against it, too, *you* may join with *me*."

Gerin remained of the opinion that one god's son, no matter how arrogant, was not going to prove a match for all the soldiers and, if what Aragis said was true, all the mages of the Empire of Elabon. But he did not feel like quibbling about definitions with Ferdulf. Instead, he held out his hand. Aragis clasped it. A moment later, the demigod set his warm little palm over both their hands. Gerin had made a good many unlikely alliances in his time. This one struck him as being as improbable as any.

Balser Debo's son looked mutinous. "By the gods, lord king, why should I furnish you with twenty chariot crews? All the fighting you aim to do will be off my land."

"That's not the point." Gerin might have borrowed his hard, harrowing smile from Aragis the Archer. "The point is that you owned yourself my vassal. True, you did it because you wanted me to help protect you. But that doesn't mean your obligations go away when the danger to your holding disappears. I have the right to ask this of you, and ask it I do."

"It's outrageous!" Balser exclaimed. "Why should I send my men off to fight farther south than they'd ever have any natural reason to go?"

"Because if you don't, they're likelier to be fighting here sooner or later anyhow," Gerin answered. "The idea, if we can bring it off, is to beat the Empire as far south as we can. If we can do that, the imperials may never get up here at all."

If all the fighting turned out to be in the south, Aragis'

lands would suffer far more than his own. That might end up giving him a decisive edge on the Archer: so declared the calculating part of his mind that never slept.

"I suppose *my* twenty men are going to make the difference between beating the imperials and losing to them," Balser said scornfully.

"By themselves? I doubt it, or else we're in worse trouble than I think," Gerin said. "But if you leave yours home and Widin Simrin's son leaves his home and Adiatunnus leaves his home . . . You didn't much like the idea of Adiatunnus' leaving his men home when you thought Aragis was going to land on you like a load of rocks, did you?"

Balser had the decency to turn red. "All right, I see what you're saying, lord king. Bah! To the five hells with me if I like it."

"Oh, I'm just dancing with glee myself at the idea of taking on the Elabonian Empire. Dancing with bloody glee!" The Fox did a few rather awkward steps.

Balser stared at him. Kings were supposed to be serious, even solemn, people. Gerin didn't fit the bill. He hadn't intended to be a king. He hadn't intended to be a prince, or a baron. If he wasn't always what the world thought he was supposed to be, that was the world's hard luck.

But he wasn't always a funny man, either. "One more thing for you to think about," he told Balser: "How many men do I have on your lands right now?"

That got through to his new and now reluctant vassal. Balser looked as if he'd bitten into a pear about three days after it should have been tossed into a swill bucket for the pigs. "Lord king, when I became your vassal, you promised you'd respect my rights," he said reproachfully.

"So I did," Gerin agreed. "And, when you became my vassal, you promised you'd live up to your duties. This is one of them. I am within my rights to ask it of you. You are not within your rights to refuse it to me."

Plainly, Balser Debo's son did not agree. As plainly, he couldn't do anything about it. "Very well." He spat out the words one by one. "Twenty chariots and their crews, to go with you when you leave my land."

"I do thank you for them," the Fox said. "They will help.

And there's one other thing you need to remember: the sooner you furnish them to me, the sooner we will be able to leave your land, and the sooner we stop eating your storerooms empty."

"Ah," Balser said. "I was wondering if you'd be able to come up with a reason for me to give you the crews and cars in a hurry. You have, by the gods."

"I thought that might be so," Gerin said.

Balser sighed. "Get caught up in the quarrels of neighbors bigger than you are and you find they make you do things and then expect you to like it."

"I don't expect you to like it," Gerin told him. "I do hope you'll see the need." He got a shrug from Balser, which was about as much as he'd thought the baron would give him. Then he shrugged, too: the Elabonian Empire was forcing him into a position not far from the one in which he'd put Balser. He hoped he'd have better luck than Balser getting out of it.

Aragis the Archer studied Gerin's assembled forces. "I'll tell you this much, Fox," he said: "I'm gladder to have you with me than I would have been fighting you. You've got more men here than I thought you could raise."

"I've never picked a quarrel with you," Gerin answered. "I wasn't picking a quarrel with you over Balser's holding, either, however you chose to take it. But I wasn't going to back away, either."

"Leave that aside, since I'm not such a fool as to call my ally a liar," Aragis said, which let him call the Fox a liar even as he said he was doing no such thing. "You've put a lot of men on horseback here, too. You always were one to try things no one would have looked for."

"Maybe." Gerin raised an eyebrow. "You came here all by your lonesome, and you say I do things nobody would look for? What would have kept me from dropping you off Balser's wall on your head?"

Aragis shrugged. "I counted on your good sense. Biggest worry I had was that some of your troopers would do me in before I got the chance to tell you what the Empire was up to. But your men are well disciplined, too—maybe not quite so tight as mine, but well enough."

"Your idea of discipline is to make your men fear you worse than any foe," the Fox said.

"Well, of course," Aragis said, as if surprised Gerin contemplated discipline of any other sort. "It's worked, too. Tell me it hasn't."

Gerin couldn't tell him that. Whether it would work for Aragis' successor was a different question. Maybe Aragis didn't care. Maybe he thought one of his sons was as fierce as he—an alarming idea if ever there was one.

"My way works, too," Gerin said, and Aragis could not deny that. The Fox went on, "We'll see—or our sons will see, or our grandsons—whose way ends up working better."

By way of reply, Aragis only grunted. Gerin hadn't expected much more from him. Other times he'd talked with Aragis about anything further away than the immediate future, he'd got only incomprehension in return. Within Aragis' range of vision, he was most effective; beyond it, he didn't seem to see at all.

"How determined did the imperials seem to be about taking back the northlands?" the Fox asked Aragis. "If we give them one set of lumps, or maybe two, will they go back over the High Kirs and leave us alone? Or do you think they'll keep coming after us no matter what we do?"

"I don't know the answer to that," Aragis answered. "I do know one thing: if we don't give them a set of lumps, we've lost the cursed fight." He paused, as if waiting for Gerin to disagree with him. When Gerin didn't say anything, the Archer picked up again: "They're every bit as arrogant as I remember them being, and that's saying a lot."

"So it is," Gerin agreed. "Down in the City of Elabon, they'd look down their noses at you for wearing trousers instead of robes, and for coming straight out and saying what you mean instead of talking all around it from four different directions at once." He looked up at the sound of hoofbeats. "And a good day to you, Rihwin. What can I do for you?"

Atop his horse, the noble from the City of Elabon tossed his head in anger more assumed than real. "I heard that last remark of yours, lord king, and I desire you to know that it filled my heart with resentment, that I reject it as a slanderous and scurrilous assault on my former homeland, that it bears not even the slightest relation to truth of any sort, and that, furthermore, your syntax in framing the said remark, being both slipshod and leaden, causes me to—"

"—Prove the point of everything I was saying?" Gerin suggested.

"Oh, I am wounded. Wounded!" Rihwin cried, clapping a hand over his heart. Gerin snorted. By the expression on Aragis' face, he wouldn't have put up with Rihwin's flamboyant nonsense for a moment. There were times when Gerin wondered why he put up with his fellow Fox's nonsense himself. But, over years, Rihwin had—narrowly—convinced him he was worth keeping around.

And then his friend did his best to unconvince him. Rihwin's face took on a look almost of transfiguration. In soft, reverent tones, he said, "With the Empire returned to the northlands once more, surely commerce between us and the long-sundered south will soon revive."

As soon as Rihwin spoke of commerce, Gerin knew what he had in mind. Gerin would have liked to see commerce revived, too, commerce in books and fine cloth and other such luxuries the northlands had trouble producing for itself. Rihwin, however, would be thinking of only one such luxury. "You don't mean commerce. What you mean is wine."

"And wherefore, I pray you, should I not?" Rihwin demanded.

"For one thing, you get into trouble when you drink wine," Gerin answered. "You get into trouble when you drink ale, too, but you get into worse trouble when you drink wine. For another, with wine comes Mavrix, lord of the sweet grape. Do you truly want more dealings with him?"

That did give Rihwin pause. The first time he'd ever invoked Mavrix, just before the werenight, the Sithonian god had permanently taken away his ability to work magic. Their meetings since had not been marked with any great warmth, either; Mavrix disliked and distrusted not only Gerin but also anyone who had anything to do with him.

But Rihwin was made of stern stuff—either that or he had a marvelously selective memory. He said, "It should be all right, lord king, and for the chance to taste wine once more, what risk could be too great?" He struck a melodramatic pose on horseback.

"I like wine well enough," Aragis said, "but ale suits me." He stuck out his chin and folded his arms across his chest in a different sort of melodrama, the pantomime of demanding obedience.

As Gerin could have told him, getting obedience out of Rihwin the Fox was an uphill fight. Loftily, Rihwin observed, "Some people are of the opinion that, for no better reason than something's suiting them, it should suit everyone, a proposition easily demonstrated to be fallacious."

Aragis blinked. Gerin watched him sort through Rihwin's sentence a clause at a time. He watched him scowl when he got to the end of it. "Some people," Aragis rumbled, "are of the opinion that anyone else cares about their opinions to the extent of dumping a pisspot."

"Yes, some people are," Rihwin agreed. He and Aragis glared at each other. Gerin would have bet the two of them were likely to rub each other the wrong way. When he made bets of that sort, he usually proved right. When he bet something would go well, on the other hand, he was wrong dishearteningly often.

That afternoon, his army reached the border between Balser's holding and the lands Aragis the Archer ruled. The border guards cheered. "Kick Aragis the Arrogant's arse!" one of them shouted. The rest offered even more creative advice. They all cheered Gerin.

Aragis tapped his driver on the shoulder. His chariot broke out of the swarm and rattled over to the border station. One of the guards recognized him, and went from jeering to white-faced and shaky in the space of a heartbeat. At his whispered comment, the other warriors shut up one by one.

"I thought I would give you the chance to say to my face what you say to my back," Aragis told them. "I see you have not the belly for it. This surprises me not at all." At his order, his driver took him back up alongside Gerin.

"That took nerve," the Fox said. In his own cold-blooded way, Aragis had style.

The Archer shrugged. "Most men are dogs. They yap loud enough when nothing bigger and fiercer is around. When challenged, though, they sniff your backside and then roll over."

"Use them as men and you'll find them likelier to behave as men," Gerin said. Aragis shook his head. They rode on in silence after that. Gerin would have been happier had he been more nearly certain he was right and his royal rival wrong.

IV

Gerin had not been down in the lands over which Aragis the Archer ruled for more than twenty years. For some time, he'd been busy far closer to Fox Keep. Then, after his attention reached so far south, the only way he could have come was at the head of an invading army. Here he was at the head of an army, but, to what would have been his astonishment up until a couple of days before, he wasn't invading.

Before the Empire of Elabon withdrew beyond the High Kirs, the lands closer to the mountains had been more nearly a true part of the Empire than the raw frontier up by the River Niffet. Some of the villages hereabouts had almost deserved to be called towns. Close by the Elabon Way, especially, trade had flourished. It was, in fact, the condition to which the Fox aspired to lift his own holdings.

And Aragis, who had such splendid underpinnings for his kingdom, was letting them slip. Maybe Gerin remembered these lands as having been more prosperous than they really were because he'd been so much younger the last time he'd been through them. But he didn't think so. He hadn't been so young as all that. He could see signs of change, too, and not for the better.

Several villages had buildings standing empty—not just houses, but smithies and potters' works and taverns as well. Some had fallen down into rubble. Some were being torn down to patch other buildings still in use. And only weeds and bushes grew in the blank spaces between houses where others had presumably stood.

Some fields weren't being cultivated, either. In them, scruffy wheat and barley fought what was going to be a losing fight against brambles and saplings and plain, ordinary grass. "You don't seem to have quite so many people as you did," Gerin remarked to Aragis, sounding as casual as he could.

"Just have to make sure the ones who are left work harder to take up the slack." Past that, Aragis was indifferent. Gerin wanted to grab him by the front of the tunic, lift him into the air, and shake some sense into him. *What are you doing, you fool?* he wanted to shout. *Don't you see that, if this goes on a while longer, the peasants you have left won't be able to feed all your warriors? Then it won't matter how strong your armies are, or would be, because you won't be able to keep them in the field.*

Aragis wouldn't listen. Aragis wouldn't have the vaguest idea what he was talking about. Aragis would get angry. Knowing all that, Gerin walked away instead of screaming at him.

Van followed the Fox. "If you could have seen the look on your face there when the Archer said, 'So what?'—" the outlander began.

"If he saw it, he didn't know what it meant." Gerin kicked at the dirt. "If he had known what it meant, he wouldn't have let this happen to his lands in the first place." Gerin kicked again. "I wouldn't have had to fight him. In another few years, all this would have fallen under its own weight."

"Maybe," Van said. "Or maybe, if he heard the creaking, he would have fought you. If he won, he'd have your lands to ruin over the next twenty years. Even if he lost, he wouldn't have so many fighters to feed."

Gerin studied him. "That's a cold-blooded way of looking at things. It's more the way I'd look at them than how I'd expect you to."

"And who's been living beside you in Fox Keep these twenty years and more?" Van returned. He shook his head. "I wouldn't have thought that way when I first came there, not when I swam the Niffet with the Trokmoi shooting arrows at me till I got out of range. I'd spent so many years wandering, I didn't expect I'd ever put down roots." His head went back and forth again. "Never would have thought I'd stay attached to the same woman so long, either."

"You don't let that worry you, not when you're off someplace where Fand can't see what you're up to."

"And so what?" Van said. "If I get the itch, by the gods, I scratch it." His chuckle was mordant. "And if I didn't, I'd get no credit for holding back. One campaign we fought over in the southwest, years ago this was, I kept my prong in my breeches the whole time, and when I got back to Castle Fox I said as much to my lady love. What happened? Do you remember what happened, Fox?"

"Sorry," Gerin answered. "You and Fand have had enough dustups that that one doesn't stick in my mind."

"No, eh? Well, it does in mine. She thought I was lying, is what she thought. That put more fire under her cookpot than she gets when I tell her about all the pretty girls I rumple. So I ask you: what am I supposed to do?"

"I don't know," the Fox said. As far as he could see, Van and Fand quarreled as much because they enjoyed quarreling as because they really had anything about which to quarrel. He'd suggested as much to the outlander once or twice. Van had agreed with him, which was alarming, and had done exactly nothing to change his ways, which Gerin found even more alarming.

Dagref trotted by on horseback. He waved to the Fox and to Van. Loping along beside the horse, barely visible over the beast's back, was the fuzzy-bearded youngster Gerin had noticed once or twice before as the army moved south. He didn't wave. *Has to be from some keep out in the middle of nowhere*, Gerin thought. *The king's son isn't far from his own age, so he can be easy with him, but with the king and his old friend—no.*

Van said, "One of these days before long, Kor will be coming with us when we go to war, too. Won't be long, not the way time goes by now."

"You're right about that," Gerin said. "He'll be something to watch out for on the battlefield, too."

"That he will," Van said proudly. "My size, or most of it, and Fand's temper, or worse. I tell you the truth, the gods had better help anybody fool enough to stand in his way by the time he's seventeen. And if Maeva were a lad, I'd have two grand warriors to leave behind me when I go." He scratched his chin. "I wonder how many brats I've got that I don't know the first thing about? A few, I shouldn't wonder, but I've never been like Rihwin, ready to keep track of 'em all."

"Rihwin's almost as good at keeping track of his bastards as Carlun is at keeping track of beans," Gerin agreed. He spotted his fellow Fox not far away, and raised his voice a little: "The only thing Rihwin can't keep track of is Rihwin."

"Are you speaking to me or of me or against me?" Rihwin asked. "In sooth, I was but enjoying a vision, a memory of days long past, and nights as well, nights spent in the pursuit of knowledge, nights spent comparing the color and bouquet of one glorious vintage against another, and—"

"—Mornings spent wishing you were dead," Gerin broke in. Rihwin looked indignant. With his flexible features, every expression he assumed was, in a small way, a work of art. Gerin took no notice of him, but pressed ahead: "All you remember about wine is the parts of the drinking of it you enjoyed. The parts that weren't so much fun, you forget."

Rihwin shook his head. "There was," he insisted, "nothing about drinking wine that failed of enjoyment for me. I was a connoisseur." He struck a pose of exaggerated estheticism that would have made Mavrix proud.

"Fanciest word for *drunk* I ever heard," Van said.

Rihwin looked indignant all over again, giving a rendering full of even more virtuosity than the previous one. Before he could protest out loud, though, Gerin spoke up in agreement with the outlander: "You weren't much of a connoisseur the day we met you down in that horrible dive in the City of Elabon, the one not far from the Sorcerers' Collegium. What you were was somebody trying to climb into a wine jar through the little hole in the neck, and you didn't care a lick about the vintage you were drinking."

"After all these years, I must confess to remembering little about the occasion," Rihwin said with dignity.

"Yes, passing out will do that to you, won't it?" Gerin replied.

"You were as cold as a carp on a snowbank," Van added.

"If you grand and magnificent gentlemen, who of a certainty have been sober every moment of every day of your lives, insist on reviling me and casting imputations upon my character, I shall be forced to take myself off and drown my sorrows—in ale, worse luck." Rihwin marched away, nose in the air.

Behind him, Gerin and Van both started to laugh. "There's nothing we can do with him," Gerin said, and his voice held only admiration. "Not a single thing."

"How about a good swift kick in the arse?" Van suggested.

"If all the knocks Rihwin's taken over the years haven't let in any sense, one more kick won't do the job," Gerin said, and Van laughed again. Nonetheless, Gerin kept a thoughtful eye on Rihwin the Fox. When Rihwin got particularly vehement on the subject of wine, strange things had a way of happening. Gerin didn't want strange things to start happening. Life, at the moment, was quite complicated enough without them. Unfortunately, he had not the slightest idea what he could to do prevent them.

Most of Aragis' warriors were down in the southern part of his lands, keeping an eye on the forces of the Elabonian Empire. Even so, more detachments joined the army the Fox was leading. Aragis' peasants and villagers might have had their troubles, but his kingdom did seem to support an astonishing number of soldiers, every one of them well armed, well equipped, and to all appearances a rugged customer.

"I would have put even more men into the south against the Empire," Aragis remarked to Gerin when yet another contingent of his warriors came rattling up in their chariots to join the army, "but I had to hold a good many back to fight you in case you decided to jump on me and then worry about the Empire."

"To the five hells with me if you don't have enough fighting men to tackle two big wars at once," Gerin said.

"If your Trokmê neighbor had decided to forget he was your vassal, you wouldn't have brought so many of your own troopers down to Balser's holding." Aragis spoke with as much certainty as if he'd announced that Math moved through the sky more slowly than Tiwaz.

Since he was right, Gerin changed the subject: "Who's commanding the force you've got facing the Empire?"

"My eldest son, Aranast, with Marlanz Raw-Meat to hold him steady should he falter," Aragis answered. "Aranast has never tried leading that big an army before. If he's up to it, well and good. If he's not, I don't aim to let him throw away the kingdom."

"That's sensible," Gerin agreed, though he wondered how happy Aranast was at having Marlanz looking over his shoulder. Then something else occurred to him: "The first time you sent Marlanz up to treat with me, you had an older man with him, too, to hold him to the road if he tried wandering off."

"You have your son with you here," Aragis said, nodding to Dagref. "One day, he'll lead men on his own. For now, he's still learning."

Gerin nodded, but still thought the two principles not quite the same. Dagref plainly lacked the experience he needed to lead now. In a while, he would as plainly have it. Aragis seemed to make a habit of using a man with such experience alongside one who was just on the edge of having it. The idea was a long way from the worst one Gerin had ever met.

That evening, as the steadily growing army was encamping by the side of the Elabon Way, a chariot came pounding up the highway, wheels clattering on stone paving, the driver whipping on the horses to wring every last drip of speed from them.

The fellow in the car with him sprang down as soon as the chariot halted. "Lord king—" he gasped, and then paused for a moment to catch his breath. He was swaying a little; if he'd come a long way in a chariot going hells for leather, solid ground probably felt unsteady under his feet. Gerin came over to hear what he had to say. Aragis frowned at that, but said nothing. The messenger resumed: "Lord king, uh, lord kings, there's an imperial coming behind me. You'll meet him on the road tomorrow, I've no doubt, but I can tell you what he's going to say."

"Good," Aragis said briskly, and Gerin nodded. "Say on, Sandifer." The Archer glanced at the Fox and shrugged a small shrug, acknowledging that this business concerned both of them.

Sandifer said, "Lord, uh, kings, he's going to give you ten days to disperse your forces, or else there will be war: voluminous war, I heard him say, whatever that means."

"It means he talks like a southerner," Gerin said. "They like to throw in a fancy word every now and then, whether they use it the right way or not."

"I heard that," Rihwin called.

"If they want volumes of war," Aragis said, ignoring Rihwin (as did Gerin), "we'll give them enough to fill the Fox's library."

That wasn't using *voluminous* the right way, either, but Gerin was not inclined to undertake literary criticism on his fellow king's utterances. "If it comes to war—no, when it comes to war," he said, "do you aim to go back into your keeps and make the Empire dig you out one castle at a time?"

"Only if I have to," Aragis answered at once. "If I were fighting the imperials alone, I might do that, for they'd have far more strength than I do by myself. But they'd ravage the countryside, so that even beating them back now might mean losing to you next year. My lands shield yours here, you'll notice."

"That's what you get for living south of me." Gerin scratched his head. Aragis could see that having the Elabonian Empire devastate his territory would weaken him to the point where he'd have trouble withstanding the Fox. He wasn't stupid, nor anything close to it. But the idea that he was doing to his own lands over the course of years what the Empire would do in a single campaigning season had never entered his mind. It wasn't immediately apparent, and so wasn't there at all for him.

The Archer said, "With you beside me, Fox, I aim to fight those imperial bastards as hard as I can and as far south as I can. One thing I will say about you: now that you've said you will fight alongside me, I don't think you'll turn on me instead of the Empire. There are others in the northlands to whom I'd not trust my back."

Gerin bowed slightly. When it came to judging how things ran in the short term, Aragis was as good as anyone he'd ever know—as good as he was, probably. Could he trust Aragis at his back? The only answer he could come up with was . . . *sometimes*. He said, "Knowing which enemy to pick counts for a good deal."

"Oh, indeed." Aragis bared his teeth in one of his alarming smiles. "Did I not rely on you to understand the Elabonian Empire was more dangerous to both of us than we are to each other? Did I not put my life in your hands on that understanding and no more?"

"You did." Gerin wondered whether he would have done that in reverse if, say, the Gradi had been on the point of beating him five years earlier. Maybe. Maybe not, too. Because Aragis lived so close to the here-and-now, every crisis was liable to seem a matter of life and death to him. Gerin was better at waiting than his hard-charging fellow king.

"We cast defiance in the envoy's teeth, then, and smash the Empire's army on the battlefield." Aragis' eyes had a fierce falcon's glint in them, too. He believed every word of what he was saying. Maybe that would help him make his belief real. Maybe it would make him try to do more than he really could. Gerin shrugged. He'd find out soon.

When the chariot bearing the envoy of the Elabonian Empire and those in which his retinue rode came into view, Gerin felt—not for the first time since leaving Fox Keep—he'd fallen back in time through close to half his life. Not since his last trip down to the City of Elabon, more than twenty years before, had he seen men dressed in the flowing robes the imperials south of the High Kirs affected.

Adiatunnus saw them, too, and did not know what to

make of them. "Is the Empire after sending women to treat with us the now?" he asked, not quite in jest.

"No, that's just their style down there," the Fox answered. "And they shave not only their cheeks and chins, the way you Trokmoi do, but their upper lips as well. I did it myself, when I lived down in the city."

"But you had the sense to go back to a better way," Adiatunnus said.

Gerin shrugged. "Sometimes different is just different, not better or worse."

He looked around for Ferdulf. When he spied the little demigod, he waved for him to come over. Ferdulf came, looking suspicious. More often than not, Gerin was doing his best to make him go away. "What do you want?" Ferdulf growled.

"See those fellows up ahead?" The Fox pointed. "That's the envoy from the Elabonian Empire and his friends."

Ferdulf's lip curled in splendid scorn. "So? What do you want me to do about it? Miserable imperial—" His voice faded down into a scatological mumble.

That was just what Gerin wanted. "They probably won't like you any better," he said with a grin he did not show: Ferdulf seemed to have forgotten he too was an Elabonian. "They're the ones who hold down Sithonia, after all."

"I wonder what I can do to them," Ferdulf mused. Dagref looked back over his shoulder at Gerin. Gerin wished he hadn't done it; the look might have alerted Ferdulf to the notion that he was being manipulated. If Dagref did have to give Gerin a look, though, a look of approval was the one the Fox wanted. Dagref, as his father had learned to his own discomfiture, was better than anyone else at manipulating Ferdulf.

Up came the Elabonian chariots. The one in the lead had a shield painted in green and white stripes mounted on the pole between the two horses: a shield of truce. That chariot and the one behind it pulled away from the rest and approached the army that had set out from Fox Keep. "I am Efilnath the Earnest," the fellow in the fanciest robe called, "commissioner to his majesty Crebbig I, Emperor of Elabon. I see here Aragis the Archer, who presumes to make the error of styling himself king. Rumor has it that others in the province are equally rash. Be any such others present, that I might treat with and dismiss all such false claimants simultaneously?"

"I am Gerin the Fox," Gerin announced, "king of the north. I am here in alliance with Aragis. I note, Efilnath, that if you call claims false and say ahead of time you will dismiss them, you are not treating with those who make them, only disposing of them. I also note that they—and we—are not to be disposed of so readily."

He wondered who Crebbig I was. On his last journey down to the City of Elabon, Hildor III had reigned there: an indolent excuse for a monarch. Whatever Crebbig's faults—and, being a man, he was bound to have them—indolence did not seem to be among their number.

"As the Elabonian Empire does not recognize that this land has ever been anything but an imperial province, so naturally we cannot recognize any men styling themselves kings, save in recognizing them as rebels and traitors," Efilnath said.

Aragis the Archer growled something angry under his breath. Gerin was about to growl something out loud when his eye chanced to fall on one of the men in the chariot behind Efilnath's. The fellow was nothing special to look at—not too tall, not too wide, not too handsome—and wore a robe that would have been altogether ordinary in the City of Elabon. Nonetheless, perhaps by the way he carried himself, perhaps by a certain look in his eye, Gerin knew him for what he was: a wizard from the Sorcerers' Collegium.

And he recognized Gerin, too—not as an equal, as one who had completed the same arduous training, but as one who had some part of it. Those oddly compelling eyes of his widened, just a little; plainly, he had not expected to come across anyone in the northlands who shared even a fragment of his arcane expertise. Gerin understood that. The Elabonians south of the High Kirs reckoned the northlands a barbarous backwater. He knew they had a point, but not so much of one as they thought they did.

He smiled at the wizard, a bleak display of acknowledgment and warning. The Elabonian got down from his chariot and hurried over to Efilnath's. He whispered in the envoy's ear. Whatever he said—and the Fox had a pretty good notion of what it would be—Efilnath seemed unimpressed. "Come what may, a backwoods baron remains a backwoods baron," he said, a distinct sniff in his voice.

"Oh, Ferdulf," Gerin called sweetly, "come and say hello to these nice people, would you please?"

"What nice people?" Ferdulf snarled. "All I see is a bunch of Elabonians who think they're smarter than they really are—idiots who think they're halfwits."

As if his rumbling baritone wouldn't have been enough to alert the southerners that he was something out of the ordinary, he also strolled along a couple of feet off the ground. Efilnath gaped at him. So did the wizard, in a different, more intensely concentrated way. "Who are you?" he demanded, and then, a moment later, "What are you?"

By way of reply, Ferdulf stuck out his tongue. It went out improbably far. The tip wiggled like a serpent's tongue for a moment. Then he drew the whole thing back in with a wet *plop*. He smiled unpleasantly at the Elabonian sorcerer.

Sweetly still, Gerin said, "Lord Efilnath, lord wizard—"

"Call me Caffer," the wizard said. As the Fox knew, it was not his real name. Wizards warded those, to keep enemies from working magic with them.

"Lord Efilnath, lord Caffer, then," Gerin resumed, "allow me to present you to Ferdulf, the son of Mavrix, who, when he is not accompanying me, dwells in the village by Fox Keep."

"A son of the lord of the sweet grape, here?" Efilnath exclaimed. "Impossible!"

"Not impossible," Caffer said. "It is truth." He and the Elabonian envoy conferred again, more urgently this time.

Gerin hoped the idea that Ferdulf was at least in some measure under his control would get through to the imperials. Ferdulf didn't help, remarking, "And a bloody boring hole that village is, too."

"Yield to the Empire's might, pay the tribute long owed us, and all shall be forgiven concerning these usurpations of authority you have perpetrated," Efilnath said with what he obviously thought was true generosity. "Return to your own barony, abandon any false claims to suzerainty over your neighbors, and live under the beneficent splendor of Crebbig, justly styled the Magnificent."

"Pay twenty years' tribute?" Gerin shook his head. "Not likely, not when the Elabonian Empire wasn't here for a day of that time."

"Twenty years' tribute, yes," Efilnath said, "plus whatever you may have owed prior to that time. Our records indicate that you northern barons were shockingly lax in paying your dues even before such time as we temporarily fell out of touch with you."

"That's a nice way to put it," Gerin said. "Before you forgot all about us, you mean. Before you left us to the tender mercy of the Trokmoi, you mean. Before you weren't here to help us fight the monsters or the Gradi, you mean. And if you go away again now, you'll expect us to pay you again for being gone, won't you?"

Ignoring the sarcasm, Efilnath said, "You did not, as I have noted, contribute your fair share before we temporarily fell out of touch with you."

With a shrug, Gerin answered, "It all depends on how you look at things. I never saw any imperial soldiers on the Niffet helping me hold the Trokmoi at bay. If the crops failed, I never saw any grain hauled up from south of the High Kirs to help us. I don't know about you, Efilnath, or about your Emperor Crebbig, either, but I'm not in the habit of paying for what I don't see."

"Crebbig is your Emperor as well as mine." Efilnath sounded shocked—artfully shocked—that Gerin could imagine otherwise.

Caffer broke in: "Speak to me of the Gradi, lord baron. South of the High Kirs, we know less of them than we would like."

"The Fox's style is *lord king*, even as is mine," Aragis said. "Best you remember it, lest he take your rudeness to heart and avenge himself on you."

Aragis was likelier than Gerin to do something like that. Gerin started to say he wasn't offended, but then checked himself. Why not give the imperials something else to worry about? He laughed scornfully instead. "I'll answer," he said.

"They think they can rule this province, and they don't even know who lives in it."

"They temporarily fell out of touch, that's all," Dagref said. He struck the perfect tone. It wasn't even scorn. It said the Empire's envoy and wizard didn't rate scorn, only amused disdain.

It struck home, too. In a voice less suave than he had used before, Efilnath demanded, "Lord baron, will you then yield to the authority of the Emperor Crebbig and beg his forgiveness for the autonomy you have usurped?"

"In a word, no," Gerin answered. "This would look to be a word you people don't know well, since your comrade heard it from Aragis without listening to it."

Ferdulf's yawn was as extravagant and as anatomically unlikely as the distance to which he'd stuck out his tongue. "Go away, you foolish people," he said. "You only prove how dull Elabonians can be." And then, without warning, all the gentleness disappeared from his mockery. "Begone. Get out of this land. You have no right to it. I, a god's son, so declare."

Efilnath flinched. Gerin would have flinched, too, had an angry demigod growled at him. But the Empire's envoy was not without spirit. "The gods of Elabon say otherwise, and I serve them and the Emperor."

"What do you suppose the gods of Elabon do say, Father?" Dagref whispered to Gerin. "Efilnath and his friends here are Elabonian, but so are we. How do the gods choose one side or the other?"

"My guess is, they probably don't," the Fox whispered back. The gods of Elabon, from everything he'd seen, intervened in human affairs as little as they possibly could. Most of the time, that suited him fine. Against the Gradi, whose own gods were as aggressive as they were, he'd wished the Elabonian deities had done more. Now, he'd be just as well pleased to have them keep on doing nothing in particular.

While he and Dagref talked, Efilnath and Caffer were also holding their own low-voiced colloquy. Gerin couldn't make out what the Elabonian envoy was saying. Whatever it was, Caffer agreed with it: he nodded several times, each more vigorously than the one before.

"Quit jabbering, the two of you," Ferdulf growled at the men from south of the High Kirs. "I told you once, get out of here. Now I tell you twice. Leave while you can still take your clothes with you, which is better luck than the last imperial envoy had, isn't it?"

Now Efilnath nodded to Caffer. The wizard pointed in Ferdulf's direction. His lips moved. So did his right hand, in passes Gerin knew he would never be able to match for swift fluidity. As Aragis had said, this was a mage from the Sorcerers' Collegium, the most highly trained and skilled band of sorcerers this part of the world knew.

Ferdulf shouted in rage. "Try and silence me, will you?" he roared, and suddenly, despite staying the same size, seemed much larger and fiercer than he had a moment before. He pointed two fingers at Caffer, a vulgar gesture straight from the alleys of the City of Elabon.

It was a vulgar gesture with power behind it. Caffer staggered, and had to snatch at the rail of Efilnath's chariot to keep from falling. He looked astonished that his sorcery had failed. The one flaw Gerin had sometimes noted in trained Elabonian wizards was a belief that, because they could do so many things, they could do everything.

But Ferdulf looked astonished, too. He, evidently, had expected to flatten the Elabonian wizard.

"Enough, both of you!" Gerin said sharply. "We met here behind a shield of truce. Shall we fall to blows now, and save the waiting?"

"No," Efilnath said. Caffer gave a shaky nod to show he agreed with his superior. Ferdulf, on the other hand, looked ready—looked eager—to continue the battle of powers. Gerin glared at him. He glared back. His eyes blazed with more power than the Fox had ever seen in them. Resolutely, Gerin kept staring. To his everlasting relief, Ferdulf finally nodded, too.

"Go back to your soldiers, then," Gerin told the imperial envoy. "When we meet again, we shall be at war."

"I said this earlier, to your other ambassador," Aragis added. "Now my fellow king confirms it. If you want this land, you will have to take it from us—and from the god's son here." He beamed at Ferdulf. Gerin had never seen him beam before. It was, when you got down to it, a pretty alarming sight.

"We have powers of our own," Caffer said. His voice wasn't as certain and bright as a new-stamped coin, though. After that first clash with Ferdulf, doubts had entered his mind. Doubt was the enemy of strong sorcery. The thought made Gerin beam, too, in Caffer's direction. The mage from the City of Elabon looked as if he could have done without that sunny smile.

Efilnath the Earnest tapped his driver on the shoulder. The fellow steered the horses in as tight a circle as he could. They went off the Elabon Way for part of it, their hooves kicking up clumps of dirt and grass. Then they got back on the road and clattered off down the paving stones. In precise order of precedence, the rest of the chariots in Efilnath's party followed, Caffer jumping up into his car when it came past him.

As that car rolled away, Caffer looked back over his shoulder at Gerin—or perhaps at Ferdulf, who stood nearby. Ferdulf snarled, like one tomcat warning another to go away. Caffer stared steadily back at him—a stare that proclaimed *I will not be cowed*—until the soldiers in another chariot got between him and Mavrix's son.

"It will be war." Aragis the Archer spoke with a certain somber satisfaction. "If the imperials will not heed words, let them heed the flight of arrows and the thunder of chariotry."

"It will be war," Gerin agreed. He looked around. "I don't think Efilnath or his men were paying much attention to our riders. That's to the good, in my view. May they prove an unpleasant surprise for the imperials."

"So may it be," Aragis said, though sounding more as if he hoped it would be so than as if he expected it.

"Let's follow the imperials as close as we can," Gerin said. "If they're as proud of themselves as they always used to be, they'll expect us to cower and wait for them to come to us. The more we can rock them back on their heels, the better off we'll be."

"Oh, aye, no doubt of that. If I'd had only a few more men of my own—or if I hadn't worried that you'd jump me instead of joining me, I'd have done as much myself,"

Aragis said. He turned his harsh gaze on the Fox. "And now for what you'd likely call an interesting question: who commands?"

"Interesting indeed," Gerin said, almost as lightly as he'd hoped he could. "Well, it's easy enough to answer: you do."

"Just like that?" The Archer stared. He'd been ready for an argument.

But Gerin said, "Just like that. For one thing, this is your land. You know it, and I don't. For another, you also know—or you'd better know—I'll take my men out of the fight if you try to harm them with your orders. That should be enough to keep you honest, or close to it."

Aragis weighed the words, then nodded with his usual abrupt decision. "Very well. Let it be so. Had you insisted on taking the lead, I likely would have yielded, but I'd have given you a harder time than you sound as though you'll give me."

"That also crossed my mind." Gerin grinned at the other king in the northlands. "I didn't feel like arguing with you every time I turned around, either. Life is too short for that. You're a perfectly good general; I've seen as much. I doubt we'd do a whole lot better with me giving orders than with you."

"Why do you make me think you've won a victory when I see you yielding?" Aragis asked suspiciously.

"Sometimes you can do both at once," Gerin told him. The Archer shook his head, like a man bedeviled by gnats he couldn't see. The only victories he understood were the ones where he went out and smashed something. Gerin nodded to himself. With luck, there would be plenty of that sort. *There had better be*, he thought.

More and more of Aragis' men joined the army as it moved south in the wake of the imperial envoy and his entourage. At Gerin's suggestion—to which the Archer agreed after a sour look—the newcomers rode at the head of the army. "That way," Gerin said blandly, "if the imperials have spies in your land, they'll have a harder time spotting all our riders."

"If the Elabonians have spies in our land, I'll crucify them." Aragis obviously meant what he said. Down south of the High Kirs, the Empire crucified miscreants. The headsman's axe mostly settled them in the northlands. But, for spies, Gerin would not have been surprised in the least to learn that Aragis might take the trouble to run up crosses.

Marlanz Raw-Meat sent a charioteer back to Aragis and Gerin to let them know the imperial envoy had passed his army and returned to the host the Elabonian Emperor had sent into the northlands. "And," the messenger added, "he says the horseman you sent to warn him this Efilnath was coming got there ahead of the cursed imperial even though he went cross-country, as a chariot couldn't do. No man afoot could have run fast enough to outdo a car, either."

"Isn't that fine?" Gerin said.

"Isn't that splendid? Isn't that magnificent?" Rihwin the Fox said.

"Oh, shut up," Aragis the Archer said. Gerin and Rihwin both laughed at him till he looked so fierce, they stopped. Rihwin probably wouldn't have stopped even then, but Gerin contrived to tread on his toes. He wanted Aragis angry at the Elabonian Empire, not at his own allies.

He might make Rihwin stop laughing. Making Rihwin shut up was another matter. In his best didactic tones, Rihwin lectured Aragis: "So you see, lord king, judicious employment of men riding horses does in good sooth have the potential to smite the foe when and where he least expects it."

"I see a man who talks too bloody much, is what I see," Aragis rumbled, and worked a small miracle: Rihwin did fall silent. Aragis kept right on scowling, not so much at Rihwin as at the world around him: "We're going to eat this country empty, curse it."

"Could be worse," Gerin said cheerfully.

"Oh? How?" The scowl remained, now turned full force on Gerin.

He said, "Easy enough. Could be the imperials eating your countryside empty. For that matter, could be the imperials burning out your countryside so nobody'd be able to eat from it."

Aragis pondered that, then looked surprised. "Well, you're right. It could be worse," he said gruffly. "That doesn't make this any too good, though."

"I didn't say it did." Gerin resolutely kept his tone light. That wasn't too hard for him. His land wasn't facing invasion—yet. His land wasn't facing being eaten empty—his land had already had an army feeding off it, when he'd thought he was going to war against Aragis rather than the Elabonian Empire.

The next afternoon, Gerin's force came up to the encampment where Aragis' main army kept an eye on the imperials. Marlanz Raw-Meat rode out to greet the Fox. "Well met, lord king," he said, clasping Gerin's hand. "I'm happier to see you fighting with me than fighting against me, if you know what I mean, heh, heh."

"Oh, yes," Gerin said. "I never wanted to fight a war with your king, either, and now I won't." *I'll fight a war with the Elabonian Empire instead, and I would have wanted that even less, had it occurred to me not to want it.*

Marlanz said, "Lord king, I present to you Aranast Aragis' son."

"Lord king," Aranast said politely, bowing. He looked like Aragis, right down to the cast of features that warned nobody had better disagree with him for any reason whatever. Gerin didn't think he had the force of character that would let him back up that cast of features, but he wasn't very old yet, either. He couldn't have had more than a couple of years on Duren.

Thinking of Duren made the Fox wish he'd accepted more support from his own eldest son. He hadn't thought he'd need it against Aragis the Archer. The Elabonian Empire had rather greater resources than his rival king. He didn't know what part of those resources the Empire had committed or would commit to reconquering the northlands, but he'd find out soon enough.

Aranast said, "We've all . . . heard a great deal about you, lord king."

"That's nice," Gerin said blandly, playing the simpleton to see how Aragis' son would respond.

Aranast drew back half a pace, struggling to reconcile

the ruler who'd held his father at bay for two decades with this fellow who sounded as if he had not a brain in his head. After a moment, he smiled a smile that matched any of Aragis' for icy precision. "Much of what we've heard is how self-effacing you are. I see that's so."

All right, then: he wasn't a fool. That disappointed the Fox. With a smile of his own, Gerin said, "If I wanted to stay in hiding, I wouldn't have come south."

"We're glad you did, whatever your reasons were," Marlanz said hastily. "The Empire won't be so glad." He paused. "Is . . . that Ferdulf . . . with you?" As he had up at Fox keep, he spoke of the demigod as if Ferdulf were some kind of wild animal.

"Oh yes, he's here," Gerin answered.

"Good!" Marlanz said with heartfelt relief—one of the rare times Ferdulf had ever inspired that emotion, or indeed any emotion save inchoate, or sometimes not so inchoate, fury in anyone.

As if to prove he was there, Ferdulf strolled over, rose into the air till he could look Marlanz in the face, and said, "I remember you. You're the man who's made out of raw meat."

"Most men are," Marlanz replied with what Gerin thought of as commendable calm. He stared back at Ferdulf. "I expect you are, too."

"Well, yes," the little demigod admitted, "but not raw meat of such a gross and repellent sort as yours or the Fox's here; of that I'm comfortably certain."

"No doubt you're right," Gerin said in a voice of elaborate unconcern. "When you go in the bushes, it's daisies and violets that come out, not the stuff that makes them grow."

Ferdulf gave him a look full of such concentrated loathing, he had to brace himself to stand against it. The demigod stalked off through the air. "He does dislike the Empire more than he dislikes us, doesn't he?" Marlanz asked anxiously. "I had hoped he would, ever since I learned the imperials were coming over the mountains."

"He did, anyhow," Gerin said, which made Marlanz look more anxious still and Aranast downright alarmed. The Fox laughed. "It will be all right. He and I have been carving chunks off each other for as long as he's been around. He's used to it. He'll get over it. But he despises the Elabonian Empire with a fine bright loathing that should be good for a long time to come."

"Do you plan to move straight against the Empire, lord king?" Marlanz asked the Fox.

Gerin pointed to Aragis. "You'd better put that to your own overlord, Marlanz," he replied. "He's in overall command here."

Aranast looked as if he'd already assumed that. Marlanz looked surprised, then tried to look as if he hadn't. It didn't work: Aranast had noticed. Marlanz would probably be unhappy after Aragis found a chance to speak with him in private. Had the Archer been operating against Gerin, he would have been delighted. Since they were on the same side, he wasn't.

Aragis said, "They are here. They have no business being here. My fellow king agrees they have no business being here." He turned his fierce gaze on Gerin, as if daring him to disagree. He couldn't disagree. Aragis came to a conclusion as obvious to him as a Sithonian geometer found the proof of two triangles' congruence: "And so, we attack."

A mounted scout came galloping back to the army of the northlands. "Lord kings!" he shouted to Gerin and Aragis, who rode at the head of their conjoined forces. "The imperials aren't far south—just back of the next rise south from the one I rode over here. They're in column, but they aren't asleep—look like they can deploy in a hurry whenever they take a mind to."

"We'll hit them anyhow," Aragis said. At his order, his driver reined in. Gerin had Dagref pull to a stop beside his fellow king. Aragis waved to gain the attention of the troopers behind him. "Left and right!" he shouted. "Form line of battle! Left and right!"

Cheers rose, from his men and Gerin's both. They were going to get the fighting so many of them craved. The Fox hadn't understood anyone's being eager for battle, not since his first one, but a lot of people were. The warriors peeled off across the fields to either side of the Elabon way to make a ragged line that would only get more ragged as they advanced against the Empire.

"What about the horsemen?" Gerin asked, when Aragis didn't give them any special orders.

The Archer frowned. "That's right," he said—sure enough, he'd forgotten about them. After a moment's thought, he issued the command: "Let them go off around to the right. Maybe they can take the imperials in the flank, since they won't be looking for anything like that."

He spoke as if he didn't expect that to happen, as if he was sending Rihwin's riders out of the way so he could get on with the main battle. Gerin didn't try to change his mind. No matter why he'd issued the order, it made good sense. Gerin waved for Rihwin, drew his attention, and relayed it.

"Aye, lord king, we shall essay it," Rihwin replied. He glanced over to Aragis the Archer with an expression that said he too knew Aragis didn't expect much. "Perhaps we shall disabuse doubters of their dubiety."

"Talk fancy like that when you get near the imperials," Aragis said. "Maybe they'll think you're one of them long enough to help you hurt 'em."

"I shall, lord king, and I thank you for the suggestion," Rihwin said. He surveyed Aragis with respect no less real for being grudging.

But the Archer hadn't finished: "If you don't fool them, maybe you can bore them to death."

"Thank you again, lord king, so much," Rihwin said tightly. He rode off to rally his men and take them in the direction Aragis had commanded. Gerin wondered whether Aragis had insulted him for the sake of being insulting or to inspire him to fight harder. Gerin also wondered whether Aragis bothered drawing such distinctions.

"Where's that Ferdulf?" Aragis demanded, looking around. "I want him front and center against the Empire."

Front and center Ferdulf came. He and Aragis made allies more unlikely than Gerin and Aragis. "Back over the mountains with them!" Ferdulf shouted, and rose above the front rank like a living battle standard. The troopers—especially Aragis' men, who knew him only as a demigod and not as an obnoxious brat—raised a cheer.

"Forward!" Aragis shouted. With another cheer, with a rumble of wheels and squeaks from ungreased axles, the chariots rolled ahead.

In the car with Gerin and Dagref, Van said, "Ah, well, another brawl." He hefted his spear. "Now to make the other fellows sorry their mothers ever bore 'em."

Aragis shouted again: "Our cry is, 'The northlands!' " A third cheer rang out from his men and the Fox's, louder than either of the other two.

Gerin set a hand on Dagref's shoulder. "Drive as I command you, or as seems best to you if I'm too busy fighting to give you any orders. The gods keep you safe."

"And you, Father. And all of us," Dagref answered. Then he frowned. His back was to Gerin, but the Fox recognized the expression by the way his son's shoulders hunched forward a little. After his usual pause for thought, Dagref went on, "But, of course, the gods won't keep all of us safe. Why make the prayer, then?"

If Dagref was worrying over philosophical questions, he wasn't likely to panic when the fighting started. Gerin had never gone into battle with that sort of preparation. He didn't think Duren had, either. But if philosophy helped keep his eldest by Selatre on a steady course, the Fox would not complain.

Over the first low rise rolled the army. The chariots were just coming down the far slope when over the crest of the second rise the scout had mentioned came the lead chariots of the force the Elabonian Empire had sent out to reclaim the northern province it had abandoned a generation before.

At the sight of their foes, Gerin's men and Aragis' raised a great shout: derision and hatred all commingled. "Hold the line steady!" Aragis yelled. "By Father Dyaus, I'll cut the balls off the first chariot crew I see charging ahead all on their lonesome. Hold steady."

And the line did hold steady. In the short run, fear worked well enough to keep men obedient. More and more imperial chariots came up over the crest of the second rise. They were deploying as they advanced; their line got wider as the Fox watched. He wished his men and Aragis' had been closer to them, to hit them before they shook themselves out into line. Wishing got him what wishing usually got.

Dagref said, "All their chariots look just alike. Isn't that peculiar?"

"Not when you think about it," Gerin answered. "Down in the City of Elabon, the Empire has an armory where smiths and carpenters and such make weapons for the whole imperial army. They have a pattern for spears and a pattern for helmets and a pattern for chariots, too. It's not the way it is here, where each keep will have its own carpenter or wheelwright with his own notions about how to do things."

"Then these cars will likely be better than some of ours but worse than others," Dagref said. "If they keep on making them to the same pattern long enough while we test worse against better, sooner or later all of ours will be better than theirs."

"Or else we'll try something different altogether." Gerin looked west to see if he could spot Rihwin's troop of horsemen. He was, on the whole, glad to discover he couldn't: trees screened them from what would momentarily become the battlefield. If they got round that screen, they were liable to give the imperials a nasty surprise.

"Elabon! Elabon! Elabon!" The foe was shouting, too, in rhythmic unison very different from the great incoherent roar that came from the men of the northlands. The imperials were much more uniform in appearance than Gerin and Aragis' troopers, each of whom equipped himself as he could afford and as he thought best. The men from south of the High Kirs put the Fox in mind of the warriors Ros the Fierce had used to conquer this province in the first place, a couple of hundred years before. That comparison worried him; Ros' warriors, by all accounts, had been as tough as any ever made.

"This'll be the biggest chariot fight I've ever seen," Van said as more and more imperials came over the rise.

"Biggest chariot fight this part of the world has ever seen," Gerin answered, "unless there were bigger ones when we Elabonians conquered it in the first place." No sooner were the words *we Elabonians* out of his mouth than he found them odd. He thought of himself as an Elabonian.

He spoke the Elabonian language. He worshiped Elabonian gods. He revered Elabonian civilization (not least the parts borrowed or stolen from Sithonia). And now he was going to do his best to defeat the soldiers of the Elabonian Empire.

Of course, they'd kill him if he didn't. That was a powerful argument in favor of fighting.

Ferdulf floated high overhead, screaming abuse at the imperial army. Gerin didn't know what the little demigod could do beyond screaming abuse. Even that would help, with his being so obviously supernatural. Maybe Ferdulf didn't know himself whether he could do anything. Maybe he wouldn't know till he tried it and it either worked or it didn't.

To Dagref, Gerin said, "If you see the Empire's wizards, steer toward their cars. If we can get rid of them, we help our own cause more than we do by putting paid to ordinary troopers." Dagref nodded.

Gerin reached over his shoulder, pulled an arrow from his quiver, and set it to his bowstring. The two armies were closing fast. Already the first few arrows had begun to fly. They fell far short of their targets. There were always soldiers who couldn't wait till they had some reasonable chance of hitting something before they started to shoot.

Closer and closer came the enemy cars. Gerin's own mouth felt dry. His heart pounded. He understood why the overeager troopers had begun to shoot too soon. It made them feel the battle had started and the waiting was over. Beside the Fox in the jouncing car, Van was muttering, "Come on. Come on. Come on." Gerin didn't think he knew he was doing it. He wanted to get into the fight, too, but carried no bow.

Straight ahead was an imperial with a gilded corselet and helmet. That made him an officer of some sort, and also a good target. Gerin set himself, drew the bow to his ear in one smooth motion, and let fly. The bowstring lashed the leather brace on his wrist. He grabbed another arrow, nocked it, and let fly again.

The officer in the gilded armor did not fall. Shooting from a chariot took a lot of luck, even for the best of warriors. Of course, with enough shafts in the air, some of them were bound to be lucky. Here and there, screams rose from both lines. Men crumpled and fell out of their cars as those bounded over the fields. Horses crashed down, too, sending chariots slewing sideways and, once or twice, crashing into one another and bringing more men to ruin.

Buzzing like an angry bumblebee, an arrow flew past the Fox's ear. He shook his head, as if at a veritable insect. Indeed: with enough shafts in the air, some *were* bound to be lucky—and unlucky for him. An old, pale scar puckered his left shoulder. He knew what wounds were like.

"Here we go," Van said. Aragis wasn't being subtle about what he did: he was throwing his army straight at the imperial forces. Maybe he thought they would break and flee—they were effete southerners, after all. The commander the Elabonian Emperor had sent over the mountains was taking the same approach to the warriors from the northlands. Maybe he thought they would break and flee—they were half-barbarous rebels, after all.

Neither side broke. Neither side fled. Neither side did much in the way of maneuvering. Gerin aimed for the driver of the chariot that was thundering toward him. His arrow caught the luckless Elabonian right in the neck. The fellow dropped the reins and clutched at himself as he fell out of the chariot. A wheel thumped over him. He lay very still.

One of the bowmen in that imperial chariot snatched for the reins. He missed. They dragged along the ground. The horses, no longer under anyone's control, slowed from gallop to walk. Dagref steered past them, so close that Van was able to use his heavy spear. He let out a great shout of fierce glee as he watched the imperial soldier crumple.

Some of the chariots of the opposing sides shot past one another. Others pulled up to avoid collisions. The fight turned into a melee. What had been neat lines turned into a confused jumble of chariots and horses. Some men kept on shooting arrows at their foes. Others, at closer quarters, drew swords and axes and slashed away at one another.

"Pull back, in the Emperor's name!" an imperial officer

shouted to his men. "We'll form line again and smash through these savages."

But the troopers of the Elabonian Empire could not pull back and re-form. They were locked together with the warriors from the northlands as tightly as if held in a lover's embrace.

"Smash 'em!" Aragis yelled. "Smash 'em to pieces!" Gerin wondered how he'd grown so strong with no better notion of strategy than that. Maybe ferocity had had more to do with it than strategy. Any of Aragis' men who gave ground would have to face him afterwards. That meant giving ground was anything but a sure way to escape from danger.

An imperial chariot pulled close to the one Dagref was driving. One of the warriors in it turned and cut at Gerin with his sword. The Fox leaned away from the blade, which flew past him. He snatched an axe out of a bracket set into the side of his chariot and smashed it into the trooper's ribs. It bit through the scales of his corselet. Blood gushed from the wound. With a bubbling shriek and an outraged expression, the soldier toppled.

Van boomed laughter. "You do that once every fight, Captain, seems like," he said. "They never expect you to be left-handed, and that's a mistake they never get to make twice."

Gerin started to answer, but shouted "Watch yourself!" instead. An imperial trooper with an axe ran toward the chariot from the side. Many horses on both sides were down; many drivers had been hit; many chariots had overturned. Some men kept fighting on foot.

Van jumped down from the car and, with a roar that might have sprung from a longtooth's throat, rushed at the soldier of the Elabonian Empire. The soldier was close to a foot shorter than the enormous outlander, whose helm and the nodding horsehair crest above it made him seem taller still. When Van thrust with his spear, the imperial did not wait to try conclusions with him, but spun on his heel and ran away to find a foe for whom he was more nearly a match. Shouting laughter, Van sprang back into the chariot.

Dagref managed to get out of the press and send the

car, at Gerin's direction, toward several imperial chariots whose crews were pressing hard against some of Aragis' men and some of his own. A couple of the Empire's chariots also pulled loose and quickly moved to block his path.

Suddenly, Ferdulf flew down from the sky and screeched in the faces of the imperials' horses. One team ran wild, thundering out of the fight. The other team didn't run at all. The horses reared and screamed in terror. The Elabonian warriors clung to the rails of their car. That was all they could do to keep from being spilled out onto the ground.

That also made them easy meat for Gerin and Van. The Fox shot one at close range; Van speared another. The third did dive out of the chariot then, and so preserved himself.

"Well done!" Gerin shouted to Ferdulf. "Keep it up—you'll drive them crazy."

Floating in midair, Ferdulf grinned at the Fox, who, with the Elabonian Empire as the new standard of comparison, looked better to the obnoxious little demigod than he ever had before. "I've found something else new to do to them, too," Ferdulf said.

He drifted up above the fight, tugged his tunic up over his belly, and . . . It wasn't really something new. It was the disgusting game he'd been playing at Fox Keep when Marlanz Raw-Meat came to visit. Then, it had been nothing but disgusting. Now, if a soldier of the Elabonian Empire unexpectedly got pissed on from out of the sky, he was liable to be distracted for a few crucial moments, during which he could neither attack nor defend himself very well. Several soldiers paid with their lives for such distraction.

Ferdulf seemed to have an unlimited supply of his nasty weapon. Gerin had never thought that one of a demigod's attributes might be the ability to piss endlessly without having to load up on water or ale. That was not the sort of ability on which the Sithonian mythologizers and their Elabonian imitators dwelt. They had their minds on higher things. Ferdulf didn't.

Another attribute of his, one the mythologizers might actually have mentioned in writing, was his uncanny ability to avoid arrows. He got plenty of chances to use that ability, too. Plenty of outraged imperials sent shafts his way, and he was not floating so high as to be anything but an easy target. Nevertheless, every arrow missed. Gerin couldn't tell whether the arrows went wide or Ferdulf dodged. However that worked, none struck home. He took unpleasant revenge on the men who shot at him, too.

And then, with a squawk of surprise and indignation, he tumbled out of the sky not far from the Fox. "Oh, a pestilence!" Gerin exclaimed. "Caffer or one of their other cursed wizards found a spell that would bite on him after all. Dagref!"

"Aye, Father," Dagref said, and then looked back over his shoulder at Gerin. "Are you really sure you want to rescue him?"

"Don't tempt me, lad," Gerin said. He would have liked it better had the words come out of his mouth sounding more like a joke. But, while he wouldn't have cared to explain himself to either Ferdulf or Mavrix, the idea of leaving the Sithonian god's irksome little bastard to his fate held an appalling appeal.

Even though Ferdulf wasn't flying, arrows still wouldn't strike him. They dug into the ground all around his little feet, but none pierced his flesh. "Finish him!" an imperial shouted—sure enough, there was Caffer, looking indecently pleased with himself.

"Steer toward the sorcerer!" Gerin shouted, and shot an arrow at Caffer. The wizard deflected it with an absent-minded pass. He could not do so without effort, though, as Ferdulf could, and, while he was momentarily distracted, the demigod floated off the ground. As soon as the arrow had gone by, the mage from the City of Elabon renewed his spell, and Ferdulf, shouting in fury, found his feet on the ground again.

Gerin shot at Caffer once more. Once more, the wizard made him miss. An imperial warrior jumped out of a chariot and ran toward Ferdulf, who, after another leap into the air while Caffer was otherwise engaged, had again returned to earth. Cursing, Van sprang down and dashed to the demigod's aid. Unlike the other trooper, this one stood and fought.

The Fox had scant time to watch that fight. Dagref, by

then, had driven quite close to Caffer's car, close enough for him to snap his whip at the wizard. The whip wasn't so easy to deflect as Gerin's arrows had been. Caffer did manage to evade it, then howled a spell. The lash changed to a serpent in Dagref's hands. The serpent hissed, twisted, and tried to bite.

That, however, did not work so well as Caffer had hoped. Like a lot of boys his age, Dagref was fond of snakes. This one was bigger than any Gerin had seen around Fox Keep, but that did not seem to faze his son. Dagref grabbed it behind the head. He had to use both hands to control its writhing length. Gerin snatched up the reins to keep the horses from running wild.

"Thank you, Father," Dagref said. Then he shouted to Caffer: "You made it—now see how you like it!" He threw the snake into the wizard's car.

Caffer had had a spell handy for turning whip to snake. He did not seem to have one for turning a snake back into a whip. He and his driver and the warrior in the chariot with them all shouted and stomped and slashed at the serpent, which, like every other serpent, proved extremely reluctant to expire.

Dagref took the reins back from Gerin as calmly as if nothing had happened. The Fox shot a third arrow at Caffer. The wizard knew nothing of this one till it rammed its way between two ribs and pierced him almost to its fletching. He straightened up and screamed, a long wail of agony and surprise mixed. Since men, like snakes, could prove reluctant to die, Gerin shot him again, this time in the face. He spilled out of the chariot like a sack of peas.

With a shout of joy, Ferdulf floated above the field once more. Gerin looked around to see if Van needed help against his foe. The imperial warrior lay on the ground, thrashing toward death. Van's spear dripped blood. "Fool was brave," the outlander said as he got back into the chariot, "but that doesn't make him any less a fool."

"Father, I'm sorry, but I haven't got a whip any more," Dagref said.

"Considering what you did with it, I think I'll forgive you," the Fox answered, his voice dry. "That was quick thinking."

Dagref's shoulders went up and down in a shrug. "I didn't see anything better I could do with the thing."

Van looked around the field, then nudged Gerin. "Fox, are we winning this confounded fight or losing it?"

Gerin looked, too. "To the five hells with me if I know," he said. "They aren't running, and we aren't running, and we're all mashed together." With a certain sardonic pride, he added, "The fights I make are *neater* than this, anyhow. Aragis has no sense of tidiness."

"You can tell him that when everything here is done," Van said with a grin. "Wait till I'm around, though, if you'd be so kind. I want to hear what he says to you afterwards."

Dagref managed to keep the chariot moving as he wanted even without a whip to speed the horses along. What to do on the battlefield did not come naturally to him, as it did, say, to Van, and to Duren, too. But he thought well, and did not let himself get rattled. All that counted, too.

And he managed to keep everything that was and should be going on straight in his mind, which a good many men who reckoned themselves great captains had trouble doing. He said, "Shouldn't Rihwin and his horsemen ride in from the flank sometime soon?"

"Father Dyaus!" Gerin exclaimed. His head whipped around toward the west. "I'd forgotten all about them. Where are they, anyhow?"

Van looked west, too. "Probably in amongst the trees," he said, "trying to figure out which side is which. Like you said, Fox, this is about as untidy a brawl as I've ever seen."

"Well, one way for them to neaten things up would be to attack right about now," Gerin said. "Our men know who they are, and the imperials don't, except to figure out that they aren't friends, and—"

He shut up. Neither Dagref nor Van was paying attention to him. They were both staring west. Gerin took another look in that direction, too. His sour expression disappeared, to be replaced by an enormous grin. Sounding more serious than he often did, Van said, "You ever by any chance think of going into the prophet business?"

"I leave that to my wife and farseeing Biton, thanks," Gerin answered.

Regardless of whether or not he'd foretold their arrival, Rihwin's riders approached the battlefield at something close to a gallop. Gerin's men, and Aragis', cheered. The imperials either cursed or laughed.

More slowly than he should have, the officer who led the Elabonian Empire's army figured out that the horsemen, however peculiar they looked to him, might represent a real threat. He detached a squadron of chariots from his main force—no easy task, considering how heavily engaged against the men of the northlands his army was—and sent them against the new foes on horseback.

When other imperials weren't trying to kill him, Gerin watched with great interest the clash of the old way and the new. To his vast astonishment, it went exactly as Rihwin the Fox had predicted it would. He'd known Rihwin more than twenty years; in all that time, he couldn't recall thinking such a thing before. What he thought now was that Rihwin had picked a splendid time to be right.

The chariots thundered across the fields toward the horsemen, bumping and jouncing as they always did. The warriors in the bumping, jouncing cars shot arrows at Rihwin's men. Rihwin's men shot back. Not only that, they rode around the chariots as if the latter were nailed to the ground. They shot back at the imperials from all directions at once; anyone who tried to lift a shield against a shaft coming from the right was apt as not to be pierced by one coming from the left or the rear.

Dagref said, "We're watching the end of a whole way of fighting. I didn't think it would happen quite so easily."

"Neither did I," Gerin said.

"Neither did anybody," Van said.

But happen it did. Before long, the chariots the imperial commander had sent out against the horsemen were swept off the field as if by a broom. Rihwin's riders began showering the men in the main imperial force with arrows. Some rode close, to use sword and spear against their foes.

Where the men of the Elabonian Empire had fought Gerin and Aragis' chariots to a standstill, the shock of the new alarmed them far more than its actual effect on the battlefield and the number of horsemen would have warranted. At first by ones and twos and then in larger numbers, they broke off the fight and withdrew to the south. They weren't routed; they fought back fiercely when the men of the northlands pursued. But they weren't going to fight on that field any more, either.

Rihwin rode up to Gerin. His sword had blood on it. So did his face; an arrow had nicked one cheek. But his face also bore an enormous grin. Gerin didn't blame him—he'd earned the right to grin. "How about that, lord king?" Rihwin said. "How *about* that?"

"Well, how about it?" Gerin asked, deadpan. Rihwin stared, then started to laugh. So did Gerin. Why not? They'd won.

"It's a battle," Gerin said for the eighteenth—or was it the twenty-third?—time that afternoon. "It's not the war."

This particular time, he happened to be talking with Adiatunnus. The Trokmê chieftain gave him an impatient look, as if he were quibbling over trifles. "They're licked the now, and we'll see them no more, is it not so?"

"No, curse it, it's not so," the Fox said wearily. "Or rather, it's so that we beat them, but there's no way of knowing whether that means they've had enough or whether we'll be in another battle day after tomorrow."

Adiatunnus said, "You're after telling me, then, that the Elabonians from over the mountains are even more stubborn nor the lot of you kerns we Trokmoi have been coping with all along?"

"As stubborn as we are, anyhow: we're a branch off that trunk," Gerin said. "The other part of the bargain is, they're drawing on the resources of a land bigger than this province, and all of it under the rule of one man; it's not split into fragments the way the northlands are. If the Emperor orders this army to keep fighting, it will. If he orders another army up over the High Kirs, we'll have to fight that one, too."

"Maybe this whole business of civilization isna the fun I thought it was." Adiatunnus walked off shaking his head.

Gerin went back to what he had been doing: helping to care for the injured. Study and more practice than he wished he'd got had left him as good a battlefield surgeon as anyone else in the northlands. He dug out arrowheads, stitched up slashes, helped set a couple of broken bones, and urged anyone with any sort of wound to wash it out with ale. "It helps clean," he said, "and a clean wound is less likely to go bad than a dirty one."

"Wine would be better," said an imperial trooper who had been pitched out of his chariot and captured while he was stunned.

"So it would, if we had any," the Fox agreed. Spotting Ferdulf strolling along not far away, he waved and called the demigod's name.

Rather to his surprise, Ferdulf came to him. "What do you want?" Mavrix's son asked, sounding less hostile than Gerin was used to. Maybe Ferdulf had figured out that he ought to be grateful. And maybe the Fox would flap his arms and fly to Fomor. He'd borrowed the image from the Trokmê tongue; Fomor was the name the woodsrunners gave the moon Elabonians called Tiwaz.

Hoping to take advantage of what passed for good nature with Ferdulf, Gerin said, "Do you have any healing powers, by any chance?" Mavrix had great power over flesh, but Gerin thought it wiser not to mention that, lest Ferdulf grow angry at being reminded, however indirectly, that he was only half a god.

The question seemed to take Ferdulf by surprise. "I don't know," he answered. "I don't think I ever tried. Why should I try, anyhow? Even if I can, all I'd be doing would be healing Elabonians, and I don't like Elabonians."

"You'd be healing warriors who could fight against the Elabonian Empire again," Gerin pointed out.

"There is that," Ferdulf admitted grudgingly. His small shoulder shrugged. "Oh, all right, I'll see what I can do. I don't know if I can do anything, you know. Sometimes, when I try to do something, I find I can. Sometimes I can't. That makes me angry."

"Be angry at the Empire, for causing these wounds in

the first place," Gerin suggested. "Don't be angry at our men who are hurt. It's not their fault."

"No?" Ferdulf said. "If they were better soldiers, maybe they wouldn't have got hurt to begin with." But, having said that, he went over to a man who was cursing as blood from a wounded arm slowly soaked the bandage wrapped around the injury.

"What's he going to do?" The soldier looked at Ferdulf as dubiously as the demigod was looking at him.

Ferdulf reached out and touched the bandage. The warrior exclaimed in delight. Ferdulf exclaimed, too, and jerked his hand away. He grabbed at his own arm, in the spot where the warrior had been wounded. His lower lip stuck out in petulant dismay. "It hurts! It hurts as if the arrow had gone into me."

"But it took my pain away," the warrior said. "While you were holding me, it didn't hurt any more, and I thought I felt it getting better, if you know what I mean. But when you took your hand off the wound, it hurt again."

"And I stopped hurting," Ferdulf said, as if that were much more important. To him, no doubt, it was.

Gerin said, "Could you try a little more, even so? This would be a great help in the war against the Empire, if you could do it."

"It hurts," Ferdulf repeated. Gerin, though, had chosen the right hook with which to catch his fish. Ferdulf might have been reluctant, but he set his hand on the warrior's wound once more. The fellow let out a great, luxuriant sigh as his pain vanished again. Ferdulf grimaced and whimpered, but did not let go.

Then the soldier said, "Dyaus Allfather, will you look at that?" With his good arm, he pointed to the demigod.

Gerin stared. Forming on Ferdulf's little arm, even as he watched, was what looked as if it would be a wound of the same sort as the trooper had suffered. Gently, the Fox said, "Ferdulf, you don't have to go on any more. In fact, it might be better if you didn't."

When Ferdulf looked down at himself, he gasped and jerked his hand away from the wounded man. Along with Gerin and the warrior, he stared at his arm. Slowly, what would have become a wound faded from his flesh.

"You made mine better, little fellow, and I thank you for it," the soldier said. "It doesn't hurt near so much now. But I wouldn't have wanted you to go on any more, not when you were going to start bleeding yourself any minute there."

"Too high a price to pay," Gerin said regretfully. He clapped Ferdulf on the back as if the little demigod were a man. "You did what you could, and I thank you for trying."

"If I were all god, I could have done it." Ferdulf scowled. No, that thought was never far from his mind. "I feel the power in me, but I can't keep it from doing what it does to me. My body won't bear what it should."

The Fox suspected that problem would plague him all his life, which was liable to be a very long life indeed. Being only a man, Gerin had only human abilities, which did not overtax his merely human frame. Ferdulf's abilities outstripped the body containing them, as if a squirrel, say, were to be suddenly endowed with human intellect.

While Gerin was pondering that, Aragis the Archer came up to him. He looked as happy as he ever did, which wasn't very. "Your men fought well, Fox," he said, nodding to Gerin. "Better than I thought they would, and I've never thought they couldn't."

"I understand that, or you'd have attacked me," Gerin said, to which the Archer, unabashed, nodded again. Gerin went on, "Nothing wrong with the way your soldiers did their job, either, but I've always known any men you led would fight hard."

"If they didn't, *you'd* have attacked *me*," Aragis said. That was what he would have done, and he judged others by his own standards. After a few heartbeats, he added, "You got more out of those riders than I thought you would, too. Always up for something new." What came next was half bark, half chuckle. "Keeps your neighbors on their toes."

Gerin raised an eyebrow and grinned a lopsided grin. "That's the idea."

"Oh, I know. I understand as much," Aragis said. "Even so, I never thought you'd put a woman on horseback." He turned that coughing chuckle loose again. "Women are for being ridden, not for riding."

"What in the five hells are you talking about now?" Gerin demanded. "I haven't got any women—"

And Aragis threw back his head and guffawed. Gerin was as astonished as if the High Kirs had suddenly stood up on little spindly legs to dance a sprightly Trokmê dance. "By the gods, there's something you didn't know," the Archer said. "Haw, haw, haw! Who would have guessed it? The Fox with something going on right under his nose, and he had never a clue. Haw, haw!" He wiped his streaming eyes.

The last time something had gone on under Gerin's nose without his noticing, Elise had run off with the horseleech. After close to half a lifetime, that memory remained bitter as horseradish. Holding his voice under tight control, he said, "You'd better tell me just what you mean."

"I mean what I say." Aragis' face bore an utterly uncharacteristic grin. "I generally do, which is more than some people I might mention can claim. And what I say is this—if one of your riders tries to piss standing up, it'll run down her leg. And if you didn't notice, you ought to take your eyes to a smith and get 'em sharpened."

"You're not joking," Gerin said slowly. That was foolish, and he knew it. As far as he could tell, Aragis never joked. The Fox pointed toward the riders, who, as they usually did, stayed a little apart from the rest of the warriors. "Show me this woman you say is there."

"Father Dyaus, if you don't know a woman when you see one—" Aragis didn't merely guffaw, he giggled. Gerin wondered if a demon had taken possession of him. It would have to be a very silly demon, to get a giggle past Aragis' lips. The Archer took him by the arm. "All right, come on, then. If you need showing, I'll show you. While I'm about it, shall I tell you how to make children, too?"

"I have the hang of that, thanks," Gerin said through clenched teeth. "Now do as you said you would."

"Come on, then." Aragis was still chuckling as he headed for Rihwin's riders. Gerin, following, fumed. The Archer's head went this way and that. Gerin was about to start jeering when Aragis' arm shot out. "There, by the gods. Talking to your own son, she is. Did he bring her along to keep himself amused on campaign?"

"That's not a—" The words clogged in Gerin's throat. The rider standing there talking with Rihwin was the very young-looking fellow with the very fuzzy beard he'd noticed a couple of times on the way south from Fox Keep. He'd thought that an improbable beard for such a young man to have. Now that he took a closer look, he saw it was improbable because it wasn't real. Recognizing that it wasn't real, he took a closer look at the face under it. "Maeva!" he exclaimed.

Van's daughter whipped her head around. Dagref spun toward his father and Aragis, then, resigned, turned back to face Maeva. Gerin caught a few words of what he was saying: "—bound to happen sooner or later."

"Well, Fox," Aragis said, chuckling still, "is that a woman, or have you forgotten what they look like?"

"That is a woman," Gerin agreed seriously. "That is a woman who, now that you've found her out, is liable to kill you for doing it."

Aragis started to laugh some more, then looked at him. The Archer looked at Maeva, too. She stood a couple of digits taller than he did, and was wider through the shoulders, too. And, as Gerin had recognized her face, Aragis recognized her name. "Considering who her father is, you're likely the one who isn't joking now," he said.

"Not even a little bit," the Fox answered. "I tell you, my fellow king, I shouldn't want her angry at me." He raised his voice: "Maeva, come here, if you'd be so kind. Dagref, you'd better come, too. You seem to have known what was going on."

"Yes, I knew, Father," Dagref said with impressive artificial calm. "What of it? You never forbade Maeva to come on campaign with us, and—"

"I never thought I'd have to forbid her to come on campaign with us," Gerin said, "because I never thought she'd do it."

Dagref talked right through him: "—and she killed at least one imperial, and wounded three more. If that doesn't show she can hold her own on the field, what *does* she have to do to prove it?"

Gerin started to answer that, then stopped when he

realized he had no good answer handy. He turned to Maeva. "What will your father say when he finds out you've come to war?"

She shrugged, which only made her shoulders seem wider. "He'll probably shout and scream at me," she answered, "but what *can* he say now? I'm here, and I've already fought. He would have done the same thing. He *did* do the same thing, back when he was my age."

"Younger," Gerin said absently. "But he was a man. You're—"

"—Here and alive and with a dead foeman," Dagref put in. "That is what you were going to say, isn't it, Father?"

Aragis snorted. Gerin gave him a dirty look and Dagref another. Then the Fox spotted a tall, nodding horsehair crest of crimson. He waved in that direction. Van waved back. Gerin waved again, this time to bring his friend over. "I'm not going to say anything right now," he said as Van ambled toward him. "I'll leave that to Maeva's father."

Maeva herself gave him a look he would sooner not have had. But she stood straight and waited for Van to arrive. He towered over her, but he towered over almost everyone. "Hello, Fox," he boomed. "What do you need me for now? I was just about to . . ."

He followed Gerin's glance toward Maeva. For a moment, the Fox didn't think he'd recognize her under the false whiskers she'd stuck to her face. Gerin was ready to twit Van for that before remembering he hadn't penetrated Maeva's disguise, either. And then Van did. His gray-blue eyes got very wide. He started to say something, but all that came out of his mouth was a wordless, coughing croak of astonishment.

"Hello, Father," Maeva said. By then, she had her voice under control. It was a strong contralto that could easily have been mistaken for the treble of a youth whose voice hadn't broken—although such a youth probably wouldn't have sprouted so thick a beard.

Still, Gerin wasn't altogether astonished she'd managed to pull off the imposture. Most people saw what they expected to see, heard what they expected to hear. Maeva was as big as a man, she was in a place where only men were expected to be, she handled her weapons like a man, so what else but a man was she likely to be? *An illustration of the difference between what's likely and what is*, the Fox thought.

Van finally found words: "What are you doing here?" They weren't the best words, perhaps, but Gerin would have been hard pressed to come up with better on the spur of the moment.

Maeva had had the chance to compose herself. "Why, spinning thread and baking bread, of course," she answered with irony she must have learned from Dagref.

Van stared and spluttered. Dagref, sounding helpful when in fact he was anything but, said, "She's one of Rihwin's riders. She killed an imperial, and wounded a couple of more."

"What will your mother say?" Van demanded of his daughter. That made Gerin stare. He couldn't ever remember hearing Van use Fand's name in such a fashion before.

Evidently, Maeva couldn't, either. With a shrug, she replied, "When you go on campaign, you don't pay attention to what Mother says. Why do you think I'm going to?"

Listening with an analytical ear, Gerin admired that. It assumed Maeva had as much business going on campaign as anyone else. The Fox waited to see if Van would accept, or even notice, that unspoken assumption.

The outlander shook his head, like a bear bedeviled by bees. "It's not the same, not the same at all," he said. "Fine woman that your mother is, there's only so long I can stand being in the same place with her."

"Do you think it's any different for me?" Maeva asked.

Van coughed, then turned red beneath his bronzed hide. "Well, aye, it's some different," he answered, and let it go at that rather than explaining how it was different. That would have involved explaining how adultery ranked alongside fighting as his favorite campaign sports. He coughed again, then said, "Now that I know you're here, I'll say you've had your fun, and now you're to go back to Fox Keep where you belong."

Maeva set her chin. "No," she said, a reply remarkable for simplicity and succinctness.

Somehow, the shade of red Van turned was different this

time. "I am your father, I'll have you know, and what I tell you, that you shall do."

"No," Maeva said again. "Did you pay any attention to what your father told you once you'd killed your first man?"

"He was dead by then," Van said, an answer that was not really an answer. He turned to Gerin. "You're the king, Fox. If you tell her to go home and keep herself safe, she'll have to do it."

Gerin suffered his own coughing fit then. In all the years he'd known Van, the outlander had never appealed to his authority till now. Thoughtfully, he said, "I don't know. Isn't a lone girl on the road liable to face more danger than one in the middle of our own army?"

"She can take care of—" Van began, and then, a couple of words too late, stopped in his tracks.

Dagref, as was his way, drove home the logical flaw with a mallet: "If she can take care of herself, what point to sending her home?"

Maeva sent him a grateful look. The one Van sent him was anything but. Gerin said, "I don't think you're going to win this one, old friend. If she were a boy, you wouldn't be trying."

"But she's no boy, which is the point to the business," Van said stubbornly. "I know soldiers, and—"

"Wait." The Fox held up a hand. "I know Maeva, too. Don't you think anyone who tried to touch her if she didn't care to be touched would end up a eunuch like the priests of Biton, and that bloody quick?"

Van kept frowning. "Not right," he said again. "Not even close to right." After a moment, Gerin figured out what was likely troubling him. No doubt Maeva could protect herself if she didn't want to be touched. What if she *did* want to be touched, though? That had to be in Van's mind.

Aragis said, "You're not going to send her home." He sounded as if this was the first time he'd imagined that possibility.

Gerin bowed to him. "Lord king, there she is." He pointed to Maeva. "If you think you can order her home and make it stick, go ahead. Me, I don't like to waste orders that won't be obeyed. It weakens every other order I give after that."

"One way to do it would be to forbid her from any future fighting here," Aragis said, "and to post guards around her to make sure she cannot join it."

He was not a fool. He would never have done so well for himself had he been a fool. Maeva's face fell. Gerin could indeed do that. Van saw as much, too. Where his daughter wilted, he beamed. "That's the way, by the gods," he said, and bowed to Aragis. "I thank you, Archer. That's just the way."

"Oh, yes, a splendid suggestion," Dagref said. Had Gerin loosed his own sarcastic tones quite so freely when he was younger? On reflection, he decided he had. No wonder no one had liked him much. Dagref went on, "Not only does it take one proved fighter out of the army, it takes half a dozen or however many more out to watch her and make certain she doesn't do what she's already shown she's good at doing."

Maeva had eyed him with a certain speculation back at Fox Keep. He hadn't noticed then. If he didn't notice now, he was blind. Besides, his education in such things had advanced since then.

But maybe he didn't after all, for Aragis was eyeing him, too. "I am a king, young fellow," the Archer said coldly. "Do you cast scorn on me?"

"On you, lord king? Of course not," Dagref answered. "But a king can spout foolishness like anyone else. If you don't believe me, listen to my father for a while."

Aragis pursed his lips, then turned back to Gerin. "If that one can fight as well as he talks, he will be dangerous—if you let him live."

"Honh!" Van broke in. "We've said the same thing about Ferdulf, close enough. No wonder those two get on pretty well."

Dagref took no notice of that. He spoke to Gerin, who hadn't managed to get a word in edgewise about Aragis' suggestion: "Father, one of the things you always talk about is giving people the chance to do what they're good at. Why else would you have made Carlun your steward?"

"Because you weren't old enough yet to do the job?" the Fox suggested, perhaps a fourth in jest.

His son ignored him. His son was good at ignoring him,

and getting better. "Why else do you teach peasants to read and write? If Maeva's good at fighting and wants to do it, why shouldn't she have the chance?"

"You can't get maimed with a pen and a scrap of parchment in your hands, curse it," Van said.

Gerin still hadn't said anything. No matter what he did say, he realized, he was going to make people he cared about unhappy. He hated having to speak in circumstances like that. Too many times, though, he had no choice. This was one of them. Slowly, he said, "Maeva *has* proved what she can do. That she came south with us proves she wanted to do it. Much as I'd like to, I can't see any justice in sending her back."

"Thank you, lord king," Maeva said quietly. Dagref looked as pleased as if he'd invented her. Van looked like a thunderstorm about to spill over. Maeva went on, "Now I peel this fuzz off my face."

"Were I you, I wouldn't," Gerin said. "With the beard, you look like any other northern warrior, near enough. Without it, the imperials will see you're something out of the ordinary and take special care against you. That's the last thing you ever want on the battlefield. I've got rid of a good many foes who didn't think I was dangerous till too late."

"I don't know," Van said. "I want 'em afraid of me." With his tall-plumed helm, his gleamingly polished corselet of solid bronze, and his great size and bulk, he smashed Gerin's principle to smithereens. He had the strength and skill to get away with it, too.

Dagref said, "A lot of the southerners shave their faces. They might not take Maeva for a woman, just for a northerner who does likewise."

"If you'll remember, son," Gerin said with a certain relish, "I didn't say they were liable to take her for a woman. I said they were liable to take her for something out of the ordinary. A man from north of the High Kirs without a beard is out of the ordinary, too."

"Why, so he is," Dagref said. "You're right, Father." He was not least disconcerting because he had no trouble admitting he was wrong.

Gerin rubbed his own chin. He'd shaved his face when

he came back up from the City of Elabon, but harsh, ceaseless teasing had made him—and Rihwin, too—conform in outward appearance, if not in what lay beneath.

"Thank you, lord king," Maeva said again. "I will do everything I can to show myself a worthy warrior for you."

"I shall have words for you presently, young lady," Van said, and stomped off. Somehow, that particular salutation seemed out of place when aimed at someone in a leather shirt with bronze scales sewn into pockets on it.

"You handled that smoothly," Aragis said to Gerin; the Fox supposed he meant it for a compliment. "I wouldn't have decided as you did, but I can see how and why you did it, which I never would have guessed when I spied . . . your new warrior." With a nod to Maeva that might have been ironic or might not, he took himself off, too.

Maeva went back toward the rest of the riders. Gerin expected Dagref to follow her, but the youth stayed. "I want to thank you, Father, for keeping Maeva with the army," he said. "If you'd ordered her back to Fox Keep, I would have used the promise I won from you to make you change your mind."

"Would you?" Gerin said, and his son nodded. Half the Fox—maybe more than half—wished he *had* ordered Maeva back. That would have rid him of the promise at a price he could afford. Now— Who could say what Dagref would come up with now? Gerin eyed his son in a speculative way. "You must think a lot of her, if you'd give up the promise for that."

"She's like a sister to me," Dagref said. Then, a moment later, he turned pink. With characteristic honesty, he corrected himself: "Maybe not quite like a sister." He didn't so much leave as flee. Rubbing his chin once more, Gerin stared after him.

The next morning, Gerin's men and Aragis' moved south after the imperials. The pursuit went slowly. Gerin had expected it would, but it was even slower than he'd looked for. In their withdrawal, the soldiers of the Elabonian Empire had manhandled boulders onto the Elabon Way and scattered caltrops not only on the road but in the fields to either side of it.

"We may have won a battle, Fox, but we haven't won the war," Aragis the Archer said. "They'll be ready to take us on again before long."

"I thought as much from the way they pulled back," Gerin answered. "I said so, to whoever would listen. Nobody much listened. I wish I'd been wrong."

Every so often, he would roll past wreckage of the army he had beaten: a chariot fallen to pieces; a dead horse; a hastily dug grave, brown against the green of the fields, to mark the final resting place of some imperial trooper who'd died slowly instead of quickly. Every time he spotted a grave, he wondered if Maeva had seen it. That probably didn't matter. No one her age believed anything bad could happen to her. The years taught you otherwise, sooner or later—more often sooner.

A rider came trotting back from around a bend in the road. "Lord king!" he shouted, and then, remembering himself, "Lord kings!"

"What have the imperials gone and done now?" Gerin asked.

"Lord king," the scout answered, seeming relieved to be speaking to a single sovereign, "lord king, there's a wall across the road."

Gerin pictured a barricade of rocks and logs, perhaps with a few dismounted archers behind it to give approaching warriors a greeting less friendly than they might have wanted. "Did you ride around it?" he asked. "Do they have an ambush somewhere back of it?"

"Couldn't ride around it, lord king," the horseman said. "It's too wide to ride around." He stretched out his arms as far as they would go.

"What's he talking about?" Aragis demanded irritably.

"I don't know," the Fox admitted. "Best thing I can think for us to do is go have a look for ourselves." He tapped Dagref on the shoulder. "Forward. We'd better find out."

As soon as the chariot rounded the bend, he saw the horseman had been telling the truth. His own visualization had been at fault. The wall was of red brick, about ten feet high, and stretched off to east and west as far as the eye could see. Van said, "The imperials couldn't have built that."

"Of course not," Gerin agreed, "or their soldiers couldn't have, anyway. It's sorcerous, without a doubt."

"Maybe it's an illusion," Van said hopefully. "Maybe if we go up to it, we can go right through it."

It looked very solid. Of course, an illusion that didn't look solid wouldn't have been much of an illusion. Gerin jumped down from the chariot. He walked up to the brick wall and slapped it with the palm of his hand. It felt very solid, too. Suddenly suspicious, he closed his eyes and walked forward. He bumped his nose, not too hard, because he wasn't going too fast.

He opened his eyes. He was staring at bricks, up so close they were blurry. He backed away. The bricks became sharp and clear. They didn't disappear, no matter how hard he wished they would.

More and more of the army came round the bend in the road. Gerin heard the exclamations of surprise that rose from his men and Aragis'. Some were just exclamations of surprise. He could deal with those. He was surprised himself. Others, though, ones that came mostly from his men, were full of confidence that he could get rid of the wall in short order.

Van had his own ideas about how to do that. Saying, "Don't be shy with the cursed thing," he shouted for a hammer. When he got one—a stout bronze-headed tool that looked about as deadly as the mace he carried—he slammed it into the wall with all his strength. Nothing happened, except that he grunted in pain and rubbed at his shoulder. "Didn't even dent it," he said in disgust.

"You wouldn't," Gerin said. "It's magical."

"Really?" Van said, packing enough sarcasm into the word to prove he'd lived a good many years in Fox Keep.

Aragis the Archer said, "This is why I wanted you with me, Fox, not against me."

Gerin glared at him. "Why? So I can look like an idiot in front of your men and mine both?" Aragis' expression was one of stolid incomprehension. He was convinced Gerin was a marvelous mage. Nothing would unconvince him except watching the Fox fail. In that case, he was liable to get unconvinced in a hurry. Hoping to sidestep the issue, Gerin looked around and shouted, "Ferdulf!"

"What do *you* want?" the little demigod demanded. He was back to being surly. Most of the time, Gerin wouldn't have let that bother him. Now he would have been glad for a little of the grudging gratitude Ferdulf had shown right after the battle against the Empire.

Since he didn't have it, he went ahead without: "Can you fly up over the wall and tell us what's on the other side of it?"

"Grass," Ferdulf said. "Trees. Cows. Elabonians. Go far enough and there are mountains. I don't need to fly over it to tell you that."

Gerin exhaled through his nose. *I will not let the little divine bastard get my goat*, he thought. With as much patience as he could, he said, "Knowing exactly where the imperials are might be good for us. We'll probably fight them again once we get past the wall, you know."

"Oh, all right," Ferdulf said sulkily, and hopped up into the air. What happened next made everyone who saw it exclaim in surprise and alarm. As Ferdulf rose, so did the wall in front of him.

He exclaimed, too—angrily. He didn't much care about obeying Gerin. Having the Elabonian Empire thwart him was something else again. But as fast as he flew, as high as he flew, whichever way from side to side he flew, the wall rose to keep him from passing over it. When he flew lower, it shrank, as if it, or the wizard in charge of it, could sense exactly how high he was at any given moment.

When he returned to the ground, the wall went back to being what it had been before he started flying: ten feet high, and very solid-looking. Gerin rubbed his nose. It felt as solid as it looked.

"You ought to knock it down," Ferdulf said. "A wall like that has no business existing in the first place."

"Van didn't have much luck. And if it's magical, I'm not sure we *can* knock it down," Gerin said. "For instance, how thick is it?"

"I don't know," Ferdulf answered. "I think you're pretty thick yourself, though, if you stand here and let it baffle you."

Rihwin the Fox came riding over to Gerin. "Nice piece of work, isn't it?" he said with the tones of one admiring a fellow professional's achievement even when that achievement inconvenienced him. He'd studied sorcery down in the City of Elabon till a jape played on a senior wizard got him expelled from the Sorcerers' Collegium. Despite that expulsion, he'd been a better mage than Gerin up to the moment when Mavrix took away his sorcerous powers. He still knew magic well, even if he couldn't work it any more.

"I'd like it better if it weren't so nice," Gerin said.

"Oh, but it's as pretty a use of the law of similarity as I've ever seen," Rihwin protested, "not only in building the wall, but also in making detection of the keystone—or rather, in this case, the key brick—as difficult as possible."

"What nonsense is he spouting now?" Aragis demanded irritably.

Gerin took no notice of his fellow king. "Father Dyaus," he whispered. "I do believe you're right."

"Of course I'm right," Rihwin said. "When have you ever known me to be mistaken, pray tell?"

"Only when you open your mouth," Gerin replied, which reduced Rihwin to irate splutters. Gerin ignored those, too. He walked up to the wall and examined it brick by brick. Sure enough, each brick was identical to all its neighbors: not just similar to them, but identical. Each one had a chip near the center, each had a scratch at the upper left-hand corner, and each, over to the right, had embedded in it a tiny crystal or flake of mica that sparkled when the light caught it at the right angle. "Isn't that interesting?" he murmured.

"Now you're the one full of drivel," Aragis complained. "Tell me at once what's going on."

"One of their wizards took a brick and sorcerously duplicated it about as many times as there are drops of water in the Niffet," Gerin answered. "If I could find out which brick is the real one, I wouldn't have any trouble—well, not much trouble—making the wall disappear."

"Ah," Aragis said, and then, "All right. I was beginning to wonder whether you were able to talk sense or not. I see you are. Good. As I told you, I wanted you on my side because of the wizardry you know. Now—find that brick and get rid of it."

Rihwin had the grace to give Gerin a sympathetic look. "It's not quite so easy as that, I'm afraid," Gerin said. "One of these bricks along the bottom row is sure to be *the* brick, but which one? Go ahead, lord king—you tell me which one it is."

"You're the wizard," Aragis said. "You're the one who's supposed to know things like that. Now get to work, curse it." He might have been ordering a lazy serf to spread manure over a field.

"I can't tell which brick it is by looking, any more than you can," Gerin said. "That means I've got a couple of thousand to choose from. And that's liable to mean we'll be here for a while."

"Can we go around the bloody thing?" Aragis asked.

"Maybe," Gerin said, "but I wouldn't bet anything I cared to lose on it. My guess is that, if the wall can go up and down to keep Ferdulf from flying over it, it'll go from side to side to keep us from getting by it."

"That makes more sense than I wish it did," Aragis said. "How do you go about finding out which brick is *the* brick, then?"

"You have not put forward an easy question, lord king," Rihwin the Fox said. "The essence of the law of similarity centering on resemblance, distinguishing between prototype and likeness is by its nature a daunting task."

"If it were easy, the cursed imperials wouldn't have bothered running up the wall in the first place," Aragis retorted. He folded his arms across his chest and looked over toward Gerin. "Well?"

"Well, my fellow king, much as I hate to disappoint you—and to disappoint myself, I might add—I haven't the faintest idea which one is *the* brick," Gerin answered. "I told you that once already. Maybe I can figure out some sort of sorcerous test, though the gods only know how long that'll take or whether it'll work. You'd need a god to tell you which one brick out of thousands is the real one and . . ." His voice trailed away. "You'd need a god—or maybe a demigod. How about it, Ferdulf?"

"You want something *more* from me?" Ferdulf said indignantly. His sigh declared that he was put upon far beyond anything his powers might have made acceptable.

"There are times when I wonder why the gods ever bothered creating mortals in the first place."

"Some Sithonian philosophers wonder whether mortals didn't create gods instead of the other way round," Gerin said, which made Ferdulf, despite being descended from a Sithonian deity, give him a horrible look. He wished he'd kept his mouth shut. Since he hadn't, he went on in smoothly ingratiating tones: "Be that as it may, can you use your own great powers to see what we cannot? It would give you another chance to have a go at the Elabonian Empire, and embarrass the imperial wizard who put up the wall thinking it would stop us so easily."

"Oh, all right." Even in agreement, Ferdulf was petulant. In that, he took after his father. He floated up a foot or so into the air and drifted along to the west a couple of hundred yards. "It's this one right here." He didn't raise his voice—or Gerin didn't think he did—but it came as clear as if he'd been standing by the Fox. A helpful soldier ran forward and set his hand on the brick after Ferdulf left it.

Gerin trotted over to it, ignoring the weight of his bronze-and-leather armor. To look at, it was just another brick in the wall. He'd expected nothing different. He turned to Van, who'd followed him. "Will you do the honors?"

"I will, and gladly," the outlander answered. He smashed at the brick with the bronze-headed hammer. When a chip flew from it, chips flew from all the others along the wall. Soldiers cheered. Van hit the brick again and again, till it cracked in three places. The rest of the bricks cracked, too. Van pushed at one of the pieces with his foot. It came away from the rest of the brick—and the wall vanished.

About a hundred feet behind it stood a fellow in a fancy robe who looked absurdly surprised to be staring all at once at the entire army of the northlands. "That's a wizard!" Gerin exclaimed as the man turned to run. "Don't let him get away."

"I'll take care of that," Van growled. He snatched up a piece of the brick he had broken and flung it at the sorcerer. It caught him between the shoulderblades. He went down on his face with a dismayed squawk. Before he could get to his feet again, Dagref and a couple of other men who'd run after him jumped on him and frogmarched him back to Gerin and Aragis.

"Hello," the Fox said mildly. "I gather you're to blame for this latest bit of unpleasantness?" The wizard didn't answer. Gerin clicked his tongue between his teeth in mock dismay. "And I remembered manners south of the High Kirs being so much smoother than they are here in the northlands. Tell us what to call you, anyhow."

"Lengyel." The sorcerer replied to that without hesitation. It was, after all, only his use-name, not his hidden true name.

"Well, Lengyel, suppose you start answering my questions," Gerin said, still sounding mild but looking anything but.

"Well, Lengyel, suppose you start answering questions or we'll see how long you last up on a cross," Aragis added. "You'll have a cursed hard time working magical passes with your hands nailed to the wood." Sounding mild was beyond the Archer, but he did seem more matter-of-fact than menacing. To Gerin, at least, that made him more frightening, not less.

It seemed to have the same effect on Lengyel, who did not look to be in a good position to work passes anyhow, not with Dagref jamming one arm up behind his back and the other held tight against his side. After licking his lips, the wizard said, "Tell me what you want to know."

"You were the fellow who made this wall?" the Fox repeated.

"Yes," Lengyel said, and then spoke in some exasperation: "And I certainly did not expect a pack of semibarbarous backwoods bumpkins to penetrate its secret quickly. I did not expect you to penetrate them at all, in fact."

"You keep a civil tongue in your head if you want to keep any tongue in your head," Aragis said, in about the tone Gerin would have used to tell Blestar to get down off the table.

"Don't worry about it, Archer," Gerin told him. "That's how the Empire thinks of the northlands. It's how the Empire has always thought of the northlands. Since the Empire hasn't had anything to do with us for the past twenty years, you can't expect them to have changed their minds during that time."

"How did—?" Lengyel's face suddenly twisted in pain. "Stop that!" he hissed.

"Then you stop wiggling your fingers," replied Dagref, who had given the wizard's arm a yank. "I don't know what sorcery you were trying, and I don't care to find out, either."

Lengyel bowed his head. For the first time, he seemed to realize the sorcerous wall hadn't come down and he hadn't been caught by a lucky accident. "You northerners are . . . more clever than I'd expected," he said slowly.

"We're clever enough to know we're better off out of the Empire than in it, anyhow," Gerin said. "Of course, you don't have to be very clever to figure out that paying taxes and not getting anything for them—no soldiers when the barbarians come over the border, no grain when the harvest fails—isn't the best bargain in the world."

"You people have paid no taxes the past twenty years, and you didn't pay many before that," Lengyel returned. "Why you deserve to be rewarded for not doing what you should have is beyond me."

"Even when we did pay, back a long time ago, the City of Elabon forgot everything this side of the High Kirs," Gerin said.

"That isn't the point," Aragis said. "The point is, where in the five hells is the imperial army we thrashed? Once we thrash it again, and maybe one more time after that, you southerners will figure out that you ought to leave us alone."

"This is the territory of the Empire of Elabon," Lengyel said. "We shall not abandon what is ours."

"I think you'd be wise to answer King Aragis," Gerin said. "If you don't answer, he's liable to get insistent, and you wouldn't care for that. Believe me, Lengyel—you wouldn't."

Lengyel looked at Aragis. He licked his lips again. Gerin hadn't said what Aragis would do to him if sufficiently displeased. He'd figured Lengyel's imagination would come up with something more horrific than anything he might suggest. If studying Aragis' hard face didn't start a frightened imagination working at a gallop, nothing ever would.

To make matters worse, Aragis smiled. The Fox would not have wanted to be on the receiving end of that smile. By all appearances, Lengyel didn't, either. His larynx worked a couple of times before he said, "The army—my army—will be most of a day's journey south of here, no doubt regrouping to face you reb—uh, you northerners—once more, and this time come away victorious."

"No doubt," Gerin said dryly. "Now—will the other wizards with the army know this wall has fallen, or will we be able to give them a surprise greeting?"

Lengyel licked his lips again. Gerin saw evasion forming in his eyes. Dagref must have sensed the same thing, for he gave the wizard's arm another jerk upwards. "Aii!" Lengyel yelped. "Have a care. You'll break it."

"Answer my father, then," Dagref said pleasantly.

"Yes." Lengyel's voice was sullen. "They will know."

"Too bad," Gerin said. "I'd have like to drop in on them unannounced. But, as Aragis has said, we will beat them, one way or another."

Van pointed at Lengyel. "What are we going to do with him now? Keeping a cursed wizard captive in our midst could mean trouble for us."

"So it could," Gerin said. "I hope it won't, though." He raised his voice: "Ferdulf!"

"What do you want to annoy me with now?" Ferdulf asked, as touchy as he usually was. He drifted through the air toward the Fox—and toward the captured imperial wizard. Lengyel's eyes almost bugged out of his head as he stared at the demigod. Ferdulf went on, "What do you think I'm able to do that you're too stupid to manage for yourself?"

"I want you to keep an eye and an ear and whatever other senses you happen to need on this fellow here." The Fox pointed at Lengyel. "If he tries to make a nuisance of himself with magic, stop him. If you can't stop him, shout for the guards. I expect they'll stop him for good."

"Yes, I'll do that," Ferdulf said, a look of nasty anticipation on his face. "I don't like Elabonian wizards, not even a little. I don't like what they can do, either." He hadn't cared for landing with a thump in the middle of the battle between the imperials and the men of the northlands. He hadn't been able to do anything about it, though, not till Gerin dealt with Caffer by means altogether unsorcerous.

Much as the late, unlamented (certainly by the Fox) Caffer had, Lengyel asked, "What manner of creature is this . . . Ferdulf, is that right?"

Before Gerin could answer, Ferdulf shouted, "I am not a creature, wretch! You are the creature. And a miserable creature you are, too, I'll have you know. I am the son of a god. Kindly grant me the respect due my station."

Lengyel was not in a good position to grant anyone respect, and Dagref and his other captors did not loose their grip on him anyway. The wizard spoke to Gerin: "He won't be enough to hold back the might of the Empire of Elabon. Nothing will be enough to hold back the might of the Empire of Elabon. Do what you will with me for saying so, but it remains true."

"No, it remains your opinion," Gerin answered. "My opinion—and I know the Empire better than you know the northlands, I assure you—is that you have no idea what you're talking about." He nodded to his son. "Take him away."

By the time two more days had passed, Gerin began to wonder how well he'd really known the Elabonian Empire after all. The imperials responded to defeat far more resolutely than he'd expected. They hadn't relied only on their sorcerous wall, but had had scouts and skirmishers out south of it. The skirmishers, when they clashed with Gerin's men, fought hard.

"They wouldn't have acted like this in Hildor's day," Aragis said. "Of course, in Hildor's day they stayed down in Cassat under the mountains and didn't bother with the rest of the northlands at all. This new Emperor of theirs must be a real meat-eater."

"I'm afraid you're right," the Fox said gloomily. Ahead in the distance, the latest party of imperial skirmishers fled back toward their own main force, some of Rihwin's riders and a few chariots offering pursuit. Gerin clicked his tongue between his teeth. "I hope they aren't trying to lure our people into an ambush."

"You don't think they would, do you?" Dagref sounded far more alarmed and far less rational than usual.

Gerin needed only a moment to understand why: Maeva was liable to be among the riders. If he said something about that, he'd only make his son angry at him as well as worried. What he did say was, "Well, it's not beyond the bounds of the possible, you know."

Dagref nodded. "Yes, that's true," he admitted, as much to himself as to the Fox. "I hope they don't, though."

"All right, son. I hope they don't, too," Gerin said. "I do want to remind you, our captains didn't get to be captains because they were so generous and trusting, they'd follow the enemy wherever he went without another thought in their heads."

"Yes, that's also true," Dagref said. "Of course, if all captains were as clever as you make out, no ambush would ever work, and we know that's not so."

Van boomed laughter. "He's got you there, Fox. I never thought I'd see the day when you were outlogicked, but your sprout can do it now and then."

"You're right," Gerin said, and let it go at that. Van evidently hadn't figured out what Dagref had: that his daughter was liable to be riding into danger. Gerin supposed that meant Dagref had outlogicked the outlander, too. Had he been Dagref's age himself, he would have pointed it out. Being the age he was, he kept quiet. Not all the things the years had brought were welcome, but discretion often came in handy.

Before long, the riders and chariots returned. No ambuscade had awaited them, and, for that matter, Maeva was not among them. Dagref had the grace to look sheepish. Some little while later, as the chariot rattled south along the Elabon Way, Van let out several startled oaths.

"What's biting you?" Gerin asked.

"What? Nothing. Never mind." Van shook his head and looked determined not to answer. The Fox decided pushing him right then would probably be a bad idea. The outlander had taken a while to work out what Dagref saw right away, was his guess, and didn't care for it any more than Dagref had.

Nothos, Elleb, and Tiwaz were in the sky when the army camped that night, the first pale moon a thin crescent, swift-moving Tiwaz a much fatter one, almost at first quarter, and ruddy Elleb a couple of days before full. Rihwin said, "I think they'll fight us again soon, tomorrow or the day after. If they wait much longer, we'll be down to Cassat."

"You're likely right," Gerin said. He caught one yawn, then let another one loose. "They won't fight us tonight, though. With the ghosts abroad, traveling by night will be more dangerous to them than we would."

"There you speak sooth, lord king," Rihwin answered. He yawned, too. "I shall have a good night's rest, the better to lay waste the imperials come morning, and the better to forget I was once a man from south of the mountains myself."

"Yes, you had better forget that, hadn't you?" Gerin said pointedly. He yawned again. "Me, I'm going to forget everything but my bedroll."

Morning dawned bright and clear. It also dawned without Lengyel. Both his guards were asleep and remained so despite repeated efforts to shake them awake. "Some drug or other, I judge," Gerin growled, examining the prostrate men with no small annoyance. "Maybe he had it secreted on his person, or maybe he found an herb he could use when he went behind a bush. Either way—" He raised his voice to a shout: "Ferdulf!"

"What *now*?" the demigod demanded, drifting over from some distance away.

"The wizard escaped," the Fox snapped.

"I didn't know anything about it," Ferdulf said. He looked at Lengyel's unconscious guards, too. "He didn't use magic to do it. That's what I was looking for. That's what you told me to look for, if you'll recall."

Gerin exhaled angrily. "I don't care if the whoreson bored them to sleep reading bad poetry. I didn't want him loose."

"That's not what you said," Ferdulf replied with considerable aplomb. "I can't keep track of everything at once, you know. I'm only superhuman."

In the abstract, Gerin admired the line. He had scant time to worry about the abstract. "Since you let him get away—"

"I did no such thing," Ferdulf retorted.

"You were charged with keeping him here," Gerin said.

"I was charged with making sure he did not escape by magic," the demigod said. "I did as I was charged, and he did not escape by magic. If a couple of witless mortals let him up and wander off when he didn't even have to bother with sorcery, that's hardly my problem, now is it?" He folded his skinny arms across his narrow chest and floated off the ground till he was staring the Fox straight in the eye.

The expression on his face ached for a slap. Regretfully, Gerin held off from delivering it. Instead, keeping his voice light, he said, "It depends on how you look at things, I suppose. If you don't mind taking the chance that his magic will do worse things to you than Caffer's did, you may be right."

Ferdulf might have had a god for a father, but he wasn't much better than any other four-year-old at looking ahead to the likely consequences of things he did—and things he didn't do. He was unhappy enough at what Gerin said to let his feet scuff the dirt once more. "All right—what should I do about that?" he asked in tones much less toplofty than he usually used.

"Now that he has escaped, can you use your powers to hunt him down, or to help some troopers hunt him down?" Gerin asked.

"I don't think so." Ferdulf frowned. "Or maybe I can. I could try, anyway." Gerin nodded.

He rose into the air now, till he drifted high above the encampment like a bad-tempered cloud. He twisted his body so that he faced due west, then slowly began bearing ever more to the south. Gerin wondered what sort of sense he was using to feel for the vanished Lengyel. Had it been a sense the Fox possessed, he could have done the search himself.

Up in the sky, Ferdulf suddenly stiffened. He dropped a few feet, as he had a way of doing when he wasn't paying full attention to his flying. Were he wholly divine, no doubt he wouldn't have had to worry about such things. Were he wholly divine, Gerin would have had to worry much more about him.

"There!" he called down to the Fox, pointing southwest. "He's going that way."

That way was the direction in which Gerin was almost certain the bulk of the imperial army lay. "How far away is he?" he shouted up to Ferdulf. "Can you tell?"

"Hard to be sure," Ferdulf answered. "I wasn't sure I could find him at all, you know."

"Yes, yes," Gerin said. "But is it worth my while to send a few men after him, or has he got back safe to the enemy's main camp?"

The little demigod dropped a few feet more. "I can't tell," he said, sounding angry at Gerin, Lengyel, and himself. "I wish I could, but I can't."

"A pestilence," Gerin muttered. "I wish you could, too." He looked around for Aragis. The Archer wasn't far away. "Shall we send men after the wizard?" Gerin asked him. "Were it up to me, I'd say yes, but you're the overall commander. If you want to hold back and let him go, I won't quarrel."

"Are you daft?" Aragis growled. "Of course, send men after him. Bringing him back is worth the risk. Send some of your riders. It's the sort of thing they'd be good for—they're faster than men afoot, and they can go places where chariotry can't. Chase him till he wishes he'd never run away."

"Good enough." As Gerin shouted for Rihwin, he reflected that the best way to fight Aragis was liable to be leading him into a trap, a place where he'd think he had an easy victory, but where in fact more foes waited than he'd expect. For the moment, though, he was an ally.

"How many men would you have me send, lord king?" Rihwin asked. "And shall I take Ferdulf?"

"If he'll go with you, certainly," Gerin answered. "That'll make it harder for Lengyel to turn your troopers into toads." He raised an eyebrow. "You're going to lead this chase yourself?"

"By your leave, I am," Rihwin said. "Since I could not even detect the presence of a woman warrior among my men, I'd fain reassure myself that I am on occasion capable of seeing beyond the end of my nose."

"Fair enough," Gerin told him. "But don't just have your eyes open for Lengyel. Remember, the imperials are liable to be waiting for you somewhere out there, too." He hesitated, then asked, "And how did Maeva seem to you?—as a warrior, I mean."

"Oh, I understood you; you need not fret over that." Rihwin looked chagrined. "Had Aragis not noticed what she was, I doubt I should have done so. This, you must follow, disturbs me for not one but two reasons: first, that she performs in every way so much like a man, and second, that I of all people simply failed to note her femininity."

"And what would you have done if you had?" Gerin asked, and then answered his own question: "If she didn't make you sing soprano for trying to do that, her father would have."

"I do not molest women who find my attentions unwelcome," Rihwin replied with dignity. "Given the number who find those attentions most welcome, I have no need to bother, or bother with, the others." What with the number of bastards he'd fathered over the years, that comment held no small grain of truth. With more dignity still, he went on, "In any event, the charms of a woman—or, I should say, a girl—of that age hold little appeal for me."

"All right, I'm persuaded," Gerin said. "Now go off and—"

But Rihwin, once begun, was not so easily headed. "Maeva may well be attractive to someone with fewer years than myself. Your son, for example, immediately springs to mind."

"Aye, he does, doesn't he?" Gerin said, which seemed to disconcert Rihwin—maybe he'd expected indignant denials. Gerin waved his fellow Fox forward. "Go on, get after that wizard. Don't stand around gabbing all day."

Rihwin and a squadron of his riders went trotting south a few minutes later. Ferdulf went along with them. Gerin wouldn't have wanted to be an imperial mage the little demigod flushed out of hiding. On the other hand, he wouldn't have wanted to be Rihwin using Ferdulf as a hunting hound, either. Most hunting hounds had the sovereign virtue of not talking back.

Rihwin and his men had been gone only moments when someone spoke to Gerin in a reedy tenor: "Lord king?"

He turned and found himself facing a fuzzy-bearded youth. He needed a heartbeat to remember the beard was false and the tenor in fact a contralto. "What is it, Maeva?" he asked cautiously.

"When you sent the riders out just now," Van's daughter asked, "did you tell Rihwin not to put me in that squadron?"

"No," Gerin answered. "Maybe I would have if it had occurred to me, but it didn't. I didn't tell him anything one way or the other. Did he say I did?"

"No, he didn't say that," Maeva said. "But when he didn't choose me, I wondered. Can you blame me?"

"I suppose not," the Fox admitted. "If you're going to do this, though, there's something I want you to think about, all right?"

"What?" Either in her own proper person or disguised as a man, Maeva was no one to trifle with.

"This," Gerin said: "Just because you *can be* chosen to do this, that, or the other thing doesn't mean you *will be* chosen all the time or that you *have to be* chosen. It may just mean you *weren't* chosen this one time, and you *may be* the next."

Maeva considered that with almost the grave intensity Dagref might have shown. At last, she said, "All right, lord king, that's fair enough, as far as it goes. But if I'm *never* chosen for anything dangerous, then it doesn't go far enough. If that happens, I'll get angry." Her eyes blazed, as if to warn that getting her angry was not a good idea.

Being acquainted with her parents, Gerin could have—indeed, had—figured that out for himself. He considered her words in turn. "You're with the army, Maeva. You're fighting. If you think none of the imperials could have killed you in the last battle, maybe I should send you home after all."

She tossed her head, a feminine gesture odd when combined with the false beard stuck to her chin and cheeks. "Nobody knew—well, nobody but Dagref knew—who I was, what I was. I was just another trooper. It's not going to be like that any more. It can't be like that any more. I wish it could."

"I'm not going to send you back, no matter how much your father wishes I would," Gerin said. "That means you're going forward. You'll get more fighting, believe me you will." He paused. "What will your mother think when you come home?" Fand was formidable, but not in the same way Maeva was.

"My mother? You heard me tell my father I didn't worry about that much, but . . ." Maeva thought it over. "My mother would probably say I didn't need to put on armor and carry a bow if I wanted to fight with men."

Gerin laughed. "Yes, that probably is what she'd say." He wondered whether Maeva knew he and Fand had been lovers for a while, in the dark time between Elise's leaving him and his meeting Selatre. If she did, he wondered what she thought. He saw no way to ask. He didn't really want to find out. Some curiosity was better left unsatisfied.

He let out a small snort. Rihwin would surely disagree with him there. But then, Rihwin didn't believe in holding back on anything.

"What's funny now, lord king?" Maeva asked.

"Sometimes the things you don't do are as important as the things you do," he answered. Maeva cocked her head to one side, no doubt wondering how that could possibly be amusing. Would Dagref have understood? Maybe. Maybe not, too. The Fox couldn't think of anyone else so young who might have.

When Gerin didn't seem inclined to explain further, Maeva went off scratching her head. He was unoffended. He'd sent his vassals off bemused more times than he could count. Most of those times had worked out all right. That gave him reason to hope this one would, too.

He peered south and kicked at the dirt. He also hoped Rihwin's chase after Lengyel would work out all right, but he had no particular reason to believe it would. Rihwin could perform far better than anyone who knew him only slightly might imagine. He could also perform far worse. Until he did whatever he did on any given day, no one could guess what that would be.

Trees blocked Gerin's view; he couldn't see as far as he would have liked. He couldn't see Ferdulf in the air any more, either. What was happening, out there where he couldn't see? How foolish had it been to let Rihwin and Ferdulf, each erratic by himself, go off together? How sorry would he be when he found out how foolish he'd been?

Was that a bird in the sky, down there to the south? No—no bird had ever flown with such a smooth, effortless motion. That was Ferdulf. (And what did the birds think of the little demigod who invaded their domain? Gerin would have bet they found him as annoying as everyone else did.) He was coming this way. And, out from behind those trees, here came horsemen.

They had people on foot with them. Gerin took that for a good sign. Also promising was the way Ferdulf kept flying down and darting into the faces of the men on foot, as if they were chariot horses of the soldiery of the Elabonian Empire. The Fox wondered if Ferdulf was doing anything disgusting to them from on high. That didn't seem the best way to treat . . . prisoners, he supposed they were.

Gerin trotted toward the returning horsemen. So did Aragis. So did a good many ordinary soldiers. A lot of people were still curious to learn what the riders could do.

A horseman detached himself from the rest and approached the Fox at a rapid trot. After a moment, Gerin saw it was Rihwin. "We have him!" Rihwin shouted as soon as he was close enough for his voice to carry.

The soldiers cheered. Gerin clapped his hands together. Aragis looked astonished, and didn't bother hiding it. Gerin called, "Who are all the others you have there?"

"A round dozen of the fanciest whores off the streets of the City of Elabon," Rihwin answered. Gerin blinked. The soldiers burst into louder cheers. Rihwin waved them down. "Would it were so, but alas, it isn't. They're imperial troopers at whose forward camp Lengyel was staying. They offered no resistance, for we not only outnumbered them two to one but also came on them by surprise, thanks going almost entirely to the aid Ferdulf furnished."

"You probably wouldn't have been able to do it in chariots, would you?" Gerin asked, and Rihwin shook his head.

Aragis said, "I never denied horsemen had their uses, Fox. I even said this was one of them. Don't twit me here." He didn't sound so angry as he might have; he couldn't have expected Rihwin to succeed as fully as he had.

Here came Lengyel, looking even more dejected than he had when the men of the northlands captured him the first time. "Hello again," Gerin greeted him. "Aren't you glad we're barbarians and don't know what we're doing?"

"Delighted, I'm sure," Lengyel said sourly, which made Gerin respect him for the first time as a man rather than simply as a dangerous sorcerer.

Rihwin said, "And, lord king—lord kings—we have booty that may prove as valuable and delightful as our victory itself has been." He pointed to the mounts of some of his riders; the animals had skins tied on behind the horsemen. Grinning, he went on, "Here we find precious treasure scarcely seen in the northlands for a generation of men."

"Rihwin, you didn't—" Gerin began.

"Oh, but lord king, my fellow Fox, I did," Rihwin broke in. "Did you think that, after so long, I could resist the allure of so much splendid, glorious, magnificent wine?"

VI

"You idiot," Gerin said to Rihwin. "You clodpoll. You jackanapes. You bungler. You cretin. You jobbernowl. You madman. You fool. You loon. You twit. You lout. "You—"

"Thank you, lord king; I have by now some notion of your opinion, so you need not elaborate further," Rihwin said.

"Oh, but I was just warming up," Gerin said. "I hadn't even begun to discuss your ancestry, if any, your habits, and how lovingly the demons of the five hells will roast you after you die—which may be far sooner than you think, for I'm bloody tempted to murder you myself."

"Be reasonable, my fellow Fox," Rihwin said, a request to which Gerin might usually be expected to respond well. "Could you imagine I would pour the blood of the sweet grape out onto the uncaring ground rather than bringing it home in triumph?"

"And what about the lord of the sweet grape, Rihwin?" Gerin shouted, too furious for reason to hold any appeal. "What about Mavrix? Do you want to deal with Mavrix? Do you want Mavrix to deal with you? What happens when Mavrix and Ferdulf make each other's acquaintance? How far away would you like to be when that happens? Can you get to a place so far away?"

"I don't know," Rihwin said, an answer more inclusive than specific.

"Why didn't you bother thinking about any of those things ahead of time?" Gerin demanded, though he knew the answer only too well: at the sight of wine, anything resembling thought had fled from Rihwin's head.

Rihwin said, "Lord king, imagine if you'd been without a woman for most of the last twenty years and then found not one but half a dozen beautiful maids, all of them not only willing but eager. Would you leave them behind? Would you spill *their* blood out on the ground instead of enjoying them?"

"It's not the same, and don't you try to distract me," Gerin said. "You haven't exactly been pining away; you've made do quite well with ale."

"A man who wants women can, without them, make do with boys," Rihwin replied. "He can even, if his temper runs that way, make do with sheep. Making do, though, will not stop him from wanting women."

"I ought to spill this wine right now," Gerin grated.

He'd meant that to alarm Rihwin. Instead, it made the transplanted southerner brighten. "You mean you *shan't* spill it out?"

"Not right now," Gerin answered reluctantly. "Not till I think it through, which is a cursed lot more than you ever bothered doing."

"Blessings upon you, lord king!" Rihwin cried in fervent tones. He seized Gerin's hand, which alarmed his overlord. Then he kissed it, which alarmed Gerin even more. "Have no fear," Rihwin said, his eyes sparkling with amusement. "I am not one of those who, wanting boys, make do with women, of that you may rest assured." He changed notes yet again: "Er, lord king—*why* aren't you going to spill the wine out on the ground?"

Gerin let out a weary sigh. "Because I've seen, more often than it suits me—much more often than it suits me—that you and wine and the will of the gods are somehow all tied together. The only reason I can think of to make it so is that your head is altogether empty inside, which means they have no trouble filling it with their desires."

"I loved the blood of the sweet grape long before I made Mavrix's acquaintance," Rihwin said. "I should have been as glad not to make that acquaintance, and I should have gone on loving wine had I not made it."

"All of that is no doubt true," Gerin replied. "None of it has anything to do with how many pits of wheat are buried around the village by Fox Keep, and none of it, I fear, has anything to do with why you found that wine and why you decided to bring it back here to our camp."

"This may be so, lord king," Rihwin said. "Let us assume it is so. If it be so, if I act at the will of the gods rather than pursuant to my own will, how is it you are furious with me, when I was but the empty-headed conduit through which they manifested their will?"

"Because—" Gerin stood there with his mouth hanging open, realizing he had no good answer. At last, he said, "Because you're handy, curse it," adding a moment later, "and because you'd have brought back that wine even without a god whispering in your ear, and you bloody well know it."

"Such a claim is all the better for proof," Rihwin said loftily. "If you do not purpose spilling the wine, what will you do with it?"

"Set a guard over it so you can't guzzle it," Gerin replied at once, and watched Rihwin's face fall. "And so no one else can, either," he said for good measure, but that did little to cheer his fellow Fox.

"You take all the fun out of life," Rihwin complained.

"I hope so," Gerin said, which made Rihwin angrier yet.

The wine stayed under guard. Rihwin kept right on grumbling. He wasn't the only one, either. Most of those grumbles, Gerin simply ignored. He couldn't ignore the ones from Aragis the Archer.

"Well, go ahead, my fellow king," the Fox said. "If you want to see what will happen, go ahead. If you want to meet Mavrix face to face, go ahead. You're a king. You can do as you please—till a god tells you otherwise, anyhow."

"Suppose I drink it and nothing happens?" Aragis demanded.

"Then you get to call me a fool," Gerin said. "Suppose

you drink it and something happens? Will there be enough left of you for me to call a fool?"

Aragis muttered something into his beard that Gerin didn't catch. The Archer stomped off, making a point of kicking at the grass at every stride. He did not drink any wine. Gerin thought about teasing him, then thought better of it.

And then he got a request for wine from someone else, in a fashion he had not expected. Ferdulf came up to him in as nearly a polite way as he'd ever seen from the demigod. "May I please have a taste of the blood of the grape?" he asked.

Gerin stared. As far as he could remember, he'd never heard *please* from Ferdulf before. Not least because of that, he didn't say *no* right away. Instead, he asked, "Why do you want it?"

"Why do you think?" Ferdulf replied, with some—but not all—of his usual irritating sense of superiority. Gerin had an answer, or thought he did, but didn't speak it. He waited. The arrogance leaked out of the demigod. In a voice much smaller than Ferdulf usually used, he said, "If I drink wine, perhaps it will bring my father thither."

That was the possibility that had occurred to the Fox, too. It was not one that much appealed to him, whatever Ferdulf thought of it. "If your father does come," he asked cautiously, "what would you do?"

Ferdulf looked confused and unhappy, as opposed to malicious and intent on making everyone around him unhappy, his more usual aspect. "I don't know," he answered, something else he hardly ever said. "I think I'd like to ask him why he brought me into the world and what he intends of me, though—that for a beginning, and who can say from there?"

Why did he start you? Gerin thought. *As best I can tell, for no better reason than to annoy me.* Mavrix had certainly succeeded there. Aloud, the Fox said, "Why are you asking leave of me? You have the strength to overcome the guards I've set—I'm sure of it."

"Oh, yes," Ferdulf said carelessly. "But I know it might cause trouble, so I thought I had better ask before I do anything."

That didn't sound like Ferdulf, either. If nothing else in the world intimidated him, Mavrix did. Gerin said, "I don't really think the time is ripe now. Tell me the truth: do you?"

The little demigod sagged. "Maybe not," he said, and walked off with his feet on the ground, his head down. Then, suddenly, he turned back, hopping half his height into the air as he did so. "If my father were to be summoned, though, would he not take our side against the Empire of Elabon, which has inflicted such indignities on Sithonia over the centuries?"

"He might," the Fox admitted, and let it go at that: adding more would have reminded Ferdulf that the men of the northlands were as much Elabonians as the imperials. He went on in a different vein, saying, "Remember what the imperial wizard told us, though—the Empire of Elabon has ruled Sithonia for all those years, and the Sithonian gods haven't been able to do anything about it except slander the imperials. That being so, how much good will Mavrix do us?"

Ferdulf descended to the ground once more. He didn't answer, but went off in the direction he'd chosen before his afterthought. Gerin concluded he didn't think Mavrix would do much good. Seeing a humble Ferdulf was as novel an experience as any the Fox had had lately.

He looked in the direction of the wineskins and the guards around them. They'd drawn a fair-sized crowd. At first, that alarmed him. Then he relaxed a little. If a lot of people were hanging about the wine, that would make it harder for any one man—Rihwin's smiling face popped into his mind—to sneak away with any of the blood of the grape.

While the Fox was thinking thus, Van came up to him and said, "By all the gods, Captain, it's been a long time since I slugged down any wine. If I could just undo the tie on one of those skins, now— Wait, Fox! What in the five hells do you think you're doing, looking at me like that? Curse it, Fox, put your sword back in its sheath. Have you gone mad?"

"No, it's the whole world around me," Gerin answered. Van examined him closely for signs he was joking. By the way the outlander walked off shaking his head, he didn't find any.

The next morning, the army of the northlands rolled through another of those villages that had trembled on the edge of being towns and were now falling back unmistakably into the lesser status. Gerin had no time to do anything but mournfully note as much, for, a couple of bowshots south of the village, imperial scouts riding chariots with fast horses began pelting his men and Aragis' with arrows.

"Ha!" Aragis exclaimed. "They aren't as smart as they think they are." Without waiting for Gerin's advice, he shouted, "Rihwin! Forward the riders!"

"Aye, lord king," Rihwin said, and shouted orders of his own.

Out rode the horsemen. Gerin looked to see if he could spot Maeva among them, but had no luck. By the way Dagref's head followed the evolutions of the riders, he was looking for Maeva, too.

With roughly equal numbers, the horsemen routed the charioteers, as they had at the first big battle between the imperials and men of the northlands. The riders were faster and more maneuverable than their foes. They shot no worse than the men in the chariots. Before long, those chariots streamed back toward the southwest in headlong retreat.

"I think we ought to form line of battle," Gerin told Aragis. "We're liable to run into the whole imperial army any time now."

Aragis frowned. "If we don't run into the imperials, moving forward that way will slow us down." After a bit of thought, though, he nodded. "Let it be as you say. If we do run into them before we're ready, they'll make us sorry for it." As he had before the earlier battle with the forces of the Elabonian Empire, he halted the army and shouted, "Left and right! Form line of battle! Left and right!"

As they had then, his men and Gerin's cheered. That still left the Fox bemused, though he supposed he should have been used to it. Why didn't they think forming line of battle meant they were about to get maimed or die painful, lingering deaths? If they thought like that, and if their opponents fought the same way, nobody would fight wars. And then . . .

And then—what? Then they would not die painful, lingering deaths in battle, which was not, as Gerin's logical mind noted, the same as saying they would not die painful, lingering deaths. Fever might take them from life raving, or they might die of a wasting sickness that ate them from the inside out, or they might fall over from a fit of apoplexy and linger, perhaps for years, unable to speak and with half their bodies dead in life.

When you got down to it, there weren't any good way ways to die, only bad ones and worse ones. When measured with that ruler, perhaps dying on the battlefield looked less appalling.

Gerin looked up to Ferdulf, who floated over the army light as thistledown. Demigods, unlike the divine half of their parentage, weren't immortal. They commonly outlived ordinary mortals, and they commonly died in ways ordinary mortals might envy, such as dropping off to sleep and never waking up. The Fox wondered if the chance of dying was in Ferdulf's thoughts now. He doubted it; no ordinary four-year-old gave such things a thought.

Then Aragis shouted, "Riders to the right and left. We'll hit the imperials on both flanks this time, and see if we can't cave 'em in."

The horsemen who hadn't joined Rihwin in his assault on the imperials cheered as they rode to take the positions to which Aragis had ordered them. Gerin felt like cheering, too. To his fellow king, he said, "You're learning."

Aragis gave him a wintry look before answering, "The first time your father set a sword in your hand, did you know straightaway everything you could do with it? Now you have given me a new weapon, and I am beginning to discover what it may be good for."

"Fair enough," Gerin said. "Better than fair enough, in fact. A great many people, when they come across something new, will either pretend it isn't there or try to use it as if it were old and familiar, regardless of whether it's really anything like the old and familiar."

"A lot of people are fools." Cold contempt filled the Archer's voice. "Tell me you've not seen that in your years as baron and prince and king and I'll call you a liar to your face."

"I can't do it," Gerin answered. "The difference between us, I think, is that you scorn men for being fools and I find them funny—at least, I do my best to find them funny. The gods know it's not always easy."

"Easy?" Aragis snorted. "It's not worth doing, you ask me." Gerin hadn't expected him to say anything different. The Archer's arrogance had taken him a long way: as long a way as it could have taken him, unless he overthrew Gerin and ruled as king of the whole of the northlands, or unless he crossed over the mountains and cast Crebbig I down from his throne.

"We're all different," Gerin observed with profound unoriginality.

"So we are," Aragis said. "Sometimes I think you're light-minded as a Trokmê. Then I look at what you do, not what you say, and I think you're hiding behind a mask. All these years, and I still haven't figured out what to make of you." He sent the Fox an accusing stare.

"Good." Gerin let it go at that. Keeping Aragis off balance had probably gone a long way toward keeping the two of them from fighting a war.

Before they could take it any further, Ferdulf whizzed down toward them, pointing southwest and shouting, "If that's not the imperial army beyond the next rise, it's a herd of elephants." A moment later, mounted scouts came back with the same news.

Aragis, for once, looked at Ferdulf with approval unalloyed. "He gave us the news faster than the riders did." He took on a thoughtful expression. "Warfare would be a different business if both sides had people up in the air spying on the foe. I wonder if you could fight at all if the other bastard knew what you were going to do as you did it."

"You could, unless I miss my guess," Gerin answered. "You'd just have to make it look as if you were going to do one thing while you really intended to do something else."

Aragis studied him now for some time without saying anything. When he finally spoke, it was in tones of reluctant admiration: "Aye, and belike you'd find some way to do just that, too. You *are* a sneaky demon, no mistake."

He shouted and waved to his troopers and the Fox's, who weren't forming their battle line fast enough to suit him. In the car with Gerin, Dagref said, "How could the Archer not have seen that subterfuge would be necessary if each side could observe the other's preparations for combat?"

"Because he doesn't think as fast as you do," Gerin said, "and he doesn't like to play with hypotheticals in his mind. I'll tell you this, though, son: if he really did have to worry about people spying on him from the air, his dispositions would be the lyingest ones you ever saw."

"That's a fact," Van agreed. "If it's real, Aragis is good with it. If it's not real, he doesn't worry about it."

"Foolishness," Dagref said with a sniff, flicking the reins to bring the horses up to a trot. "The hypothetical has a way of becoming real without warning. Before it happened, who would have thought the Elabonian Empire would come roaring back over the High Kirs to trouble us?"

"I didn't think that would happen myself," Gerin said, "and I'd be just as glad if it hadn't happened, too, believe me." The Elabon Way swung wide, and he got his first glimpse of the imperial army. "But they're here, and we're going to have to deal with them."

Van said, "By the gods, we've taught them something like respect. They aren't swarming toward us the way they did in the first fight. Then they thought they could ride right over us and make us run. They know better now, the stinking whoresons."

"Yes," Gerin said, not altogether contented with the change in the imperials' tactics. He wanted his enemies to go right on being stupid. It made them much easier to deal with. He also glanced over at the outlander. "And look who's talking about the Elabonian Empire as if he'd been born in the northlands and spent his whole life listening to people running it into the ground."

"Go howl," Van said with dignity. "It's a fight, and I'm on *this* side, so of course the imperials are a pack of bastards. If I were over on *that* side, everybody from the northlands would be a filthy rebel. There. Doesn't that make sense?"

"More than I like," Gerin answered. He watched Rihwin's horsemen swing wide to right and left to take the imperial army in the flank. The imperials didn't send squadrons of chariotry out against them to try to hold them up. They'd learned better than that, too. What they hadn't learned, the Fox saw with rising glee, was that, if they didn't stop the riders, they were going to get both wings of their army smashed up in a hurry.

Dagref saw the same thing at the same time. "What do they think they're doing?" he demanded, like a schoolmaster faced with unprepared pupils.

"They're trying to throw the fight away," Van said. "I'll let 'em. Anybody thinks I'll complain if they make my work easy is plumb daft."

He started to elaborate—Gerin knew it was a theme on which he would be able to elaborate for a good long while—but then grunted in surprise and shut up. Some of the horses had gone down just as they were nearing bow range of the imperials' flanks.

"Is that magic, Father?" Dagref asked.

"Do you know, I don't think so," the Fox replied. "If I had to guess, I'd say the imperials have strewn some caltrops around to either side of their position to help ward their flanks. They work against chariot horses, so I don't suppose there's anything that would keep them from working against horses with men on top of 'em."

Some of Rihwin's riders did get through, and started plying the men of the Elabonian Empire with arrows. But some hung back, and even those who didn't had to ride more slowly. They were an annoyance, then, not a devastation, as they might have been.

Seeing as much, the imperials cheered. Horns blared along their line. Now they rolled forward: they would not receive the attack of the chariots from the northlands while standing still themselves.

Men on both sides shouted, Gerin and Aragis' troopers as individuals, the imperials in the fierce unison that had seemed so effective in the first battle. Arrows flew.

As always, the first few fell short. But the range between the two armies closed rapidly. Men began to cry out; horses began to scream. Here and there, chariots overturned, spilling soldiers onto the ground.

"Any place in particular, Father?" Dagref asked as Gerin, arrow set to bowstring, looked around for his first target. "The other king doesn't seem to take much care in the way he arranges things, does he?"

That held an unmistakable sniff. Before Gerin could reply, Van laughed and said, "Being the son of your father has spoiled you, lad. Aragis had given us a decent field and a good chance to win if we fight hard, and I've seen plenty of captains who lived to grow old and fat even though they were in the habit of handing their men a lot less."

Dagref sniffed again. He had high standards, and was too young to have realized the trouble most mortals had meeting such standards. Pointedly, he said, "You still haven't answered me, Father."

"Steer for anybody who looks to have fancy armor or a fine team of horses," the Fox said. "Most men of high rank enjoy showing off."

"Honh!" Van said. His cast-bronze corselet and plumed helm were without a doubt the most distinctive gear on the field.

"You heard me." Gerin's armor was not gilded, nor even polished; the leather that secured the bronze plates in place was scuffed and patched. But all the leather and all the plates were sound. The horses Dagref drove were undersized and rough-coated, but they had more endurance than most. They were descended from a pony off the plains of Shanda for which Van had traded while accompanying Gerin and Elise down to the City of Elabon more than twenty years before. That horse had been even smaller and uglier, but it was tougher than any other Gerin ever knew.

Obediently, Dagref pointed the team at an imperial whose armor was bright with gold paint and who wore a crimson cloak that fluttered behind him. Gerin let fly. The officer of the Elabonian Empire threw both hands in the air and tumbled out the back of the chariot.

"Well shot!" Van shouted. Though refusing to use the

bow in battle, he would not hold back praise from others who used it well.

Dagref guided the horses toward another imperial who looked more splendid than his fellows. Gerin shot at the foe—and missed. However good a shot he was, however much practice he had shooting from the pitching platform of a chariot, he missed more often than he hit. Disappointed but not devastated, he reached over his shoulder for another shaft.

Thunk! An arrow smote the leftward horse of the team, just back of the animal's left foreleg. The horse went down as if clubbed; the arrow must have pierced its heart. Its fall fouled the other horse. The chariot tipped, jounced along on one wheel for a couple of frantic heartbeats, and then overturned, spilling onto the ground all three men in the car.

Gerin heard himself shouting as he flew through the air. He'd gone out of chariots before. He tried to tuck himself into a ball, to land as softly as he could. Even so, the soft ground slammed against him as if it were granite. His helmet spun off his head and bounced away. Pain shot through his right side, which took most of the impact. But, when he tried to scramble to his feet, he discovered he could. Nothing broken, then. That was something—or would be, if he could stay alive long enough to appreciate how lucky he was.

He was, he discovered, still holding his bow. No—he was still holding a piece of his bow. Unlike him, it had broken when it hit the ground. He threw down the chunk in his hand and yanked out his sword. Then he looked around to see how Van and Dagref were. Both of them were on their feet, too, and seemed sound, so for the moment they, like he, were lucky.

How long their luck—and his—would last remained problematical. *Not very long* seemed the likeliest guess. The chariots of the Elabonian Empire were very close now, and getting closer every heartbeat. One of them thundered straight toward Dagref, who, being slim and beardless and without sword or spear, looked to be the easiest target of the three downed warriors.

Gerin ran—slowly, favoring his right leg—to his son's

aid. Dagref proved not to need any aid. With him, as with the Fox, looks turned out to deceive. Though he had no sword or spear, he'd held on to the whip he used to urge on his team (a replacement for the one Caffer had turned into a snake). He waited till the Elabonian chariot was terrifyingly close, then lashed out with the whip, striking one of the horses on its soft, tender nose.

The animal screamed in shock and pain. It stopped dead and tried to rear. The driver kept it from doing that, but the chariot thundered past Dagref instead of riding him down. And, as it went past, the whip lashed out again. The driver screamed as loud as the horse had. He clutched at his eyes. The other two imperials in the car clutched at the reins he'd dropped.

Neither one of them could make a clean grab. That was unfortunate for them, because they got only the one chance. Dagref cracked the whip again. One of them shrieked. He shrieked again a moment later when Van speared him in the side—shrieked and crumpled. Gerin scrambled up into the chariot. The surviving unwounded imperial was an archer who carried only a dagger for self-defense. He didn't stay unwounded long. He scrambled over the rail of the car and ran off howling and dripping blood.

Killing the driver seemed unfair, since he still had both hands clapped to his face. In the middle of a battle, though, *fair* was a flexible notion. Gerin thrust home hard, threw the driver's thrashing body over the side, and seized the reins. He started to shout for Van and Dagref, but they were already up in the car with him.

With a flourish, he handed his son the reins. "I think you know what to do with these," he said.

"He knows what to do with all sorts of things," Van said, an enormous grin on his face. "Don't you, Dagref the Whip?"

"Who, me?" Dagref looked absurdly pleased with himself. A man could get an ekename any number of ways. If he was very fair or very fat, he might have one before he could toddle. Or he might be called his father's son his whole life long. Earning an ekename on the battlefield didn't happen to everyone. It didn't happen to many, in fact.

"Dagref the Whip," Gerin agreed. "Better than Dagref the Surly, or Dagref the Brown Study, or—"

"Since the whip is still in my hand," Dagref remarked pointedly, "a prudent man would save such suggestions for another time."

"A prudent man wouldn't have done a lot of the things I've done over the years," Gerin said.

"You're the most prudent man I know, Fox," Van said.

"That may be true, but it doesn't say much for the rest of the people you know," Gerin retorted. Fand immediately came to mind, but the Fox was prudent enough not to mention her. Instead, he said, "How prudent is it, for that matter, to ride around in a chariot when none of us has a bow?"

"You should have grabbed the one that imperial had before you pitched him out of the car," Van said.

"Aye, that would have been prudent," Gerin agreed, "if only I'd thought of it at the time. Can't think of everything at once, though, no matter how much I wish I could."

Van said, "Well, since we haven't got one, we'll have to pretend we're some of Rihwin's riders, and see how close we can get to the imperials. I've always liked that kind of fighting better, anyhow."

"Why am I not surprised?" Gerin murmured. Being so big and so strong, the outlander naturally excelled at close-quarters fighting. A man with a bow, though, might hurt him before he had the chance to do damage of his own.

Dagref took the discussion between his father and his father's friend as an instruction for him, and guided the chariot toward the nearest one full of imperials. The men of the Elabonian Empire, seeing a car that looked like their own, took a fatal moment too long to realize the warriors inside were foes. Van speared one of them, Dagref kept using the whip to wicked effect, and, by the time the brief fight was done, Gerin once more had a bow to call his own.

He reached over his shoulder to snatch an arrow out of his quiver. An imperial screamed like a longtooth a moment later, and clutched at the side of his thigh. The Fox shot another arrow. This one missed. He reached back yet again—and found the quiver empty.

He scowled. The quiver had been nearly full before he spilled out of the chariot. Before he . . . He growled a curse. Most of the arrows must have gone flying from the quiver when he hit the ground. He hadn't even noticed. He'd had rather more urgent things on his mind, such as staying in one piece.

"Come on, Fox," Van said. "Why aren't you shooting at the whoresons?"

"I'll tell you what," Gerin answered. "As soon as you figure out how to spear them without any spear, I'll shoot them without any arrows."

"What?" The outlander stared. Then his face cleared. "Oh. Aye. We did go arse over soup-pot there, didn't we? Well, all right, we'll have to keep on doing the way we did just now, won't we?"

"Sooner or later, everyone will start running out of arrows," Dagref said.

"Oh, indeed." Gerin nodded. "The next interesting question is whether people will run out of arrows before one gets stuck in one of us. That's an interesting question in any fight."

"Interesting. Oh, aye. Heh." Van snorted, then spat. In a way, that was disgust. In another way, it was bravado. Not many warriors on the field, Gerin would have guessed, had enough saliva in their mouths to spit. He was a long way from sure he did himself. He worked his cheeks experimentally.

Then he stopped worrying about whether he could spit. There ahead, sure as sure, was a gap in the imperials' line, where chariots had swung right and left around one that had overturned, and then hadn't closed up again. He looked around. Not far from him—how they'd got there, he hadn't noticed—were a good many chariots full of Trokmoi. He waved to them. A couple of the woodsrunners aimed arrows at him. They lowered them when he shouted in their own language: "Through there, now"—he pointed—"and we'll be after carving a great chunk from the southron spalpeens."

"Do you want me to go through that gap and hope the barbarians will follow?" Dagref asked. By his tone, he'd heard ideas he liked much better.

But Gerin said, "That's just what I want you to do."

"Be a mite embarrassing if the Trokmoi decide they'd sooner be rid of you than of the cursed imperials," Van remarked. What he meant was, *If that happens, we're going to get killed.* Gerin couldn't recall the last time he'd heard such a protest so elegantly phrased.

He stopped worrying about that, too. "Go on," he told Dagref. "Quick, now, before they close up the hole."

"All right." His son urged the horses forward. The Fox shouted when the chariot did force its way between two manned by soldiers of the Elabonian Empire. The imperials hesitated before trying to block his path: as had happened once already, they thought anyone in a chariot from south of the High Kirs was bound to be a comrade.

As had happened once already, they discovered they were mistaken. Gerin laid open the face of one of the imperial troopers on his left, a cut that took the enemy doubly by surprise because he delivered it with his left hand. On the other side of the car, Van speared an imperial archer out of a chariot. The fellow looked comically surprised, or would have had he not also been in agony.

"Well, I think that's drawn their notice," Dagref said.

"I bloody well knew it would draw their notice," Gerin answered as an arrow hissed past his ear. "What I want to know is, has it drawn the woodsrunners in after us? If it hasn't . . ." He let that hang. If it hadn't, Van was right—they would get killed.

He looked back over his shoulder . . . and whooped with glee. The Trokmoi *were* behind him, and more of them than he'd expected. Often, what looked suicidally stupid to an Elabonian looked like fun to a Trokmê. Gerin was heartily glad of that, not least because it meant the imperials wouldn't be concentrating on him alone. They'd have other things on their minds, such as stopping the penetration before it split their whole army in two. Sometimes distraction was better than victory. Sometimes they were one and the same.

Chariots were at close quarters now, everyone hacking and stabbing and shooting at everyone else. The men of the Elabonian Empire seemed to feel a slight superstitious awe of the Trokmoi, who must have been much discussed but never seen during the years when the Empire stayed south of the High Kirs. Superstitious awe, however, had a way of lasting no longer than the first successfully blocked blow. After that, it was just man against man.

For their part, the Trokmoi went after the imperials with almost unholy glee. The woodsrunners had no more use for Elabonians than Elabonians had for them. But, by now, they'd dwelt south of the Niffet for a generation. To them, Gerin's men were only partly hated southrons. They were also neighbors, sometimes friends, sometimes even in-laws.

None of those palliatives applied to the warriors from south of the mountains. They were the enemy, pure and simple. The Trokmoi laid into them with an appalling lack of concern for what might happen to themselves, so long as they could get in a few more licks at the foe.

Because the woodsrunners were so fierce, the imperials needed a disproportionate number of men to hold them in check. And, because they were making a move that would be important if it succeeded, the imperials threw those men at them. That didn't help their position along the rest of the line, which was what Gerin had had in mind.

"There!" As he had before, he aimed Dagref toward a gap between a couple of imperial chariots. "If we get through there and bring a few Trokmoi after us, we really have cut the whoresons in two."

"Aye, Father." Dagref urged the horses forward. Wild whoops proclaimed that the Trokmoi were still following the Fox.

The imperials he faced knew they were holding an important part of the line. They could hardly help knowing it, with so many foes bearing down on them. One of them let fly with an arrow. Behind Gerin, a Trokmê shrieked. The Fox had a perfect shot at the imperial—or would have had one, with any arrows in his quiver.

And then the imperial cried out and clutched at his flank, from which a shaft sprouted. To have hit him at that angle, it couldn't have come from straight ahead. Gerin turned his head to the right. Recognizing him, some of Rihwin's horsemen waved. He waved back, an enormous grin on his face.

"We've got 'em!" Van shouted. "By all the gods, we've got 'em in the mill. All we have to do now is crumble 'em from grain to flour."

"It'll be harder work than that," Gerin said. "The grain in the mill doesn't try to break the millstones."

"Is this really the time for literary criticism?" Dagref asked.

"Possibly not," Gerin admitted. An imperial who had been thrown out of his chariot flung a stone at him. It clanged off his shoulder, which started to throb. Maybe that was literary criticism, maybe it wasn't. Whatever it was, Van's spear responded to it most pointedly. The imperial was never heard to comment on a metaphor again.

With part of their army cut off and surrounded, the rest of the forces of the Elabonian Empire began falling back. As they had before, the imperials retreated with a professional competence the men of the northlands, Trokmoi and Elabonians both, would have been hard pressed to match. They held their ranks and kept fighting instead of running every which way, which was the more usual response to defeat north of the High Kirs. They didn't seem to be saying, *We're beaten! Gods preserve us!* It was more as if they meant, *All right, you've got the better of us this time, but it was probably just luck. See what happens when we meet again.*

Thinking thus, Gerin said, "What worries me is, this is the second time we've beaten them, not the first. Don't you think they ought to be getting used to the idea that they don't fight as well as we do?"

Dagref said, "They're probably getting used to the idea that they're going to need reinforcements from over the mountains."

"I wish you hadn't said that," Gerin told his son. "Where are we going to get reinforcements if they do? Father Dyaus, where are we going to get reinforcements even if they don't? It's a bloody miracle that Aragis and I are on the same side as things are."

"What do we do if they should send another army over the High Kirs?" Dagref asked.

"Either fight it out or surrender and go back to cheating the Empire out of the tribute it thinks it deserves, the way I did in the old days," Gerin answered. Here he was, winning a battle, and Dagref had managed to make him think he was losing. Pointedly, he went on, "Let's tend to one thing at a time, if you please. If we manage to botch what we're doing now, the Empire won't need to think about sending reinforcements."

"That's sensible, Father," Dagref allowed after his usual pause for thought.

"Nice of him to admit it, eh, Fox?" Van said with a chuckle.

Dagref started to say something else. Gerin cut him off, and the outlander, too. "Take it up *after* the fight's over with," he said. "Meanwhile, let's see what we can do to get it over with faster." He raised his voice to a shout: "Imperials! Give yourselves up and I promise you your lives!"

One of the men in the surrounded pocket of charioteers asked, "And who are you, that we should care about your promise?"

"Gerin the Fox, king of the north," he answered; every once in a while, wearing unobtrusive gear had disadvantages as well as good points. If he'd dressed like a king, they would have known who he was. If he'd dressed like a king, though, they might have done a better job of trying to kill him.

"What will you do with us if we yield ourselves?" the imperial inquired.

That was a good, relevant question. Gerin wished he didn't have to come up with a reply on the spur of the moment. "If you yield now," he said, "I'll disarm you and send you north and settle you in peasant villages—one or two of you in each one, because I don't want you plotting against me. It's the best I can do. Will you take it? Otherwise, you'll die right here, either that or be used as slaves if you give up later and we decide to let you live. What do you say?"

The imperial who'd been asking questions threw down his bow and took off his helmet. "Good enough for me," he said at once.

His comrades started throwing down their weapons, too. Once Gerin saw they were going to yield, he detailed a small number of men to take charge of them, then led the rest south in pursuit of the bigger part of the imperial army.

Before long, he caught up with Aragis the Archer. "Ha!" Aragis said. "I wondered what happened to you, Fox. You disappeared for a while there, and I thought I might be the only king left in the northlands, but I see it isn't so." He plainly wouldn't have been broken-hearted had Gerin died, but he didn't seem broken-hearted to find him alive, either. That struck the Fox as a reasonable reaction. No flies on Aragis, either; the next thing he said was, "That's not the chariot you started out with today."

"So it isn't," Gerin agreed. "They kept trying to kill us out there, and they came closer to doing a proper job of it than I would have liked." Not wearing royal regalia had probably saved his neck.

"Ha," Aragis said again, this time evidently intending it for laughter rather than a greeting. "What they do a proper job of is getting off a battlefield once they've lost the main fight." He waved ahead. "Look at the order they're keeping. If they fought that well *in* the battle, they might win."

Gerin unrolled an imaginary scroll and made as if to read its title: "The triumphal retreats of the Elabonian Empire, being a relation of the manner in which the said Empire was won by its armies' going backwards."

"Ha," Aragis said for a third time. "That's not half bad. If only the bastards would go to pieces once we licked them, we'd drive 'em over the mountains and be rid of 'em once for all."

"Only if they decided not to reinforce," Dagref said.

Aragis studied the youth for a long moment, then shook his head. "He's got as nasty a way of looking at the world as you do, Fox."

"Worse," Gerin answered. He glanced toward his son. Dagref preened. That was the only word for it—he unmistakably preened.

Van pointed ahead to the imperial army. "They *are* going to break away from us, and to your five Elabonian hells with me if I see anything we can do about it."

"Best thing to do is give up the pursuit if we can't break 'em," Gerin said. "If we spread ourselves too thin chasing them, they're liable to counterattack, and then they'd steal a victory on the cheap."

"I hate to say it, but I fear you're right," Aragis said. "We'll gather ourselves up, and then we'll hit 'em another lick in a few days. Sooner or later, they ought to figure out they can't beat us." He gave Dagref a pointed look. Dagref as pointedly ignored it. That made Aragis laugh a genuine laugh. To Gerin, he said, "He will be formidable, won't he?"

"I expect so," the Fox answered. "Of course, he's had practice not paying attention to me." Dagref preened again.

Aragis began shouting orders to bring the army to a halt. When he saw they would be obeyed, he turned back to Gerin. "Where has that Ferdulf of yours got to? I didn't see much of him in the fight."

"Neither did I," Gerin said. "He must have been doing something of his own, unless I miss my guess. He's *his* Ferdulf, not mine; if you don't remember that, he'll make you pay."

Aragis grunted. "I'll remember. Men, now—men you order to do something, and if they don't do it you make them. How are you supposed to make a demigod pay if he doesn't feel like doing it?"

"I've spanked him once or twice," Gerin said, sounding much, much more casual talking about it afterwards then he'd felt doing it.

He succeeded in impressing Aragis. "I always knew you were brave," the Archer said. "Up till now, I never thought you were stupid." Aragis looked Gerin up and down. "Maybe I was wrong."

"Maybe you were," the Fox said. "I'm allied with you, aren't I?" Aragis chewed on that for a little while, then started to laugh. So did Gerin. Why not? They'd just won another battle.

Going back to the field, Gerin found laughter harder to come by. The dead back there, some of them men he'd known most of his life and others, not so old, men he'd known all their lives—they were every bit as dead as if he'd been defeated. The only consolation he found was that not so many of them were dead as if he'd been defeated. That might suffice for him. He didn't think it would for them.

Nor did victory ease the torment of the wounded. They still screamed or groaned or wailed or hissed or stood or lay silent, biting their lips against the pain till blood ran from the corners of their mouths. There would have been more of them whom the Fox knew and liked had the imperials won, but that didn't help the ones who had been hurt. Moreover, wounded men who'd fought for the Elabonian Empire didn't look or sound any different from those who'd followed Gerin or Aragis.

As he had at the earlier battle, Gerin did what he could to help the wounded, extracting arrows, washing cuts out with ale despite the curses of the men who'd acquired those cuts, and, once or twice, quietly cutting the throat of a man who could not live but would, without help, be a long, slow, painful time dying. He hated that, but hated their suffering more.

Presently, he came upon a young fellow with a fuzzy beard who was limping around with a bloody bandage on his right calf. No, not a fellow; though his own arms were bloody to the elbow, Gerin's stomach did a slow lurch. "Maeva!" he exclaimed.

"Hello, lord king," she said, her voice a little wobbly but firmer than a lot of others he'd heard. "They wanted to draw the shaft, but I wouldn't let them. I know you have a good hand for such things." She sat down on the ground, pale yet determined.

"I'll do the best I can," the Fox said. She'd given him a compliment, but not one of a sort he'd ever wanted to get. In the hope that talking would keep her mind off the pain, he asked, "How did it happen?"

She looked at him as if he'd asked a very stupid question. On reflection, he realized he had. "How do you think?" she asked irritably. "I was riding along, doing what I was supposed to be doing, and my leg started to hurt. When I looked down, I saw why—an arrow was sticking out of it."

He nodded. Of itself, one of his hands went to the other shoulder. He'd felt that same absurd surprise when he'd been shot. Then it had started to hurt. He reached down and undid the bandage, saying, "Let's see what we've got."

It was about what he'd expected. Whoever had slapped the bandage on Maeva had also cut the shaft of the arrow off short so it wouldn't be in the way. That was as it should have been, but it kept the Fox from gauging how deep in the meat of her calf the arrowhead lay. "Can you pull it out?" Maeva asked.

"I'd rather not," he answered, his voice troubled. "The imperials use barbed arrowheads, same as we do. Pulling it back will make the wound a lot worse."

"What will you do, then?" Maeva sounded calm, but ragged at the edges. She was liable to start screaming any time. Gerin didn't hold that against her, or blame it on her sex. He'd heard plenty of wounded men scream on the battlefield. He'd been a wounded man screaming on the battlefield.

He used his knife to cut her trousers away from the wound so he could feel of it. He also cut the checked wool on the inner side of her calf. When he gently pressed there, he felt something hard under his fingertip. He grunted. Maeva flinched and hissed and let out a small fragment of a shriek before she could bite down on it.

"It's almost through," he said. "Actually, that's pretty good. If I push it all the way through, the head will be out, and then the rest of the shaft will come with it without much trouble." He was telling the truth. He knew he was telling the truth. He'd had plenty of practice sounding cheerful with wounded men, too. Somehow, this was different. It was harder.

"Go ahead," Maeva said, her voice more ragged now. She set herself. Gerin had set himself, too, before they started working on that shoulder. It hadn't done him much good. He didn't think it would do her much good, either.

He set his hand on the stub of the arrow and pushed hard—soonest over, he'd found, was best. Maeva did shriek then. He'd expected she would; pain deliberately inflicted was harder to bear than that which came by accident.

The barbed bronze arrowhead stabbed out through her skin. Though it was slick with her blood, Gerin seized it and drew the shaft after it. "There," he said. "It's done—well, almost." He carried a jar of ale with him. When he poured it on both wounds in Maeva's leg, she screamed again, and tried to kick him. "Easy," he told her. "Now I'm going to bandage it again."

He did, with fresh rags. Blood started soaking into them from the old wound and the new. Maeva took a long, shuddering breath. "Thank you," she said. "It's . . . better now. I'm sorry I made so much noise."

"I didn't hear anything," Gerin assured her. He knew it wasn't necessarily better yet. The wound could still go bad, in which case she would be very sick and might even die. He'd done what he could do, and made himself sound reassuring: "It won't be long before you're on your feet and running hard again. It didn't cut the tendon; you wouldn't have been on both feet if it had. You should heal nice and clean."

"Thank you, lord king," she said. That made him feel worse rather than better. If he hadn't let her stay and fight, she would have been angry instead of grateful—but she would have been unwounded. He knew which way he would rather have had her. But, as if picking that thought from his mind, Maeva went on, "I'm glad you gave me the chance to fight, even if it turned out like this. Next time, I hope I'll be luckier."

Gerin looked down at his hands. They had her blood on them, literally and now, he supposed, figuratively as well. He kept trying to think of her as just another warrior; he'd had plenty of wounded young men tell him more or less the same thing she'd said a moment before. Try as he would, it wasn't easy. That thought kept recurring.

"Fox!" a deep voice boomed, from over on another part of the battlefield. "Where in the five Elabonian hells have you gone and got to now?"

"Here!" Gerin answered, and waved. Maeva was frantically shaking her head. Had Gerin thought before he waved, he wouldn't have done it. Too late now: Van was already on the way over, crimson horsehair plume nodding above him to make him even more unmistakable than he was already.

"Hullo, Fox," he called, still from some distance away. "Patching up another—" By the way the outlander's voice cut off, Gerin knew exactly when his friend realized exactly whom he was patching up. Van came the rest of the way at a pounding trot. He stooped beside his daughter. "What happened?" he demanded, a question no more useful than Gerin's had been.

"Arrow," she said, doing her best to make light of it. "The king says it should heal well."

"Through the meat of the calf," Gerin said when Van looked a query his way. "No tendon cut—I'm sure of that. She should heal clean." *The gods willing*, he added to himself. Maybe saying it over and over would help make the gods more willing.

Van was still looking at him, not with a question in his eyes any longer but with rising anger. Gerin had seen him aim that look at scores, likely hundreds, of enemies over the years. The Fox had never had it aimed at him. *Run* went through his mind, as it was no doubt meant to do. Van growled, "If it hadn't been for you, Fox—"

That Gerin had had the identical thought would have done little to console the outlander. Gerin was sure of it. But, before Van could say anything more, Maeva broke in sharply: "Leave him be, Father. How old were you when you took your first wound?"

"Sixteen or so," Van answered. "I was lucky for a while. I've made up for it since." That was, if anything, an understatement. He bore a great many scars. Gerin wondered how he'd ever survived one wound that had gashed his chest and belly.

"Well, then," Maeva said, as if that said everything that needed saying.

But Van shook his head. "It's not the same, chick," he said: the same thought that had been troubling the Fox.

"Why not?" Maeva said. "I fought well enough—oh, maybe not so well as you, Father, because I'm not the size you are, even though I'm not small. I kept fighting after I got hurt, too; it wasn't bad enough to make me quit the field."

"What am I supposed to do?" Van sounded plaintive, something he very rarely did. He looked to Gerin. "Curse it, Fox, help me. She sounds like I did when I was the same age."

"And why are you so surprised at that?" Gerin asked. "She's your daughter, after all. Dagref sounds more like me than I ever thought anyone could. He sounds more like me than I ever thought anyone would want to."

"Oh, aye, I can see that," Van said. Gerin laughed. Dagref, perhaps fortunately, was nowhere nearby. Van went on, "But it's not the same." He'd said that before, and sounded most sincere. He still did. "Dagref's your son. Of course he'll follow in your track."

"Am I not your child because I have no stones?" Maeva asked.

Before Van could answer, Gerin said, "I've seen men with beards down to their belts who had less in the way of stones than you do, Maeva."

"Thank you, lord king," she said quietly.

Van glared at Gerin. "Fat lot of help you are," he growled, and stomped off shaking his head.

"Thank you, lord king," Maeva said again, more firmly this time. "I think you're a great deal of help."

"I know you do," Gerin answered. "The trouble is, I still don't know whether I'm supposed to be helping you or your father." He gave her a sudden, sharp bow. "And I have other wounded to help. If I am supposed to treat you like a soldier—and I'm still a long way from sure that I am—then I have to go on, as I would from another soldier."

"Why, of course, lord king," she said, as if surprised he could imagine thinking any other way. That surprised him in turn, and made him begin to believe he might in fact be able to think of her as a soldier.

Gerin sat up on his blanket. "Something's wrong," he said, his voice blurry with sleep. He looked around. The campfires were lower than they had been, though sentries still fed them to help hold the night ghosts at bay—not that the ghosts hadn't had their glut of blood earlier that day. Snores rose from sleeping soldiers in an unmelodious chorus. Injured men groaned against their pain.

Everything seemed to be as it should. But Gerin had not been dreaming when he thought something was wrong; he was sure of that. He did not know how he was sure, only that he was. He looked around again. Again, he could find nothing amiss.

He started to lie down once more, then checked himself. He looked around yet again, this time for Rihwin the Fox. Wherever there was trouble, Rihwin usually wasn't far away. That was especially true when wine was involved. Gerin hadn't had to worry about wine for a good many years. Now he did. Worrying about wine meant worrying about Rihwin.

But no: there Rihwin lay, not twenty feet off, snoring as unmusically as anyone else. Gerin let out a small sigh of relief. If Rihwin had no part in whatever trouble brewed, odds were it wouldn't be so bad. Years of experience had led Gerin to believe as much, at any rate.

He yawned and lay flat again. Despite the yawn, despite Rihwin's snores, sleep would not come. "Something's wrong," he said again, quietly this time, and got to his feet. He would not find any rest till he made sure that prickly feeling of unease in his mind was imagination and nerves.

He breathed a little easier when he saw Dagref, too. Dagref probably would not make trouble on his own. He knew precisely what sort of trouble Dagref and Maeva would make together, though. He would not have wanted to make that sort of trouble while wounded, but, with both of them so young, who could tell what they were liable to do? But they couldn't very well do anything with Dagref sprawled asleep on a blanket.

A sentry was laying branches on a fire. He looked up when he heard Gerin's footsteps. "Is everything all right, lord king?" he asked.

"I don't know," Gerin answered. "I'm trying to find out." He prowled on.

Lengyel the wizard was liable to cause trouble, too. Lengyel had already caused trouble, as a matter of fact. Gerin stalked over to where he stayed under guard. The guards were alert. So was Gerin, when he saw that Lengyel, instead of lying there asleep, was sitting up looking at him.

"No, lord king, he hasn't done anything," one of the wizard's guards assured the Fox. "He wakes up in the night sometimes—has to piss, you know. He's often a goodish while dropping off afterwards."

"Is he?" Gerin gave Lengyel a hard stare. "Probably looking for another chance to get away."

"If I found one, I should be a fool not to take it," the sorcerer said. "I regret to admit I have not found it. Your men have been more careful than I had expected." He made a sour face. "Very little on this side of the High Kirs has been as I expected."

"We never expected to see imperials on this side of the High Kirs at all," Gerin said. "We'd have been just as happy if you people had gone on minding your own business, too, instead of poking your snouts into ours."

Even as he spoke, he wondered if he was telling the truth. If the imperial army had stayed south of the mountains, he would have been fighting Aragis instead. By what the men of the Elabonian Empire had shown thus far, the Archer would have made a more troublesome foe. On the other hand, Gerin had no guarantee that the Elabonian Emperor wouldn't send another army over the High Kirs to give this one a hand.

In musing tones, he said, "Tell me what this Crebbig I is like." He chuckled into the darkness, thinking how much he sounded like the imperials asking him about Ferdulf.

"His imperial majesty is bold and valiant and splendid and terrible, beloved of his friends, a terror to his enemies—"

"Wait." Gerin held up a hand. Lengyel sounded as if he could go on like that for days without ever saying anything that mattered. Gerin said, "Let's try it another way: is Crebbig Hildor's son? If he's not, what was he before his backside landed on the throne down there in the City of Elabon?"

"How could you not know these things?" Lengyel asked in surprise.

"No trouble at all," the Fox answered. "Very much the same way as you were ignorant about everything that has anything to do with the northlands. The difference is, I know that I don't know, where you hadn't a clue."

That drew an indignant sniff from Lengyel; wizards, knowing so much about wizardry, naturally assumed they knew a lot about everything else, too. Primly, the sorcerer said, "You exaggerate, I assure you."

"No, I don't." Gerin held up a hand. "Wait. Never mind. It doesn't matter. Just answer my questions about Crebbig."

"Very well." Lengyel did not and would not call him *lord king*, holding to the official imperial view that there were no kings north of the High Kirs, only rebels ruling against the authority of the City of Elabon. The wizard went on, "No, Crebbig is not the son of the Emperor Hildor III, who is now beloved among the gods."

"Dead, you mean," Gerin said, and Lengyel nodded. The Fox asked, "Did Crebbig give him some timely help in becoming beloved among the gods?" Lengyel nodded again. This time, so did Gerin. "Good. Now we're getting somewhere. What was the murderous usurper doing before he slaughtered his way to the top of the heap?"

"I resent the imputation contained within your words," Lengyel said.

"I don't care," Gerin said cheerfully. "Resent all you like. You serve him. I don't, and I won't. Now answer my question: what was Crebbig the Killer doing before he got to be Elabonian Emperor?"

Lengyel gave him another reproving look for that highly unofficial ekename. He ignored it. He was good at ignoring such looks, having had practice with his children. Seeing it fail, Lengyel said, "The Emperor was formerly commander of the Elabonian garrison occupying the city-states of Sithonia."

"Was he?" Gerin said. "Now, isn't that interesting?" Crebbig would have had a good-sized army behind him when he rebelled; Elabon kept a large garrison in Sithonia for the good and sufficient reason that Elabon needed a large garrison in Sithonia. Down through the centuries of Elabonian occupation, the Sithonians had never given up plotting and scheming and conniving and occasionally rising up against their imperial overlords—and, being Sithonians, had never given up betraying one another to their imperial overlords, either.

It was also interesting, the Fox realized a moment later, because of the Sithonian connections in his own life. He hadn't actually seen a man from one of the city-states east of the Greater Inner Sea since he'd come back from the City of Elabon more than twenty years before, but since then he'd had more dealings with Mavrix than he'd ever wanted, and Mavrix had saddled him with Ferdulf, and . . .

"Father Dyaus," he whispered, and left Lengyel so quickly, the wizard and the guards all stared after him. He didn't care. Something was indeed liable to be wrong, and he thought he finally knew what sort of something, too.

His nostrils twitched when he got close to where he was going. He hadn't smelled that smell in a long time, but he knew what it was. Rich, fruity . . . He couldn't have mistaken it for anything else.

Guards stood around the wine Rihwin the Fox had captured from the imperials, as guards had stood around Lengyel. The wizard's guards hadn't been able to keep him from escaping once, and the guards here hadn't been able to keep somebody from getting into the wine. Gerin's nose told him as much, though the guards didn't seem to notice anything out of the ordinary. "Hello, lord king," one of them greeted him. "What brings you here?"

"Trouble." Gerin pointed. "Don't you see, someone's got past you and in among the wineskins? Can't you smell the spilled blood of the sweet grape?"

Once he showed them they had been befooled, they exclaimed angrily and snatched out their swords. Before then, they'd been oblivious. "Curse the imperial wizard to the hottest of the five hells," said the fellow who'd greeted Gerin. "His spells must have stolen our wits away."

"That's not Lengyel in there." Gerin frowned. "All things considered, I rather wish it were."

Ferdulf looked up from the wine he'd been drinking. "Bother!" he said, glaring at the Fox. "Why didn't my glamour take you, too?"

"It's always harder if someone already knows what he's looking for," Gerin said. "Do you know what you're looking for, there with the wine?"

"My father," Ferdulf said.

"I thought we'd agreed that wasn't a good idea," Gerin told him.

"Aye, we did," Ferdulf, that most unchildlike baritone

still as clear as if he'd never begun to drink. "And then I stopped agreeing, and I decided to do something about not agreeing."

"What you should have done was come to me," Gerin said. "You didn't agree by yourself. You shouldn't have broken the agreement by yourself, either."

Ferdulf shrugged. "It takes two to make an agreement, but only one to be rid of it. You'd have tried to talk me out of this, and—"

"You'd best believe I would," Gerin broke in. Mavrix was the last person—force, god—the Fox wanted to see right now. No one, not Gerin, not Ferdulf, probably not Mavrix himself, could begin to guess what he'd do.

"But I don't want to be talked out of it," Ferdulf said. "The more I thought about that, the more certain I got. And so . . ." He raised a drinking jack to his lips. His throat worked. "That's very fine." It was sure to be only rough army wine, barely worth drinking, but he cared nothing for objectivity. "My father certainly made something better here than boring old ale."

"Ale suits me well enough," Gerin answered sincerely, "though I would be the last to deny wine is fine, too. I've drunk a deal of wine, and drunk it with enjoyment." The last thing he wanted to do was offend Mavrix, if by some mischance the god should be listening and choose to manifest himself here.

He succeeded in offending Ferdulf instead. "Trimmer!" the little demigod sneered, drinking again. "This is good, but that isn't bad—bah! You haven't much time, mortal man. You should be all one thing or all another, not a bit of this and a bit of that."

Gerin shook his head. "I have something of everything in me. If I left something out, that would be the waste."

Ferdulf stared at him. The demigod's eyes caught and reflected what little light there was like a cat's. "You don't answer as you should," he complained. "You don't think as you should. As best I can tell, my father put me on earth where he did for no better reason than to have you torment me."

"I doubt that." Gerin had always thought Mavrix had sired Ferdulf on Fulda for no better reason than to torment him.

If Ferdulf hadn't drawn the same conclusion, Gerin didn't intend to point it out to him. Life with the demigod had proved interesting enough as things were.

For his part, Ferdulf was not thinking about about his relationship with the Fox. "I want my father!" he shouted, loud enough that the cry should have awakened the entire camp—but only Gerin and the guards around the wine seemed to hear him. "I want my father!" He poured wine down his throat from a skin almost as large as he was.

Alarm prickled through Gerin. "Don't do that," he said urgently. "Come on, Ferdulf, give me the skin."

"I want my father!" Ferdulf shouted again.

The space around the wineskins seemed to . . . expand. "My son, I am here," Mavrix said.

VII

"Father!" Ferdulf cried in delight.

Gerin trotted out his halting Sithonian: "I greet you, lord of the sweet grape." He bowed low, looking at the Sithonian god of wine and fertility from under his eyelids.

Mavrix, as usual, wore supple fawnskin. A wreath of grape leaves kept his long, dark hair off his forehead. Ferdulf's eyes had flashed; Mavrix glowed all over, raiment and all. The only darkness in him was his eyes, twin pits of deepest shadow in his effeminately handsome face.

"Well," he said now, voice echoing inside Gerin's head as if the Fox heard him with mind rather than with ears, "I have not been north of the mountains in some little while. I cannot say this benighted excuse for a country has improved much since I last saw it, I must tell you."

"What do you mean?" Now Ferdulf sounded indignant. "*I'm* here, and I wasn't the last time you came to Fox Keep."

"Well, yes," Mavrix admitted. He seemed something less than delighted to make his son's acquaintance. "Even so—"

"The Gradi don't trouble the northlands these days," Gerin put in. He carefully did not add, *No thanks to you*. Mavrix had tried to stand against Voldar, the ferocious chief goddess of the Gradi, but had not been strong enough. Baivers, the Elabonian god of barley and brewing, had held off Voldar and the rest of the Gradi pantheon, along with considerable help from the fearsome deities of the monsters under Biton's cave. Gerin wondered whether Mavrix despised Baivers or the monsters' gods more.

"Well, yes." If anything, Mavrix sounded even less thrilled than he had with Ferdulf. "Even so—"

Ferdulf ran over to him and caught him by the hand. "Father!" he cried again.

Mavrix inspected him. If the Sithonian god was impressed, he concealed it exceedingly well. "Yes, I am your father," he said. "You summoned me, so I came. Now what do you want?"

He sounded like Gerin granting a brief audience to a man for whom he could not spare any more time: he wanted Ferdulf to come to the point so he could get back to whatever he had been doing. Ferdulf caught that, too. "Here I am, the son you got on my mother," he exclaimed. "Have you no praise for me? Have you no words of wisdom?"

Words of wisdom were the last thing Gerin would have asked of Mavrix. If the Sithonian god had chosen to give him any, he would have reckoned true wisdom likely to lie in ignoring them. Here and now, the issue did not arise, for Mavrix only shrugged; the sinuous motion put Gerin in mind of a serpent. "I may be your father," the god said, "but I am not your nursemaid."

Ferdulf reeled back as if Mavrix had slapped him. However heartless Mavrix's words sounded, Gerin thought they did hold good advice. At least they told Ferdulf in no uncertain terms that he could not rely on Mavrix for anything but his existence.

Whatever else they did, they infuriated the little demigod. "You can't ignore me!" he shouted. His feet came off the ground. He shot through the air at Mavrix like an angry arrow.

In his right hand, the Sithonian god bore a wand wreathed in ivy and vine leaves and topped with a pinecone. The thyrsus looked like a harmless ornament. In Mavrix's hands, though, it was a weapon more deadly than the longest, sharpest, heaviest spear any human warrior could carry.

Mavrix tapped Ferdulf with the wand. Ferdulf groaned and crashed to the ground. "A child who annoys his father gets the stick, as he deserves," the god said to the demigod.

Ferdulf was used to having more supernatural power than anyone around him. He rose into the air again and hurled himself at his sire. "You can't do that to me!" he cried.

"Oh, but I can," Mavrix answered, and tapped his son with the thyrsus again. Again, Ferdulf hit the ground, more heavily this time than before. "You need to understand that. Just because I came when you called, you have not the right to abuse me, nor shall you ever." Ferdulf moaned and lay in a heap. Alert as a longtooth, Mavrix stood there watching him. A faint rank odor, of wine lees and old corruption, floated from the god, making Gerin's nose twitch.

Slowly, with another groan, Ferdulf sat up. "Why did you come when I called?" he asked in a voice full of despair. "I hoped you would see me and be proud of me. I hoped—" He shook his head, as if to clear it.

"What a naive little creature you are," Mavrix said, which brought one more groan from Ferdulf. The Sithonian god turned to Gerin. "I should have thought he would have learned better, dwelling by you as he does. For a mortal, you have a moderate amount of sense."

"Even if he is a demigod, he's only four years old," Gerin said, concealing his own bemusement at hearing anything even remotely resembling praise from Mavrix.

Ferdulf heard it, too, heard it and did not like it. "How dare you talk to him, talk to this, this *man*, more kindly than you do to me?"

"I dare because I am a god. I dare because I am your father," Mavrix returned evenly. By early appearances, Ferdulf annoyed him even more than the Fox did. His dark, dark eyes stared at, stared through, his son. "How dare *you* presume to question *me*?"

"I am flesh of your flesh, blood of your blood," Ferdulf said. "If I have not got the right, who has?"

"No one," Mavrix answered. "Now be quiet for a little while."

Ferdulf tried to speak, but produced only squeaks and grunts, not intelligible words. Gerin was impressed he could do even so much; when Mavrix commanded silence of a mortal man, silence was what he got. Seeing Mavrix relatively well-disposed to him, the Fox asked, "Lord of the sweet grape, what aid can you give me against the Elabonian Empire?"

At that, Ferdulf did fall silent. He wanted to hear the answer, too, being anything but enamored of the Empire.

Mavrix looked troubled. That troubled Gerin. Sithonian legend spoke of what a coward Mavrix was. But what was on the god's face did not look like fear to the Fox. It looked like resignation. That troubled Gerin more.

"I can do less than you might hope," Mavrix said at last. "If I could do more than you might hope, do you think I would not have done it for fair Sithonia rather than for this grapeless and otherwise unattractive wilderness?"

"But—" Gerin shook his head. "You Sithonian gods are still very much a part of your own country, while the gods of Elabon hardly seem to notice this world any more: one has to shout to get their attention, you might say."

Mavrix nodded. "That is so. And, once gained, their attention is frequently not worth having." He sniffed scornfully.

"As may be," Gerin said, not wanting to disagree openly with the Sithonian god of wine and fertility. Once he'd summoned Baivers, the Elabonian god had done more for him than Mavrix had. In any case, that wasn't what he wanted to know. He asked, "With the gods of Sithonia immanent in the world while those of Elabon are not, how have the Elabonians"—he carefully did not say *we Elabonians*—"ruled your land so long?"

"That is a cogent question—a painfully cogent question," Mavrix said. "The best reply I can give is that the folk of Sithonia, while they have a great many gifts from their gods, conspicuously lack that of governing themselves. Elabonians, on the contrary, have next to no discernible gifts of any sort . . . save only that of government. It would take a stronger god than any known in Sithonia to make its people unite."

Regretfully, Gerin nodded. That fit too well with what

the imperial wizards had told him. "Is there nothing you can do?" he said, wondering, *What good is an impotent god, especially an impotent fertility god?*

"I have already done all you require of me, and more besides," Mavrix answered. "Without my son—who may, by the way, speak again—you would have no hope whatever of repelling the forces of the Elabonian Empire. With him, you have that hope. Nothing in the mundane world is altogether certain, however, either for gods or for men. Do not be smug; do not be overconfident; you may yet lose this fight, too."

"You're talking in riddles," Gerin said accusingly. "I thought you despised Biton."

"And so I do," Mavrix said with a curl of the lip. "But how am I to speak with certainty when I cannot see everything that lies ahead?"

Gerin wondered if he ought to go up to Ikos to hear what the farseeing god had to say. Maybe he'd made a mistake, not doing that when Duren suggested it. He wondered when—and if—he'd have the chance to leave the army and try to puzzle out one of Biton's notoriously ambiguous oracular verses.

Ferdulf said, "But what must I *do* to drive the Empire out of the northlands?"

"*I* don't know," Mavrix answered. "I haven't the faintest idea. I don't much care, either, if the truth be known. That anyone would be mad enough to wish to live in a land where the grape grows not is beyond me." He turned his head toward Ferdulf. "You will manage, I expect—unless, of course, you don't." A sigh rippled out of him. "For some reason, I am frequently disappointed in my offspring. It must be the fault of the mortal women on whom I sire them."

"Nothing is ever your fault, is it?" Ferdulf said, a thought also in Gerin's mind but one he found it politic not to mention. "When things go your way, you take the credit; when they go wrong, someone else gets the blame."

"You, for example, my charming child, are entirely to blame for that unseemly temper of yours," Mavrix returned, which, to Gerin, proved only that the Sithonian fertility god was not so perceptive as he thought he was.

Ferdulf started to curse him. Gerin had heard some fancy curses in his time, but very few to match the ones spewing from the little demigod's lips. When the Fox closed his eyes for a moment, he could easily imagine he was listening to a veteran abusing a man he'd hated for twenty years.

If the abuse bothered Mavrix, he didn't show it. On the contrary: he beamed at Ferdulf as if proud of him. "I love you, too, dear son of mine," he said when the demigod finally paused for breath. He stuck out his tongue even farther than Ferdulf could have—and then he was gone.

Ferdulf kept on cursing for quite some time, even though only Gerin stood beside him near the wineskins. Without warning, he stopped cursing and burst into tears.

"I was afraid something like this might happen," Gerin said, as consolingly as he could. "That's why I didn't want you to try summoning your father."

"He didn't care." Ferdulf spoke in tones of astonished disbelief. "He just didn't care. I am his son—and he didn't care."

"He's a fertility god," Gerin answered. "He's had lots of sons—and lots of daughters, too. He doesn't see much reason why a new one should particularly matter to him."

"I hate him," Ferdulf snarled. "I'll hate him forever. He'd better not show his ugly face around here again, or I'll make him sorry, that's what I'll do."

"Easy," Gerin said. "Easy. You don't want to talk that way about your father, no matter who he is. You especially don't want to talk that way about your father when he's a god."

"I don't care what he is," Ferdulf said, and then began to cry again. "I'll pay him back for not caring about me if it's the last thing I ever do."

"If you try that, it's liable to be the last thing you ever do," Gerin said.

Ferdulf ignored him. The little demigod kept crying as if his heart would break—no, as if it were already broken. The men guarding the wine stared at him. They were Gerin's subjects, and knew about Ferdulf. They no more expected this behavior from him than they expected the

Fox to go on a four-day drunk and rumple every peasant girl he could get his hands on.

Gerin stared at Ferdulf, too. After staring, he did what he would have done for any other crying child: he walked over, squatted beside Ferdulf, and put his arms around the demigod. Even as he did it, he wondered how foolish he was being. Like any other crying child, Ferdulf could do all sorts of unpleasant things if he didn't feel like being held. Unlike any other crying child, he could do all sorts of dangerous things if he didn't feel like being held.

But all he did was throw his own arms around the Fox and bawl till he had no more tears left. When sobs subsided into sniffles and hiccoughs, Gerin said, "Why don't you go find your blanket now? I don't think anything more will happen here around the wine tonight." He devoutly hoped—and that seemed to be the right word, too—nothing more would happen around the wine tonight.

"All right," Ferdulf said. "But I will have my revenge. You wait and see if I don't." Off he went, hardly more than half as tall as a grown man but showing a determination few grown men could—or would have wanted to—match.

When the Fox straightened up, his knees clicked. He glanced over to the guards, who were staring after Ferdulf. "The less you talk about what happened just now, the happier I'll be," he said. "The happier I am, the happier you'll be. Do you understand that?"

"Aye, lord king," they chorused.

As Gerin walked back toward his blanket, he was gloomily certain the secret wouldn't hold. He counted himself lucky Mavrix hadn't gone and roused the whole camp. That would have created a fine chunk of chaos, which the Sithonian god often enjoyed.

He lay down. He wondered how he was supposed to go back to sleep after some of that chaos—to say nothing of a despondent demigod—landed in his own lap. He looked up at the stars and the moons. Tiwaz and Elleb were in the sky, both of them moving from full toward third quarter. Even Elleb, which had risen after Tiwaz, floated high in the southeast. Sunrise couldn't be too far away.

Gerin yawned. With his luck, he thought, he'd have just dozed off when the sun came over the horizon. And, sure enough, that was exactly what happened.

Rihwin the Fox set hands on hips and looked indignant. He had a good deal of practice looking indignant; along with innocence no sucking babe could match, it was an expression he donned frequently. This time, though, Gerin would have been willing to bet at least most of the ire was real.

"You quaffed the wine without inviting *me*?" Rihwin demanded, as if unable to imagine an act more heinous.

Gerin shook his head. "I didn't quaff a bit of it," he replied. "Ferdulf did. And, sure enough, Mavrix came. Did you really want to make his acquaintance again? Do you think he would have wanted to make yours?"

Rihwin brushed that aside with an airy wave of the hand, a gesture that came from south of the High Kirs. "Wine was quaffed, and I quaffed none of it?" he said. "Where, I pray you, is the justice in that? I found the wine, I brought the wine back to the camp, I—"

"—Pant after the wine the way an old lecher pants after a young virgin," Gerin broke in. "That is what you meant to say, isn't it?"

"Well, possibly I might have chosen other words to the same effect," Rihwin said with a disarming grin—another expression he'd practiced . . . and had need to practice. "But, lord king, unlike the lecher, I have done without for fifteen years—and, now that the wine is a virgin no longer, how can you begrudge my having it, too?"

"I might have known better than to try a figure of speech against you," Gerin said. "Of course you'd turn it upside down and throw it back at me."

Now Rihwin looked smug. He didn't need to practice that expression; it came naturally. "You cannot in logic deny me," he said.

And Gerin nodded. "You're right. I cannot in logic deny you," he admitted. "But I'm going to go right on denying you just the same—and denying myself and Van and Aragis and everyone else. If Mavrix came for Ferdulf, he's liable to come again, and I'd just as soon he didn't."

"But this is unjust!" Rihwin cried. "It has behind it no rational force."

"Yes?" Gerin said. "And so?" Rihwin simply stared at him. Gerin stared back. *He'd* had a lot of practice at keeping his features impassive. What with Rihwin, Ferdulf, his own children, Fand, and many others, he'd needed that kind of practice. Rihwin dropped his eyes. Not smiling, Gerin said, "Go on—get ready to move out. We're not done with the imperials, you know: not anywhere close."

Off Rihwin went. Every line in his body proclaimed mute outrage. Dagref, who had been standing by listening to the exchange, remarked, "He *will* try to get into the wine, you know."

"And the sun will come up tomorrow," Gerin agreed wearily. "Tell me something I couldn't figure out for myself. He stayed away from it as long as he did because no one else could get at it, either. Now that Ferdulf has—"

"But Ferdulf is a demigod, and son to the god of wine," Dagref said. "Doesn't Rihwin see any distinction between that case and his own?"

"The only thing Rihwin sees is his own thirst," Gerin answered. "That worries me, too, but I can only do so much about it. The best way I've come up with to make sure he stays away from the blood of the sweet grape is to keep him too busy to get near the wineskins."

That being so, he sent Rihwin out on patrol with a couple of squadrons of his riders. Whatever else Rihwin was, no one had ever accused him of being dull-witted. He had no trouble seeing what Gerin was doing or why he was doing it, and gave his fellow Fox a sour look. But, since Gerin's order also made perfectly good sense in military terms, Rihwin could do nothing about it but obey.

Maeva did not ride out with Rihwin and the others who fought on horseback. Gerin would have given Rihwin a kick in the fundament had he sent any wounded warrior into action without dire need. Maeva still looked offended at being left behind. "How does the leg feel?" he asked her. "Tell me the truth, now."

A more experienced warrior probably would have lied despite that admonition. Maeva was young enough and serious-minded enough to heed it. "Sore," she confessed.

He set a hand on her forehead. "Hold still," he said when she tried to pull away. "You're not feverish. Is your leg hot around the wound?"

"A little," she said, and then, in a very firm voice, "but only a little."

"All right," he answered. "That sounds like it's healing as it should. Stay off it as much as you can. The less strain you put on it, the faster it will get better." *And the sooner you'll have a scar that will startle your husband on his wedding night*, he thought, *or maybe some other young man on a warm spring night a good deal sooner than that.* If he'd said what was in his mind, he would have embarrassed them both. By keeping his mouth shut, he managed to embarrass only himself. Shaking his head, he went off to get the army moving faster as they broke camp.

He soon saw again that the imperials, while they had now lost two battles, were still very much in the fight. They had so many chariots out to slow down the northerners' march, Rihwin sent a rider back to ask for reinforcements. "They'll smash us up if you don't send more men forward, lord kings," the messenger said.

"We'll send more men forward, by the gods," Aragis snarled. "We'll send the whole cursed army forward, see if we don't." He shouted orders.

Gerin frowned. That wasn't how he would have handled things; it struck him as sticking his head into a longtooth's mouth and inviting the beast to bite down. Scouts went ahead of an army to develop the opposition, to see what was out there. Moving up with the entire force meant the scouts didn't have the chance to do their job and invited an ambush.

He started to protest, then made himself keep quiet. This was what he'd bought when he agreed Aragis should have command of the whole host. He could not claim the Archer was holding back his own men and endangering only Gerin's. Aragis was sending everyone into the fight. He was sending everyone into the fight so aggressively that, if the imperials did have an ambush set, it might not do them much good. He didn't seem to have many ideas as a general, but he knew what to do with the ones he had.

And the imperials proved not to have set a trap after all. Their chariots had been skirmishing briskly with Rihwin's horsemen, but drew back when so much support for the riders made its appearance.

"There—you see, Fox?" Aragis said, more than a little complacently. "We *will* drive them back to Cassat, and, once we've done that, we'll drive them over the mountains and out of the northlands for good."

"By the gods, maybe we will." Gerin heard the bemusement in his own voice. He wouldn't have believed it when the war began, but he was starting to believe it now. One more victory over the forces of the Elabonian Empire, and he didn't see how the imperial forces could sustain themselves on this side of the High Kirs any more.

"Of course we will." Aragis didn't seem to have any doubts. Aragis never seemed to have any doubts about anything. Maybe he didn't have doubts because he was right so often. Maybe he didn't have doubts because nobody dared tell him he was wrong, which wasn't quite the same thing.

"What's Cassat like these days?" Gerin asked. "I haven't been through it since just after the Empire closed off the High Kirs."

"You remember what a sad place it was then?" Aragis said. "Remember how it pretended to be the capital of a province that didn't want to have anything to do with it?"

"That I do," Gerin said. "Dyaus only knows what the governor they'd sent there had done to get himself shipped into exile—no, wait, I remember, it was something to do with getting an army chopped to pieces, wasn't it? Whatever it was, he hated everything that had anything to do with the northlands." That wasn't quite true. The imperial functionary had had quite a yen for Elise. So had Gerin, in those days. She'd disabused the governor with a knife to his throat. Disabusing Gerin had taken longer, and hurt worse by the time the job was through, too.

"Didn't he, though?" Aragis said. "Well, like I say, Cassat was a sad place then, and that was with traffic going over the mountains into the Empire. When the imperials closed the pass, the place didn't have any reason for being at all. What it reminds me of nowadays is a night ghost that wails because it isn't what it used to be—it isn't much of anything, just the remnant of something that was alive once upon a time."

Gerin gave him a look out of the corner of his eye. "You'd better be careful, Archer, or you're going to end up writing poetry."

"Heh," Aragis said. "You're a funny fellow. Order those horsemen of yours forward again, and we'll get on with this business. The gods only know how much I want to get back to my own holdings. Without anybody to keep an eye on 'em, the peasants are sure to be sitting around with their thumbs up their arses."

"They can't sit idle all the time," Gerin said. "They have to eat this winter, too. They know it."

"Aye, and they'll start thinking of that about two days before harvest time, too," Aragis said. "Meanwhile, the weeding and the manuring won't have gone on half so well as they should. Instead of working, they'll be swilling ale and screwing each other's wives."

"They might as well be barons," the Fox murmured.

Van turned a snort into a cough in the nick of time. Dagref's shoulders hunched, as they would have done at the start of a laugh, but he managed to hold it in. "What was that?" Aragis said sharply.

"Never mind," Gerin told him. "You already think I'm too bloody light-minded. Where do we go from here?"

"After the imperials," the Archer replied without hesitation. "We bring them to battle wherever they will stand, either in front of Cassat or behind it, we smash them, and we run them back over the mountains. If they want to come up into our country to trade, well and good. If they come here again with edged bronze in their hands, we'll give them a new set of lumps and send them home again."

"Maybe we will," Gerin said, as he had before. Listening to Aragis made him believe it, anyhow.

Aragis certainly believed it. "We *will*," he declared in such ringing tones that almost everyone within earshot turned his head toward him. "Put your men on the left, Fox; I shall put mine on the right. We'll meet behind the imperials. With the circle closed around them, we'll make sure not many ever do get back over the High Kirs to tell the tale."

He had, perhaps automatically, assigned himself the place of greater honor. "Let it be as you say," Gerin answered; honor mattered less to him, and results more, than to most of his fellows. He was also pleased to see Aragis coming up with a plan more sophisticated than the sort of headlong charge the Trokmoi might have used.

He wondered if he should have been pleased to see the Archer coming up with better plans. Even if they routed the forces of the Elabonian Empire, they would still be left looking at each other across a border that made Aragis acutely unhappy. The more like an idiot Aragis performed, the happier the Fox should have been. And so he would have been, but for the small detail that Aragis' ineptitude, if any, also endangered him.

He did find one question to put to the Archer: "You don't want to start mixing your men and mine together more? They've fought two battles on the same side by now. They should know they can trust one another against the imperials."

But Aragis shook his head. "I don't want to change what's worked well already. Your men have brothers and cousins and friends fighting alongside them, and so do mine. They'll fight better in front of warriors they know, and they'll fight better being certain in their bones the warriors close by them will come to their rescue if they get into trouble."

"I think the Archer has the right of it, Fox," Van said.

"Well, maybe he does," Gerin allowed. "In fact, I suppose he does. His way, the only place we'll have to worry about the kind of trouble he has in mind is at the join of the two armies."

"Just so," Aragis said. "Besides, while your men will obey me and mine will obey you, each force will obey its own sovereign better. Less chance for treachery my way, too. I don't fear it, not after these two fights, but I don't care to leave myself open to it, either."

Gerin started to tell him he was being absurd, but stopped with the words unspoken. Aragis wasn't being absurd. He was being sensibly cautious. Now that Gerin thought about it, he didn't want to leave himself open to treachery from the Archer, either. Keeping his men together reduced the risk of it.

Aragis saw him start to speak and then stop, too. The Archer nodded, as if Gerin had proved his point. In a way, Gerin had. Aragis said, "We are allies against a common danger, not friends. I do not see how we can be friends, you and I."

"Once we drive the Empire back south of the High Kirs—" Gerin began, and then stopped again. The two of them would have been rivals had the Empire not cleared the passes through the mountains; they would have been at war had the Empire not done so. He'd thought as much only moments before. If the Empire left the northlands, what would keep them from being at each other's throats once more? Nothing he could see.

"Allies," Aragis repeated. "Not friends. So long as we remember it, we should do well enough. We've done well enough so far."

"Allies," Gerin agreed. Did he sound mournful or relieved? Even he couldn't tell. Were Aragis his friend, he might well sleep easier of nights. On the other hand, who could sleep easy knowing he was the sort of person able to make friends with Aragis the Archer?

That evening, after the army encamped, Rihwin fell on his knees before Gerin. "Lord king, I implore you, let me taste of the blood of the sweet grape!" he cried.

"What in the five hells do you think you're playing at, Rihwin? Get up, for pity's sake." Gerin shook his head. "Anyone would think I were a pretty little peasant wench you were trying to wheedle into bed."

"Truly, lord king, I suffer for lack of wine as I would suffer for lack of a friendly wench's caresses," Rihwin replied as he climbed to his feet. He winked at Gerin. "And, as truly, I have wheedled a good many pretty peasant wenches into bed with just such words."

"I don't doubt it for a moment," Gerin said. "They probably lie down with you just to make you shut up."

"It could be," Rihwin admitted, not a bit abashed—but then, Rihwin was seldom abashed. "I did not inquire as to why they did it, I confess." He gave Gerin a sidelong look. "I would not inquire why you did it, either, lord king. You have my solemn word."

Gerin exhaled angrily. "To the crows with your solemn word. You do know, do you not, that Mavrix came visiting when Ferdulf drank of the wine you captured? Of course you do; I told you myself. Now I ask you again, do you want to meet the god?"

"Yes, I do know that." Rihwin looked troubled. "I forgot where I heard it, though, and dismissed it as nothing more than camp gossip."

"Of course you did," Gerin snapped. "It wasn't what you wanted to hear, so you bloody well ignored it. You have a way of doing that with things you don't want to hear. Unfortunately, it happens to be true. One more time, sirrah, and answer me yea or nay, if you please: do you care to try conclusions with Mavrix?"

"I don't care," Rihwin said. "He's taken my magic from me. What more can he do, short of taking my life? And if he should take my life, I shall die happy with the taste of wine on my lips. It's a better way to go than most I can think of."

"That depends on what sort of end he feels like giving you." But Gerin threw his hands in the air. "All right, by the gods, go ahead and drink. You've worn me down—if I were a peasant girl, I'd be taking off my skirt right now. On your head be it, though, and I hope all your bastards are well provided for. If you want to be a cursed fool—if you insist on being a cursed fool—I don't suppose I have the right to stand in your way."

Rihwin seized his hand and kissed it. Gerin yanked it back with a startled oath. Rihwin said, "You are a prince among men—no, a king among men." He winked. "Will you not come and drink with me, that we may greet Mavrix together?"

Greeting Mavrix was about the last thing Gerin wanted to do. Nevertheless, he said, "I'll come with you, all right. If you think I trust you with wine while you're out of my sight, you're even crazier than I think you are—and that, believe me, would take some doing."

"Rail at me and insult me as much as you like, so long

as you don't stand between me and the blood of the sweet grape." Rihwin hurried away, to return a moment later with his drinking jack, which dripped. "I have rinsed it in the stream to remove whatever dregs of ale might have remained within."

"Good for you," Gerin said. "Let's go. Let's get this over with."

The guards around the wine began to raise their swords to keep Rihwin away from that which they protected; Gerin had given them very firm orders about that. Then the guards exclaimed in surprise, seeing Gerin stalking along behind him. Gerin countermanded the orders.

"Are you sure, lord king?" one of the guards asked.

"No, I'm not sure," Gerin answered. "The only thing I'm sure of is that Rihwin has wine where his wits ought to be, and he's whined so much I'm going to let him drink some. That will settle that—one way or another."

Rihwin sniffed at Gerin's assessment of him. He poured his jack full, brought it up to his face, and sniffed. His expression grew blissful as he savored the bouquet. "Truly I bless thee, lord of the sweet grape," he murmured. He drank.

Gerin waited for the sky to fall, or at least for Mavrix to appear in all his rather effeminate glory. The sky did not fall. Mavrix did not appear. Nothing whatever out of the ordinary happened, in fact. Rihwin tilted back his head so as to drain the last drop of wine from the jack. He wiped his mouth on his sleeve, a slightly puzzled expression stealing over his face.

"Well?" Gerin demanded. He looked around. Still no sign of Mavrix.

Rihwin kept on looking puzzled. He stared down at the drinking jack, as if it had somehow betrayed him. "It's very fine, lord king," he said slowly. "In sooth, I do prefer it to ale, as I had been certain I should. It's very fine indeed, as I say, and yet . . ." His voice trailed off.

"Not so fine as you remember it, eh?" Gerin said.

"No," Rihwin said in a small voice. "In my mind, I had built up the idea of what it was like, the idea of what it would be like, and, having gone without for so long, I suppose I kept building it and building it, until at the last

I had erected a structure taller and wider than the foundation of truth would support."

"And it just came crashing down on you?" Gerin had not expected to find himself feeling sympathetic to Rihwin, any more than he'd expected to find himself feeling sympathetic to Ferdulf when the demigod's encounter with his father failed to turn out as he'd hoped. But Gerin's friend seemed so uncharacteristically crestfallen, he couldn't help himself.

Rihwin let out a small, sad sigh. "Even so, lord king. Have you ever wanted a beautiful woman who would not give herself to you? Your imaginings of what she would be like grow ever more heated, until at last, in them, she puts to shame Astis the goddess of love."

"And if, after that, you do end up having her after all, what do you find out?" Gerin said. "You find out she's only another woman."

"It has happened to you!" Rihwin exclaimed.

"Not since I was very young," Gerin answered. "You always expect great things when you're very young." He sent Rihwin a pointed look. "Most people get over it after a while."

"So kindly," Rihwin murmured. "So generous. So much like finding a wasp by thrusting your foot into the boot wherein it had chosen to pass the night. Well, I shall have my revenge."

"Of course you will," Gerin said. "You come out with four times as many outrageous things as I do. One of them is bound to skewer me before long."

But that was not the sort of revenge Rihwin had in mind. He filled the drinking jack with wine for a second time and, instead of draining it himself, pressed it into Gerin's startled hands. "Here, lord king. You have gone without longer than I. Taste of the sweet grape and measure it against *your* memory."

"Curse you, Rihwin," Gerin muttered. If he drank, he was liable to draw Mavrix's notice, which was one of the last things he wanted to do. But if he refused to drink, he was liable to offend the Sithonian god of wine, which was another of the last things he wanted to do. After a brief mental debate as to which was the worse risk, he decided he had better drink. "I bless thee, Mavrix, lord of the sweet grape," he said in his seldom-used Sithonian, and raised the jack to his lips.

The wine was sweet, not sour like beer. As Rihwin had, he'd remembered that. He did not think it was very good wine; what army was in the habit of sending a fine vintage with its troopers? But, even if it had been good wine, it would have been worth trading for, but not worth ecstasies.

He said as much, looking around warily again lest Mavrix suddenly appear. Wherever the Sithonian god chose to manifest himself, he did not spring into being in the camp.

Rihwin sighed again. "Lord king, I fear you have the right of it. Only wine! What a sad thing to say—every bit as sad, I think, as your, 'Only another woman'!"

"Maybe it is," Gerin said absently. He kept looking this way and that, waiting for Mavrix to appear and do something appalling. The god gave no sign of his presence. Gerin didn't know whether to be relieved or suspicious. He ended up being both at once, as if someone had shot an arrow at him from arm's length and missed.

Rihwin figured out what he was doing. Rihwin was not a fool. No. Gerin shook his head. Rihwin was not stupid—there was a difference. "Waiting for the lord of the sweet grape to come and turn us inside out?" he asked.

"You deserve to be turned inside out," Gerin snapped. He ran his tongue over his lips; a few little drops of wine remained in his mustache. Their taste made him nervous all over again.

"Why?" Rihwin said. "For thinking it would be safe and proving it?"

"For taking the chance," Gerin said. "The risk wasn't worth the reward. You got yourself a jack of wine, but you put your neck on the line to get it."

Rather to Gerin's surprise, that succeeded in embarrassing Rihwin. "I thought the wine was worth my neck," Rihwin said. "Perhaps—I say only *perhaps*, mind you—I was wrong."

"You got by with it," Gerin said. "I don't know that you deserved to get by with it, but you did, so let it go."

Hearing Rihwin admit he might have made a mistake made Gerin back off a bit, too.

And then Rihwin said, "Now that we know we may safely partake of the blood of the sweet grape, what say we empty the wineskins as fast as we can, to remove further danger?"

"What say we don't?" Gerin answered dryly. "We don't *know* we can safely drink wine whenever we want. All we do *know* is, we got by with it once." Rihwin stuck out his tongue. Gerin ignored him and let out a long sigh. "And I don't think we'd better get rid of all the wine, whether by drinking it or any other way. We may need to summon Mavrix one day, and wine is best for that." He could hear the reluctance in his own voice, but the words needed saying.

The reluctance got through to Rihwin, but so did the sense of what Gerin said. "Very well, lord king; let that be as you say. My own craving, having been slaked once, shall not be so desperate as it has been till now."

"Here's hoping you're right," Gerin said. "But it's liable to be as much in Mavrix's hands as it is in yours." Rihwin gave him a horrified look. He pretended not to see it, and slapped his friend from south of the High Kirs on the back. "Let's get what rest we can. I think we may fight in the morning."

They didn't fight the next morning, nor the next afternoon, either. Gerin began to wonder if the imperials were going to fall back not just to Cassat but through it. If that was so, they might have given up on their efforts to reunite the northlands to the Elabonian Empire.

But then, the morning after that, Rihwin's riders came back to report that the imperial army was drawn up in battle array, awaiting attack. "We'll give it to them," Aragis declared. "One more win and they're gone for good." He shouted orders for the advance.

"Do you think he's right, Father?" Dagref asked as he steered the chariot out in front of the warriors who acknowledged Gerin as their overlord.

"As a matter of fact, I do," the Fox answered. "Beating an army once and seeing it keep its spirit—that can happen, no doubt about it. Beating an army twice and seeing it keep its spirit—when the imperials managed it, that surprised me. If we beat them three times running, I don't see how they can keep from running themselves."

Van nodded. "I think you have the right of it, Captain. I don't suppose I've ever seen soldiers with so much discipline in all my days, but discipline only takes a soldier so far. If it keeps taking him into fights where he can't hope to win, it'll break like a dropped pot."

"That does make good logical sense." Dagref looked back over his shoulder at Gerin. "Haven't you tried to thump it into my head that battles don't always make good logical sense?"

"I think I ought to thump your head on the principle of the thing," Gerin said. "Keep your attention on where we've going, if you please, not on where we've been."

Out ahead of the chariots, and out wide of them as well, rode Rihwin's horsemen. Among them was Maeva, who found sitting a horse easier than walking around. Gerin almost mentioned her to Dagref, because that would have made sure his son looked ahead at all times. He refrained, though, not wanting to remind Van that Maeva was in the fight and had already been hurt once.

Above and ahead of the army of the northlands flew Ferdulf. The demigod had been subdued since meeting his father. He seemed exuberant enough now, though, stabbing out his hand to show the position of the imperial army and then making several lewd gestures in the direction of the men from south of the High Kirs. Gerin's troopers whooped.

The Fox saw the army of the Elabonian Empire a couple of minutes later. He nodded in reluctant admiration. The imperials looked as steady now as they had at the first clash. They'd lost more men than Gerin and Aragis had; having started with an army about the same size as that of the northlands, they were now at a disadvantage. They didn't seem worried, though. As soon as they spied their foes' chariotry, they began their war cry: "Elabon! Elabon! Elabon!"

"Gerin!" the men from the northlands shouted, and "Aragis!" and anything else they could think of. The

Trokmoi who rode with the Fox let out a chorus of yips and yowls that might have burst from the throats of wolves.

Maybe those howls were what made Dagref say, "We sound like an army of barbarians."

"And the imperials sound like civilized men?" Gerin asked. His son nodded. The Fox said, "Well, maybe they are. But I'll tell you this: a civilized man doesn't smell any better four days dead than a Trokmê with mustachios that droop down to his collarbones."

"That's a fact," Van agreed. "And another fact is, you'll die just as dead from a civilized man's sword as from a barbarian's—if the silly bugger knows what to do with it, of course."

"Also true," Gerin said. He raised his voice to ask Dagref, "What do you think of these new horses?"

They were still using the team from the imperial chariot onto which they'd forced themselves during the most recent fight. Dagref answered, "They haven't the endurance of the beasts we brought down from Fox Keep—that's certain. But I do think they may run faster for a short burst. That could prove useful. They're easier-tempered beasts than the ponies we had, which is pleasant."

The Fox grunted. If anything, his son had told him more than he'd wanted to know. That was typical of Dagref. He loved detail, and assumed everyone else did, too. With Gerin, that assumption was usually good. Now, though, he had too much on his mind to want a whole lot more rattling around in there.

"Elabon! Elabon! Elabon!" The drivers of the imperial chariots cracked their whips above the backs of their mounts and sent them bounding toward the men of the northlands. Gerin admired their spirit, in the same sort of way in which he admired the courage of the Trokmoi: which is to say, he admired it without seeing that it made much sense. They'd been beaten twice. What on earth made them think the result would be any different this time, especially since they were now outnumbered?

Whatever it was, here they came. Arrows flew toward Gerin and his followers. Some of his men began shooting back, even if they were out of range. He'd told them not to do that, but not everybody thought when he fought.

Nocking an arrow, Gerin waited for a good target to present itself. The imperial officers still persisted in wearing fancy gear to let their men see at a glance who they were. That that also let their foes see at a glance who they were never seemed to enter their heads. Gerin sent two of them tumbling out of their chariots, one right after the other.

Men and horses on both sides went down. One imperial chariot came to grief in front of another, which collided with it and came to grief, too. Along with looking for officers, Gerin sent shafts at drivers and at horses. That last wasn't sporting, and he knew it. He didn't care. If the horses went down, the chariots couldn't roll.

Order and discipline didn't hold long. Once the chariots were in among one another, the tactics of the captains on either side didn't matter much. It was a melee, everyone smashing away at whoever was close by and happened to be shouting the wrong battle cry.

Gerin tried to do something about that, yelling for some of his troopers to overlap the end of the imperial line. The imperials stretched, too, and didn't stretch so thin as to let him shatter them. His mouth twisted. This didn't look like a day on which anything would come easy.

Then Ferdulf dived down to horrify the horses of an imperial chariot. They ran so wild, Dagref had to steer smartly to escape a collision. Van speared the driver out of the enemy car, which meant it would keep right on going wild.

Dagref was no demigod, but he could also make himself unloved by the imperials' horses. His lash made them scream and turn aside from the chariot he drove. One of the drivers who fought for the Elabonian Empire drew back his arm to do likewise to the team Dagref drove. Before he could snap the whip, Gerin shot him in the shoulder. He howled and cursed and dropped the whip, but somehow managed to hang on to the reins. That made Gerin curse in turn.

"How are we doing?" Van shouted. He looked as if he was doing pretty well for himself. His face wore a fierce grin. Blood trails dripped down the shaft from his long, leaf-shaped bronze spearhead. No blood dripped from him.

"Doing well, I think," Gerin answered. He looked around. "The imperials are having to bend back to keep us from getting around behind them, so their line is a bow now—it isn't a line any more. And you can bend a bow only so far. After that, it snaps."

"Aye." Van peered toward the other wing. "Aragis' men seem to be giving the southerners a hard time, too. Say what you will about that fellow, the men he leads can fight."

"I've never doubted that," Gerin said. "He wouldn't be dangerous to me if he weren't dangerous to everyone else who got in his way, too." He hesitated, then admitted, "I suppose I have to say I didn't expect him to be as dangerous as he is."

Dagref said, "If he happened to suffer an unfortunate accident just at the moment when the imperials were routed and running for the High Kirs, I don't think my heart would break."

"Neither would mine," Gerin said. Then, a bit slower than he should have, he realized what else his son had been saying. "If Aragis has an unfortunate accident, it won't be on account of me."

"All right," Dagref said equably. Gerin stared at his son's back. The youth could indeed be formidable to everyone around him when he grew up. As a matter of fact, he was already formidable to everyone around him.

"You keep your eyes open, Fox," Van said, "because I don't think Aragis' heart would break if you had an unfortunate accident along about the time the imperials were hightailing it for the mountains, either. And Aragis doesn't believe in live and let live, not even a little bit."

Gerin could hardly argue with that. Aragis had about as much forbearance in him as a pike swimming in the Niffet. Any other fish he saw was either his size, bigger . . . or breakfast. But the Fox replied, "I didn't get to be as old as I am by closing my eyes, you know."

"Oh, yes, I do know that," Van said. "But if you want to keep on getting older, don't shut 'em now."

Instead of shutting his eyes, Gerin used them to gape at Ferdulf whizzing around the battlefield, stirring up chaos in the ranks of the imperials. He flew untroubled. Whatever magics the wizards from the Sorcerers' Collegium were using to try to bring him down, they weren't working, not today. And, because they weren't working, the little demigod was making life miserable for the men from south of the High Kirs.

Life, or at least the battle, was pretty miserable for them anyhow. Gerin and Aragis' men did not beat them easily, but beat them they did. Both ends of the imperial line bent back and back now. Gerin began thinking Aragis' dream would come to pass. If his own men met the Archer's behind the imperials, precious few soldiers would have the chance to get back over the mountains and let Crebbig I know what had happened to them. The officers of the Empire realized as much; their shouts grew ever more urgent and desperate.

Gerin shouted, too: "Press them hard! Don't let them have a moment's breather. If we smash them here, they're ruined for good. Press them."

Press them the men of the northlands did. The imperials fought hard, but, though they managed to press forward here and there, overall kept going back and back. Three arrows, one of them Gerin's, hit an officer who was rallying them. They all struck within heartbeats of one another; the Fox was by no means sure his smote first.

Van whooped as he watched the imperial topple from his car. "He's hit so many times, he doesn't even know which way to fall, the poor sod. You've got your troopers thinking the same way you do, Captain."

"Anyone who can't see that an able officer needs killing is probably too stupid to go on breathing, let alone be worth anything in a fight," Gerin answered with a shrug.

Dagref said, "It would be a wonder, Father, if your followers haven't learned something from you, as long as you've been leading them."

Van whooped again. "Have you ever been called old more politely, Fox?"

"That's not what I—" Dagref began.

"Never mind. I know what you meant," his father said. "I also know Van was trying to rattle you, not me, because he knows you're the easier mark."

"I deny everything," Van said.

"There!" Dagref was triumphant. "Even Van sounds a bit like you, Father, and I'll bet he didn't before he came to Fox Keep."

That was true. Van and Gerin had remarked on it, too. Neither of them remarked on it now, perhaps for fear of making Dagref even more insufferable about his own cleverness than he was already.

Then shouts came from the far rear of the bending imperial line. Gerin leaned forward, trying to make out what they were. A moment later, he let out a shout of his own: "Our men and Aragis' have joined hands. We've got 'em in the barrel—now we pound 'em flat."

His men shouted, too, as they realized they'd surrounded the army of the Elabonian Empire. Most of the shouts were threats aimed at the imperials. But the men from south of the High Kirs stolidly fought on, doing their foes as much harm as they could.

"I think they're too stupid to know how badly beaten they are," Van said.

"You could be right," Gerin allowed. "If you are, though, it's not the worst way for a soldier to be."

Ferdulf kept on flying above the imperials and diving down to dismay them. As before, arrows refused to strike him. He rose on high and dove, rose on high and dove. Then he rose and, instead of diving on the imperials, flew straight to Gerin. "Watch out!" the little demigod shouted, pointing to the southwest. "Watch out!"

"What is it?" Gerin demanded, wishing Ferdulf had been more specific.

And then, when Ferdulf was specific, the Fox wished he hadn't been: "There's another imperial army, as big as this one or maybe bigger, heading straight for us. We're going to get smashed like a bug between two rocks."

In remarkably self-possessed tones, Dagref said, "Well, now we know why the imperials who are already here didn't panic when we surrounded them."

"Don't we?" Gerin agreed sourly. Unlike Aragis, the general in command of the Elabonian Empire's newly reinforced forces was capable of real strategy. He'd set out this tempting army here, certain the men of the northlands would leap on it like a starving longtooth. And the men of the northlands had leaped—and now they were going to pay for it.

Ferdulf hovered in front of Gerin's face like the gadfly he was. "What are you going to do?" he screeched. "What are we going to do?"

"We're going to get licked, that's what we're going to do," Van said.

Ferdulf screeched again, this time wordlessly. "He's right, of course," Gerin said, which made Ferdulf screech at him. Ignoring the racket, the Fox went on, "Only question left now is how badly we get licked. Ferdulf, go tell Aragis what you just told me. He's on the right; he'll get hammered harder than my troopers will."

"I don't want to talk to Aragis." Ferdulf stuck out his lower lip. "He's nasty."

"Go talk to Aragis!" Gerin shouted. Ferdulf flew off. Gerin hoped he flew off in obedience rather than in a fit of the sulks, but wouldn't have bet anything he minded losing on it.

"We ought to pull back now," Dagref said.

"I know. But we can't." Gerin grimaced. "If we save ourselves like that, we leave Aragis in the lurch."

"Why shouldn't we?" Dagref asked. "He'd do it to us."

"Mm, I think not, not here," Gerin answered. "If he goes under altogether, or if I do, that leaves the other one to face the whole weight of the Empire by himself. That doesn't strike me as something I want to do."

"Well, maybe," Dagref said grudgingly.

Gerin didn't find out whether Ferdulf told the Archer the second imperial army was on the way. It mattered little. Aragis could not have remained in doubt very much longer. The new cry of "Elabon! Elabon! Elabon!" pierced the rest of the battlefield noise like a knifeblade piercing flesh.

"Elabon! Elabon! Elabon!" The surrounded imperials answered the war cry with one of their own.

As soon as he realized he was trapped rather than trapper, Aragis pulled away from the battle without the slightest concern for what that might do to Gerin. The Fox was less infuriated at finding his prediction wrong than he would have been otherwise, for Aragis was the one stuck between the two imperial forces. Most of the pressure fell on him. Gerin was able to break off his part of the fight without too much trouble.

And then, having broken off, he ordered his troopers forward in one last charge against the imperial force he and Aragis had lately surrounded. That made those imperials turn aside from their assault on the Archer to repel him. Van sighed. "Helping Aragis get loose, are you?"

"See any better ideas?" Gerin asked.

The outlander sighed again. "No, but I wish I did. You're hurting yourself while you're helping him."

"Don't remind me." Gerin stared across the field. Aragis did seem to be pulling back, not being surrounded—the fate he and Gerin and inflicted, though not for long enough, on the first army from south of the High Kirs. Seeing that Aragis' men would not be immediately cut off and destroyed satisfied the Fox that he'd done his duty by his ally. "Now back!" he shouted. "Now we get away."

He didn't know how hard the imperials would press his retreating force. They had the numbers now to press him and Aragis at the same time, if they so chose. The lunge they made after his men turned out to be halfhearted. For one thing, they remained intent on trying to break Aragis, against whom they could bring more warriors to bear than against Gerin. For another, most of Rihwin's horsemen—as many as were able—fell back on Gerin's force rather than on Aragis'. The imperial chariotry had great—perhaps even exaggerated—respect for the riders, whose feints and countercharges looked to intimidate them and keep them from pressing harder than they did.

Rihwin himself rode back to Gerin with an anxious expression on his face. "I pray the wine is safe, lord king," he said.

"It's not the biggest thing on my mind right now," Gerin said, in lieu of getting down from the chariot to find a rock with which to hit Rihwin in the head. "I'm more worried about everything else the supply wagons carried. Most of them were on Aragis' side of the field. Without journeybread and sausage and cheese and whatnot, we're going to have to start foraging all over the countryside if we want to stay alive."

"Wine is also important," Rihwin insisted, "it being our

best conduit, as you yourself said, to hope and beg for divine aid from Mavrix."

"Not a good hope," Gerin said, but the comment held enough sense to keep him from again wishing to clout his fellow Fox. He sighed. "All right, Rihwin, have it your way. I hope the wine is safe, too. Now let me get back to running this retreat, if you please."

Rihwin sketched a salute. "Lord king, I obey." His eyes twinkled. "When I feel like it, I obey." He rode off before Gerin could find an answer.

The one thing of which the Fox was glad was that his men still showed fight. That let him conduct the sort of retreat the imperials had made before: a retreat with teeth in it. His lines weren't so neat as the ones the men from the Elabonian Empire had maintained, but they weren't pushing him so hard as he'd pushed them. That evened things out. As the imperials had broken free of his pursuit, so his army broke free of theirs.

"Where now?" Van asked. "What now?"

Those were indeed the relevant questions. Gerin took the second one first, not because he had an answer but because he didn't: "I haven't the faintest notion of *what now*, except to get away in the best way we can, so the imperials still have to do some fighting after the battle we just lost. Have to see what sort of shape we're in, have to see what sort of shape Aragis' men are in, have to see if the Empire lets us rejoin them. Maybe I stop being a king and go back to being a baron."

"Would you do that, Father?" Dagref asked, some concern in his voice: if Gerin was not a king, Dagref never would be.

"I might, if I didn't think the Empire would nail me to a cross for taking a title they say I have no right to," the Fox replied. "Being a king—by the gods, even being a baron—never meant all that much to me of itself. The best part of it always has been that it's given me the power I need to make people leave me and mine alone. But I don't think his usurping majesty, Crebbig I, will want anyone around who's dared defy his glory, and so I'm better off to keep on fighting."

"That's the way of it," Van agreed. "You keep standing

till they knock you down and you can't get up any more." He looked around. "We'll be on our feet again before too long. Now—the other question I put to you. *Where* now?"

"Northeast, the way we're going," Gerin replied without hesitation. "With all these big villages that are almost little towns around, the farmers down here are plainly growing more than they can eat by themselves. If we have to forage off the countryside, let's forage off countryside that'll give us enough to be worth taking."

"Makes sense to me," the outlander said.

"Besides," Gerin said, "even if I don't know what's happened to most of our supply wagons, I saw taverns in some of those towns. Tonight, I'm going to drink something better than water."

"Not enough better, if you listen to Rihwin," Van said.

"If you listen to Rihwin, you'll hear any number of things that aren't so," Gerin said. "You'll hear any number of things that may be so but probably aren't. You'll hear any number of things that are so but don't matter at the moment. And, I don't deny, you'll hear some things that do matter. But winnowing the grain from the chaff is often more trouble than it's worth."

"You have the right of that." Van rumbled laughter. Then his heavy-featured face grew bleak. "I've not seen Maeva since the fighting started. Have you set eyes on her, Captain?"

"No," Gerin answered. He did not like the way Van looked at him—it was as if the outlander were measuring him for a grave.

But then Dagref said, "She's in the retreat with the rest of us. I saw her off on what would have been our left when we were facing the imperial army; I suppose it's our right now that we've turned our backs on them. She must have been one of the riders who got farthest around the flank of the first imperial force, before the other one made us break off."

"Ah, that's good to hear," Van said, and his features cleared.

"Sounds like your child, too, to be at the fore of the fighting," Gerin said, also more than a little relieved.

"It does, doesn't it?" Now Van looked proud and puzzled

at the same time. "Who would have thought a girl child would take after me so, though? I never did, not for a moment."

Dagref looked back over his shoulder. "If you don't mind my saying so, you should have. She's been practicing with bow and sword and spear since she's been big enough to hold them in her hands. She's kept working with them, too, to get to be as good as she is. Why would she do all that if she didn't intend to use them in war one day?"

"When you ask it that way, lad, I have no good answer for you," the outlander said with a sigh. "I thought it was a childish thing in her, I suppose, and that she would put it aside when she turned into a woman, and take up the things of a woman instead."

"That didn't happen," Dagref said. "If you'd been paying attention, you'd have noticed she's been a woman for a year, and she hasn't come close to putting aside her practice. She's worked harder than ever, as a matter of fact."

"Has she?" Van's tone was surprised, not so much at the news, perhaps, as at how emphatically Dagref gave it to him. "You've been paying close attention, haven't you?"

"Well, of course I have," Dagref answered. "I've been practicing a good deal myself, you know. If I didn't notice what people did around me, I wouldn't be much use to anyone, would I?"

Van grunted and subsided. Perhaps he was even convinced. Dagref had spoken most convincingly. He might even have believed what he was saying himself. Over the years, Gerin had seen a great many people talk themselves into believing what wasn't so.

Thoughtfully, the Fox shook his head. He was of the opinion that Dagref was concealing from Van rather than deluding himself. He was also of the opinion that Dagref had made special note of Maeva practicing because she was Maeva, not because she was practicing. He'd also caught Maeva noticing Dagref, which made life . . . less than dull.

The sun sank toward the western horizon. The imperials stopped harassing Gerin's rear guard and drew back. He hadn't thought they would do anything else, but he hadn't thought they would bring a second army over the

High Kirs, either. If Aragis had been generous instead of greedy and given the Fox the right instead of the left, the Archer would have had the easier retreat and Gerin would have had to contend with two forces at once. He wondered if Aragis was thinking the same thing at the moment.

Up ahead sat one of those not-quite-towns common here close to the High Kirs. Gerin ordered his men to encamp a couple of bowshots from it. He wasn't worried about feeding them, not tonight. Most of them would have bread or sausage or something on their persons, and those who didn't would be able to get something.

He did need some sort of sacrifice against the night ghosts, though. He walked up toward the village, Dagref at his side. Van stayed behind to talk with Maeva, who'd come through unhurt. Dagref had wanted to do that, too, but Van's presence persuaded him to take himself elsewhere.

When Gerin got to the village, he wondered if anyone would be there at all. His army had passed nearby on the way south, and so had the imperials before them. To his relief, he found that, if the inhabitants had fled as warriors briefly approached the place, they were back now. They were also willing, he discovered, to sell him a couple of sheep.

"How did you keep somebody from stealing them?" he asked.

"Oh, we managed," answered the man who had them. Three words summed up generations of dealing with nobles and warriors, always being the weaker but somehow getting through.

Admiring that resilience, Gerin said, "Well, come to the tavern and have a jack of ale with my son and me."

"I'll take you up on that," the villager said. He led the Fox and Dagref into the tavern, which wasn't too clean but likewise wasn't too dirty. "Three ales," he told the woman who looked to be in charge of the place. He pointed to Gerin. "This fellow here is doing the buying."

She nodded and filled three jacks. She was somewhere in early middle age, brown hair—beginning to go gray—pulled back from her pale face and tied behind her. In the growing gloom inside the tavern, Gerin couldn't make out what color her eyes were.

She carried the jacks over to the table where he, his son, and the villager sat. She didn't set them down till the Fox put money on the table. Then she nodded and said, "Here you are."

Gerin's head came up, so suddenly that Dagref and the villager stared. He knew her voice. Her eyes were green. He still could not see them, but he knew. Hoarsely, he spoke her name: "Elise."

VIII

She set the tarred-leather drinking jacks on the table very slowly and carefully, as if they were cut rock crystal that might shatter at a touch. Gerin felt as if he might shatter at a touch, too.

"Here, what's this?" the villager said. "The two of you know each other? How in the five hells do you know each other?"

"We manage," Gerin said, his voice still ragged. Dagref's eyes were wide as rounds of flatbread.

"Aye, we do." Elise sounded as much taken aback as the Fox did. Turning to him, she said, "I didn't know your face. I didn't know who you were till I heard you speak."

"Nor I you," he answered. He scratched at his beard. He knew how gray it was. "It's been a long, long time."

"Yes." She looked from him to Dagref and back again. Slowly, some small question in her voice, she said, "Surely this isn't Duren. He would be older."

"You're right." Gerin nodded. "This is Dagref, my older son by Selatre, my wife since a few years after you . . . you left. Did you know that Duren is lord of the holding that belonged to your father?"

Elise shook her head, which meant she was hearing of the death of her father, Ricolf the Red, for the first time.

"No. I didn't know," she answered. "News moves slowly, when it moves at all. How long—? How—?"

"Five years ago now," the Fox answered. "A fit of apoplexy. From everything I heard, it was as easy as such things can be. Duren has the holding firmly in his hands these days."

"Does he?" Elise still looked dazed. She had plenty to be dazed about. Gerin was feeling dazed, too. He also felt as if he'd tumbled twenty years back through time, into a part of his life long closed off from that in which he was living now and had been since he'd found Selatre.

The villager who'd come into the tavern with Gerin and Dagref gulped his ale. "Well, I'd best be off," he said, and got up from his stool and hurried out into the sunset.

Dagref, by contrast, stared in fascination from Gerin to Elise and back again. The Fox thought his son's ears curled forward to hear the better, but that might have been his imagination. He hoped it was. Quietly, he said, "Son, why don't you take the sheep back to the camp, so they're sacrificed before the sun goes down?"

"But—" Dagref began. He stopped, then tried again: "But I want to—" Then he realized that what Gerin had phrased as a polite request was in fact an order, and one that brooked no contradiction. The glare Gerin sent his way helped him realize that. Regretfully, resentfully, sulkily, and very, very slowly, he did as his father bade him.

Elise's laugh was nervous. "He wanted to hear everything," she said.

"Of course he did," Gerin said. "And once he'd heard it, he'd know it all, and be able to give back any piece of it you wanted, as near word for word as makes no difference. He'd even understand most of it."

"He takes after you," Elise murmured. By her tone, she didn't altogether intend that as a compliment.

Gerin started to get angry. Before he let the anger show, he saw that half of it—maybe more than half of it . . . no, certainly more than half of it—was all the things he hadn't been able to say since she'd disappeared, now trying to crawl out of his throat at once. With an effort, he crammed them back. "How have you been?" he asked, a question that seemed unlikely to throw oil on the fire.

"How do I look?" she answered. Everything she said seemed to have a bitter edge to it.

"As if you've seen hard times," Gerin said.

She laughed again. "What do you know of hard times? You've always been a baron in a keep, or a prince, or a king. Your belly's been full. People do what you tell them to do. Even your son does what you tell him to do."

"And who says the gods no longer give us as many miracles as we'd like?" Gerin said. Once, a long time before, his sarcasm had amused her. Now she just tossed her head, waiting for him to say something of consequence. Holding back the anger was harder. With an edge in his own voice, he said, "I'm sorry it's been hard for you. It didn't have to be, you know. You could—"

"Could what?" Elise broke in. "Could have stayed? That would have been harder yet. Why do you think I left?"

"My best guess always was that you left because you got bored and wanted something new and didn't much care what it was," Gerin answered. "As long as it *was* new, that would suit you."

"You were the prince of the north," Elise said. "You were having a fine time being the prince of the north—such a fine time, you forgot all about me. I was good enough for a brood mare, and that was that."

One side of Gerin's mouth twisted in what was not a smile. "I needed to do everything I did, you know. If I hadn't done what I did, odds are neither one of us would be here hashing this out now. The Trokmoi would have swallowed up a lot more land than they did."

"That's likely so." Elise nodded. "I never said you weren't good at what you did. I just said you paid more attention to it than you did to me—except when you wanted to take me to bed, of course. And you didn't pay all that much attention to me then."

"Not fair," he said. He hadn't seen her for twenty years, and yet she knew how to get under his skin as if they'd never been apart. "I never looked anywhere else. I never wanted to look anywhere else."

"Of course not," Elise said. "Why would you? I was handy. 'Come here, Elise. Take off your skirt.' "

"It wasn't like that," Gerin insisted.

"Oh, but it was," she said.

They glared at each other. Gerin was convinced he remembered things just as they'd been. Elise, obviously, was as convinced her memory was straight and his crooked. He had no records, not for something like that. He sighed. "It's done. It's over. You made sure it would be over. Have you been happier since than you would have been if you'd stayed with me? I hope so, for your sake."

"Decent of you to say so, though talk is cheap. I've seen how cheap talk is, over the years." She pursed her lips. "Have I been happier than I would have been if I'd stayed behind? Every once in a while, much happier. All together? I doubt it."

The answer held a certain bleak honesty. Gerin sighed again. He was tempted to walk out, walk back to the encampment, and spend the rest of his life pretending he'd never run into the woman who'd borne his oldest son. But that thought brought up another one, one he needed to ask about for Duren's sake: "Do you have any other children?"

"I had two, both girls," she answered, and then looked down at the ground. "Neither one of them lived to be two years old."

"I'm sorry," Gerin said.

"So am I," she said, even more bleakly than before. When she raised her head once more, unshed tears glittered in her eyes. "You know you take a chance loving them, but you can't help it."

"No, you can't," Gerin said. "I've had three since who lived. We lost one."

"You've been lucky," Elise said soberly. She studied him for a moment, then repeated herself in a different tone of voice: "You've been lucky."

"Yes, of course I have," he replied. "I've been steady, too."

He could see she didn't understand what he was talking about. When he'd known her, she'd been ready to turn her world upside down at a moment's notice. That was how the two of them had come together. He doubted she'd changed much since. That made her steady, in an unsteady way.

"You've been lucky," she said yet again. "You sound as if you were even lucky enough to find a woman whose temper matches yours. I didn't think there was any such creature."

"You threw me aside," he said. "Of course you wouldn't think anyone else might want me."

"That's not—" Elise paused. She *was* relentlessly honest. "Well, maybe it is true, but not all true."

"However you like." Gerin shrugged. He could feel how tight a grip he had on his temper. It struggled and writhed in that grip, too, the way Van did when they wrestled together. As the Fox did with Van, he felt it liable to escape at any moment. To try to hold it in check, he asked, "Did you find a man who matched your temper?"

"Several of them," she answered. Given how steadily changeable she was, that saddened the Fox a little but didn't surprise him. Elise scowled. "The latest one threw me over, the son of a whore, for a woman who couldn't have been more than half his age. If he hadn't left this place in a hurry, I'd have slit his throat for him, or maybe slit him somewhere else."

She sounded like Fand. Gerin thought she would have done it if she'd got the chance, as Fand would have. He asked, "How is what this fellow did to you any different from what you did to me?"

He probably shouldn't have said that. He realized as much as soon as the words were out of his mouth, which was, of course, too late. Elise had been scowling at the latest man to disappear from her life. Now she scowled at Gerin. "I never pretended Prillon didn't exist."

"I never pretended you didn't exist," Gerin returned.

"Ha!" Elise tossed her head. The tone flayed meat from the Fox's bones. He hadn't had that tone aimed at him in a long time. She went on, "No one is so blind as the person who thinks he sees everything."

"That's true," Gerin agreed. He saw that she was applying it to him. She had not a clue that it also applied to her. Even after his remark, she didn't apply her own comment to herself. The Fox shrugged. He hadn't expected that she would, not really.

"It hardly seems fair," she said. "I've struggled all this

time, and what have I to show for it? Nothing to speak of. And you—you've just gone on and on and on."

"You were the one who left," Gerin answered with yet another shrug. "I didn't put you on a boat in the middle of the Niffet and heave you over the side. I would have . . ." He broke off. He wouldn't have been happier had she stayed. For a little while, he might have been. Over the long haul of years, he was happier the way things had turned out.

Her mouth tightened. She must have realized what he'd been about to say, and why he hadn't said it. "You may as well go," she said. "There's nothing left at all, is there?"

"No," he answered, even if that wasn't quite true. The thing that had been dead inside him for twenty years stirred, like a ghost at sunset. But even ghosts, drawn by the boon of blood, that tried to give good advice only howled unintelligibly, like the wind. A man who listened to the wind instead of his own mind and heart deserved to be called a fool. Gerin pretended not to hear this ghost, too.

"Would you like another jack of ale?" Elise asked with brittle politeness.

"Thank you, no." He'd seldom been so tempted to drink till he couldn't see. He thought for a moment, then said, "If you like, I'll send a messenger up to Duren, to ask if he wants you to come stay at the keep that was your father's?"

"It's Duren's through me," Elise said angrily. "Why shouldn't I simply go and stay there, if I so choose?"

Gerin ticked off points on his fingers. "Item: I am not the lord of that holding. Duren is. Item: I do nothing to take a hand in his affairs without his leave. Item: you left Fox Keep when he was barely able to toddle. Why are you sure he'd want to see you now?"

"I am his mother," Elise said, as if to a halfwit.

Gerin shrugged.

Her eyes blazed. "I remember why I left Fox Keep, too. You are the most cold-blooded man the gods ever set on the face of the earth."

Gerin shrugged again.

That made Elise angrier. "To the five hells with you,"

she snapped. "What would happen if I left on my own and traveled to my father's holding—my son's holding—by myself?"

She would put herself in danger, traveling alone. After the life she'd lived, she had to know that. After the life she'd lived, she also had to be good at coming through danger. And she might find herself in danger if she stayed here, too. "The imperials are liable to be coming through this place in a few days," he warned.

"I'm not afraid of them," Elise answered. "I have kin south of the High Kirs, too, you know."

"So you do," Gerin said. "If they happen to feel like it, I suppose the imperials could give you an escort to the country south of the mountains—maybe even down to the City of Elabon."

His voice held a sardonic bite. Elise, though, chose to take him seriously. "Maybe they would," she said. "Why shouldn't they? I'm kin to nobles close to the Emperor."

Nobles close to the man who had been the Emperor, Gerin thought. *How they stand with Crebbig I is anyone's guess. How glad they'll be to see you is anyone's guess, too. They weren't very glad when you came calling on them before the werenight.*

He didn't get the chance to say any of those things. Before he could, Elise went on, "And then I'd be living in the capital of the Elabonian Empire and you'd be stuck here in the northlands. How would you like that?"

She was gloating, loving the idea. She knew how he'd longed for the life of the City of Elabon when he'd been together with her. He still longed for it. But the longing wasn't a vital part of him any more, even if it did stir in his heart now and again. Like her, it had become a piece of his past, and he was satisfied to leave it so.

He said, "I've spent most of the time since you left me trying to make the northlands into the sort of place where I might want to live. Up around Fox Keep, I haven't done too badly. I'm happy enough to stay where I am. If you'd sooner go down to the City of Elabon, go ahead."

Elise glared at him. That wasn't the answer he was supposed to give, nor the way he was supposed to respond. He was supposed to get angry, to shout and act jealous.

Elise didn't quite know what to do when he failed to perform as expected.

He got to his feet. "I'm going to go. If you like, I *will* send a messenger up to Duren. I owe you so much, at least. If you want me to, perhaps you'd better come along with me." He didn't like that, not even a little, but saw no other choice. "The gods only know what sort of shape this village will be in after the imperials come through here."

"The only woman in among your army?" she said coldly. "No, thank you. No, indeed."

"You wouldn't be the only woman," the Fox answered. "Van's daughter Maeva is along, riding a horse under Rihwin's command."

That startled Elise. She could fight; Gerin knew as much. She'd never dreamt of making a life of soldiering, though. After a moment, her eyes went hard again. "No, thank you," she repeated. "I'd sooner take my chances with the Elabonian Empire."

"Have it your way," Gerin said. "You were always bound and determined to do that anyhow, weren't you?"

"Me?" Elise exclaimed. "What about you?"

"You know what the trouble is?" the Fox said sadly. "The trouble is, we're both right. That's probably one of the things that helped split us apart."

Elise shook her head. "Don't blame me for that. You did it."

"However you like." Gerin sighed. "Goodbye, Elise. I don't wish you ill. If you're still here after we drive the imperials out of the northlands, think again about finding out whether Duren wants to see you."

"Maybe I'll ask the imperials to take me up to his holding—my holding," she said. "They're going forward. You're not."

His face froze. "Goodbye, Elise," he said again, and left the tavern. At the edge of the village, he looked back over his shoulder. She was not standing in the doorway, watching him go. He hadn't really expected she would be.

"Captain, why in the five hells aren't you getting drunk?" Van demanded. "Something horrible like that happened to me, I wouldn't be able to turn both eyes in the same direction for the next three, four days."

"When I first set eyes on her, I thought that was just what I was going to do," the Fox answered. "But do you know what? It's been so long, she's not important enough to me for me to want to do that."

Van's eyes got wide. "That may be the saddest thing anybody ever said."

Gerin thought about it. "I don't know. *Not* getting over her in all this time would be worse, don't you think?"

"She's . . . not much like Mother, is she?" Dagref spoke very slowly, picking his words with obvious care. He didn't want to offend the Fox, who had, after all, fathered his half-brother on Elise, but he also didn't want to speak well of her. He balanced the one and the other better than most youths his age could have done.

Gerin considered the question as carefully as Dagref had asked it. "Some ways yes, some ways no," he replied at last. "She's a very bright woman, the same as your mother is. But I don't think Elise is ever happy with what she has. If it's not perfect, it's not good enough for her."

"That's foolish," Dagref said.

Van guffawed. "This from the lad who, if you tell a dirty story twice and say the whore was awkward the first time and then that she was clumsy the next, will call you on the difference then and there."

Dagref had the grace to blush, or perhaps the embers got a little more ruddy. He said, "Actually, I think you called her stumblefooted the first time I heard that story, didn't you?"

"Stumblefooted? I never—" Van broke off and glared at Dagref. "You're having me on. Do you know what I do to people who try having me on?"

"Something dreadful and appalling, or you wouldn't be telling me about it," Dagref returned, unabashed.

"What *are* we going to do about him, Fox?" Van said.

"To the five hells with me if I know," Gerin answered. "The way I look at it, it's the world's lookout as much as Dagref's."

"The way I look at it, you're right," Van said.

Dagref didn't rise to that, as he might have a couple

of years before. Nor did he let himself be diverted, asking, "If she's different from my mother, why did you marry her?"

"It seemed like a good idea at the time," the Fox replied. Dagref folded his arms across his chest, not about to let an answer like that be fobbed off on him. It was a pose Gerin had assumed many times with larcenous peasants, stubborn nobles, and his own children. Having it aimed at him made him chuckle in spite of everything. He said, "You can't always know ahead of time how you'll get along with somebody. You can't always know ahead of time *if* you'll get along with somebody."

"That's so," Van agreed. "Take a look at Fand and me."

"Oh, nonsense," Gerin said, glad to be talking about someone else's marriage instead of his own. "You knew perfectly well that you and Fand didn't get along."

"Aye, true enough." The outlander's grin was on the sheepish side. "But we make a sport of fighting, if you know what I mean. Most of the time, we make a sport of fighting, I should say. Some of it, now, some of it turns real."

"I don't understand." Dagref turned to Gerin. "Why would you want to fight with someone you love, someone you're living with?"

"Why are you asking me?" the Fox said. "I don't want to do that. He does." He pointed at Van. "It's the first time I've ever heard him say so out loud, though."

"To the crows with you." Van spoke without much rancor. "You want so much peace and quiet, Fox, you want life to be dull all the bloody time."

"No." Gerin shook his head; this was an old argument, and one in which he could take part without bruising. "I just don't want life to blow up in my face, the way a pot of bean stew will if you leave it in the fire with the lid on too tight for too long."

"Sometimes life does blow up in your face, though," Dagref said, a truth as self-evident as any at the moment. "What are you going to do about . . . this woman?" Again, he took a little thought to find the phrase he wanted.

"Nothing," Gerin replied, which made both Dagref and Van stare at him. He went on, "I won't send her up to Duren without finding out whether he wants to have anything to do with her. I offered to bring her along with the army so she'd find out as soon as I did whether he wants her to come up to his holding, but she said no to that."

Van coughed. "If she hangs around here, she won't know for a goodish while what Duren has to say, because the imperials aren't going to stop following us. They'll be here day after tomorrow at the latest."

"I don't think that was the biggest worry in her mind," Gerin answered. "She has relatives south of the High Kirs. You've met one of them—remember?"

"Aye, now that you remind me of it. Some sort of fancy noble, gave the Emperor advice." Van frowned in concentration. "Valdabrun—that's what his name was. He had a mistress I wouldn't have minded tasting at all."

"That's the name," Gerin agreed. "Now me, I'd forgotten about his leman till you called her to my mind."

"You were too busy staring at Elise to have much room left in your mind for other women," the outlander said. Gerin would have got angry at him had he not been telling the truth.

Dagref said, "If her family were advisors to the old Emperor, what does this new Emperor think of them?"

"I don't know," Gerin answered. "That also crossed my mind. I don't think it crossed Elise's, and by then I wasn't going to bring it up. If she goes south of the High Kirs, she's gone, that's all. I won't miss her, not a bit." And that was true, or almost true. He'd missed her more than he'd imagined possible, back in the days just after she first left him. Occasional echoes of that feeling had kept cropping up through the years, even after he'd been happily yoked to Selatre for a long time.

Was one of those echoes cropping up now? If it was, he didn't intend to admit it, even to himself. He waited for Van or Dagref to challenge him. Van, after all, had known Elise, while Dagref had few compunctions about asking questions, no matter how personal.

But neither of them said anything. He realized neither of them was going to say anything. A small sigh of relief escaped him. They'd let him off the hook.

✧ ✧ ✧

Ferdulf flying above them, Gerin's men rolled north through the village the next morning. The Fox wondered if Elise would come out and watch them go, as some of the villagers did. He didn't see her. Once he'd passed through, he decided that was just as well.

Now, instead of screening the army's advance, Rihwin's riders covered the retreat. They did a better job of that than Gerin had thought when he gave them the duty. Rihwin came trotting up to him to report: "The imperials keep dogging us, aye, lord king, but not very hard. We've taught them respect, I think, for they are never sure if we might gallop out at them from some unexpected direction."

"That's good," Gerin said. "If we'd taught them so much respect that they stopped dogging us altogether, that would be even better."

"It would also be too much to ask for," Rihwin pointed out.

"Oh, I wasn't asking for it," Gerin said. "If I did, no one would pay me any attention. But it *would* be better."

"Er—yes," Rihwin said, and soon found an excuse to rejoin his riders.

Van chuckled. "That was well done, Captain. Not easy to confuse Rihwin—not least, I expect, on account of he's so often confused on his own—but you managed." The outlander lost his smile. "Have to tell you, though, I'm a bit on the confused side myself. What are we doing now, and why are we doing that instead of something else?"

"What are we doing?" the Fox repeated. "We're falling back—that's what. Why are we doing it? I can think of three reasons offhand." He ticked them off on his fingers: "If we don't fall back the imperials will smash us here. That's one. If we do fall back, maybe the imperials will string themselves out or give us some chance to hit part of them from ambush. That's two. And, as we're falling back, we're falling back into country that hasn't been foraged too heavily, so we won't starve, which we would, and pretty bloody quick, if we stay where we are. Three."

"Aye, well, there is that." Van looked around. "Falling

back toward land Aragis rules, if we're not on that land already. Don't know how happy he'll be if we take everything that isn't tied down and cut the lashings off what is tied down so we can take that, too."

Gerin looked around. "To the five hells with me if I know where Aragis' southern border is. Maybe we'll find boundary stones, maybe we won't. To the five hells with me if I care, either. If Aragis thinks I'm going to starve to death to keep from bothering his serfs' precious crops, to the five hells with him, too."

Over his shoulder, Dagref said, "If the threat lay by the Niffet, he'd eat you out of house and home without a second thought."

"Well, the gods know that's true," Gerin said. Now he looked straight ahead, north and a little east, a thoughtful expression on his face. "Ikos is just on the other side of Aragis' holdings, too. I've never had cause to go to the Sibyl by the southern route, but maybe I will." He nodded, more decisively than he'd thought he would. "Yes, indeed. Maybe I will."

Dagref said, "In the learned genealogies, they say Biton is a son of Dyaus Allfather, but—"

Gerin held up his hand. "But that's Elabonians writing for Elabonians below the High Kirs," he finished. "Biton is truly a god of this land here, and everyone who lives in the northlands knows it."

"Even so," Dagref said. "Compared to the gods of the Gradi, Baivers, god of brewing and barley, is a god of this land, even though we Elabonians brought him here a couple of hundred years ago when we conquered this province. Because he is a god of this land, you were able to use him against the gods of the Gradi. From that, it would follow logically—"

"—that I might use Biton against the Elabonian Empire." Gerin interrupted once more. "Yes."

"I thought you might not have seen it," Dagref said, a little sulkily.

"Well, I did." Gerin clapped his son on the back. "Don't let it worry you. The two of us think a lot alike—"

"You're both sneaky," Van put in.

"Thank you," Gerin and Dagref said in the same breath,

which made the outlander stare from one of them to the other. Gerin continued, "As I was saying before we were disturbed by a breath of wind there—"

"Honh!" Van said.

"—the two of us think a lot alike, but I've been doing it longer, so it's likely I'll come up with a lot of the same notions you do," Gerin went on imperturbably. "That shouldn't disappoint you, and it shouldn't stop you from telling me what's on your beady little mind—"

"Honh!" Now Dagref interrupted, doing a surprisingly good impression of Van.

Gerin talked through him as he'd talked through the outlander: "—because you never can tell, you might come up with something I've missed." He took a deep breath, triumphant at finally managing to complete his thought.

"Fair enough, Father." Dagref heaved his shoulders up and down in a sigh. "Hard sometimes, being a smaller, less detailed copy of the man you've already become. It makes me feel rather like an abridged manuscript."

"No, not an abridged one," Gerin said. "You just have a lot more blank parchment left at the end of your scroll than I do, that's all."

"Hmm." Dagref contemplated that. "Well, all right—maybe so." He flicked the reins and urged the horses up to a better pace.

"By the things you've said, Fox, I know what the difference between you and him is," Van remarked.

"Tell me," Gerin urged. Dagref's back expressed mute interest.

"I will," Van said. "The difference is, Fox, that your father had no more idea what to do with you than a crow would with a chick that came out of the egg with white feathers instead of black. Is that so, or am I lying?"

"It's so, sure enough," Gerin agreed. "My brother was a warrior born, everything my father could have wanted. My father hadn't the slightest notion what to make of me. I might be the first real live scholar spawned in the northlands in better than a hundred years."

"And yet you're a king, while your father died a baron, so you never can tell," Van said. "But my point is, Dagref's the second real live scholar spawned in the northlands. You have a notion of what you've got there, while your father had never a clue with you."

"Ah," Gerin said. "Well, there's some truth in that, sure enough. How about it, Dagref? Do you like it better that I can guess along with you some of the time, or would you rather I had never a clue?"

Dagref looked back over his shoulder at the Fox again. "I can guess along with you some of the time, Father. What in the world makes you think you can guess along with me?" Van guffawed. Gerin felt his ears heat.

Riders and charioteers fanned out through the countryside around the village by which Gerin had chosen to camp for the night. They brought back cattle and sheep and ducks and chickens. "Had to let the air out of a shepherd before he'd cough up his beasts," one rider said, patting his bow so as to leave no possible doubt about what he meant.

Under other circumstances, Gerin would have been angry at him for alienating the peasantry. As things were, the Fox hardly noticed the comment. He had his sword in his left hand, and was wondering if he'd have to start carving chunks off the village headman, who was doing his best to act like an idiot from birth.

"No," the fellow said, "we don't have no grain stored in pits. We don't have no beans in pits, neither."

"That's very interesting," Gerin said, "very interesting indeed. I suppose you get through every winter by not eating during most of it."

"Seems that way, a lot of the time," the headman answered sullenly.

"Well, all right." Gerin's voice was light and blithe. "I suppose we'll just have to burn this place down so all these houses here don't get in our way while we're searching."

The headman sent him a look full of loathing and led him over to the storage pits, which had been concealed by grass growing over them. "I thought you had a name for being soft alongside Aragis," the peasant grumbled.

"Only goes to show you can't always trust what you hear, doesn't it?" the Fox returned with a smile. The village headman's glare held even more hate than it had before.

Having got what he wanted, Gerin generously affected not to notice. Keeping his army fed was at the moment more important than keeping Aragis' peasants happy.

That was his opinion, at any rate. He discovered the next day that Aragis had a different one. A chariot bearing the Archer's son, Aranast, came jouncing over a side road toward Gerin's army. When Aranast had made his way up alongside the Fox, he spoke without preamble: "Lord king, my father forbids you from foraging on the countryside while in lands whose overlord he is."

"Does he?" Gerin answered. "That's nice."

Aranast took off his bronze, potlike helm and scratched his head. "Does that mean you will obey this prohibition?"

"Of course not," Gerin replied. "If he can teach me how to subsist on no food while I cross his lands, I might try it. Otherwise, though, I'll do what I have to do to get through them."

"You dare go against my father's stated will?" Aranast's eyes went round and wide and staring. No one in Aragis' lands had dared go against his stated will for many years. Though Aranast gave signs of being a fairly formidable fellow in his own right, he seemed astonished anyone might imagine going against his father's stated will.

"I just said so. Weren't you listening?" Gerin asked politely. "He's not my suzerain, so I'm under no obligation to obey him, and he's told me to do something impossible, which means I'd be an idiot to obey him. Do I look like an idiot to you, young fellow?"

Aranast didn't answer that, which might have been just as well. His frown did its best to be severe to the point of threatening. People were no doubt much more in the habit of calling him things like *prince* and *heir* and maybe *your highness* than *young fellow*. Taking a deep breath, he said, "My father entered into alliance with you in good faith. He did not enter into it to give you leave to plunder his holdings."

"Oh, don't be a pompous twit," Gerin said, which flicked Aranast on his vanity much harder than *young fellow* had done. The Fox went on, "I told you once, I don't aim to let myself starve. If I were plundering, though, I'd have booty with me, wouldn't I? I'm feeding myself and I'm feeding my men. Would you like some roast mutton?"

"Generous of you to offer me what already belongs to my father," Aranast remarked. Dagref was much younger, but would have done the sarcasm better than Aranast even so. Still, the effort was there.

Gerin rewarded it with sarcasm of his own: "Glad you think so." That drew another glare from Aragis' son. "Where is your father, anyhow?" the Fox asked.

"West of here," Aranast answered. "The imperials still press him hard. Some of them are between him and you. I had to thread my way past them to deliver his word to you, and to have you set it aside as being of no account."

"It was a foolish word to deliver, and you can tell him I said so. He might be better off if more people let him know when he was being foolish," Gerin said. "But he sees no hope of linking with me again?"

"He does not, being too sore beset," Aranast answered. "He hoped you might rejoin him, and also expressed the hope that you would use your skill at magic to good effect in the struggle against the Empire."

"I'll do everything I can," Gerin said with a sigh. Aragis persisted in believing he could do things he couldn't. He held up a forefinger. "Has Aragis also forbidden the imperials from plundering his holdings?"

Aranast shook his head. "No, for he did not think it would do any good. You, however, are not his enemy, unless you choose to make yourself so."

"Or unless he makes me one by insisting I do things I can't," Gerin said. "A man who asks too much of his friends starts finding out he doesn't have so many friends as he thought he did."

"I will take your words back to my father, that he may judge them for himself," Aranast said stiffly.

"Fine," the Fox told him. "Tell him this, too: if he wants to fight a war against me after we beat the Empire, I'll be ready, the same as I was ready to fight a war against him before I knew the imperials were on this side of the High Kirs."

He kept astonishing Aranast. "You challenge my father?" Aragis' son said. "No one challenges my father."

"I've done it for more than twenty years, as he's challenged me all that time," Gerin answered. "Tell him I'm doing what I have to do here, no more—and no less."

Still scowling, still muttering to himself, Aranast Aragis' son got back into his chariot and rattled off toward the west, toward whatever was left of Aragis' army. "Well, he doesn't lack for nerve, that's certain," Van said, eyeing the dust the horses' hooves and the chariot's wheels kicked up from the track along which it traveled.

"Who doesn't?" Gerin asked. "Aragis or Aranast?"

"Both of 'em, now that I think on it," the outlander replied. Gerin watched that receding plume of dust, too. After a moment, he nodded.

Getting livestock and grain from the peasants who lived under Aragis' rule turned out to be, for the most part, easier than Gerin had expected. The majority of village headmen had lived so long under the Archer, they seemed to have forgotten the possibility of cheating an overlord. "Take what you will, lord," one of them told Gerin. "Whatever you take, you'd do worse to us if we tried to hide it from you." The men and women who came up to listen to him talking with the Fox nodded. Aragis, evidently, had given lessons of that sort.

A few villages, though, appeared to have no substance whatsoever: only huts and whatever was ripening in the fields. Gerin's men found no livestock even on searching the nearby woods, and the headmen at such places staunchly denied having grain pits anywhere by their huts.

"Do what you want with me," one said. "I can't give you what I haven't got."

"You should be careful saying things like that," Gerin told him. "If you said them to Aragis or his men, they'd do it."

The headman pulled off his tunic and stood there in his wool trousers. He turned his back on the Fox. Long, pale ridged scars crisscrossed it. "Laid the whip on himself, he did," he said with something that sounded almost like pride. "He didn't come away with anything here, either, on account of there isn't anything to come away with."

After seeing those scars, Gerin gave up and went on to the next village, whose headman proved more tractable. The Fox remained unconvinced the serfs he'd just left had as little as they'd shown, but lacked both time and inclination to check as hard as he might have otherwise. He also knew a certain amount of admiration for their headman. Anyone who could stand up to Aragis had more than the common amount of nerve.

Every so often, the imperials hounding the Fox's force would press forward. A couple of the skirmishes were sharp, but the men from south of the High Kirs made no effort to get close to his army, stay close to it, and hound it to death, which was what he would have done to theirs had it not been reinforced. He wondered how Aragis fared, with more imperials after him. The Archer had sent no more messengers to him after Aranast's unsuccessful mission.

Keeps dotted the landscape, as they did throughout the northlands. Most of the nobles who dwelt in them had gone to fight under Aragis. These days, the castles housed striplings, graybeards, and noblewomen who were often more determined than the menfolk left behind. Some of the keeps opened their gates to share what they had and let Gerin and some of his officers sleep in real beds. Some—very often, those where petty barons' wives seemed to be in charge—stayed shut up tight against his force, as if against enemies.

"If you're friends, you won't be offended that we don't let you in, because you'll understand why we don't," one of those women called from the walkway around the wall of the keep she was running. "And if you're foes masquerading as friends—well, to the five hells with you, in that case."

Gerin didn't push her any further. For one thing, he would have had to lay siege to the keep to get inside if she wouldn't let down the drawbridge. For another, what she said made perfectly good sense from her point of view.

Van thought so, too, saying, "By the gods, if Fand were running a keep, that's the sort of defiance she would shout."

"You're likely right." Gerin raised an eyebrow. "Maybe Maeva gets it from both sides of the family."

"Aye, maybe she—" Van broke off three words too late, and gave the Fox a dirty look. "And maybe you talk out of both sides of your mouth."

"Maybe I do, when there's a need, but not this time," Gerin said. "I've said the same thing all along here."

Van rumbled something, down deep in his chest. Maybe it was just a discontented noise; maybe it was an oath in one of the many languages he'd picked up in his travels. Whatever it was, he changed the subject: "What's the road up to Ikos from the south like?"

"I've never taken it myself, so I can't tell you for certain," Gerin answered. "I hear, though, that it's easier than jogging west off the Elabon Way because it doesn't go through that haunted forest in the hill country there."

"I won't miss that forest a bit, thank you very much," Van said with a shudder. "There's things in there that don't think men have any business going through on the roads. The gods help you if you wander off under the trees, or if you're stupid enough to try spending the night there."

"You're right," the Fox said. "I wouldn't want to do either of those things."

"Sounds like an interesting place," said Dagref, who'd never been through the forest.

Van laughed. So did Gerin, as much in awe as in mirth. "A lot of places sound interesting, when you hear people talking about them at a nice, safe distance," he observed. "Visiting them, you'll find, is a lot less interesting than hearing people talk about them at a nice, safe distance."

"You've been into the forest," Dagref said. "You've been in it a good many times, and you must have always come out the other side, or else you wouldn't be here at a nice, safe distance talking about it."

"Logic," Gerin agreed gravely. "But doing it once, or even doing it a few times, doesn't mean I'm anxious to do it again. Unlike some people I could name, I've never been wild for adventure for adventure's sake. One of the things that make adventure adventure is that somebody or something is trying to kill you, and I'm usually against that."

"Oh, I'm against anybody or anything trying to kill me, too," Van said. "Best way to stop it, I've always thought, is to kill whoever or whatever it is first."

Gerin shook his head. "The *best* way to stop it is not to put yourself in a place where anybody or anything can try to kill you in the first place."

"A long life and a boring one," Van said with a sneer.

"This argument strikes me as being moot, seeing that we have an imperial army on our tail and another on our left that's dogging Aragis—that we hope is dogging Aragis," Dagref said.

"A long, boring life," Van repeated. "Nothing to do but futter women and sit around drinking ale." He paused, as if listening to what he'd just said. Then he stuck an elbow in Gerin's ribs, almost hard enough to pitch him out of the chariot. "Well, it could be worse."

Aragis' holdings ran up close to the southern end of the valley in which lay the village of Ikos and Biton's shrine. Not even Aragis had been so arrogant as to claim that valley as his own.

Guardsmen from the temple patrolled the road that led up into Ikos. They did not bother on the road that ran west off the Elabon Way; the strange trees and stranger beasts of the forest through which that road ran guaranteed its safety better than men with bronze weapons and armor of leather and bronze could hope to do. Here, though, on an open dirt track, they were needed.

One of them recognized Gerin. "Lord king!" he exclaimed in no small surprise. "Why do you come to Ikos by this route?" After a moment, he phrased that differently: "*How* do you come to Ikos by this route?"

"Having an army from south of the High Kirs on my trail might have something to do with it," the Fox answered, at which the temple guards exclaimed in dismay. Biton might have—surely would have—seen that, but he hadn't told them anything about it. Gerin went on, "Aragis and I made alliance, as you may have heard, which is what I was doing down in the direction of the mountains in the first place."

"We had heard you had he had made common cause, aye, but rumors of the foe have been many and various," the soldier answered.

"It's the Empire. Even though we'd forgotten about it

up here, it never forgot about us, worse luck," Gerin said. "The imperials have beaten Aragis, too, and they're chasing him somewhere off to the west of here. How do you suppose the farseeing god would feel about being shoved back into a pantheon headed up in the City of Elabon?"

"If the Empire tries such a thing, there will be trouble," the guardsman said positively. He himself looked to be an Elabonian in blood, but several of the soldiers with him were plainly of the folk who had lived in the northlands before the Elabonian Empire first came over the High Kirs a couple of centuries before. They were slimmer than Elabonians, with wide cheekbones and delicate, pointed chins. Selatre, who had formerly been Biton's Sibyl at Ikos, had that look to her.

One of those men asked, "And why do you come to Ikos now, lord king?" His Elabonian was fluent enough, but had a half-lisping, half-hissing accent to it: traces of the language the folk of the old blood still sometimes spoke among themselves.

"Partly because I'm in retreat," Gerin admitted, "but also partly because I would hear what the farseeing god has to say about this—if lord Biton has anything to say about it."

The guardsman who had spoken first said, "You cannot bring your whole host into the valley to camp. It may be that they shall be permitted to traverse the valley, but they may not encamp in it."

"Why not?" Gerin asked. "Biton protects his own shrine. Even if we wanted to plunder, we wouldn't dare."

"But Biton's protection reaches less certainly to the villages around the sacred precinct," the temple guard replied. "We would not have them plundered. Surely, with your numbers, you can overcome us here, but what sort of welcome will you have from the god if you do?"

"A point," Gerin said. "A distinct point. Very well. It shall be as you say. I'd sooner have my men foraging off Aragis' lands than those here in the valley, anyhow."

"So, lord king, would we," the guardsman said. "You being allied to him, I hope you will forgive my saying so, but Aragis the Archer has not always made the most comfortable of neighbors."

"He hasn't always made the most comfortable of neighbors for me, either," the Fox answered, "and he has fewer reasons to keep from stepping on my toes than to keep from stepping on Biton's. Or rather, Biton can do a better job of stepping on Aragis' toes than I can."

"If he's not gone to war with you in all these years, lord king, he thinks you can do something along those lines," the guard said.

"You flatter me outrageously," Gerin said. He enjoyed flattery. There was, he told himself, nothing wrong with enjoying it. The trick was not to take it too seriously. When you started believing everything people told you about how clever you were, you proved you weren't so clever as they said.

He gave his army their orders. The men seemed content enough to rest where they were. "If the imperials try to bring us to battle, lord king, we'll make 'em sorry they were ever born," one of them said, which raised a cheer from the rest. Since the bulk of the force from south of the High Kirs was chasing Aragis, the Fox thought his men did have a decent chance of doing just that.

When he started forward, up into Biton's valley, Adiatunnus surprised him by coming ahead, too. "By your leave, lord king, I'm fain to be after seeing the Sybil myself," the Trokmê chieftain said. "The oracle here was a famous one, you'll know, even back in the days when I and all my people dwelt north of the Niffet."

"Yes, I did know that." Gerin nodded.

"But there's summat else you might not ha' known," Adiatunnus said. "Back before Balamung the wizard, the one you slew, now, back before he led us south over the river, some of our chieftains came down to Ikos to hear whether 'twould be wise to go with that uncanny kern. But they were never heard of again that I recall, puir wights."

"As a matter of fact, I knew that, too," the Fox answered. "They tried to kill me here. Van and I—and Elise, too—killed all of them but one. He decided moving against me wouldn't be a good notion, but Balamung caught him and burned him in a wicker cage."

"Ah, I mind me I heard summat o' that, now that you

speak of it," Adiatunnus said. "But you'll not mind if I come with you the now?"

"Not unless you plan on trying to murder me inside the temple, the way those other Trokmoi did," Gerin replied.

"Nay, though I thank you for the offer," Adiatunnus said, which made Gerin snort. Adiatunnus went on, "I've had my chances, that I have, and the putting of you in the ground for good and all, I've found, is more trouble nor it's turned out to be worth."

"For your sweet and generous praises, far beyond my deserts, I thank you most humbly," the Fox said, and Adiatunnus snorted in turn. With a sigh, Gerin turned to Rihwin. "If the imperials do pitch into us, you're in command till I can get back. Send word to me straightaway, and try not to wreck the army till I can come and join the celebration."

Rihwin gave him a sour look. "For *your* sweet and generous praises, lord king, I thank you." Gerin chuckled and dipped his head, conceding the round to his fellow Fox.

When Dagref drove the chariot up toward the temple to Biton, Adiatunnus followed close in his own car. Above them floated Ferdulf. The temple guardsmen stared up at him with interest and curiosity. So did Gerin. He said, "Are you sure you want to visit the Sibyl and the farseeing god? Biton and your father don't get on well." That would do for an understatement till a better one came along, which he didn't think would happen soon.

Ferdulf turned a fine semidivine sneer his way. "Why should I care what my father thinks or does?" he returned. "Since he has no room in his life for *me*, do his views on others—even other gods—matter?"

"I told him he shouldn't have got into the wine," Gerin murmured to Van.

The outlander rolled his eyes. "A man's own children don't listen to him. Why should anyone else's children?"

"Whose son is that?" one of the guardsmen asked, pointing up to Ferdulf.

"Mavrix's," Gerin answered. "The Sithonian wine god got him on one of my peasant women."

"Is it so?" The warrior's eyes widened. "But Mavrix and the lord Biton worked together in driving the monsters off the surface of the earth and back into the caverns under Biton's shrine."

"So they did," Gerin agreed. "And it was the most quarrelsome cooperation you've ever seen in all your born days."

They drove past several neat little villages and the fields surrounding them. The peasants in the valley of Ikos were all freeholders, owing allegiance to no overlord save Biton. That arrangement had always smacked of anarchy to the Fox, but he, like Aragis, fought shy of trying to annex the valley. If Biton tolerated freeholders here, Gerin would, too.

Ferdulf flew down and hovered alongside Gerin like a large, bad-tempered mosquito. In confidential tones, he asked, "Do you think the farseeing god will be able to tell me how to take vengeance on my father?"

"I have no way of knowing that," Gerin said. "If I were you, though, Ferdulf, I wouldn't get my hopes too high."

"He's all god," Ferdulf muttered. "It's not fair."

"No, it probably isn't," Gerin admitted, "but I don't know what you can do about it, either."

White against greenery, the marble walls of Biton's shrine gleamed ahead. The earthquake that had released the monsters had also overthrown it, but Biton's own power restored it at the same time as Biton and Mavrix recontained the monsters.

"Isn't that pretty?" Adiatunnus said, and then, in speculative tones, "Doesn't look so strong as the wall of a proper keep, though. And I've heard the god keeps all manner of pretties inside, though."

"So he does," Gerin said, "and it's worth your life to try to steal any of them. Biton has a special plague he uses to smite people who walk off with what's his. I've seen one or two he's killed with it. It's not a pretty way to go."

Adiatunnus looked thoughtful, but no less acquisitive, as they drew near the temple compound. Back in the days when he was newly over the Niffet, he likely would have assumed Gerin was lying and tried to steal. He would have paid for it then. He would pay for it now if he tried it, too. Gerin didn't think he would be so foolish.

Outside the gates, attendants took charge of the two

chariots. No others waited there. The shrine did not draw the crowds it had before the earthquake, let alone before the days when folk came from all over the Elabonian Empire, and even from beyond its borders, to gain the Sibyl's oracular responses.

A plump priest with a eunuch's smooth face led the travelers into the temple compound. Ferdulf had been drifting along a couple of feet off the ground. As soon as he passed through the entranceway, he descended to the earth with a thump that staggered him. He glared toward the temple ahead. "He's a full god, too," he growled resentfully, "so I have to do what he wants. Not what I want. Still not fair."

Adiatunnus and the couple of Trokmoi with him paid no attention. They were gaping at the treasures on display in the courtyard, chiefest among them the statues of the Elabonian Emperors Ros the Fierce, who had conquered the northlands for the Empire, and of his son, Oren the Builder, who had erected the temple now standing above the entrance to the Sibyl's cavern. Both statues were larger than life, both starkly realistic, and both made of ivory and gold.

Gerin's voice was dry as he gave Adiatunnus good advice: "Pull your tongue back in, there, and stop drooling on the grass."

"Och, 'tis no easy thing you ask of me, Fox darling," the Trokmê chieftain said with a sigh. His eyes flicked from the statues to stacked ingots to great bronze bowls supported on golden tripods. "I'd heard of these riches, but the difference between the hearing of them and the seeing of them with the eyes of a man himself, it's the difference 'twixt hearing of a pretty woman and lying with her. And these won't be all the gauds, either, I'm thinking."

"You're right about that, too," Gerin said. "There's plenty more in the caverns off the route to the Sibyl's throne." Adiatunnus sighed again, as at the thought of the pretty woman he would never meet.

He glowered at the frieze on the entablature above the colonnaded entrance to the temple itself. It showed Ros the Fierce driving back Trokmoi with Biton's aid. Adiatunnus did not approve of anything depicting Elabonians beating

Trokmoi. Gerin didn't suppose he could blame his vassal for that.

They went into the temple. Adiatunnus and the two woodsrunners with him exclaimed again, this time at the rich marbles of the columns, the fancy woods that had gone into the pews, and the gold and silver candelabra throwing sheets of light over them.

Ferdulf exclaimed, too, but he was pointing at the cult statue of Biton that stood near the opening into the caverns below the shrine. The statue was not an anthropomorphic representation of the farseeing god, as were the rest of the images in the compound. Instead, it was a column of black basalt utterly plain except for scratches that might have been eyes and a jutting phallus. "How old is it?" Ferdulf whispered; in this place, even he showed a certain amount of respect for the god who ruled here.

"I wouldn't even try to guess," Gerin answered. "It's been a shrine for a long, long time, even if it didn't used to be as pretty as we Elabonians made it after we came up here."

"Not *we* Elabonians," Ferdulf said testily. "I am no Elabonian, for which I thank all the gods, Biton very much included."

Gerin made his voice sweet as clover honey: "On your mother's side, you are." He cherished the horrible look the demigod gave him. Perhaps he shouldn't have yielded to the temptation; reminding Ferdulf of his background was liable to make him less willing to oppose the Elabonian Empire. Turning aside every temptation, though, made life too dull to stand.

The priest waved the suppliants to the pews. "Pray to the lord Biton," he urged. "Pray that your question will be phrased in such a way as to make his answer, which shall be true, also meaningfully true for you."

That, Gerin thought, was good advice. The Sibyl's oracular responses were often obscure, clearer after the event than beforehand. He tried to clear his mind of all his worries so he could ask a question that would have as unambiguous an answer as possible.

Just for a moment, he looked up at the cult statue. He'd done that on other visits to Biton's shrine. Those crudely carved eyes would seem to come alive for a heartbeat, to look back into his. He wondered if that would happen again. It did—and then some. For an instant, no more, he saw the god as he had seen him in the little shack back at Fox Keep where he undertook his sorceries. Biton might have been a handsome man, but for the eye in the back of his head that showed when he twisted his neck preternaturally far. And then he was gone, back into the basalt.

"That statue—that *is* the god," Ferdulf whispered—had he seen the apparition, too? "That's not his image—that *is* the god. It's how he looks when he isn't thinking about how he looks, and when people aren't thinking about how he looks."

"Maybe it is," Gerin said. Philosophers had always wondered whether gods were as they were because people conceived of them as being that way, or if people conceived of gods as they did because the gods essentially were like that. The Fox suspected such arguments would go on forever.

"Have you composed your mind?" the eunuch priest asked. Gerin nodded. The priest smiled. "Then come with me. We shall go down below the ground, down to the cave of the Sibyl, where Biton shall speak through her."

He tried to make it sound mysterious and exotic. It *was* mysterious and exotic, but Gerin had gone many times into the cavern below the temple to see the Sibyl—and for other, darker, purposes. He climbed to his feet, saying, "Let's get on with it." The plump eunuch in his fancy robes looked disappointed that the Fox and his comrades were not trembling with awe, but took a torch and led them all to the mouth of the cave.

Elabonian workmen had put steps down from the cave mouth after a prominent visitor years before tripped, fell, and broke his ankle. Soon, though, Gerin's feet trod the natural stone of the cavern. Generations of suppliants seeking guidance from the Sibyl had worn a path in the rock, but it was a path more visible in torchlight than smooth beneath the feet.

Every so often, torches flaming in sconces added their light to that of the burning brand the priest carried. A cool breeze made the flames flicker. "Isn't that strange, now?" Adiatunnus murmured. "I always thought the air inside a cave would be still and dead as a corp."

"It is the power of the god," the priest said.

"Or else it's something natural that we don't understand," Gerin put in. The priest glared at him, eyeballs glittering in the torchlight. Gerin looked back steadily. Biton didn't seem inclined to smite him for blasphemy. With a disappointed sniff, the priest resumed the journey down to the Sibyl's cave.

Other paths led off that one; other caverns opened onto it. Biton's priesthood used some of them to store treasures. The Trokmoi exclaimed at the gleaming precious metals the torches briefly revealed. Of course, they also exclaimed at the beautiful but largely worthless bits of shining rock crystal set here and there in the walls of the cavern.

And some entrances to Sibyl's underground chamber were bricked up and sealed not only with masonry but also with potent magical charms. Some of the bricks, baked with round tops like loaves of bread, were almost immeasurably ancient.

Ferdulf shivered as he came to one such wall. "Monsters dwell behind these bricks," he murmured.

"That's so," Gerin agreed: "monsters like Geroge and Tharma. They have an understanding of sorts with us now, which is why some of these charms have been set aside here. They could come forth, but they don't: their gods are in our debt for launching them against the gods of the Gradi."

"A mad venture," the priest said. Adiatunnus nodded; the torchlight made the shadow of his bobbing head dip and swirl. Since Gerin was inclined to agree with them, he didn't argue.

Before he was quite ready, they came to the Sibyl's cave. Biton's priestess sat on a throne that looked as if it had been carved from a single black pearl, which glowed nacreously when light fell on it. She herself wore a plain tunic of undyed linen. The eunuch priest went up to her, set a hand on her shoulder, and murmured something too low for Gerin to catch. Had the fellow been a whole man, he would not have been permitted to touch her; not only did Sibyls remain lifelong maidens, they were not allowed even to touch true men.

The Sibyl looked something like Selatre—not close enough to be near kin, but plainly of the same blood. She eyed Gerin with curiosity; perhaps the priest had told her who he was—no reason for her to remember his face, with his last visit five years in the past—and reminded her that he was wed to the woman who'd preceded her on the Sibyl's throne. Was she wondering what that would be like?

If she was, she didn't show it. "You have your question?" she asked the Fox.

"I do," he answered. "Here it is: how may the Empire of Elabon be made to give up its claims to the northlands and withdraw its forces south over the High Kirs?" He'd phrased it carefully, not asking what he could do to make that happen. Perhaps it would happen without him. Perhaps it would not happen at all. He forced himself to shove that thought aside.

He had scarcely uttered the last word when the Sibyl stiffened. She thrashed on the throne, limbs splayed awkwardly. Her eyes rolled up in her head till only the whites showed. When she spoke again, it was not in her own voice, but in Biton's, a deep, virile baritone:

"The foe is strong, up to no good—
To rout him will take bronze and wood.
You must not find the god you seek:
'Twould make your fate a sour reek.
They snap and float and always trouble,
But without them fortune turns to rubble."

IX

As soon as Ferdulf left the temple compound, he hopped into the air and let out a luxurious sigh of relief. "My feet were getting tired," he said, and then, to Gerin, "Well, was that obscure enough to suit you?"

"And to spare," the Fox answered. "I've had difficult omens from Biton and the Sibyl before, but never one close to that."

"As best I could see, it was meaningless, not difficult," Dagref said.

"But can you see as far as the farseeing god?" Gerin asked.

Dagref only shrugged. Adiatunnus said, "I'm with the colt, lord king. When you hear summat without plain sense in it, more often the reason is that it's senseless than too clever for words, I'm thinking."

More often than not, Gerin would have made the same argument. Here, he said, "I've seen Biton be right a good many times when everyone would have thought he was wrong. I'm not going to say he's wrong here, not now."

"Why do we hope we don't find a god?" Van demanded. "If we're seeking one, shouldn't we hope we do find him?"

"And which god would you be seeking?" Adiatunnus added. " 'Twouldn't be Biton his own self, or we're ruined or ever we start. But he wouldna say who it was, did you see?"

"Obscure. Ferdulf had the right word for it," Gerin said. "Sooner or later, we *will* have the meaning laid out before us."

"Aye, likely when it's too late to do us any good," Van said.

"That is the way of oracles sometimes," the Fox agreed. "But you never know till you try."

"And now that we have gone and tried and got nothing to speak of for it, what are we to be doing next?" Adiatunnus asked. "Shall we bring our army through the valley of Ikos?—on the promise we willna linger, mind."

"I don't want to do that," Gerin said. "I don't think the god wants us to do that. If it's that or stay out and be destroyed, then I might, but not before. I still have a fighting chance of beating the imperials, and no one who opposes a god straight up will do anything but lose."

"You say that," Dagref said, "you who have probably outdone more gods in more different ways than anyone else alive."

"But never straight up," Gerin said. "The way to deal with gods is to trick them, or else to make them do what you want by showing them it gives them some advantage, too, even if that's just that it lets them score off a rival; or else to use a rival either to beat the god who's angry at you or to distract the other god so he doesn't care about you any more."

"That's what you did with the Gradi gods," Dagref said, and Gerin nodded.

"So it is," he answered. "The brawl I got them into has worked out better—which is to say, it's lasted longer—than I ever dared hope."

"Puts me in mind of something that happened to me a good many years ago, back in my wandering days," Van said as they waited for the attendants to bring back their chariots.

"Probably something that didn't happen," Ferdulf said, "if it's anything like most of your stories."

Van glared at him. "I ought to pop you like the blown-up pig's bladder you are," he growled.

Ferdulf rose into the air. "I am the son of a god, and you would be wise to remember it, lest we discover who pops whom." He was not much more than half as tall as the outlander, and couldn't possibly have weighed a quarter as much, but that little body held power of a different sort from Van's brute strength.

Glaring still, Van said, "I don't care whose son you are, you bigmouthed little weed—I'd like to see you show that even one of my stories, even one, mind you, has the smallest bit of falsehood in it."

Ferdulf fell a few inches, a sign of dismay or chagrin. "How am I supposed to show that?" he demanded. "I wasn't born yet when you were having these adventures you tell lies about, and I haven't been to the preposterous places where you had them."

"Then why don't you shut up?" Van asked sweetly. "Why don't you shut up before you open your mouth so wide, you fall right in?"

Now Ferdulf glared. Before he could say anything, Adiatunnus said, "I'm fain to hear the outlander's tale. He's never dull, say what else you will of him." His comrades nodded; Van's stories had long been popular along the border.

"Shall I go on, then?" Van asked. When even Ferdulf did not say no, go on he did: "This was out in the Weshapar country, east of Kizzuwatna and north of Mabalal. The Weshapar have the most jealous god in the world. He's so crazy, he won't even let them call him by his name, and he has the nerve to claim he's the only real god in the whole wide world."

"Foosh, what a fool of a god he is," Adiatunnus than. "What does he think of the gods of the folk who are lucky enough not to be after worshiping him?"

"He thinks they aren't real at all—that the people around the Weshapar country are imagining them," Van answered.

"Well! I like that!" Ferdulf said indignantly. "I'd like to fly over his temple and piss on it from on high. Maybe he would think that was his imagination, too. Or else I could—"

"Do you want to say what you would do, or do you want to hear what this god and I did do?" Van gave Mavrix's son a dirty look. The attendants fetched the chariots then; everyone but Ferdulf got into them. He floated along beside the one Dagref drove.

"Oh, go on." Now Ferdulf sounded very much like his father, which is to say, petulant.

"Thank you, most gracious demigod." From living with Gerin, Van had learned to be sardonic when it suited him. It didn't suit him very often, which made him more dangerous when it did. While Ferdulf sputtered and fumed, the outlander went on, "This god of the Weshapar put me in mind of a jealous husband. He was always sneaking around keeping an eye on his people to make sure they didn't worship anyone but him, and—"

"Wait," Dagref said. "If this strange god said none of the other gods around him was real, how could people worship them? They wouldn't be worshiping anything at all. Logic."

"I don't think this god ever heard of logic, and I'm starting to wish I'd never heard of you," Van said. "Between you and Ferdulf, we'll be all the way back with the rest of the army before I'm through. Anyhow, there I was, on the way through the Weshapar country—it's hills and rocks and valleys, hot in the summer and cold as all get-out in the winter—trading this for that, doing a little fighting on the side to help keep myself in food and trinkets, when one of the Weshapar chieftains got on the wrong side of this god."

"How'd he do that?" Gerin asked.

"To the five hells with me if I know," Van answered. "A god like that, any little thing will do the trick, same as a jealous husband will think his wife is sleeping with somebody else if she sets foot outside the front door." He sighed. Maybe he was thinking of Fand, though he wasn't a jealous husband of the type he'd described—and though he gave her plenty of reason for jealousy, too. Gathering himself, he went on, "Like I say, I don't know what Zalmunna—this Weshapar chief I was talking about—did to get his god angry at him, but he did something, because the god told him he had to cut the throat of his son to make things right—and to show he really did reverence that foolish god."

"And did this Zalmunna spalpeen tell him where to head in?" Adiatunnus asked. "I would ha' done no other thing but that."

"But you and your people hadn't been worshiping this god for who knows how many generations," Van said. "Zalmunna was in a state, I'll tell you. He was in an even worse state because his son was all ready to let himself be used like a goat or a hog, too. If the god wanted him, he was ready for it. Ready?—no, he was eager as a bridegroom wedding the loveliest wench in the countryside."

"You would think he would have had better sense," Dagref said.

"No, lad—*you* would think he had better sense, because you have better sense yourself," Van said. "What you haven't figured out yet is how many people are fools, one way or another. What you haven't figured out is how many people are fools one way *and* another."

"I wonder why they are," Dagref said, a question aimed not so much at Van as at the world around him.

The world around him did not answer. Van went on, "Like I say, the lad was ready to be offered up like a beast. Most of the Weshapar were ready for him to be offered up, too. They were used to doing what their god told them. He was their god. How could they do anything else? Even Zalmunna was thinking he might have to do it. He didn't want to, you understand, but he didn't see that he had much choice.

"We got to talking the night before he was supposed to go into this overgrown valley where that god had his shrine and kill the boy. He'd got himself drunk, the same way you would have if this was happening to you. He knew what I thought of his god, which was not much, so he came to me instead of to any of the rest of the Weshapar.

"Well, since their god was as jealous as he was, and as stupid as he was . . . like I say, we got to talking. When the time came for him to take his son down into the valley, I went along. His son didn't want me to come. He was fussing and fuming like anything. Sometimes, though you can't pay much attention to what these brats say."

Dagref ignored him. Ferdulf stuck out his tongue at him.

Van grinned. "Miserable little excuse for a shrine this god had, too—nothing but a few piled-up stones and a shabby stone table for the throat-cutting business. We got there, and the god's voice came from out of the stones. 'Get on with it,' he said, and he sounded like my old grandfather about two days before he died.

"Zalmunna laid his son down on the stone table. He took out his knife. Before he used it, though, I hit his son in the side of the head with a little leather sack full of sand and pebbles. The lad went out like a torch you'd stick in a bucket of water. I'd led a sow along, too. I lifted her up onto the table instead of Zalmunna's son, and Zalmunna cut her throat."

"What happened next?" Gerin asked. "The god didn't strike you dead." He took a long, careful look at the outlander. "At least, I don't think he did."

"Honh!" Van said. "What happened was, that god said, 'There. You see? Next time you'd better pay attention to me.' He felt Zalmunna's son stop thinking, you understand, and then there was blood all over the place. It was just like we'd hoped: he thought Zalmunna really had killed the boy. I slung Zalmunna's son over my shoulder and carried him back to the Weshapar village we'd started out from."

"What happened when he woke up?" Gerin asked.

"To the five hells with me if I know," Van repeated. "I clouted him a good one; he was still quiet as a sack of mud when we got back to the village. Zalmunna started shouting up a storm about what an idiot their god was and how he'd fooled him and how they should all quit worshiping him and on and on and on. Me, I thought that looked like a pretty fair time to find somewhere else to go, so away I went."

"And what might that ha' been, pray?" Adiatunnus asked. "Are you after telling us you were fain to keep clear o' the quarrels 'twixt a god and his folk?"

"Now that you mention it, yes," Van said. "The Fox will tell you I've done a stupid thing or three in my time, but he'll also tell you I've never done anything outright daft in all my born days."

"Oh, I will, will I?" Gerin said. "This, I have to let you know, is news to me."

"Go howl," Van said. "Anyhow, a couple of days after that, I felt myself a pretty fair earthquake—say, about like the one that turned Ikos topsy-turvy and let the monsters out, though I was right on top of that one and a ways away from the one I'm talking about now. It would have hit hardest in the Weshapar country, unless I miss my guess."

"You think the god caused it?" Dagref said.

"Well, Zalmunna couldn't very well have done it," Van replied, "though he was angry enough to, if only he could. I can't tell you, even now, whether the Weshapar still follow their nasty little jealous god, or whether they've all gone over to the ones their neighbors follow."

"I would that," Adiatunnus said. "If you must be worshiping gods, now, better to follow the bunch that let you have a good time, I'm thinking."

Dagref had another question: "If all these—Weshapar, was it?—did fall away from the jealous god, would he shrivel up and die for lack of worship?"

"It's a good question," Van said, "but I'd be lying if I claimed I knew the answer to it, for I don't. But if it's not what Zalmunna was hoping for, I'd be astonished."

"It's not a good question," Ferdulf growled. "Not even slightly. It's a wicked question, and a wicked idea. Gods are immortal—it's one of the things that make them gods. How can an immortal die?"

Gerin asked a question of his own: "Suppose you're a god, and no one worships you for a thousand years or so—how would you like that? Would you be hungry? If you weren't dead, wouldn't you rather be?"

Ferdulf considered that. "It's not something my father need fear," he said at last. "People will always worship a god who gives them wine, a god who gives them the pleasures that go with fertility, a god who aids them in all manners of creation."

"That's so," Gerin said, understanding from Ferdulf's answer why the little demigod had been so upset. The Fox thought Ferdulf's father would live forever, too; Ferdulf had named good reasons he would stay popular among men. Wistfully, Gerin wished Dagref's father would live forever, too.

✧ ✧ ✧

"Bronze and wood." Van touched his sword hilt, then set his hand on the chariot rail. "Here we have the one thing and the other. Now we have to go forth and lick the cursed imperials."

"You make it sound so easy," Gerin said, his voice dry.

"It *was* easy," Van said. "Twice in a row, it was easy. Why shouldn't it be once more?"

"You're forgetting something," Gerin replied, even more dryly than before. "The two battles we won, Aragis and I were together, and together we matched the number of imperials we were fighting. They have more men now, and they've split us in two. Attacking when you're outnumbered doesn't strike me as the best idea I've ever heard."

"And have you got a better one?" the outlander asked.

And Gerin didn't. The imperials had not pressed the pursuit so hard as they might have. While he wasn't eager to attack them, they still weren't eager to attack him, either. Those two victories he and Aragis had won over them made them wary even with the advantage of numbers. Even so . . .

"We're going to get hungry pretty soon if we don't do anything but stay where we are," Van said, driving home the point. "It's either knock 'em back and find some new land to forage over or else fall back into the valley of Ikos—and farseeing Biton isn't going to be happy about that."

"I know." Now Gerin's voice was somber. "His guardsmen couldn't have made that much plainer, could they?" He sighed. "If it's fighting the Elabonian Empire or fighting the farseeing god, there's not much choice, is there?"

Rihwin's riders in the van, the Fox's army moved out the next day. Those of Aragis' vassals who had not gone to war along with their king held their keeps shut tight against Gerin. They were holding their keeps shut against everyone. They no doubt wished Gerin and the imperials would all go away and leave them at peace, or as close to it as they had known while living under Aragis' rule. No matter what they wished, they had not the strength to enforce their wishes.

The Fox's forward move seemed to catch the imperials by surprise. The riders drove back the scouts the forces of the Elabonian Empire had posted to keep an eye on them. They killed a few, too, and captured several more.

Maeva, beaming from ear to ear, brought one of those prisoners back to the Fox—and, not coincidentally, to her father and Dagref. "I caught him myself," she said, pride ringing in her voice.

The prisoner looked indignant, perhaps at being captured by a woman, perhaps at being captured at all. The latter, it proved, for he burst out, "You cursed rebels are a tougher nut to crack than they told us you were going to be when we came over the mountains. They said some of you would want to come back under the City of Elabon, and the rest wouldn't be able to fight."

"People say all sorts of stupid things," Gerin answered. "The trick is knowing whether they're stupid. For instance, I'll know if you lie, because I've already asked these questions to other prisoners. How many men have you got? . . ."

He got the answers he wanted. They largely agreed with the answers he'd had from other imperials his men had captured. The soldiers of the Elabonian Empire outnumbered his own men, but not overwhelmingly. He had some reason to hope he could knock them back on their heels.

"What will you do with me?" the prisoner asked.

"What will you do with me, *lord king*?" Dagref and Maeva spoke together, in the tones they would have used to reprove younger siblings who'd said something stupid. They looked at each other, both seeming surprised and pleased.

"What will you do with me, lord king?" For his part, the prisoner seemed grateful enough to be corrected with words rather than with something hard slammed against the side of his head.

"Take him back that way, Maeva," Gerin said, pointing over his shoulder. "Don't do anything to him as long as he behaves himself. If he doesn't behave himself . . . well, the ghosts will have fresh blood to drink tonight." To the captured imperial, he went on, "I don't quite know what we'll end up doing with you. We may let you farm on a peasant village, but I won't lie to you—you may end up in the mines. It depends on where we can get the most and the most useful work out of you."

"Lord king, if it's use you're after, I know something of smithcraft," the prisoner said.

"If that turns out to be true, you won't go to the mines," Gerin said. "And if it turns out not to be true, you will, for having lied." The imperial didn't quail, from which Gerin concluded he was either telling the truth or had some small practice lying. "Take him away, Maeva."

"I do thank you for getting her out of the brawling for a while," Van said.

"You're welcome, for whatever it may be worth," Gerin answered, his voice mild; he understood what was in the outlander's mind.

Dagref, on the other hand, spoke to Van in the same hectoring tones he'd used on the prisoner Maeva had taken: "You do understand, don't you, that she gets to go out of the brawling now because she was in it before?"

"Oh, aye, I understand that, lad," Van said, manfully resisting the temptation to break Dagref over his knee or offer him some other form of great bodily harm. "Now if you want to ask me whether I like the idea or not, I may just have a different answer for you. Aye, I may."

For a wonder, the brittle edge in his voice got through to Dagref, who suddenly made himself very busy steering the chariot. Gerin caught Van's eye and raised an eyebrow. Van coughed a couple of times. They both laughed.

"Stop talking about me," Dagref said without looking back, which only made his father and Van laugh harder.

More prisoners came back as the Fox's advance drove in the scouts the imperials had set up to keep an eye on him. He was mournfully certain his horsemen and chariots were not capturing all those scouts. He pushed south and west harder, to hit the main imperial army before the foe was ready for him.

Instead of finding the imperial force concentrated to receive his men, he found it scattered in detachments. He hit them one after another, glad of his good fortune. They would skirmish with him and then draw off, retreating toward the west every time. The peasants in the eastern part of Aragis' kingdom did not seem delighted to have him foraging from the countryside rather than the soldiers of the Elabonian Empire.

Some of them, in fact, probably would have preferred to have the imperials remain. Being strangers in the northlands, and unused to some of the ways of the peasants there, the men from south of the High Kirs missed stores that Gerin and his men had no trouble sniffing out. They'd dealt with the local peasants all their lives, and knew their tricks.

Flatbread made from coarse-ground flour baked in the hot ashes of a campfire was not the most appetizing meal, but it kept a man going. Van said, "We may run those buggers right out of here yet. If they keep giving us ground, by the gods, we'll take it."

"So we will," Gerin said, gnawing on flatbread. He kept looking toward the west. His expression was glum.

Van noted that. "You ought to be glad we've broken out of that cramped little stretch of ground where they'd pinned us back. If you are, you've not told your face of it."

"I am glad. We would have got hungry after a bit. But I'm not delighted. You see what they're doing, don't you?"

"Running," Van said with a sniff.

"Running, aye," the Fox said. "But running with a purpose." Van let out an interrogative grunt. Gerin explained: "They're keeping themselves between Aragis and us. They don't want us joining up with him until their other force has hit him hard, unless I miss my guess."

"Ah." Van took a bite of flatbread, too. He chewed on the bread and the idea at the same time. By the look on his face, he didn't much care for the taste of either. He tried to make the best of things: "Well, they'll be the ones with the harder foraging now."

But the Fox shook his head. "I have my doubts about that. If they can bring two armies up over the High Kirs, they'll have a supply train with 'em, too, to keep them fed." He listened to his own words. A smile slowly stole over his face. "And they've gone and let us out."

Van's smile spread till it matched Gerin's. "Wagons and wagons full of good things to eat—that's what you're saying, isn't it, Fox?"

"Good things to eat," Gerin agreed. "Probably more

wine, to help Rihwin get drunk. Probably arrows and such, too. All sorts of things we could use. All sorts of things we'd be happier if the imperials didn't have. And they're falling back toward the west, to keep us away from Aragis the Archer."

"Don't they realize you'd think of the supply train?"

"Do you know, I don't believe they do," Gerin said. "To them, after all, I'm just a backwoods half-barbarian." He winked. "But I'll tell you something: I'm going to show them they're wrong."

"This will be grand fun," Van boomed as the chariot jounced along the stretch of the Elabon Way Gerin's counterattack had opened up. "Grand fun for us, I should say—the imperials won't like getting a door slammed on their prongs even a little bit."

"Wouldn't much care for that myself." Gerin had all he could do not to clutch at himself at the very idea. "But aye, if it goes as we hope, it'll do us some good and make life harder for our chums from south of the mountains."

He'd taken as many of Rihwin's riders as he could while still leaving enough to scout for the main mass of warriors he'd left behind. He'd also taken the chariots with the fastest horses and those with the fiercest crews, including a good many of Adiatunnus' Trokmoi. Set the prospect of booty in front of the woodsrunners and they'd go after it the way a pack of hounds would run baying down the scent track of a stag.

He glanced east. Somewhere not far over there, beyond forests and low hills, lay the village where Elise had her tavern. Gerin wondered what had happened when the imperials went through there after him.

A rider came galloping north up the Elabon Way toward his force. "Wagons!" the fellow was shouting. "Wagons!" When he was sure the Fox had heard him, he pointed in the direction from which he had come.

"Let's go," Gerin said, and waved his men forward. They whooped with glee. The troopers in chariots urged their teams ahead. The riders booted their mounts up from slow trot to quick. Sure enough, as soon as the paved highway rose a little, the Fox saw the ox- and donkey-drawn wagons coming toward him. The riders were already whooping and reaching over their shoulders for arrows.

The drivers saw Gerin's oncoming men at about the same time as he spotted them. They had a few chariots along to protect them against bandits, but not nearly enough to hold back a force like the one Gerin had assembled. The charioteers did what they could: they rolled up the highway in a spoiling attack to try to give the wagon crews time to form a defensive circle.

Gerin was having none of that. "Roll past them!" he shouted. "Don't let them slow us down. Once we get in among the wagons, we'll be able to throw the chariots into the bag, too."

Arrows flew as the imperials tried to delay his troopers. A couple of men on either side tumbled out of their cars. But then, despite shouts of scorn and dismay from the warriors from south of the High Kirs, the Fox and his followers were by, speeding on toward the wagons.

A fierce grin stretched his mouth wide: the circle remained incomplete. His men knew they had to make sure it stayed incomplete, too. They broke in among the wagons. Some of the men from the chariots dismounted and set upon the wagon drivers. The drivers fought back as best they could, but they were not armored, and many of them carried nothing more lethal than knives.

Pointing to the havoc the dismounted chariot crews were wreaking, Van said, "Wouldn't be so easy for riders to do that."

"You're right—it wouldn't," Gerin agreed. "But men on horses can do things men in chariots can't, too: more things, unless I miss my guess." He raised his voice. "There go a couple, Dagref. See if you can run them down before they make it into the trees."

"Aye, Father." Dagref steered the chariot after the closer of the two fleeing drivers. As it pulled alongside the fellow, Van swung his mace. Its wicked spiked bronze head slammed home with a meaty thunk. The driver shrieked and crumpled.

"I would have let him yield," Gerin said mildly.

"He wasn't yielding," the outlander answered. "He was running."

As if the other driver had heard him, he stopped running and threw up his hands. Gerin waved for him to head back toward the Elabon Way. He obeyed, but, as soon as Dagref turned the chariot aside, he whirled and sprinted for the trees and got in among them before the chariot crew could do anything about it. Gerin shot an arrow at him, but missed.

"There, you see?" Van said. "Try and be generous and look at the thanks you get."

"He's not as smart as he thinks he is," Gerin said as the chariot bounced back to the highway. "If he comes out, either we'll scoop him up or Aragis' peasants will put paid to him. He'll have a thin time either way."

"That's not the point," Van said. "The point is, we should have put paid to him, and we cursed well didn't."

Since he was right, Gerin didn't try to argue with him. Instead, he said, "Let's see if we can keep their chariot escort from getting away and letting the rest of the imperials know we've made their wagons disappear."

His shouts pulled other chariots from the northlands away from the wagons and into the pursuit. He and his men caught up with what he thought was the last imperial chariot a mile or so up the Elabon Way. Seeing they would be overhauled, the driver and the two warriors with him jumped out and ran for the woods, as the wagon drivers had done. Unlike the wagon drivers, they didn't get there.

"Now, let's get these wagons back to our camp," the Fox said. "We haven't got time to waste. The faster we move 'em up along the road, the less the chance the Empire will have of getting them back."

Some of the wagon drivers had surrendered. Gerin was glad of that, because his own men, while skilled with horses, had less practice with donkeys and oxen. The animals obeyed better when they saw what their fellow beasts were doing under drivers who knew how to make them work.

Rihwin rode up alongside Gerin. "I wonder what all we've captured." For a wonder, he didn't say, *I wonder how much wine we've captured*.

"Same sort of things we'd have along for our own

troopers, I expect," Gerin answered. "Journeybread and sausage and onions and cheese—anything that keeps well. Dried fruit, too, maybe. There's a name for dried grapes." He snapped his fingers. "Raisins, that's what they call them."

"Raisins," Rihwin agreed. "It's been a very long time since I've had raisins." He still didn't say anything about wine, which Gerin had made a point of not mentioning. Gerin eyed him suspiciously, as if wondering whether he was coming down with some peculiar ailment. *Maturity?* Gerin wondered, trying again to find a name. He shook his head. If Rihwin hadn't caught that yet, he probably never would.

Van said, "Have to see what they've got in these wagons besides food, too. Sheaves of arrows, like you said. Those'll come in handy for us. Maybe swords. Maybe metal fittings for chariots, too. Those'd be nice."

"Let's move faster," Gerin said again.

"Captain, trying to hurry a donkey bothers you more than it does the donkey," Van said. "The only way I know to hurry oxen is to fling 'em off a cliff. What's that the Trokmoi say? Don't fash yourself—there you are. We're making the best time we can."

"It's not good enough," Gerin fretted. He knew his friend was right. He couldn't help worrying and barking and snapping anyhow. Eventually, more of his own riders came down to screen the wagons from any possible imperial revenge. Only then did he relax.

His troopers cheered when the wagons came into camp. When they started going through them, they found about what they'd expected, including one wagon full of wineskins. Gerin stalked around that wagon, glum as a man with a toothache. "What in the five hells do we do with it?" he asked the air.

Dagref was close enough to hear him. "My view is, we ought to drink it. If Mavrix didn't come up to the northlands in a cloud of purple smoke when Rihwin drank, why should he care about Widin Simrin's son drinking, or Adiatunnus, either, for that matter?"

"I don't know why he might care about Widin or Adiatunnus," the Fox answered. "I haven't the faintest idea.

If he does care, though, is the risk in drinking worth the chance we're taking?"

"No way to tell ahead of time, of course," Dagref admitted. "But then, Mavrix would surely be insulted if we spill the wine, and might be insulted if we *don't* drink it. Risks everywhere."

"You so relieve my mind," Gerin said, at which Dagref bowed, as if to a compliment.

Ferdulf came swaggering up to the wagon, walking with his feet far enough off the ground to let him look Gerin the the eye. "You've found more of my father's spoiled grape juice, have you?" he demanded.

"If that's what you want to call it, yes," Gerin answered cautiously. "Why?"

"Because I still aim to pay him back, that's why," Ferdulf said. "And now I know how to do it, too."

"Wait!" Gerin said, and grabbed at the demigod. He missed—Ferdulf must have known he was going to try it. With a mocking laugh, Ferdulf floated up into the air. Gerin leaped after him, which proved how alarmed he was. He didn't leap high enough or fast enough.

From above his head, Ferdulf mocked him. "You can't stop me this time. Nobody can stop me this time." He pointed a forefinger at the wine and muttered under his breath. Gerin couldn't hear all of it, but part of it was, "Take that, Father, and I hope you choke on it!"

"*Stop* it!" Gerin said urgently, but Ferdulf had no intention of stopping it, not for him, not for anybody. He was going to do what he was going to do, and if the Fox didn't like it, too bad for the Fox.

What if Mavrix didn't like it? That, obviously, was what Ferdulf hoped would happen. He wanted the Sithonian god of wine to come up to the northlands. Maybe he even wanted Mavrix to punish him. Getting a rise out of his father might have looked better to him than the indifference Mavrix had shown at their first meeting.

He drifted down to the ground, a brat doing an imitation of a snowflake. "Go ahead," he told Gerin. "Drink all the wine you like. I hope you and your troopers enjoy it."

"What have you done?" the Fox demanded.

Ferdulf gave him a nasty smile. "You'll find out." And

off he went, before Gerin could make up his mind to try to shake some truth out of him.

"What do you think he's done?" Dagref asked.

"Something horrible," Gerin snapped. "What does he ever do? I ought to make Rihwin open a skin and find out what's gone wrong: he's wild for wine, so he should be the one to see how wild the wine's got. Doesn't that sound like justice to you, Dagref?"

His son didn't answer. With a question like that, a long answer meant *no*. No answer at all meant *no*, too. With a sigh, Gerin went and got a tarred-leather drinking jack. He took a wineskin out of the wagon, undid the tie at the neck, and poured the jack full.

He hadn't raised it to his lips when Rihwin called, "Oh no you don't, my fellow Fox. I was all but supernaturally patient, not even speaking of the blood of the sweet grape, but if you're going to go ahead and quaff—"

"Justice," Dagref said, and sighed.

"Here." Gerin pressed the jack into Rihwin's outstretched hand. "Since you want it so much, it's only fitting that you should have it. Go right ahead, my fellow Fox. Quaff."

Rihwin should have been suspicious when Gerin yielded so easily. But he wasn't. "I not only want it," he declared, "I deserve it." He took a big mouthful—and then sprayed out as much of it as he could, coughing and choking on what had gone down his throat. "Feh!" he said. "Vinegar!"

"Well, that's something of a relief," Gerin said. "I was afraid it would be donkey piss."

"Thank you so much," Rihwin snarled. "And you went ahead and let me drink it."

"No," Gerin said. "I did not *let* you drink it. You insisted on doing it. 'I deserve it,' you said. In my opinion, you were correct. You did deserve it. If you hadn't been so greedy, you would have let me taste, or you would have let me tell you Ferdulf had done something to the wine. But no—you went ahead and took what you wanted and enjoyed it less than you might have done. I'd say, both as your friend and as your king, that you have no complaint coming."

Rihwin wiped his mouth on his sleeve, which couldn't

have done much good. "And I'd say, both as your friend—for some indecipherable reason or other—and as your subject, that you haven't the faintest notion of what you're talking about." He wiped his mouth again.

"Maybe you should go drink some ale," Dagref suggested. "That would get rid of some of the taste."

"Aye, maybe I should go and—" Rihwin gave Gerin's son a horrible look. "You take altogether too much after your father." He strode away, his back as stiff as an offended cat's.

"Thank you," Dagref called after him, which only made his back grow stiffer—it wasn't what he'd wanted to hear. Dagref turned to Gerin. "He'll be a while getting over that."

"So he will," Gerin agreed. "So he ought to be." He scowled at the wagon, then let out a long sigh. "We can pickle all the cabbages and cucumbers we like, but we're not going to be drinking wine."

"That's so," Dagref agreed. "I wonder why Mavrix hasn't descended on us in a cloud of fury. He's not usually one to ignore insults, is he?"

"No, he's usually one to pay them back," Gerin answered. "That's why my heart fell into my sandals when Ferdulf decided to take his petty revenge."

"Well, why isn't Mavrix here, then?" Dagref demanded, as if his father were somehow responsible for the absence of the Sithonian god of wine and fertility.

"If I knew, I would tell you," Gerin answered. "Maybe he's finally decided he doesn't care what happens here in the northlands any more. That would be nice, wouldn't it? Or maybe he's raising a rebellion down in Sithonia, and doesn't have time to fret about this part of the world for a while."

"But didn't you say he told you he didn't think the Sithonians *could* successfully rise against the Elabonian Empire?" Gerin asked.

"Yes, I did say he told me he didn't think they could," Gerin answered, and stuck out his tongue at his son. "Doesn't mean he wouldn't try to raise one anyhow. The Sithonians have revolted against the Empire a good many times over the years, even if they've always lost."

"If the Sithonians are revolting," Dagref said, both thoughtfully and with malice aforethought, "that could be very convenient for us."

"We're guessing, you know," Gerin said. Dagref nodded. Gerin went on, "We're guessing with our hearts, not our heads." He sighed. "It would be nice, but we don't dare believe it. It's like believing a pretty girl you've never seen will come looking for you. It happens every once in a while, maybe, but not often enough that you can expect it for even a heartbeat."

"I understand," Dagref said. "What happens anywhere else doesn't matter anyhow, not unless we beat the imperials here."

"That's also true," Gerin said. "In fact, that's *the* truth about this war. And we were on the point of doing it, too, till they threw another army into the fight. Nasty and rude of them, if anyone wants to know what I think. They want to win, too, worse luck. Very inconsiderate."

"Can't trust anyone any more, can you?" Dagref asked.

"Who said I ever did?" the Fox returned.

The next morning, Ferdulf was loud and triumphant and obnoxious: in other words, not far removed from his usual self. "I gave my father a proper black eye," he boasted, "and he hasn't had the nerve to come do anything to me. I guess he sees who's boss in the northlands now."

"You've done better guessing," Gerin told him.

Ferdulf stuck his nose in the air. Following that nose, the rest of him floated off the ground. "I do not have to stay here to listen to myself being insulted," he said haughtily, and drifted away like an indignant dandelion puff.

"He hasn't the faintest notion how big a fool he is," Van said.

"Fools never do," Gerin answered. "That's what makes them fools."

"Strange, thinking of a half-god as a fool," the outlander said, "but Ferdulf gives us plenty of chances to do it."

"So he does," Gerin said. He could easily think of a few gods he'd met whom he considered fools, but he didn't mention that. Whether gods were fools or not, they were vastly stronger than mortals. A man insulted a god, even a god as cowardly as Mavrix, at his peril. A demigod insulted a god, even a god who was his father, at his peril. Ferdulf hadn't figured that out—another proof Ferdulf was a fool.

"What now?" Van asked.

"I don't know what we can do but keep on with what we've been doing," Gerin answered. "If we can keep riders moving along the Elabon way, the imperials are going to have a harder time supplying their armies up here. And if we can keep pushing back the outposts of that force that was dogging us, maybe we'll be able to join hands with Aragis."

"Aye, maybe we will," Van said. "And maybe, once we do, we ought to count the fingers on the hand we join with his, too."

Gerin, once more, would have argued with his friend more had he agreed with him less. The men from the northlands did drive in a couple of more imperial positions, which gave them new land from which to forage. The men from the Elabonian Empire hadn't been on the land long enough to pick it bare, nor were they as good at the job as Gerin and his followers. Combining what they took from the land with what they captured from the imperial supply column, the warriors from the northlands were for the moment comfortable.

He ate sausages and gnawed on chunks of journeybread and tried to decide what to do next: probably about the same thing as his imperial opposite number was doing.

He could do one thing his opposite number couldn't: he could send riders west to slide around the imperial forces between him and Aragis. Men on horseback could go at least as fast as men in chariots, and could go crosscountry on tracks and through fields and woods chariotry couldn't use.

Maeva was not one of the riders he sent toward Aragis. As she had before when she wasn't chosen for a duty, she complained. He did his best to look down his nose at her; it wasn't easy, not when they were very much of a height. "You're right," he said. "I didn't pick you. So what?"

"It's not fair," she insisted. "I deserve to go into danger the same as any other rider."

"You deserve to have your backside walloped," the Fox said, now truly starting to get annoyed. "And 'It's not fair!' is the battle cry children use. I'm tired of it from you. If you want to be a warrior, act like one when you're not in the middle of a fight, not just when you are."

"You're holding me back because I'm a woman," Maeva said.

"No, I'm holding you back because you're a girl," Gerin said. She stared at him, astonished and furious at the same time. He went on, "This is your first campaign, remember? Take a look at the riders I sent west. What do you notice about them, pray tell?"

"They're all men," Maeva said angrily.

"That's right," Gerin agreed. "They're all men. There isn't a boy among them. They've all been riding horses as long as you've been alive; a couple of them have been riding horses as long as anyone in the northlands has been doing it. They've all done a lot of fighting, and a lot of fighting from horseback. If you're still in the army ten or twelve years from now" *—if I'm still alive ten or twelve years from now—* "you'll have a real chance of getting sent on a ride like this."

He wondered how Maeva would take that kind of dressing-down. Fand would have flown into a fury at him. Van would have been angry, too, but not with the same sort of deadly rage. But Gerin had a great many years on Maeva, which made her take him more seriously than either of her parents would have done. "Very well, lord king," was all she said before going off disappointed but not obviously irate.

Watching her go, the Fox nodded in reluctant approval. He almost wished she had thrown a tantrum; that would have given him the excuse he needed to send her home. But she offered him no such excuse, however much having one would have pleased him and delighted Van. All things considered, she'd taken the tongue-lashing . . . like a soldier.

No sooner had that comparison crossed his mind than he wished it hadn't. Too late. He'd started thinking of Maeva as a soldier even before he saw how well she handled herself when she was wounded. He couldn't very well change his mind now.

Not all the riders he sent out came back. Before any of them came back, he had to try to withstand an assault from the imperials, who had begun to concentrate against him once he started rolling up their outposts. Their commander was about as unsubtle as Aragis the Archer. He simply gathered his force and rolled toward where he thought Gerin had the bulk of his army. He turned out to have a pretty good notion of that, too.

Mounted scouts brought the Fox the word. "They can't be a quarter of an hour behind us, lord king, coming down that road there," one of the riders said, pointing west along the dirt road up which he'd come.

"Well, all right." Gerin's grimace held annoyance, but no real surprise. He'd poked the men from south of the High Kirs; they were going to hit back if they could—and they could. He surveyed the ground through which the road ran. It was mostly open country—grain fields and and meadows—with a forest of oaks and elms off to the left. "We'll stay right here," he said. "It's as good a spot as any, and better than most."

"I think you're doing the right thing, Father," Dagref said. "We've shown that, man for man, we're more than a match for the imperials."

"So we have," Gerin agreed. "Unfortunately, they've shown they've got more men than we do."

He started shouting orders, shaking his men out from line of march into line of battle. He barely had time to post a couple of dozen chariot crews in among the trees, with orders to burst forth against the enemy's flank and rear when the time seemed ripe, before a rising dust cloud and horn calls through it announced the imperials were at hand.

"Elabon! Elabon! Elabon!" the men of the Empire shouted, as if to leave no doubt who they were. Gerin's men were not in any doubt: his riders plied the leading chariots from the Elabonian Empire with arrows and javelins. The horsemen in front of them kept the imperials from charging as ferociously as their commander probably would have liked. The men from south of the High Kirs were still learning how to face mounted foes.

One thing they'd learned was that, when there were

enough of them, their foes had to give way. Archers shooting from tightly bunched chariots put enough arrows in the air to discourage anyone—on foot, on horseback, or in other chariots—from doing much to hinder their passage.

Seeing their numbers—sure enough, they were going to have more men in the fight than he did—Gerin waved and yelled to extend his line to either side and lap round them. If he could hit them from three sides at once, those numbers wouldn't do them much good: his troopers could slay men in the middle of that rumbling herd of chariots without their having the chance to do him any harm.

"There's a lot of them, Captain," Van said.

"I'd noticed that myself," Gerin answered. "We scraped together all the men we could, Aragis and I. The Empire of Elabon is bigger than the northlands, and has more people, too. They've sent a bigger force over the mountains than we can hope to equal."

"Most places, that's a recipe for a lost war for the side that doesn't have the big army," the outlander said.

"Thank you so much," the Fox snapped. "I never would have realized that if you hadn't pointed it out to me."

"Glad to help, Captain," Van said imperturbably.

He did not stay imperturbable after an arrow ticked off the side of his helm, scratching a brighter line on the brightly polished bronze. He cursed and bellowed and brandished his spear at the imperials, though he couldn't have had the slightest idea which of them had shot at him.

Gerin started shooting at the soldiers and horses of the Elabonian Empire in front of him. One way to reduce the odds his men faced was to kill or disable as many of the imperials as he could. One of his shafts struck the right-hand horse of a team square in the breast. The horse went down. The chariot slewed leftwards, colliding with the car and team next to it. They slewed away in turn. Because the main body of the imperial was so tightly packed, they ran into the team on their left, too: one arrow fouling three chariots, half a dozen horses, and nine men.

"Well shot," Van said, seeing what the Fox had done.

"Thank you." The Fox sounded modest, letting the shot speak for itself. "Come on, men!" he shouted. "Lay into them."

Lay into them the men from the northlands did. The imperials' charge slowed as collisions and casualties took their toll of the cars in the front ranks. The fight became a melee, the sort of struggle in which Gerin's troopers had consistently proved to own the advantage.

Gerin shot an arrow at an imperial officer with a red cloak draped around his shoulders. The fellow was inconsiderate enough to lean to one side at the moment the shaft hissed past him. Gerin cursed. "How in the five hells am I supposed to get rid of the imperials if they keep trying not to get killed?" he demanded of no one in particular.

Dagref, as usual, had an answer: "Pretty rude of them, isn't it, Father? They aren't behaving the way the enemy—whoever the enemy is—usually does when the minstrels sing their songs."

"To the five hells with the minstrels, too," Gerin growled. He had a couple of reasons for despising minstrels. First and foremost was that one who had practiced that calling had kidnapped his eldest son fifteen years before. But the way they distorted the truth to fit into what made a good song grated on him, too.

He wondered how the historians who recorded events down in the City of Elabon would mention this clash. To them, of course, he and his followers would be that highly variable creature, the enemy—*rebels*, they'd call the warriors of the northlands, and *semibarbarians allied to true barbarians*. He knew their style. Being the enemy, he probably wouldn't get any credit from the historians no matter what he did. If he lost, that he was the enemy would be enough to explain a great deal. If he won, they'd chalk it up to guile or trickery, not courage.

As long as he won, he didn't care how they chalked it up. He wondered what sort of guile or trickery he could use to rouse the future historians' ire.

Looking around the crowded field, he didn't see much opportunity for anything of the sort. His men did have some advantage of position, but the imperials had the advantage of numbers. They seemed at least as liable to win as did the men of the northlands.

He sighed. He hadn't wanted this particular battle, not

here, not now. He sighed again. Life had given him any number of things he didn't want. The trick was to get through them as well and as quickly as he could, to have the best chance to return to what he did in fact want.

He shot at that imperial officer again—and missed again, at a range from which he should not have missed. He cursed in disgust. The fellow seemed to lead a charmed life, though Gerin knew of no magic that would keep an arrow from piercing a man if properly aimed.

Arrows would not pierce Ferdulf, but Ferdulf's immunity was not the sort to which an ordinary man could readily aspire. Ferdulf swooped down on the officer from the Elabonian Empire, for all the world like a ill-mannered hawk. He shouted in the officer's ears. He waved hands in front of the officer's face. He flipped up his tunic in front of the driver's face, giving the fellow a charming view of a semidivine backside.

With such distractions, the officer couldn't do much in the way of commanding and the driver couldn't do much in the way of driving. Both men, and the soldier in the car with them, did their best to grab, shoot, or otherwise get rid of Ferdulf. They paid so much attention to him, they didn't notice their chariot was about to collide with another till it did. The officer and the soldier fell out the back of the car. The driver got yanked over the front rail and under the horses' hooves. Ferdulf flitted off to work more mischief elsewhere on the field.

Gerin looked toward the forest in which he'd placed those couple of dozen chariots. He wished he had them in the fight, either bursting from ambush or simply in the line with the rest of his men. The imperials weren't doing anything fancy, but he didn't have enough men to drive them back. That was becoming more and more obvious as the fight wore along. All the imperials had to do was stolidly keep on fighting and odds were he'd lose unless he came up with something spectacular. For the life of him, he had no idea what that might be.

He looked toward the oaks again. He didn't want to send a messenger over there; that was liable to draw the imperials' attention to the wood, which was the last thing he wanted.

A moment later, he changed his mind about that. Truly, the last thing he wanted was to be hacked to bloody pulp in the chariot. A car full of imperials pulled alongside of his. One of them cut at him with a sword. The blade turned slightly, so that the flat thudded against his ribs.

He hissed in pain anyhow, and snatched out his own sword. He and the imperial traded strokes till their chariots pulled apart from each other. He thought he would have beaten the fellow had they fought longer; being left-handed, he hadn't had to bring the sword across his body as they battled. But what might have been didn't matter. The truth was, the trooper remained alive and hale to fight someone else.

Gerin wondered how hale he was himself. Breathing hurt but didn't stab, so he doubted he'd broken ribs. He could go on fighting. He laughed, which also hurt. Even if he had broken ribs, he had to go on fighting.

Dagref snapped his whip at one of the horses harnessed to another imperial chariot drawing near. The horse screamed and reared and flinched aside, despite the driver's best effort to force an attack.

"You *are* getting good with that thing," Van said in admiring tones, and then half spoiled the compliment by adding, "You must have got the practice flaying the hide off folk with your tongue."

"I haven't the faintest notion what you're talking about," Dagref replied with more dignity than a stripling had any business owning.

"I know, lad," Van said. "That's the trouble." Dagref's dignity, this time, consisted of pretending he hadn't heard. He didn't bring that off quite so well as he had the dispassionate answer.

More seriously, Gerin said, "Maybe you ought to start practicing with a longer lash than most drivers carry, son. You're better with it than most, that seems plain, so you ought to get as much advantage from it as you can."

"Now that's not a bad idea, Father," Dagref said. "I've had the same thought myself, as a matter of fact."

Had he? Gerin studied his back, which was remarkably uncommunicative. Maybe he had. One thing Dagref was never short on was ideas. He seldom lied, either, unless he found an immediately expedient reason for doing so. The Fox couldn't see one here.

He also couldn't see anything that looked like victory—certainly not for his side. The soldiers of the Elabonian Empire kept on fighting, no matter what he did to them. Every once in a while, in fist fights, Gerin had seen a man whom no blow would put down. Sooner or later, even if that kind of fellow wasn't a particularly good fighter, he would win by wearing down his foe.

That, he thought worriedly, was what he faced here. He was hurting the imperials worse than they were hurting him—he could see that much. The trouble was, they could afford it better than he could. Their captain had brought more men to the battle than he'd thought at first, and he'd known from the beginning he was outnumbered.

He looked over toward the trees again. He waved, on the off chance that anyone over there was looking in his direction and could recognize him at a considerable distance through the dust the chariots and horses had kicked up. A sudden thrust at the flank and rear of the imperials would be extremely welcome about now. The longer the men he'd concealed in the forest delayed, the greater the effect of that thrust would be. He knew as much. If they delayed much longer, though, the battle would be lost.

Van looked in the same direction. "Maybe they're waiting for an invitation, like shy maids hanging back from the dance."

"There won't be any dance left if they don't come soon," Gerin said.

Then he shouted. Out from among the oaks burst the chariots he'd stationed there. On toward the imperials they thundered, picking up speed with every lengthening stride of their horses. The crews in the cars shouted like men possessed. Arrows flew ahead of the chariots.

The imperials shouted, too, in dismay. Their whole line shook as Gerin's men took them from an unexpected direction. "Come on!" the Fox shouted, to all his warriors whom the men of the Elabonian Empire had been pressing back. "Now is our chance to beat those bastards!"

As soon as the words were out of his mouth, he wished he'd phrased that differently. It was all too accurate for comfort. He'd hoped the flank attack would win him the battle. Instead, it was doing exactly what he'd said—it was giving him a chance to win. That it was doing no more than giving him a chance told him with unpleasant clarity how much trouble he'd been in.

"Forward!" he shouted. Forward his line went, instead of moving back. Forward—for a little while. Then the imperial resistance stiffened. Had he had a hundred chariots in the wood, he might have thrown the men of the Elabonian Empire into confusion enough to let him crush them. But, had he had a hundred chariots in the wood, he was likelier to have weakened the rest of his force so much, the battle would have been lost before they could think about a flank attack.

Dagref drove the chariot past a car full of imperials. Van speared the horse closest to him. Spouting blood, the beast screamed and foundered. Dagref's slash made the driver scream, too, and clutch at his neck. Gerin shot one of the archers in the car. The other dove out before anything dreadful could happen to him.

"That's as near a clean sweep as makes no difference," Van said as the archer ran for his life.

"You'll talk differently if he shoots you from ambush," Gerin said.

"If he shoots Uncle Van from ambush, he probably won't talk at all," Dagref said over his shoulder.

"To the five hells with logic, and with both of you, too," Van said. He looked around. "Now we get down to it. Are we going to lick these whoresons, or are they going to lick us?"

Gerin looked around, too. What had been an advance was stalled. The imperials had managed to contain the band that had attacked them from the forest. Without much fuss, without much style, but with plenty of men, they pressed ahead with the fight. He'd mauled them. He had indeed hurt them worse than they'd hurt him, much worse. They kept coming anyhow.

He didn't know what he was supposed to do about that. It wasn't how warfare usually worked up here in the northlands. Finding foes stubborn enough to keep fighting no matter how badly battered they were wasn't easy anywhere. A lifetime of experience and as much reading as he'd been able to do convinced him of the truth there.

He had just reached that unhappy conclusion when Dagref said, "I don't think we can force them back, Father."

"I don't, either," Gerin said. "They have too many men—that's all there is to it. Anything even close to equal numbers, and we'd beat them. We've proved that. But we haven't got equal numbers, and we can't get them."

"Well, what do you aim to do, then, Fox?" Van asked.

"I've got two unpleasant choices," Gerin answered. "I can give up this battle, admit we've lost, retreat, and yield the field to the imperials. Or I can keep on fighting, do the best I can, and watch them chew my army to pieces one bite at a time."

"You're right—those are both nasty choices," Van said.

"If you see any others, please let me know," Gerin said. Van grunted while he thought, then shook his head. Gerin sighed. "Too bad. I was hoping you would."

Dagref said, "What will you do, Father?"

"What would *you* do?" Gerin returned. The battle was lost, one way or the other, but he might at least get a lesson out of it. It wasn't so dreadfully lost that a moment spent here would matter one way or the other.

"I'd hold the army together," Dagref answered at once. "Maybe they'll divide their force or send out detachments we can pick off, the way they did before, or leave themselves open to ambush. If we still have an army, we can take advantage of that. If we let them grind us here like flour, we're finished."

"You're my son, all right. For better and for worse, we think alike. I'm going to see if the imperials will the satisfied with a win and let us go." Gerin raised his voice in a reluctant shout: "Pull back, men of the northlands! Pull back!"

The imperials made no more than a token pursuit—certainly less than he would have made were roles reversed. He thought the commander facing him was the one who'd led the first imperial force into the northlands. The other one, with the larger part of Crebbig I's army, had more drive and more imagination—and was facing Aragis, who, while surely a driver, imagined very little.

Gerin had scant time to worry about Aragis. He had scant time to worry about anything except making certain he put enough distance between his army and that of the Elabonian Empire to let his men camp safely. That, with some effort, he managed.

Adiatunnus came up to him after the army halted. "And what do we do now?" the Trokmê chieftain asked.

"To the crows with me if I know," Gerin answered.

X

What the army did, over the next several days, was retreat. Gerin fought a number of sharp skirmishes with the imperials. He never had any trouble pushing back their advance parties. Whenever the main force came up to support the scouts, though, he had to fall back himself.

Before long, he found himself with no choice but to abandon the swath of Aragis' country in which his army had been foraging. He cursed at having to do it, but it was either that or move south and let the imperials get between him and his own homeland. He resolved not to do that no matter what. If the Elabonian Empire wanted him out of his own holdings, the imperials would have to come and dig him out one keep at a time, just as Aragis would have had to do if he'd beaten him in the field.

"Good thing we stole their supply train," Van said as he gnawed sausage of an evening.

"Anything that keeps us going is good," Gerin said. "We'll have a hard time doing it again, worse luck—they've pushed us a long ways back from the Elabon Way now."

"See any chance of turning loose a decent counter-attack?" the outlander asked, taking another bite.

"I wish I did," Gerin said. "This fellow isn't leaving himself open, though. He doesn't fight like a Trokmê or one of our crack-brained barons up here. I wish he would just charge straight ahead without looking where he's going. It would make life a lot simpler. But he doesn't want to do that. Slow but sure, that's him."

"Doesn't seem stupid, anyhow," Van said. He looked back over his shoulder, toward the northeast. "If he keeps coming, he's liable to push us back into the valley of Ikos whether we want to go there or not."

"That thought had also crossed my mind," Gerin said unhappily. "If we have to go back through there, we'll go back through there, that's all. Biton is the farseeing god. If he can't see far enough to figure out that we're doing what we have to do, not what we want to do, he's not as smart as I think, nor as smart as he thinks he is, either."

Van grunted. "Gods aren't gods because they're smart, Fox. They're gods because they're strong."

"I wish I could say you were wrong," Gerin replied. "The trouble is, I know too well you're right."

He looked around. Where was Dagref? Last time he'd noticed his son, the lad had been eating sausage and journeybread not far away. He didn't see Dagref now. He'd waited for some pungent comment from him about gods and whether they were strong or smart, and now, almost disappointed, realized he'd have to do without.

A moment later, he stopped worrying about Dagref, for Rihwin the Fox strode importantly up to him and said, "Lord king, I'm sure I know how all our troubles may be solved."

Rihwin was enough to worry about any time. Rihwin sure was sure to make Gerin worry. "I'm glad you're sure," he said, his voice as polite as he could make it. "That doesn't necessarily mean you're right, of course. Some people have trouble understanding the difference."

Rihwin looked wounded, an admirable artistic effort. "Lord king, you have no call to make fun of me."

"Why doesn't he?" Van asked in tones of genuine curiosity. "You leave yourself open to it often enough."

"And to the five hells with *you*," Rihwin replied with dignity.

Gerin held up a hand. "Never mind. Enough wrangling. How, my fellow Fox, may all our troubles be solved?"

Rihwin raised an eyebrow. He knew irony when he heard it. For that, if not for a number of other things, Gerin gave him credit. But he answered as if Gerin had meant his sardonic question soberly: "We need divine aid against the men from south of the High Kirs."

"You're a man from south of the High Kirs," Van pointed out.

"Wait." Gerin forestalled the outlander. He fixed Rihwin with a baleful stare. "Why do I think I already know the god whose aid you are going to tell me we must seek?"

"Because he is one of the gods whom you know best, perhaps?" Rihwin said. "Because he has come to your aid and to the aid of the northlands before? Because he is a god who has no reason to love the Elabonian Empire and a great many reasons to loathe it? Those must be the reasons you have in mind—is it not so, lord king?"

"Mm, possibly," Gerin allowed. "That Mavrix is also lord of the sweet grape and what comes from the sweet grape also enters my mind, for some reason or other. Why do you suppose that might be?"

"I haven't the faintest notion," Rihwin replied.

Van guffawed. "If you were as innocent as you sound, you'd still be a virgin at your age, and that, at least, you're not."

Rihwin ignored him, which wasn't easy. "Lord king," he said, addressing himself directly to Gerin, "do you deny, can you deny, Mavrix is our best hope among the gods?"

"Of course I deny it," Gerin answered. "So would you, if you had any sense, though all the gods know *that's* too much to ask for. Biton is a god of this country. Mavrix is even more an imported interloper than we Elabonians are."

"Biton is also aloof," Rihwin said. "The only way you got him to move against the monsters was with Selatre's help and with the added irritation of an appeal to . . . Mavrix." He looked triumphant.

Gerin let out a long, exasperated breath. "Rihwin, if you want another cup of wine, take another cup of wine. If you think the risk is worth it, go ahead. If you get away with it, well and good. If Mavrix tears your head off, my view is that you bloody well asked for it. But don't go wrapping your own desires in a scheme you claim will benefit all of us."

"I should like to drink wine again, aye," Rihwin said, "but I am no longer mad for it, as I was before I slaked my thirst and my desire not long ago. And when I slaked my thirst not long ago, let me remind you, Mavrix made no appearance of any sort, your jittery predictions to the contrary notwithstanding. I propose enlisting him in our cause regardless of whether or not, in the accomplishment thereof, I once more taste the blood of the sweet grape."

"Well—a disinterested Rihwin. Now I've seen everything," Gerin said. Rihwin looked—no, not indignant. Rihwin looked angry. Gerin, for once, did not think the expression was donned for the occasion, to be casually discarded at need. He thought he'd struck a nerve.

All Rihwin said, though, was, "Are you sure *you* are disinterested in this matter, lord king, or are you prejudiced against me because of events now past?"

"Honh!" Van said. "Who wouldn't be? Some of the things you've done would make the hair stand up on a bald man."

But Rihwin's question brought Gerin up short. He prided himself on viewing the world around him as disinterestedly as he could. Anyone who could be anything close to disinterested about Rihwin, though, needed divine detachment, not that afforded to mere mortal men. Slowly, Gerin said, "You're like the boy who says that, just because he's pushed his sister into the mud half a dozen times, there's no reason to think he'll do it again."

"Not so," Rihwin said. "Unlike that boy, whom some of my bastards assuredly resemble, I have learned my lesson. I urge you to summon Mavrix, regardless of whether I play any role whatever in the summoning, and also regardless of whether I get to drink wine then or afterwards." After a bow to Gerin, he strode off.

"Bugger me with a pine cone," Van said. "Now I've seen everything, too."

"If I thought you were wrong, I would argue with you," Gerin answered. He scratched his head. "Much to my own surprise, I'm willing to believe my fellow Fox means what he says. That brings me to the next question on the list: is what he says a good notion or a foolish one?"

"Having the help of a god is is better than not having the help of a god," Van said. "That's a general working rule. Of course, Mavrix is the sort of god who has a way of showing you that general working rules aren't all they're cracked up to be, isn't he?"

"That's putting it mildly," the Fox said. "And there's this foolish feud Ferdulf has chosen to pick with him, too. If Mavrix does come here, it's more likely to be to warm Ferdulf's backside than to give us a hand against the Empire."

"But if he did come to help us—" Van said.

"Aye," Gerin said. "If he did." He looked around again for Dagref. When he realized why he was doing that, he blinked in surprise. He admired the wits of few men enough to ask them for their views. Without his quite noticing it, his son had become one of that small, select group.

Dagref did come back to the fire. "Mavrix?" he said when Gerin asked him about trying to summon the Sithonian god. "Mavrix . . . hmm." It was almost as if he had never heard of the god of wine and fertility.

Gerin clicked his tongue between his teeth in annoyance. "Yes, Mavrix. You remember—fawnskins, thyrsus, tongue like a frog's."

"Oh, yes, of course I remember," Dagref said. But even that sounded absent-minded, nothing like the sharp comeback he would usually have given. He yawned, rubbed his eyes, and yawned again.

"Oh, by the gods!" Gerin snapped. "Did you go and jump into an alepot? Is that why you're acting as if you haven't got two sticks of sense to rub together?"

"I'm not drunk," Dagref said. Gerin eyed him. With some reluctance, he decided his son was telling the truth. After one more yawn, Dagref went on, "I am tired. Am I allowed to be tired?"

"You weren't acting that tired before you went off to wherever you went off to," the Fox grumbled. "Since you weren't, you can give me an answer to my question before you lie down on your blanket: should I seek Mavrix's aid or not?"

"I don't see why you shouldn't *seek* it," Dagref answered. "You might be better off if you don't get it, though. That's what the oracle Biton gave would seem to mean, wouldn't it?" He hesitated. "If, of course, Biton was talking about Mavrix and not some other god altogether."

Gerin grunted, then said, "All right, go to sleep. You've earned it. You've given me something new to think about, I admit."

Dagref unfolded his blanket, wrapped himself in it, and was snoring very shortly thereafter. Gerin eyed him and scratched his head. His son didn't reek of ale, and had spoken and thought clearly enough when he decided to put his mind to it. But that mind had been somewhere else, somewhere far away. The Fox let out a puzzled grunt. That wasn't like Dagref.

But his son, once he chose to pay attention—some attention—to what he was saying, had indeed given him something new to think about. The idea of summoning a god in the hope that he would ignore the summons hadn't occurred to the Fox. He doubted it would have occurred to him, either. Dagref had a sideways way of looking at the world that could come in handy sometimes, no doubt about it.

"Ah, but the next question is, what happens if we summon dear Mavrix and he does decide to lend a hand?" Gerin murmured. That could prove embarrassing. Biton had plainly said—as plainly as the god ever said anything, anyhow—he would be better off if he got no divine help when he asked for it. What *would* he do if Mavrix pitched in against the forces of the Elabonian Empire?

After some thought, Gerin smiled. If Mavrix did decide to aid him, he could summon some other god, so that his failure there would bring him into conformity with the oracle. He glanced over to Dagref. That had an underhanded quality to it his sleeping son would appreciate.

Then he glanced over at Dagref again, in sudden sharp suspicion. If a young man disappeared for a while and then came back tired and with his mind far away from whatever his father was talking about, one obvious explanation sprang to mind.

That it was obvious didn't make it true. Gerin looked

this way and that to see if he could spy Maeva. He couldn't, which proved nothing one way or the other. The only ways to prove anything would be to catch the two of them in the act (if there was any act in which to catch them) or to have her belly start to swell—and even that wouldn't prove who the father was.

Van lay snoring a few feet from Dagref. For Dagref's sake, Gerin hoped Van's mind didn't work the way his own did.

Next evening, Rihwin's eyes got big and round. "Do you mean what you say, lord king?" he breathed.

"Of course not," Gerin snapped. "I'm lying to build your hopes up." He snorted in exasperation. "Yes, I mean what I say, curse it. I've thought things through, and I've decided you had a good idea there after all. We shall try to summon the lord of the sweet grape to our aid."

He wished he'd looked up before he spoke. Ferdulf, drifting overhead, had been close enough to hear. The demigod dove down to screech in his face: "You want my father here again? I forbid it!"

"You can't forbid it," Gerin said. "You can make my life difficult—the gods know you do make my life difficult—but you can't stop me. Ferdulf, I *am* going to do this. What you do afterwards is your affair and Mavrix's."

"He'll be sorry if he comes here," Ferdulf said darkly.

"You'll be sorry if he comes here and you try annoying him," Gerin answered. "He's stronger than you are, and you'd do well to remember it."

Ferdulf stuck out his tongue. "I'm not afraid of him. Bring him on. He'll regret it, he will."

Gerin shrugged and forbore to argue any more. People had an amazing ability to put unpleasant truths out of their minds. The Fox saw that also applied to demigods. For that matter, it probably applied to gods, too.

"Shall we now summon the lord of the sweet grape to the northlands without any further delay?" Rihwin said with a sidelong glance at Ferdulf.

Ferdulf sneered. "I'll delay you, all right. I'll turn all the wine you have left into vinegar, the same as I did with that wagonload you captured from the imperials."

"No, you won't," Gerin said, much as he might have told Blestar he wouldn't jump off the palisade walkway back at Fox Keep.

"And what's to stop me?" Ferdulf said, sticking out his tongue again.

"If you turn that wine to vinegar," Gerin said deliberately, "I will use the vinegar to call your father, it being the best I have for the purpose, and I will tell him why I could use nothing better. Then we can all find out what he chooses to do about that."

Ferdulf's glare came close to scorching him where he stood. "How could a mere mortal prove so hateful?" he demanded.

"Practice," Gerin answered. "Come on, let's get on with this."

He had Rihwin do the actual honors, drinking a cup of wine and imploring Mavrix to appear. His fellow Fox was the one who most wanted the Sithonian god to come forth. Gerin himself would have been just as glad—gladder—to have Mavrix stay down in Sithonia. The only reason Ferdulf wanted to see his father was to harass him.

"We summon thee, lord of the sweet grape," Rihwin called, sipping the wine he and his riders had captured from the warriors from south of the High Kirs. He didn't shudder with ecstasy, as he had before he'd drunk his first cup of wine in so many years. He simply drank, without making a fuss about it. Gerin took that for a good sign.

"Well, where is he?" Ferdulf said nastily when Mavrix did not forthwith appear. "Is he asleep? Is he drunk? Is he off buggering a pretty boy, or perhaps a pretty lamb?"

"You would do well, I think, to watch your tongue," Gerin said.

Ferdulf stuck it out farther than any man could have, and, for good measure, waggled the end of it. "There," he said indistinctly—he didn't bother pulling it back in before he started talking. "I'm watching it. It isn't doing very much, though."

"Heh," Gerin said—the sound of a laugh, without the mirth.

Rihwin drank more wine and called on Mavrix again. The Sithonian god stayed wherever he was; he did not come to that part of the northlands. Rihwin looked unhappy. So did Gerin, though he did not feel that way.

"Maybe he won't come. Maybe he won't hear us." Rihwin sounded as disappointed as he looked

"Maybe he won't." Gerin also sounded as disappointed as he looked, but, again, he did not feel that way.

"Maybe he's afraid of me." Ferdulf sounded arrogant. He was a demigod. He had reason to be arrogant most of the time. He did not, in Gerin's view have reason to be arrogant when he was talking about making a god afraid. Maybe, when he was older, Ferdulf would figure that out for himself. Maybe he would stay arrogant as long as he lived. Maybe, if he stayed arrogant around gods, he wouldn't live so long as he expected.

Rihwin drank yet again. "We implore thee, lord of the sweet grape, to favor us with thy presence," he said.

When nothing happened, Gerin began, "Well, all right, you've had yourself some wine, Rihwin, but the lord of the sweet grape doesn't—"

And then the lord of the sweet grape did. Glowing softly, Mavrix appeared before Gerin, Rihwin, and Ferdulf. The Sithonian god did not look happy. Mavrix, in fact, looked intensely annoyed. "Well, what is it now?" he asked in a peevish voice. "You keep bellowing in my ear until I can hardly hear myself think. Rudeness, that's what it is."

"Welcome, lord of the sweet grape," Gerin said. Now that Mavrix was here, he had to make the best of it. "We have summoned you to the northlands once more to implore you for aid against the Elabonian Empire, and—"

"And to take your much-used backside out of here, and never come back again," Ferdulf broke in.

"Is that so?" Mavrix said. Between *that* and *so* he moved from where he had been to right next to Ferdulf, apparently without crossing the intervening space. He seized his son. Ferdulf squalled and tried to get away, but could not. Mavrix gave Ferdulf a harder, more thorough spanking than Gerin had ever dared administer. "This is for the filthy tongue in your head." After a brief pause, he walloped his son again, harder than ever. "And this is for presuming to tamper with the blood of the sweet grape—so much wine wasted, so much wine men will never drink."

In an aside to Gerin, Rihwin muttered, "I'd do that to Ferdulf for wasting a wagonload of wine, too, if only I dared."

"Mavrix has the power to do it," Gerin whispered back.

Presently, Mavrix left off chastising Ferdulf, who collapsed in a weeping puddle. The Sithonian god turned his fathomless black eyes on the Fox. "What were you saying before we endured that tasteless interruption?"

"Lord Mavrix, I was saying that I hoped you might change your mind and aid me against the forces of the Elabonian Empire," Gerin replied.

"No," Mavrix said. He then repeated himself several times, at increasing volume: "*No*. NO. *NO!* Does that adequately acquaint you with my feelings in this matter?"

"But why not, lord?" Rihwin asked.

"Why?" Mavrix screeched—yes, he was exercised, and Gerin felt a certain amount of relief that Rihwin had beat him to the question. Since this whole summoning had been his fellow Fox's idea, let the oh-so-clever fellow take the heat for it. And heat there was. Mavrix continued, high and shrill, "I am not required to tell you anything, you pustule on the backside of this backwoods nest of barbarians!"

"I know you are not required to do anything of the sort, lord," Rihwin said: for a wonder, he had the sense to walk very small. "I thought you might, in your great generosity, deign to tell me, that's all."

"Well," Mavrix said, somewhat mollified by a mortal's flattery. "You are trying. But then, you are trying, too, if you take my meaning." He stuck out his tongue at Rihwin, but then drew it back in. "All right. All right. If you must know, if you *must*, one reason I have no interest whatever in coming to your aid is on account of what this little wretch did." He dug his foot into Ferdulf's ribs in what was half a poke, half a kick.

"I didn't do half of what I wish I could," Ferdulf snarled.

Mavrix ignored him, which was probably his good fortune. The Sithonian god went on, "Don't you think there's a basic rudeness involved in insulting a deity and then beseeching him for aid? Don't you?"

"Lord, I did not insult you," Rihwin said. "Gerin the Fox

did not insult you. We are the ones who seek your aid, not your son."

Gerin would have been just as well pleased—better than just as well pleased—had Rihwin not mentioned him. But, when Mavrix turned those deep, deep black eyes his way, he found he had no choice but to nod. "Assuredly, lord, I offered you no insult," he said, and that was true—he, unlike Ferdulf, knew better than to insult a god.

"I don't care," Mavrix said sniffily. "My son insulted me, and he associates with you. Therefore, you might as well have insulted me."

That was breathtakingly unfair. Had Gerin really wanted Mavrix's aid, he would have protested loud and long. Since he didn't, he contented himself with saying, "I myself would never do such a thing, and I cannot control everyone who associates with me." He gave Rihwin a pointed stare.

"I don't care," Mavrix repeated. "I am insulted, and one of yours insulted me. You get nothing from me in return."

"I'm not one of his!" Ferdulf shouted. "I'm yours."

"He showed me a pleasant peasant wench to tempt me to his keep," Mavrix answered, pointing at Gerin. "I let myself be tempted . . . and then I let myself be tempted. You, Ferdulf, are the result."

Ferdulf's curses, aimed impartially at Gerin and Mavrix, were loud and fierce and vile. In point of fact, Rihwin, who had a more intimate acquaintance with the charms of peasant women than did Gerin, had chosen Fulda, who'd proved tempting to Mavrix. Gerin refrained from mentioning that. Ferdulf was quite upset enough as things were.

Rihwin said, "What other reasons have you for refusing, lord?"

"None I need discuss with you," Mavrix said haughtily. "None I intend discussing with you. Whatever they may be, they are mine, and no business of yours in any particular."

He'd said pretty much the same thing about his first reason, which made Gerin, whose curiosity never rested, ask, "Can we not persuade you to explain yourself?"

Maybe Mavrix would have explained himself, maybe he

wouldn't. Before he could speak, though, Ferdulf broke in: "Can we not persuade you to bugger off? Can we not persuade you to take a flying futter at fast Fomor, as the Trokmoi say? Can we not persuade you to—?"

Gerin did not get a chance to find out what else Ferdulf might have wanted to persuade his father to do, because Mavrix gave the demigod another licking, more savage than either of the first two. Demigod Ferdulf might have been, but he was not strong enough to withstand punishment from a god. He wailed and shrieked and made noises not far different from those any child might have made after a drubbing from its father.

Through that racket, Mavrix said to Gerin, "You see how it is. This north country is unpleasant enough without the insults. With them, it is intolerable. I go, and, if fate be kind, I shall not return." He vanished.

"Well," Gerin said to Rihwin, "so much for that."

"Er—yes, lord king," Rihwin answered. "I think it shall be some long while before I once more seek to have aught to do with Mavrix, lord of the sweet grape." He sketched a salute and strode off, shaking his head.

That left Gerin alone with Ferdulf, not a position he would have chosen. But the choice was not his to make. He thought about walking off, as Rihwin had. Ferdulf, after all, had been the author of his own troubles. The Fox was mildly surprised to discover himself not hardhearted enough to leave the battered little demigod by himself in his pain.

"Are you all right?" he asked Ferdulf.

"You can bugger off, too," Ferdulf growled. "You're laughing at me. You hate me. Everybody hates me."

"Not quite everybody," Gerin answered, "though that certainly isn't from any lack of effort on your part. You seem to go out of your way sometimes to make yourself hateful."

"Go away," Ferdulf said. "You're not my father. I haven't got a father. As far as I'm concerned, he isn't real. He doesn't exist."

"You were scandalized about the foolish god of the Weshapar, who said the same thing about his neighbor gods," Gerin said. "Do you think it sounds any wiser coming out of your mouth?"

"I don't care," Ferdulf said. "I just don't care. You had a proper father, a father who cared about you."

Gerin burst into laughter so bitterly raucous, it made Ferdulf stare. The Fox said, "What in the five hells do you know about it? My father thought he could cure me of books and make me a warrior with the back of his hand. It was only when he finally figured out he was wrong that he shipped me over the High Kirs to be rid of me."

"But you ended up a warrior anyhow," Ferdulf said.

"So I did," Gerin said. "But that was my doing, not his—and I didn't waste his time and mine with a pack of childish tricks and tries for revenge."

"I am not a child," Ferdulf said. "I am a demigod."

"You are a demigod," the Fox agreed. "But you're also a child. That's what makes things so difficult for everyone around you."

"Good," Ferdulf said, and drifted away, apparently none the worse for wear from the beatings Mavrix had given him and just as apparently intent on taking no notice whatever of Gerin's sermon. The Fox sighed. He didn't suppose he should have been surprised.

"Aye, lord king, that's how it is," Fandil Fandor's son said as he rubbed down his horse. "I got around the imperials with no great trouble, but it didn't do me as much good as I would have liked. It didn't do you as much good as you'd like, either." He patted the horse's neck. "I will tell you this, though—I had no trouble getting through the bastards and back again."

"Wonderful," Gerin said sourly. "But, once you did get through, you found that Aragis had gone to earth?"

"That's what I said, lord king." Fandil returned to rubbing the horse's back. Gerin sympathized with the animal. Fandil's father had been called Fandor the Fat. Fandil was more along the lines of *the Chubby*, but Gerin wouldn't have wanted to try carrying him on his back.

"He doesn't plan on doing any more fighting out in the open, then?" Gerin persisted.

"Not if he can help it," Fandil answered. "He and his army are holed up in the strongest keeps they can find, and he doesn't think the imperials can pry him out of them before winter comes and they get too hungry to stay in the field. If they tear up the countryside but then go home, what does he care? He's ahead of the game."

"His peasants aren't," Gerin said, but that only made him laugh at himself. As long as the imperials went away, Aragis didn't care what happened to the peasantry. Gerin supposed he had to sympathize with that, but Aragis didn't care what happened to the peasantry any other time, either.

Fandil said, "Looks like the imperials are settling down to the sieges, too. Don't know whether they'll try knocking down walls or just sit there and starve the places out one at a time—if they can."

"If they can," Gerin agreed. "The one thing I'm sure of is that Aragis wouldn't put his men into castles that are easy to take, and he wouldn't put them into castles that don't have plenty in their cellars, either."

"You know best about that, lord king," Fandil said. "But what it looks like to me is, we're on our own over here."

Gerin sighed. "It looks that way to me, too, Fandil. We've been on our own over here all along, and we haven't done any too well so far."

"You'll come up with something." Gerin might not have confidence, but Fandil, like a lot of his men, did.

"I hope so," Gerin said. "To the crows with me if I have the faintest notion what it is, though." Fandil didn't seem to hear that, any more than Aragis had heard Gerin when he said he wasn't a sorcerer. Not for the first time, nor for the five hundredth, either, he wondered why people didn't pay more attention to what other people said. They already had their own ideas, and that seemed to be enough for them.

The next morning, he and Van and Dagref rode out along the picket line of horsemen he kept west of his force to warn him if the imperials decided to come at him again. For the moment, the men of the Elabonian Empire were holding back. They had pickets out, too, in chariots, to warn of any sudden move Gerin might make against them.

"They're not bad fellows," one of Rihwin's riders said, pointing toward an imperial chariot perhaps a quarter of a mile away. "For business like this, they don't bother us and we don't bother them. When the time comes to really fight again, they'll really go after us, I suppose, and we'll do our best to fill 'em full of arrow holes, but what's the use till then?"

"None I can see," Gerin allowed. "It's a pretty sensible way of going about things, when you get down to it."

He glanced over at Van. In the outlander's younger days, odds were he would have thundered out something about killing the foe whenever you found any chance to do it. Had Gerin had Adiatunnus with him, the Trokmê chieftain probably would have said the same thing now. But Van only shrugged and nodded, as if to say the horseman's words made good sense to him, too. Little by little, he was mellowing.

A couple of riders farther along the line, Maeva patrolled a stretch of meadow. "No, lord king," she said when Gerin asked her, "I haven't seen anything out of the ordinary." As the earlier rider had, she pointed toward an imperial chariot out of arrow range to the west. "They're keeping an eye on us, same as we're keeping an eye on them."

"All right," Gerin said. "Right at the moment, I'm not sorry things are quiet. We need the time to pull ourselves back together."

"They're probably thinking the same thing about us, lord king," Maeva answered seriously. "We had to pull back, aye, but we bloodied them."

"They have more room to make mistakes than we do, though," Van said. "By the gods, we didn't make any mistakes I could see in that last fight, and we lost it anyhow."

Dagref said nothing at all. That was unusual enough to make Gerin keep an eye on his son, as Maeva kept an eye on the force from the Elabonian Empire and as the imperials kept an eye on Gerin's army. For his part, Dagref was keeping an eye on Maeva. As best Gerin could tell from watching the back of his son's head, Dagref's eyes did not leave her.

She kept looking at him, too. *Well, well*, the Fox thought. *Isn't that interesting?* Gerin looked over at Van again, too. The outlander was also eyeing his daughter, but not, Gerin judged, with that kind of suspicion. Van was still trying to figure out why in blazes she wanted to take the field, and not worrying about anything else.

Life would get even more interesting if Maeva's belly started to bulge. Gerin had had that thought before. He wondered whether Dagref worried about such things. He might well not have himself at that age. A man and a woman—or a boy and a girl—could enjoy each other a good many ways without running the risk. Did Dagref know about them? He had little in the way of real experience, but who could guess what all he'd heard, what all he'd read? Who could guess what all Maeva knew, either?

Still shaking his head, Gerin tapped Dagref on the shoulder. "Let's get moving," he said. With obvious reluctance—obvious to the Fox, at any rate, and probably to Maeva, too—Dagref flicked the reins. The horses began to walk, and then to trot.

Dagref was not so unsubtle as to look back over his shoulder at Maeva. Gerin, however, could look back with no fear of rousing Van's suspicions, and he did. Sure enough, Maeva was staring after the chariot. Maybe that was because it held her father. Gerin wouldn't have bet on it, though, not anything he couldn't afford to lose.

After he'd finished the tour of his pickets and convinced himself the imperials weren't going to take him by surprise, he had Dagref drive back to camp. When he returned, Rihwin and Ferdulf were in the middle of a screaming row, each plastering the other with names that stuck like glue. Van descended from the chariot and tried to break up the fight, with the result that both Rihwin and Ferdulf turned on him.

Gerin hadn't tried to interfere between his friend and the little demigod, knowing that was what would happen if he did. He'd had a sufficiency—indeed, an oversupply—of people shouting at him lately, and saw no need to encourage more. If Van was of the opinion he hadn't been getting his own fair share of abuse, he was, in Gerin's view, welcome to it.

Van's furious bass roar blended with Ferdulf's baritone and Rihwin's higher, lighter voice to produce discord in three-part disharmony. Dagref rolled his eyes. "You'd think

Uncle Van would have better sense than to get mixed up in that," he said.

"Aye, good sense is hard to come by among these parts, isn't it?" Gerin said.

He didn't think he was being much more than his usual sardonic self. His son's mind, though, worked in the same channel as his own. Dagref whirled around and gave him a look half stricken, half relieved. "You know, don't you?" he said.

"I *know* now," Gerin said. "I'd wondered for a while, aye."

"You don't think Van knows, do you?" Dagref asked in some alarm—not enough, as far as Gerin was concerned, but some.

"If he did know," the Fox answered, "do you think he'd waste his time yelling at Rihwin and Ferdulf?"

"A point," Dagref said, still not happily.

"You had better be careful," Gerin said—useless advice to most youths, but Dagref was not—in some ways was not—cut from the usual cloth. "If you get her with child, you'll think the five hells had come crashing down on you, no matter how much fun you're having now."

"Another point," Dagref admitted. "There are—" He paused and coughed and might have blushed a little as he searched for words. "There are . . . ways of doing things where we don't have to worry about that."

"Yes, I know about those ways," Gerin said, nodding. "I wasn't sure whether you did."

"Er—I do," Dagref said, and stopped there.

Gerin was content to stop there, too. He couldn't very well keep an eye on his son, not in this matter he couldn't. He could—and did—hope Dagref and Maeva would stay content to stop with substitutes when they found themselves alone together. Whatever Maeva did, she threw herself into it wholeheartedly. In that, she very much resembled both her parents. That meant Gerin would have to rely on Dagref's good sense, and on Dagref's having good sense at a time when good sense was supposed to go flying out the door.

With any other lad of Dagref's age, it would have been the most forlorn of forlorn hopes. Gerin studied his son.

He still didn't think the odds were any too good, but he didn't think they were hopeless, either. He sighed. Whatever the odds were, he had no choice but to accept them.

He rubbed his chin. That wasn't strictly true. "Maybe I ought to send Maeva home, to keep this from getting any further out of hand than it is already."

Dagref looked stricken. "Don't do that, Father. You didn't send her home for anything she did, so it wouldn't be fair to send her home for anything I'm doing."

"Unless you're violating her by force, which I doubt you would do and doubt you could do, you're not doing it altogether by yourself," the Fox pointed out, at which Dagref blushed again. In musing tones, Gerin went on, "Maybe I should send you home instead."

"I hope you don't send either of us," Dagref said. "If you have to send one of us, though, send me."

Gerin slapped him on the back. "That's well spoken, for I know you aren't trying to get away from the fighting. But I do think I'll leave you both here." He found one other question to ask: "What will you do if Van finds out?"

He didn't think Dagref would be able to come up with any answer for that. But Dagref did, and promptly, too: "Run."

"Well, all right," Gerin said with a startled laugh. "That's probably the best thing you could do, though I don't know if you'll be able to run far enough or fast enough."

"Have to try." Dagref risked a wry smile that reminded Gerin achingly of himself. "Maybe he won't be able to decide whether to set out after me first or Maeva, and we'll both be able to get away."

"Maybe." Gerin laughed again. Van, though, was too automatically competent a warrior to dither at a time like that. He would settle on one of Dagref or Maeva—probably Dagref—first and then the other. The Fox hoped his son wouldn't have to learn that from experience.

After a few days, scouts brought back word that the imperials looked to be getting ready to push forward again. Gerin clicked his tongue between his teeth, far from a happy sound. "I knew it was coming," he said with a sigh. "I'd have been happier if it hadn't come so soon, though."

"What will we do, lord king?" a scout asked.

"Fight, I suppose." Gerin sighed again. "The only other choice we have is letting ourselves get pushed back into the valley of Ikos, and I don't want to do that. With everything else that's gone wrong in this campaign, I don't need to have Biton angry at me, too."

"We lost the last time we tried to withstand the imperials," Dagref pointed out. "Why should this time be any different?"

"Last time, they picked the ground—or they didn't leave me much choice, which amounts to the same thing," the Fox answered. "They struck faster and harder than I thought they would. We have better warning this time. I'm going to fight where I want to fight, by the gods."

"What sort of ground are you thinking of?" Dagref asked.

"I have a place in mind, as a matter of fact," Gerin said. "It's a long, thin stretch of meadow, with really heavy woods on either side. Off to the left, beyond the woods, there's a little hill I intend to screen off with a good many of Rihwin's riders. Do you see what's in my mind?"

"I think so," Dagref answered. "You want to put men back there and trap the imperials between your two forces, don't you?"

"That's what I'm planning, yes," Gerin agreed. "Now I have to hope the imperials don't see it as clearly as you've done."

But the imperials, to his loud, vehement, and profane dismay, did see the trap, and refused to fall into it. When his riders picked off one of the scouts from south of the High Kirs, he found out why. "We've got Swerilas in command of us now," the prisoner said. "Swerilas the Slippery, men call him. He sent Arpulo Werekas' son back west to take charge of the sieges against Gerin—"

"I'm Gerin," Gerin said.

"Against Aragis, then. I can't keep you rebels straight," the captured imperial said. "Swerilas figured that was the easier part of the job, so he gave it to Arpulo. You've caused Arpulo trouble; Swerilas decided he needed to deal with you himself."

"Were it not for the honor he shows me, it's a compliment I could do without," Gerin murmured, and then,

"Swerilas the Slippery, eh? He'd be the fellow who was in charge of your second army, wouldn't he?"

"Aye," the prisoner said. "Arpulo led the first."

Gerin scowled. His life had just got more difficult. He had Arpulo's measure, even if he'd lacked the manpower to beat him in their latest clash. But Swerilas . . . an ekename like *the Slippery* was all too close to *the Fox*, and Swerilas had shown that he had more than a few ideas of his own. Gerin would have been happier fighting a bruiser who didn't think very well.

After he sent the prisoner away, he decided he might have been lucky that Swerilas had stayed out of his trap rather than letting himself go in with his eyes open and then smashing out in both directions at once. Gerin's force was inferior to his in numbers. Against an average commander like Arpulo, the Fox had no qualms—well, few qualms—about dividing even an inferior force. Against someone who knew what he was doing, as Swerilas plainly did, dividing his force was asking to be destroyed in detail.

With another scowl, Gerin did his best to come up with a new plan. Against Swerilas, he had fewer options than he'd had against Arpulo. And Swerilas, no doubt, would be able to think of more unpleasant things to do to him than would have crossed Arpulo's fierce but unimaginative mind.

Gerin dispatched all his horsemen to harass Swerilas' scouts, to drive them back on the main body of imperials, and to disrupt the imperials' foraging as much as he could. "You riders are the one force we have that the imperials don't know everything about," he told Rihwin the Fox. "We'll wring every particle of advantage we can out of that."

"Aye, lord king," Rihwin said. "We shall fall on the men of the Elabonian Empire like a whirlwind. We shall trouble them with continuous attacks from all directions, until they weepingly regret ever having stirred north of the High Kirs."

That was as grandiloquent as anything Gerin had heard lately, even from Rihwin. But Rihwin, fortunately, was almost as long on fighting talent as he was on bombast. Gerin thumped him on the shoulder. "Aye, that's good.

That's what I want from you. The harder he has to work against your horsemen, the less leisure he'll have to do anything against the main army here."

"I shall think on this with gratitude as the imperials chew my force to pieces," Rihwin replied, bowing.

"Go howl," Gerin said. "I don't want you to get chewed to pieces. I'm counting on you not to let yourself and your force get chewed to pieces. By the gods, I don't want to fight a pitched battle with this Swerilas. I want you to keep him running every which way, so he's too busy and hot and bothered to come and fight a pitched battle with the whole army."

"Oh, I understand you, lord king," Rihwin said. "Whether what you want and what Swerilas wants are one and the same remains to be seen."

"That's true in any fight," Gerin said. "I'll move forward as far as I can with the bulk of my force. If you do get in trouble, I'll support you as best I can." He set a hand on Rihwin's shoulder again. "Do your best not to get in too much trouble, would you?"

"How can you say such a thing about me?" Rihwin drew back in an artful display of indignation. "Have I ever been anything in all my days save staid and sedate?" He had an excellent straight face.

"No, never," Gerin agreed soberly. Both men laughed then.

Rihwin said, "Will you let Ferdulf come along with me? It will be easier to annoy the imperials if I have the best notion I can of where they are, where they're moving, and what they want to try to do to me."

"If you can talk Ferdulf into going with you, you're welcome to him," Gerin answered. His grin was distinctly sardonic. "In fact, you're welcome to him as a general principle."

"As a general principle, I don't want him, thanks." Rihwin's grin closely matched Gerin's. "Didn't you hear us going at each other a few days ago?"

"Most of the northlands heard you, I should think," Gerin said.

"I daresay. You can understand me, then. As a flying spy, though, he has his uses."

"Whether he'll want anything to do with you, of course, remains to be seen," Gerin said. "He's liable not to be very happy with you, you know, after the rough handling Mavrix gave him—you were the one who was bound and determined to summon the Sithonian god."

"Yes, that's what Ferdulf was screeching about before," Rihwin said, "but I'll take my chances now."

"You certainly will," Gerin agreed, at which Rihwin gave him a dirty look. Gerin went on, "Talk with him, though. If, after he's done insulting you some more, he decides to go along, I think you're right—he'll be quite useful to you as a flying spy."

"After something close to half a lifetime with you and Van of the Strong Arm, I shan't let insults from a bad-tempered baby demigod faze me," Rihwin said. Off he went, ostentatiously ignoring the sour stare Gerin sent after him.

Sure enough, he managed to persuade Ferdulf to accompany the force of riders. After the shouting Ferdulf put up when he made the request, though, Gerin wouldn't have blamed Rihwin if he'd buried Mavrix's son upside down in the ground. That, at least, would have made Ferdulf shut up.

Watching the little demigod wheel and swoop above the horsemen, Gerin was also just as well pleased not to be under there, in the same way he would have been just as well pleased not to be under a flock of crows with griping bowels. The crows would have let fly—or let fall—at random. Ferdulf, if the evil mood took him, could aim.

Van was not watching Ferdulf as the riders trotted away. He was trying to spot Maeva among the warriors on horseback, and not having much luck. Turning to Gerin, he said, "I still wish you'd made her go home."

"She's doing what she wants to do, you know," the Fox answered. "You couldn't stop it more than another couple of years at the most."

"That would be good," Van said. "In a couple of years, likely enough, we wouldn't be worrying about the imperials any more."

"Unless we'd already lost to them, of course," Gerin replied. "No, wait—I take your point. But we would be worrying about Aragis or the Trokmoi or the Gradi or *somebody*, by the gods. If Maeva wanted to fight somebody, she'd find somebody to fight. And if you didn't feel like letting her, she'd fight *you*."

"Maybe. Maybe." The prospect didn't make Van look any happier. "But that's not the only thing I fret about. Come on, Fox—you know what soldiers are like."

"Well, what if I do?" the Fox said. "Anyone who tried to take anything she didn't feel like giving would regret it as long as he lived, and that might not be long, either. We've been over this ground before, you know."

"Oh, aye." The outlander let out a long, sad sigh. "Why couldn't she have just stayed home and come to notice Dagref, say? We could have married them off, and that would have been an end to it."

Gerin didn't gape like a fool. He didn't burst into hysterical laughter. He didn't even suffer a coughing fit. The effort he needed to keep from doing any of those things would have let him lift the temple at Ikos over his head and throw it from one end of the valley to the other.

In an offhand tone that somehow wasn't more elaborately casual than it should have been, he answered, "If they like the idea, you wouldn't see me complaining. We'll have to see if we can make it seem as if they're the ones who came up with it, not us."

"Truth that," Van said, one of the turns of phrase he'd learned from the Trokmoi that still occasionally showed up in his speech. "If anybody older than I was came up with a notion back when I was a sprat, I didn't want anything to do with it." He cocked his head to one side and studied the Fox. "And you! You must have been a terror when it came to listening to your elders."

"Who, me?" Gerin did his best to look like innocence personified. His best, evidently, wasn't good enough, for Van guffawed.

"Aye, you, Captain," he said. "Go on and look sweet all you fancy. My guess is, you weren't any more ready to pay the least bit of attention to what your father told you than Dagref is for you."

"My father hit me harder and more often than I've hit Dagref," Gerin said after a brief pause for thought. "That made me more likely to listen, but I think less likely to agree."

Van smacked a fist into the palm of his other hand. "Sometimes you'll settle for getting them to listen that way."

"You say that *now*," Gerin said. "What did you say *then*?"

"Ahh, what difference does that make?" the outlander replied with a grin. "I was just a brat then, wet behind the ears. Of course, I wouldn't have believed that if anybody told it to me, mind you."

Rihwin began sending back prisoners and the occasional wagon pilfered from the imperials and news of what Swerilas the Slippery was up to. "The Empire's general looks to be pulling all his men back into a knot," one of Rihwin's riders reported, "the same way a snail will go back into its shell if you poke it in one of its little horns." He held up a couple of fingers, imitating a snail.

"The creatures have their eyes at the ends of those stalks," Gerin said, a fact he'd picked up in the City of Elabon. He'd never had occasion to trot it out in all the many years since, but his fiendishly tenacious memory hadn't let him forget it.

Now that he finally did get to use it, he discovered the horseman didn't believe him. With a laugh, the fellow said, "That's funny, lord king."

"I mean it," Gerin said indignantly. "If those little black dots on the ends of the stalks aren't eyes, where would a snail keep 'em?"

"How am I supposed to answer a question like that?" the rider said. "The whole world knows snails have no eyes."

"But they do," the Fox insisted. He couldn't persuade the horseman he wasn't joking. Finally, in disgust, he sent him back to Rihwin. Gerin was still fuming when he turned to Van, who had listened to the last part of his exchange with the scout. "Can you believe the stubborn ignorance of that man?"

Van chuckled. He shook his head, but not in the way Gerin would have wanted. "Oh no you don't, Captain," the outlander said. "You can try and confuse a rider from some backwoods keep as much as you like, but you're not going to do it to me, by the gods. When you come right down to it, that fellow was right—everybody knows snails don't have any eyes."

Gerin snarled a curse and stalked off.

He snarled another curse a couple of days later, when the imperials mauled a detachment of Rihwin's riders. The damage done was bad enough that Rihwin felt he had to come back himself to explain. "They outwitted me," he said, sounding angry and embarrassed at the same time. "They had a small band showing, making their way through wheatfields. But more of them were lurking in the trees. As soon as we were well engaged with the decoys, out they swarmed."

"That's . . . unfortunate," Gerin said. He looked down his nose at Rihwin. "It's also unfortunate that you let yourself be fooled by the sort of trick we've used so often ourselves."

"I didn't expect it of the imperials," Rihwin said, a little sullenly. "One of the reasons I came north of the High Kirs all those years ago, if you'll remember, is because interesting things happen here while all stays stodgy south of the mountains. The way the Emperor's men fought in this campaign had given me little reason to change my view."

"Except for the forces commanded by this Swerilas the Slippery," Gerin said. "He beat us when we were almost down to Cassat, and he did it the same way he did here: he stuck out one force, and then he struck with another one we didn't expect. If bait looks too juicy to be true, my fellow Fox, it likely is."

"But it didn't look too juicy to be true." Rihwin angrily kicked at the dirt. "By the gods, you would have sent in the riders with no more hesitation than I showed. It was a chance encounter, nothing more."

"No, it *seemed* a chance encounter—or you wouldn't have been ambushed," Gerin said. "He must have set it up by gauging where your detachment was, which way they were headed, and how fast." He kicked at the dirt, too. "Which means Swerilas is very slippery indeed."

"I want another crack at him," Rihwin said. "No one does that to me, not without paying for it."

"Unfortunately, someone did do it to you," Gerin

answered, "and I don't want you charging after the imperials all wild for revenge. Swerilas will be waiting for something like that."

For a wonder, he got through to Rihwin. "Aye, belike you're right," Rihwin said. "It's just what a man from the City of Elabon would expect in the northlands—let the locals make fools of themselves, and then count on them to make bigger fools of themselves trying to recover."

"Of course, odds are he didn't know he was facing another man from south of the High Kirs," Gerin said.

"Go ahead—rub salt in the throbbing wound." Rihwin struck a pose of affronted dignity. Then it collapsed, and he chuckled. "Speaking of men from south of the High Kirs, lord king, did I tell you we've captured my cousin?"

"No." Gerin raised an eyebrow. "How did that happen?"

"Usual sort of way," Rihwin answered. "He got wounded in the shoulder—doesn't look too bad—fell out of his chariot, and we scooped him up. When I found out his name was Ulfilas Batwin's son, I asked about his family, because my uncle's son Batwin is a man of about my age. And sure enough, we are first cousins, once removed."

"You've been removed by twenty years and a mountain range, too," Gerin said. He sighed and put an arm around Rihwin. "All right. You walked into this one. It's over. Don't do it again." He laughed. "I sound as if I'm talking to one of my sons, don't I? One of these days, maybe, just maybe, you'll grow up. One of them has done it, and the second is on the way."

"I resent the imputation." Rihwin looked affronted again.

"Go ahead," Gerin said cheerfully. "I'll probably have to keep right on lecturing you till they shovel dirt over one of us or the other."

"You could shut up instead," Rihwin suggested. They laughed, both knowing that Gerin shutting up was about as likely—or rather, as unlikely—as Rihwin growing up.

Ferdulf came flying toward Gerin's main force. "Here he comes!" the demigod shouted. "That cursed horse turd of a Swerilas is heading this way, and I don't think he's coming to invite you to take ale with him."

"Well, I can't say I'm surprised," Gerin answered. He

couldn't say he was truly ready to meet Swerilas' assault, either, but volition didn't play any great role here. "How far away is he, and how are the horsemen doing at holding him back?"

"He'll be here in a couple of hours' time, maybe less," Ferdulf answered. "The riders are doing what they can, but they can't stop the son of a sow all by themselves. He's got too many men. He's got too many chariots, too."

"I know that," Gerin said discontentedly. "He's got too many men and too many chariots for this whole army."

"Well, what are you going to do about it?" Ferdulf screeched.

"The best I can," Gerin answered.

"*That's* not good enough," Ferdulf said. "You have to beat him. If you don't beat him, the northlands are ruined."

"If I don't beat him, I'm ruined," the Fox said. "The possibility remains that I may not beat him." He clicked his tongue between his teeth. "If I don't, I'll just have to go on from there."

"You make it sound so easy." Scorn laced Ferdulf's voice. "Where will you go on from there, pray tell?"

"I don't know," Gerin admitted. "I hope I don't have to find out." Ferdulf stared at him. A trifle irritably, he went on, "I'm not a god, Ferdulf. I'm not even related to a god. I don't know what's going to happen next. All I can do is the best I can, and see what happens. I told you that already."

"What a sloppy arrangement," Ferdulf said. "And what, if you would be so generous as to tell me, is the best you can do?"

Gerin had been thinking it over while the demigod carped at him. "I'm going to keep my men in one compact mass and hit the imperials as hard a blow as I can. I don't dare divide my army against Swerilas. He has too many men and too many brains for me to take the chance. What I hope is that I'll catch him trying to do something fancy and punish him before he can pull all of his forces together." He brightened a little. "Go fly off and tell me how he's deploying. That way, I'll have some notion of what I'm up against."

"You're out of your head," Ferdulf replied with mournful

certainty, but away he flew. Gerin sighed and began shouting orders.

The men formed up as quickly as he could have wanted. None of them showed any particular eagerness for the fight ahead, not even Adiatunnus' Trokmoi. Maybe that meant they were veterans who didn't need to scream like fiends to go out and fight well. Maybe it meant they had no particular hope of victory. Gerin hoped it was the one and not the other.

Far faster than he should have, given where Swerilas' force was, Ferdulf came whizzing back. "What now?" Gerin asked in alarm. Had the imperial general stolen a march on him?

But Ferdulf answered, "If you're going to fight in one large, ugly lump, are you fain to have me tell Rihwin bring his horsemen back so they can take their lumps with the rest of you?"

"Oh, by the gods!" Gerin exclaimed, mentally kicking himself for having sent the demigod off too soon. "Yes, and thank you, Ferdulf. I'm in your debt. I admit it."

"You're in my debt, you owe your son a promise, you owe the imperials a thrashing—do you think you can deliver on any of these?" Ferdulf flew away before the Fox had a chance to reply.

He sent his men forward, toward that field he'd found that was well suited to the size of his force. As the main force advanced, Rihwin's riders began joining them. Gerin posted the horsemen as a screen in front of the main body of chariotry and on either flank.

"Is that Maeva?" Van pointed off to the right. He answered his own question: "Aye, it is." He waved, then muttered in disappointment. "She didn't see me, curse it."

Dagref's head was turned in that direction. He nodded. "It is Maeva, though, and she seems all right." He was better than he had been a little while before at sounding casual about it.

Gerin looked west down the dirt road that ran through the field. he nodded. Here came the imperials, exchanging arrows with the last of his horsemen. Like his own troops, the men of the Elabonian Empire were already deployed in line of battle, sweeping down the road and along the open country to either side. Catching them in column would have been sweet, but Swerilas, with his sobriquet, was too alert to have let that happen.

"Elabon! Elabon! Elabon!" the imperials shouted. Gerin, for one, was heartily sick of that battle cry. His own men yelled the usual northlands assortment of war cries and insults back at their foes.

"Forward!" Gerin put everything he had into his own shout. He wanted to be moving to receive the imperials' charge, not standing still, waiting to be overrun.

Dagref flicked the reins and cracked the whip above the horses' backs. They went from walk to trot to gallop. One wheel of the car hit a stone. The chariot flew into the air and came back to earth with a crash. Neither Gerin nor Van nor Dagref did anything more than shift weight back and forth.

Gerin looked to see if he could pick out Swerilas the Slippery among the imperials. He couldn't. Swerilas was slippery enough not to deck himself out in raiment that made him a target. The Fox shook his head in disappointment. He hadn't seen any other imperial officers that canny.

He started shooting anyhow. If he couldn't find the best target, he'd hit what he could. He didn't think Swerilas had sent an outflanking party off to either wing; if the imperial general had done such a thing, Ferdulf would have reported it—or so the Fox devoutly hoped. That made it a straightforward slugging match, army against army: the same sort of fight Arpulo had waged. Like the general he'd replaced, Swerilas had greater numbers.

But Swerilas quickly proved himself a better general than Arpulo. Arpulo had let Gerin's men get round his flanks and attack his force from three sides at once. Swerilas, by contrast, made his own battle line wide and kept trying to lap round Gerin's force to the right and left. Very much unlike Arpulo, he knew what he had and what to do with it.

Unhappily, Gerin extended his own line. He knew what Swerilas was trying to do: make him thin his force enough to let the imperials find or create a weak spot and punch on through. If they did that, they could split his army in two and destroy one of the parts at their leisure.

Other than retreat, the only counter he could find was doing it to them before they had a chance to do it to him. That meant thinning his line even more than he'd done already, to collect a force with which he could strike. Crew by crew, his chariotry remained better than that of the Elabonian Empire. Without that being true, he couldn't have done what he did. Even with its being true, he gripped the rail of the chariot hard, knowing the risk he took.

"Forward!" he shouted again. Dagref steered the car toward what looked like the weakest part of the imperial line.

For a brief, shining moment, he thought his striking force would break through. The imperials still had a respect for the Trokmoi just short of dread. Adiatunnus' howling warriors did make them hesitate. But Swerilas, unlike Gerin, did not have to stint one part of his line to send reinforcements to another. He brought enough men in against Gerin's striking force to keep it from piercing his army through and through.

"Well, what do we do now?" Van yelled in Gerin's ear once the attack had plainly bogged down.

"Good question," Gerin answered. Dagref maneuvered smartly to keep the imperials from getting a chariot to either side of his own at the same time. The maneuver brought the horses around so they were facing more nearly the way they had come than the way they'd been going. Gerin shot an arrow at one of the imperials closest to him, and wounded the trooper in the arm. But there were still too many soldiers from the Elabonian Empire close by. With a weary curse, the Fox said, "Now we go back. I don't see what in the five hells else we can do, not if we want to keep the army in one piece."

He managed the retreat as well as he could. By then, he'd had more practice managing retreats than he'd ever wanted. He'd never had to manage one against Swerilas the Slippery before, though. Swerilas did what he would have done himself in the same place: pushed hard and tried not merely to beat the army from the northlands but to wreck it.

Gerin had hoped to be able to make a stand back at his camp, but the leading imperials were too closely mingled with his rear guard to make that possible. They were pressing Gerin and his men too hard to make any stand possible for some time. Gerin had everything he could do to keep the imperials from getting ahead of his men and cutting off their line of retreat.

He did succeed in doing that much—that little, he thought of it at the time—but Swerilas drove him almost to the southern opening of the valley of Ikos before the light finally failed. By all indications, Swerilas aimed to keep right on driving him when morning came, too. He looked north. Temple guards no doubt waited at the mouth of the valley. He didn't care. But for Ikos, he had nowhere to go.

XI

A guardsman held his shield horizontally across his body to bar the road into the valley of Ikos. "The lord Biton forbids the entry of large bodies of armed men into the land surrounding his sacred precinct," the fellow said.

Gerin answered, "If the lord Biton punishes me for bringing my army into his land, then he will, that's all." He turned and waved his battered army forward. "Get moving, boys!"

"The god will know of your action!" the guard bleated as chariots began rolling past him and his spear.

"He's the farseeing god, so of course he will," the Fox replied. "He'll also know why we're doing it, which is more than you do. Swerilas the Slippery and the Elabonian army are on our tail. You're going to have more company than us, and worse company than us, too."

"Biton preserve us!" the guardsman said.

"That would be nice," Gerin agreed, "but don't count on it too much, because it's liable not to happen."

The guard glared at him. "Why did you have to lead the imperials here? Why couldn't you have fled in some other direction than this one?"

"It's hard to flee straight toward the fellow who's just made you do it," Gerin pointed out. "And it was either come here or head off east toward the plains of Shanda. Somehow, I don't think I'm cut out to be a nomad."

"But we've been free of the Empire for many years," the temple guard moaned. "Will the officious priests from south of the mountains stick their long snouts into the way we run our affairs, as I have heard they did in the long-ago and far-off days?"

"Very likely they will," Gerin said. "That's what they're good for: sticking their noses into things, I mean. That's what they'll do if they win, anyhow. But my army is still in one piece, even if we have lost some fights. We may beat the imperials yet."

"Farseeing Biton grant it be so!" the guard answered. "Very well, then: I give you leave to pass into this valley, unless the farseeing god should himself choose to overrule me."

"Thanks," the Fox said. He'd intended to take his army into the valley of Ikos whether the guardsman gave him leave or not. If the temple guard had been so foolish as to refuse to give his leave, Biton's temple probably would have had to get along without him from then on. Gerin figured he could square it with the god; what use would a farseeing deity have for such a stupid guard?

"We shall not grant leave to the imperials," the temple guard declared. "If they enter, they shall enter in Biton's despite, and shall face his punishment."

"Will you fight against the men of the Elabonian Empire?" Gerin asked. "Will you fight alongside us to protect the northlands?"

"That will be Biton's judgment to make, not mine," the guardsman said. "If the god orders it, we shall assuredly fight. If the god orders otherwise, we shall likewise obey him."

I haven't the faintest idea, was what he meant, though his phrasing was a good deal more polished than that. He hadn't come right out and said no. Gerin supposed that would have to do.

Into the valley of Ikos rode his battered troopers. Had the imperials been a little luckier—and he knew it would have taken no more than that—his army would have been cut off before it got to the valley, cut off and destroyed.

The imperials would have more chance to do that soon enough.

For now, though, rest. Time to see to the wounded, time to see to the horses and chariots, time to curl up in a blanket and sleep a sleep that seemed not far removed from death. Gerin looked forward to that kind of sleep—looked forward to it with a hopeless longing, because he would be too busy to enjoy anywhere near so much of it as his men did.

As usual after a battle, he did what he could for the men who had been hurt. He did some horse-doctoring, too. That was harder, and in a way more discouraging. His men had a notion of why and how they'd taken wounds. To the horses, everything was a nasty surprise.

Gerin was washing a cut on a horse's rump with ale when Rihwin came up to him. The horse quivered and let out a whuffling snort, but did not try to bolt or kick. "That's a good fellow," the Fox said. The rider holding the horse's head stroked its nose and murmured, "There's a brave fellow. That's my beauty." The words meant little, the tone much.

With a sigh, Gerin turned to Rihwin. "And what can I do for *you*?" His tone meant much, too, but in a far less gentle way.

Rihwin answered, "Lord king, I should like to know what our next movement against the imperials will be."

"Should you?" Gerin said. Rihwin nodded. With a grimace, Gerin went on, "Well, by the gods, so should I. The only thing I can think of doing, though, is to keep on with what we're already doing, which is to say, retreating."

"Back toward our own lands, you mean," Rihwin said.

Gerin exhaled in exasperation. "You must have been listening to that lackwit of a temple guard. It's very hard to retreat *toward* the enemy; the technical term for that is *advance*."

"For which wisdom I thank you, O font of knowledge," Rihwin said, not about to be outdone in sarcasm, "but that was not precisely what I had in mind. As you know, only one road leads from the valley of Ikos to lands under your illustrious suzerainty, and it is a road perhaps something less than conducive to rapid travel."

"Ah," Gerin said, and nodded. "Now I understand. You're not happy about the notion of traveling through the haunted woods, eh?"

"To put with as much abridgment as I can muster, lord king, no," Rihwin said. "Are you?"

"Not so you'd notice," Gerin answered. "But if it's a choice between that and staying here so the imperials can finish wrecking us, I know which direction I'll go. All I can do is hope my men and I come out on the other side. If we do, maybe we can smash in the head of the imperials' column as they come after us."

"That would be good," Rihwin said without much conviction. He didn't think it would happen, then.

"Better still," Gerin said in a spirit of experimentation, "would be meeting the imperials here in the valley of Ikos and driving them back."

Plainly, Gerin didn't think that would happen, either. "Yes, that would be better, lord king," he agreed. "Not likely, perhaps, but better without a doubt. How do you aim to produce a victory when lately we've known nothing but defeat?"

"I don't know," Gerin admitted, which seemed to nonplus Rihwin more than anything else he might have said. "The best we can hope for now, it seems to me, is to hope the imperials haven't the stomach for a long, hard campaign and give up and go home."

"We might have had a better hope for that had we gained the aid of the lord of the sweet grape," Rihwin said.

"That's not what Biton said, but then you've never been much interested in any opinion but your own."

Rihwin scowled at him; a moment later, though, the eyes of the man from south of the High Kirs widened. "You demon from the hottest hell," he whispered. "You let me go through the danger of summoning Mavrix hoping and expecting I would fail, and you said never a word."

"I understand how surprising it must be for you to discover there are people who can on occasion keep their mouths shut," Gerin replied sweetly. "You really should try it sometime. It can be useful."

"To the crows with utility, and to the crows with you, too," Rihwin said. His effort to stalk off in impressive fury was hampered when he bumped into Van. Like everyone else who bumped into the outsized outlander, he bounced off. He kept stalking after that, but it wasn't the same.

Van shook his head. "I see you were rattling his cage again."

"Twice," Gerin answered. Then he corrected himself. "No, I take that back. He rattled his own cage once, when he figured out I wasn't too unhappy that he hadn't managed to get Mavrix to help us after all."

"What did he do, say you were trying to use him as a sacrifice, the way the god of the Weshapar wanted Zalmunna to sacrifice his son?"

"He didn't use that example, no, but that was the general tone, as a matter of fact." The Fox laughed. Laughing felt good. It also let him take his mind off the unpleasant fact that he still had no idea how to stop the imperials. But when he stopped laughing, that fact remained—and it seemed to be laughing at him, laughing and showing fangs as long as sharp as those of a longtooth.

Maybe it was laughing at Van, too. He said, "Come morning, that Swerilas the Slimy is going to start nipping at our tails again."

"Slippery," Gerin said. "Swerilas the Slippery, no matter how slimy he is. But . . ." He hesitated, then spoke in some surprise: "I may just know what I'm going to do about him. Aye, by the gods—and by one god in particular—I may just."

Sure enough, Swerilas pushed his men forward not long after the sun came up. The temple guards did resist them. So did a rear guard of Gerin's men. But the imperials were too many to be withstood for long, and in Swerilas had a leader who grew angry with anything less than victory.

Gerin fed more men into the fight, not so much in expectation of stopping Swerilas as to slow him down. And, had Swerilas not already been a suspicious sort, failure to try to hold him off would have made him one. Slowing him down also let Gerin's main force forage among the prosperous villages of the valley of Ikos as they retreated toward the Sibyl's shrine.

The temple guards peeled off to defend the temple from

its marble outwalls. Gerin ordered his own men to keep on retreating. Dagref gave his father a curious look. Then, all at once, it vanished from his face. "Biton's temple holds a lot of rich things, doesn't it?" he remarked.

"Oh, there might be a few in there, I suppose," Gerin answered, his voice elaborately casual. "Why? Do you think that might be interesting to the imperial soldiers and their officers?"

"It just might," his son said, imitating his tone with alarming precision. "The one thing about which the men of the northlands always complain is how the Elabonian Empire squeezed wealth out of them like a man squeezing whey out of a lump of cheese."

"Biton isn't the sort of god who fancies being squeezed," Van put in.

"You know that," Gerin said. "I know that. The question is, does Swerilas the Slippery know that? And the other question is, if he does know, does he care? He has wizards with him. He has the backing of the Elabonian gods, or thinks he does. Maybe he won't care a fig's worth, and think he can take whatever he pleases."

"Wouldn't that be nice?" Van said dreamily. "We've seen the plague Biton sends down on people who try robbing his shrine. All those blisters and things—it's not pretty, not even a little bit. Fox, don't you think this Swerilas would look mighty fine all blistered up?"

"Since I've never met him, I don't know how ugly he is already," Gerin replied. "But any old imperial covered in blisters would look pretty good to me right now."

North of the Sibyl's shine lay the town that catered to visitors to the valley who came seeking oracular responses. The town was not what it had been in Gerin's younger days. Traffic for the Sibyl had diminished when the Elabonian Empire severed itself from the northlands, and diminished again after the earthquake that loosed the monsters on the earth. Many of the inns and taverns and hostels that had served travelers were empty. Some were wrecks that had gone unrepaired since the quake fifteen years before. Grass grew where others had once stood.

The innkeepers whose establishments survived viewed the arrival of Gerin's army with the same delight that serfs would have shown over the arrival of a swarm of locusts, and for similar reasons: they feared the troopers were going to eat them out of house and home, and they were right.

"Is this justice, lord king?" one of them wailed as Gerin's soldiers gobbled bread and roasted meat and guzzled ale.

"Probably not," the Fox admitted. "But we're hungry and we're here and we're bloody well going to eat. If we win this war, I'll pay you back next year—by all the gods I swear it. If we lose, you can send the bill to Crebbig I, the Elabonian Emperor."

"Then I'll root for you," the innkeeper said. "You have a good name for not telling too many lies. I wouldn't wipe my arse with a promise from somebody on the far side of the mountains, not that I even have a promise from the whoreson to wipe my arse with."

Gerin thought it likely the innkeeper would see the imperials at first hand before too long. As he'd hoped, Swerilas had slowed his aggressive pursuit of the men from the northlands when he came in sight of Biton's shrine. Rihwin's riders had no trouble holding the imperials away from the town of Ikos, not for the time being.

Taking advantage of that, the Fox put as many of his men in real beds as he could. The summer's fighting had worn down his troopers; the more rest they got now, the better they would perform when they had to climb into their chariots again.

He slept outside rolled in a blanket himself, which perplexed Adiatunnus. "Where's the point to kinging it if you canna be after enjoying yourself?" the Trokmê chieftain demanded. He hadn't been slow about claiming the pleasures of a bed.

Gerin shrugged. "I'm all right. Some of the men with small wounds need mattresses worse than I do."

"Maybe that's so, and maybe it's not," Adiatunnus said. "Most o' these lads are half your age—half my age, too, forbye—and think naught of a night in the open. If you say you don't creak of a morning, you're a better man than I am—or else you're a liar."

"I do creak," Gerin admitted, "but I don't creak too badly. And half the time I'll creak when I get up out of a bed in the morning, too. I'm at the age when creaking is part of being alive. I'm used to it. I don't love it, but I can't do anything about it."

"Nor I," Adiatunnus said sadly. "Nor I. But I creak less if I'm rising from soft straw or wool, sure and I do, and so I'll take a bed when I find one. A bed is better when you're after finding a friendly barmaid, too."

"However you like," Gerin said with another shrug. Like Van, Adiatunnus wenched whenever he found a chance.

He laughed at the Fox now. "You canna be saying you're so old, it stirs in your breeches no more. When it does, why not let it out to play? Plenty o' girls'd lie down with you just for the sake of saying they'd bedded a king."

"I don't want—" Gerin stopped. What he'd been about to say wasn't true. He wasn't immune from wanting an attractive woman when he was away from Selatre. What he did, or rather didn't, do about it was something else again. He changed the direction in which the sentence had been going: "I don't want to complicate my life. How many bastards have you got?"

"A good many, I'll allow," the Trokmê answered, laughing again. "Not so many as Rihwin, I expect, but I had fun getting every one of 'em."

"All right," Gerin said. "I don't begrudge you the way you live your life. Why can't you let me lead mine as suits me best?"

Adiatunnus scowled again. "How can I be having a proper quarrel with you when you willna get angry?"

"My quarrel is with Swerilas the Slippery, not with you," Gerin replied. "You're my ally and my vassal; he's my foe." He grinned a lopsided grin. "And when we were young, neither of us would have believe that could be so, not for a minute we wouldn't."

"Truth that," Adiatunnus said. "Och, how we hated the very name of yourself on the far side of the Niffet! Too good you were, too good by half, at tying us all in knots whenever we thought to raid over the river. And then, we we did at last lodge ourself on this side, who but you did so much against us and kept so many from crossing? And now you are my overlord, and we have the same enemies, as you say. Aye, 'tis strange and more than strange."

"If I can put up with the likes of you," Gerin said, "I

shouldn't—and I don't—mind putting up with a blanket on the ground."

"Sure it was for your kindness and sweet spirit I first named you king," Adiatunnus said. He walked off shaking his head and laughing.

The next morning, Maeva, her face glowing with self-importance, came riding back from the line against the imperials with the fat eunuch who had taken Gerin down to the Sibyl's cave. "He says he must have speech with you, lord king."

"I'm glad enough to speak with him," Gerin answered, and turned to the priest. "How now?"

Awkwardly, the eunuch prostrated himself before Gerin, as if before an image of farseeing Biton. "Lord king, you must save the god's shrine from desecration!" he cried.

"Get up," the Fox said impatiently. When the priest had risen, Gerin went on, "Who says I must?"

"If you do not save the shrine, lord king, the arrogant wretches from south of the High Kirs will plunder it of the accumulated riches of centuries." The priest seemed on the point of bursting into tears.

For his part, though, Gerin had hoped the accumulated riches in and around Biton's temper would make Swerilas forget about him for a while. And so he repeated, "Who says I must save the shrine? Is it a command sent straight from Biton himself?" If it was, he might have to obey it, however little he wanted to.

But the priest shook his head, the loose, flabby flesh of his jowls swinging back and forth. "Biton has been mute in this matter," he said in his sexless voice. "But you, lord king, are well known for the great respect you have always shown the farseeing god."

"If the farseeing god ordered me to try to drive the men of the Elabonian Empire from his temple, I would do it, or do my best to do it," Gerin answered, on the whole truthfully. "Since he does not, though, let me ask a question of my own: why do you think I retreated past the Sibyl's shrine and made my base here in the town of Ikos?"

"I wondered, lord king," the eunuch priest replied. "I thought surely you would defend us with all your power."

"With all my power." Gerin heard the bitterness in his

own voice. "If I had the power to stop the imperials, why would I have retreated into the valley of Ikos in the first place? Why would I have retreated through it? Why will I have to retreat out of it if the imperials attack me again?"

The priest stared at him. "But you are the chiefest warrior in all the northlands. How could you be beaten?"

"More easily than I'd like, as a matter of fact," Gerin answered. "When the Elabonian Empire sends more men against me than I can withstand, they beat me. Nothing complicated about it at all. And you can be glad Aragis the Archer isn't here to hear you call me the chiefest warrior, too. He'd disagree with you, and he isn't pleasant when he disagrees."

He might as well not have spoken. The priest didn't interrupt him, but plainly didn't pay any attention to his words, either. The fellow went on, "And you are the favorite of the farseeing god as well. How could it be otherwise, when you are wed to Biton's former Sibyl?" He sighed, perhaps admiring the close relationship with Biton he thought being married to Selatre gave Gerin, perhaps—as he was a eunuch—admiring Gerin for being married at all.

And, where he had not before, he gave Gerin pause. *Did* being married to Selatre give him any special obligations? It had given him advantages in the past, and accounts had a way of balancing. Even so, he hardened his heart and shook his head, saying, "If the farseeing god wants anything from me, he can tell me himself. I'll do what I can then. Without orders from the god, though, I'm not going to throw myself and my army away. Have you got that?"

The eunuch stared at him out of large, dark, tragic eyes. "I have indeed, lord king," he said. "I shall take your words back to my comrades in Biton's holy priesthood, that they may learn nothing shall suffice to rescue them from the rapacious clutches of the Elabonian Empire."

Gerin's children sometimes tried to make him feel guilty by taking that tone of voice. It didn't work for them, and it didn't work for the eunuch priest, either, though the Fox didn't laugh at him as he often did at his offspring. "If Biton wants his temple to stay unplundered, I expect he can manage that without me."

"I console myself with the hope that you are right," the priest replied, "but I have seen little to persuade me of it." He turned and waddled south, back toward the temple.

"Thanks, Maeva," Gerin said, watching him go. "You did the right thing to bring him to me, even if we can't help him now."

"I wish we could," Maeva said.

"So do I," Gerin said, "but if we could beat Swerilas' army any time we chose, don't you think we would have done it by now? Go on back and keep an eye on the imperials. They did slow down for the temple, the way I hoped they would. Sooner or later, they'll start again."

"Aye, lord king." She sketched a salute and rode after the eunuch priest.

The imperials did not move that day. Gerin hoped for thunderbolts from the temple, but none came. Glad at least for the respite, he wrapped himself in his blanket and went to sleep. While he slept, he dreamt.

It might have been the strangest dream he'd ever had. He kept seeing everything in it from an enormous distance, so he could make out nothing clearly. At the same time, he felt an overpoweringly strong sense of urgency. It was almost as if he were seeing the very edge of an important dream truly intended for someone else.

He kept trying to get closer to the center of the dream, to learn why it seemed so important. Try as he would, though, he could not. His dream-self ground its teeth in frustration. He might have stood at the bottom of some deep, smooth-sided hole too deep from him to climb out of it. But he had to climb out of it, no matter what.

When he woke, he was on his knees, his hands up over his head. He stared around in confusion at the inns and houses of Ikos, and at the campfires around which most of his soldiers slept. For a moment, they seemed far less real than the dream he'd just lost.

He bit his lip. He'd missed something important. He knew he'd missed something important. He hated missing anything important. In the straits he was in, he couldn't afford to miss anything important. He couldn't do anything about it, though.

Maybe if he lay down and fell back to sleep, the dream

would return. They sometimes did. Maybe, too, he would find himself closer to the heart of the matter. He bit his lip. He didn't like maybes. But, with no better choice, he lay down. Eventually, he slept. So far as he remembered, he dreamt nothing more for the rest of the night.

In the morning, Dagref and Ferdulf were missing. Gerin didn't fret so much over the demigod. For one thing, he thought Ferdulf likely able to take care of himself. For another, the camp was a good deal quieter without Ferdulf around.

But Dagref—for Dagref to run off struck Gerin as highly unlikely. And then, all at once, it didn't. Dagref could have had a perfectly good reason for slipping out of camp, a reason named Maeva. That he should have been so foolish as not to come back before things started stirring was another matter, one over which Gerin intended to have some pointed conversation with him.

The Fox couldn't even lose his temper, not so thoroughly as he would have liked, unless he wanted to alert Van to the reason he was upset. The outlander, seeing he was worried but not fully grasping why, said, "To the five hells with me if I like the notion of Dagref and Ferdulf going off together. Who can guess what mischief they're liable to get into till they go and do it?"

And that gave Gerin something new to worry about. He'd been thinking so much about Dagref and Maeva together, the prospect of Dagref and Ferdulf together had entirely escaped his mind. That was an oversight on his part, he realized. "You don't suppose they've gone off to conquer the imperials all by their lonesome, do you?"

He hadn't intended Van to take him seriously. But the outlander said, "The gods only know what they've gone off to try and do. *I* don't think they *can* conquer the bloody imperials by themselves, seeing as the whole lot of us haven't been able to do that. What *they* think they can do—who knows?"

"Who knows?" Gerin echoed mournfully. Dagref was at the age where he thought anything was possible. As for Ferdulf, almost anything *was* possible around him.

Since his driver had gone off, Gerin borrowed a horse

from Rihwin's men and rode, slowly and carefully, down to the horsemen who were holding the line against Swerilas' imperials. The Fox wished he'd put in more time on horseback over the years. He managed a simple ride well enough, but wouldn't have wanted to try to fight while mounted.

One advantage of going by horse rather than by chariot was that he went by himself. Without Van along, he didn't have to come up with fancy and fanciful explanations for why he wanted to see Maeva. But he got no satisfaction from seeing her, nor did it seem that Dagref had got any satisfaction from her the night before.

"No, lord king," she said, her eyes widening. "I haven't seen either Dagref or Ferdulf. Why do you think Dagref would have come to me?"

"For the obvious reasons," he answered, and watched her flush. "He's not back at the camp, and he didn't tell me he was going anywhere. My first guess was that that meant a tryst with you."

"If it meant a tryst, it wasn't with me." Now Maeva sounded dangerous for reasons that had only a little to do with warfare.

"If it didn't mean a tryst with you, I don't think it meant a tryst with anyone," Gerin said. Maeva relaxed—a little, and grudgingly. The Fox scratched his head. "If it didn't mean a tryst with you, I don't know what it did mean."

All at once, he remembered the peculiar dream he'd had, the dream where he'd been on the fringes of things and unable to figure out what was going on no matter how important figuring out what was going on was. Maybe he'd had to stay on the fringes of things because the dream had truly been aimed at Dagref. The two of them had both remarked on how much they thought alike; Gerin didn't find it unreasonable that he should catch the edge of a dream meant for his son. That, though, only raised the next interesting question: who or what was aiming dreams at Dagref?

Two answers came to mind—the imperials and Biton. No, three, for Mavrix might have done it, too, which would, or could, have accounted for Ferdulf's absence—assuming, of course, Ferdulf's absence was connected to Dagref's.

"Too much I don't know," Gerin muttered with a sigh.

"What's that, lord king?" Maeva asked. "Is Dagref all right?"

"I don't know that, either," Gerin said. Awkwardly, he swung up onto the horse and rode back to the town of Ikos.

He hoped against hope Dagref would be there when he got back. He even hoped Ferdulf would be there when he got back. If that wasn't a mark of desperation, he didn't know what was.

But neither Dagref nor Ferdulf was there. "Where in the five hells have they gone? What in the five hells do they think they're doing?" he asked of Van, who had already shown he didn't know the answers, either.

"We'll just have to see if the imperials ask us for ransom," the outlander said. "If they've got Ferdulf, as far as I'm concerned they can keep him."

"There are people who would say the same about Dagref," Gerin said gloomily, "but I'm not any of them. If they have him, I'll pay what they want to get him back."

"The price they want is liable not to be gold or copper or tin," Van said. "It's liable to be a bended knee."

"Whatever the price is, I'll pay it," Gerin answered. "Do you think I'm so much in love with having people call me 'lord king' that I'd throw away my son so they'd keep on doing it?"

"No," Van said at once. "And if you were fool enough to throw your son away, no one would call you 'lord king' afterwards anyhow, for everybody would sicken at being led by such a man."

"Here's hoping you're right," Gerin said. He had his doubts, but did not pass them on to the outlander. Van would surely sicken of being led by such a man, but plenty of truly vicious people had gone on to long and successful reigns. The Fox, though, had no desire to emulate them.

He wondered if Dagref and Ferdulf hadn't gone south after all, if instead they'd chosen to head west along the track through the haunted woods back toward lands within Gerin's suzerainty. He had trouble imagining why they would want to do such a thing—the fighting here would be over long before they could bring back reinforcements—

but he had trouble imagining why they would go see the imperials, too.

He slammed one balled-up fist into the palm of the other hand. What *had* that dream been? If he'd been able to see more of it . . .

Some time in the middle of the morning, his son and Ferdulf came walking into the town of Ikos: up from the south, not from the forest and hills to the west. No one escorted them, which Gerin took to mean that no one had seen them while they were coming from wherever they had been.

That was his first to the two of them: "Where were you?"

Neither answered right away. Dagref's silence was thoughtful. Silence from Ferdulf struck Gerin as most uncharacteristic. At last, Dagref said, "We went down to see Swerilas the Slippery."

"Just like that?" Gerin said. "You didn't have any trouble getting through my pickets? You didn't have any trouble getting through the imperials' pickets? You went right ahead and walked in to have a chat with Swerilas?"

"Aye, we did," Ferdulf said. The unemphatic nod he gave lent credence to his words.

"We did," Dagref echoed, sounding a bit surprised about it. "We had no trouble doing it. I knew we would have no trouble doing it. I had a dream that told me we would have no trouble doing it, and it was a true dream."

"Ha!" Gerin said. "I was right. The dream was aimed at you. I had it, too, or rather the ragged fringe of it."

"Did you?" Now Dagref looked interested. "I thought you might have, or someone might have. I thought someone on the outside was trying to look in, you might say."

"I didn't notice anyone else when I had the dream," Ferdulf said with more than a trace of hauteur. "I was alone, communing with the god."

"Which god?" Gerin asked. "Your father?"

"Not likely," Ferdulf exclaimed. "My wretch of a father communes with his hand on my fundament, not with a dream in my mind."

"With whom, then?" the Fox demanded.

"Why, with Biton, of course," Ferdulf said, and Dagref

nodded. "He did indeed tell us to go to see Swerilas the Slippery—who is truly as oleaginous an article as I have ever set eyes on—and so we did. Biton has more power than I could hope to oppose, and I daresay more power than my father, too."

Gerin didn't know whether that last was true or not. Either way, it wasn't his problem. He kept on trying to find out about the things that were his problem: "And what did you tell Swerilas when you saw him?"

"Why, we told him to attack your army, of course, and not to waste any more time doing it." Ferdulf and Dagref spoke together, smilingly confident they had done the right thing.

"You told him *what*?" Gerin shouted. "How could you tell him that? Why would you tell him that?"

"It was what farseeing Biton told us to tell him," Ferdulf and Dagref chorused. Only after the words were out of his mouth did Dagref's smile slip on his face. "I wonder why Biton told us to tell him that."

"To ruin me?" Gerin suggested. "I can't think of any other reason, can you? If Swerilas attacks me, he'll push this army right along the path through the haunted wood west of here. He'll probably push us to pieces, too, trying to get onto that one path. How are we supposed to hold him off? We haven't got the men to hold him off. Don't you know that?"

"We do know that," Dagref said. "Of course we know that. We knew it then, too." Ferdulf nodded. "It didn't seem to matter then, though," Dagref added in some perplexity, and Ferdulf nodded again.

"Why does Biton hate me?" Gerin didn't direct the words at his son and the little demigod, but at the indifferent sky.

"He doesn't hate you, Father." Now Dagref tried to sound reassuring. "Why would he hate you? My mother was his Sibyl on earth."

"Maybe he hates me for taking her away from him." But Gerin frowned and shook his head. Biton had never shown any sign of disliking his match with Selatre. But if this wasn't such a sign, what was it? He couldn't answer that question, so he found another one to ask Dagref and

Ferdulf: "What else did the farseeing god tell you to tell Swerilas?"

"Nothing much," Dagref answered. "We were supposed to make it plain to him that we came with Biton's message, but we didn't have any trouble convincing him of that."

"I'll bet you didn't," Gerin said. He thought for a while, then asked, "Did Biton tell the two of you to tell *me* anything? Why he decided to do this to me might be interesting to learn, in a morbid sort of way."

"You?" Ferdulf had some of his arrogance back. "Why on earth would the god want us to speak to *you*? If he had wanted you to know anything, he would have sent you a dream. But he didn't, did he? He left you on the outside looking in, didn't he? No, he wanted nothing to do with the likes of you."

Gerin didn't get insulted, as he might have done. He just shrugged and said, "Well, the god might have sent a dream straight to Swerilas the Slippery, too, but he didn't choose to do that, so I thought I'd ask about this."

"Nothing for you," Ferdulf repeated. "Nothing, do you hear?"

"Ferdulf, you need never doubt that, when you say something, people do hear you," Gerin said. "They may sometimes—they may often—wish they didn't, but they do."

He'd hoped that would make Ferdulf glower at him. Instead, the little demigod's childlike face took on an altogether unchildlike look of satisfaction. As far as Ferdulf was concerned, the Fox had paid him a compliment.

Dagref frowned. "Wait," he said. "There was something. I think there was something."

"No, there wasn't," Ferdulf said indignantly. "I just told him there wasn't. I ought to know. I'm half a god myself, and the better half at that. If I say there wasn't anything, there wasn't, and that's flat."

"Maybe we didn't have exactly the same dream," Dagref said. "Maybe I got this because I'm my father's son."

"Maybe you think you have this because what's really between your ears is rock, not brains," Ferdulf retorted, and stuck out his tongue.

Dagref remained unperturbed, which perturbed Ferdulf.

"Whatever the reason, there was something," the youth said. He turned to Gerin. "Here it is, for whatever it maybe be worth: it's something like, *Pick the right path, stay on the right path, don't go off the right path no matter what*."

"What a stupid message," Ferdulf said. "You must have made that up yourself. Why would a god say anything that foolish?"

"I don't know," Dagref answered. "I've certainly heard a demigod say a good many foolish things lately."

Ferdulf did glower at that. Gerin said, "What path?"

His son shrugged. "I couldn't begin to tell you. Until you asked, I didn't even know I had any message for you at all."

"Maybe it's the path through the wood west of here," Gerin said. But then he shook his head. "I really don't see how it could be. There's only the one path through that wood. No right or wrong about it: you're either on the path or in the forest, and if you're in the forest, well, too bad for you. So what in the five hells is Biton talking about?"

"Something you're too ignorant to understand," Ferdulf said.

"I'm too ignorant to understand a great many things," the Fox said. "Why I put up with you immediately springs to mind."

Before Ferdulf could find a retort to that, a horseman came galloping up from the south. "Lord king!" he cried. "Lord king! The imperials are attacking, lord king!"

After that, everything seemed to happen at once. The Fox shouted for his men to form a battle line in front of the town of Ikos. They were still forming it when Rihwin's riders came back to them. "Sorry, lord king," one of the horsemen said, wiping at a bleeding cut on his forehead. "There's just too many of the cursed buggers for us to hold back, and they're coming hard, too."

"Swerilas has a way of doing that," Gerin answered absently.

"Now what?" Ferdulf exclaimed. "Now what?" He hopped up into the air. Anyone might do that while excited. Ferdulf, though, was not just anyone. He didn't come down again.

Dagref answered him before Gerin could: "Now we fight. What else can we do? Even if you float like a pig's bladder, you wits should be better than the ones a bladder, or even a pig, comes with." Ferdulf's venomous glare showed that even the Fox would have had a hard time being more pungently sarcastic.

"Aye," Gerin said. "Now we fight. Now we . . ." His voice trailed away. He looked from Dagref to Ferdulf and back again. After stroking his beard for a moment, he walked over to Dagref and kissed him on the cheek. Then he did the same with Ferdulf.

"What was that in aid of, Father?" Dagref asked. Ferdulf's comments were a good deal more pungent, but had the same general meaning.

"Understanding," Gerin answered. "At least, I hope it's understanding." *If it's not understanding, if it's anything but understanding, I'm in even more trouble than I was already—and here I'd been thinking that couldn't possibly happen.* He didn't say that out loud. What he did say was, "Come on. We have to meet that temple-robbing whoreson of a Swerilas with edged bronze before—"

"Before what, Father?" Dagref broke in.

"Before anything else happens," the Fox said—not the sort of reply calculated to satisfy his son. Satisfying his son was not the most urgent matter on his mind right then, though.

Dagref gave him an irked stare. "You're being as deliberately obscure as the Sibyl when Biton speaks through her," he complained. "You're . . ." And then, as his father's had done, his voice trailed away. "Wouldn't that be interesting?" he murmured.

"What *are* the two of you talking about?" Ferdulf sounded even more irritable than usual.

"You're a demigod. Use your semidivine wisdom to figure it out," Gerin told him. "While you're at it, why don't you fly up and tell me what Swerilas is trying to do to us?"

"You don't need me for that. You can see him from here," Ferdulf answered, which was depressingly true. But the little demigod did pop into the air, perhaps as much for the chance that gave him to wave his backside at Gerin and Dagref as for any other reason. Off he flew.

"I hope you're not wrong, Father," Dagref said.

"So do I," Gerin said. "Believe me, so do I."

Before the Fox could say any more—not that there was much more to say—Van came rushing up demanding to know why in the five hells he and Dagref weren't in the chariot yet, and why they weren't charging forward to smash Swerilas into some large number of small pieces. "We do have to try, Father," Dagref added.

"I know we do," Gerin answered. "Well, let's be about it, then." He stepped up into the chariot, where Van was already waiting and fuming. So did Dagref, who flicked the reins and got the horses moving.

Van gave Gerin a dubious look. "Are you going fey on us, Captain?" he demanded. "Do you think we're as done as a slab of beef over a fire? Are you riding out expecting to be killed?"

Gerin shook his head. "No. Very much the opposite, as a matter of fact. I don't think we're going to win this battle, but I haven't lost hope for the war. In fact, I have more than I did a little while ago."

Now the outlander's stare was quizzical. After a moment, he shrugged. "All right—you've got some sort of scheme cooking in that beady little mind of yours. I don't need to know what it is right now. As long as it's something, and you haven't given up on us."

"I've never quite done that," Gerin said. "I've come close a few times over the years, but I've never given up."

Ahead of his force of chariotry, Rihwin's riders and some of the temple guards were righting to slow the force Swerilas the Slippery led. "Elabon! Elabon! Elabon!" the imperials shouted, their war cries ringing through those of the men from the northlands.

"Let's hit 'em!" Gerin yelled to his own troopers. He plucked an arrow from his quiver, let fly, and pitched an imperial out of the chariot. His men cheered. They didn't seem to have any particular hope of victory, either, but they went into the attack with a will.

And, for a while, they drove the imperials back toward Biton's shrine. "Temple robbers!" was the shout Biton's guards raised. They fought with a fury that made them stronger than their numbers. Rihwin's riders strove mightily to keep the warriors from the Elabonian Empire off balance. Gerin began to wonder what he would do if his army beat the foe. That would mean he'd been wrong in the way he'd thought things would go.

He shrugged. "It wouldn't be the first time I've been wrong," he muttered.

"What's that, Fox?" Van asked.

"Nothing much, believe me," Gerin answered.

Just out of bowshot of the wall of the temple, the momentum of his counterattack faded. Swerilas had too many men and was too good a leader to let an inferior force beat him. His men rallied and began to push not only forward but out to either wing. The Fox's troopers had to fall back to keep from being outflanked and cut off.

Gerin stayed calmer about this retreat than he had during earlier fights in which the imperials had used their numbers to gain the upper hand. "You know something," Van said. "What is it?"

"Saying I *know* something probably pushes things further than they should go," the Fox answered. "I have some ideas, though."

"Ah, that's good. That's fine." Van beamed. He didn't even ask what the idea were. Instead, he stuck a finger in his friend's face. "There, you see? Didn't I tell you you'd come up with something. And you, walking around with a rain cloud over your head, you told me I was wrong. You told me I was crazy."

"I don't know whether you were wrong or not," Gerin said. "In case you're wondering, though, I still think you're crazy."

When he ordered the army to fall back through the town of Ikos without making a stand protected by the houses and other buildings, Van shook his head and said, "You don't need to wonder if I'm crazy. I'm the one who needs to wonder whether you're daft."

"Maybe I am," Gerin said. "We'll know pretty soon."

North of the town, he had two choices left: he could fall back to the top of the valley and try to break out through the rugged hills to either side, or he could swing to the west and take the one narrow, winding road through the ancient wood that lay between the valley and the

Elabon Way. Without hesitation, he swung his men to the west.

"Stay on this path!" he shouted to the warriors. "By all the gods, and by farseeing Biton most especially, stay on this path!"

"What other path could they go on, Fox?" Van said. "There's only the one, after all. We've been along it, going east and west, often enough to know."

"Take another look," Gerin suggested.

Van did, and his eyes widened. As soon as he'd finished staring to either side, he stared at Gerin. "I'm *not* daft," the outlander said. "I know I'm not daft that particular way, anyhow. If you tell me there used to be half a dozen roads climbing up toward the forest, I'll call you a liar to your face. I know better. They didn't used to be here."

"Unless I'm the one who's gone mad, they weren't here yesterday," Gerin answered. "That doesn't mean they're not here now, though." He raised his voice to shout again: "Stay on this road, men! No matter what happens, stay on this road!"

"How do you know this is the right one, Father?" Dagref asked.

Gerin gave him a harried look. "I don't," he answered in a low voice. "But I think it is, and that will have to do." He let out another yell "Stay on this road, by the gods!"

"But, lord king, they're outflanking us!" one of his men cried in a frightened voice. The trooper pointed to either side. Sure enough, Swerilas the Slippery, with the luxury of numbers, was dividing his force, sending parts of it along the new paths that had appeared to either side of the one on which Gerin and his men traveled. Never having been in the valley of Ikos before, Swerilas did not, could not, know they were new.

"Stay on the path!" Gerin shouted again. He looked ahead. The wood was getting closer and closer. A few imperials—enough to plug the gap should his army try to reverse its course—followed the men of the northlands along the road they were using. Most, though, hurried along the other paths that led into the wood.

Van chuckled, but even the bluff outlander sounded a little nervous now. "I know what Swerilas is thinking," he said. "I know just what he's thinking, the son of a pimp."

"So do I," Gerin said. "He's thinking these roads will all come together inside the forest. He's thinking he'll rush men along some of them, get ahead of us, cut us off, and wreck us once and for all. If you look at things from his point of view, it's a good plan. It's better than a good plan, in fact. Or it would be."

"Aye," Van said in a hollow voice. "It would be."

As he spoke, Dagref drove the chariot in under the trees. It was one of the last cars that belonged to the men of the northlands to enter the wood west of the valley of Ikos. "Stay on the path," Gerin called to the riders and chariot crews ahead. "For your lives, stay on the path! Ride through to the end of the wood, and we'll see what happens then."

He hoped they heard him. He hoped they *could* hear him. He didn't know, not for certain. Sound had a different quality here under these great, immeasurably ancient trees. The rattle and squeak of the chariot axle, the clop of the horses' hooves, seemed distant, attenuated, as if not quite of this world. He could hardly hear the noise from other cars at all.

Light changed, too. As it filtered down through the branches interlaced overhead, it became green and shifting, making distances deceptive and hard to gauge. Gerin imagined seeing underwater would be something like this. The green was not the usual shade it would have been in a forest, either. The Fox could not have said how it was different, but it was. He noticed that whenever he entered this strange place. Maybe it was because so many of the trees and bushes in this place grew nowhere else in the world. But maybe, too, it was because the rest of the world did not fully impinge on this place.

Gerin tapped Dagref on the shoulder. "Stop the car," he said.

His son obeyed. The last few chariot crews who had been behind them went past. The men in those cars gave Gerin curious and alarmed looks. Dagref looked curious, too, and perhaps a little alarmed. "If we wait here very long, Father, the imperial vanguard will be be upon us," he said.

"Will they?" Gerin shook his head. "You may be right, but I don't think so. Listen."

Obediently, Dagref cocked his head to one side. So did Van. So did the Fox. He could hear, ever more faintly, his own men hurrying west through the old and haunted wood. That was all he could hear, but for a few soft padding noises from beasts he had heard before but of which he had never seen anything save, once or twice, green eyes.

"Where are the imperial whoresons?" Van sounded indignant. "They should be rattling along close behind us. Dagref is right; they ought to be coming upon us any time now. And they're racing along those other paths, too, the funny ones to either side of us. We should hear them there, too. By the gods, how could we miss 'em? But I don't hear a bloody thing." He dug a finger in his ear, as if that might help. "Where are they?"

"I don't know." Gerin didn't hear the imperials, either. As Van said, he should have. Nor could he hear his own men, not any more. All he heard now was his own breathing, that of Dagref and Van, and the horses' panting and the jingle of their harness. "Turn back," he told his son. "Swing the chariot around and go back toward Ikos."

"I will, Father," Dagref said, "but only if you're sure you want me to."

"Go on," Gerin said. Shaking his head a little, Dagref flicked the reins and clucked to the horses. He was obviously reluctant. So were the animals. They rolled their eyes and snorted and flicked their ears. But they obeyed Dagref, and he obeyed Gerin. The chariot turned on the path, which was barely wide enough to let it do so, and rolled back toward the east.

It did not roll far. No sooner had it rounded the first turn in the road than there was no more road. Trees and bushed blocked the way, looking as if they'd been growing there for the past hundred years. Dagref stared. "How could we have come up this path if there's no path to come up?"

Before Gerin could answer, Van said, "The trees in this wood aren't to be trusted, and that's a fact. They move around some kind of way—I've seen it before. Never like this, though. Never like this."

"He's right," the Fox said. "I've never seen it like this, either, though, because . . ." His voice trailed off. *Something* was watching him from the cover of the bushes. He couldn't tell what—or who—it was. He couldn't even make out its eyes, as he could sometimes spot those of the strange creatures that dwelt inside this haunted wood. But he knew it was there.

Something passed from it to him—and to Dagref and Van. It wasn't a message in words. Had it been, though, it would have required only two: *go away*. Dagref swung the chariot back toward the west. Now the horses seemed glad to run. They scurried away from that new-risen barrier. Gerin blamed them not in the least.

Softly, Van said, "I wonder what's going on behind those trees. I wonder what's going on other places in the forest. Something quiet, but not something, I'd guess, that's making the imperials very happy."

"I'd say you're likely right," Gerin agreed. "No matter how slippery Swerilas the Slippery is, I think he's just run into something he's not going to be able to slip out of again."

"I wish I knew what was happening to the imperials," Dagref said.

He had every bit of Gerin's relentless itch to know. He had only a small part of his father's years to temper that itch. Still, Gerin found the right question to ask: "Do you want to know badly enough to step off the road?"

Dagref thought that over, then shook his head. He didn't spend much time thinking, either.

Gerin wondered what would happen if, quite suddenly, the road ahead closed off as the road behind had done. Whatever it was, he didn't think he would be able to do much about it. He hoped it would be quick.

But then he heard the rattle and squeak of chariots in front of him. Without his saying a word, Dagref urged the horses up to a quicker trot. They soon caught up with the cars at the rear of his force. The men in those chariots exclaimed to Gerin and his companions. "Lord king!" one of them said. "We didn't think you'd be coming this way again when you stopped there."

"Well, here I am," the Fox answered, determinedly making his voice sound as normal as he could. "Now, are you glad or sorry?"

"Oh, glad, lord king!" the trooper said, and others echoed him. "How far behind are the imperials, would you say?"

Dagref and Van both looked at Gerin. He, in turn, looked for the best reply he could give. "Farther than you'd think," he said at last, and then, liking the sound of the words, repeated them: "Aye, farther than you'd ever think."

The warriors took the literal meaning and missed his tone. "That's good," one of them said. "Maybe the bastards'll take a wrong turning and get lost in these stinking woods."

"Maybe they will," Gerin said, again with irony his men did not catch. When he spoke again, though, he was not being ironic at all: "I only hope we don't get lost in them ourselves."

"Don't see how we could," a trooper said. "It's just the one road, and it looks like it runs straight on through. Doesn't get much simpler than that." Gerin didn't say anything. He and Van and Dagref looked at one another again. Then that trooper spoke once more, in puzzled tones: "I wonder what happened to the rest of the imperials, the ones who went down those other paths."

"So do I," Gerin said solemnly. "So do I."

He was relieved when the trooper turned out to be right: the road stayed straight, and the men of the northlands emerged from the wood into bright afternoon sunshine. Rihwin, who had been one of the first men out, was forming them into a line of battle to resist the imperials. "If we hit them hard," he was shouting when Gerin came out of the wood, "we'll have the effective advantage of numbers, for most of them will still be back under the trees."

"Are you going to tell him, Father?" Dagref asked softly.

Gerin shook his head. "I don't know for a fact, not yet," he said. "The event will tell better than I could, anyhow."

Ferdulf came flitting over. "Do you know that I had to ride in a chariot like an ordinary mortal all the way through those ugly woods?" he demanded. "Well? Do you?"

"You seem to have survived," Gerin answered dryly. Ferdulf glared, then floated off in a snit.

The army waited, and waited, and waited. At last, as the

sun began to set, the troopers made camp. No imperials came out of the wood, then or ever.

When morning came, the Fox rode into the forest again. He had no trouble traversing it. It seemed as normal as it ever did, perhaps even a little closer to normal than he'd ever known it before. Or perhaps the strangeness that dwelt within was sated for a time.

Presently, Van said, "We're farther in now than we were yesterday when we turned around and the track was gone, aren't we?"

"Aye, I think so," Gerin answered, and Dagref nodded. After a moment, the Fox added, "It's still here now. Or rather, it's here again now. Anyhow, it's as if the thing never went away, isn't it?"

"Isn't it, though?" Van fixed Gerin with an accusing stare. "You knew this was going to happen, didn't you?"

"This?" Gerin shook his head. "I had no idea *this* would happen. I did hope *something* would happen if the imperials came into this forest, and I was lucky enough to be right."

"Not, *if the imperials came into this forest*," Dagref said. "The proper phrase is, *if the imperials came into this wood*."

"What in the five hells difference does it make?" Van said. "The forest—the wood. So what? You're not a bard, to complain the one doesn't scan and the other does." He paused. Dagref looked very smug but didn't say anything, rare restraint for a lad his age. Gerin didn't say anything, either. That extended silence warned Van he was missing something. Though not quite so quick as either Gerin or Dagref, he was nobody's fool. After a moment, he snapped his fingers. "The oracle!"

Dagref grinned. Gerin just nodded. "Aye, the oracle," he said.

Van slapped him on the back, almost hard enough to pitch him out of the chariot. "You sneaky son of a whore," he said in admiring tones. "You *sneaky* son of a whore. When the Sibyl talked about 'bronze and wood,' I thought sure she meant swords and spears and arrowheads on the one hand and chariots on the other. Who wouldn't have thought that?"

"It's what I thought first, too, and I'm not ashamed to admit as much," Gerin said. "And we kept fighting the imperials, and they kept kicking us in the teeth. It's not surprising, when you get down to it—they had twice as many men as we did, near enough."

"Nothing like being proved wrong over and over again to make you think you might have misinterpreted an oracle," Dagref observed, sounding appallingly like his father. "You had already fulfilled one condition of the verse, when Rihwin summoned Mavrix but the god refused to aid us."

"Even so," Gerin said, nodding.

"One piece of the verse still puzzles me, though," Dagref said. " 'They snap and float and always trouble'? What on earth was the farseeing god talking about there?"

Gerin looked at Van. The outlander was looking back at him. He couldn't have said which of them started laughing first. Dagref let out an indignant snort. Laughing still, Gerin said, "That part of the oracular response seemed pretty plain to me, even at the time."

"To me, too," Van added.

"Well, I don't follow it," Dagref said, getting angrier by the moment. "And furthermore, let me tell you—"

"No, let me tell you," the Fox broke in. "You're doing the snapping now. You don't float, but someone you know does."

Dagref stopped and stared. "Ferdulf and me?" he said in a voice much smaller than the one he usually used. Gerin nodded. Dagref's eyes got even wider. "How did the god find a place for Ferdulf and me in his prophecy?"

Van laughed. "You're not the most promising material, lad, but there's no accounting for what a god's liable to do."

Dagref turned his head to give the outlander a dirty look over his shoulder. He opened his mouth. By the expression on his face, Gerin knew what he was going to say: something along the lines of, *You may not think I'm so much, but your daughter has different ideas.*

Without the least hesitation, Gerin kicked Dagref in the ankle. Instead of saying what he'd been about to say, Dagref let out a startled yip. "On this road of all roads," Gerin said, "you'd better keep your eyes ahead of you and your mind on what you're doing—and nowhere else."

He couldn't have been much less subtle if he'd walloped Dagref over the head with a branch. For a wonder, Van didn't notice that he was giving a ponderous hint. For an even bigger wonder, Dagref did.

Then, a moment later, the Fox forgot all about the indiscretion from which he'd saved Dagref. Through the clop of the horses' hooves, though the squeak of the axle and the rattle of the wheels of the car, he caught the noise of another chariot—a chariot headed west, straight toward him.

"Stop the chariot," he told Dagref, and reached over his shoulder for an arrow. His hand shook as he set the shaft on his bowstring. His heart pounded. Cold sweat burst out on his forehead. After the disaster that had befallen the army of the Elabonian Empire in this haunted wood, who was—who could be—riding through it now? Or was the right question, what could be riding through the haunted wood now?

On came the other chariot, steady and confident as if it owned not just the road but the rest of the wood, too. Van muttered something under his breath. It wasn't in Elabonian. It wasn't in any language Gerin understood. Beneath his sun-bronzed skin, the outlander was pale. He didn't know who or what was liable to be in that other car, either, and he didn't seem to like any of the possibilities that occurred to him.

Dagref clutched the whip till his knuckles whitened. "Is it—the master of this place, Father?" he whispered.

"I don't know," Gerin whispered back. "I don't know if this place *has* any one master. If it does, I don't know if he's the sort of master who rides in a chariot. But I think we're about to find out."

Around a slight twist in the path came the other car. Gerin, Dagref, and Van all shouted the instant they spotted it. The driver of the other team shouted, too, in horrified surprise. So did his passenger, who threw his hands in the air, bleating, "I yield! Spare me, by the gods!"

"Why, it's only a couple of imperials," Gerin said in slow wonder. "Did you lugs come into this wood yesterday?"

Could they have survived when all their comrades . . . disappeared?

But both imperials shook their heads. "By the gods, no!" the passenger said. "We are not fighting men; we are but harmless couriers."

Gerin stared. The imperial couriers he'd known had been ready-for-aughts who delivered their messages come what might. These fellows were a disgrace to the breed—either that, or it had gone badly downhill over the generation during which it hadn't operated north of the High Kirs.

"And what message were you delivering to Swerilas the Slippery?" he asked. When the couriers hesitated before speaking, he went on, "You can tell me now, or we can take the message pouch off your body and read what's inside it." He aimed his bow at the driver's face. "Which will it be? You haven't got much time to make up your minds."

Neither courier was armed with anything more than a knife at his belt. They must have thought they were traveling through safe country, and that Swerilas had crushed Gerin by now. The Fox grinned. They hadn't known everything there was to know.

"We'll talk," the passenger said at once. The driver might have said something different if he hadn't been looking at an arrow from a range almost short enough to make his eyes cross. As things were, he nodded glumly. The passenger went on, "You'll probably like the news anyhow."

"How do we know till we hear?" Gerin didn't lower the bow. "Speak up."

And the courier did: "We were sent here to recall both lord Swerilas and lord Arpulo to duties more urgent than suppressing these semibarbarous northlands. All the empire's forces are needed in more vital provinces, for the Sithonians are risen in furious revolt."

XII

Back at the encampment west of the haunted wood, Gerin examined the order the imperial couriers would have given to Swerilas the Slippery. The one of them had summed up that order well enough: Crebbig I was abandoning the reconquest of the northlands because, as he wrote, "the wicked, treacherous, underhanded Sithonians and their effete and effeminate gods have banded together in a malicious conspiracy to overthrow our rule in Sithonia, an effrontery we do not propose to and shall not tolerate."

If ever two men had been bewildered, the couriers were they. That Swerilas' opponents had captured them was one thing, and quite bad enough. That Swerilas' army had vanished off the face of the earth was something else again, and a great deal worse, too.

Gerin wasted no time on explanations with them. For one thing, he was far from certain of explanations himself. For another, he had matters more urgent to worry about than whether a couple of prisoners were contented.

"Do you see?" he said to Rihwin the Fox. "Mavrix did have other things on his mind besides the northlands. No wonder he didn't feel like helping us, and no wonder he didn't thank you for jogging his elbow."

"Very well, lord king," Rihwin said. "Seen in retrospect,

you plainly have the right of it. But you could not see in retrospect at the time, and neither could I. Why twit me over it, when I was doing the best I could?" That was such a good question, Gerin didn't answer it.

He did ask Ferdulf, "What do you think of your father now?"

"I think he is an odious, sniveling, drunken degenerate who chanced to do you a good turn for reasons that had nothing whatever to do with you, but only with his own selfish desires," Ferdulf answered.

That was nothing if not forthright. It was so forthright, in fact, that it pitched the Fox into a coughing fit. "Oh, come now," he said when he could speak again. "I've hardly ever heard Mavrix snivel."

Ferdulf pondered that for a few heartbeats. When he was done pondering it, he laughed one of the few laughs Gerin had ever heard from him. Then he floated away, a contented little demigod—contented, typically, because someone else had just been insulted.

Dagref came up to Gerin. "Father, between our army and Aragis', we outnumber the imperials. And, since Arpulo is ordered to withdraw anyhow—"

"—We can beat him about the head and shoulders while he's going," Gerin broke in. "Yes, I intend to do that. If the imperials lose one of their armies here in the northlands and have the other cut to pieces, it's likely to be a good long while before they poke their noses over the High Kirs again, regardless of whether they put down the Sithonian uprising or not."

"Ah, that's fine. That's very fine." Dagref looked relieved. "I was just wondering if, with so many things going on so fast, that one might have slipped past you. I'm glad it didn't."

"No, I managed to keep up there," Gerin answered. "Haven't moved against Arpulo yet, but I do intend to. After that, I have two other things on the list, and then, the gods willing, I think we can head back up toward the Niffet."

"Ah." Dagref raised an eyebrow. "And those are—?"

His father started ticking them off on his fingers. "First, I need to see how things stand with Aragis the Archer.

Don't forget, we came south to fight a war with him, not with the Elabonian Empire. If the imperials have hurt his lands enough, it'll be a good long while before he can think of tangling with us again, too. If not, we'll start a new verse of the old song next spring."

Dagref nodded. "Aye, I saw that one myself. It's the only one I saw, as a matter of fact. What's the other?"

"I want to send someone to that village off the Elabon Way and find out what Elise intends to do," the Fox answered. "If she wants to go to Duren's holding, I'll send her. If she's gone there on her own, she's liable to be aiming to stir up trouble between your half brother and me."

"Do you think she could?" Dagref asked, wide-eyed. He'd always been slightly in awe of Duren, as younger brothers often are of older ones.

"I don't think so," Gerin answered, "but I don't know. Nor do I want to be unpleasantly surprised. Now that I know where she is, I want to keep an eye on her." He didn't think Elise would like that, but he wasn't going to lose much sleep over whether she did or not.

He'd finished his explanation, but Dagref didn't go away. Instead, the youth took a deep breath and said, "Father, I know how I want to use the promise I won from you as we were coming south."

"Do you?" Gerin said, hoping, he was doing a good enough job of disguising apprehension as polite curiosity.

"I do." Dagref sounded very determined. Hearing how determined he sounded should have made the Fox proud. As a matter of fact, it did make him proud. It also made him more than a little frightened.

"I suppose you intend to tell me," he said when his son showed no sign of doing anything of the sort.

"Oh. Yes. Of course." Dagref snapped his fingers and looked annoyed at himself. "That's right. You do need to know." He took another deep breath; maybe he too was less steady than he wanted to seem. After letting it out and inhaling again, he said, "When the time comes, I want you to speak to Van about Maeva for me."

"Is that all?" Gerin asked, now trying to hide surprise. Dagref nodded. The Fox set a hand on his shoulder. "I'll do it." He took a deep breath of his own. "I'd do it anyhow.

If you like, you can have your promise back and save it for something else you want."

Dagref weighed that. "You've been worried about what I'd ask for, haven't you?" he asked. The Fox nodded; he could hardly do otherwise. Dagref rubbed his chin, on which some of the down was beginning to darken. "And yet you'd let me hold on to the promise and still speak to Van?"

"I just said so, didn't I?" Gerin wondered how much he'd regret it.

But Dagref was shaking his head. "That wouldn't be right. I gave it up freely, for something that matters to me—well, you know how much it matters to me."

"Yes, I do." Whether it would matter so much to Dagref in half a year, or in five years . . . who could tell, before the event? Farseeing Biton, surely, but no one of lesser powers.

Dagref made motions as if to push his father away. "That wouldn't be right," he repeated. "Do what I asked you to do, and that will put us at quits."

"No." Now Gerin shook his head. "That will make us square. I don't want the two of us to be at quits."

"That's fair enough, Father. Neither do I." Dagref looked at Gerin out of the corner of his eye. "If I did, I could easily have asked for something else." He didn't say *something more*, not with Maeva on his mind, but that was what he meant, and Gerin knew it.

"So you could." Gerin admitted what he could scarcely deny. "Since you decided not to, can we get on with the business of running the imperials back to their side of the mountains?"

"Oh, I suppose we can," Dagref said, so magnanimous his father felt like kicking him in the teeth. Then they both laughed. Why not? They were both getting what they wanted.

Arpulo Werekas' son was still in the process of pulling together the detachments he had on Aragis' lands when Gerin struck him. The Fox's army drove in a series of Arpulo's bands and siege parties; the last thing Arpulo had expected was that Swerilas and his whole force would completely disappear from the scene. Whether he had expected it or not, though, it had happened. His withdrawal became an undignified scamper.

As Arpulo fell back from one keep he had been besieging after another, Aragis' soldiers who had been trapped inside those keeps came forth and joined Gerin in pushing the imperials ever farther south. They accepted the Fox's orders without complaint, and obeyed him far more readily than his own troopers often did.

"I know why that is," Van said with a sly grin. "They're still used to the Archer, who'd have their guts for garters if they tried telling him no. They don't know how soft you are."

"Hmm," Gerin said. "How am I supposed to take that?" He held up a hand. "Never mind. I don't really want to know. I'll just ask you this: if I'm so soft, why has no one ever raised a successful revolt in twenty-odd—and a lot of them were very odd—years?"

"Nothing hard about that, Captain," the outlander answered. "Who'd follow a rebel against you? Whoever the son of a whore was, he'd be more trouble than you ever were. And so everyone's been on your side all along."

"Oh, indeed," the Fox replied. "And that, of course, is why I've never fought a single, solitary war in all the time since I became baron of Fox Keep."

"Well . . ." Van paused to think. At last, he said, "Not all your neighbors know you as well as they should, that's what it is." Gerin snorted. Van was unabashed, but then Van was usually unabashed.

The next day, Arpulo's men withdrew from around the castle where Aranast Aragis' son was leading the defenders. Aranast was glad to be able to come out. He was glad to join in helping to chase the imperials out of his father's dominions. He was appalled at the way his father's vassals obeyed the Fox.

"You are not their sovereign, lord king," he told Gerin that evening as the army encamped. "You have no business requiring them to act as you desire."

"Fine," Gerin said cheerfully. "In that case, you can go back to your keep and stay there, too."

"That is not what I meant." Had Aranast's back got any

stiffer, he would have turned to stone. "These men are vassals to my father, King Aragis the Archer. It is fitting and proper for your own vassals to grant you all due obedience. It is neither fitting nor proper for the vassals of another sovereign to grant you the aforesaid obedience, nor for you to claim it."

Gerin felt like marching around behind Aranast and giving him a boot in the arse, that being a likelier avenue to admit sense than his ears. Regretfully abandoning the idea, the Fox said, "When we were campaigning against the imperials before, I acknowledged your father as the overall commander. I wasn't his vassal when I did it. The world didn't end. It won't end now, either, if his men obey me for a while."

"My father will not approve," Aranast said.

"If he has any sense, he will," Gerin replied. "I don't know how much that proves, I will admit. Besides, your father is still besieged down there"—he pointed south—"and so they can't very well obey him for the time being. Do please remember, I'm the one who got rid of Swerilas the Slippery and won my half of the war. I did that before the imperials retreated, before they knew they were even supposed to retreat. What did your father do? Locked himself up in a keep, that's what."

"That's unfair," Aranast said. "He was heavily beset, and facing the larger half of the imperial army—against which he struck some strong blows."

"Good for him," Gerin said. "I have no complaint about anything he did. No, I take that back—for him to send you to tell me not to presume to forage off the countryside struck me as excessive, and does to this day. When he comes out of his castle, he's welcome to take his men back, for all of me. In the meanwhile, I intend to get some use out of them."

Aranast sputtered and fumed. He remonstrated with some of his father's vassals. "Gerin the Fox has a higher rank than yours, Prince Aranast," one of them told him. "If you expect us to obey you, shouldn't you also expect us to obey him?" That made Aragis' son sputter and fume even more, but he gave the noble no answer.

The imperials had trampled down a good many fields

of wheat and barley in Aragis' dominions, and stolen a lot of livestock. Now that they were withdrawing from the northlands, they set fires in the fields behind them, both to hamper Gerin's pursuit and to leave Aragis' vassals and serfs as hungry and weak as they could.

Aranast cursed Arpulo with bitter hatred. So did Aragis' retainers who rode with the Fox. So did Gerin. Arpulo was conducting a coldbloodedly vicious retreat, doing as much harm as he could before he finally went south over the High Kirs.

But only the Fox's long experience as a ruler, a man whose every action was on display before his fellows, let his curses sound sincere. Inwardly, he was something less than downhearted at seeing how much Aragis would have to do in the lands he already ruled before he could contemplate going to war against anyone else.

Just before sunset, the riders Gerin had sent to the village where Elise was keeping a tavern caught up with his army. "You haven't got her with you," Gerin noted. "Did she refuse to come?"

"No, lord king," one of them answered. "She wasn't there."

Gerin scowled. "Where did she go? Did any of the villagers know? Did she go south into the Empire, or north to Duren's holding?"

"No one knew, lord king," the rider said. "One day she was there, as she'd been for the past little while. Next morning, she was gone. The villagers made it plain she was not in the habit of telling them what she intended doing before she did it."

"I believe that," Gerin said. "She was never in the habit of telling anyone what she intended doing before she did it."

He paced back and forth, discontented with the world. He'd hoped to have an unambiguous answer about the woman he'd once loved, but the world hadn't been generous enough to give him one. For her sake and his own, he hoped Elise had gone down over the mountains, not up to her son's holding. Not only would the road up to Duren's be full of refugees and brigands and deserters from Aragis' army and Gerin's and the imperials', and thus dangerous for her, she might make the road dangerous for Gerin if she reached the keep and inflamed Duren against him.

Gerin wondered again if she could do that. In the end, he had to shrug and shake his head. He simply did not know.

By that time the next day, he'd stopped worrying about a woman he'd seen for an hour or so over a twenty-year span. He had more urgent—perhaps not more important, but more urgent—concerns: his army came up to the keep in which Aragis the Archer had been besieged.

Aragis proved not to be in the castle. "Oh, no, lord king," said the steward, a pudgy fellow named Wellas Therthas' son. "He went south in pursuit of Arpulo when the imperials broke off their encirclement yesterday."

"Sounds like him," Gerin agreed. He eyed Wellas. "You could have stayed besieged a lot longer before they starved you out, couldn't you?"

"Oh, aye, lord king," Wellas answered. "But how could you have known that, to bring it out so sure and certain?" He eyed the Fox, too, with a mixture of respect and wonder.

"Call it a good guess, if you like," Gerin said. If Wellas was still plump after a good many days shut away from the outside, the siege couldn't have caused the defenders too much in the way of hardship. Gerin didn't want to come right out and say that, though, having no reason to hurt the steward's feelings.

The Fox rode after his fellow king. Wellas thoughtfully helped supply the army with journeybread, sausage, and smoked meat from the castle storerooms, proving the keep had indeed been far from running out of supplies. Gerin was quickly glad to have the extra food: the imperials had set more fires behind their line of march, and he could have done little in the way of foraging.

For that very reason, he met Aragis coming back up the Elabon Way. The Archer looked disgusted. "Good to see you, Fox," he growled, though *good* was not a word that would have fit his humor. "We can do this better together than I could by myself—I haven't the men for a proper pursuit, and I just went after that bastard of an Arpulo as soon as he pulled out: didn't realize he'd burn everything behind him as he went." His lean face—not much leaner than when Gerin had seen him last—was streaked with soot and smoke.

"He does seem to be doing that," Gerin said, nodding. "A farewell present since he can't stay, you might say."

"So I gather." Aragis looked more disgusted than ever. "I've been penned up in there, away from everything that looks like news. What in the five hells happened? Did Crebbig I, his ever so illustrious majesty, have the generosity to drop dead?"

"No such luck, I'm afraid," Gerin answered. "The Sithonians are revolting again, and he's called his men back over the mountains."

"Ah, is that what it is? So we'll be rid of Swerilas as well as Arpulo, eh?" Aragis nodded, too. "I won't miss either of them a bit, and that's the truth." His gaze suddenly sharpened. "What are you doing here, Fox? I mean *here* in particular. Why aren't you chasing Swerilas' men instead of Arpulo's? For that matter, where are Swerilas' men? Why didn't they come down and join their friends?"

"They were chasing me," Gerin answered. "They tried chasing me through the wood west of Biton's shrine in the valley of Ikos. Do you know that wood?" Aragis' eyes widened in his filthy face. Gerin took that for agreement. He went on, "They rode into the wood. They didn't ride out." He explained the oracular response he'd had from Biton's Sibyl, and how he interpreted it.

" 'Bronze and wood,' " Aragis repeated. "I would have taken that to mean swords and chariots, or maybe spearheads and spearshafts. That the wood might be *a* wood . . . I doubt I'd have thought of that."

"I almost didn't, either," Gerin said. "Even when I did think of it, I was a long way from sure I was right—but I was in so much trouble, I had nothing to lose by finding out."

Aragis pointed at him. "Did I not say that, when the time came, you would have some sorcery ready to wreck the foe?"

"You said it," Gerin agreed. "That you said it doesn't

make it true. Rihwin summoned Mavrix, except that Mavrix didn't feel like being summoned. Biton gave his oracular response—all I did was hear it. When Dagref and Ferdulf went off to see Swerilas, I didn't know anything about it. If I had known anything about it, I would have stopped it if I could. I don't know exactly what happened in the haunted wood, and I don't think I ever will know. By the gods, I don't think I want to know, either. The only thing *I* did in all of that was ask Biton for the oracular response, and I didn't know what I'd get when I did."

"Everything you say is true—taken one thing at a time." Aragis let out a long, angry breath. "But it's only true taken one thing at a time. Put it all together and you were at the center of it, the way a spider sits at the center of its web. Tell me that, when Rihwin summoned Mavrix, you weren't hoping he would fail. Go ahead and tell me—I want to see how good a liar you are."

"Not good enough, evidently," Gerin said. "If you already know the answers, why ask the questions?"

"Because I wanted to find out if what I thought was true: that you were in the middle, taking advantage of everything that happened around you." He glared at the Fox like an angry wolf. "And you were, and I curse you for it."

Calmly, Gerin folded his arms across his chest. "I haven't taken advantage of *every* tiny thing that happens around me. I hope I am on my way toward doing that, though. In aid of which, shall we discuss the matter of suzerainty over the holding of Balser Debo's son?"

Aragis looked around. Had more of his men been close by than Gerin's, the Fox thought he would have ordered them to attack on the instant. But more of Gerin's troopers stood near the two kings, and they looked alert. Aragis' earlier glare had been mild to the point of benignity compared to the one he gave Gerin now. "You see what the imperials have done to my lands," the Archer ground out.

"Yes, I see that," Gerin said.

"You see they've hurt my fighting force worse than yours," Aragis persisted.

"Yes, I see that, too," Gerin said, nodding.

"And so, because I am weakened, you think to gain at my expense," Aragis said.

"Of course I do," Gerin said. "I'm not gaining anything I didn't think was rightfully mine beforehand, though. How hard would you have squeezed me if things were the other way round? You know the answer to that as well as I do: you'd take as much as you could get away with. I've said it before, Aragis: unless you make yourself so, you're not my enemy. You've spend twenty years not believing me. Will you believe me now?"

"Because I am hurt here, you think to drop the hammer on me," Aragis said, as if the Fox had not spoken.

"You're repeating yourself," Gerin said. "The words are different; the meaning is the same. You ought to try listening to me instead. If you don't want to listen to me, by the gods, I'm tempted to drop the hammer on you just to get you to pay attention for once in your life."

Aragis turned the color of molten copper. "No one has presumed to speak to me in that fashion for a very long time," he growled.

"Oh, I believe *that*," Gerin said. "You're the sort who hands a fellow his head if he has the nerve to tell you something to your face. That will make your vassals shut up around you, I must say. But it'll also make you miss things you ought to hear. You're not strong enough to hand me my head if I tell you something to your face, so you can bloody well listen to me instead."

He wondered if he oughtn't to hurt Aragis as badly as he could, to keep the Archer from trying for revenge as soon as he saw the chance. The only sure way of doing that, though, was killing Aragis now. He didn't have the stomach for it. Murder was not a political tool he kept in his chest.

Just for a moment, Aragis' hand dropped down toward the hilt of his sword. He checked the movement before he touched the hilt. Like a bear bothered by bees, he shook his head. "Slaughtering you might solve the problem, but you haven't—quite—done anything to deserve it," he said.

"For which polite qualification I do thank you," Gerin said. "I thought about stretching you out bleeding on the ground, too." He grimaced. "This being a king is a nasty business sometimes."

"So is being a baron. So is anything above being a serf,"

Aragis said, "and being a serf is a nasty business, too, in a different way. It's a nasty business all the time, with no letup ever. If I have a choice between taking orders and giving them, I know which one's for me."

"If I had a choice, I'd sooner do neither," the Fox replied. Aragis stared at him in blank incomprehension. He'd been sure Aragis would do something like that: as the Archer himself admitted, he liked giving orders. With a sigh, Gerin went on, "Since I don't have a choice, I'd sooner be on the top than on the bottom. I won't say different."

"You'd better not," Aragis said. "And I'll tell you one other reason I didn't try to let the air out of you there."

"You'd answer to Dagref," Gerin said.

He'd meant it for a joke, or mostly for a joke. Aragis, however, gave him a very odd look, a look as nearly frightened as the Fox had ever seen on his face. "How did you know that?" Aragis whispered. "How *could* you know that? To you, he'd be only a youth."

"Oh, Dagref is a youth, all right," Gerin answered, "but it's been a long time since I thought of him as *only* an anything. If I don't strangle him in the next two or three years, he'll go far, that one will."

He scratched his head. Did that mean he'd made up his mind about the succession? Maybe he had. Duren was doing a perfectly fine job as baron of the holding that had been his grandfather's, but how much did he look beyond it? Dagref had a wider view. But Dagref was also much younger, and had never actually ruled a barony or anything else. Who could tell what he'd be like when he was seventeen? So maybe Gerin hadn't made up his mind about the succession after all. Maybe.

"Back to matters at hand," he said, as much to himself as to Aragis. "Balser Debo's son wants me as his overlord. I have accepted him as my vassal. I don't want a war, but I was ready to fight to keep that holding as part of my domain before the imperials came, and I am still ready. So." He turned away, picked up a long, thin broken branch that had fallen out of a load of firewood, and used it to draw a circle in the dirt around Aragis' feet. "Shall we have peace, or shall we fight? Answer me one way or the other before you step out of that circle."

Aragis' eyes looked about ready to bug out of his head. "Of all the high-handed—" he spluttered. "You have not the right to use me so. No one has the right to use me so."

He started to stride out of the circle, but stopped when Gerin held up a hand and said, "I have the right, and it's one even you understand."

"What is it?" Aragis demanded.

"Simple—I'm stronger than you are," Gerin answered. "Now—peace or war? If you step out of the circle without naming one or the other, we shall have war right now, I promise."

To some degree, he was running a bluff. He was far from sure that, if he suddenly shouted for his men to attack the Archer's, they would obey him. But he was also far from sure how many of Aragis' men would fight hard for their overlord.

Aragis must have been making the same calculations, and coming up with answers not far removed from his own. "You are an arrogant son of a whore," he ground out, to which the Fox bowed as at a compliment. "May you toast your toes in the hottest of the five hells forever." Gerin bowed again. Aragis bared his teeth in another wolf's smile before going on, "But you *are* stronger than I am, curse you. Take the holding of Balser Debo's son. Keep it. I hope you choke on it, but I will not fight you for it." He stepped out of the circle.

Gerin wondered if he was lying. If he was, he would be made to pay for it, that was all. He had done as the Fox required. Trying to hold him to more—even trying to get an oath from him—would be too much in the way of arrogance.

"We've beaten the imperials," Gerin said. "Now, if the time does come, we can settle things that have to do with the northlands between ourselves—and, if the Empire puts down the revolt in Sithonia and decides to have another go at us, we can still fight side by side. Remember, I am not taking anything that was yours; you weren't Balser's suzerain. You wanted him to become your vassal, aye, but he never did."

"Hmp." If Aragis was mollified, he wasn't about to let

Gerin know it. Had the sandal been on the other foot, Gerin wouldn't have let him know it, either. But the Archer had got a better deal from him than he would have got from from the Elabonian Empire, and he had to know as much. If Crebbig I sent another army north, the Archer was unlikely to be inclined to throw in with it.

"We aren't friends—we've never been friends," Gerin said, "but we've had our borders march for a lot of years without going to war against each other, and that's something a good many friends can't say. I'd sooner see it go on than end."

"Hmp," Aragis said again. He turned and walked away. He'd said he wouldn't fight the Fox over Balser's holding. If he meant that, everything would be fine. If he didn't . . . Gerin sighed. If he didn't, there would be another war, that was all.

Another war. Gerin was mildly amazed at how little the prospect bothered him. After so many wars, what would one more be? And maybe Aragis would live up to his word after all. Stranger things had happened. "Not many," Gerin muttered, "but a few. They really have." He might even have meant it. He hoped with all his heart that he did mean it.

As Gerin's men began pulling back from the lands over which Aragis the Archer ruled as king, Aragis said not another word about his foraging on the countryside. Gerin took that for a good sign. He did not take the state of the countryside for a good sign. Aragis and his vassals were going to have a hungry time of it over the winter. Maybe that would leave the Archer too weak to fight come spring. Maybe, on the other hand, it would leave him with no choice but to fight come spring.

"How will you know, Father?" Dagref asked.

"Oh, it's a simple enough business," the Fox answered. "If he attacks me, he does. If he doesn't, he doesn't, that's all."

"Yes, that is simple," Dagref agreed, "but what I meant was, how will you know beforehand?"

"If he does choose to attack me, I may not know beforehand," Gerin said. "I may get signs beforehand that tell me he isn't going to war, though. If his harvest is as it looks now, his serfs are liable to rise against him. If they do, he'll be too busy dealing with them to worry about me."

"I'll say he will," Van put in. "He's been grinding his peasants' faces in the dirt for a long time. If they rise up, they'll try to pay him back all at once."

"Some of his vassals may decide to rise against him, too," Gerin went on. "He's a demon of a warlord, but that's not all that goes into the mix for making a good king. Maybe some of his barons will decide as much, anyhow."

"Maybe you'll help some of them decide as much," Dagref said.

"Hmm. Maybe I will, if I can do it so that Aragis doesn't figure out I'm doing it," Gerin said. He thumped his son on the back. "One fine day, you're going to make all your neighbors, whoever they may be, very uncomfortable." He was liable to make all his friends very uncomfortable, too, but that was another matter.

Gerin sent riders north to Duren, not only to let him know what had happened in the war against the Elabonian Empire but also to tell him the Fox had met Elise. That was, of course, something Duren was liable to know already. Gerin instructed the riders to bring word back to him if Elise was at Duren's keep. He wondered what he'd do if she was. He wondered whether he could do anything if she was. He had his doubts.

Balser Debo's son received him like a hero. Gerin listened to his new vassal's fulsome praise with but half an ear; he'd heard such praise delivered many times before, and heard it done better, too. As often as not, he knew what Balser was going to say three sentences before he said it. That let his mind dwell on more interesting things.

There were some. Chief among them was the way Rowitha the serving girl had come out into the courtyard and was staring so intently at Dagref. Dagref might have stared back at Rowitha, too, if Maeva hadn't been standing by Van, only a few feet away. As things were, Dagref alternated between a polite smile and doing his best to pretend Rowitha didn't exist.

That was a tricky bit of juggling; a man three times Dagref's age would have had a hard time bringing it off with aplomb. He did about as well as could have been expected: better than most his age would have done, Gerin thought, because he habitually showed less of what was in his mind than most.

Maeva was watching Rowitha, too, watching her, not much liking what she was seeing, and liking it less by the moment. She'd slept out with the rest of the riders when Gerin's army was on its way south. Only a couple of people, Gerin certainly not among them, had known what she was then. Things were different now.

But Maeva couldn't very well keep Dagref from going over and talking with Rowitha after Balser finally finished blathering, not without giving more away to Van than would have been wise. She had to stand and stare and do her best not to fume too openly. Her best wasn't so good as Dagref's had been.

Rowitha, now, Rowitha didn't have to hold anything back, and she didn't. She listened to Dagref's low-voiced explanation, or part of it, and then hauled off and slapped him, a ringing report that made all heads in the courtyard turn his way. He stood, his cheek turning red—actually, his whole face turning red, but his cheek turning redder—while she stomped away.

"Haw, haw, haw!" Van boomed. "Well, there's something that'll happen to most men a time or twelve before they shovel dirt on 'em. The lad may be starting a little early, but then, thinking back, he may not, too."

Maeva, by contrast, hurried over and put her arm around Dagref's shoulder. Remembering his promise to his son, Gerin spoke to Van: "You said you'd hoped her eye might fall on Dagref if she'd stayed back at Fox Keep. Maybe it's fallen on him anyhow."

"Maybe it has," Van agreed, in tones polite but imperfectly delighted. He was probably wondering how long ago Maeva's eye had fallen on Dagref, and what might have happened since. Turning a thoughtful frown toward Gerin, the outlander continued, "We'll have to speak of this further when we get back to Fox Keep, I expect."

"I expect we will," Gerin agreed. He also expected he would have to dicker with Fand. As if in anticipation, his head started to ache.

Dagref came over to him, the mark of Rowitha's palm and fingers still printed on his cheek. "Father," he said, "would you mind if I asked you to spend as little time here in Balser's holding as you possible can?"

"No, I wouldn't mind that." Gerin hid a smile. "We *do* have to head north."

"That's good," Dagref said. "That's very good." He looked around to see if the serving girl had reappeared. Not spotting her, he relaxed a little.

"You know, if you ask Balser to make sure your lady love—excuse me, your former lady love—doesn't come inside the castle as long as you're here, he'll likely find her something else to do," Gerin said.

"Do you think so?" Dagref looked astonished. Gerin felt pleased with himself, though he didn't show it: Dagref wasn't used to asking special favors just because of who he was. Then his son went on, "Would you do it for me?"

Gerin was less pleased with that. "If *you* do it, I said," he replied. "You're the one who wants the wench out of your hair. When we were here last, I didn't do anything to get any wenches into my hair."

"You are the soul of virtue," Dagref said sourly. "Besides, Mother would be in your hair if you did anything like that. I didn't have anyone special in my life when Rowitha and I—" He coughed a couple of times, finishing, "But I do now, you see." Gerin only shrugged, which left his son dissatisfied.

Maybe Dagref talked to Balser and maybe he didn't. In either case, Maeva ate in the great hall with Gerin and Van and Dagref, and Rowitha did not make an appearance there. Dagref did his best to pretend Rowitha had never existed. Maeva, by contrast, kept looking around for her. She still dressed like a warrior, with a sword on her belt. Maybe Rowitha had noticed that instead of getting orders from Balser. Gerin did not inquire. It was not his business.

Van kept watching Maeva watching out for Rowitha. He kept muttering things that weren't quite words and that didn't quite get past his beard and mustaches. He was, it seemed, drawing his own conclusions, and not much caring for the pictures they made. Every now and then, he would glance over toward Dagref, too, and then mutter some more.

"This was a match you said you wanted," Gerin reminded him, continuing to keep his promise. "I think it's a good one, too, for whatever it may be worth to you."

"Eh?" Whatever Van had been thinking, it wasn't about how good a match Dagref and Maeva might make. Now, very visibly, he did. He grunted instead of muttering—progress, of a sort. At last, he came out with real words: "Oh, aye, Fox, I don't doubt you're right, or I don't doubt it too much, anyhow. But good match or bad, I didn't look for it so bloody *soon*."

"That I understand. Neither did I, though I might have noticed a sign or two even back at Fox Keep." Gerin slapped his friend on the back. "There isn't one cursed thing in life that doesn't happen too bloody *soon*, especially when it happens to our children."

Van thought that over. He'd had enough ale to make thinking take a while. Slowly and deliberately, he nodded. "Tell your fancy Sithonian philosophers to go on home, Fox," he said. "Once you've said that, you don't need to say any more."

Gerin approached Duren's keep with more than a little apprehension. His riders had come back to let him know Elise hadn't been there then, but he would still have to tell his son by her about their meeting. And strife between Duren and Dagref was one more thing that was liable to come too bloody soon. If it *ever* came, that was too bloody soon for him.

Duren's vassal barons had been anything but delighted about accepting him as their overlord. Gerin had wondered if they would see his own preoccupation with the south as an opportunity to rise against his son. That hadn't happened; everything looked peaceful as he led his army up the Elabon Way toward Duren's keep. Either Duren's vassals had thought the Fox would win and punish them for rebelling against his son, or else they'd figured Duren could put them down by himself. Gerin hoped for the latter.

"Who comes to the castle of Duren Ricolf's grandson?" a sentry shouted as the Fox's army drew within hailing distance. The question had a certain formal quality to it—either it was Gerin, or someone was about to lay siege to the keep. But, Duren not owing his father homage and fealty, he treated with him as one equal with another.

"I am Gerin the Fox, king of the north, returning from my campaign against the Elabonian Empire," Gerin answered, again as one equal to another.

"Congratulations on your victory, lord king," the sentry said. The Fox's messengers would have told of that. Without any orders Gerin heard, the drawbridge began to lower. "Enter into the keep of Duren Ricolf's grandson. The baron eagerly awaits you."

Sure enough, Duren stood just inside the wall. He looked to be about ready to burst, waiting for Gerin to dismount from his chariot. When the Fox and Van and Dagref did get down, Duren couldn't at once ask Gerin what was so plainly on his mind, either; he had to go through polite greetings first.

Then those greetings turned more interesting than Duren might have thought they would be. He gave Dagref a long, long look as the two of them clasped hands. "You were on your way to turning into a man when you came down from Fox Keep. Now, unless I'm much mistaken, you've gone and done it." Duren sounded almost accusing.

Dagref answered, "Well, now I've done more of the things men do than I had then, anyhow." He looked at his half brother out of the corner of his eye. "I even picked up an ekename. I don't know if it will stick, but I don't know that it won't, either."

"What is it?" Duren asked warily. He used no ekename—styling himself *Ricolf's grandson* had helped him gain control of the holding formerly his grandfather's.

"Dagref the Whip." Dagref was still holding the lash he'd used to urge on the horses and with such effect against the imperials. He hefted it, to show the source of the sobriquet. Duren looked something less than delighted. Then he looked astonished, for Maeva came up and placed herself alongside Dagref in a marked manner. Gerin, who had become something of a connoisseur of astonishment, and who had seen—and caused—a great deal of it over the years, judged that Duren's had at least three flavors: seeing Maeva there at all, seeing her there as a warrior, and seeing her there so solidly beside Dagref.

When Duren turned away from Dagref and Maeva, he spoke plaintively to his father: "Fall out of touch for even a little while, and things go all strange by the time you get another look at them."

"Even if you don't fall out of touch, things have a way of going all strange behind your back," Gerin answered, also more than a little plaintively.

"Father, you speak nothing but the truth," Duren said. "Come into my great hall—come into my great hall, all of you—and have some ale. And then"—he looked toward Gerin—"then I will hear about my mother." He spoke the last word slowly, and with some hesitation, for which the Fox could hardly blame him.

As they were walking into the castle, Gerin said, "Elise didn't come up here, then? She told me she might."

"She didn't." Now Duren's voice was flat, uninflected. He went on, "If she set out this way, she never got here. Do you suppose something happened to her along the way? That would be terrible."

Gerin wasn't convinced it would be so terrible as all that, but he understood how his son had to feel. The idea that something might have happened to Elise when she was on her way to see him for the first time since abandoning him as an infant had to eat at Duren. As consolingly as he could, Gerin said, "She's been traveling through the northlands for a lot of years, and she's always been able to take care of herself. I think it's likelier that she went south to visit her kin down in the Empire. She was talking about that, too."

He did not mention the other possibility that had occurred to him: that Elise might have suffered misfortune at the hands of the imperial warriors who'd come through her village after his own army retreated out of it. Some soldiers did whatever they pleased in their foes' country. Elise was no longer young and beautiful, but she wasn't ancient and ugly, either. She might not have gone—she might not have had the chance to go—anywhere at all.

Perhaps fortunately, Duren's mind was running in a

different channel. In an indignant voice, he said, "I'm her kin, too."

"That's so," Gerin agreed, "but one thing about your mother was always plain, as long as I knew her—and now, too, from the little I saw of her—and that is that she was going to do what she was going to do, and she wasn't about to listen to anyone who tried to tell her anything different."

"What would she say about you?" It wasn't Duren who asked the question but the avidly curious Dagref.

"Most likely, she would say that I never cared what she wanted to do, and that I never wanted to do anything interesting myself," Gerin answered, doing his best to be just.

"Would she be telling the truth?" Dagref asked.

"Well, I don't think so," the Fox said, "but I don't expect that she thinks I'm telling the truth about her now, either. Truth is easy enough to find when you're talking about things you can see or count on your fingers. It gets a lot harder when you're trying to figure out why people are the way they are and how they truly are. Half the time, they don't know themselves."

"Hmm," Dagref said, plainly unconvinced. "I always know *precisely* why I do what I do."

Maeva nodded vigorous agreement, as much because he was very young as because she was enamored of Dagref. Gerin and Van laughed. Duren looked thoughtful, as if wondering which side was right.

"Is that so?" Van rumbled. Dagref nodded. He might not always have been right about such things, but he was always sure. Van cocked his head to one side and said, "Then tell me *precisely* why you've formed an attachment with my daughter." He stared down at the Fox's son.

Dagref did *precisely* what Gerin could have done in the same circumstances: he spluttered and turned red and said nothing intelligible. Maeva set her hand in his. Most times, that would have steadied him. Here, it only seemed to make matters worse.

"Well, Father, how, *precisely*, did you beat the imperials?" Duren asked. "Not everything your couriers told me was as clear as it might have been." Maybe he was helping ease his half brother off the hook, in which case he had more charity in him than his father would have had at the same age. Or maybe, having learned everything he could—surely not close to everything he wanted—about his mother, he was just moving along to the larger events that had taken place down toward the High Kirs.

Gerin told him the oracular verse the Sibyl at Biton's temple had delivered, how he'd interpreted it, and the role Dagref and Ferdulf had played in fulfilling it. That made Duren give Dagref another sharp look. Dagref looked back with a bland, blank expression he might have stolen from Gerin's face. He wasn't immune to discomfiture, but he got over it in a hurry.

Getting no satisfaction there, Duren turned to Gerin and said, "By what I have seen and heard of Dagref and what I have seen and heard of Ferdulf, the two of them must be . . . lively together."

"And so they are," Gerin agreed. "They're pretty bloody lively apart from each other, too."

"I can see that." Duren gave Dagref another measuring, speculative stare, which his half brother returned. Duren turned back to the Fox. "We need to talk, the two of us."

"The three of us," Dagref corrected.

Gerin shook his head. "I need to talk to both of you. I need to do it with each one separately. My mind's not made up about any of these things, and I don't expect it to be any time soon."

"It should be—I'm your eldest," Duren said. With no small bitterness, he went on, "But I'm not your son by Mo—by your wife, who raised me. I can see how that makes a difference."

"Less than you think," Gerin answered. "Selatre has never once pushed me to shove you aside and put him in your place. She knows you'd do well. And I know you'd do well, come to that. I'm also coming to know Dagref would do well, too."

"If no one shortens him by a head, he would," Van put in.

"And what will you do?" Duren asked. "Split the kingdom between us?"

"I couldn't find a better recipe for civil war if I brought

a cook up from the City of Elabon," Gerin said with a shudder. "Remember the barony north of you that used to be Bevon's, and how all his sons squabbled over it for years? Whatever else I do, I aim to make sure that doesn't happen with or to everything I've spent so long building up."

"What does that leave, then?" Duren asked. "What will one of us do if you leave the whole kingdom to the other?"

"It could be that you'd stay content with this barony if Dagref held the kingdom." Gerin held up a hand before either of his sons could say anything. "And it could be that Dagref might want to study down in the City of Elabon while you took on the burden—and it *is* a burden, believe me—of ruling. That would depend on what the Empire decides to do about the northlands, of course."

"And there's Blestar to figure into all this," Dagref said. "He's only a little fellow now, but I was only a little fellow when you went off to take over this holding, Duren."

"I'd almost forgotten about Blestar," Duren admitted. "Not forgotten he was there, but forgotten he could mean something in all this."

"I hadn't," Gerin said. "The gods only know now how he'll turn out when he's a man, though. As a boy, he's better natured than either of the two of you was, not that that's saying much."

Duren and Dagref joined in giving their father a dirty look. That didn't bother the Fox, who wanted the half brothers as united as they could be: if in annoyance at him, fair enough.

Dagref said, "Do you really suppose, Father, that the Empire would let me go down to the City of Elabon to study?"

Before Gerin answered that, he let his eyes flick to Maeva for a moment. By her expression, she didn't realize she had a rival in learning, very possibly a rival more dangerous than any woman, no matter how beautiful, no matter how passionate. Gerin smiled a little. If she didn't realize it yet, she would before too long.

And Dagref had asked a good question. The Fox gave it the best answer he could: "If the Empire decides to take another shot at conquering us, then you won't be able to go south of the High Kirs, no. But the revolt in Sithonia and the drubbing the imperials took up here are liable to make them think twice. My guess is, that's more likely. Crebbig I may never recognize Aragis and me as kings, but I don't think he'll come up and try to knock us over again, either."

Dagref and Duren both thought that over. Duren said, "What do you expect from Aragis after this?"

"I hope he'll lick his wounds for a while," Gerin answered. "He has plenty of them. He also has plenty of vassals who've seen me, which means they've seen that a man doesn't have to be a bronze-arsed son of a whore to make a proper ruler. If some of them rise up, or if the serfs on Aragis' land decide they've had enough of being squeezed to bits, then Aragis will find he has the same sorts of troubles as Crebbig."

"You'd weep and wail over that, wouldn't you?" Van said, setting a finger by the side of his nose.

"So I would," Gerin said dryly. "I'd weep till my eyes were all red and swollen." He let out an exaggerated sob. Everyone laughed.

Some time later, after roasted mutton and fresh-baked bread and berry tarts and a good many jacks of ale, Duren waved for Gerin to walk out from the great hall into the court between the outer wall and the castle itself. Darkness had fallen. Tiwaz, a medium-fat crescent, hung low in the southwest; ruddy Elleb, just past first quarter, shone in the south; pale Nothos, nearly full, climbed above the eastern wall. Math would not rise for another hour or two.

Duren said, "I wish you'd found out more about my mother—either more, or nothing at all."

"I understand," Gerin said, setting a hand on his shoulder. "But we do what we can do, not what we wish we could do. I didn't expect to find out anything at all. I didn't even know her till she spoke, nor she me." He started to add, *Maybe she'll turn up one day*, but decided that would do more harm than good. Duren was no doubt thinking it, too, but the gulf between thinking something and saying it yawned wide and deep.

"Now I wish I'd come along with you," Duren said.

"Maybe it's just as well you weren't there. We've all

changed a good deal, these past twenty years. Last time your mother saw you, you were making messes on the floor." That was not his principal concern. His principal concern was how much damage Elise might do if she turned Duren against him. He still didn't know whether she could, but he still didn't want to find out, either.

"I've changed," Duren said. "My mother must have changed, or she wouldn't have gone away from you."

"Honh!" Gerin said, borrowing the useful not-quite-word from Van.

Before he could add anything to it, Duren went on, "But you, Father, you've hardly changed at all."

"You only say that because you're watching me with a son's eyes," Gerin answered. "I'm like anybody else. I'm soup in a pot, and the years boil away more and more of the water, so my flavor gets stronger and saltier, the same way my beard keeps right on getting grayer. The longer you live, the more you go about the business of turning into yourself."

Duren didn't fully follow that. Gerin hadn't expected that he would. Duren said, "I suppose I'll have to go on as best I can. I don't see what else I can do. Do you, Father?"

"I don't think there is anything else you can do," Gerin told him. "Nothing useful, anyhow: pining away over might-have-beens doesn't help." He clicked his tongue between his teeth. "Other thing I'll say is, you're Elise's son, aye, but you're my son, too, or you wouldn't think that way. Remember it."

"I always do," Duren answered. Not quite for the first time, Gerin thought that, whatever happened to his kingdom, he'd leave some good behind.

Dagref urged the horses up from a walk to a trot. The chariot swung around the curve in the road that brought Fox Keep into sight. "It's still there, and it's still mine," Gerin said.

"A lot of people have tried taking it away from you," Van said. "You've made 'em all sorry. They mostly know better now."

"I wish they did," Gerin said. "I wish they had for a long time. I'd have lived a more peaceable life if it were so."

Van snorted, a wordless expression of his opinion about what a peaceable life was worth. Gerin ignored him.

The drawbridge swung down over the ditch around the palisade as soon as the folk inside Fox Keep recognized Gerin and the warriors who still accompanied him: those who did not dwell at his keep had already peeled off and headed for their own homes. As he had to Duren's keep, he'd sent riders ahead to his own, so people knew he was returning, if not in triumph, at least in something close to it.

Men and women—and Geroge and Tharma with them—came spilling out over the drawbridge. Van pointed. "There's Fand," he said gloomily. "Now I'm for it. She'll have to hear about every time I dropped my drawers for some hussy since I rode out of here, and she'll make me pay for all of 'em."

Sure enough, Fand charged out ahead of most of the rest of the people, so far ahead that Ferdulf, feeling mischievous, dove on her—and just missed spitting himself on a knife she pulled from her belt and thrust at him. He darted away, shouting abuse. Fand screeched back.

But, for once after an army returned from campaign, she did not screech at Van. Instead, she ran toward Rihwin's riders and screeched at Maeva for going off and fighting without letting her know she'd done it.

"Well, isn't this nice?" Van said, beaming. "I come home to peace and quiet, at least aimed at me." The smile slipped. "It won't last. It can't last. It never lasts—but I'll enjoy it while it does."

Maeva, plainly, did not enjoy it. "Mother," she said, "I'm home safe. I've killed a couple of men, and I'm home safe." Gerin noted she did not mention taking a wound of her own.

She did not impress Fand, either. "Och, you've killed, have you now? If that was all you wanted, you could have waited till some lustful young spalpeen tried putting his hands where they don't belong, then stuck a knife 'twixt his ribs whilst he was after trying to stick summat else 'twixt your legs."

"I have no trouble taking care of myself there, either," Maeva answered. "No one will ever do anything to me that I don't want."

Van rumbled something deep in his chest. In front of Gerin, Dagref's ears turned pink. And Fand, who though hot-tempered was far from a fool, exclaimed, "And who's been doing things to you that you do want, now?"

Maeva did not answer, not in front of everyone. But Gerin had no doubt she would before too long—and Van knew, and a good many others who could tell Fand. Maybe she would approve of the match. Maybe she wouldn't, too. Gerin would find out in due course.

"Ride on into the keep," he told Dagref. "Easier to sort everything out in there than out here."

"Aye, Father," Dagref said. As the chariot made its slow way forward through the crowd, he and Gerin both waved to Selatre, and to Clotild and Blestar as well. Van waved to Kor. His son looked furiously jealous of Maeva, who'd had the chance to go out and fight and kill. Maeva let her hand fall to the hilt of her sword, which only infuriated Kor even more. Gerin, who'd had his older sibling flaunt privileges, too, knew a certain amount of sympathy for the boy.

He jumped down from the chariot as it slowed to a halt. Not too far away, Fand was still shouting at Maeva: "Why couldn't you go saving yourself for a nice lad like that Dagref, say, instead of letting some rough soldier ha' his way with you? The shame of it, now!"

Dagref jumped down after Gerin, as soon as a stable boy had taken charge of the horses. "Well, we won't have too much trouble there, will we?" he murmured. "Not if she wishes Maeva had saved herself for me, I mean."

"There's always going to be trouble with Fand," Gerin answered, also quietly. "The only question is, how much? By the sound of that, there shouldn't be too much. Of course, when she finds out you and Maeva are already . . . well, something more than friends, there'll be a row over that, too, I expect."

Dagref sighed. "You're probably right—people get so excited over these things."

Before Gerin could respond to that, Selatre and Clotild flung themselves onto him, while Blestar was flinging himself onto Dagref. Gerin kissed his wife and daughter. Blestar didn't want kisses. He wanted every single solitary detail of Dagref's adventures, he wanted the details on the spot, and not even his older brother's astonishingly retentive memory looked likely to be good enough to satisfy him.

Clotild, having got her share of kisses and hugs from her father, tried to get some from Dagref, too, which put him off his stride in his narration, which made Blestar shout at Clotild. Gerin laughed. "It's so *good* to be home," he said.

Selatre laughed, too. Then she glanced at him sidelong. "I hope you'll say that tonight and sound more as if you mean it," she said, adding, "If we can find somewhere to be alone, that is."

"The library," Gerin whispered in her ear, "even if Ferdulf is liable to fly up and peek through the window, and even if Dagref is liable to figure out why we keep that rolled-up bolt of cloth in there. But the library, even so. Yes indeed." He slipped his arm around her waist. She molded herself to him.

"Dagref will figure that out, will he?" Selatre asked. Gerin nodded. His wife clicked her tongue between her teeth. "Time does go on, doesn't it?"

"Doesn't it, though?" Gerin said. He hesitated, then spoke of something he had not entrusted to the riders who'd come up to Fox Keep ahead of him: "I was passing through a village down in the land Aragis rules, and I happened to run into Elise there."

Just for a heartbeat, the name did not register with Selatre; it was not one the Fox had been in the habit of using often. Then it did, and her eyes widened. "Duren's mother," she said in a voice that showed nothing whatever.

"Aye, Duren's mother," Gerin said. "I don't know where she is now, or what she's doing." He explained how he'd told Elise of Ricolf's passing, how she'd spoken of going south over the High Kirs, and how she had not come back to the barony that had been her father's and now was her son's. "And if you think I'm sorry that she hasn't, you're very much mistaken."

"No, I don't think that." Selatre still held her voice under tight restraint. That restraint was revealing in itself. After a little while, she said, "I never thought you would see her again."

"Neither did I," Gerin answered, "and I would have been just as well pleased if I hadn't, believe me."

Something in Selatre eased. The Fox hadn't noticed how tensely she was holding herself—almost like a bow strung and drawn—till she stopped doing it. She said, "I'm sorry, but I can't help worrying about these things. You did find her before you found me, after all."

His hand still rested on the curve of her hip. He squeezed, just for a moment. "And do you want to know what she taught me?" he asked. Selatre's nod was wary. He said, "She taught me to know when I was well off, because she gave me a standard of comparison, you might say."

Selatre thought about that for a moment, then threw her arms around his neck. After she finished kissing him, she said, "You just made me want to drag you up to the library right now."

"Why?" Gerin asked innocently. "Did you come up with a new codex while I was away on campaign?"

Selatre snorted and planted an elbow in his ribs. "When you choose, you can be most absurd," she said. Best of all, and one of the many reasons he was so fond of her, was that she made it sound like a compliment.

"How have things been while I was gone?"

"On the whole, very well," Selatre answered. "The weather has been good, and the harvest looks promising." She and Gerin both glanced toward the west. The Gradi still had their foothold in the northlands, out where the Niffet flowed into the Orynian Ocean, but they'd stayed quiet since their gods got embroiled with Baivers and the gods of the monsters who dwelt in some of the caves below Biton's shrine. If that fight ever ended, the gods of the Gradi and the Gradi themselves might prove troublesome again. It hadn't happened yet, though. With luck, it wouldn't happen for many years to come.

"On the whole, you say." Gerin knew when his wife had things to add, even if she tried to paint as bright a picture as she could.

She nodded now. "Yes, on the whole. The one worrisome thing I can think of is that, if Tharma isn't carrying pups—and I don't think she is, right now—it's not from lack of effort, if you understand what I'm saying."

Gerin sighed, loud and long. "Well, we've been waiting for that to happen for quite a while, so I can't say I'm surprised. The gods only know what I'll do about it if she does bear pups or cubs or babies or whatever you want to call them, but I can't say I'm surprised."

"The gods who may know best what you should do if Tharma gives birth are busy fighting the Gradi gods," Selatre said.

"Oh, the monsters' gods?" Gerin said, and his wife nodded. He went on, "I was thinking of them in a different connection a moment ago. I suppose you're right. And, for that matter, Maeva's lucky—or careful, one—not to be coming home great with child herself."

Selatre's eyes widened. "You mean Fand wasn't just shouting to hear herself shout, the way she does so often?"

"Not this time," the Fox answered. He hesitated, then spoke one word more: "Dagref."

Selatre's eyes got wider still. "But he's not old enough. She's not old enough, either, come to that." Then she counted on her fingers and frowned. "Time does run away, doesn't it? They could, I suppose, but I wish they wouldn't."

"So do I," Gerin said. "Outside of wishing, though, I haven't the faintest idea what to do about it but let it run its course and see what comes of that. Van and Fand both seem to think a match between the two of them would be good, and I don't mind one, either. How about you?"

"If it's what they want, I don't mind," his wife said. "I wouldn't want it right away, though. They aren't old enough to know their own minds. Let's see what they think two or three years from now."

"That sounds good to me," Gerin agreed. "My guess is, Van and Fand won't mind, either. Whether Dagref and Maeva will put up with waiting two or three more years, though, is another question. If they stay attached to each other, they'll just get more attached, if you know what I mean."

"I suppose so," Selatre said. "When I was their age, though, I was waiting for the old Sibyl to die. I was to be a maiden, and had no chance to form an attachment to any male." She took his arm in hers, so that his also brushed against the side of her breast. "I've made up for it since."

"That's good." Gerin let it go there. He couldn't say he wondered if he would be around in two or three more years, because saying as much would bring up the question of the succession, and the succession was the one thing he'd ever found that he did not care to discuss with Selatre.

No, she'd never urged him to name Dagref over Duren. He didn't think she would urge him to do that, but he didn't want to set temptation in front of her, either. If Dagref kept growing as well as he had lately—and if no one hit him over the head with a rock for being so maddeningly right all the time—the decision might shape itself. If Dagref made everyone want to hit him over the head with a rock, even if no one did, the decision would shape itself, too, the other way.

If neither of those things happened, Gerin would have to shape things himself. He shook his head. He would have to try to shape things himself. Whatever choice he made, by the very nature of things he wouldn't be around to enforce it. That would be up to his sons, and to Selatre if she outlived him, and to all his vassals: many of them, these days, the sons of the men who'd first given him homage and fealty, some the grandsons.

"No matter how long you last," he murmured, far more to himself than to Selatre, "sooner or later things fall from your hands."

His wife thought along with him, as she often did. "They don't fall and break, though. Someone catches them and carries on. You did, when the Trokmoi killed your father and your brother." She said no more than that. She didn't suggest that someone would catch the affairs of Gerin's kingdom when they did fall from his hands. Suggesting such a thing was as much as implying that someone should be Dagref.

Gerin thought about Duren competently running his barony, about Dagref fighting well and also falling in what might be love with Maeva. "You're right," he said. "One way or another, things do go on. Pretty soon, they'll be in someone else's hands."

"Not pretty soon, I hope. And whosever hands they're in, your mark will be on them," Selatre said.

He considered that, then slowly nodded. "I suppose it

will. I helped keep the Trokmoi from overrunning all the northlands—and the ones who did settle south of the Niffet are mostly my vassals these days. I kept the monsters from breaking out, too: all except Geroge and Tharma, anyhow. If I didn't drive the Gradi from the northlands, I pinned them back against the ocean. And I could be wrong, but I don't *think* the Elabonian Empire will trouble us again any time soon. The gods know I haven't been perfect, but I've done pretty well. When you think how things can go for a man, I'll take that." He nodded once more. "Aye, I'll take that."

IF YOU LIKE . . .
YOU SHOULD ALSO TRY . . .

Lackey's "SERRAted Edge" series . . . . . . Rick Cook, *Mall Purchase Night*

Dungeons & Dragons™ . . . . . . "Bard's Tale"™ Novels

Star Trek . . . . James Doohan & S.M. Stirling, *The Rising* and *The Privateer*

Star Wars . . . . Larry Niven, David Weber
The "Wing Commander"™ series

Jurassic Park . . . . Brett Davis, *Bone Wars* and *Two Tiny Claws*

Casablanca . . . . Larry Niven, *Man-Kzin Wars II*

Elves . . . . Ball, Lackey, Sherman, Moon, Cook, Guon

Puns . . . . Rick Cook, Spider Robinson
Harry Turtledove, *The Case of the Toxic Spell Dump*

Alternate History . . . . Gingrich and Forstchen, *1945*
James P. Hogan, *The Proteus Operation*
Harry Turtledove (ed.), *Alternate Generals*
S.M. Stirling, "Draka" series
Eric Flint & David Drake, "Belisarius" series
Eric Flint, *1632*

SF Conventions . . . . Niven, Pournelle & Flynn, *Fallen Angels*
Margaret Ball, *Mathemagics*
Jerry & Sharon Ahern, *The Golden Shield of IBF*

Quests . . . . Mary Brown, Elizabeth Moon, Piers Anthony

Greek Mythology . . . . Roberta Gellis, *Bull God*